THE COMPLETE
HAMMER'S
SLAMMERS
Volume 1

Baen Books By David Drake

THE COMPLETE
HAMMER'S SLAMMERS
Volume 1

BY
DAVID DRAKE

THE COMPLETE HAMMER'S SLAMMERS, VOL. 1

Copyright © 2009 by David Drake.
"Introduction" © 2006 by Gene Wolfe.
"Foreword: Becoming a Professional Writer by Way of Southeast Asia" © 1988 by David Drake. Originally published in *The Butcher's Bill*.
"Under the Hammer" © 1974 by David Drake. Originally published in *Galaxy*, November 1974.
"The Church of the Lord's Universe" © 1979 by David Drake. Originally published in *Hammer's Slammers*.
"But Loyal to His Own" © 1975 by David Drake. Originally published in *Galaxy*, October, 1975.
"Powerguns" © 1979 by David Drake. Originally published in *Hammer's Slammers*.
"Caught in the Crossfire" © 1978 by David Drake. Originally published in *Chrysalis 2*.
"Cultural Conflict" © 1979 by David Drake. Originally published in *Destinies*, January, 1979.
"The Bonding Auth" © 1979 by David Drake. Originally published in *Hammer's Slammers*.
"Hangman" © 1979 by David Drake. Originally published in *Hammer's Slammers*.
"Table of Organization and Equipment, Hammer's Regiment" © 1979 by David Drake. Originally published in *Hammer's Slammers*.
"Standing Down" © 1979 by David Drake. Originally published in Hammer's Slammers.
"Code-Name Feirefitz" © 1984 by David Drake. Originally published in *Men of War*.
"The Interrogation Team" © 1986 by David Drake. Originally published in *There Will be War Vol. 5*.
"The Tank Lords" © 1986 by David Drake. Originally published in *Far Frontiers Vol. 6*.
"Liberty Port" © 1987 by David Drake. Originally published in *Free Lancers*.
"Night March" © 1997 by David Drake. Originally published in *The Tank Lords*.
"The Immovable Object" © 1998 by David Drake. Originally published in *Caught in the Crossfire*.
"The Irresistible Force" © 1998 by David Drake. Originally published in *The Butcher's Bill*.
"A Death in Peacetime" © 2005 by David Drake.
"Afterword: Accidentally and by the Back Door" © 2005 by David Drake.

A Baen Book

Baen Publishing Enterprises
P.O. Box 1403
Riverdale, NY 10471
www.baen.com

ISBN: 978-1-4391-3309-5

Cover art by Kurt Miller

First Baen printing, October 2009

Distributed by Simon & Schuster
1230 Avenue of the Americas
New York, NY 10020

Library of Congress Cataloging-in-Publication Data

Drake, David.
  The complete Hammer's slammers / by David Drake.
    p. cm.
  ISBN 978-1-4391-3309-5 (v. 1 : trade pbk.)
  1. Science fiction, American. I. Title.
  PS3554.R196A6 2009
  813'.54--dc22
                                    2009024675
Printed in the United States of America

10 9 8 7 6 5 4 3 2 1

CONTENTS

INTRODUCTION

BY GENE WOLFE

It is remarkable—though never remarked—how few writers have been soldiers in wartime. Kipling, who wrote of soldiers and soldiering as well as anyone ever has, was never himself a soldier. I believe I am correct in saying that Hemmingway was never a soldier, although he drove an ambulance and was wounded in combat. Avram Davidson presents a peculiar case; as a Marine medic in World War Two he was technically a sailor, although he wore a Marine uniform and treated wounded Marines in the South Pacific. Subsequently he jumped through all sorts of legal hoops to stay out of the Israeli Army while fighting Arabs, since service in the army of a foreign nation would have cost him his US citizenship.

Such are the exceptions—some of the few writers at the edge of military service who were, or may have been, shot at. *The Red Badge of Courage* is often called the greatest of all war novels; Stephen Crane did not take part in the Civil War, although he interviewed many men who did.

David Drake is a writer of the rarest kind. He knows soldiers because he has been one, and knows war because he has been there. He knows more: he knows how to speculate plausibly about the future of soldiering and the future of war.

People who know as little of science fiction as most science fiction writers know of war believe that the business of science fiction is to predict the future—to extrapolate rationally from present trends, and, especially, present fads.

We should thank God that it is not. Rational extrapolation is a pistol, effective only at short ranges and not very effective there. The duty of science fiction is to tell us not what will be, but what might be, what the future *may* hold, what human reactions to it are likely, and what results are apt to ensue—socially, economically, militarily, romantically, and in every other department of life.

More and better than any other writer, David Drake does this for the wars of the future and the men and women who will fight them. Like every science fiction writer, he assumes that certain technological developments have taken place. He also assumes, as all who write science fiction are forced to, that certain others have *not* taken place. (He is, of course, fully capable of making a different set of assumptions and writing a good story around those.) Self-appointed experts may disagree with the assumptions of the Hammer's Slammers stories. They know exactly what war in the far future will be like. That there will be no war, or that wars will be fought entirely by robots while human beings sit around hoping not to die at the end. Or whatever. We should ask them and all such experts whether they have made their fortunes in the stock market. If there really were people capable of predicting what life—and death—will be like a thousand years from now, they would be capable of predicting what those things will be like just a few years from now, wouldn't they? Of predicting it and making shrewd investments. After all, there are men who can jump a one-foot ditch but cannot jump a three-foot ditch; but there are no men who can jump a three–foot ditch but cannot jump a one-foot ditch. Prediction is a rifle, less accurate as the range increases.

We can argue with any assumption found in any science fiction story. It will give us a good bull session, and perhaps even a bit of enlightenment. Still, we cannot rationally deny these assumptions. In science, it is the happy fate of human kind to know what is possible but not what is impossible. In 1946, anyone who said that all the wars to come in the Twentieth Century would be non-nuclear would have been laughed to scorn.

On what basis, then, can we judge a science fiction writer's assumptions? (Assuming that they seem relatively plausible.) Reading any story in this book will supply the answer. Good science fiction assumptions are those that lead to a good science fiction story.

Ah, but what is a good science fiction story? That is a question we might debate endlessly. I can no more give you a definitive answer than the next reader of David Drake's next book can. But by references to Dave's stories in this one, I can illustrate my own opinions. I will try to do it without hurting those stories for you—the last thing I want to do is deprive you of the pleasures this book affords.

First, a good science fiction story gives us that famed sense of wonder. The intricacies of future tank warfare do that for me, and you will find plenty of those here.

Second, a good science fiction story gives us a place to stand on, something that checks with our own experience. At some point in the story, we need to say to ourselves, "Why, I've been there!" Or, "I knew her!" Or, "That's just how it was for me!"

I find a number of these in the stories in this book, and so will you. My favorites—my own dear pets among them all—are the open-topped combat cars the Slammers use for recon. I rode in open APCs (Armored Personnel Carriers) once, you see, and hunkered down as the shells banged and boomed outside and the shrapnel screamed overhead.

Third, a good science fiction story must be a good *story*, just as a good crime story must be a good story. It must give us someone to like who has problems we want to read about; Colonel Hammer and Danny Pritchard are obvious examples. They may be smarter than we are, and braver than we are; but they are anything but alien to us. They are human beings, and recognizably so. We like them, and can imagine ourselves standing in their boots.

Here I am going to set off on a private rant—stop me if you can. War stories written by people who know nothing of wars and even less of the men and women who fight them often tell us at great length that those men and women are dehumanized, and try their damnedest to show them like that. Soldiers are often tired enough to drop, and people tired enough to drop are seldom as quick with a quip as the cast of *M*A*S*H*. But if that level of fatigue dehumanizes them, we can forget about the next guy who gets lost in the woods for three days. After the second day he is no longer human, so why should we care?

I have known one man, a fellow soldier long ago, whom I considered dehumanized. He grasped his rifle tightly just about all the time, and although we tried to keep ammunition away from him, it was impossible where we were: that rifle almost always had a round in the chamber, and the safety was always off. Looking ahead, and looking left and right, and looking behind him without cease, he repeated: "There ain't no Chinks around here, I want to go back to Baker Company. I want to go back to Baker, there ain't no Chinks around here. There ain't no Chinks around here, I'm goin' back to Baker Company, ain't no Chinks around here." We had him instead of Baker Company because we were about a mile behind the Main Line of Resistance just then, while Baker Company was on line and manning outposts.

Also because the guys in Baker Company were threatening to kill him before he killed them. He was suicidally courageous, would never remove the filthy fatigue cap he wore under his helmet, and had other peculiarities. I once met him on a dusty road as he walked along muttering to himself and kicking a human head as boys used to kick tin cans. (If I had been as quick as I like to pretend, I would have suggested he take it to the Battalion Intelligence Officer for questioning.) When we, too, began threatening to kill him, the brass at last concluded that he was not simply angling for a Section Eight.

The point of all this is that this one soldier was unlike anyone else in our company, and was in fact certifiably and dangerously psychotic. And that he was a lone exception among the hundreds of soldiers I fought behind, beside, and now and then in front of. Ken Clough was perhaps the sanest man I have known. I watched him one day when he was caught in a mortar barrage; and just when I felt certain he had been killed, he rolled onto his back and lit a cigarette. Lieutenant Wilcox, who killed thirteen enemy in one day with a thirty-eight, was thoroughly human and as fine an officer as I ever saw.

I have been telling you about all this, because I know that some of you will not know it. I would not tell David Drake the same thing because I know that he knows it already. You will find it here, in every story he writes. Men and women do not stop being women and men because they are out where the metal flies, and that is the wonderful, the truly miraculous, thing about them. Now and then the experience even knocks a bit of the pretence and pettiness out of them, and that is the glorious thing about a real shooting war, otherwise such a mess of pain and waste.

I sat in on a late-night party once in which the subject of friendship came up, and I listened in dumbstruck incredulity as one man explained that his friends had to like the same things he did—that they must not only read the same books and magazines he did, and listen to the same music, but pretty much share his opinions of all those things. He was followed by an attractive young woman who insisted that her friends had to be of her social and economic class. At that point I made all of them shut up while I explained that a friend is someone who will give you a drink from his canteen and watch while you sleep.

You will find the waste and horror and cruelty of war in the pages that follow, and the glory of it, too, as well as the friendships formed when there's little cover or none and the enemy has the range.

Now go to it!

FOREWORD

BECOMING A PROFESSIONAL WRITER
BY WAY OF SOUTHEAST ASIA

Some years ago my son took an undergraduate history course in the Vietnam Era. He mentioned that his father had been drafted out of law school in 1969. The other students and their twenty-seven-year-old professor were amazed; they "knew" that college students weren't drafted.

I was in the Duke Law School Class of 1970 when LBJ removed the graduate student deferment in 1968 and I was drafted along with nine more of its hundred and two guys. There were only two women in our class, a sign of the times that changed abruptly afterwards.

I'd been a history and Latin major as an undergraduate. I'd been against the war in a vague sort of way but I'd never protested or done anything else political except vote once, since the voting age was twenty-one. There was never any real question about me refusing to serve, though believe me I wasn't happy about it.

While a student I'd sold two fantasy short stories for a total of $85. I used what I knew about: historical settings and monsters based on H. P. Lovecraft's creepy-crawlies. I was proud of the sales, but writing was just a hobby.

Because I scored high on an army language aptitude test I was sent to Vietnamese language school at Fort Bliss, then for interrogation training at Fort Meade. Finally to Nam, where I was assigned to the

7

Military Intelligence detachment of a unit I'd never heard of: the 11th ACR, the Blackhorse Regiment.

My service wasn't in any fashion remarkable, and nothing particularly bad happened to me. I was in the field for a while with 2nd squadron just after the capture of Snuol; then with 1st squadron; and for the last half of the tour I was back in Di An, probably the safest place in Viet Nam, as unit armorer and mail clerk. The Inspector General was due, and apparently I was the only person in the 541st MID who knew how to strip a .45 down to the frame. (Military Intelligence doesn't seem to get many people who shot in pistol competitions in civilian life.)

And then I went back to the World. Seventy-two hours after I left Viet Nam I was sitting in the lounge of Duke University Law School, preparing to start my fourth semester. Because nothing awful had happened to me, I was honestly convinced that I hadn't changed from when I went over.

As I sat there, two guys I didn't know (my class had already graduated) were talking how they were going to avoid Viet Nam. One of them had joined the National Guard, while the other was getting into the Six and Six program that would give him six months army in the US, followed by five and a half years in the active reserves.

These were perfectly rational plans; I knew better than they did how much Nam was to be avoided. But for a moment, listening to them, I wanted to kill them both.

That gave me an inkling of the notion that maybe I wasn't quite as normal as I'd told myself I was.

I finished law school and got a job lawyering. I kept on writing, which after the fact I think was therapy. I didn't have anybody to talk to who would understand, and I'm not the sort to go to a shrink. I don't drink, either (which I think was a *really* good thing).

I had much more vivid horrors than Lovecraft's nameless ickinesses to write about now. I wrote stories about war in the future, assuming that the important things wouldn't change. The stories weren't like earlier military SF. Instead of brilliant generals or bulletproof heroes, I wrote about troopers doing their jobs the best way they could with tanks that broke down, guns that jammed—and no clue about the Big Picture, whatever the hell that might be. I kept the tone unemotional: I didn't tell the reader that something was horrible, because nobody had had to tell me.

It was very hard to sell those stories because they were different. They didn't fit either of the available molds: "Soldiers are spotless heroes," or the (then more-popular) "Soldiers are evil monsters." Those seemed to be the only images that civilians had.

But the funny thing is, when the stories were published they gained a following. Part of it was guys who'd been there, "there" being WW II, Korea, and later the Gulf as well as Viet Nam. Some of the fans, though, were civilians who could nonetheless tell the difference between the usual fictions and stories by somebody who was trying to tell the truth he'd seen in the best way he could.

Some civilians really wanted to understand. I guess that as much as anything helped me get my own head straighter over the years.

After I got back to the World I'd just done what was in front of me. I didn't think about the future, because I suppose I'd gotten out of the habit of believing there was one. When I raised my head enough to look around—almost to the day ten years after I rode a tank back from Cambodia—I quit lawyering and got a part-time job driving a city bus while continuing to write. I didn't quit lawyering "to write" (though I'd already had two books published) but because I realized the work was making me sick.

At this point something unexpected happened. Publishers were setting up new SF lines. Editors already knew that I would write them a story that people wanted to read; my first book, *Hammer's Slammers*, had succeeded beyond the editor's wildest dreams. (I didn't realize that for some years afterwards.) I got literally all the work I could do. The only limitation on how many books I could sell was the number of books I could write.

I've told you that Nam gave me a need to write and also gave me something real to write about. It gave me a third thing: service with that unit I'd never heard of; the 11th ACR. I'd been part of a professional outfit whose people did their jobs with no excuses, no matter what the circumstances.

There are writers who spend more time making excuses for why they can't write than they do writing. I could've become one of them, but that attitude wouldn't have cut any ice in the Blackhorse. Instead I just got on with my job, and since 1981 I've supported my family as a full-time freelance writer.

I'm successful now because I learned professionalism in the Blackhorse and carried that lesson over to the work I do in civilian life—which happens to be writing SF. The lessons people learned in Nam probably cost more than they were worth—even to the folks like me who got back with nothing worse than a couple boil scars from the time I was in the field. They were valuable lessons nonetheless.

If any of the folks reading this were with Blackhorse, thank you for what you taught me. I'm proud to have been one of you.

Dave Drake
david-drake.com

UNDER THE HAMMER

"Think you're going to like killing, boy?" asked the old man on double crutches.

Rob Jenne turned from the streams of moving cargo to his unnoticed companion in the shade of the starship's hull. His own eyes were pale gray, suited like his dead-white skin to Burlage, whose ruddy sun could raise a blush but not a tan. When they adjusted, they took in the clerical collar which completed the other's costume. The smooth, black synthetic contrasted oddly with the coveralls and shirt of local weave. At that, the Curwinite's outfit was a cut above Rob's own, the same worksuit of Burlage sisal that he had worn as a quarryhand at home. Uniform issue would come soon.

At least, he hoped and prayed it would.

When the youth looked away after an embarrassed grin, the priest chuckled. "Another damned old fool, hey, boy? There were a few in your family, weren't there . . . the ones who'd quote the *Book of the Way* saying not to kill—and here you go off for a hired murderer. Right?" He laughed again, seeing he had the younger man's attention. "But that by itself wouldn't be so hard to take—you were leaving your family anyway, weren't you, nobody really believes they'll keep close to their people after five years, ten years of star hopping. But your mates, though, the team you worked with . . . how did you explain to them why you were leaving a good job to go on contract? 'Via!' " the priest mimicked, his tones so close to those of Barney Larsen, the gang boss, that Rob started in surprise, "you get your coppy ass shot off, lad, and it'll serve you right for being a fool!"

"How do you know I signed for a mercenary?" Jenne asked, clenching his great, calloused hands on the handle of his carry-all. It was everything he owned in the universe in which he no longer had a home. "And how'd you know about my Aunt Gudrun?"

"Haven't I seen a thousand of you?" the priest blazed back, his eyes like sparks glinting from the drill shaft as the sledge drove it deeper into the rock. "You're young and strong and bright enough to pass Alois Hammer's tests—you be proud of that, boy, few enough are fit for Hammer's Slammers. There you were, a man grown who'd read all the cop about mercenaries, believed most of it . . . more'n ever you did the *Book of the Way,* anyhow. Sure, I know. So you got some off-planet factor to send your papers in for you, for the sake of the bounty he'll get from the colonel if you make the grade—"

The priest caught Rob's blink of surprise. He chuckled again, a cruel, unpriestly sound, and said, "He told you it was for friendship? One a these days you'll learn what friendship counts, when you get an order that means the death of a friend—and you carry it out."

Rob stared at the priest in repulsion, the grizzled chin resting on interlaced fingers and the crutches under either armpit supporting most of his weight. "It's my life," the recruit said with sulky defiance. "Soon as they pick me up here, you can go back to living your own. 'Less you'd be willing to do that right now?"

"They'll come soon enough, boy," the older man said in a milder voice. "Sure, you've been ridden by everybody you know . . . now that you're alone, here's a stranger riding you, too. I don't mean it like I sound . . . wasn't born to the work, I guess. There's priests— and maybe the better ones—who'd say that signing on with mercenaries means so long a spiral down that maybe your soul won't come out of it in another life or another hundred. But I don't see it like that.

"Life's a forge, boy, and the purest metal comes from the hottest fire. When you've been under the hammer a few times, you'll find you've been beaten down to the real, no lies, no excuses. There'll be a time, then, when you got to look over the product . . . and if you don't like what you see, well, maybe there's time for change, too."

The priest turned his head to scan the half of the horizon not blocked by the bellied-down bulk of the starship. Ant columns of stevedores manhandled cargo from the ship's rollerway into horse-and ox-drawn wagons in the foreground: like most frontier worlds, Burlage included, self-powered machinery was rare in the back country. Beyond the men and draft animals stretched the fields, studded frequently by orange-golden clumps of native vegetation.

"Nobody knows how little his life's worth till he's put it on the line a couple times," the old man said. "For nothing. Look at it here on Curwin—the seaboard taxed these uplands into revolt, then had to spend what they'd robbed and more to hire an armored regiment. So boys like you from—Scania? Felsen?—"

"Burlage, sir."

"Sure, a quarryman, should have known from your shoulders. You come in to shoot farmers for a gang of coastal moneymen you don't know and wouldn't like if you did." The priest paused, less for effect than to heave in a quick, angry breath that threatened his shirt buttons. "And maybe you'll die, too; if the Slammers were immortal, they wouldn't need recruits. But some that die will die like saints, boy, die martyrs of the Way, for no reason, for no reason . . .

"Your ride's here, boy."

The suddenly emotionless words surprised Rob as much as a scream in a silent prayer would have. Hissing like a gun-studded dragon, a gray-metal combat car slid onto the landing field from the west. Light dust puffed from beneath it: although the flatbed trailer behind was supported on standard wheels, the armored vehicle itself hovered a hand's-breadth above the surface at all points. A dozen powerful fans on the underside of the car kept it floating on an invisible bubble of air, despite the weight of the fusion power unit and the iridium-ceramic armor. Rob had seen combat cars on the entertainment cube occasionally, but those skittering miniatures gave no hint of the awesome power that emanated in reality from the machines. This one was seven meters long and three wide at the base, the armored sides curving up like a turtle's back to the open fighting compartment in the rear.

From the hatch in front of the power plant stuck the driver's head, a black-mirrored ball in a helmet with full face shield down. Road dust drifted away from the man in a barely visible haze, cleansed from the helmet's optics by a static charge. Faceless and terrible to the unfamiliar Burlager, the driver guided toward the starship a machine that appeared no more inhuman than did the man himself.

"Undercrewed," the priest murmured. "Two men on the back deck aren't enough for a car running single."

The older man's jargon was unfamiliar but Rob could follow his gist by looking at the vehicle. The two men standing above the waist-high armor of the rear compartment were clearly fewer than had been contemplated when the combat car was designed. Its visible armament comprised a heavy powergun forward to fire over the head of the driver, and similar weapons, also swivel-mounted, on either side to command the flanks and rear of the vehicle. But with only two men in the compartment there was a dangerous gap in the circle of fi re the car could lay down if ambushed. Another vehicle for escort would have eased the danger, but this one was alone save for the trailer it pulled.

Though as the combat car drew closer, Rob began to wonder if the two soldiers present couldn't handle anything that occurred. Both were in full battle dress, wearing helmets and laminated back and breast armor over their khaki. Their faceplates were clipped open. The one at the forward gun, his eyes as deep-sunken and deadly as the three revolving barrels of his weapon, was in his forties and further aged by the dust sweated into black grime in the creases of his face. His head rotated in tiny jerks, taking in every nuance of the sullen crowd parting for his war-car. The other soldier was huge by comparison with the first and lounged across the back in feigned leisure: feigned, because either hand was within its breadth of a powergun's trigger, and his limbs were as controlled as spring steel.

With careless expertise, the driver backed his trailer up to the conveyor line. A delicate hand with the fans allowed him to angle them slightly, drifting the rear of the combat car to edge the trailer in the opposite direction. The larger soldier contemptuously thumbed a waiting horse and wagon out of its slot. The teamster's curse brought only a grin and a big hand rested on a powergun's receiver, less a threat than a promise. The combat car eased into the space.

"Wait for an old man," the priest said as Rob lifted his carry-all, "and I'll go with you." Glad even for that company, the recruit smiled nervously, fitting his stride to the other's surprisingly nimble swing-and-pause, swing-and-pause.

The driver dialed back minusculy on the power and allowed the big vehicle to settle on the ground without a skip or a tremor. One hand slid back the face shield to a high, narrow nose and eyes that alertly focused on the two men approaching. "The Lord and his martyrs!" the driver cried in amazement. "It's Blacky himself come in with our newbie!"

Both soldiers on the back deck slewed their eyes around at the cry. The smaller one took one glance, then leaped the two meters to the ground to clasp Rob's companion. "Hey!" he shouted, oblivious of the recruit shifting his weight uncertainly. "Via, it's good to see you! But what're you doing on Curwin?"

"I came back here afterwards," the older man answered with a smile. "Born here, I must've told you . . . though we didn't talk a lot. I'm a priest now, see?"

"And I'm a flirt like the load we're supposed to pick up," the driver said, dismounting with more care than his companion. Abreast of the first soldier, he too took in the round collar and halted gape-mouthed. "Lord, I'll be a coppy rag if you ain't," he breathed. "Whoever heard of a blower chief taking the Way?"

"Shut up, Jake," the first soldier said without rancor. He stepped back from the priest to take a better look, then seemed to notice Rob. "Umm," he said, "you the recruit from Burlage?"

"Yessir. M-my name's Rob Jenne, sir."

"Not 'sir,' there's enough sirs around already," the veteran said. "I'm Chero, except if there's lots of brass around, then make it Sergeant-Commander Worzer. Look, take your gear back to the trailer and give Leon a hand with the load."

"Hey, Blacky," he continued with concern, ignoring Rob again, "what's wrong with your legs? We got the best there was."

"Oh, they're fine," Rob heard the old man reply, "but they need a weekly tuning. Out here we don't have the computers, you know; so I get the astrogation boys to sync me up on the ship's hardware whenever one docks in—just waiting for a chance now. But in six months the servos are far enough out of line that I have to shut off the power till the next ship arrives. You'd be surprised how well I get around on these pegs, though. . . ."

Leon, the huge third crew member, had loosed the top catches of his body armor for ventilation. From the look of it, the laminated casing should have been a size larger; but Rob wasn't sure anything larger was made. The gunner's skin where exposed was the dense black of a basalt outcropping. "They'll be a big crate to go on, so just set your gear down till we get it loaded," he said. Then he grinned at Rob, teeth square and slightly yellow against his face. "Think you can take me?"

That was a challenge the recruit could understand, the first he could meet fairly since boarding the starship with a one-way ticket to a planet he had never heard of. He took in the waiting veteran quickly but carefully, proud of his own rock-hardened muscles but certain the other man had been raised just as hard. "I give you best," the blond said. "Unless you feel you got to prove it?"

The grin broadened and a great black hand reached out to clasp Rob's. "Naw," the soldier said, "just like to clear the air at the start. Some of the big ones; Lord, testy ain't the word. All they can think about's what they want to prove with me . . . so they don't watch their side of the car, and then there's trouble for everybody."

"Hammer's Regiment?" called an unfamiliar voice. Both men looked up. Down the conveyor rode a blue-tunicked ship's man in front of what first appeared to be a huge crate. At second glance

Rob saw that it was a cage of light alloy holding four . . . "Dear Lord!" the recruit gasped.

"Roger, Hammer's," Leon agreed, handing the crewman a plastic chit while the latter cut power to the rollers to halt the cage. The chit slipped into the computer linkage on the crewman's left wrist, lighting a green indicator when it proved itself a genuine bill of lading.

There were four female humanoids in the cage—stark naked except for a dusting of fine blue scales. Rob blinked. One of the near-women stood with a smile—Lord, she had no teeth!—and rubbed her groin deliberately against one of the vertical bars.

"First-quality Genefran flirts," Leon chuckled. "Ain't human, boy, but the next best thing."

"Better," threw in Jake, who had swung himself into the fighting compartment as soon as the cage arrived. "I tell you, kid, you never had it till you had a flirt. Surgically modified and psychologically prepared. Rowf!"

"N-not human?" Rob stumbled, unable to take his eyes off the cage. "You mean like *monkeys?*"

Leon's grin lit his face again, and the driver cackled, "Well, don't know about monkeys, but they're a whole lot like sheep."

"You take the left side and we'll get this aboard," Leon directed. The trailer's bed was half a meter below the rollerway so that the cage, though heavy and awkward, could be slid without much lifting.

Rob gripped the bars numbly, turning his face down from the tittering beside him. "Amazing what they can do with implants and a wig," Jake was going on, "though a course there's a lot of cutting to do first, but those ain't the differences you see, if you follow. The scales, now—they have a way—"

"Lift!" Leon ordered, and Rob straightened at the knees. They took two steps backward with the cage wobbling above them as the girls—the flirts!—squealed and hopped about. "Down!" and cage clashed on trailer as the two big men moved in unison.

Rob stepped back, his mouth working in distaste, unaware of the black soldier's new look of respect. Quarry work left a man used to awkward weights. "This is foul," the recruit marveled. "Are those really going back with us for, for . . ."

"Rest 'n' relaxation," Leon agreed, snapping tiedowns around the bars.

"But how . . ." Rob began, looking again at the cage. When the red-wigged flirt fondled her left breast upward, he could see the implant scars pale against the blue. The scales were more thinly spread where the skin had been stretched in molding it. "I'll *never* touch something like that. Look, maybe Burlage is pretty backward about . . . things, about sex, I don't know. But I don't see how anybody could . . . I mean—"

"Via, wait till you been here as long as we have," Jake gibed. He clenched his right hand and pumped it suggestively. "Field expedients, that's all."

"On this kinda contract," Leon explained, stepping around to get at the remaining tiedowns, "you can't trust the local girls. Least not in the field, like we are. The colonel likes to keep us patrol sections pretty much self-contained."

"Yeah," Jake broke in—would his cracked tenor never cease? "Why, some of these whores, they take a razor blade, see—in a cork you know?—and, well, never mind." He laughed, seeing Rob's face.

"Jake," Sergeant Worzer called, "shut up and hop in."

The driver slipped instantly into his hatch. Disgusting as Rob found the little man, he recognized his ability. Jake moved with lethal certainty and a speed that belied the weight of his body armor.

"Ready to lift, Chero?" he asked.

The priest was levering himself toward the starship again. Worzer watched him go for a moment, shook his head. "Just run us out to the edge of the field," he directed. "I got a few things to show our recruit before we head back; nobody rides in my car without knowing how to work the guns." With a sigh he hopped into the fighting compartment. Leon motioned Rob in front of him. Gingerly, the recruit stepped onto the trailer hitch, gripped the armored rim with both hands, lifted himself aboard. Leon followed.

The trailer bonged as he pushed off from it, and his bulk cramped the littered compartment as soon as he grunted over the side.

"Put this on," Worzer ordered, handing Rob a dusty, bulbous helmet like the others wore. "Brought a battle suit for you, too," he said, kicking the jointed armor leaning against the back of the compartment, "but it'd no more fit you than it would Leon there."

The black laughed. "Gonna be tight back here till the kid or me gets zapped."

"Move 'er out," Worzer ordered. The words came through unsuspected earphones in Rob's helmet, although the sergeant had simply spoken, without visibly activating a pickup.

The car vibrated as the fans revved, then lifted with scarcely a jerk. From behind came the squeals and chirrups of the flirts as the trailer rocked over the irregularities in the field.

Worzer looked hard at the starship's open crew portal as they hissed past it. "Funny what folks go an' do," he said to no one in particular. "Via, wonder what I'll be in another ten years."

"Pet food, likely," joked the driver, taking part in the conversation although physically separated from the other crewmen.

"Shut up, Jake," repeated the blower captain. "And you can hold it up here, we're out far enough."

The combat car obediently settled on the edge of the stabilized area. The port itself had capacity for two ships at a time; the region it served did not. Though with the high cost of animal transport many manufactures could be star-hopped to Curwin's back country more cheaply than they could be carried from the planet's own more urbanized areas, the only available exchange was raw agricultural produce—again limited to the immediate locality by the archaic transport. Its fans purring below audibility, the armored vehicle rested on an empty area of no significance to the region—unless the central government should choose to land another regiment of mercenaries on it.

"Look," the sergeant said, his deep-set eyes catching Rob's, "we'll pass you on to the firebase when we take the other three flirts in next week. They got a training section there. We got six cars in this patrol, that's not enough margin to fool with training a newbie.

But neither's it enough to keep somebody useless underfoot for a week, so we'll give you some basics. Not so you can wise-ass when you get to training section, just so you don't get somebody killed if it drops in the pot. Clear?"

"Yessir." Rob broke his eyes away, then realized how foolish he must look staring at his own clasped hands. He looked back at Worzer.

"Just so it's understood," the sergeant said with a nod. "Leon, show him how the gun works."

The big black rotated his weapon so that the muzzle faced forward and the right side was toward Rob and the interior of the car. The mechanism itself was encased in dull-enameled steel ornamented with knobs and levers of unguessable intent. The barrels were stubby iridium cylinders with smooth, 2 cm bores. Leon touched one of the buttons, then threw a lever back. The plate to which the barrels were attached rotated 120 degrees around their common axis, and a thick disk of plastic popped out into the gunner's hand.

"When the bottom barrel's ready to fire, the next one clockwise is loading one a these"—Leon held up the 2 cm disk—"and the other barrel, the one that's just fired, blows out the empty."

"There's a liquid nitrogen ejector," Worzer put in. "Cools the bore same time it kicks out the empty."

"She feeds up through the mount," the big soldier went on, his index finger tracing the path of the energized disks from the closed hopper bulging in the sidewall, through the ball joint and into the weapon's receiver. "If you try to fire and she don't, check this." The columnar finger indicated but did not move the stud it had first pressed on the side of the gun. "That's the safety. She still doesn't fire, pull this"—he clacked the lever, rotating the barrel cluster around one-third turn and catching the loaded round that flew out. "Maybe there was a dud round. She still don't go, just get down outa the way. We start telling you about second-order malfunctions and you won't remember where the trigger is."

"Ah, where is the trigger?" Rob asked diffidently.

Jake's laughter rang through the earphones and Worzer himself smiled for the first time. The sergeant reached out and rotated the gun. "See the grips?" he asked, pointing to the double handles at the back of the receiver. Rob nodded.

"OK," Worzer continued, "you hold it there"—he demonstrated—"and to fire, you just press your thumbs against the trigger plate between 'em. Let up and it quits. Simple."

"You can clear this field as quick as you can spin this little honey," Leon said, patting the gun with affection. "The hicks out there"—his arm swept the woods and cultivated fields promiscuously—"got some rifles, they hunted before the trouble started, but no powerguns to mention. About all they do since we moved in is maybe pop a shot or two off, and hide in their holes."

"They've got some underground stockpiles," Worzer said, amplifying Leon's words, "explosives, maybe some factories to make rifle ammo. But the colonel set up a recce net—spy satellites, you know—as part of the contract. Any funny movement day or night, a signal goes down to whoever's patrolling there. A couple calls and we check out the area with ground sensors . . . anything funny then— vibration, hollows showing up on the echo sounder, magnetics— anything!—and bam! we call in the artillery."

"Won't take much of a jog on the way back," Leon suggested, "and we can check out that report from last night."

"Via, that was just a couple dogs," Jake objected.

"OK, so we prove it was a couple dogs," rumbled the gunner. "Or maybe the hicks got smart and they're shielding their infrared now. Been too damn long since anything popped in this sector."

"Thing to remember, kid," Worzer summed up, "is never get buzzed at this job. Stay cool, you're fine. This car's got more firepower'n everything hostile in fifty klicks. One call to the firebase brings in our arty, anything from smoke shells to a nuke. The rest of our section can be here in twenty minutes, or a tank platoon from the firebase in two hours. Just stay cool."

Turning forward, the sergeant said, "OK, take her home, Jake. We'll try that movement report on the way."

The combat car shuddered off the ground, the flirts shrieking.

Rob eyed them, blushed, and turned back to his powergun, feeling conspicuous. He took the grips, liking the deliberate way the weapon swung. The safety button was glowing green, but he suddenly realized that he didn't know the color code. Green for safe? Or green for ready? He extended his index finger to the switch.

"Whoa, careful, kid!" Leon warned. "You cut fifty civvies in half your first day and the colonel won't like it one bit."

Sheepishly, Rob drew back his finger. His ears burned, mercifully hidden beneath the helmet.

They slid over the dusty road in a flat, white cloud at about forty kph. It seemed shockingly fast to the recruit, but he realized that the car could probably move much faster were it not for the live cargo behind. Even as it was, the trailer bounced dangerously from side to side.

The road led through a gullied scattering of grain plots, generally fenced with withies rather than imported metal. Houses were relatively uncommon. Apparently each farmer plowed several separate locations rather than trying to work the rugged or less productive areas. Occasionally they passed a rough-garbed local at work. The scowls thrown up at the smoothly running war-car were hostile, but there was nothing more overt.

"OK," Jake warned, "here's where it gets interesting. Sure you still want this half-assed check while we got the trailer hitched?"

"It won't be far," Worzer answered. "Go ahead." He turned to Rob, touching the recruit's shoulder and pointing to the lighted map panel beside the forward gun. "Look, Jenne," he said, keeping one eye on the countryside as Jake took the car off the road in a sweeping turn, "if you need to call in a location to the firebase, here's the trick. The red dot"—it was in the center of the display and remained there although the map itself seemed to be flowing kitty-corner across the screen as the combat car moved—"that's us. The black dot"—the veteran thumbed a small wheel beside the display and the map, red dot and all, shifted to the right on the panel, leaving a black dot in the center—"that's your pointer. The computer feeds out the grid coordinates here"—his finger touched the window above the map display. Six digits, changing as the map moved under the centered black dot, winked brightly. "You just put the black dot on a bunker site, say, and read off the figures to Fire Central. The arty'll do all the rest."

"Ah," Rob murmured, "ah . . . Sergeant, how do you get the little dot off that and onto a bunker like you said?"

There was a moment's silence. "You know how to read a map, don't you kid?" Worzer finally asked.

"What's that, sir?"

The earphones boomed and cackled with raucous laughter. "Oh my coppy ass!" the sergeant snarled. He snapped the little wheel back, re-centering the red dot. "Lord, I don't know how the training cadre takes it!"

Rob hid his flaming embarrassment by staring over his gunsights. He didn't really know how to use them, either. He didn't know why he'd left Conner's Stoneworks, where he was the cleanest, fastest driller on the whole coppy crew. His powerful hands squeezed at the grips as if they were the driver's throat through which bubbles of laughter still burst.

"Shut up, Jake," the sergeant finally ordered. "Most of us had to learn something new when we joined. Remember how the ol' man found you your first day, pissing up against the barracks?"

Jake quieted.

They had skirted a fence of cane palings, brushing in once without serious effect. Russet grass flanking the fence flattened under the combat car's downdraft, then sprang up unharmed as the vehicle moved past. Jake seemed to be following a farm track leading from the field to a rambling, substantially constructed building on the near hilltop. Instead of running with the ground's rise, however, the car cut through brush and down a half-meter bank into a broad-based arroyo. The bushes were too stiff to lie down under the fans. They crunched and howled in the blades, making the car buck, and ricocheted wildly from under the skirts. The bottom of the arroyo was sand, clean-swept by recent runoff. It boiled fiercely as the car first shoomped into it, then ignored the fans entirely. Somehow Jake had managed not to overturn the trailer, although its cargo had been screaming with fear for several minutes.

"Hold up," Worzer ordered suddenly as he swung his weapon toward the left-hand bank. The wash was about thirty meters wide at that point, sides sheer and a meter high. Rob glanced forward to see that a small screen to Worzer's left on the bulkhead, previously dark, was now crossed by three vari-colored lines. The red one was bouncing frantically.

"They got an entrance, sure 'nough," Leon said. He aimed his powergun at the same point, then snapped his face shield down. "Watch it, kid," he said. The black's right hand fumbled in a metal can welded to the blower's side. Most of the paint had chipped from the stenciled legend: grenades. What appeared to be a lazy overarm toss snapped a knobby ball the size of a child's fist straight and hard against the bank.

Dirt and rock fragments shotgunned in all directions. The gully side burst in a globe of black streaked with garnet fire, followed by a shock wave that was a physical blow.

"Watch your side, kid!" somebody shouted through the din, but Rob's bulging eyes were focused on the collapsing bank, the empty triangle of black gaping suddenly through the dust—the two ravening whiplashes of directed lightning ripping into it to blast and scatter.

The barrel clusters of the two veterans' powerguns spun whining, kicking gray, eroded disks out of their mechanisms in nervous arcs. The bolts they shot were blue-green flashes barely visible until they struck a target and exploded it with transferred energy. The very rock burst in droplets of glassy slag splashing high in the air and even back into the war-car to pop against the metal.

Leon's gun paused as his fingers hooked another grenade. "Hold it!" he warned. The sergeant, too, came off the trigger, and the bomb arrowed into the now-vitrified gap in the tunnel mouth. Dirt and glass shards blew straight back at the bang. A stretch of ground sagged for twenty meters beyond the gully wall, closing the tunnel the first explosion had opened.

Then there was silence. Even the flirts, huddled in a terrified heap on the floor of their cage, were soundless.

Glowing orange specks vibrated on Rob's retinas; the cyan bolts had been more intense than he had realized. "Via," he said in awe, "how do they dare . . . ?"

"Bullet kills you just as dead," Worzer grunted. "Jake, think you can climb that wall?"

"Sure. She'll buck a mite in the loose stuff ." The gully side was a gentle declivity, now, where the grenades had blown it in. "Wanna unhitch the trailer first?"

"Negative, nobody gets off the blower till we cleaned this up."

"Umm, don't want to let somebody else in on the fun, maybe?" the driver queried. If he was tense, his voice did not indicate it. Rob's palms were sweaty. His glands had understood before his mind had that his companions were considering smashing up, unaided, a guerrilla stronghold.

"Cop," Leon objected determinedly. "We found it, didn't we?"

"Let's go," Worzer ordered. "Kid, watch your side. They sure got another entrance, maybe a couple."

The car nosed gently toward the subsided bank, wallowed briefly as the driver fed more power to the forward fans to lift the bow. With a surge and a roar, the big vehicle climbed. Its fans caught a few pebbles and whanged them around inside the plenum chamber like a rattle of sudden gunfire. At half speed, the car glided toward another fenced grainplot, leaving behind it a rising pall of dust.

"Straight as a plumb line," Worzer commented, his eyes flicking his sensor screen. "Bastards'll be waiting for us."

Rob glanced at him—a mistake. The slam-spang! of shot and ricochet were nearly simultaneous. The recruit whirled back, bawling in surprise. The rifle pit had opened within five meters of him, and only the haste of the dark-featured guerrilla had saved Rob from his first shot. Rob pivoted his powergun like a hammer, both thumbs mashing down the trigger. Nothing happened. The guerrilla ducked anyway, the black circle of his foxhole shaped into a thick crescent by the lid lying askew.

Safety, *safety!* Rob's mind screamed and he punched the button fat-fingered. The rifleman raised his head just in time to meet the hose of fire that darted from the recruit's gun. The guerrilla's head exploded. His brains, flash-cooked by the first shot, changed instantly from a colloid to a blast of steam that scattered itself over a three-meter circle. The smoldering fragments of the rifle followed the torso as it slid downward.

The combat car roared into the field of waist-high grain, ripping down twenty meters of woven fencing to make its passage. Rob, vaguely aware of other shots and cries forward, vomited onto the floor of the compartment. A colossal explosion nearby slewed the car sideways. As Rob raised his eyes, he noticed three more swarthy riflemen darting through the grain from the right rear of the vehicle.

"Here!" he cried. He swiveled the weapon blindly, his hips colliding with Worzer in the cramped space. A rifle bullet cracked past his helmet. He screamed something again but his own fire was too high, blue-green droplets against the clear sky, and the guerrillas had grabbed the bars while the flirts jumped and blatted.

The rifles were slamming but the flirts were in the way of Rob's gun. "Down! Down!" he shouted uselessly, and the red-haired flirt pitched across the cage with one synthetic breast torn away by the bullet she had leaped in front of. Leon cursed and slumped across Rob's feet, and then it was Chero Worzer shouting, "Hard left, Jake," and leaning across the fallen gunner to rotate his weapon. The combat car tilted left as the bow came around, pinching the trailer against the left rear of the vehicle—in the path of Worzer's powergun. The cage's light alloy bloomed in superheated fireballs as the cyan bolts ripped through it. Both tires exploded together, and there was a red mist of blood in the air. The one guerrilla who had ducked under the burst dropped his rifle and ran.

Worzer cut him in half as he took his third step.

The sergeant gave the wreckage only a glance, then knelt beside Leon. "Cop, he's gone," he said. The bullet had struck the big man in the neck between helmet and body armor, and there was almost a gallon of blood on the fl oor of the compartment.

"Leon?" Jake asked.

"Yeah. Lord, there musta been twenty kilos of explosive in that satchel charge. If he hadn't hit it in the air . . ." Worzer looked back at the wreck of the trailer, then at Rob. "Kid, can you unhitch that yourself?"

"You just *killed* them," Rob blurted. He was half-blinded by tears and the afterimage of the gunfire.

"Via, they did their best on us, didn't they?" the sergeant snarled. His face was tiger striped by dust and sweat.

"No, not them!" the boy cried. "Not them—the girls. You just—"

Worzer's iron fingers gripped Rob by the chin and turned the recruit remorselessly toward the carnage behind. The flirts had been torn apart by their own fluids, some pieces flung through gaps in the mangled cage. "Look at 'em, Jenne!" Worzer demanded. "They ain't human but if they was, if it was *Leon* back there, I'd a done it."

His fingers uncurled from Rob's chin and slammed in a fist against the car's armor. "This ain't heroes, it ain't no coppy game you play when you want to! You do what you got to do, 'cause if you don't, some poor bastard gets killed later when he tries to. "Now get down there and unhitch us."

"Yes, sir." Rob gripped the lip of the car for support.

Worzer's voice, more gentle, came through the haze of tears: "And watch it, kid. Just because they're keeping their heads down don't mean they're all gone." Then, "Wait." Another pause while the sergeant unfastened the belt and holstered handgun from his waist and handed it to Rob. Leon wore a similar weapon, but Worzer did not touch the body. Rob wordlessly clipped the belt, loose for not being fitted over armor, and swung down from the combat car.

The hitch had a quick-release handle, but the torquing it had received in the last seconds of battle had jammed it. Nervously aware that the sergeant's darting-eyed watchfulness was no pretense, that the shot-scythed grainfield could hide still another guerrilla, or a platoon of them, Rob smashed his boot heel against the catch. It held. Wishing for his driller's sledge, he kicked again.

"Sarge!" Jake shouted. Grain rustled on the other side of the combat car, and against the sky beyond the scarred armor loomed a parcel. Rob threw himself flat.

The explosion picked him up from the ground and bounced him twice, despite the shielding bulk of the combat car. Stumbling upright, Rob steadied himself on the armored side.

The metal felt odd. It no longer trembled with the ready power of the fans. The car was dead, lying at rest on the torn-up soil. With three quick strides, the recruit rounded the bow of the vehicle. He had no time to inspect the dished-in metal, because another swarthy guerrilla was approaching from the other side.

Seeing Rob, the ex-farmer shouted something and drew a long knife. Rob took a step back, remembered the pistol. He tugged at its unfamiliar grip and the weapon popped free into his hand. It seemed the most natural thing in the world to finger the safety, placed just as the tribarrel's had been, then trigger two shots into the face of the lunging guerrilla. The snarl of hatred blanked as the body tumbled facedown at Rob's feet. The knife had flown somewhere into the grain.

"Ebros?" a man called. Another lid had raised from the ground ten meters away. Rob fired at the hole, missed badly. He climbed the caved-in bow, clumsily one-handed, keeping the pistol raised. There was nothing but twisted metal where the driver had been. Sergeant Worzer was still semi-erect, clutched against his powergun by a length of structural tubing. It had curled around both his thighs, fluid under the stunning impact of the satchel charge. The map display was a pearly blank, though the window above it still read incongruously 614579 and the red line on the detector screen blipped in nervous solitude. Worzer's helmet was gone, having flayed a bloody track across his scalp as it sailed away. His lips moved, though, and when Rob put his face near the sergeant's he could hear, "The red . . . pull the red tab . . ."

Over the left breast of each set of armor were a blue and a red tab. Rob had assumed they were decorations of some sort. He shifted the sergeant gently. The tab was locked down by a cotter pin which he yanked out. Something hissed in the armor as he pulled the tab, and Sergeant Worzer murmured, "Oh Lord. Oh Lord." Then, "Now the stimulant, the blue tab."

After the second injection sped into his system, the sergeant opened his eyes. Rob was already trying to straighten the entrapping tube. "Forget it," Worzer ordered weakly. "It's inside, too . . . damn armor musta flexed. Oh Lord." He closed his eyes, opened them in time to see another head peak cautiously from the tunnel mouth. "Bastard!" he rasped, and faster than he spoke he triggered his powergun. Its motor whined spitefully though the burst went wide. The head disappeared.

"I want you to run back to the gully," the sergeant said, resting his eyes again. "You get there, you say 'Fire Central.' That cuts in the arty frequency automatic. Then you say, 'Bunker complex . . .'" Worzer looked down. " 'Six-one-four, five-seven-nine.' Stay low and wait for a patrol."

"It won't bend!" Rob snarled in frustration as his fingers slid again from the blood-slick tubing.

"Jenne, get your ass out of here, *now*."

"Sergeant—"

"Lord curse your soul, get out or I'll call it in myself! Do I look like I wanna live?"

"Oh, Via . . ." Rob tried to reholster the pistol he had set on the bloody floor. It slipped back with a clang. He left it, gripping the sidewall again.

"Maybe tell Dad it was good to see him," Worzer whispered. "You lose touch in this business, Lord knows you do."

"Sir?"

"The priest . . . you met him. Sergeant-Major Worzer, he was. Oh Lord, *move it*—"

At the muffled scream, the recruit leaped from the smashed war-car and ran blindly back the way they had come. He did not know he had reached the gully until the ground flew out from under him and he pitched spread-eagled onto the sand. "Fire Central," he sobbed through strangled breaths, "Fire Central."

"Clear," a strange voice snapped crisply. "Data?"

"Wh-what?"

"Lord and martyrs," the voice blasted, "if you're screwing around on firing channels, you'll wish you never saw daylight!"

"S-six . . . oh Lord, yes, six-one-four, five-seven-nine," Rob singsonged. He was staring at the smooth sand. "Bunkers, the sergeant says it's bunkers."

"Roger," the voice said, businesslike again. "Ranging in fifteen."

Could they really swing those mighty guns so swiftly, those snub-barreled rocket howitzers whose firing looked so impressive on the entertainment cube?

"On the way," warned the voice.

The big tribarrel whined again from the combat car, the silent lash of its bolts answered this time by a crash of rifle shots. A flattened bullet burred through the air over where Rob lay. It was lost in the eerie, thunderous shriek from the northwest.

"Splash," the helmet said.

The ground bucked. From the grainplot spouted rock, smoke, and metal fragments into a black column fifty meters high.

"Are we on?" the voice demanded.

"Oh, Lord," Rob prayed, beating his fists against the sand. "Oh Lord."

"Via, what is this?" the helmet wondered aloud. Then, "All guns, battery five."

And the earth began to ripple and gout under the hammer of the guns.

SUPERTANKS

Tanks were born in the muck and wire of World War One. Less than sixty years later, there were many who believed that technology had made the behemoths as obsolete as horse cavalry. Individual infantrymen of 1970 carried missiles whose warheads burned through the armor of any tank. Slightly larger missiles ranged kilometers to blast with pinpoint accuracy vehicles costing a thousand times as much. Similar weaponry was mounted on helicopters which skimmed battlefields in the nape of the earth, protected by terrain irregularities. At the last instant the birds could pop up to rip tanks with their missiles. The future of armored vehicles looked bleak and brief.

Technology had dragged the tank to the brink of abandonment. Not surprisingly, it was technology again which brought the panzers back. The primary breakthrough was the development of portable fusion power plants. Just as the gasoline engine with its high horsepower-to-weight ratio had been necessary before the first tanks could take the field, so the fusion unit's almost limitless output was required to move the mass which made the new supertanks viable. Fusion units were bulky and moderately heavy themselves, but loads could be increased on a fusion-powered chassis with almost no degradation of performance. Armor became thick—and thicker. With the whole galaxy available as a source of ores, iridium replaced the less effective steels and ceramics without regard for weight.

Armor alone is not adequate protection. Stationary fortresses can always be battered down—as the French learned in 1940, having forgotten the lesson Caesar taught their ancestors at Alesia two millennia before. Caterpillar treads had given the first tanks cross-country ability; but at the cost of slow speed, frequent breakage, and great vulnerability to attack. Now that power was no longer a factor, even the armored bulk of a tank could be mounted on an air cushion.

The air-cushion principle is a very simple one. Fans fill the plenum chamber, a solid-skirted box under a vehicle, with air under pressure. To escape, the air must lift the edges of the skirts off the ground—and with the skirts, the whole vehicle rises. Fans tilt with the velocity and angle of attack of the blades determining the amount and direction of thrust. The vehicle skims over surfaces it does not touch.

On tanks and combat cars, the lift was provided by batteries of fans mounted on the roof of the plenum chamber. Each fan had its own armored nacelle. Mines could still do considerable damage; but while a single broken track block would deadline a tracked vehicle, a wrecked fan only made a blower a little more sluggish.

Successful protection for the supertanks went beyond armor and speed. Wire-guided missiles are still faster, and their shaped-charge warheads can burn holes in any practical thickness of any conceivable material—if they are allowed to hit. Reconnaissance satellites, computer fire control, and powerguns combined to claw missiles out of the air before they were dangerous. The satellites spotted missile launchers usually before they fired and never later than the moment of ignition. Fire control computers, using data from the satellites, locked defensive weaponry on the missiles in microseconds. And a single light-swift tribarrel could hose any missile with enough fire in its seconds of flight to disintegrate it.

Hand-launched, unguided rockets—buzzbombs—were another problem, and in some ways a more dangerous one despite their short range and small bursting charges. Individual infantrymen fired them from such short ranges that not even a computer had time enough to lay a gun on the little rockets. But even here there was an answer—beyond the impossible one of killing every enemy before he came within two hundred meters.

Many armored vehicles were already fitted with a band of antipersonnel directional mines just above the skirts. Radar detonated the mines when an object came within a set distance. Their blast of shrapnel was designed to stop infantry at close quarters. With only slight modification, the system could be adapted against buzzbombs. It was not perfect, since the pellets were far less destructive than powergun bolts, and the mines could not be used in close terrain which would itself set them off. Still, buzzbombs were apt to be ill-aimed in the chaos of battle, and a tank's armor could shrug off all but a direct hit by the small warheads.

So tanks roamed again as lords of battle, gray-gleaming phoenixes on air cushions. Their guns could defeat the thickest armor, their armor could blunt all but the most powerful attacks. They were fast enough to range continents in days, big enough to carry a battery of sensors and weaponry which made them impossible to escape when they hunted. The only real drawback to the supertanks was their price.

A tank's fire control, its precisely metered lift fans, the huge iridium casting that formed its turret—all were constructs of the highest sophistication. In all the human galaxy there were probably no more than a dozen worlds capable of manufacturing war tools as perfect as the panzers of Hammer's tank companies.

But Hammer paid for the best, man and tank alike; and out of them he forged the cutting edge of a weapon no enemy seemed able to stop.

THE BUTCHER'S BILL

"You can go a thousand kays any direction there and there's nothing to see but the wheat," said the brown man to the other tankers and the woman. His hair was deep chestnut, his face and hands burnt umber from the sun of Emporion the month before and the suns of seven other worlds in past years. He was twenty-five but looked several years older. The sleeves of his khaki coveralls were slipped down over his wrists against the chill of the breeze that had begun at twilight to feather the hillcrest. "We fed four planets from Dunstan—Hagener, Weststar, Mirage, and Jackson's Glade. And out of it we made enough to replace the tractors when they wore out, maybe something left over for a bit of pretty. A necklace of fireballs to set off a Lord's Day dress, till the charge drained six, eight months later. A static cleaner from Hagener, it was one year, never quite worked off our power plant however much we tinkered with it. . . .

"My mother, she wore out too. Dad just kept grinding on, guess he still does."

The girl asked a question from the shelter of the tank's scarred curtain. Her voice was too mild for the wind's tumbling, her accent that of Thrush and strange to the tanker's ears. But Danny answered, "Hate them? Oh, I know about the Combine, now, that the four of them kept other merchants off Dunstan to freeze the price at what they thought to pay. But Via, wheat's a high bulk cargo, there's no way at all we'd have gotten rich on what it could

35

bring over ninety minutes' transit. And why shouldn't I thank Weststar? If ever a world did me well, it was that one."

He spat, turning his head with the wind and lofting the gobbet invisibly into the darkness. The lamp trembled on its base, an overturned ration box. The glare skipped across the rusted steel skirts of the tank, the iridium armor of hull and turret; the faces of the men and the woman listening to the blower chief. The main gun, half-shadowed by the curve of the hull, poked out into the night like a ghost of itself. Even with no human in the tank, at the whisper of a relay in Command Central the fat weapon would light the world cyan and smash to lava anything within line of sight of its muzzle.

"We sold our wheat to a Weststar agent, a Hindi named Sarim who'd lived, Via, twenty years at least on Dunstan but he still smelled funny. Sweetish, sort of; you know? But his people were all back in Ongole on Weststar. When the fighting started between the Scots and the Hindi settlers, he raised a battalion of farm boys like me and shipped us over in the hold of a freighter. Hoo Lordy, that was a transit!

"And I never looked back. Colonel Hammer docked in on the same day with the Regiment, and he took us all on spec. Six years, now, that's seven standard . . . and not all of us could stand the gaff, and not all who could wanted to. But I never looked back, and I never will."

From the mast of Command Central, a flag popped unseen in the wind. It bore a red lion rampant on a field of gold, the emblem of Hammer's Slammers, the banner of the toughest regiment that ever killed for a dollar.

"Hotel, Kitchen, Lariat, Michael, move to the front in company columns and advance."

The tiny adamantine glitter winking on the hilltop ten kays distant was the first break in the landscape since the Regiment had entered the hypothetical war zone, the Star Plain of Thrush. It warmed Pritchard in the bubble at the same time it tightened his muscles. "Goose it, Kowie," he ordered his driver in turn, "they want us panzers up front. Bet it's about to drop in the pot?"

Kowie said nothing, but the big blower responded with a howl and a billow of friable soil that seethed from under the ground effect curtain. Two Star in the lead, H Company threaded its way in line ahead through the grounded combat cars and a company from Infantry Section. The pongoes crouched on their one-man skimmers, watching the tanks. One blew an ironic kiss to Danny in Two Star's bubble. Moving parallel to Hotel, the other companies of Tank Section, K, L, and M, advanced through the center and right of the skirmish line.

The four man crew of a combat car nodded unsmilingly from their open-topped vehicle as Two Star boomed past. A trio of swivel-mounted powerguns, 2cm hoses like the one on Danny's bubble, gave them respectable firepower; and their armor, a sandwich of ceramics and iridium, was in fact adequate against most hand weapons. Buzzbombs aside, and tankers didn't like to think about those either. But Danny would have fought reassignment to combat cars if anybody had suggested it—Lord, you may as well dance in your skin for all the good that hull does you in a firefight! And few car crewmen would be caught dead on a panzer— or rather, were sure that was how they would be caught if they crewed one of those sluggish, clumsy, blind-sided behemoths. Infantry Section scorned both, knowing how the blowers drew fire but couldn't flatten in the dirt when it dropped in on them.

One thing wouldn't get you an argument, though: when it was ready to drop in the pot, you sent in the heavies. And nothing on the Way would stop the Tank Section of Hammer's Slammers when it got cranked up to move.

Even its 170 tonnes could not fully dampen the vibration of Two Star's fans at max load. The oval hull, all silvery-smooth above but of gouged and rusty steel below where the skirts fell sheer almost to the ground, slid its way through the grass like a boat through yellow seas. They were dropping into a swale before they reached the upgrade. From the increasing rankness of the vegetation that flattened before and beside the tank, Pritchard suspected they would find a meandering stream at the bottom. The brow of the hill cut off sight of the unnatural glitter visible from a distance. In silhouette against the pale bronze sky writhed instead a grove of gnarled trees.

"Incoming, fourteen seconds to impact," Command Central blatted. A siren in the near distance underscored the words. "Three rounds only."

The watercourse was there. Two Star's fans blasted its surface into a fine mist as the tank bellowed over it. Danny cocked his powergun, throwing a cylinder of glossy black plastic into the lowest of the three rotating barrels. There was shrieking overhead.

WHAM

A poplar shape of dirt and black vapor spouted a kay to the rear, among the grounded infantry.

WHAM WHAM

They were detonating underground. Thrush didn't have much of an industrial base, the rebel portions least of all. Either they hadn't the plant to build proximity fuses at all, or they were substituting interference coils for miniature radar sets, and there was too little metal in the infantry's gear to set off the charges. With the main director out, Central wasn't even bothering to explode the shells in flight

"Tank Section, hose down the ridge as you advance, they got an OP there somewhere."

"Incoming, three more in fourteen." The satellite net could pick up a golf ball in flight, much less a two hundred kilo shell.

Pritchard grinned like a death's head, laying his 2cm automatic on the rim of the hill and squeezing off. The motor whirred, spinning the barrels as rock and vegetation burst in the blue-green sleet. Spent cases, gray and porous, spun out of the mechanism in a jet of coolant gas. They bounced on the turret slope, some clinging to the iridium to cool there, ugly dark excrescences on the metal.

"Outgoing."

Simultaneously with Central's laconic warning, giants tore a strip off the sky. The rebel shells dropped but their bursts were smothered in the roar of the Regiment's own rocket howitzers boosting charges to titanic velocity for the several seconds before their motors burned out. Ten meters from the muzzles the rockets went supersonic, punctuating the ripping sound with thunderous slaps. Danny swung his hose toward the grove of trees, the only landmark visible on the hilltop. His burst laced it cyan. Water, flash-heated within the boles by the gunfire, blew the dense wood apart in blasts of steam and splinters. A dozen other guns joined Pritchard's, clawing at rock, air, and the remaining scraps of vegetation.

"Dead on," Central snapped to the artillery. "Now give it battery-five and we'll show those freaks how they should've done it."

Kowie hadn't buttoned up. His head stuck up from the driver's hatch, trusting his eyes rather than the vision blocks built into his compartment. The tanks themselves were creations of the highest technical competence, built on Terra itself; but the crews were generally from frontier worlds, claustrophobic in an armored coffin no matter how good its electronic receptors were. Danny knew the feeling. His hatch, too, was open, and his hand gripped the rounded metal of the powergun itself rather than the selsyn unit inside. They were climbing sharply now, the back end hopping and skittering as the driver fed more juice to the rear fans in trying to level the vehicle. The bow skirts grounded briefly, the blades spitting out a section of hillside as pebbles.

For nearly a minute the sky slammed and raved. Slender, clipped-off vapor trails of counter-battery fire streamed from the defiladed artillery. Half a minute after they ceased fire, the drumbeat of shells bursting on the rebels continued. No further incoming rounds fell.

Two Star lurched over the rim of the hill. Seconds later the lead blowers of K and M bucked in turn onto the flatter area. Smoke and ash from the gun-lit brushfire shoomped out in their downdrafts. There was no sign of the enemy, either Densonite rebels or Fosters crew—though if the mercenaries were involved, they would be bunkered beyond probable notice until they popped the cork themselves. "Tank Section, ground! Ground in place and prepare for director control."

Danny hunched, bracing his palms against the hatch coaming. Inside the turret the movement and firing controls of the main gun glowed red, indicating that they had been locked out of Pritchard's command. Kowie lifted the bow to kill the tank's immense inertia. There was always something spooky about feeling the turret purr beneath you, watching the big gun snuffle the air with deadly precision on its own. Danny gripped his tribarrel, scanning the horizon nervously. It was worst when you didn't know what Central had on its mind . . . and you did know that the primary fire control computer was on the fritz—they always picked the damnedest times!

"Six aircraft approaching from two-eight-three degrees," Central mumbled. "Distance seven point ought four kays, closing at one one ought ought."

Pritchard risked a quick look away from where the gun pointed toward a ridgeline northwest of them, an undistinguished swelling half-obscured by the heat-wavering pall of smoke. Thirteen other tanks had crested the hill before Central froze them, all aiming in the same direction. Danny dropped below his hatch rim, counting seconds.

The sky roared cyan. The tank's vision blocks blanked momentarily, but the dazzle reflected through the open hatch was enough to make Pritchard's skin tingle. The smoke waved and rippled about the superheated tracks of gunfire. The horizon to the northwest was an expanding orange dome that silently dominated the sky.

"Resume advance." Then, "Spectroanalysis indicates five hostiles were loaded with chemical explosives, one was carrying fissionables."

Danny was trembling worse than before the botched attack. The briefing cubes had said the Densonites were religious nuts, sure. But to use unsupported artillery against a force whose satellite spotters would finger the guns before the first salvo landed; aircraft—probably converted cargo haulers—thrown against director-controlled powerguns that shot light swift and line straight; and then nukes, against a regiment more likely to advance stark naked than without a nuclear damper up! They weren't just nuts—Thrush central government was that, unwilling to have any of its own people join the fighting—they were as crazy as if they thought they could breathe vacuum and live. You didn't play that sort of game with the Regiment.

They'd laager for the night on the hilltop, the rest of the outfit rumbling in through the afternoon and early evening hours. At daybreak they'd leapfrog forward again, deeper into the Star Plain, closer to whatever it was the Densonites wanted to hold. Sooner or later, the rebels and Fosters Infantry—a good outfit but not good enough for this job—were going to have to make a stand. And then the Regiment would go out for contact again, because they'd have run out of work on Thrush.

"She'll be in looking for you pretty soon, won't she, handsome?"

"Two bits to stay."

"Check. Sure, Danny-boy, you Romeos from Dunstan, you can pick up a slot anywhere, huh?"

A troop of combat cars whined past, headed for their position in the laager. Pritchard's hole card, a jack, flipped over. He swore, pushed in his hand. "I was folding anyway. And cut it out, will you? I didn't go looking for her. I didn't tell her to come back. And she may as well be the colonel for all my chance of putting her flat."

Wanatamba, the lean, black Terran who drove Fourteen, laughed and pointed. A gold-spangled skimmer was dropping from the east, tracked by the guns of two of the blowers on that side. Everybody knew what it was, though. Pritchard grimaced and stood. "Seems that's the game for me," he said.

"Hey, Danny," one of the men behind him called as he walked away. "Get a little extra for us, hey?"

The skimmer had landed in front of Command Central, at rest an earth-blended geodesic housing the staff and much of the commo hardware. Wearing a wrist-to-ankle sunsuit, yellow where it had tone, she was leaning on the plex windscreen. An officer in fatigues with unlatched body armor stepped out of the dome and did a double take. He must have recollected, though, because he trotted off toward a bunker before Danny reached the skimmer.

"Hey!" the girl called brightly. She looked about seventeen, her hair an unreal cascade of beryl copper over one shoulder. "We're going on a trip."

"Uh?"

The dome section flipped open again. Pritchard stiffened to attention when he saw the short, mustached figure who exited. "Peace, Colonel," the girl said.

"Peace, Sonna. You're such an ornament to a firebase that I'm thinking of putting you on requisition for our next contract."

Laughing cheerfully, the girl gestured toward the rigid sergeant. "I'm taking Danny to the Hamper Shrine this afternoon."

Pritchard reddened. "Sir, Sergeant-Commander Daniel Pritchard—"

"I know you, trooper," the colonel said with a friendly smile. "I've watched Two Star in action often enough, you know." His eyes were blue.

"Sir, I didn't request—that is . . ."

"And I also know there's small point in arguing with our girl here, hey, Sonna? Go see your shrine, soldier, and worse comes to worst, just throw your hands up and yell 'Exchange.' You can try Colonel Foster's rations for a week or two until we get this little business straightened out." The colonel winked, bowed low to Sonna, and reentered the dome.

"I don't figure it," Danny said as he settled into the passenger seat. The skimmer was built low and sleek as if a racer, though its top speed was probably under a hundred kays. Any more would have put too rapid a drain of the rechargeables packed into the decimeter-thick floor—a fusion unit would have doubled the flyer's bulk and added four hundred kilos right off the bat. At that, the speed and an operating altitude of thirty meters were more than enough for the tanker. You judge things by what you're used to, and the blower chief who found himself that far above the cold, hard ground—it could happen on a narrow switchback—had seen his last action.

While the wind whipped noisily about the open cockpit, the girl tended to her flying and ignored Danny's curiosity. It was a hop rather than a real flight, keeping over the same hill at all times and circling down to land scarcely a minute after takeoff. On a field of grass untouched by the recent fire rose the multi-tinted crystalline structure Pritchard had glimpsed during the assault. With a neat spin and a brief whine from the fans, the skimmer settled down.

Sonna grinned. Her sunsuit, opaquing completely in the direct light, blurred her outline in a dazzle of fluorescent saffron. "What don't you figure?"

"Well, ah . . ." Danny stumbled, his curiosity drawn between the girl and the building. "Well, the colonel isn't that, ah, easy to deal with usually. I mean . . ."

Her laugh bubbled in the sunshine. "Oh, it's because I'm an Advisor, I'm sure."

"Excuse?"

"An Advisor. You know, the . . . well, a representative. Of the government, if you want to put it that way."

"My Lord!" the soldier gasped. "But you're so young."

She frowned. "You really don't know much about us, do you?" she reflected.

"Umm, well, the briefing cubes mostly didn't deal with the friendlies this time because we'd be operating without support . . . Anything was going to look good after Emporion, that was for sure. All desert there—you should've heard the cheers when the colonel said that we'd lift."

She combed a hand back absently through her hair. It flowed like molten bronze. "You won on Emporion?" she asked.

"We could've," Danny explained, "even though it was really a Lord-stricken place, dust and fortified plateaus and lousy recce besides because the government had two operating spacers. But the Monarchists ran out of money after six months and that's one sure rule for Hammer's Slammers—no pay, no play. Colonel yanked their bond so fast their ears rang. And we hadn't orbited before offers started coming in."

"And you took ours and came to a place you didn't know much about," the girl mused. "Well, we didn't know much about you either."

"What do you need to know except we can bust anybody else in this business?" the soldier said with amusement. "Anybody, public or planet-tied. If you're worried about Foster, don't; he wouldn't back the freaks today, but when he has to, we'll eat him for breakfast."

"Has to?" the girl repeated in puzzlement. "But he always has to—the Densonites hired him, didn't they?"

Strategy was a long way from Danny's training, but the girl seemed not to know that. And besides, you couldn't spend seven years with the Slammers and not pick up some basics. "OK," he began, "Foster's boys'll fight, but they're not crazy. Trying to block our advance in open land like this'd be pure suicide—as those coppy freaks—pardon, didn't mean that— must've found out today. Foster likely got orders to support the civvies but refused. I know for a fact that his arty's better'n what we wiped up today, and those *planes* . . ."

"But his contract . . .?" Sonna queried.

"Sets out the objectives and says the outfit'll obey civie orders where it won't screw things up too bad," Danny said. "Standard form. The legal of it's different, but that's what it means."

The girl was nodding, eyes slitted, and in a low voice she quoted, " ' . . .except in circumstances where such directions would significantly increase the risks to be undergone by the party of the second part without corresponding military advantage.'" She looked full at Danny. "Very . . . interesting. When we hired your colonel, I don't think any of us understood that clause."

Danny blinked, out of his depth and aware of it. "Well, it doesn't matter really. I mean, the colonel didn't get his rep from ducking fights. It's just, well . . . say we're supposed to clear the Densonites off the, the Star Plain? Right?"

The girl shrugged.

"So that's what we'll do." Danny wiped his palms before gesturing with both hands. "But if your Advisors—"

"We Advisors," the girl corrected, smiling.

"Anyway," the tanker concluded, his enthusiasm chilled, "if you tell the colonel to fly the whole Regiment up to ten thousand and jump it out, he'll tell you to go piss up a rope. Sorry, he wouldn't say that. But you know what I mean. We know our job, don't worry."

"Yes, that's true," she said agreeably. "And we don't, and we can't understand it. We thought that—one to one, you know? —perhaps if I got to know you, one of you . . . They thought we might understand all of you a little."

The soldier frowned uncertainly.

"What we don't see," she finally said, "is how you—"

She caught herself. Touching her cold fingertips to the backs of the tanker's wrists, the girl continued, "Danny, you're a nice . . . you're not a, a sort of monster like we thought you all must be. If you'd been born of Thrush you'd have had a—different—education, you'd be more, forgive me, I don't mean it as an insult, sophisticated in some ways. That's all.

"But how can a nice person like you go out and kill?"

He rubbed his eyes, then laced together his long, brown fingers. "You . . . well, it's not like that. What I said the other night—look, the Slammers're a good outfit, the best, and I'm damned lucky to be with them. I do my job the best way I know. I'll keep on doing that. And if somebody gets killed, OK. My brother Jig stayed home and he's two years dead now. Tractor rolled on a wet field but Via, coulda been a tow-chain snapped or old age; doesn't matter. He wasn't going to live forever and neither is anybody else. And I haven't got any friends on the far end of the muzzle."

Her voice was very soft as she said, "Perhaps if I keep trying . . ."

Danny smiled. "Well, I don't mind," he lied, looking at the structure. "What is this place, anyhow?"

Close up, it had unsuspected detail. The sides were a hedge of glassy rods curving together to a series of peaks ten meters high. No finger-slim member was quite the thickness or color of any other, although the delicacy was subliminal in impact. In ground plan it was a complex oval thirty meters by ten, pierced by scores of doorways which were not closed off but were foggy to look at.

"What do you think of it?" the girl asked.

"Well, it's . . ." Danny temporized. A fragment of the briefing cubes returned to him. "It's one of the alien, the Gedel, artifacts, isn't it?"

"Of course," the girl agreed. "Seven hundred thousand years old, as far as we can judge. Only a world in stasis, like Thrush, would have let it survive the way it has. The walls are far tougher than they look, but seven hundred millennia of earthquakes and volcanoes . . ."

Danny stepped out of the skimmer and let his hand run across the building's cool surface. "Yeah, if they'd picked some place with a hotter core there wouldn't be much left but sand by now, would there?"

"Pick it? Thrush was their home," Sonna's voice rang smoothly behind him. "The Gedel chilled it themselves to make it suitable, to leave a signpost for the next races following the Way. We can't even imagine how they did it, but there's no question but that Thrush was normally tectonic up until the last million years or so."

"Via!" Danny breathed, turning his shocked face toward the girl. "No wonder those coppy fanatics wanted to control this place. Why, if they could figure out just a few of the Gedel tricks they'd . . . Lord, they wouldn't stop with Thrush, that's for sure."

"You still don't understand," the girl said. She took Danny by the hand and drew him toward the nearest of the misty doorways. "The Densonites have well, quirks that make them hard for the rest of us on Thrush to understand. But they would no more pervert Gedel wisdom to warfare than you would, oh, spit on your colonel. Come here."

She stepped into the fuzziness and disappeared. The tanker had no choice but to follow or break her grip; though, oddly, she was no longer clinging to him on the other side of the barrier. She was not even beside him in the large room. He was alone at the first of a line of tableaux, staring at a group of horribly inhuman creatures at play. Their sharp-edged faces, scale-dusted but more avian than reptile, stared enraptured at one of their number who hung in the air. The acrobat's bare, claw-tipped legs pointed 180 degrees apart, straight toward ground and sky. Pritchard bunked and moved on. The next scene was only a dazzle of sunlight in a glade whose foliage was redder than that of Thrush or Dunstan. There was something else, something wrong or strange about the tableau. Danny felt it, but his eyes could not explain.

Step by step, cautiously, Pritchard worked his way down the line of exhibits. Each was different, centered on a group of the alien bipeds or a ruddy, seemingly empty landscape that hinted unintelligibly. At first, Danny had noticed the eerie silence inside the hall. As he approached the far end he realized he was conscious of music of some sort, very crisp and distant. He laid his bare palm on the floor and found, as he had feared, that it did not vibrate in the least. He ran the last twenty steps to plunge out into the sunlight. Sonna still gripped his hand, and they stood outside the doorway they had entered.

The girl released him. "Isn't it incredible?" she asked, her expression bright. "And every one of the doorways leads to a different corridor—recreation there, agriculture in another, history—everything. A whole planet in that little building."

"That's what the Gedel looked like, huh?" Danny said. He shook his head to clear the strangeness from it.

"The Gedel? Oh, no," the girl replied, surprised again at his ignorance. "These were the folk we call the Hampers. No way to pronounce their own language, a man named Hamper found this site is all. But their homeworld was Kalinga IV, almost three days transit from Thrush. The shrine is here, we think, in the same relation to Starhome as Kalinga was to Thrush.

"You still don't understand," she concluded aloud, watching Danny's expression. She sat on the edge of the flyer, crossing her hands on the lap of her sunsuit. In the glitter thrown by the structure the fabric patterned oddly across her lithe torso. "The Gedel association—it wasn't an empire, couldn't have been. But to merge, a group ultimately needs a center, physical and intellectual. And Thrush and the Gedel were that for twenty races.

"And they achieved genuine unity, not just within one race but among all of them, each as strange to the others as any one of them would have been to man, to us. The . . . power that gave them, over themselves as well as the universe, was incredible. This—even Starhome itself—is such a tiny part of what could be achieved by perfect peace and empathy."

Danny looked at the crystal dome and shivered at what it had done to him. "Look," he said, "peace is just great if the universe cooperates. I don't mean just my line of work, but it doesn't happen that way in the real world. There's no peace spending your life beating wheat out of Dunstan, not like I'd call peace. And what's happened to the Gedel and their buddies for the last half million years or so if things were so great?"

"We can't even imagine what happened to them," Sonna explained gently, "but it wasn't the disaster you imagine. When they reached what they wanted, they set up this, Starhome, the other eighteen shrines as . . . monuments. And then they went away, all together. But they're not wholly gone, even from here, you know. Didn't you feel them in the background inside, laughing with you?"

"I . . ." Danny attempted. He moved, less toward the skimmer than away from the massive crystal behind him. "Yeah, there was something. That's what you're fighting for?"

You couldn't see the laager from where the skimmer rested, but Danny could imagine the silvery glitter of tanks and combat cars between the sky and the raw yellow grass. Her eyes fixed on the same stretch of horizon, the girl said, "Someday men will be able to walk through Starhome and understand. You can't live on Thrush without feeling the impact of the Gedel. That impact has . . . warped, perhaps, the Densonites. They have some beliefs about the Gedel that most of us don't agree with. And they're actually willing to use force to prevent the artifacts from being defiled by anyone who doesn't believe as they do."

"Well, you people do a better job of using force," Danny said. His mind braced itself on its memory of the Regiment's prickly hedgehog.

"Oh, not us!" the girl gasped.

Suddenly angry, the tanker gestured toward the unseen firebase. "Not you? The Densonites don't pay us. And if force isn't what happened to those silly bastards today when our counter-battery hit them, I'd like to know what is."

She looked at him in a way that, despite her previous curiosity, was new to him. "There's much that I'll have to discuss with the other Advisors," she said after a long pause. "And I don't know that it will stop with us, we'll have to put out the call to everyone, the Densonites as well if they will come." Her eyes caught Danny's squarely again. "We acted with little time for deliberation when the Densonites hired Colonel Foster and turned all the other pilgrims out of the Star Plain. And we acted in an area beyond our practice— thank the Lord! The key to understanding the Gedel and joining them, Lord willing and the Way being short, is Starhome. And nothing that blocks any man, all men, from Starhome can be . . . tolerated. But with what we've learned since . . . well, we have other things to take into account."

She broke off, tossed her stunning hair. In the flat evening sunlight her garment had paled to translucence. The late rays licked her body red and orange. "But now I'd better get you back to your colonel." She slipped into the skimmer.

Danny boarded without hesitation. After the Gedel building, the transparent skimmer felt almost comfortable. "Back to my tank," he corrected lightly. "Colonel may not care where I am, but he damn well cares if Two Star is combat ready." The sudden rush of air cut off thought of further conversation, and though Sonna smiled as she landed Danny beside his blower, there was a blankness in her expression that indicated her thoughts were far away.

Hell with her, Danny thought. His last night in the Rec Center on Emporion seemed a long time in the past.

At three in the morning the Regiment was almost two hundred kilometers from the camp they had abandoned at midnight. There had been no warning, only the low hoot of the siren followed by the colonel's voice rasping from every man's lapel speaker, "Mount up and move, boys. Order seven, and your guides are set." It might have loomed before another outfit as a sudden catastrophe. After docking one trip with the Slammers, though, a greenie learned that everything not secured to his blower had better be secured to him. Colonel Hammer thought an armored regiment's firepower was less of an asset than its mobility. He used the latter to the full with ten preset orders of march and in-motion recharging for the infantry skimmers, juicing from the tanks and combat cars.

Four pongoes were jumpered to Two Star when Foster's outpost sprang its ambush.

The lead combat car, half a kay ahead, bloomed in a huge white ball that flooded the photon amplifiers of Danny's goggles. The buzzbomb's hollow detonation followed a moment later while the tanker, cursing, simultaneously switched to infrared and swung his turret left at max advance. He ignored the head of the column, where the heated-air thump of powerguns merged with the crackle of mines blasted to either side by the combat cars; that was somebody else's responsibility. He ignored the two infantrymen wired to his tank's port side as well. If they knew their business, they'd drop the jumpers and flit for Two Star's blind side as swiftly as Danny could spin his heavy turret. If not, well, you don't have time for niceness when somebody's firing shaped charges at you.

"Damp that ground-sender!" Central snapped to the lead elements. Too quickly to be a response to the command, the grass trembled under the impact of a delay-fused rocket punching down toward the computed location of the enemy's subsurface signaling. The Regiment must have rolled directly over an outpost, either through horrendously bad luck or because Foster had sewn his vedettes very thickly.

The firing stopped. The column had never slowed and Michael, first of the heavy companies behind the screen of combat cars, fanned the grass fires set by the hoses. Pritchard scanned the area of the firefight as Two Star rumbled through it in turn. The antipersonnel charges had dimpled the ground with shrapnel, easily identifiable among the glassy scars left by the powerguns. In the center of a great vitrified blotch lay a left arm and a few scraps of gray coverall. Nearby was the plastic hilt of a buzzbomb launcher. The other vedette had presumably stayed on the commo in his covered foxhole until the penetrator had scattered it and him over the landscape. If there had been a third bunker, it escaped notice by Two Star's echo sounders.

"Move it out, up front," Central demanded. "This cuts our margin."

The burned-out combat car swept back into obscurity as Kowie put on speed. The frontal surfaces had collapsed inward from the heat, leaving the driver and blower chief as husks of carbon. There was no sign of the wing gunners. Perhaps they had been far enough back and clear of the spurt of directed radiance to escape. The ammo canister of the port tribarrel had flash-ignited, though, and it was more likely that the men were wasted on the floor of the vehicle.

Another hundred and fifty kays to go, and now Foster and the Densonites knew they were coming.

There were no further ambushes to break the lightless monotony of gently rolling grassland. Pritchard took occasional sips of water and ate half a tube of protein ration. He started to fling the tube aside, then thought of the metal detectors on following units. He dropped it between his feet instead.

The metal-pale sun was thrusting the Regiment's shadow in long fingers up the final hillside when Central spoke again. You could tell it was the colonel himself sending. "Everybody freeze but Beta-First, Beta-First proceed in column up the rise and in. Keep your intervals, boys, and don't try to bite off too much. Last data we got was Foster had his antiaircraft company with infantry support holding the target. Maybe they pulled out when we knocked on the door tonight, maybe they got reinforced. So take it easy—and don't bust up anything you don't have to."

Pritchard dropped his seat back inside the turret. There was nothing to be seen from the hatch but the monochrome sunrise and armored vehicles grounded on the yellow background. Inside, the three vision blocks gave greater variety. One was the constant 360 degrees display, better than normal eyesight according to the designers because the blower chief could see all around the tank without turning his head. Danny didn't care for it. Images were squeezed a good deal horizontally. Shapes weren't quite what you expected, so you didn't react quite as fast; and that was a good recipe for a dead trooper. The screen above the three-sixty was variable in light sensitivity and in magnification, useful for special illumination and first-shot hits.

The bottom screen was the remote rig; Pritchard dialed it for the forward receptors of Beta-First-Three. It was strange to watch the images of the two leading combat cars trembling as they crested the hill, yet feel Two Star as stable as 170 tonnes can be when grounded.

"Nothing moving," the platoon leader reported unnecessarily. Central had remote circuits, too, as well as the satellite net to depend on.

The screen lurched as the blower Danny was slaved to boosted its fans to level the downgrade. Dust plumed from the leading cars, weaving across a sky that was almost fully light. At an unheard command, the platoon turned up the wick in unison and let the cars hurtle straight toward the target's central corridor. It must have helped, because Foster's gunners caught only one car when they loosed the first blast through their camoufl age.

The second car blurred in a mist of vaporized armor plate. Incredibly, the right wing gunner shot back. The deadly flame-lash of his hose was pale against the richer color of the hostile fire. Foster had sited his calliopes, massive 3cm guns whose nine fixed barrels fired extra-length charges. Danny had never seen a combat car turned into Swiss cheese faster than the one now spiked on the muzzles of a pair of the heavy guns.

Gray-suited figures were darting from cover as if the cars' automatics were harmless for being outclassed. The damaged blower nosed into the ground. Its driver leaped out, running for the lead car which had spun on its axis and was hosing blue-green fire in three directions. One of Foster's troops raised upright, loosing a buzzbomb at the wreckage of the grounded car. The left side of the vehicle flapped like a batwing as it sailed across Danny's field of view. The concussion knocked down the running man. He rose to his knees, jumped for a handhold as the lead car accelerated past him. As he swung himself aboard, two buzzbombs hit the blower simultaneously. It bloomed with joined skullcaps of pearl and bone.

Pritchard was swearing softly. He had switched to a stern pickup already, and the tumbled wreckage in it was bouncing, fading swiftly. Shots twinkled briefly as the four escaping blowers dropped over the ridge.

"In column ahead," said the colonel grimly, "Hotel, Kitchen, Michael. Button up and hose 'em out, you know the drill."

And then something went wrong. "Are you insane?" the radio marveled, and Danny recognized that voice, too. "I forbid you!"

"You can't. Somebody get her out of here."

"Your contract is over, finished, do you hear? Heavenly Way, we'll all become Densonites if we must. This horror must end!"

"Not yet. You don't see—"

"I've seen too—" The shouted words cut off .

"So we let Foster give us a bloody nose and back off? That's what you want? But it's bigger than what you want now, sister, it's the whole Regiment. It's never bidding another contract without some-body saying, 'Hey, they got sandbagged on Thrush, didn't they?' And nobody remembering that Foster figured the civvies would chill us—and he was right. Don't you see? They killed my boys, and now they're going to pay the bill.

"Tank Section, execute! Dig 'em out, panzers!"

Danny palmed the panic bar, dropping the seat and locking the hatch over it. The rushing-air snarl of the fans was deadened by the armor, but a hot bearing somewhere filled the compartment with its high keening. Two Star hurdled the ridge. Its whole horizon flared with crystal dancing and scattering in sunlight and the reflected glory of automatic weapons firing from its shelter. Starhome was immensely larger than Danny had expected.

A boulevard twenty meters wide divided two ranks of glassy buildings, any one of which, towers and pavilions, stood larger than the shrine Danny had seen the previous day. At a kilometer's distance it was a coruscating unity of parts as similar as the strands of a silken rope. Danny rapped up the magnification and saw the details spring out; rods woven into columns that streaked skyward a hundred meters; translucent sheets formed of myriads of pinhead beads, each one glowing a color as different from the rest as one star is from the remainder of those seen on a moonless night; a spiral column, free-standing and the thickness of a woman's wrist, that pulsed slowly through the spectrum as it climbed almost out of sight. All the structures seemed to front on the central corridor, with the buildings on either side welded together by tracery mazes, porticoes, arcades—a thousand different plates and poles of glass.

A dashed cyan line joined the base of an upswept web of color to the tank. Two Star's hull thudded to the shock of vaporizing metal. The stabilizer locked the blower's pitching out of Danny's sight picture. He swung the glowing orange bead onto the source of fire and kicked the pedal. The air rang like a carillon as the whole glassy facade sagged, then avalanched into the street. There was a shock of heat in the closed battle compartment as the breech flicked open and belched out the spent case. The plastic hissed on the floor, outgassing horribly while the air conditioning strained to clear the chamber. Danny ignored the stench, nudged his sights onto the onrushing splendor of the second structure on the right of the corridor. The breech of the big powergun slapped again and again, recharging instantly as the tanker worked the foot trip.

Blue-green lightning scattered between the walls as if the full power of each bolt was flashing the length of the corridor. Two Star bellowed in on the wake of its fire, and crystal flurried under the fans. Kowie leveled their stroke slightly, cutting speed by a fraction but lifting the tank higher above the abrasive litter. The draft hurled glittering shards across the corridor, arcs of cold fire in the light of Two Star's gun and those of the blowers following. Men in gray were running from their hiding places to avoid the sliding crystal masses, the iridescent rain that pattered on the upper surfaces of the tanks but smashed jaggedly through the infantry's body armor.

Danny set his left thumb to rotate the turret counterclockwise, held the gun-switch down with his foot. The remaining sixteen rounds of his basic load blasted down the right half of Starhome, spread by the blower's forward motion and the turret swing. The compartment was gray with fumes. Danny slammed the hatch open and leaned out. His hands went to the 2cm as naturally as a calf turns to milk. The wind was cold on his face. Kowie slewed the blower left to avoid the glassy wave that slashed into the corridor from one of the blasted structures. The scintillance halted, then ground a little further as something gave way inside the pile.

A soldier in gray stepped from an untouched archway to the left. The buzzbomb on his shoulder was the size of a landing vessel as it swung directly at Danny. The tribarrel seemed to traverse with glacial slowness. It was too slow. Danny saw the brief flash as the rocket leaped from the shoulder of the other mercenary. It whirred over Two Star and the sergeant, exploded cataclysmically against a spike of Starhome still rising on the other side.

The infantryman tossed the launcher tube aside. He froze, his arms spread wide, and shouted, "Exchange!"

"Exchange yourself, mother!" Danny screamed back white-faced. He triggered his hose. The gray torso exploded. The body fell backward in a mist of blood, chest and body armor torn open by four hits that shriveled bones and turned fluids to steam.

"Hard left and goose it, Kowie," the sergeant demanded. He slapped the panic bar again. As the hatch clanged shut over his head, Danny caught a momentary glimpse of the vision blocks, three soldiers with powerguns leaping out of the same towering structure from which the rocketeer had come. Their faces were blankly incredulous as they saw the huge blower swinging toward them at full power. The walls flexed briefly under the impact of the tank's frontal slope, but the filigree was eggshell thin. The structure disintegrated, lurching toward the corridor while Two Star plowed forward within it. A thousand images kaleidoscoped in Danny's skull, sparkling within the wind-chime dissonance of the falling tower.

The fans screamed as part of the structure's mass collapsed onto Two Star. Kowie rocked the tank, raising it like a submarine through a sea of ravaged glass. The gentle, green-furred humanoids faded from Danny's mind. He threw the hatch open. Kowie gunned the fans, reversing the blower in a polychrome shower. Several tanks had moved ahead of Two Star, nearing the far end of the corridor. Gray-uniformed soldiers straggled from the remaining structures, hands empty, eyes fixed on the ground. There was very little firing. Kowie edged into the column and followed the third tank into the laager forming on the other side of Starhome. Pritchard was drained. His throat was dry, but he knew from past experience that he would vomit if he swallowed even a mouthful of water before his muscles stopped trembling. The blower rested with its skirts on the ground, its fans purring gently as they idled to a halt.

Kowie climbed out of the driver's hatch, moving stiffly. He had a powergun in his hand, a pistol he always carried for moral support. Two Star's bow compartment was frequently nearer the enemy than anything else in Hammer's Slammers.

Several towers still stood in the wreckage of Starhome. The nearest one wavered from orange to red and back in the full blaze of sunlight. Danny watched it in the iridium mirror of his tank's deck, the outline muted by the hatch-work of crystal etching on the metal.

Kowie shot off-hand. Danny looked up in irritation. The driver shot again, his light charge having no discernible effect on the structure.

"Shut it off," Danny croaked. "These're shrines."

The ground where Starhome had stood blazed like the floor of Hell.

THE CHURCH OF
THE LORD'S UNIVERSE

Perhaps the most surprising thing about the faith that men took to the stars—and vice versa—was that it appeared to differ so little from the liturgical protestantism of the nineteenth and twentieth centuries. Indeed, services of the Church of the Lord's Universe— almost always, except by Unitarians, corrupted to "Universal Church"—so resembled those of a high-flying Anglican parish of 1920 that a visitor from the past would have been hard put to believe that he was watching a sect as extreme in its own way as the Society for Krishna Consciousness was in its.

The Church of the Lord's Universe was officially launched in 1985 in Minneapolis, Minnesota, by the merger of 230 existing protestant congregations—Methodist, Presbyterian, Episcopalian, and Lutheran. In part the new church was a revolt against the extreme fundamentalism peaking at that time. The Universalists sought converts vigorously from the start. Their liturgy obviously attempted to recapture the traditional beauty of Christianity's greatest age, but there is reason to believe that the extensive use of Latin in the service was part of a design to avoid giving doctrinal offense as well. Anyone who has attended both Presbyterian and Methodist services has felt uneasiness at the line, "Forgive us our debts/trespasses . . ." St. Jerome's Latin version of the Lord's Prayer flows smoothly and unnoticed from the tongue of one raised in either sect.

But the Church of the Lord's Universe had a mission beyond the entertainment of its congregations for an hour every Sunday. The priests and laity alike preached the salvation of Mankind through His works. To Universalists, however, the means and the end were both secular. The Church taught that Man must reach the stars and there, among infinite expanses, find room to live in peace. This temporal paradise was one which could be grasped by all men. It did not detract from spiritual hopes; but heaven is in the hands of the Lord, while the stars were not beyond Man's own strivings.

The Doctrine of Salvation through the Stars—it was never labeled so bluntly in Universalist writings, but the peevish epithet bestowed by a Baptist theologian was not inaccurate—gave the Church of the Lord's Universe a dynamism unknown to the Christian center since the days of Archbishop Laud. It was a naive doctrine, of course. Neither the stars nor anything else brought peace to Man; but realists did not bring men to the stars, either, while the hopeful romantics of the Universal Church certainly helped.

The Universalist credo was expressed most clearly in the *Book of the Way*, a slim volume commissioned at the First Consensus and adopted after numerous emendations by the Tenth. The *Book of the Way* never officially replaced the Bible, but the committee of laymen which framed it struck a chord in the hearts of all Universalists. Despite its heavily Eastern leanings (including suggestions of reincarnation), the *Book* spoke in an idiom intelligible and profoundly moving to men and women who in another milieu would have been Technocrats.

While the new faith appealed to men and women everywhere, it by no means appealed to every man and woman. By their uncompromising refusal to abandon future dreams to cope with present disasters—the famines, pollution, and pogroms of everyday— the Universalists faced frequent hatred. During the Food Riots of 2039, three hundred Universalists were ceremonially murdered and eaten in a packed amphitheater in Dakkah, and there were other martyrs as well. But the survivors and their faith drove on. Their ranks swelled every time catastrophe proved Man was incapable of solving his problems on Earth alone.

Thus, when Man did reach the stars, the ships were crewed in large measure by Universalists. Those who had prayed for, worked for, and even sworn by the Way of the Stars, *Via Stellarum*, were certain to be among the first treading it. On Earth, the Church of the Lord's Universe had been a vocal minority; in the colonies spreading like a bacterial culture through the galaxy, Universalists were frequently in the majority.

There were changes. Inevitably, fragmentation followed success as centuries and the high cost of interstellar communication made each congregation a separate entity. But the basic thrust of the Church, present peace and safety for Mankind, remained even when reality diluted it to lip service or less. Mercenaries were recruited mostly from rural cultures which were used to privation—and steeped in religion as well. Occasionally a trooper might feel uneasy as he swore, "Via!" for the Way had been a way of peace.

But mercs swore by blood and the martyrs as well; and few had better knowledge of either blood or innocent victims than the gunmen of the mercenary companies.

BUT LOYAL TO HIS OWN

"It just blew up. Hammer and his men knew but they didn't say a thing," blurted the young captain as he looked past Secretary Tromp, his gaze compelled toward the milky noonday sky. It was not the sky of Friesland and that bothered Captain Stilchey almost as much as his near-death in the ambush an hour before. "He's insane! They all are."

"Others have said so," the councillor stated with the heavy ambiguity of an oracle replying to an ill-phrased question. Tromp's height was short of two meters by less than a hand's-breadth, and he was broad in proportion. That size and the generally dull look on his face caused some visitors looking for Friesland's highest civil servant to believe they had surprised a retired policeman of some sort sitting at the desk of the Secretary to the Council of State.

Tromp did not always disabuse them.

Now his great left hand expanded over the grizzled fringe of hair remaining at the base of his skull. "Tell me about the ambush," he directed.

"He didn't make any trouble about coming to you here at the port," Stilchey said, for a moment watching his fingers writhe together rather than look at his superior. He glanced up. "Have you met Hammer?"

"No, I kept in the background when plans for the Auxiliary Regiment were drafted. I've seen his picture, of course."

"Not the same," the captain replied, beginning to talk very quickly. "He's not big but he, he moves, he's alive and it's like every time he speaks he's training a gun on you, waiting for you to slip. But he came along, no trouble— only he said we'd go with a platoon of combat cars instead of flying back, he wanted to check road security between Southport and the firebase where we were. I said sure, a couple hours wasn't crucial. . . ."

Tromp nodded. "Well done," he said. "Hammer's cooperation is very important if this . . . business is to be concluded smoothly. And"—here the councillor's face hardened without any noticeable shift of muscles—"the last thing we wanted was for the good colonel to become concerned while he was still with his troops. He is not a stupid man."

Gratification played about the edges of Stilchey's mouth, but the conversation had cycled the captain's mind back closer to the blast of cyan fire. His stomach began to spin. "There were six vehicles in the patrol, all but the second one open combat cars. That was a command car, same chassis and ground-effect curtain, but enclosed, you see? Better commo gear and an air-conditioned passenger compartment. I started toward it but Hammer said, no, I was to get in the next one with him and Joachim."

Stilchey coughed, halted. "That Joachim's here with him now; he calls him his aide. The bastard's queer, he tried to make me when I flew out. . . ."

Puzzlement. "Colonel Hammer is homosexual, Captain? Or his aide, or. . . ?"

"No, Via! Him, not the—I don't know. Via, maybe him, too. The bastard scares me, he really does."

To statesmen patience is a tool; it is a palpable thing that can grind necessary information out of a young man whose aristocratic lineage and sparkling uniform have suddenly ceased to armor him against the universe. "The ambush, Captain," Tromp pressed stolidly.

With a visible effort, Stilchey regained the thread of his narrative.

"Joachim drove. Hammer and I were in the back along with a noncom from Curwin—Worzer, his name was. He and Joachim threw dice for who had to drive. The road was supposed to be clear but Hammer made me put on body armor. I thought it was cop, you know—make the staffer get hot and dusty.

"Via," he swore again, but softly this time. "I was at the left-side powergun but I wasn't paying much attention; nothing really to pay attention to. Hammer was on the radio a lot, but my helmet only had intercom so I didn't know what he was saying. The road was stabilized earth, just a gray line through hectares of those funny blue plants you see all over here, the ones with the fat leaves."

"Bluebrights," the older man said dryly. "Melpomone's only export; as you would know from the briefing cubes you were issued in transit, I should think."

"Would the Lord I'd never *heard* of this damned place!" Stilchey blazed back. His family controlled Karob Trading; no civil servant—not even Tromp, the Gray Eminence behind the Congress of the Republic—could cow him. But he was a soldier, too, and after a moment he continued: "Bluebrights in rows, waist high and ugly, and beyond that nothing but the soil blowing away as we passed.

"We were half an hour out from the firebase, maybe half the way to here. The ground was dimpled with frost heaves. A little copse was in sight ahead of us, trees ten, fifteen meters high. Hammer had the forward gun, and on the intercom he said, 'Want to double the bet, Blacky?' Then they armed their guns—I didn't know why—and Worzer said, 'I still think they'll be in the draw two kays south, but I won't take any more of your money.' They were laughing and I thought they were going to just . . . clear the guns, you know?"

The captain closed his eyes. He remembered how they had stared at him, two bulging circles and the hollow of his screaming mouth below them, reflected on the polished floorplate of the combat car. "The command car blew up just as we entered the trees. There was a flash like the sun and it *ate* the back half of the car, armor and all. The front flipped over and over into the trees, and the air *stank* with metal. Joachim laid us sideways to follow the part the mine had left, cutting in right behind when it hit a tree and stopped. The driver raised his head out of the hatch and maybe he could have got clear himself . . . but Hammer jumped off our deck to his and jerked him out, yanked him up in his armor as small as he is. Then they were back in our car. They were firing, everybody was firing, and we turned right, into the trees, into the guns."

"There were Mel troops in the grove, then?" Tromp asked.

"Must have been," Stilchey replied. He looked straight at the older man and said, very simply, "I was behind the bulkhead. Maybe if I'd known what to expect . . . The other driver was at my gun, they didn't need me." Stilchey swallowed once, continued: "Some shots hit on my side. They didn't come through, but they made the whole car ring. The empties kept spattering me, and the car was bouncing, jumping downed trees. Everything seemed to be on fire. We cleared the grove into another field of bluebrights. Shells from the firebase were already landing in the trees; the place was targeted. And Worzer pulled off his helmet and he spat and said, 'Cold meat, Colonel, you couldn't a called it better.' Via!"

"Well, it does sound like they reacted well to the ambush," Tromp admitted, puzzled because nothing Stilchey had told him explained the captain's fear and hatred of Hammer and his men.

"Nice extempore response, hey?" the aide suggested with bitter irony. "Only Hammer, seeing I didn't know what Worzer meant, turned to me, and said, 'We let the Mels get word that me and Secretary Tromp would take a convoy to Southport this morning. They still had fifty or so regulars here in Region 4 claiming to be an infantry battalion, and it looked like a good time to flush them for good and all.'"

Tromp said nothing. He spread his hands carefully on the citron-yellow of his desktop and seemed to be fixedly studying the contrast. Stilchey waited for a response. At last he said, "I don't like being used for bait, Secretary. And what if you'd decided to go out to the firebase yourself? I was all right for a stand-in, but do you think Hammer would have cared if you were there in person? He won't let anything stand in his way."

"Colonel Hammer does seem to have some unconventional attitudes," Tromp agreed. A bleak smile edged his voice as he continued: "But at that, it's rather fortunate that he brought a platoon in with him. We can begin the demobilization of his vaunted Slammers with them."

The dome of the Starport Lounge capped Southport's hundred-meter hotel tower. Its vitril panels were seamless and of the same refractive index as the atmosphere. As a tactician, Hammer was fascinated with the view: it swept beyond the equipment-thronged spaceport and over the shimmering billows of bluebright, to the mountains of the Crescent almost twenty kilometers away. But tankers' blood has in it a turtle component that is more comfortable on the ground than above it, and the little officer felt claws on his intestines as he looked out.

No similar discomfort seemed to be disturbing the other men in the room, all in the black and silver of the Guards of the Republic, though in name they were armor officers. "Had a bit of action today, Colonel?" said a cheerful, fit-looking major. Hammer did not remember him even though a year ago he had been Second in Command of the Guards.

"Umm, a skirmish," Hammer said as he turned. The Guardsman held out to him one of the two thimble-sized crystals he carried. In the heart of each flickered an azure fire. "Why, thank you—" the major's name was patterned in the silver highlights below his left lapel "—Mestern."

"No doubt you have seen much worse with your mercenaries, eh, Colonel?" a voice called mockingly from across the room.

Karl August Raeder lounged in imperial state in the midst of a dozen admiring junior officers. He had been the executive officer of the Guards for the past year— ever since Hammer took command of the foreign regiment raised to smash the scattered units of the Army of Melpomone.

"Mercenaries, Karl?" Hammer repeated. A threat rasped through the surface mildness of his tone. "Yes, they cash their paychecks. There may be a few others in this room who do, hey?"

"Oh . . ." someone murmured in the sudden quiet, but there was no way to tell what he meant by it. Raeder did not move. The blood had drawn back to yellow his smooth tan, and where the cushions had borne his languid hands they now were dimpled cruelly. Two men in the lounge had reached officer status in the Guards without enormous family wealth behind them. Hammer was one, Raeder was the other.

He strained at a breath. In build, he and Hammer were not dissimilar: the latter brown-haired and somewhat shorter, a trifle more of the hourglass in his shoulders and waist; Raeder blond and trim, slender in a rapier sort of way and quite as deadly. His uniform of natural silk and leather was in odd contrast to Hammer's khaki battledress, but there was nothing of fop or sloven in either man.

"Pardon," the Guardsman said, "I would not have thought this a company in which one need explain patriotism; there are men who fight for their homelands, and then there are the dregs, the gutter-sweepings of a galaxy, who fight for the same reason they pimped and sold themselves before our government—let me finish, please!" (though only Hammer's smile had moved) "—misguidedly, I submit, offered them more money to do what Friesland citizens could have done better!"

"My boys are better citizens than some born on Friesland who stayed there wiping their butts—"

"A soldier goes where he is ordered!" Raeder was standing.

"A *soldier*—"

Dead silence. Hammer's sentence broke like an axed cord. He looked about the lounge at the twenty-odd men, most of them his ex-comrades and all, like Raeder, men who had thought him mad to post out of the Guards for the sake of a combat command. Hammer laughed. He inverted the stim cone on the inside of his wrist and said approvingly, "Quite a view from up here. If it weren't such a good target, you could make it your operations center." As if in the midst of a normal conversation, he faced back toward the exterior and added, "By the way, what sort of operations are you expecting? I would have said the fighting here was pretty well over, and I'd be surprised at the government sending the Guards in for garrison duty."

The whispering that had begun when Hammer turned was stilled again. It was Raeder who cleared his throat and said in a tone between triumph and embarrassment, "Colonel Rijsdal may know. He . . . he has remained in his quarters since we landed." Rijsdal had not had a sober day in the past three years since he had acceded to an enormous estate on Friesland. "No doubt we are to provide proper, ah, background for such official pronouncements as the Secretary will make to the populace."

Hammer nodded absently as if he believed the black and silver of a parade regiment would over-awe the Mels more effectively than could his own scarred killers, the men who had rammed Frisian suzerainty down Mel throats After twelve regiments of regulars had tried and failed. But the Guards were impressively equipped . . . and all their gear had been landed.

Five hundred worlds had imported bluebright leaves, with most of the tonnage moving through Southport. The handful of Frisian vessels scattered on the field looked lost, but traffic would pick up now that danger was over. For the moment, hundreds of Guard vehicles gave it a specious life. In the broad wedge of his vision Hammer could see two rocket batteries positioned as neatly as chess pieces on the huge playing surface. The center of each cluster was an ammunition hauler, low and broad-chassied. Within their thin armor sheetings were the racks of 150mm shells; everything from armor-piercing rounds with a second stage to accelerate them before impact, to antipersonnel cases loaded with hundreds of separate bomblets. The haulers rested on the field; no attempt had been made to dig them in.

The six howitzers of each battery were sited about their munitions in a regular hexagon, each joined to its hauler by the narrow strip of a conveyor. In action the hogs could kick out shells at five-second intervals, so the basic load of twenty rounds carried by the howitzer itself needed instant replenishment from the hauler's store. Their stubby gun-tubes gave them guidance and an initial boost, but most of the acceleration came beyond the muzzle. They looked grim and effective; still, it nagged Hammer to see that nobody had bothered to defilade them.

"A pretty sight," said Mestern. Conversation in the lounge was back to a normal level.

Hammer squeezed the last of his stim cone into the veins of his wrist and let the cool shudder pass through him before saying, "The Republic buys the best, and that's the only way to go when a battle's hanging on it. Not that you don't need good crews to man the gear."

Mestern pointed beyond the howitzers, toward a wide-spaced ring of gun trucks. "Latest thing in arty defense," he said. "Each of those cars mounts an eight-barrel powergun, only 30mm but they're high-intensity. They've got curst near the range of a tank's 200—thirty, forty kilometers if you've that long a sight line. With our radar hook-up and the satellite, we can just about detonate a shell as soon as it comes over the horizon."

"Nice theory," Hammer agreed. "I doubt you can swing the rig fast enough to catch the first salvo, but maybe placing them every ten degrees like that . . . where you've got the terrain to allow it. The Mels never had arty worth cop anyway, of course."

He paused, not sure he wanted to comment further. The grounded tanks and combat cars of the regiment were in an even perimeter at the edge of the circular field. Their dull iridium armor was in evident contrast to the ocher soil on which they rested. "You really ought to have dug in," Hammer said at last.

"Oh, the field's been stabilized to two meters down," the major protested innocently, "and I don't think the Mels are much of a threat now."

Hammer shook his head in irritation. "Lord!" he snorted. "The Mels aren't any threat at all after this morning. But just on general principles, when you set up in a war zone—*any* war zone—you set up as if you were going to be hit. Via, you may as well park your cars on Friesland for all the good they'd do if it dropped in the pot."

"The good colonel has been away from soldiers too long," whipped Raeder savagely. "Major Mestern, would you care to enlighten him as to how operations can be conducted by a real regiment—even though a gutter militia would be incapable of doing so?"

"I don't . . . think . . ." Mestern stuttered in embarrassment. His fingers twiddled an empty stim cone.

"Very well, then I will," the blond XO snapped. Hammer was facing him again. This time the two men were within arm's length. "The Regiment of Guards is using satellite reconnaissance, Colonel," Raeder announced sneeringly. "The same system in operation when you were in charge here, but we are *using* it, you see."

"We used it. We—"

"Pardon, Colonel, permit me to explain and there will be fewer needless questions."

Hammer relaxed with a smile. There was a tiger's certainty behind its humor. "No, your pardon. Continue."

Hammer had killed two men in semi-legal duels fought on Friesland's moon. Raeder chuckled, unconcerned with his rival's sudden mildness. "So," he continued, "no Mel force could approach without being instantly sighted."

He stared at Hammer, who said nothing. If the Guardsman wanted to believe no produce truck could drop a Mel platoon into bunkers dug by a harvesting crew—spotting the activity was no problem, interpreting it, though—well, it didn't matter now. But it proved again what Hammer had known since before he was landed, that a lack of common sense was what had so hamstrung the regular army that his Slammers had to be formed.

Of course, "common sense" meant to Hammer doing what was necessary to complete a task. And that sometimes created problems of its own.

"Our howitzers can shatter them ninety kilometers distant," Raeder lectured on, "and our tanks can pierce all but the heaviest armor at line of sight, Colonel." He gestured arrogantly toward the skyline behind Hammer. "Anything that can be seen can be destroyed."

"Yeah, it's always a mistake to underrate technology," agreed the man in khaki.

"So," Raeder said with a crisp nod. "It is possible to be quite efficient without being—" his eyes raked Hammers stained, worn coveralls "—shoddy. When we hold the review tomorrow, it will be interesting to consider your . . . force . . . beside the Guard."

"Via, only two of my boys are in," Hammer said, "though for slickness I'd bet Joachim against anybody you've got." He looked disinterestedly at the drink dispenser. "We'll all be back in the field, as soon as I see what Tromp wants. We've got a clean-up operation mounted in the Crescent."

"There is a platoon present now," the Guardsman snapped. "It will remain, as you will remain, until you receive other orders."

Hammer walked away without answering. Bigger men silently moved aside, clearing a path to the dispenser. Raeder locked his lips, murder-tense; but a bustle at the central dropshaft caused him to spin around. His own aide, a fifteen-year-old scion of his wife's house, had emerged when the column dilated. Rather than use the PA system built into the lounge before it was commandeered as an officer's club, messages were relayed through aides waiting on the floor below. Raeder's boy carried a small flag bearing the hollow rectangle of Raeder's rank, his ticket to enter the lounge and to set him apart from the officers. The boy might well be noble, but as yet he did not have a commission. He was to be made to remember it.

He whispered with animation into Raeder's ear, his own eyes open and fixed on the mercenary officer. Hammer ignored them both, talking idly as he blended another stim cone into his blood. The blond man's face slowly took on an expression of ruddy, mottled fury.

"Hammer!"

"The next time you determine where my boys will be, Colonel Raeder, I recommend that you ask me about it."

"You traitorous scum!" Raeder blazed, utterly beyond curbing his anger. "I closed the perimeter to everyone, *everyone!* And you bull your way through my guards, get them to pass—"

"Pass *my* men, Lieutenant Colonel!" Hammer blasted as if he were shouting orders through the howling fans of a tank. All the tension of the former confrontation shuddered in the air again. Hammer was as set and grim as one of his war-cars.

Raeder raised a clenched fist.

"Touch me and I'll shoot you where you stand," the mercenary said, and he had no need to raise his voice for emphasis. As if only Raeder and not the roomful of officers as well was listening, he said, "You give what orders you please, but I've still got an independent command. As of this moment. That platoon is blocking a pass in the Crescent, because that's what I want it to do, not sit around trying to polish away bullet scars because some cop-head thinks that's a better idea than fighting."

His body still as a gravestone, Raeder spoke. "*Now* you've got a command," he said thickly.

The wing of violence lifted from the lounge. Given time to consider, every man there knew that the battle was in other hands than Raeder's now—and that it would be fought very soon.

The dropshaft hissed again.

Joachim Steuben's dress was identical in design to his colonel's, but was in every other particular far superior. The khaki was unstained, the waist-belt genuine leather, polished to a rich chestnut sheen, and the coveralls themselves tapered to follow the lines of his boyish-slim figure. Perhaps it was the very beauty of the face smoothly framing Joachim's liquid eyes that made the aide look not foppish, but softly feminine.

There was a rich urbanity as well in his careful elegance. Newland, his home-world, was an old colony with an emphasis on civilized trappings worthy of Earth herself. Just as Joachim's uniform was of a synthetic sleeker and less rugged than Hammer's, his sidearm was hunched high on his right hip in a holster cut away to display the artistry of what it gripped. No weapon in the lounge, even that of Captain Ryssler—the Rysslers on whose land Friesland's second starport had been built—matched that of the Newlander for gorgeous detail. The receiver of the standard service pistol, a 1cm powergun whose magazine held ten charged-plastic disks, had been gilded and carven by someone with a penchant for fleshy orchids. The stems and leaves had been filled with niello while the veins remained in a golden tracery. The petals themselves were formed from a breathtakingly purple alloy of uranium and gold. It was hard for anyone who glanced at it to realize that such a work of art was still, beneath its chasing, a lethal weapon.

"Colonel," he reported, his clear tenor a jewel in the velvet silence, "Secretary Tromp will see you now." Neither he nor Hammer showed the slightest concern as to whether the others in the lounge were listening. Hammer nodded, wiping his palms on his thighs.

Behind his back, Joachim winked at Colonel Raeder before turning. The Guardsman's jaw dropped and something mewled from deep in his chest.

It may have been imagination that made Joachim's hips seem to rotate a final purple highlight from his pistol as the dropshaft sphinctered shut.

When the Guards landed, all but the fifteenth story of the Southport Tower was taken over for officers' billets. That central floor was empty save for Tromp, his staff, and the pair of scowling Guardsmen confronting the dropshaft as it opened.

"I'll stay with you, sir," Joachim said. The guards were in dress blacks but they carried full-sized shoulder weapons, 2cm powerguns inferior only in rate of fire to the tribarrels mounted on armored vehicles.

"Go on back to our quarters," Hammer replied. He stepped off the platform. His aide showed no signs of closing the shaft in obedience. "Martyrs' *blood*!" Hammer cursed. "Do as I say!" He wiped his palms again and added, more mildly, "That's where I'll need you, I think."

"If you say so, sir." The door sighed closed behind Hammer, leaving him with the guards.

"Follow the left corridor to the end—sir," one of the big men directed grudgingly. The colonel nodded and walked off without comment. The two men were convinced their greatest worth lay in the fact that they were Guardsmen. To them it was an insult that another man would deliberately leave the Regiment, especially to take service with a band of foreign scum. Hammer could have used his glass-edged tongue on the pair as he had at the perimeter when he sent his platoon through, but there was no need. He was not the man to use any weapon for entertainment's sake.

The unmarked wood-veneer door opened before he could knock. "Why, good afternoon, Captain," the mercenary said, smiling into Stilchey's haggardness. "Recovering all right from this morning?"

"Go on through," the captain said. "He's expecting you."

Hammer closed the inner door behind him, making a soft echo to the thump of the hall panel. Tromp rose from behind his desk, a great gray bear confronting a panther.

"Colonel, be seated," he rumbled. Hammer nodded cautiously and obeyed.

"We have a few problems which must be cleared up soon," the big man said. He looked the soldier full in the face. "I'll be frank. You already know why I'm here."

"Our job's done," Hammer said without inflection. "It costs money to keep the Sl—the Auxiliary Regiment mobilized when it isn't needed, so it's time to bring my boys home according to contract, hey?"

The sky behind Tromp was a turgid mass, gray with harbingers of the first storm of autumn. It provided the only light in the room, but neither man moved to turn on the wall illuminators. "You were going to say 'Slammers,' weren't you?" Tromp mused. "Interesting. I had wondered if the newscasters coined the nickname themselves or if they really picked up a usage here . . ."

"The boys started it . . . It seemed to catch on."

"But I'm less interested in that than another word," Tromp continued with the sudden weight of an anvil falling. " 'Home.' And that's the problem, Colonel. As you know."

"The only thing I could tell you is what I tell recruits when they sign on," Hammer said, his voice quiet but his forehead sweat-gemmed in the cool air. "By their contract, they became citizens of Friesland with all rights and privileges thereof . . . Great Dying *Lord*, sir, that's what brought most of my boys here! Look, I don't have to tell you what's been happening everywhere the past ten years, twenty—there are thousands and thousands of soldiers, good soldiers, who wound up on one losing side or another. If everybody that fought alongside them had been as good, and maybe if they'd had the equipment Friesland could buy for them . . . I tell you, sir, there's no one in the galaxy to match them. And what they fight for isn't me, I don't care what cop you've heard, it's that chance at peace, at stability that their fathers had and their father's fathers, but they lost somewhere when everything started to go wrong. They'd *die* for that chance!"

"But instead," Tromp stated, "they killed for it."

"Don't give me any cop about morals!" the soldier snarled.

"Whose idea was it that we needed control of bluebright shipments to be sure of getting metals from Taunus?"

"Morals?" replied Tromp with a snort. "Morals be hanged, Colonel. This isn't a galaxy for men with morals, you don't have to tell me that. Oh, they can moan about what went on here and they have—but nobody, not even the reporters, has been looking very hard. And they wouldn't find many to listen if they had been. You and I are paid to get things done, Hammer, and there won't be any blame except for failure."

The soldier hunched his shoulders back against the chair. "Then it's all right?" he asked in wonder. "After all I worried, all I planned, my boys can go back to Friesland with me?"

Tromp smiled. "Over my dead body," he said pleasantly. The two men stared at each other without expression on either side.

"I'm missing something," said Hammer flatly. "Fill me in."

The civilian rotated a flat datavisor toward Hammer and touched the indexing tab with his thumb. A montage of horror flickered across the screen—smoke drifting sullenly from a dozen low-lying buildings; a mass grave, reopened and being inspected by a trio of Frisian generals; another village without evident damage but utterly empty of human life—

"Chakma," Hammer said in sudden recognition. "Via, you ought to thank me for the way we handled that one. I'd half thought of using a nuke."

"Gassing the village was better?" the councillor asked with mild amusement.

"It was quiet. No way you could have kept reporters from learning about a nuke," Hammer explained.

"And the convoy runs you made with hostages on each car?" Tromp asked smilingly.

"The only hostages we used were people we knew—and they knew we knew"—Hammer's finger slashed emphasis—"were related to Mel soldiers who hadn't turned themselves in. We cut ambushes by a factor of ten, and we even had some busted when a Mel saw his wife or a kid riding the lead car. Look, I won't pretend it didn't happen, but I didn't make any bones about what I planned when I put in for transfer. This is bloody late in the day to bring it up."

"Right, you did your duty," the big civilian agreed. "And I'm going to do mine by refusing to open Friesland to five thousand men with the training you gave them. Lord and Martyrs, Colonel, you tell me we're going through a period when more governments are breaking up than aren't—what would happen to *our* planet if we set your animals loose in the middle of it?"

"There's twelve regiments of regulars here," Hammer argued.

"And if they were worth the cop in their trousers, we wouldn't have needed your auxiliaries," retorted Tromp inflexibly. "Face facts."

The colonel sagged. "OK," he muttered, turning his face toward the sidewall, "I won't pretend I didn't expect it, what you just said. I owed it to the boys they . . . they believe when they ought to have better sense, and I owed them to try . . ." The soldier's fingers beat a silent tattoo on the yielding material of his chair. He stood before speaking further. "There's a way out of it, Secretary," he said.

"I know there is."

"No!" Hammer shouted, his voice denying the flat finality of Tromp's as he spun to face the bigger man again. "No, there's a better way, a way that'll work. You didn't want to hire one of the freelance regiments you could have had because they didn't have the equipment to do the job fast. But it takes a government and a curst solvent one to equip an armored regiment—none of the privateers had that sort of capital."

He paused for breath. "Partly true," Tromp agreed. "Of course, we preferred to have a commander—" he smiled "—whose first loyalty was to Friesland."

Hammer spoke on, choking with his effort to convince the patient, gray iceberg of a man across from him. "Friesland's always made her money by trade. Let's go into another business—let's hire out the best equipped, best trained—by the Lord, *best*—regiment in the galaxy!"

"And the reason that won't work, Colonel," Tromp rumbled coolly, "is not that it would fail, but that it would succeed. It takes a very solvent government, as you noted, to afford the capital expense of maintaining a first-rate armored regiment. The Melpomonese, for instance, could never have fielded a regiment of their own. But if . . . the sort of unit you suggest was available, they could have hired it for a time, could they not?"

"A few months, sure," Hammer admitted with an angry flick of his hands, "But—"

"Nine months, perhaps a year, Colonel," the civilian went on inexorably. "It would have bankrupted them, but I think they would have paid for the same reason they resisted what was clearly overwhelming force. And not even Friesland could have economically taken Melpomone if the locals were stiffened by—by your Slammers, let us say."

"Lord!" Hammer shouted, snapping erect, "Of course we wouldn't take contracts against Friesland."

"Men change, Colonel," Tromp replied, rising to his own feet. "Men die. And even if they don't, the very existence of a successful enterprise will free the capital for others to duplicate it. It won't be a wild gamble anymore. And Friesland will *not* be the cause of that state of affairs while I am at her helm. If you're the patriot we assumed you were when we gave you this command, you will order your men to come in by platoons and be disarmed."

The smaller man's face was sallow and his hands shook until he hooked them in his pistol belt. "But you can't even let them go then, can you?" he whispered. "It might be all right on Friesland where there wouldn't be any recruiting by outsiders. But if you just turn my boys loose, somebody else will snap them up, somebody else who reads balance sheets. Maybe trained personnel would be enough of an edge to pry loose equipment on the cuff. Life's rough, sure, and there are plenty of people willing to gamble a lot to make a lot more. Then we're where you didn't want us, aren't we? Except that the boys are going to have some notions of their own about Friesland. . . . What do you plan, Secretary? Blowing up the freighter with everybody aboard? Or will you just have the Guards shoot them down when they've been disarmed?"

Tromp turned away for the first time. Lightning was flashing from cloud peak to cloud peak, and the mass that lowered over the Crescent was already linked to the ground by a haze of rain. "They put us in charge of things because we see them as they are, Colonel," Tromp said. The vitril sheet in front of him trembled to the distant thunder. "Friesland got very good value from you, because you didn't avoid unpleasant decisions; you saw the best way and took it—be damned to appearances.

"I would not be where I am today if I were not the same sort of man. I don't ask you to like this course of action—I don't like it myself—but you're a pragmatist, too, Hammer, you see that it's the only way clear for our own people."

"Secretary, anything short of having my boys killed, but—"

"Curse it, man!" Tromp shouted. "Haven't you taken a look around you recently? Lives are cheap, Colonel, lives are very cheap! You've got to have loyalty to something more than just men."

"No," said the man in khaki with quiet certainty. Then, "May I be excused, sir?"

"Get out of here."

Tromp was seated again, his own face a mirror of the storm, when Captain Stilchey slipped in the door through which Hammer had just exited. "Your lapel mike picked it all up," the young officer said. He gloated conspiratorially. "The traitor."

Tromp's face forced itself into normal lines. "You did as I explained might be necessary?"

"Right. As soon as I heard the word 'disarmed' I ordered men to wait for Hammer in his quarters." Stilchey's gleeful expression expanded to a smile of real delight. "I added a . . . refinement, sir. There was the possibility that Hammer would—you know how he is, hard not to obey— tell the guards be cursed and leave them standing. So I took the liberty of suggesting to Colonel Raeder that he lead four men himself for the duty. I used your name, sir, but I rather think the colonel would have gone along with the idea anyway."

The captain's laughter hacked loudly through the suite before he realized that Tromp still sat in iron gloom, cradling his chin in his hands.

★ ★ ★ ★

The room was a shifting bowl of reds and hot orange in which the khaki uniforms of Worzer and Steuben seemed misplaced. The only sound was a faint buzzing, the leakage of the bone-conduction speakers implanted in either man's right mastoid. Hammer, like Tromp, had left his lapel mike keyed to his aides.

"Get us a drink, Joe," Worzer asked. With the Slammers, you either did your job or you left, and nobody could fault Joachim's effectiveness. Still, there was a good deal of ambivalence about the Newlander in a unit made up in large measure of ex-farmers whose religious training had been fundamental if not scholarly. Tense, black-bearded Worzer got along with him better than most, perhaps because it had been a Newland ship which many years before had lifted him from Curwin and the Security Police with their questions about a bombed tax office.

Joachim stood and stretched, his eyes vacant. The walls and floor gave him a satanic cruelty that would have struck as incongruous those who knew him slightly. Yawning, he touched the lighting control, a slight concavity in the wall. The flames dulled, faded to a muted pattern of grays. The room was appreciably darker.

"Wanted you to do that all the time," Worzer grumbled. He seated himself on a bulging chair that faced the doorway.

"I liked it," Joachim said neutrally. He started for the kitchen alcove, then paused. "You'd best take your pistol off, you know. They'll be jumpy."

"You're the boss," Worzer grunts. Alone now in the room, he unlatches his holstered weapon and tosses the rig to the floor in front of him. It is a fixed blackness against the grays that shift beneath it. Glass tinkles in the kitchen.

Men on every world have set up stills, generally as their first constructions. Even in a luxury hotel, Worzer's habits are those of a lifetime. Hammer's microphone no longer broadcasts voices.

The door valves open.

"Freeze!" orders the first man through. He is small and blond, his eyes as cold as the silver frosting his uniform. The glowing tab of a master door key is in his left hand, a pistol in his right. The Guardsmen fanning to each side of him swing heavy powerguns at waist level, the muzzles black screams in a glitter of iridium. Two more men stand beyond the door, facing either end of the hallway with their weapons ready.

"Move and you're dead," the officer hisses to Worzer. Then, to his tight-lipped subordinates, "Watch for the other one—the deviate."

The kitchen door rotates to pass Joachim. His left hand holds a silver tray with a fruit-garnished drink on it. Reflections shimmer from the metal and the condensate on the glass. He smiles.

"You foul *beast!*" says the officer and his pistol turns toward the aide of its own seeming will. The enlisted men wait, uncertain.

"Me, Colonel Raeder?" Joachim's voice lilts. He is raising the tray and it arcs away from his body in a gentle movement that catches Raeder's eyes for the instant that the Newlander's right hand dips and—a cyan flash from Joachim's pistol links the two men. Raeder's mouth is open but silent. His eyeballs are bulging outward against the pressure of exploding nerve tissue. There is a hole between them and it winks twice more in the flash of Joachim's shots. Two spent cases hang in the air to the Newlander's right; a third is jammed, smeared across his pistol's ejection port. None of the Guardsmen have begun to fall, though a gout of blood pours from the neck of the right-hand man.

It is two-fifths of a second from the moment Joachim reached for his pistol. Worzer had been ready. He leaped as Steuben's shots flickered across the room, twisting the shoulder weapon from a Guardsman who did not realize he was already dead. The stocky Curwinite hit the floor on his right side, searching the doorway with the powergun. In the hall, a guard shouted as he spun himself to face the shooting. Joachim's jammed pistol had thudded on the floor but Worzer wasted no interest on what the aide might do—you didn't worry about Joachim in a firefight, he took care of himself. The noncom had been squeezing even as he fell, and only a feather of trigger pressure was left to take up when the Guardsman's glittering uniform sprouted above the sights.

Heated air thumped the walls of the room. The body ballooned under the cyan impact. The big-bore packed enough joules to vaporize much of a man's abdomen at that range, and the Frisian hurtled back against the far wall. His tunic was afire and spilling coils of intestine.

The boots of the remaining Guardsman clattered on the tile as he bolted for the dropshaft. Joachim snaked his head and the pistol he had snatched from Raeder through the doorway. Worzer and the big gun plunged into the corridor low to cover the other end. The shaft entrance opened even before the Frisian's outflung arm touched the summoning plate. Hammer, standing on the platform, shot him twice in the chest. The Guardsman pitched into the wall. As he did so, Joachim shot him again at the base of the skull. Joachim generally doubted other men's kills, a practice that had saved his life in the past.

Hammer glanced down at the jellied skull of the last Guardsman and grimaced. "Didn't anybody tell you about aiming at the body instead of getting fancy?" he asked Joachim. Neither man commented that the final shot had been aimed within a meter of Hammer.

The Newlander shrugged. "They should've been wearing body armor," he said offhandedly. "Coppy fools."

The colonel scooped up both the powerguns from the corridor and gestured his men back into the room. The air within stank of blood and hot plastic. Death had been too sudden to be prefaced with pain, but the faces of the Guardsmen all held slack amazement. Hammer shook his head. "With five thousand of you to choose from," he said to Joachim, "didn't they think I could find a decent bodyguard?"

The Newlander smiled. After his third quick shot, the expended disk had been too hot to spin out whole and had instead flowed across the mechanism when struck by the jet of ejection gas. Joachim was carefully chipping away at the cooled plastic with a stylus while the pistol he had taken from his first victim lay on the table beside him. Its muzzle had charred the veneer surface. "There isn't enough gas in a handgun ejector to cool the chamber properly," he said, pretending to ignore his colonel's indirect praise.

"Via, you hurried 'cause you wanted all of them." Worzer laughed. He thumbed a loaded round into the magazine of the shoulder gun he had appropriated. "What's the matter—don't you want the colonel to bother bringing me along the next time 'cause I scare away all your pretty friends?"

Hammer forced a smile at the interchange, but it was only a shimmer across lines of fear and anger. On one wall was a communicator, a flat, meter-broad screen whose surface was an optical pickup as well as a display. Hammer stepped in front of it and drew the curtain to blank the remainder of the room. His fingers flicked the controls, bringing Captain Stilchey into startled focus. Tromp's aide blinked, but before he could speak the colonel said, "We've got three minutes, Stilchey, and there's no time to cop around. Put me through."

Stilchey's mouth closed. Without comment he reached out and pressed his own control panel. With liquid abruptness his figure was replaced by the hulking power of Secretary Tromp, seated against the closing sky.

"Tell the Guard to ground arms, Secretary," Hammer ordered in a voice trembling with adrenaline. "Tell them now and I'll get on the horn to my boys—it'll be close."

"I'm sorry for the necessity of your arrest, Colonel," the big man began, "but—"

"Idiot!" Hammer shouted at the pickup, and his arm slashed aside the drapes to bare the room. "I heard your terms—now listen to mine. I've arranged for a freighter to land tomorrow at 0700 and the whole regiment's leaving on it. I'll leave you an indenture for the fair value of the gear, and it'll be paid off as soon as contracts start coming in. But the Lord help you, Tromp, if anybody tries to stop my boys."

"Captain Stilchey," Tromp ordered coolly, "sound general quarters. As for you, Colonel," he continued without taking verbal notice of the carnage behind the small officer, "I assure you that the possibility you planned something like this was in my mind when I ordered the Guards landed with me."

"Secretary, we planned what we'd do if we had to a month and a half ago. Don't be so curst a fool to doubt my boys can execute orders without me to hold their hands. If I don't radio in the next few seconds, you won't have the Guards to send back. Lord and *Martyrs,* man, don't you understand what you see back of me? This isn't some coppy parade!"

"Sir," came Stilchey's thin voice from offscreen, "Fire Central reports all satellite signals are being jammed. The armored units in the Crescent began assembling thirty— Lord! Lord! *Sir!*"

A huge scarlet dome swelled upward across the vitril behind Tromp. The window powdered harmlessly an instant later as the shock wave threw man and desk toward Hammer's image. The entire hotel shuddered to the blast.

"They're blowing up the artillery," the captain bleated. "The ammunition—" His words were drowned in the twin detonations of the remaining batteries.

Hammer switched the communicator off. "Early," he muttered. "Not that it mattered!" His face was set like that of a man who had told his disbelieving mechanic that something was wrong with the brakes, and who now feels the pedal sink to the firewall to prove him fatally correct. "Don't go to sleep," he grunted to his companions. "Tromp knows he's lost, and I'm not sure how he'll react."

But only Worzer was in the room with him.

Though Tromp was uninjured, he rose only to his knees. He had seen Captain Stilchey when the jagged sheet of iridium buzz-sawed into the suite and through him. Scuttling like a stiff-legged bear, the civilian made his way to the private dropshaft built into the room. He pretended to ignore the warm greasiness of the floor, but by the time the platform began to sink his whole body was trembling.

Ground floor was a chaos of half-dressed officers who had been on the way to their units when fire raked the encampment. Tromp pushed through a trio of chattering captains in the branch corridor; the main lobby of bronze and off-planet stonework was packed and static, filled with men afraid to go out and uncertain where to hide. The councillor cursed. The door nearest him was ajar and he kicked it fully open. The furniture within was in sleep-mode, the self-cleaning sheets rumpled on the bed, but there was no one present. The vitril outer wall had pulverized; gouges in the interior suggested more than a shock wave had been responsible for the damage.

Seen through it, the starport had become a raving hell.

Four hundred meters from the hotel, one of the anti-artillery weapons was rippling sequential flame skyward from its eight barrels. High in a boiling thunderhead at its radar-chosen point of aim, man-made lightning flared magenta: high explosive caught in flight. Almost simultaneously a dart of cyan more intense than the sun lanced into the Guard vehicle. Metal heated too swiftly to melt and sublimed in a glowing ball that silhouetted the gun crew as it devoured them. Hammer's tanks, bunkered in the Crescent, were using satellite-computed deflections to rake the open Guard positions. Twenty kilometers and the thin armor of the lighter vehicles were no defense against the 200mm powerguns.

Tromp stepped over the low sill and began to run. The field was wet and a new slash of rain pocked its gleam. Three shells popped high in the air. He ignored them, pounding across the field in a half-crouch. For a moment the whistling beginning to fill the sky as if from a thousand tiny mouths meant nothing to him either—then realization rammed a scream from his throat and he threw himself prone. The bomblets showering down from the shells went off on impact all across the field, orange flashes that each clipped the air with scores of fragments. Panic and Hammer's tanks had silenced the Guard's defensive weaponry. Now the rocket howitzers were free to rain in wilful death.

But the tanks, Tromp thought as he stumbled to his feet, they can't knock out the tanks from twenty kilometers and they can't capture the port while the Guard still has that punch. The surprise was over now. Lift fans keened from the perimeter as the great silvery forms of armored vehicles shifted from their targeted positions. The combatants were equal and a standoff meant disaster for the mercenaries.

Much of the blood staining Tromp's clothing was his own, licked from his veins by shrapnel. Incoming shells were bursting at ten-second intervals. Munitions shortages would force a slowdown soon, but for the moment anyone who stood to run would be scythed down before his third step. Even flat on his belly Tromp was being stung by hot metal. His goal, the ten-place courier vessel that had brought him to Melpomone, was still hopelessly far off . The remains, however, of one of the Guard's self-propelled howitzers lay like a cleat-kicked drink-can thirty meters distant. Painfully the councillor crawled into its shelter. Hammer's punishing fire had not been directed at the guns themselves but at the haulers in the midst of each battery. After three shots, the secondary explosions had stripped the Guard of all its ill-sited artillery.

A line of rain rippled across the field, streaking dried blood from Tromp's face and whipping the pooled water. He was not running away. There was one service yet that he could perform for Friesland, and he had to be home to accomplish it. After that—and he thought of it not as revenge but as a final duty—he would not care that reaction would assuredly make him the scapegoat for the catastrophe now exploding all around him. It was obvious that Hammer had ordered his men to disturb the spaceport as little as possible so that the mercenaries would not hinder their own embarkation. The lightly rattling shrapnel crumpled gun crews and the bewildered Guard infantry, but it would not harm the port facilities themselves or the ships docked there.

For the past several minutes no powerguns had lighted the field. The bunkered mercenaries had either completed their programs or ceased fire when a lack of secondary explosions informed them that the remaining Guard vehicles had left their targeted positions. The defenders had at first fired wild volleys at no better target than the mountain range itself, but a few minutes' experience had taught them that the return blasts aimed at their muzzles were far more effective than their own could possibly be. Now there was a lull in the shelling as well.

Tromp eased a careful glance beyond the rim of his shelter, the buckled plenum chamber of the gun carriage. His ship was a horizontal needle three hundred meters distant. The vessel was unlighted, limned as a gray shadow by cloud-hopping lightning. The same flashes gleamed momentarily on the wet turtle-backs of a dozen tanks and combat cars in a nearby cluster, their fans idling.

All the surviving Guard units must be clumped in similar hedgehogs across the port.

The big man tensed himself to run; then the night popped and crackled as a Guard tank began firing out into the storm. Tromp counted three shots before a cyan dazzle struck the engaged vehicle amidships and its own ammunition went off with an electric crash. The clustered vehicles were lit by a blue-green fire that expanded for three seconds, dissolving everything within twenty meters of its center. One of the remaining combat cars spun on howling fans, but it collapsed around another bolt before it could pull clear. There were Guardsmen on the ground now, running from their vehicles. Tromp's eyes danced with afterimages of the exploding tank, and for the first time he understood why Stilchey had been so terrified by the destruction of the car he might have ridden in.

Half a dozen shots ripped from beyond the perimeter and several struck home together. All the Guard blowers were burning now, throwing capering shadows beyond the councillor's shelter. Then, threading their way around the pools of slag, the steam and the dying fires, came a trio of tanks. Even without the scarlet wand wavering from each turret for identification, Tromp would have realized these were not the polished beauties of the Guard. The steel skirts of their plenum chambers were rusty and brushworn. One's gouged turret still glowed where a heavy powergun had hit it glancingly; the muzzle of its own weapon glowed too, and the bubbling remains of the perimeter defense left no doubt whose bolts had been more accurately directed. The fighting had been brief, Hammer's platoons meeting the disorganized Guardsmen with pointblank volleys. The victors' hatches were open and as they swept in toward the central tower, Tromp could hear their radios crackling triumphant instructions. Other wands floated across the immense field, red foxfire in the rain.

The shooting had stopped. Now, before the combat cars and infantry followed up the penetrations their tanks had made, Tromp stood and ran to his ship. His career was ruined, of that he had no doubt. No amount of deceit would cover his role in the creation of the Slammers or his leadership in the attempted suppression. All that was left to Nicholas Tromp was the sapphire determination that the national power which he had worked four decades to build should not fall with him. They could still smash Hammer before he got started, using Friesland's own fleet and the fleets of a dozen other worlds. The cost would leave even Friesland groaning, but they could blast the Slammers inexorably from space wherever they were landed. For the sake of his planet's future, the excision had to be made, damn the cost.

And after Tromp fell in disgrace in the next week or two weeks at most, there would be no man left with the power to force the action or the foresight to see its necessity. Panting, he staggered through his vessel's open lock. The interior, too, was unlighted. That was not surprising in view of the combat outside, but one of the three crewmen should have been waiting at the lock. "Where are you?" Tromp called angrily.

The lights went on. There was a body at the big Frisian's feet. From the cockpit forward stretched another hairline of blood still fresh enough to ooze. "I'm here," said a cultured voice from behind.

Tromp froze. Very slowly, he began to turn his head.

"People like you," the voice continued, "with dreams too big for men to fit into, don't see the same sort of world that the rest of us do. And sometimes a fellow who does one job well can see where his job has to be done, even though a better man has overlooked it. Anyhow, Secretary, there always was one thing you and I could agree on—lives *are* cheap."

Surely Joachim's wrists were too slim, Tromp thought, to raise his heavy pistol so swiftly.

POWERGUNS

By the twenty-first century, missile-firing small arms appeared to have reached the pinnacle of their development, and there was nothing on hand to replace them. The mass and velocity of projectiles could be juggled but they could not be increased in sum without a corresponding increase in recoil or backblast. Explosive bullets were very destructive on impact, but they had no penetration beyond the immediate blast radius. An explosive bullet might vaporize a leaf it hit near the muzzle as easily as the intended target downrange, and using explosives in heavy brush was worse than useless because it endangered the shooter.

Lasers, though they had air-defense applications, were not the infantryman's answer either. The problem with lasers was the power source. Guns store energy in the powder charge. A machine gun with one cartridge is just as effective—once—as it is with a thousand-round belt, so the ammunition load can be tailored to circumstances. Man-killing lasers required a four-hundred-kilo fusion unit to drive them. Hooking a laser on line with any less bulky energy source was of zero military effectiveness rather than lesser effectiveness.

Science lent Death a hand in this impasse—as Science has always done, since the day the first wedge became the first knife. Thirty thousand residents of Saint-Pierre, Martinique, had been killed on May 8, 1902. The agent of their destruction was a "burning cloud" released during an eruption of Mount Peléée. Popular myth had attributed the deaths to normal volcanic phenomena, hot gases or ash like that which buried Pompeii; but even the most cursory examination of the evidence indicated that direct energy release had done the lethal damage. In 2073, Dr. Marie Weygand, heading a team under contract to Olin-Amerika, managed to duplicate the phenomenon.

The key had come from spectroscopic examination of pre-1902 lavas from Peléée's crater. The older rocks had shown inexplicable gaps among the metallic elements expected there. A year and a half of empirical research followed, guided more by Dr. Weygand's intuition than by the battery of scientific instrumentation her employers had rushed out at the first signs of success. The principle ultimately discovered was of little utility as a general power source— but then, Olin-Amerika had not been looking for a way to heat homes.

Weygand determined that metallic atoms of a fixed magnetic orientation could be converted directly into energy by the proper combination of heat, pressure, and intersecting magnetic fields. Old lava locks its rich metallic burden in a pattern dictated by the magnetic ambiance at the time the flow cools. At Peléée in 1902, the heavy Gauss loads of the new eruption made a chance alignment with the restressed lava of the crater's rim. Matter flashed into energy in a line dictated by the intersection, ripping other atoms free of the basalt matrix and converting them in turn. Below in Saint-Pierre, humans burned.

When the principle had been discovered, it remained only to refine its destructiveness. Experiments were held with different fuel elements and matrix materials. A copper-cobalt charge in a wafer of microporous polyurethane became the standard, since it appeared to give maximum energy release with the least tendency to scatter. Because the discharge was linear, there was no need of a tube to channel the force as a rifle's barrel does; but some immediate protection from air-induced scatter was necessary for a hand-held weapon. The best barrel material was iridium. Tungsten and osmium were even more refractory, but those elements absorbed a large component of the discharge instead of reflecting it as the iridium did.

To function in service, the new weapons needed to be cooled. Even if a white-hot barrel did not melt, the next charge certainly would vaporize before it could be fired. Liquified gas, generally nitrogen or one of the noble gases which would not themselves erode the metal, was therefore released into the bore after every shot. Multiple barrels, either rotating like those of a Gatling gun or fixed like those of the mitrailleuse, the Gatling's French contemporary, were used to achieve high rates of fire or to fire very high-intensity charges. Personal weapons were generally semiautomatic to keep weight and bulk within manageable limits. Submachine guns with large gas reservoirs to fire pistol charges had their uses and advocates, as their bullet-firing predecessors had.

Powerguns—the first usage of the term is as uncertain as that of "gun" itself, though the derivation is obvious—greatly increased the range and destructiveness of the individual soldier. The weapons were so destructive, in fact, that even on most frontier planets their use was limited to homicide. Despite that limited usefulness, factories for the manufacture of powerguns and their ammunition would probably have been early priority items on most worlds—had not that manufacture been utterly beyond the capacity of all but the most highly industrialized planets.

Precision forming of metal as hard as iridium is an incredible task. Gas reservoirs required a null-conductive sheath if they were not to bleed empty before they even reached the field. If ammunition wafers were rolled out in a fluctuating electronic field, they were as likely to blow out the breech of a weapon or gang-fire in the loading tube as they were to injure a foe. All the planetary pride in the cosmos would not change laws of physics.

Of course, some human cultures preferred alternate weaponry. The seven worlds of the Gorgon Cluster equipped their armies— and a number of mercenary units—with fléchette guns for instance. Their hypervelocity osmium projectiles had better short-range penetration than 2 cm powerguns, and they cycled at a very high rate. But the barrels of fléchette guns were of synthetic diamond, making them at least as difficult to manufacture as the more common energy weapons.

Because of the expense of modern weapons, would-be combatants on rural worlds often delayed purchasing guns until fighting was inevitable. Then it became natural to consider buying not only the guns but men who were used to them—for powerguns were no luxury to the mercenaries whose lives and pay depended on their skill with the best possible equipment. The gap between a citizen-soldier holding a powergun he had been issued a week before, and the professional who had trained daily for years with the weapon, was a wide one.

Thus if only one side on a poor world hired mercenaries, its victory was assured—numbers and ideology be damned. That meant, of course, that both sides had to make the investment even if it meant mortgaging the planetary income for a decade. Poverty was preferable to what came with defeat.

All over the galaxy, men with the best gifts of Science and no skills but those of murder looked for patrons who would hire them to bring down civilization. Business was good.

CAUGHT IN THE CROSSFIRE

Margritte grappled with the nearest soldier in the instant her husband broke for the woods. The man in field-gray cursed and tried to jerk his weapon away from her, but Margritte's muscles were young and taut from shifting bales. Even when the mercenary kicked her ankles from under her, Margritte's clamped hands kept the gun barrel down and harmless.

Neither of the other two soldiers paid any attention to the scuffle. They clicked off the safety catches of their weapons as they swung them to their shoulders. Georg was running hard, fresh blood from his retorn calf muscles staining his bandages. The double slap of automatic fire caught him in mid-stride and whipsawed his slender body. His head and heels scissored to the ground together. They were covered by the mist of blood that settled more slowly.

Sobbing, Margritte loosed her grip and fell back on the ground. The man above her cradled his fléechette gun again and looked around the village. "Well, aren't you going to shoot me, too?" she cried.

"Not unless we have to," the mercenary replied quietly. He was sweating despite the stiff breeze, and he wiped his black face with his sleeve. "Helmuth," he ordered, "start setting up in the building. Landschein, you stay out with me, make sure none of these women try the same damned thing." He glanced out to where Georg lay, a bright smear on the stubbled, golden earth. "Best get that out of sight, too," he added. "The convoy's due in an hour."

Old Leida had frozen to a statue in ankle-length muslin at the first scream. Now she nodded her head of close ringlets. "Myrie, Delia," she called, gesturing to her daughters, "bring brush hooks and come along." She had not lost her dignity even during the shooting.

"Hold it," said Landschein, the shortest of the three soldiers. He was a sharp-featured man who had grinned in satisfaction as he fired. "You two got kids in there?" he asked the younger women. The muzzle of his fléechette gun indicated the locked door to the dugout which normally stored the crop out of sun and heat; today it imprisoned the village's twenty-six children. Delia and Myrie nodded, too dry with fear to speak.

"Then you go drag him into the woods," Landschein said, grinning again. "Just remember—you might manage to get away, but you won't much like what you'll find when you come back. I'm sure some true friend'll point your brats out to us quick enough to save her own."

Leida nodded a command, but Landschein's freckled hand clamped her elbow as she turned to follow her daughters. "Not you, old lady. No need for you to get that near to cover."

"Do you think *I* would run and risk—everyone?" Leida demanded.

"Curst if I know what you'd risk," the soldier said. "But we're risking plenty already to ambush one of Hammer's convoys. If anybody gets loose ahead of time to warn them, we can kiss our butts good-bye."

Margritte wiped the tears from her eyes, using her palms because of the gritty dust her thrashings had pounded into her knuckles. The third soldier, the broad-shouldered blond named Helmuth, had leaned his weapon beside the door of the hall and was lifting bulky loads from the nearby air-cushion vehicle. The settlement had become used to whining gray columns of military vehicles, cruising the road at random. This truck, however, had eased over the second canopy of the forest itself. It was a flimsy cargo-hauler like the one in which Krauder picked up the cotton at season's end, harmless enough to look at. Only Georg, left behind for his sickle-ripped leg when a government van had carried off the other males the week before as "recruits," had realized what it meant that the newcomers wore field-gray instead of khaki.

"Why did you come here?" Margritte asked in a near-normal voice.

The black mercenary glanced at her as she rose, glanced back at the other women obeying orders by continuing to pick the iridescent boles of Terran cotton grown in Pohweil's soil. "We had the capital under siege," he said, "until Hammer's tanks punched a corridor through. We can't close the corridor, so we got to cut your boys off from supplies some other way. Otherwise the Cartel'll wish it had paid its taxes instead of trying to take over. You grubbers may have been pruning their wallets, but Lord! they'll be flayed alive if your counterattack works."

He spat a thin, angry stream into the dust. "The traders hired us and four other regiments, and you grubbers sank the whole treasury into bringing in Hammer's armor. Maybe we can prove today those cocky bastards aren't all they're billed as. . . ."

"We didn't care," Margritte said. "We're no more the Farm Bloc than Krauder and his truck is the Trade Cartel. Whatever they did in the capital—*we* had no choice. I hadn't even seen the capital . . . oh dear Lord, Georg would have taken me there for our honeymoon except that there was fighting all over. . . ."

"How long we got, Sarge?" the blond man demanded from the stark shade of the hall.

"Little enough. Get those bloody sheets set up or we'll have to pop the cork bare-ass naked; and we got enough problems." The big noncom shifted his glance about the narrow clearing, wavering rows of cotton marching to the edge of the forest's dusky green. The road, an unsurfaced track whose ruts were not a serious hindrance to air-cushion traffic, was the long axis. Beside it stood the hall, twenty meters by five and the only above-ground structure in the settlement. The battle with the native vegetation made dugouts beneath the cotton preferable to cleared land wasted for dwellings. The hall became more than a social center and common refectory: it was the gaudiest of luxuries and a proud slap to the face of the forest.

Until that morning, the forest had been the village's only enemy. "Georg only wanted—"

"God *damn* it," the sergeant snarled. "Will you shut it off? Every man but your precious husband gone off to the siege—no, shut it off till I finish!—and him running to warn the convoy. If you'd wanted to save his life, you should've grabbed him, not me. Sure, all you grubbers, you don't care about the war—not much! It's all one to you whether you kill us yourselves or your tankers do it, those bastards so high and mighty for the money they've got and the equipment. I tell you, girl, I don't take it personal that people shoot at me, it's just the way we both earn our livings. But it's fair, it's even . . . and Hammer thinks he's the Way made Flesh because nobody can bust his tanks."

The sergeant paused and his lips sucked in and out. His thick, gentle fingers rechecked the weapon he held. "We'll just see," he whispered.

"Georg said we'd all be killed in the crossfire if we were out in the fields when you shot at the tanks."

"If Georg had kept his face shut and his ass in bed, he'd have lived longer than he did. Just shut it off!" the noncom ordered. He turned to his blond underling, fighting a section of sponge plating through the door. "Via, Bornzyk!" he shouted angrily. "Move it!"

Helmuth flung his load down with a hollow clang. "Via, then lend a hand! The wind catches these and—"

"I'll help him," Margritte offered abruptly. Her eyes blinked away from the young soldier's weapon where he had forgotten it against the wall. Standing, she far lacked the bulk of the sergeant beside her, but her frame gave no suggestion of weakness. Golden dust soiled the back and sides of her dress with butterfly scales.

The sergeant gave her a sharp glance, his left hand spreading and closing where it rested on the black barrel-shroud of his weapon. "All right," he said, "you give him a hand and we'll see you under cover with us when the shooting starts. You're smarter than I gave you credit."

They had forgotten Leida was still standing beside them. Her hand struck like a spading fork. Margritte ducked away from the blow, but Leida caught her on the shoulder and gripped. When the mercenary's reversed gun-butt cracked the older woman loose, a long strip of Margritte's blue dress tore away with her. "Bitch," Leida mumbled through bruised lips. "You'd help these beasts after they killed your own man?"

Margritte stepped back, tossing her head. For a moment she fumbled at the tear in her dress; then, defiantly, she let it fall open. Landschein turned in time to catch the look in Leida's eyes. "Hey, you'll give your friends more trouble," he stated cheerfully, waggling his gun to indicate Delia and Myrie as they returned gray-faced from the forest fringe. "Go on, get out and pick some cotton."

When Margritte moved, the white of her loose shift caught the sun and the small killer's stare. "Landschein!" the black ordered sharply, and Margritte stepped very quickly toward the truck and the third man struggling there.

Helmuth turned and blinked at the girl as he felt her capable muscles take the windstrain off the panel he was shifting. His eyes were blue and set wide in a face too large-boned to be handsome, too frank to be other than attractive. He accepted the help without question, leading the way into the hall.

The dining tables were hoisted against the rafters. The windows, unshuttered in the warm autumn and unglazed, lined all four walls at chest height. The long wall nearest the road was otherwise unbroken; the one opposite it was pierced in the middle by the single door. In the center of what should have been an empty room squatted the mercenaries' construct. The metal-ceramic panels had been locked into three sides of a square, a pocket of armor open only toward the door. It was hidden beneath the lower sills of the windows; nothing would catch the eye of an oncoming tanker.

"We've got to nest three layers together," the soldier explained as he swung the load, easily managed within the building, "or they'll cut us apart if they get off a burst this direction."

Margritte steadied a panel already in place as Helmuth mortised his into it. Each sheet was about five centimeters in thickness, a thin plate of gray metal on either side of a white porcelain sponge. The girl tapped it dubiously with a blunt finger. "This can stop bullets?"

The soldier—he was younger than his size suggested, no more than eighteen. Younger even than Georg, and he had a smile like Georg's as he raised his eyes with a blush and said, "P-powerguns, yeah; three layers of it ought to . . . It's light, we could carry it in the truck where iridium would have bogged us down. But look, there's another panel and the rockets we still got to bring in."

"You must be very brave to fight tanks with just—this," Margritte prompted as she took one end of the remaining armor sheet.

"Oh, well, Sergeant Counsel says it'll work," the boy said enthusiastically, "they'll come by, two combat cars, then three big trucks, and another combat car. Sarge and Landschein buzzbomb the lead cars before they know what's happening. I reload them and they hit the third car when it swings wide to get a shot. Any shooting the blower jocks get off, they'll spread because they won't know—oh, cop I said it. . . ."

"They'll think the women in the fields may be firing, so they'll kill us first," Margritte reasoned aloud. The boy's neck beneath his helmet turned brick red as he trudged into the building.

"Look," he said, but he would not meet her eyes, "we got to do it. It'll be fast—nobody much can get hurt. And your . . . the children, they're all safe. Sarge said that with all the men gone, we wouldn't have any trouble with the women if we kept the kids safe and under our thumbs."

"We didn't have time to have children," Margritte said. Her eyes were briefly unfocused. "You didn't give Georg enough time before you killed him."

"He was . . ." Helmuth began. They were outside again and his hand flicked briefly toward the slight notch Delia and Myrie had chopped in the forest wall. "I'm sorry."

"Oh, don't be sorry," she said. "He knew what he was doing."

"He was—I suppose you'd call him a patriot?" Helmuth suggested, jumping easily to the truck's deck to gather up an armload of cylindrical bundles. "He was really against the Cartel?"

"There was never a soul in this village who cared who won the war," Margritte said. "We have our own war with the forest."

"They joined the siege!" the boy retorted. "They cared that m-much, to fight us!"

"They got in the vans when men with guns told them to get in," the girl said. She took the gear Helmuth was forgetting to hand to her and shook a lock of hair out of her eyes. "Should they have run? Like Georg? No, they went off to be soldiers; praying like we did that the war might end before the forest had eaten up the village again. Maybe if we were really lucky, it'd end before this crop had spoiled in the fields because there weren't enough hands left here to pick it in time."

Helmuth cleared the back of the truck with his own load and stepped down. "Well, just the same your, your husband tried to hide and warn the convoy," he argued. "Otherwise why did he run?"

"Oh, he loved me—you know?" said Margritte. "Your sergeant said all of us should be out picking as usual. Georg knew, he *told* you, that the crossfire would kill everybody in the fields as sure as if you shot us deliberately. And when you wouldn't change your plan . . . well, if he'd gotten away you would have had to give up your ambush, wouldn't you? You'd have known it was suicide if the tanks learned that you were waiting for them. So Georg ran."

The dark-haired woman stared out at the forest for a moment. "He didn't have a prayer, did he? You could have killed him a hundred times before he got to cover."

"Here, give me those," the soldier said, taking the bundles from her instead of replying. He began to unwrap the cylinders one by one on the wooden floor. "We couldn't let him get away," he said at last. He added, his eyes still down on his work, "Flééchettes when they hit . . . I mean, sh-shooting at his legs wouldn't, wouldn't have been a kindness, you see?"

Margritte laughed again. "Oh, I saw what they dragged into the forest, yes." She paused, sucking at her lower lip. "That's how we always deal with our dead, give them to the forest. Oh, we have a service; but we wouldn't have buried Georg in the dirt, if . . . if he'd died. But you didn't care, did you? A corpse looks bad, maybe your precious ambush, your own lives. Get it out of the way, toss it in the woods."

"We'd have buried him afterwards," the soldier mumbled as he laid a fourth thigh-thick projectile beside those he had already unwrapped.

"Oh, of *course,*" Margritte said. "And me, and all the rest of us murdered out there in the cotton. Oh, you're gentlemen, you are."

"Via!" Helmuth shouted, his flush mottling as at last he lifted his gaze to the girl's. "We'd have b-buried him. I'd have buried him. You'll be safe in here with us until it's all over, and by the Lord, then you can come back with us, too! You don't have to stay here with these hard-faced bitches."

A bitter smile tweaked the left edge of the girl's mouth. "Sure, you're a good boy."

The young mercenary blinked between protest and pleasure, settled on the latter. He had readied all six of the tinned, gray missiles; now he lifted one of the pair of launchers. "It'll be really quick," he said shyly, changing the subject. The launcher was an arm-length tube with double handgrips and an optical sight. Helmuth's big hands easily inserted one of the buzzbombs to lock with a faint snick.

"Very simple," Margritte murmured.

"Cheap and easy," the boy agreed with a smile. "You can buy a thousand of these for what a combat car runs— Hell, maybe more than a thousand. And it's one for one today, one bomb to one car. Landschein says the crews are just a little extra, like weevils in your biscuit."

He saw her grimace, the angry tensing of a woman who had just seen her husband blasted into a spray of offal. Helmuth grunted with his own pain, his mouth dropping open as his hand stretched to touch her bare shoulder. "Oh, Lord—didn't mean to say. . . ."

She gently detached his fingers. His breath caught and he turned away. Unseen, her look of hatred seared his back. His hand was still stretched toward her and hers toward him, when the door scraped to admit Landschein behind them.

"Cute, oh bloody cute," the little mercenary said. He carried his helmet by its strap. Uncovered, his cropped gray hair made him an older man. "Well, get on with it, boy— don't keep me 'n Sarge waiting. He'll be mad enough about getting sloppy thirds."

Helmuth jumped to his feet. Landschein ignored him, clicking across to a window in three quick strides. "Sarge," he called, "we're all set. Come on, we can watch the women from here."

"I'll run the truck into the woods," Counsel's voice burred in reply. "Anyhow, I can hear better from out here."

That was true. Despite the open windows, the wails of the children were inaudible in the hall. Outside, they formed a thin backdrop to every other sound.

Landschein set down his helmet. He snapped the safety on his gun's sideplate and leaned the weapon carefully against the nest of armor. Then he took up the loaded launcher and ran his hands over its tube and grips. Without changing expression, he reached out to caress Margritte through the tear in her dress.

Margritte screamed and clawed her left hand as she tried to rise. The launcher slipped into Landschein's lap, and his arm, far swifter, locked hers and drew her down against him. Then the little mercenary himself was jerked upward. Helmuth's hand on his collar first broke Landschein's grip on Margritte, then flung him against the closed door.

Landschein rolled despite the shock and his glance flicked toward his weapon, but between gun and gunman crouched Helmuth, no longer a red-faced boy but the strongest man in the room. Grinning, Helmuth spread fingers that had crushed ribs in past rough and tumbles. "Try it, little man," he said. "Try it and I'll rip your head off your shoulders."

"You'll do wonders!" Landschein spat, but his eyes lost their glaze and his muscles relaxed. He bent his mouth into a smile. "Hey, kid, there's plenty of slots around. We'll work out something afterwards, no need to fight."

Helmuth rocked his head back in a nod of acceptance with nothing of friendship in it. "You lay another hand on her," he said in a normal voice, "and you'd best have killed me first." He turned his back deliberately on the older man and the nearby weapons. Landschein clenched his left fist once, twice, but then he began to load the remaining launcher.

Margritte slipped the patching kit from her belt pouch. Her

hands trembled, but the steel needle was already threaded. Her whip-stitches tacked the torn piece top and sides to the remaining material, close enough for decency. Pins were a luxury that a cotton settlement could well do without. Landschein glanced back at her once, but at the same time the floor creaked as Helmuth's weight shifted to his other leg. Neither man spoke.

Sergeant Counsel opened the door. His right arm cradled a pair of fléechette guns and he handed one to Helmuth. "Best not to leave it in the dust," he said. "You'll be needing it soon."

"They coming, Sarge?" Landschein asked. He touched his tongue to thin, pale lips.

"Not yet." Counsel looked from one man to the other. "You boys get things sorted out?"

"All green here," Landschein muttered, smiling again but lowering his eyes.

"That's good," the big black said, "because we got a job to do and we're not going to let anything stop us. Anything."

Margritte was putting away her needle. The sergeant looked at her hard. "You keep your head down, hear?"

"It won't matter," the girl said calmly, tucking the kit away. "The tanks, they won't be surprised to see a woman in here."

"Sure, but they'll shoot your bleeding head off," Landschein snorted.

"Do you think I care?" she blazed back. Helmuth winced at the tone; Sergeant Counsel's eyes took on an undesirable shade of interest.

"But you're helping us," the big noncom mused. He tapped his fingertips on the gun in the crook of his arm. "Because you like us so much?" There was no amusement in his words, only a careful mind picking over the idea, all ideas.

She stood and walked to the door, her face as composed as a priest's at the gravesite. "Have your ambush," she said. "Would it help us if the convoy came through before you were ready for it?"

"The smoother it goes, the faster . . ." Counsel agreed quietly, "then the better for all of you."

Margritte swung the door open and stood looking out. Eight

women were picking among the rows east of the hall. They would be relatively safe there, not caught between the ambushers' rockets and the raking powerguns of their quarry. Eight of them safe and fourteen sure victims on the other side. Most of them could have been out of the crossfire if they had only let themselves think, only considered the truth that Georg had died to underscore.

"I keep thinking of Georg," Margritte said aloud. "I guess my friends are just thinking about their children, they keep looking at the storage room. But the children, they'll be all right; it's just that most of them are going to be orphans in a few minutes."

"It won't be that bad," Helmuth said. He did not sound as though he believed it either.

The older children had by now ceased the screaming begun when the door shut and darkness closed in on them. The youngest still wailed and the sound drifted through the open door.

"I told her we'd take her back with us, Sarge," Helmuth said.

Landschein chortled, a flash of instinctive humor he covered with a raised palm. Counsel shook his head in amazement. "You were wrong, boy. Now, keep watching those women or we may not be going back ourselves."

The younger man reddened again in frustration. "Look, we've got women in the outfit now, and I don't mean the rec troops. Captain Denzil told me there's six in Bravo Company alone—"

"Hoo, little Helmuth wants his own girlie friend to keep his bed warm," Landschein gibed.

"Landschein, I—" Helmuth began, clenching his right hand into a ridge of knuckles.

"Shut it off!"

"But, Sarge—"

"Shut it off, boy, or you'll have me to deal with!" roared the black. Helmuth fell back and rubbed his eyes. The noncom went on more quietly, "Landschein, you keep your tongue to yourself, too."

Both big men breathed deeply, their eyes shifting in concert toward Margritte who faced them in silence. "Helmuth," the sergeant continued, "some units take women, some don't. We've got a few, damned few, because not many women have the guts for our line of work."

Margritte's smile flickered. "The hardness, you mean. The callousness."

"Sure, words don't matter," Counsel agreed mildly. He smiled back at her as one equal to another. "This one, yeah; she might just pass. Via, you don't have to look like Landschein there to be tough. But you're missing the big point, boy." Helmuth touched his right wrist to his chin. "Well, what?" he demanded.

Counsel laughed. "She wouldn't go with us. Would you, girl?"

Margritte's eyes were flat, and her voice was dead flat. "No," she said, "I wouldn't go with you."

The noncom grinned as he walked back to a window vantage. "You see, Helmuth, you want her to give up a whole lot to gain you a bunkmate."

"It's not like that," Helmuth insisted, thumping his leg in frustration. "I just mean—"

"Oh, *Lord*!" the girl said loudly, "can't you just get on with your ambush?"

"Well, not till Hammer's boys come through," chuckled the sergeant. "They're so good, they can't run a convoy to schedule."

"S-sergeant," the young soldier said, "she doesn't understand." He turned to Margritte and gestured with both hands, forgetting the weapon in his left. "They won't take you back, those witches out there. The . . . the rec girls at Base Denzil don't go home, they can't. And you know damned well that s-somebody's going to catch it out there when it drops in the pot. They'll crucify you for helping us set up, the ones that're left."

"It doesn't matter what they do," she said. "It doesn't matter at all."

"Your life matters!" the boy insisted.

Her laughter hooted through the room. "My life?" Margritte repeated. "You splashed all that across the field an hour ago. You didn't give a damn when you did it, and I don't give one now—but I'd only follow you to Hell and hope your road was short."

Helmuth bit his knuckle and turned, pinched over as though he had been kicked. Sergeant Counsel grinned his tight, equals grin. "You're wasted here, you know," he said. "And we could use you. Maybe if—"

"Sarge!" Landschein called from his window. "Here they come."

Counsel scooped up a rocket launcher, probing its breech with his fingers to make finally sure of its load. "Now you keep down," he repeated to Margritte. "Backblast'll take your head off if their shooting don't." He crouched below the sill and the rim of the armor shielding him, peering through a periscope whose button of optical fibers was unnoticeable in the shadow. Faced inward toward the girl, Landschein hunched over the other launcher in the right corner of the protected area. His flééchette gun rested beside him and one hand curved toward it momentarily, anticipating the instant he would raise it to spray the shattered convoy. Between them Helmuth knelt as stiffly as a statue of gray-green jade. He drew a buzzbomb closer to his right knee where it clinked against the barrel of his own weapon. Cursing nervously, he slid the flééchette gun back out of the way. Both his hands gripped reloads, waiting.

The cars' shrill whine trembled in the air. Margritte stood up by the door, staring out through the windows across the hall. Dust plumed where the long, straight roadway cut the horizon into two blocks of forest. The women in the fields had paused, straightening to watch the oncoming vehicles. But that was normal, nothing to alarm the khaki men in the bellies of their war-cars; and if any woman thought of falling to hug the earth, the fans' wailing too nearly approximated that of the imprisoned children.

"Three hundred meters," Counsel reported softly as the blunt bow of the lead car gleamed through the dust. "Two-fifty." Landschein's teeth bared as he faced around, poised to spring.

Margritte swept up Helmuth's flééchette gun and leveled it at waist height. The safety clicked off. Counsel had dropped his periscope and his mouth was open to cry an order. The deafening muzzle blast lifted him out of his crouch and pasted him briefly, voiceless, against the pocked inner face of the armor. Margritte swung her weapon like a flail into a triple splash of red. Helmuth died with only a reflexive jerk, but Landschein's speed came near to bringing his launcher to bear on Margritte. The stream of fléechettes sawed across his throat. His torso dropped, headless but still clutching the weapon.

Margritte's gun silenced when the last needle slapped out of the muzzle. The aluminum barrel shroud had softened and warped during the long burst. Eddies in the fog of blood and propellant smoke danced away from it. Margritte turned as if in icy composure, but she bumped the door jamb and staggered as she stepped outside. The racket of the gun had drawn the sallow faces of every woman in the fields.

"It's over!" Margritte called. Her voice sounded thin in the fresh silence. Three of the nearer mothers ran toward the storage room.

Down the road, dust was spraying as the convoy skidded into a herringbone for defense. Gun muzzles searched; the running women; Margritte armed and motionless; the sudden eruption of children from the dugout. The men in the cars waited, their trigger fingers partly tensed.

Bergen, Delia's six-year-old, pounded past Margritte to throw herself into her mother's arms. They clung together, each crooning to the other through their tears. "Oh, we were so afraid!" Bergen said, drawing away from her mother. "But now it's all right." She rotated her head and her eyes widened as they took in Margritte's tattered figure. "Oh, Margi," she gasped, "whatever happened to *you*?"

Delia gasped and snatched her daughter back against her bosom. Over the child's loose curls, Delia glared at Margritte with eyes like a hedge of pikes. Margritte's hand stopped halfway to the child. She stood—gaunt, misted with blood as though sunburned. A woman who had blasted life away instead of suckling it. Delia, a frightened mother, snarled at the killer who had been her friend.

Margritte began to laugh. She trailed the gun three steps before letting it drop unnoticed. The captain of the lead car watched her approach over his gunsights. His short, black beard fluffed out from under his helmet, twitching as he asked, "Would you like to tell us what's going on, honey, or do we got to comb it out ourselves?"

"I killed three soldiers," she answered simply. "Now there's nothing going on. Except that wherever you're headed, I'm going along. You can use my sort, soldier."

Her laughter was a crackling shadow in the sunlight.

BACKDROP TO CHAOS

The mercenary companies of the late Third Millennium were both a result of and a response to a spurt of empire-building among the new industrial giants of the human galaxy. Earth's first flash of colonization had been explosive. Transit was an expensive proposition for trade or tourism; but on a national scale, a star colony was just as possible as the high-rise Palace of Government which even most of the underdeveloped countries had built for the sake of prestige.

And colonies were definitely a matter of prestige. The major powers had them. So, just as Third World countries had squandered their resources on jet fighters in the twentieth century (and on ironclads in the nineteenth), they bought or leased or even built starships in the twenty-first. These colonies were almost invariably mono-national, undercapitalized, and stratified by class even more rigidly than were their mother countries. All of those factors affected later galactic history. There was a plethora of suitable words on which to plant colonies, however, so that even the most ineptly handled groups of settlers generally managed to survive. Theirs was a hand-to-mouth survival of farming and barter, though, not of spaceports shipping vast quantities of minerals and protein back to Earth.

A few of the better-backed colonies did become very successful. Most of them had been spawned by the larger nations, though a few were private ventures (including that of the Dutch consortium which founded Friesland). Success left their backers in the same situation of those whose colonies were barely surviving, however, since the first result of planetary self-sufficiency was invariably to cut ties and find the best prices available for manufactures on the open market.

There followed a spate of secondary colonization from the successful colony worlds. These new colonies were planted with a specific product in mind: a mineral; a drug; sometimes simply agriculture, freeing more valuable real estate on the homeworlds. Even a planet could be filled in a few centuries by the asymptotic population growth which empty spaces seem to engender in human beings. Secondary colonies were frequently joint efforts, combining settlers and capital from several worlds. They were a business proposition, after all, not matters of national honor.

Unfortunately for the concept, the newly mixed national and racial groups got along just as badly as their ancestors had a few centuries earlier on Earth. The planetary governments of Hiroseke and Stewart, for instance, conferred placidly with each other; but in the iridium-mining colony they had founded together on Kalan, Japanese and Scotsmen were shooting at each other within five years.

The new colonizers had thought they would be able to control their colonies without military force. Their own experience had taught them to control space transport to the new colonies. Without the ability to sell its produce in markets of its own choice, a colony could not strike off on its own—as the homeworlds had themselves done.

But a colony could be forced into a pattern of logical subservience only if its populace was willing to be logical. If instead the settlers decided to eat their own guts out through internal warfare, the colony would become as commercially valueless as Germany in 1648. Inevitably, homeworlds attempted through military force to control and unify their colonies; also inevitably, they increased the disruption by their activities.

And even if some sort of a military solution *was* imposed, there remained the question of how to deal with the defeated trouble-makers—however they were defined—to avoid a new outbreak of fighting. Ideally, they could be used as expendables in battles elsewhere. It was a course which had been followed with success often in the past—Germans in French Indo-China in 1948, and Scots borderers in Ulster in 1605, for two examples. The course required that there be other battles to fight—but there were other unruly colonies as well as backwater worlds whose produce would be useful if it could be controlled at acceptable cost. Perhaps the first case of this occurred in 2414 when Monument equipped four thousand Sikh rebels from Ramadan and shipped them to Portales to take over that planet's tobacco trade, but there were many other examples later.

And in any case, there was always someone willing to hire soldiers, somewhere. World after world armed its misfits and sent them off to someone else's backyard, to attack or defend, to kill or die—so long as they were not doing it at home. Because of the pattern of colonization, there were only a few planets that were not so tense that they might snap into bloody war if mercenaries from across the galaxy were available.

Even for the stable elite of worlds, Friesland and Kronstad, Ssu-ma and Wylie, the system was a losing proposition. Wars and the warriors they spawned were short-term solutions, binding the industrial worlds into a fabric of short-term solutions. In the long run, off-world markets were destroyed, internal investment was channeled into what were basically nonproductive uses, and the civil populace became restive in the omnipresence of violence and a foreign policy directed toward its continuance.

On rural worlds, the result was nothing so subtle as decay. It was life and society shattered forever by the sledge of war.

CULTURAL CONFLICT

Platoon Sergeant Horthy stood with his right arm—his only arm—akimbo, surveying the rippling treetops beneath him and wishing they really were the waves of a cool, gray ocean. The trees lapped high up the sides of the basalt knob that had become Firebase Bolo three weeks before when a landing boat dropped them secretly onto it. Now, under a black plastic ceiling that mimicked the basalt to the eye of the Federation spy satellite, nestled a command car, a rocket howitzer with an air-cushion truck to carry its load of ammunition, and Horthy's three combat cars. Horthy's cars—except on paper. There Lieutenant Simmons-Brown was listed as platoon leader.

One of the long-limbed native reptiles suddenly began to gesture and screech up at the sergeant. The beasts occasionally appeared on the treetops, scurrying and bounding like fleas in a dog's fur. Recently their bursts of rage had become more common—and more irritating. Horthy was a short, wasp-waisted man who wore a spiky goatee and a drum-magazined powergun slung beneath his shoulder. His hand now moved to its grip . . . but shooting meant giving in to frustration, and instead Horthy only muttered a curse.

"You say something, Top?" asked a voice behind him. He turned without speaking and saw Jenne and Scratchard, his two gunners, with a lanky howitzer crewman whose name escaped him.

"Nothing that matters," Horthy said. Scratchard's nickname was Ripper Jack because he carried a long knife in preference to a

111

pistol. He fumbled a little nervously with its hilt as he said, "Look, Top, ah . . . we been talking and Bonmarcher here—" he nodded at the artilleryman "—he says we're not supporting the rest of the Regiment, we're stuck out here in the middle of nowhere to shoot up Federation ships when the war starts."

The sergeant looked sharply at Bonmarcher, then said, "*If* the war starts. Yeah, that's pretty much true. We're about the only humans on South Continent, but if the government decides it still wants to be independent and the Federation decides it's gotta have Squire's World as a colony—well, Fed supply routes pass through two straits within hog shot of this rock." Simmons-Brown would cop a screaming worm if he heard Horthy tell the men a truth supposed to be secret, but one way or another it wasn't going to matter very long.

"But Lord and *Martyrs*, Top," Bonmarcher burst out, "how long after we start shooting is it gonna be before the Feds figure out where the shells're coming from? Sure, this cap—" he thumbed toward the plastic supported four meters over the rock by thin pillars "—hides us now. But sure as death, we'll loose one off while the satellite's still over us, or the Feds'll triangulate radar tracks as the shells come over the horizon at them. Then what'll happen?"

"That's what our combat cars are for," Horthy said wearily, knowing that the Federation would send not troops but a salvo of their own shells to deal with the thorn in their side. "We'll worry about that when it happens. Right now—" He broke off. Another of those damned, fluffy reptiles was shrieking like a cheated whore not twenty meters from him.

"Bonmarcher," the sergeant said in sudden inspiration, "you want to go down there and do something about that noisemaker for me?" Two noisemakers, actually—the beast and the artilleryman himself for as long as the hunt kept him out of the way.

"Gee, Top, I'd sure love to get outa this oven, but I heard the lieutenant order . . ." Bonmarcher began, looking sidelong at the command car fifty meters away in the center of the knob. Its air conditioner whined, cooling Simmons-Brown and the radioman on watch within its closed compartment.

"Look, you just climb down below the leaf cover and don't loose off unless you've really got a target," said Horthy. "I'll handle the lieutenant."

Beaming with pleasure, Bonmarcher patted his sidearm to make sure it was snapped securely in its holster. "Thanks, Top," he said, and began to descend by the cracks and shelvings that eternity had forged even into basalt.

Horthy ignored him, turning instead to the pair of his own men who had waited in silent concern during the exchange. "Look, boys," the one-armed sergeant said quietly, "I won't give you a load of cop about this being a great vacation for us. But you keep your mouths shut and do your jobs, and I'll do my damnedest to get us all out of here in one piece." He looked away from his listeners for a moment, up at the dull iridium vehicles and the stripped or khaki crewmen lounging over them. "Anyhow, neither the Feds or the twats that hired us have any guts. I'll give you even money that one side or the other backs down before anything drops in the pot."

Scratchard, as lean and dark as Horthy, looked at the huge, blond Jenne. There was no belief on either face. Then the rear hatch of the command car flung open and the communications sergeant stepped out whooping with joy.

"They've signed a new treaty!" he shouted. "We're being recalled!"

Horthy grinned, punched each of his gunners lightly in the stomach. "See?" he said. "You listen to Top and he'll bring you home."

All three began to laugh with released tension.

Hilf, Caller of the Moon Sept, followed his sept-brother Seida along the wire-thin filaments of the canopy. Their black footpads flashed a rare primary color as they leaped. The world was slate-gray bark and huge pearly leaves sprouting on flexible tendrils, raised to a sky in which the sun was a sizzling platinum bead. Both runners were lightly dusted with the pollen they had shaken from fruiting bodies in their course. The Tree, though an entity, required cross-fertilization among its segments for healthy growth. The mottled gray-tones of Seida's feathery scales blended perfectly with his surroundings, and his strength was as smooth as the Tree's. Hilf knew the young male hoped to become Caller himself in a few years, knew also that Seida lacked the necessary empathy with the Tree and the sept to hold the position. Besides, his recklessness was no substitute for intelligence.

But Seida was forcing Hilf to act against his better judgment. The creatures on the bald, basalt knob were clearly within the sept's territory; but what proper business had any of the Folk with rock-dwellers? Still, knowing that token activity would help calm his brothers, Hilf had let Seida lead him to personally view the situation. At the back of the Caller's mind was the further realization that the Mothers were sometimes swayed by the "maleness" of action as opposed to intelligent lethargy.

Poised for another leap, Hilf noticed the black line of a worm track on the bark beside him. He halted, instinctively damping the springiness of his perch by flexing his hind legs. Seida shrieked but fell into lowering silence when he saw what his Caller was about. Food was an immediate need. As Hilf had known, Seida's unfitness for leadership included his inability to see beyond the immediate.

The branch was a twenty-centimeter latticework of intergrown tendrils, leapfrogging kilometers across the forest. In its career it touched and fused with a dozen trunks, deep rooted pillars whose tendrils were of massive cross section. Hilf blocked the worm track with a spike-clawed, multi-jointed thumb twice the length of the three fingers on each hand. His other thumb thrust into the end of the track and wriggled. The bark split, baring the hollowed pith and the worm writhing and stretching away from the impaling claw. Hilf's esophagus spasmed once to crush the soft creature. He looked up. Seida stuttered an impoliteness verging on command: he had not forgotten his self-proclaimed mission. The Caller sighed and followed him.

The ancient volcanic intrusion was a hundred-meter thumb raised from the forest floor. The Tree crawled partway up the basalt, but the upper faces of the rock were steep and dense enough to resist attachments by major branches.

Three weeks previously a huge ball had howled out of the sky and poised over the rock, discharging other silvery beasts shaped like great sowbugs and guided by creatures not too dissimilar to the Folk. These had quickly raised the black cover which now hung like an optical illusion to the eyes of watchers in the highest nearby branches. The unprecedented event had sparked the hottest debate of the Caller's memory. Despite opposition from Seida and a few other hotheads, Hilf had finally convinced his sept that the rock was not their affair.

Now, on the claim that one of the brown-coated invaders had climbed out onto a limb, Seida was insisting that he should be charged at once with leading a war party. Unfortunately, at least the claim was true.

Seida halted, beginning to hoot and point. Even without such notice the interloper would have been obvious to Hilf. The creature was some fifty meters away—three healthy leaps, the Caller's mind abstracted—and below the observers. It was huddled on a branch which acted as a flying buttress for the high towers of the Tree. At near view it was singularly unattractive: appreciably larger than one of the sept-brothers, it bore stubby arms and a head less regular than the smooth bullets of the Folk.

As he pondered, the Caller absently gouged a feather of edible orange fungus out of the branch. The rest of the aliens remained under their roof, equally oblivious of the Folk and their own sept-brother. The latter was crawling a little closer on his branch, manipulating the object he carried while turning his lumpy face toward Seida.

Hilf, blending silently into the foliage behind his brother, let his subconscious float and merge while his surface mind grappled with the unpalatable alternatives. The creature below was technically an invader, but it did not seem the point of a thrust against the Moon Sept. Tradition did not really speak to the matter. Hilf could send out a war party, losing a little prestige to Seida since the younger brother had cried for that course from the beginning. Far worse than the loss of prestige was the risk to the sept which war involved. If the interlopers were as strong as they were big, the Folk would face a grim battle. In addition, the huge silver beasts which had whined and snarled as they crawled onto the rock were a dangerous uncertainty, though they had been motionless since their appearance.

But the only way to avoid war seemed to be for Hilf to kill his sept-brother. Easy enough to do—a sudden leap and both thumbs rammed into the brainbox. The fact Seida was not prepared for an attack was further proof of his unfitness to lead. No one would dispute the Caller's tale of a missed leap and a long fall. . . . Hilf poised as Seida leaned out to thunder more abuse at the creature below.

The object in the interloper's hand flashed. The foliage winked cyan and Seida's head blew apart. Spasming muscles threw his body forward, following its fountaining blood in an arc to the branch below. The killer's high cackles of triumph pursued Hilf as he raced back to the Heart.

He had been wrong: the aliens *did* mean war.

Simmons-Brown broke radio contact with a curse. His khakis were sweat-stained and one of the shoulder-board chevrons announcing his lieutenancy was missing. "Top," he whined to Sergeant Horthy who stood by the open hatch of the command car, "Command Central won't send a space boat to pick us up, they want us to *drive* all the way to the north coast for surface pickup to Johnstown. That's twelve hundred kilometers and anyhow, we can't even get the cars *down* off this Lord-stricken rock!"

"Sure we can," Horthy said, planning aloud rather than deigning to contradict the wispy lieutenant. Simmons-Brown was a well-connected incompetent whose approach to problem solving was to throw a tantrum while other people tried to work around him. "We'll link tow cables and . . . no, a winch won't hold but we can blast-set an eyebolt, then rappel the cars down one at a time. How long they give us till pickup?"

"Fifteen days, but—"

A shot bumped the air behind the men. Both whipped around. Horthy's hand brushed his submachine gun's grip momentarily before he relaxed. He said, "It's all plus, just Bonmarcher. I told him he could shut up a couple of the local noisemakers if he stayed below the curve of the rock and didn't put a hole in our camouflage. The Fed satellite isn't good enough to pick up small arms fire in this jungle."

"I distinctly ordered that no shots be fired while we're on detached duty!" snapped Simmons-Brown, his full mustache trembling like an enraged caterpillar. "Distinctly!"

Sergeant Horthy looked around the six blowers and twenty-three men that made up Firebase Bolo. He sighed. Waiting under commo security, between bare rock and hot plastic, would have been rough at the best of times. With Simmons-Brown added . . . "Sorry, sir," the sergeant lied straight-faced, "I must have forgotten."

"Well, get the men moving," Simmons-Brown ordered, already closing the hatch on his air conditioning. "Those bastards at Central might just leave us if we missed pickup. They'd like that."

"Oh, we'll make it fine," Horthy said, his eyes already searching for a good place to sink the eyebolt. "Once we get off the rock there won't be any problem. The ground's flat, and with all the leaves up here cutting off light we won't have undergrowth to bother about. Just set the compasses on north and follow our noses."

"Hey, Top," someone called. "Look what I got!" Bonmarcher had clambered back onto the rock. Behind him, dragged by its lashed ankles, was a deep-chested reptile that had weighed about forty kilos before being decapitated. "Blew this monkey away my first shot," the artilleryman bragged.

"Nice work," Horthy replied absently. His mind was on more important things.

The world of the Moon Sept was not a sphere but a triangular section of forest. That wedge, like those of each of the twenty-eight other septs, was dominated by the main root of a Tree. The ground at the center was thin loam over not subsoil but almost a hectare of ancient root. The trunks sprouting from the edge of this mass were old, too, but not appreciably thicker than the other pillars supporting the Tree for hundreds of kilometers in every direction. Interwoven stems and branches joined eighty meters in the air, roofing the Heart in a quivering blanket of leaves indistinguishable from that of the rest of the forest. The hollow dome within was an awesome thing even without its implications, and few of the Folk cared to enter it.

Hilf himself feared the vast emptiness and the power it focused, but he had made his decision three years before when the Mothers summoned the previous Caller to the Nest and a breeder's diet. Hilf had thrust forward and used the flowing consciousness of the whole sept to face down his rivals for the Callership. Now he thumped to the hard floor without hesitation and walked quickly on feet and knuckles to the pit worn in the center of the root by millennia of Callers. His body prone below the lips of the blond rootwood, Hilf's right claw gashed sap from the Tree and then nicked his own left wrist. Sap and pale blood oozed together, fusing Caller and Tree physically in a fashion dictated by urgency. The intense wood grain rippled from in front of Hilf's eyes and his mind began to fill with shattered, spreading images of the forest. Each heartbeat sent Hilf out in a further surge and blending until every trunk and branch-bundle had become the Tree, each member of the Moon Sept had blurred into the Folk. A black warmth beneath the threshold of awareness indicated that even the Mothers had joined.

The incident trembled through the sept, a kaleidoscope more of emotion than pictures. Seida capered again, gouted and died in the invader's raucous laughter. Reflex stropped claws on the bark of a thousand branches. Response was the Caller's to suggest and guide, not to determine. The first blood-maddened reply by the sept almost overwhelmed Hilf. But his response had been planned, stamped out on the template of experience older than that of any living sept-brother—as old, perhaps, as the joinder of Folk and Tree. The alien nature of the invaders would not be allowed to pervert the traditional response: the remainder of Seida's hatching would go out to punish the death of their brother.

The pattern of the root began to reimpose itself on Hilf's eyes. He continued to lie in the hollow, logy with reaction. Most of the sept were returning to their foraging or play, but there were always eyes trained on the knob and the activity there. And scattered throughout the wedge of the Tree were thirty-seven of the Folk, young and fierce in their strength, who drifted purposefully together.

At the forest floor the raindrops, scattered by the triple canopy, were a saturated fog that clung and made breath a struggle. Horthy ignored it, letting his feet and sinewed hand mechanically balance him against the queasy ride of the air-cushion vehicle. His eyes swept the ground habitually. When reminded by his conscious mind, they took in the canopies above also.

The rain had slowed the column. The strangely woven tree boles were never spaced too closely to pass the armored vehicles between them, but frequent clumps of spire-pointed fungus thrust several meters in the air and confused the aisles. Experience had shown that when struck by a car the saprophytes would collapse in a cloud of harmless spores, but in the fog-blurred dimness they sometimes hid an unyielding trunk behind them. The lead car had its driving lights on though the water dazzle made them almost useless, and all six vehicles had closed up more tightly than Horthy cared to see. There was little chance of a Federation ambush, but even a sudden halt would bring on a multiple collision.

The brassy trilling that had grown familiar in the past several hours sounded again from somewhere in the forest. Just an animal, though. The war on Squire's World was over for the time, and whether the Regiment's employers had won or lost there was no reason for Horthy to remain as tense as he was. Simmons-Brown certainly was unconcerned, riding in the dry cabin of his command car. That was the second vehicle, just ahead of Horthy's. The sergeant's wing gunners huddled in the fighting compartment to either side of him. They were miserable and bored, their minds as empty as their slack, dripping faces.

Irritated but without any real reason to slash the men to vigilance, Horthy glared back along his course. The stubby 150mm howitzer, the cause of the whole Lord-accursed operation, was the fourth vehicle. Only its driver, his head a mirroring ball behind its face shield, was visible. The other five men of the crew were within the open-backed turret whose sheathing was poor protection against hostile fire but enough to keep the rain out.

The ammo transporter was next, sandwiched between the hog and the combat car which brought up the rear of the column. Eighty-kilo shells were stacked ten high on its flat bed, their noses color coded with incongruous gaiety. The nearby mass of explosive drew a wince from Horthy, who knew that if it went off together it could pulverize the basalt they had been emplaced on. On top of the front row of shells where its black fuse winked like a Cyclops' eye was the gas round, a thin-walled cylinder of K3 which could kill as surely by touch as by inhalation. Everyone in the Regiment respected K3, but Horthy was one of the few who understood it well enough to prefer the gas to conventional weapons in some situations.

In part, that was a comment on his personality as well.

To Horthy's right, Rob Jenne began to shrug out of his body armor. "Keep it on, trooper," the sergeant said.

"But Top," Jenne complained, "it rubs in this wet." His fingers lifted the segmented porcelain to display the weal chafed over his floating ribs.

"Leave it on," Horthy repeated, gesturing about the fighting compartment crowded with ammunition and personal gear. "There's not enough room here for us, even without three suits of armor standing around empty. Besides—"

The gray creature's leap carried it skimming over Horthy to crash full into Jenne's chest. Man and alien pitched over the bulk-head. Horthy leaned forward and shot by instinct, using his sidearm instead of the powerful, less handy, tribarrel mounted on the car. His light finger pressure clawed three holes in the creature's back as it somersaulted into the ground with Jenne.

The forest rang as the transporter plowed into the stem of the grounded howitzer. The gun vehicle seemed to crawl with scores of the scale-dusted aliens, including the one whose spear-sharp thumbs had just decapitated the driver. Horthy twisted his body to spray the mass with blue-green fire. The hog's bow fulcrummed in the soil as the transporter's impact lifted its stern. The howitzer upended, its gun tube flopping freely in an arc while inertia vomited men from the turret.

"Watch the bloody ammo!" Horthy shouted into his intercom as a tribarrel hosed one of the aliens off the transporter in a cloud of gore and vaporized metal. Ahead, the command car driver had hit his panic bar in time to save himself, but one of the long-armed creatures was hacking at the vision blocks as though they were the vehicle's eyes. The rear hatch opened and Simmons-Brown flung himself out screaming with fear. Horthy hesitated. The alien gave up its assault on the optical fibers and sprang on the lieutenant's back.

Horthy's burst chopped both of them to death in a welter of blood.

Only body armor saved the sergeant from the attack that sledged his chest forward into the iridium bulkhead. He tried to rise but could not against the weight and the shocks battering both sides of his thorax like paired trip-hammers.

The blows stopped and the weight slid from Horthy's back and down his ankles. He levered himself upright, gasping with pain as intense as that of the night a bullet-firing machine gun had smashed across his armor. Scratchard, the left gunner, grinned at him. The man's pale skin was spattered with the same saffron blood that covered his knife.

"They've gone off, Top," Scratchard said. "Didn't like the tribarrels—even though we didn't hit much but trees. Didn't like this, neither." He stropped his blade clean on the thighs of the beast he had killed with it.

"Bleeding martyrs," Horthy swore under his breath as he surveyed the damage. The platoon's own four blowers were operable, but the overturned hog was a total loss and the transporter's front fan had disintegrated when the steel ground-effect curtain had crumpled into its arc. If there was any equipment yard on Squire's World that could do the repairs, it sure as cop was too far away from this stretch of jungle to matter. Five men were dead and another, his arm ripped from shoulder to wrist, was comatose under the effects of sedatives, clotting agents, antibiotics, and shock.

"All plus," Horthy began briskly. "We leave the bodies, leave the two arty blowers too; and I just hope our scaly friends get real curious about them soon. Before we pull out, I want ten of the high

explosive warheads unscrewed and loaded into the command car—
yeah, and the gas shell, too."

"Via, Top," one of the surviving artillerymen muttered, "why
we got to haul that stuff around?"

" 'Cause I said so," Horthy snarled, "and ain't I in charge?" His
hand jerked the safety pin from one of the delay-fused shells, then
spun the dial to one hour. "Now get moving, because we want to be
a long way away in an hour."

The platoon was ten kilometers distant when the shock wave
rippled the jungle floor like the head of a drum. The jungle had
blown skyward in a gray puree, forming a momentary bubble over a
five-hectare crater.

The Moon Sept waited for twilight in a ring about the shattered
clearing in which the invaders were halted. The pain that had
slashed through every member of the sept at the initial explosion
was literally beyond comparison: when agony gouged at the Tree,
the brothers had collapsed wherever they stood, spewing waste and
the contents of their stomach uncontrollably. Hours later the second
blast tore away ten separate trunks and brought down a hectare of
canopy. The huge silver beasts had shoved the debris to the side
before they settled down in the new clearing. That explosion was
bearable on top of the first only because of the black rage of the
Mothers now insulating the Moon Sept from full empathy with their
Tree; but not even the Mothers could accept further punishment at
that level. Hilf moaned in the root-alcove, only dimly aware that he
had befouled it in reaction. He was a conduit now, not the Caller in
fact, for the eyeless ones had assumed control. The Mothers had
made a two-dimensional observation which the males, to whom up
and down were more important than horizontal direction, had
missed: the invaders were proceeding toward the Nest. They must
be stopped.

The full thousand of the Moon Sept blended into the leaves with
a perfection achieved in the days in which there had been carnivores
in the forest. When one of the Folk moved it was to ease cramps out
of a muscle or to catch the sun-pearl on the delicate edge of a claw.

They did not forage; the wracking horror of the explosions had left them beyond desire for food.

The effect on the Tree had been even worse. In multi-kilometer circles from both blast sites the wood sagged sapless and foliage curled around its stems. The powerguns alone had been devastating to the Tree's careful stasis, bolts that shattered the trunks they clipped and left the splinters ablaze in the rain. Only the lightning could compare in destructiveness, and the charges building in the uppermost branches gave warning enough for the Tree to minimize lightning damage.

There would be a further rain of cyan charges, but that could not be helped. The Mothers were willing to sacrifice to necessity, even a Tree or a sept.

The four silvery beasts lay nose to tail among the craters, only fifty meters from the standing trunks in which the Folk waited. Hilf watched from a thousand angles. Only the rotating cones on the foreheads of each of the beasts seemed to be moving. Their riders were restive, however, calling to one another in low voices whose alien nature could not disguise their tension. The sun that had moments before been a spreading blob on the western horizon was now gone; invisible through the clouds but a presence felt by the Folk, the fixed Moon now ruled the sky alone. It was the hour of the Moon Sept, and the command of the Mothers was the loosing of a blood-mad dog to kill.

"Death!" screamed the sept-brothers as they sprang into the clearing.

There was death in plenty awaiting them.

The antipersonnel strips of the cars were live. Hilf was with the first body when it hurtled to within twenty meters of a car and the strips began to fire on radar command. Each of the white flashes that slammed and glared from just above the ground-effect curtains was fanning out a handful of tetrahedral pellets. Where the energy released by the powerguns blasted flesh into mist and jelly, the projectiles ripped like scythes over a wide area. Then the forest blazed as flickering cyan hosed across it.

The last antipersonnel charge went off, leaving screams and the thump of powerguns that were almost silence after the rattling crescendo of explosions.

The sept, the surprising hundreds whom the shock had paralyzed but not slain, surged forward again. The three-limbed Caller of the invaders shouted orders while he fired. The huge silver beasts howled and spun end for end even as Hilf's brothers began to leap aboard—then the port antipersonnel strips cut loose in a point-blank broadside. For those above the plane of the discharges there was a brief flurry of claws aimed at neck joints and gun muzzles tight against flesh as they fired. Then a grenade, dropped or jarred from a container, went off in the blood-slick compartment of number one car. Mingled limbs erupted. The sides blew out and the bins of ready ammunition gang-fired in a fury of light and gobbets of molten iridium.

The attack was over. The Mothers had made the instant assumption that the third explosion would be on the order of the two previous—and blocked their minds off from a Tree-empathy that might have been lethal. Without their inexorable thrusting, the scatter of sept-brothers fled like grubs from the sun. They had fought with the savagery of their remote ancestors eliminating the great Folk-devouring serpents from the forest.

And it had not been enough.

"Cursed right we're staying here," Horthy said in irritation. "This is the only high ground in five hundred kilometers. If we're going to last out another attack like yesterday's, it'll be by letting our K3 roll downhill into those apes. And the Lord help us if a wind comes up."

"Well, I still don't like it, Top," Jenne complained. "It doesn't look natural."

Horthy fully agreed with that, though he did so in silence. Command Central had used satellite coverage to direct them to the hill, warning again that even in their emergency it might be a day before a landing boat could be cleared to pick them up. From above, the half-kilometer dome of laterite must have been as obvious as a baby in the wedding party, a gritty red pustule on the gray hide of the continent. From the forest edge it was even stranger, and strange meant deadly to men in Horthy's position. But only the antipersonnel strips had saved the platoon the night before, and they were fully discharged. They were left with the gas or nothing.

The hill was as smooth as the porous stone allowed it to be and rose at a gentle 1:3 ratio. The curve of its edge was broken by the great humped roots that lurched and knotted out of the surrounding forest, plunging into the hill at angles that must lead them to its center. As Jenne had said, it wasn't natural. Nothing about this cursed forest was.

"Let's go," Horthy ordered. His driver boosted the angle and power of his drive fans and they began to slide up the hill, followed by the other two cars. Strange that the trees hadn't covered the hill with a network of branches, even if their trunks for some reason couldn't seat in the rock. Enough ground was clear for the power-guns alone to mince an attack, despite the awesome quickness of the gray creatures. Except that the powerguns were low on ammo, too.

Maybe there wouldn't be a third attack.

An alien appeared at the hillcrest fifty meters ahead. Horthy killed it by reflex, using a single shot from his tribarrel. There was an opening there, a cave or tunnel mouth, and a dozen more of the figures spewed from it. "Watch the sides!" Horthy roared at Jenne and Scratchard, but all three powerguns were ripping the new targets. Bolts that missed darted off into the dull sky like brief, blue-green suns.

Jenne's grenade spun into the meter-broad hole as the car overran it. If anything more had planned to come out, that settled it. Scratchard jiggled the controls of the echo sounder, checked the read-out again, and swore, "Via! I don't see any more surface openings, Top, but this whole mound's like a fencepost in termite country!"

The three blowers were pulled up close around the opening, the crews awaiting orders. Horthy toothed his lower lip but there was no hesitation in his voice after he decided. "Wixom and Chung," he said, "get that gas shell out and bring it over here. The rest of you cover the forest—I'll keep this hole clear."

The two troopers wrestled the cylinder out of the command

car and gingerly carried it to the lip of the opening. The hill was reasonably flat on top and the laterite gave good footing, but the recent shooting had left patches glazed by the powerguns and a film of blood over the whole area. The container should not have ruptured if dropped, but no one familiar with K3 wanted to take the chance.

"All plus," Horthy said. "Fuse it for ten seconds and drop it in. As soon as that goes down, we're going to hover over the hole with our fans on max, just to make sure all the gas goes in the right direction. If we can do them enough damage, maybe they'll leave us alone."

The heavy shell clinked against something as it disappeared into the darkness but kept falling in the passage cleared by the grenade. It was well below the surface when the bursting charge tore the casing open. That muted *whoomp* was lost in the shriek of Horthy's fans as his car wobbled on a column of air a meter above the hilltop. K3 sank even in still air, pooling in invisible deathtraps in the low spots of a battlefield. Rammed by the drive fans, it had permeated the deepest tunnels of the mound in less than a minute.

The rioting air blew the bodies and body parts of the latest victims into a windrow beside the opening. Horthy glanced over them with a professional concern for the dead as he marked time. These creatures had the same long limbs and smooth-faced features as the ones which had attacked in the forest, but there was a difference as well. The genitals of the earlier-seen aliens had been tiny, vestigial or immature, but each of the present corpses carried a dong the length and thickness of a forearm. Bet their girlfriends walk bow-legged, Horthy chuckled to himself.

The hill shook with an impact noticeable even through the insulating air. "Top, they're tunneling out!" cried the command car's driver over the intercom.

"Hold your distance!" Horthy commanded as five meters of laterite crumbled away from the base of the hill. The thing that had torn the gap almost filled it. Horthy and every other gunman in the platoon blasted at it in a reaction that went deeper than fear. Even as it gouted fluids under the multiple impacts the thing managed to squirm completely out. The tiny head and the limbs that waved like broomstraws thrust into a watermelon were the only ornamentation on the slug-white torso. The face was blind, but it was the face of the reptiloids of the forest until a burst of cyan pulped its obscenity. Horthy's tribarrel whipsawed down the twenty-meter belly. A sphincter convulsed in front of the line of shots and spewed a mass of eggs in jelly against the unyielding laterite. The blackening that K3 brought to its victims was already beginning to set in before the platoon stopped firing.

Nothing further attempted to leave the mound.

"Wh-what do we do now, Top?" Jenne asked.

"Wait for the landing boat," answered Horthy. He shook the cramp out of his hand and pretended that it was not caused by his panicky deathgrip on the tribarrel moments before. "And we pray that it comes before too bleeding long."

The cold that made Hilf's body shudder was the residue of the Mothers' death throes deep in the corridors of the Nest. No warmth remained in a universe which had seen the last generation of the Folk. The yellow leaf-tinge of his blast-damaged Tree no longer concerned Hilf. About him, a psychic pressure rather than a message, he could feel the gathering of the other twenty-eight septs—just too late to protect the Mothers who had summoned them. Except for the Moon Sept's, the Trees were still healthy and would continue to be so for years until there were too few of the Folk scampering among the branches to spread their pollen. Then, with only the infrequent wind to stimulate new growth, the Trees as well would begin to die.

Hilf began to walk forward on all fours, his knuckles gripping firmly the rough exterior of the Nest. "Top!" cried one of the invaders, and Hilf knew that their eyes or the quick-darting antennae of their silver beasts had discovered his approach. He looked up. The three-limbed Caller was staring at him, his stick extended to kill. His eyes were as empty as Hilf's own.

The bolt hammered through Hilf's lungs and he pitched backwards. Through the bloodroar in his ears he could hear the far-distant howl that had preceded the invader's appearance in the forest.

As if the landing boat were their signal, the thirty thousand living males of the Folk surged forward from the Trees.

THE BONDING AUTHORITY

Wars result when one side either misjudges its chances or wishes to commit suicide; and not even Masada *began* as a suicide attempt. In general, both warring parties expect to win. In the event, they are wrong more than half the time.

Employing mercenaries adds new levels of uncertainty to the already risky business of war. Too often in history a mercenary force has disappeared a moment before the battle; switched sides for a well-timed bribe; or even conquered its employer and brought about the very disasters it was hired to prevent.

Mercenaries, for their part, face the chances common to every soldier of being killed by the enemy. In addition, however, they must reckon with the possibility of being bilked of their pay or massacred to avoid its payment; of being used as cannon fodder by an employer whose distaste for "money-grubbing aliens" may exceed the enemy's; or of being abandoned far from home when defeat or political change erases their employer or his good will. As Xenophon and the Ten Thousand learned, in such circumstances the road home may be long—or as short as a shallow grave.

A solution to both sets of special problems was made possible by the complexity of galactic commerce. The recorded beginnings came early in the twenty-seventh century when several planets caught up in the Confederation Wars used the Terran firm of Felchow und Sohn as an escrow agent for their mercenaries' pay.

Felchow was a commercial banking house which had retained its preeminence even after Terran industry had been in some measure supplanted by that of newer worlds. Neither Felchow nor Terra herself had any personal stake in the chaotic rise and fall of the Barnard Confederation; thus the house was the perfect neutral to hold the pay of the condottieri being hired by all parties. Payment was scrupulously made to mercenaries who performed according to their contracts. This included the survivors of the Dalhousie debacle who were able to buy passage off that ravaged world, despite the fact that less than ten percent of the populace which had hired them was still alive. Conversely, the pay of Wrangel's Legion, which had refused to assault the Confederation drop zone on Montauk, was forfeited to the Montauk government. The Third Armistice intervened and Wrangel's troops were hunted across the face of the planet by both sides, too faithless to use and too dangerous to ignore.

Felchow und Sohn had performed to the satisfaction of all honest parties when first used as an intermediary. Over the next three decades the house was similarly involved in other conflicts, a passive escrow agent and paymaster. It was only after the Ariete Incident of 2662 that the concept coalesced into the one stable feature of a galaxy at war.

The Ariete, a division recruited mostly from among the militias of the Aldoni System, was hired by the rebels on Paley. Their pay was banked with Felchow, since the rebels very reasonably doubted that anyone would take on the well-trained troops of the Republic of Paley if they had already been handed the carrot. But the Ariete fought very well indeed, losing an estimated thirty percent of its effectives before surrendering in the final collapse of the rebellion. The combat losses have to be estimated because the Republican forces, in defiance of the "Laws of War" and their own promises before the surrender, butchered all their fifteen or so thousand mercenary prisoners.

Felchow und Sohn, seeing an excuse for an action which would raise it to incredible power, reduced Paley to Stone Age savagery.

An industrialized world (as Paley was) is an interlocking whole. Off-planet trade may amount to no more than five percent of its

GDP; but when that trade is suddenly cut off, the remainder of the economy resembles a car lacking two pistons. It may make whirring sounds for a time, but it isn't going anywhere.

Huge as Felchow was, a single banking house could not have cut Paley off from the rest of the galaxy. When Felchow, however, offered other commercial banks membership in a cartel and a share of the lucrative escrow business, the others joined gladly and without exception. No one would underwrite cargoes to or from Paley; and Paley, already wracked by a war and its aftermath, shuddered down into the slag heap of history.

Lucrative was indeed a mild word for the mercenary business. The escrowed money itself could be put to work, and the escrowing bank was an obvious agent for the other commercial transactions needed to run a war. Mercenaries replaced equipment, recruited men, and shipped themselves by the thousands across the galaxy. The new banking cartel served those needs smoothly—and maximized its own profits.

With the banks' new power came a new organization. The expanded escrow operations were made the responsibility of a Bonding Authority, still based in Bremen but managed independently of the cartel itself. The Authority's fees were high. In return, its Contracts Department was expert in preventing expensive misunderstandings from arising, and its investigative staff could neither be bribed nor deluded by a violator. Under the Authority's ruthless nurture, the business of war became as regular as any other commercial endeavor, and more profitable than most.

HANGMAN

The light in the kitchen alcove glittered on Lieutenant Schilling's blond curls; glittered also on the frost-spangled window beside her and from the armor of the tank parked outside. All the highlights looked cold to Captain Danny Pritchard as he stepped closer to the infantry lieutenant.

"Sal—" Pritchard began. From the orderly room behind them came the babble of the radios ranked against one wall and, less muted, the laughter of soldiers waiting for action. "You can't think like a Dutchman anymore. We're Hammer's Slammers, all of us. We're mercs. Not Dutch, not Frisians—"

"You're not," Lieutenant Schilling snapped, looking up from the cup of bitter chocolate she had just drawn from the urn. She was a short woman and lightly built, but she had the unerring instinct of a bully who is willing to make a scene for a victim who is not willing to be part of one. "You're a farmer from Dunstan, what d'you care about Dutch miners, whatever these bleeding French do to them. But a lot of us do care, Danny, and if you had a little compassion—"

"But Sal—" Pritchard repeated, only his right arm moving as he touched the blond girl's shoulder.

"Get your hands off me, Captain!" she shouted. "That's over!" She shifted the mug of steaming chocolate in her hand. The voices in the orderly room stilled. Then, simultaneously, someone turned

133

up the volume of the radio and at least three people began to talk loudly on unconnected subjects.

Pritchard studied the back of his hand, turned it over to examine the calloused palm as well. He smiled. "Sorry, I'll remember that," he said in a normal voice. He turned and stepped back into the orderly room, a brown-haired man of thirty-four with a good set of muscles to cover his moderate frame and nothing at all to cover his heart. Those who knew Danny Pritchard slightly thought him a relaxed man, and he looked relaxed even now. But waiting around the electric grate were three troopers who knew Danny very well indeed: the crew of the Plow, Pritchard's command tank.

Kowie drove the beast: a rabbit-eyed man whose fingers now flipped cards in another game of privy solitaire. His deck was so dirty that only familiarity allowed him to read the pips. Kowie's hands and eyes were just as quick at the controls of the tank, sliding its bulbous hundred and fifty metric tons through spaces that were only big enough to pass it. When he had to, he drove nervelessly through objects instead of going around. Kowie would never be more than a tank driver; but he was the best tank driver in the Regiment.

Rob Jenne was big and as blond as Lieutenant Schilling. He grinned up at Pritchard, his expression changing from embarrassment to relief as he saw that his captain was able to smile also. Jenne had transferred from combat cars to tanks three years back, after the Slammers had pulled out of Squire's World. He was sharp-eyed and calm in a crisis. Twice after his transfer Jenne had been offered a blower of his own to command if he would return to combat cars. He had refused both promotions, saying he would stay with tanks or buy back his contract, that there was no way he was going back to those open-topped coffins again. When a tank commander's slot came open, Jenne got it; and Pritchard had made the blond sergeant his own blower chief when a directional mine had retired the previous man. Now Jenne straddled a chair backwards, his hands flexing a collapsible torsion device that kept his muscles as dense and hard as they had been the day he was recruited from a quarry on Burlage.

Line tanks carry only a driver and the blower chief who directs the tank and its guns when they are not under the direct charge of the Regiment's computer. In addition to those two and a captain, command tanks have a Communications Technician to handle the multiplex burden of radio traffic focused on the vehicle. Pritchard's commo tech was Margritte DiManzo, a slender widow who cropped her lustrous hair short so that it would not interfere with the radio helmet she wore most of her waking hours. She was off duty now, but she had not removed the bulky headgear which linked her to the six radios in the tank parked outside. Their simultaneous sound would have been unintelligible babbling to most listeners. The black-haired woman's training, both conscious and hypnotic, broke that babbling into a set of discrete conversations. When Pritchard reentered the room, Margritte was speaking to Jenne. She did not look up at her commander until Jenne's brightening expression showed her it was safe to do so.

Two commo people and a sergeant with Intelligence tabs were at consoles in the orderly room. They were from the Regiment's HQ Battalion, assigned to Sector Two here on Kobold but in no sense a part of the sector's combat companies: Captain Riis' S Company—infantry—and Pritchard's own tanks.

Riis was the senior captain and in charge of the sector, a matter which neither he nor Pritchard ever forgot. Sally Schilling led his first platoon. Her aide, a black-haired corporal, sat with his huge boots up, humming as he polished the pieces of his field-stripped powergun. Its barrel gleamed orange in the light of the electric grate. Electricity was more general on Kobold than on some wealthier worlds, since mining and copper smelting made fusion units a practical necessity. But though the copper in the transmission cable might well have been processed on Kobold, the wire had probably been drawn off world and shipped back here. Aurore and Friesland had refused to allow even such simple manufactures here on their joint colony. They had kept Kobold a market and a supplier of raw materials, but never a rival.

"Going to snow tonight?" Jenne asked.

"Umm, too cold," Pritchard said, walking over to the grate. He pretended he did not hear Lieutenant Schilling stepping out of the alcove. "I figure—"

"Hold it," said Margritte, her index finger curling out for a volume control before the duty man had time to react. One of the wall radios boomed loudly to the whole room. Prodding another switch, Margritte patched the signal separately through the link implanted in Pritchard's right mastoid. "—guns and looks like satchel charges. There's only one man in each truck, but they've been on the horn, too, and we can figure on more Frenchies here any—"

"Red Alert," Pritchard ordered, facing his commo tech so that she could read his lips. "Where is this?"

The headquarters radiomen stood nervously, afraid to interfere but unwilling to let an outsider run their equipment, however ably. "Red Alert," Margritte was repeating over all bands. Then, through Pritchard's implant, she said, "It's Patrol Sigma three-nine, near Haacin. Dutch civilians've stopped three outbound provisions trucks from Barthe's Company."

"Scramble First Platoon," Pritchard said, "but tell 'em to hold for us to arrive." As Margritte coolly passed on the order, Pritchard picked up the commo helmet he had laid on his chair when he followed Lieutenant Schilling into the kitchen. The helmet gave him automatic switching and greater range than the bioelectric unit behind his ear.

The wall radio was saying, "—need some big friendlies fast or it'll drop in the pot for sure."

"Sigma three-niner," Pritchard said, "this is Michael One."

"Go ahead, Michael One," replied the distant squad leader. Pritchard's commo helmet added an airy boundlessness to his surroundings without really deadening the ambient noise.

"Hold what you've got, boys," the tank captain said. "There's help on the way."

The door of the orderly room stood ajar the way Pritchard's crewmen had left it. The captain slammed it shut as he, too, ran for his tank. Behind in the orderly room, Lieutenant Schilling was snapping out quick directions to her own platoon and to her awakened commander.

The Plow was already floating when Danny reached it. Ice

crystals, spewed from beneath the skirts by the lift fans, made a blue-white dazzle in the vehicle's running lights. Frost whitened the ladder up the high side of the tank's plenum chamber and hull. Pritchard paused to pull on his gloves before mounting.

Sergeant Jenne, anchoring himself with his left hand on the turret's storage rack, reached down and lifted his captain aboard without noticeable effort. Side by side, the two men slid through the hatches to their battle stations.

"Ready," Pritchard said over the intercom.

"Movin' on," replied Kowie, and with his words the tank slid forward over the frozen ground like grease on a hot griddle.

The command post had been a district road-maintenance center before all semblance of central government on Kobold had collapsed. The orderly room and officers' quarters were in the supervisor's house, a comfortable structure with shutters and mottoes embroidered in French on the walls. Some of the hangings had been defaced by short-range gunfire. The crew barracks across the road now served the troopers on headquarters duty. Many of the Slammers could read the Dutch periodicals abandoned there in the break-up. The equipment shed beside the barracks garaged the infantry skimmers because the battery-powered platforms could not shrug off the weather like the huge panzers of M Company. The shed doors were open, pluming the night with heated air as the duty platoon ran for its mounts. Some of the troopers had not yet donned their helmets and body armor. Jenne waved as the tank swept on by; then the road curved and the infantry was lost in the night.

Kobold was a joint colony of Aurore and Friesland. When eighty years of French oppression had driven the Dutch settlers to rebellion, their first act was to hire Hammer's Slammers. The break between Hammer and Friesland had been sharp, but time has a way of blunting anger and letting old habits resume. The Regimental language was Dutch, and many of the Slammers' officers were Frisians seconded from their own service. Friesland gained from the men's experience when they returned home; Hammer gained company officers with excellent training from the Groningen Academy.

To counter the Slammers, the settlers of Auroran descent had hired three Francophone regiments. If either group of colonists could have afforded to pay its mercenaries unaided, the fighting would have been immediate and brief. Kobold had been kept deliberately poor by its homeworlds, however; so in their necessities the settlers turned to those homeworlds for financial help.

And neither Aurore nor Friesland wanted a war on Kobold.

Friesland had let its settlers swing almost from the beginning, sloughing their interests for a half share of the copper produced and concessions elsewhere in its sphere of influence. The arrangement was still satisfactory to the Council of State, if Frisian public opinion could be mollified by apparent activity. Aurore was on the brink of war in the Zemla System. Her Parliament feared another proxy war which could in a moment explode full-fledged, even though Friesland had been weakened by a decade of severe internal troubles. So Aurore and Friesland reached a compromise. Then, under threat of abandonment, the warring parries were forced to transfer their mercenaries' contracts to the homeworlds. Finally, Aurore and Friesland mutually hired the four regiments: the Slammers; Compagnie de Barthe; the Alaudae; and Phenix Moirots. Mercs from either side were mixed and divided among eight sectors imposed on a map of inhabited Kobold. There the contract ordered them to keep peace between the factions; prevent the importation of modern weapons to either side; and—wait.

But Colonel Barthe and the Auroran leaders had come to a further, secret agreement; and although Hammer had learned of it, he had informed only two men—Major Steuben, his aide and body-guard; and Captain Daniel Pritchard.

Pritchard scowled at the memory. Even without the details a traitor had sold Hammer, it would have been obvious that Barthe had his own plans. In the other sectors, Hammer's men and their French counterparts ran joint patrols. Both sides scattered their camps throughout the sectors, just as the villages of either nationality were scattered. Barthe had split his sectors in halves, brusquely ordering the Slammers to keep to the west of the River Aillet because his own troops were mining the east of the basin heavily. Barthe's Company was noted for its minefields. That skill was one of the reasons they had been hired by the French. Since most of Kobold was covered either by forests or by rugged hills, armor was limited to roads where well-placed mines could stack tanks like crushed boxes.

Hammer listened to Barthe's pronouncement and laughed, despite the anger of most of his staff officers. Beside him, Joachim Steuben had grinned and traced the line of his cutaway holster. When Danny Pritchard was informed, he had only shivered a little and called a vehicle inspection for the next morning. That had been three months ago. . . .

The night streamed by like smoke around the tank. Pritchard lowered his face shield, but he did not drop his seat into the belly of the tank. Vision blocks within gave a 360-degree view of the tank's surroundings, but the farmer in Danny could not avoid the feeling of blindness within the impenetrable walls. Jenne sat beside his captain in a cupola fitted with a three-barreled automatic weapon. He too rode with his head out of the hatch, but that was only for comradeship. The sergeant much preferred to be inside. He would button up at the first sign of hostile action. Jenne was in no sense a coward; it was just that he had quirks. Most combat veterans do.

Pritchard liked the whistle of the black wind past his helmet. Warm air from the tank's resistance heaters jetted up through the hatch and kept his body quite comfortable.

The vehicle's huge mass required the power of a fusion plant to drive its lift motors, and the additional burden of climate control was inconsequential.

The tankers' face shields automatically augmented the light of the moon, dim and red because the sun it reflected was dim and red as well. The boosted light level displayed the walls of forest, the boles snaking densely to either side of the road. At Kobold's perihelion, the thin stems grew in days to their full six-meter height and spread a ceiling of red-brown leaves the size of blankets. Now, at aphelion, the chilled, sapless trees burned with almost explosive intensity. The wood was too dangerous to use for heating, even if electricity had not been common, but it fueled the gasogene engines of most vehicles on the planet.

Jenne gestured ahead. "Blowers," he muttered on the intercom. His head rested on the gun switch though he knew the vehicles must be friendly. The Plow slowed.

Pritchard nodded agreement. "Michael First, this is Michael One," he said. "Flash your running lights so we can be sure it's you."

"Roger," replied the radio. Blue light flickered from the shapes hulking at the edge of the forest ahead. Kowie throttled the fans up to cruise, then chopped them and swung expertly into the midst of the four tanks of the outlying platoon.

"Michael One, this is Sigma One," Captain Riis' angry voice demanded in the helmet.

"Go ahead."

"Barthe's sent a battalion across the river. I'm moving Lieutenant Schilling into position to block 'em and called Central for artillery support. You hold your first platoon at Haacin for reserve and any partisans up from Portela. I'll take direct command of the rest of—"

"Negative, negative, Sigma One!" Pritchard snapped. The Plow was accelerating again, second in the line of five tanks. They were beasts of prey sliding across the landscape of snow and black trees at eighty kph and climbing. "Let the French through, Captain. There won't be fighting, repeat, negative fighting."

"There damned well *will* be fighting, Michael One, if Barthe tries to shove a battalion into my sector!" Riis thundered back. "Remember, this isn't your command or a joint command. *I'm* in charge here."

"Margritte, patch me through to Battalion," Pritchard hissed on intercom. The Plow's turret was cocked thirty degrees to the right. It covered the forest sweeping by to that side and anything which might be hiding there. Pritchard's mind was on Sally Schilling, riding a skimmer through forest like that fl anking the tanks, hurrying with her fifty men to try to stop a battalion's hasty advance.

The commo helmet popped quietly to itself. Pritchard tensed, groping for the words he would need to convince Lieutenant Colonel Miezierk. Miezierk, under whom command of Sectors One and Two was grouped, had been a Frisian regular until five years ago. He was supposed to think like a merc, now, not like a Frisian; but . . .

The voice that suddenly rasped, "Override, override!" was not Miezierk's. "Sigma One, Michael One, this is Regiment."

"Go ahead," Pritchard blurted. Captain Riis, equally rattled, said, "Yes, *sir!*" on the three-way link.

"Sigma, your fire order is cancelled. Keep your troops on alert, but keep 'em the hell out of Barthe's way."

"But Colonel Hammer—"

"Riis, you're not going to start a war tonight. Michael One, can your panzers handle whatever's going on at Haacin without violating the contract?"

"Yes, sir." Pritchard flashed a map briefly on his face shield to check his position. "We're almost there now."

"If you can't handle it, Captain, you'd better hope you're killed in action," Colonel Hammer said bluntly. "I haven't nursed this regiment for twenty-three years to lose it because somebody forgets what his job is." Then, more softly—Pritchard could imagine the colonel flicking his eyes side to side to gauge bystanders' reactions—he added, "There's support if you need it, Captain—if they're the ones who breach the contract."

"Affirmative."

"Keep the lid on, boy! Regiment out." The trees had drunk the whine of the fans. Now the road curved and the tanks banked greasily to join the main highway from Dimo to Portela. The tailings pile of the Haacin Mine loomed to the right and hurled the drive noise back redoubled at the vehicles. The steel skirts of the lead tank touched the road metal momentarily, showering the night with orange sparks. Beyond the mine were the now-empty wheatfields and then the village itself.

Haacin, the largest Dutch settlement in Sector Two, sprawled to either side of the highway. Its houses were two- and three-story lumps of cemented mine tailings. They were roofed with tile or plastic rather than shakes of native timber, because of the wood's lethal flammability. The highway was straight and broad. It gave Pritchard a good view of the three cargo vehicles pulled to one side. Men in local dress swarmed about them. Across the road were ten of Hammer's khaki-clad infantry, patrol S-39, whose ported weapons half-threatened, half-protected the trio of drivers in their midst. Occasionally a civilian turned to hurl a curse at Barthe's men, but mostly the Dutch busied themselves with off-loading cartons from the trucks.

Pritchard gave a brief series of commands. The four line tanks grounded in a hedgehog at the edge of the village. Their main guns and automatics faced outward in all directions. Kowie swung the command vehicle around the tank which had been leading it. He cut the fans' angle of attack, slowing the Plow without losing the ability to accelerate quickly. The command vehicle eased past the squad of infantry, then grounded behind the rearmost truck. Pritchard felt the fans' hum through the metal of the hull.

"Who's in charge here?" the captain demanded, his voice booming through the command vehicle's public address system.

The Dutch unloading the trucks halted silently. A squat man in a parka of feathery native fur stepped forward. Unlike many of the other civilians, he was not armed. He did not flinch when Pritchard pinned him with the spotlight of the tank. "I am Paul van Oosten," the man announced in the heavy Dutch of Kobold. "I am Mayor of Haacin. But if you mean who leads us in what we are doing here, well . . . perhaps Justice herself does. Klaus, show them what these trucks were carrying to Portela."

Another civilian stepped forward, ripping the top off the box he carried. Flat plastic wafers spilled from it, glittering in the cold light: powergun ammunition, intended for shoulder weapons like those the infantry carried.

"They were taking powerguns to the beasts of Portela to use against us," van Oosten said. He used the slang term, "skepsels" to name the Francophone settlers. The Mayor's shaven jaw was jutting out in anger.

"Captain!" called one of Barthe's truck drivers, brushing forward through the ring of Hammer's men. "Let me explain."

One of the civilians growled and lifted his heavy musket. Rob Jenne rang his knuckles twice on the receiver of his tribarrel, calling attention to the muzzles as he swept them down across the crowd. The Dutchman froze. Jenne smiled without speaking.

"We were sent to pick up wheat the regiment had purchased," Barthe's man began. Pritchard was not familiar with Barthe's insignia, but from the merc's age and bearing he was a senior sergeant. An unlikely choice to be driving a provisions truck. "One of the vehicles happened to be partly loaded. We didn't take the time to empty it because we were in a hurry to finish the run and go off duty— there was enough room and lift to handle that little bit of gear and the grain besides.

"In any case—" and here the sergeant began pressing, because the tank captain had not cut him off at the first sentence as expected "—you do not, and these fools *surely* do not, have the right to stop Colonel Barthe's transport. If you have questions about the way we pick up wheat, that's between your CO and ours. Sir."

Pritchard ran his gloved index finger back and forth below his right eye-socket. He was ice inside, bubbling ice that tore and chilled him and had nothing to do with the weather. He turned back to Mayor van Oosten. "Reload the trucks," he said, hoping that his voice did not break.

"You can't!" van Oosten cried. "These powerguns are the only chance my village, my *people* have to survive when you leave. You know what'll happen, don't you? Friesland and Aurore, they'll come to an agreement, a *trade-off*, they'll call it, and all the troops will leave. It's our lives they're trading! The beasts in Dimo, in Portela if you let these go through, they'll have powerguns that *their* mercenaries gave them. And we—"

Pritchard whispered a prepared order into his helmet mike. The rearmost of the four tanks at the edge of the village fired a single round from its main gun. The night flared cyan as the 200mm bolt struck the middle of the tailings pile a kilometer away. Stone, decomposed by the enormous energy of the shot, recombined in a huge gout of flame. Vapor, lava, and cinders spewed in every direction. After a moment, bits of high-flung rock began pattering down on the roofs of Haacin.

The bolt caused a double thunderclap, that of the heated air followed by the explosive release of energy at the point of impact. When the reverberations died away there was utter silence in

Haacin. On the distant jumble of rock, a dying red glow marked where the charge had hit. The shot had also ignited some saplings rooted among the stones. They had blazed as white torches for a few moments but they were already collapsing as cinders.

"The Slammers are playing this by rules," Pritchard said. Loudspeakers flung his quiet words about the village like the echoes of the shot; but he was really speaking for the recorder in the belly of the tank, preserving his words for a later Bonding Authority hearing. "There'll be no powerguns in civilian hands. Load every bit of this gear back in the truck. Remember, there's satellites up there—" Pritchard waved generally at the sky "—that see everything that happens on Kobold. If one powergun is fired by a civilian in this sector, I'll come for him. I promise you."

The mayor sagged within his furs. Turning to the crowd behind him, he said, "Put the guns back on the truck. So that the Portelans can kill us more easily."

"Are you mad, van Oosten?" demanded the gunman who had earlier threatened Barthe's sergeant.

"Are *you* mad, Kruse?" the mayor shouted back without trying to hide his fury. "D'ye doubt what those tanks would do to Haacin? And do you doubt this butcher—" his back was to Pritchard but there was no doubt as to whom the mayor meant "—would use them on us? Perhaps tomorrow we could have . . ."

There was motion at the far edge of the crowd, near the corner of a building. Margritte, watching the vision blocks within, called a warning. Pritchard reached for his panic bar—Rob Jenne was traversing the tribarrel. All three of them were too late. The muzzle flash was red and it expanded in Pritchard's eyes as a hammer blow smashed him in the middle of the forehead.

The bullet's impact heaved the tanker up and backwards. His shattered helmet flew off into the night. The unyielding hatch coaming caught him in the small of the back, arching his torso over it as if he were being broken on the wheel. Pritchard's eyes flared with sheets of light. As reaction flung him forward again, he realized he was hearing the reports of Jenne's powergun and that some of the hellish flashes were real.

If the tribarrel's discharges were less brilliant than that of the main gun, then they were more than a hundred times as close to the civilians. The burst snapped within a meter of one bystander, an old man who stumbled backward into a wall. His mouth and staring eyes were three circles of empty terror. Jenne fired seven rounds. Every charge but one struck the sniper or the building he sheltered against. Powdered concrete sprayed from the wall. The sniper's body spun backwards, chest gobbled away by the bolts. His right arm still gripped the musket he had fired at Pritchard. The arm had been flung alone onto the snowy pavement. The electric bite of ozone hung in the air with the ghostly afterimages of the shots. The dead man's clothes were burning, tiny orange flames that rippled into smoke an inch from their bases.

Jenne's big left hand was wrapped in the fabric of Pritchard's jacket, holding the dazed officer upright. "There's another rule you play by," the sergeant roared to the crowd. "You shoot at Hammer's Slammers and you get your balls kicked between your ears. Sure as god, boys; sure as death." Jenne's right hand swung the muzzles of his weapon across the faces of the civilians. "Now, load the bleeding trucks like the captain said, heroes."

For a brief moment, nothing moved but the threatening power-gun. Then a civilian turned and hefted a heavy crate back aboard the truck from which he had just taken it. Empty-handed, the colonist began to sidle away from the vehicle—and from the deadly tribarrel. One by one the other villagers reloaded the hijacked cargo, the guns and ammunition they had hoped would save them in the cataclysm they awaited. One by one they took the blower chief's unspoken leave to return to their houses. One who did not leave was sobbing out her grief over the mangled body of the sniper. None of her neighbors had gone to her side. They could all appreciate—now—what it would have meant if that first shot had led to a general firefight instead of Jenne's selective response.

"Rob, help me get him inside," Pritchard heard Margritte say.

Pritchard braced himself with both hands and leaned away from his sergeant's supporting arm. "No, I'm all right," he croaked.

His vision was clear enough, but the landscape was flashing bright and dim with vari-colored light.

The side hatch of the turret clanked. Margritte was beside her captain. She had stripped off her cold weather gear in the belly of the tank and wore only her khaki uniform. "Get back inside there," Pritchard muttered. "It's not safe." He was afraid of falling if he raised a hand to fend her away. He felt an injector prick the swelling flesh over his cheekbones. The flashing colors died away though Pritchard's ears began to ring.

"They carried some into the nearest building," the noncom from Barthe's Company was saying. He spoke in Dutch, having sleep-trained in the language during the transit to Kobold just as Hammer's men had in French.

"Get it," Jenne ordered the civilians still near the trucks. Three of them were already scurrying toward the house the merc had indicated. They were back in moments, carrying the last of the arms chests.

Pritchard surveyed the scene. The cargo had been reloaded, except for the few spilled rounds winking from the pavement. Van Oosten and the furious Kruse were the only villagers still in sight. "All right," Pritchard said to the truck drivers, "get aboard and get moving. And come back by way of Bitzen, not here. I'll arrange an escort for you."

The French noncom winked, grinned, and shouted a quick order to his men. The infantrymen stepped aside silently to pass the truckers. The French mercenaries mounted their vehicles and kicked them to life. Their fans whined and the trucks lifted, sending snow crystals dancing. With gathering speed, they slid westward along the forest-rimmed highway.

Jenne shook his head at the departing trucks, then stiffened as his helmet spat a message. "Captain," he said, "we got company coming."

Pritchard grunted. His own radio helmet had been smashed by the bullet, and his implant would only relay messages on the band to which it had been verbally keyed most recently. "Margritte, start switching for me," he said. His slender commo tech was already slipping back inside through the side hatch. Pritchard's blood raced with the chemicals Margritte had shot into it. His eyes and mind worked perfectly, though all his thoughts seemed to have razor edges on them.

"Use mine," Jenne said, trying to hand the captain his helmet.

"I've got the implant," Pritchard said. He started to shake his head and regretted the motion instantly. "That and Margritte's worth a helmet any day."

"It's a whole battalion," Jenne explained quietly, his eyes scanning the Bever Road down which Command Central had warned that Barthe's troops were coming. "All but the artillery—that's back in Dimo, but it'll range here easy enough. Brought in the antitank battery and a couple calliopes, though."

"Slide us up ahead of Michael First," Pritchard ordered his driver. As the Plow shuddered, then spun on its axis, the captain dropped his seat into the turret to use the vision blocks. He heard Jenne's seat whirr down beside him and the cupola hatch snick closed. In front of Pritchard's knees, pale in the instrument lights, Margritte DiManzo sat still and open-eyed at her communications console.

"Little friendlies," Pritchard called through his loudspeakers to the ten infantrymen, "find yourselves a quiet alley and hope nothing happens. The Lord help you if you fire a shot without me ordering it." The Lord help us all, Pritchard added to himself.

Ahead of the command vehicle, the beetle shapes of First Platoon began to shift position. "Michael First," Pritchard ordered sharply, "get back as you were. We're not going to engage Barthe, we're going to meet him." Maybe.

Kowie slid them alongside, then a little forward of the point vehicle of the defensive lozenge. They set down. All of the tanks were buttoned up, save for the hatch over Pritchard's head. The central vision block was a meter by 30 cm panel. It could be set for anything from a 360-degree view of the tank's surroundings to a one-to-one image of an object a kilometer away. Pritchard focused and ran the gain to ten magnifications, then thirty. At the higher power, motion curling along the snow-smoothed grainfields between Haacin and its mine resolved into men. Barthe's troops were clad in sooty-white coveralls and battle armor. The leading elements were hunched low on the meager platforms of their skimmers. Magnification and the augmented light made the skittering images grainy, but the tanker's practiced eye caught the tubes of rocket launchers clipped to every one of the skimmers. The skirmish line swelled at two points where self-propelled guns were strung like beads on the cord of men: antitank weapons, 50mm powerguns firing high-intensity charges. They were supposed to be able to burn through the heaviest armor. Barthe's boys had come loaded for bear; oh yes. They thought they knew just what they were going up against. Well, the Slammers weren't going to show them they were wrong. Tonight.

"Running lights, everybody," Pritchard ordered. Then, taking a deep breath, he touched the lift on his seat and raised himself head and shoulders back into the chill night air. There was a hand light clipped to Pritchard's jacket. He snapped it on, aiming the beam down onto the turret top so that the burnished metal splashed diffused radiance up over him. It bathed his torso and face plainly for the oncoming infantry. Through the open hatch, Pritchard could hear Rob cursing. Just possibly Margritte was mumbling a prayer.

"Batteries at Dimo and Harfleur in Sector One have received fire orders and are waiting for a signal to execute," the implant grated. "If Barthe opens fire, Command Central will not, repeat, negative, use Michael First or Michael One to knock down the shells. Your guns will be clear for action, Michael One."

Pritchard grinned starkly. His face would not have been pleasant even if livid bruises were not covering almost all of it. The Slammers' central fire direction computer used radar and satellite reconnaissance to track shells in flight. Then the computer took control of any of the Regiment's vehicle-mounted powerguns and swung them onto the target. Central's message notified Pritchard that he would have full control of his weapons at all times, while guns tens or hundreds of kilometers away kept his force clear of artillery fire.

Margritte had blocked most of the commo traffic, Pritchard realized. She had let through only this message that was crucial to what they were about to do. A good commo tech; a very good person indeed.

The skirmish line grounded. The nearest infantrymen were within fifty meters of the tanks and their fellows spread off into the night like lethal wings. Barthe's men rolled off their skimmers and lay prone. Pritchard began to relax when he noticed that their rocket launchers were still aboard the skimmers. The antitank weapons were in instant reach, but at least they were not being leveled for an immediate salvo. Barthe didn't want to fight the Slammers. His targets were the Dutch civilians, just as Mayor van Oosten had suggested.

An air-cushion jeep with a driver and two officers aboard drew close. It hissed slowly through the line of infantry, then stopped nearly touching the command vehicle's bow armor. One of the officers dismounted. He was a tall man who was probably very thin when he was not wearing insulated coveralls and battle armor. He raised his face to Pritchard atop the high curve of the blower, sweeping up his reflective face shield as he did so. He was Lieutenant Colonel Benoit, commander of the French mercenaries in Sector Two, a clean-shaven man with sharp features and a splash of gray hair displaced across his forehead by his helmet. Benoit grinned and waved at the muzzle of the 200mm powergun pointed at him. Nobody had ever said Barthe's chief subordinate was a coward.

Pritchard climbed out of the turret to the deck, then slid down the bow slope to the ground. Benoit was several inches taller than the tanker, with a force of personality which was daunting in a way that height alone could never be. It didn't matter to Pritchard. He worked with tanks and with Colonel Hammer; nothing else was going to face down a man who was accustomed to those.

"Sergeant Major Oberlie reported how well and . . . firmly you handled their little affair, Captain," Benoit said, extending his hand to Pritchard. "I'll admit that I was a little concerned that I would have to rescue my men myself."

"Hammer's Slammers can be depended on to keep their contracts," the tanker replied, smiling with false warmth. "I told these squareheads that any civilian caught with a powergun was going to have to answer to me for it. Then we made sure nobody thinks we were kidding."

Benoit chuckled. Little puffs of vapor spurted from his mouth with the sounds. "You've been sent to the Groningen Academy, have you not, Captain Pritchard?" the older man asked. "You understand that I take an interest in my opposite numbers in this sector."

Pritchard nodded. "The Old Man picked me for the two-year crash course on Friesland, yeah. Now and again he sends noncoms he wants to promote."

"But you're not a Frisian, though you have Frisian military training," the other mercenary continued, nodding to himself. "As you know, Captain, promotion in some infantry regiments comes much faster than it does in the . . . Slammers. If you feel a desire to speak to Colonel Barthe some time in the future, I assure you this evening's business will not be forgotten."

"Just doing my job, Colonel," Pritchard simpered. Did Benoit think a job off er would make a traitor of him? Perhaps. Hammer had bought Barthe's plans for very little, considering their military worth. "Enforcing the contract, just like you'd have done if things were the other way around."

Benoit chuckled again and stepped back aboard his jeep. "Until we meet again, Captain Pritchard," he said. "For the moment I think we'll just proceed on into Portela. That's permissible under the contract, of course."

"Swing wide around Haacin, will you?" Pritchard called back. "The folks there're pretty worked up. Nobody wants more trouble, do we?"

Benoit nodded. As his jeep lifted, he spoke into his helmet communicator. The skirmish company rose awkwardly and set off in a counterclockwise circuit of Haacin. Behind them, in a column reformed from their support positions at the base of the tailings heap, came the truck-mounted men of the other three companies. Pritchard stood and watched until the last of them whined past.

Air stirred by the tank's idling fans leaked out under the skirts. The jets formed tiny deltas of the snow which winked as Pritchard's feet caused eddy currents. In their cold precision the tanker recalled Colonel Benoit's grin.

"Command Central," Pritchard said as he climbed his blower, "Michael One. Everything's smooth here. Over." Then, "Sigma One, this is Michael One. I'll be back as quick as fans'll move me, so if you have anything to say we can discuss it then." Pritchard knew that Captain Riis must have been burning the net up, trying to raise him for a report or to make demands. It wasn't fair to make Margritte hold the bag now that Pritchard himself was free to respond to the sector chief; but neither did the Dunstan tanker have the energy to argue with Riis just at the moment. Already this night he'd faced death and Colonel Benoit. Riis could wait another ten minutes.

The Plow's armor was a tight fit for its crew, the radios, and the central bulk of the main gun with its feed mechanism. The command vehicle rode glass-smooth over the frozen roadway, with none of the jouncing that a rougher surface might bring even through the air cushion. Margritte faced Pritchard over her console, her seat a meter lower than his so that she appeared a suppliant. Her short hair was the lustrous purple-black of a grackle's throat in sunlight. Hidden illumination from the instruments brought her face to life.

"Gee, Captain," Jenne was saying at Pritchard's side, "I wish you'd a let me pick up that squarehead's rifle. I know those groundpounders. They're just as apt as not to claim the kill credit themselves, and if I can't prove I stepped on the body they might get away with it. I remember on Paradise, me and Piet de Hagen—he was left wing gunner, I was right—both shot at a partisan. And then damned if Central didn't decide the slope had blown herself up with a hand grenade after we'd wounded her. So *neither* of us got the credit. You'd think—"

"Lord's *blood*, Sergeant," Pritchard snarled, "are you so damned proud of killing one of the poor bastards who hired us to protect them?"

Jenne said nothing. Pritchard shrank up inside, realizing what he had said and unable to take the words back. "Oh, Lord, Rob," he said without looking up, "I'm sorry. It . . . I'm shook, that's all."

After a brief silence, the blond sergeant laughed. "Never been shot in the head myself, Captain, but I can see it might shake a fellow, yeah." Jenne let the whine of the fans stand for a moment as the only further comment while he decided whether he would go on. Then he said, "Captain, for a week after I first saw action I meant to get out of the Slammers, even if I had to sweep floors on Curwin for the rest of my life. Finally I decided I'd stick it. I didn't like the . . . rules of the game, but I could learn to play by them.

"And I did. And one rule is, that you get to be as good as you can at killing the people Colonel Hammer wants killed. Yeah, I'm proud about that one just now. It was a tough snap shot and I made it. I don't care why we're on Kobold or who brought us here. But I know I'm supposed to kill anybody who shoots at us, and I will."

"Well, I'm glad you did," Pritchard said evenly as he looked the sergeant in the eyes. "You pretty well saved things from getting out of hand by the way you reacted."

As if he had not heard his captain, Jenne went on, "I was afraid if I stayed in the Slammers I'd turn into an animal, like the dogs we trained back home to kill rats in the quarries. And I was right. But it's the way I am now, so I don't seem to mind."

"You do care about those villagers, don't you?" Margritte asked Pritchard unexpectedly.

The captain looked down and found her eyes on him. They were the rich powder-blue of chicory flowers. "You're probably the only person in the Regiment who thinks that," he said bitterly. "Except for me. And maybe Colonel Hammer . . .."

Margritte smiled, a quick flash and as quickly gone. "There're rule-book soldiers in the Slammers," she said, "captains who'd never believe Barthe was passing arms to the Auroran settlements since he'd signed a contract that said he wouldn't. You aren't that kind. And the Lord knows Colonel Hammer isn't, and he's backing you. I've been around you too long, Danny, to believe you like what you see the French doing."

Pritchard shrugged. His whole face was stiff with bruises and the drugs Margritte had injected to control them. If he'd locked the helmet's chin strap, the bullet's impact would have broken his neck even though the lead itself did not penetrate. "No, I don't like it," the brown-haired captain said. "It reminds me too much of the way the Combine kept us so poor on Dunstan that a thousand of us signed on for birdseed to fight off-planet. Just because it *was* off-planet.

And if Kobold only gets cop from the worlds who settled her, then the French skim the best of that. Sure, I'll tell the Lord I feel sorry for the Dutch here." Pritchard held the commo tech's eyes with his own as he continued, "But it's just like Rob said, Margritte: I'll do my job, no matter who gets hurt. We can't do a thing to Barthe or the French until they step over the line in a really obvious way. That'll mean a lot of people get hurt too. But that's what I'm waiting for."

Margritte reached up and touched Pritchard's hand where it rested on his knee. "You'll do something when you can," she said quietly.

He turned his palm up so that he could grasp the woman's fingers. What if she knew he was planning an incident, not just waiting for one? "I'll do something, yeah," he said. "But it's going to be too late for an awful lot of people."

Kowie kept the Plow at cruising speed until they were actually in the yard of the command post. Then he cocked the fan shafts forward, lifting the bow and bringing the tank's mass around in a curve that killed its velocity and blasted an arc of snow against the building. Someone inside had started to unlatch the door as they heard the vehicle approach. The air spilling from the tank's skirts flung the panel against the inner wall and skidded the man within on his back.

The man was Captain Riis, Pritchard noted without surprise. Well, the incident wouldn't make the infantry captain any angrier than the rest of the evening had made him already.

Riis had regained his feet by the time Pritchard could jump from the deck of his blower to the fan-cleared ground in front of the building. The Frisian's normally pale face was livid now with rage. He was of the same somatotype as Lieutenant Colonel Benoit, his French counterpart in the sector: tall, thin, and proudly erect. Despite the fact that Riis was only twenty-seven, he was Pritchard's senior in grade by two years. He had kept the rank he held in Friesland's regular army when Colonel Hammer recruited him. Many of the Slammers were like Riis, Frisian soldiers who had transferred for the action and pay of a fighting regiment in which their training would be appreciated.

"You cowardly filth!" the infantryman hissed as Pritchard approached. A squad in battle gear stood within the orderly room beyond Riis. He pursed his fine lips to spit.

"Hey, Captain!" Rob Jenne called. Riis looked up. Pritchard turned, surprised that the big tank commander was not right on his heels. Jenne still smiled from the Plow's cupola. He waved at the officers with his left hand. His right was on the butterfly trigger of the tribarrel.

The threat, unspoken as it was, made a professional of Riis again. "Come on into my office," he muttered to the tank captain, turning his back on the armored vehicle as if it were only a part of the landscape.

The infantrymen inside parted to pass the captains. Sally Schilling was there. Her eyes were as hard as her porcelain armor as they raked over Pritchard. That didn't matter, he lied to himself tiredly.

Riis' office was at the top of the stairs, a narrow cubicle which had once been a child's bedroom. The sloping roof pressed in on the occupants, though a dormer window brightened the room during daylight. One wall was decorated with a regimental battle flag—not Hammer's rampant lion but a pattern of seven stars on a white field. It had probably come from the unit in which Riis had served on Friesland. Over the door hung another souvenir, a big-bore musket of local manufacture. Riis threw himself into the padded chair behind his desk. "Those bastards were carrying powerguns to Portela!" he snarled at Pritchard.

The tanker nodded. He was leaning with his right shoulder against the door jamb. "That's what the folks at Haacin thought," he agreed. "If they'll put in a complaint with the Bonding Authority, I'll testify to what I saw."

"Testify, *testify!*" Riis shouted. "We're not lawyers, we're soldiers! You should've seized the trucks right then and—"

"No, I should *not* have, Captain!" Pritchard shouted back, holding up a mirror to Riis' anger. "Because if I had, Barthe would've complained to the Authority himself, and we'd at least've been fined. At least! The contract says the Slammers'll cooperate with the other three units in keeping peace on Kobold. Just because we suspect Barthe is violating the contract doesn't give us a right to violate it ourselves. Especially in a way any *simpleton* can see is a violation."

"If Barthe can get away with it, we can," Riis insisted, but he settled back in his chair. He was physically bigger than Pritchard, but the tanker had spent half his life with the Slammers. Years like those mark men; death is never very far behind their eyes.

"I don't think Barthe can get away with it," Pritchard lied quietly, remembering Hammer's advice on how to handle Riis and calm the Frisian without telling him the truth. Barthe's officers had been in on his plans; and one of them had talked. Any regiment might have one traitor. The tanker lifted down the musket on the wall behind him and began turning it in his fingers. "If the Dutch settlers can prove to the Authority that Barthe's been passing out powerguns to the French," the tanker mused aloud, "well, they're responsible for half Barthe's pay, remember. It's about as bad a violation as you'll find. The Authority'll forfeit his whole bond and pay it over to whoever they decide the injured parties are. That's about three years' gross earnings for Barthe, I'd judge—he won't be able to replace it. And without a bond posted, well, he may get jobs, but they'll be the kind nobody else'd touch for the risk and the pay. His best troops'll sign on with other people. In a year or so, Barthe won't have a regiment anymore."

"He's willing to take the chance," said Riis.

"Colonel Hammer isn't!" Pritchard blazed back.

"You don't know that. It isn't the sort of thing the colonel could say—"

"Say?" Pritchard shouted. He waved the musket at Riis. Its breech was triple-strapped to take the shock of the industrial explosive it used for propellant. Clumsy and large, it was the best that could be produced on a mining colony whose homeworlds had forbidden local manufacturing. "Say? I bet my life against one of these tonight that the colonel wanted us to obey the contract. Do you have the guts to ask him flat out if he wants us to run guns to the Dutch?"

"I don't think that would be proper, Captain," said Riis coldly as he stood up again.

"Then try not to 'think it proper' to go do some bloody stupid stunt on your own—sir," Pritchard retorted. So much for good intentions. Hammer—and Pritchard—had expected Riis' support of the Dutch civilians. They had even planned on it. But the man seemed to have lost all his common sense. Pritchard laid the musket on the desk because his hands were trembling too badly to hang it back on the hooks.

"If it weren't for you, Captain," Riis said, "there's not a Slammer in this sector who'd object to our helping the only decent people on this planet the way we ought to. You've made your decision, and it sickens me. But I've made decisions, too."

Pritchard went out without being dismissed. He blundered into the jamb, but he did not try to slam the door. That would have been petty, and there was nothing petty in the tanker's rage.

Blank-faced, he clumped down the stairs. His bunk was in a parlor which had its own door to the outside. Pritchard's crew was still in the Plow. There they had listened intently to his half of the argument with Riis, transmitted by the implant. If Pritchard had called for help, Kowie would have sent the command vehicle through the front wall buttoned up, with Jenne ready to shoot if he had to, to rescue his CO. A tank looks huge when seen close up. It is all howling steel and iridium, with black muzzles ready to spew death across a planet. On a battlefield, when the sky is a thousand shrieking colors no god ever made and the earth beneath trembles and gouts in sudden mountains, a tank is a small world indeed for its crew. Their loyalties are to nearer things than an abstraction like "The Regiment."

Besides, tankers and infantrymen have never gotten along well together.

No one was in the orderly room except two radiomen. They kept their backs to the stairs. Pritchard glanced at them, then unlatched his door. The room was dark, as he had left it, but there was a presence. Pritchard said, "Sal—" as he stepped within and the club knocked him forward into the arms of the man waiting to catch his body.

The first thing Pritchard thought as his mind slipped toward oblivion was that the cloth rubbing his face was homespun, not the hard synthetic from which uniforms were made. The last thing Pritchard thought was that there could have been no civilians within the headquarters perimeter unless the guards had allowed them; and that Lieutenant Schilling was officer of the guard tonight.

Pritchard could not be quite certain when he regained consciousness. A heavy felt rug covered and hid his trussed body on the floor of a clattering surface vehicle. He had no memory of being carried to the truck, though presumably it had been parked some distance from the command post. Riis and his confederates would not have been so open as to have civilians drive to the door to take a kidnapped officer, even if Pritchard's crew could have been expected to ignore the breach of security.

Kidnapped. Not for later murder, or he would already be dead instead of smothering under the musty rug. Thick as it was, the rug was still inadequate to keep the cold from his shivering body. The only lights Pritchard could see were the washings of icy color from the night's doubled shock to his skull.

That bone-deep ache reminded Pritchard of the transceiver implanted in his mastoid. He said in a husky whisper which he hoped would not penetrate the rug, "Michael One to any unit, any unit at all. Come in please, any Slammer."

Nothing. Well, no surprise. The implant had an effective range of less than twenty meters, enough for relaying to and from a base unit, but unlikely to be useful in Kobold's empty darkness. Of course, if the truck happened to be passing one of M Company's night defensive positions . . . "Michael One to any unit," the tanker repeated more urgently.

A boot slammed him in the ribs. A voice in guttural Dutch snarled, "Shut up, you, or you get what you gave Henrik."

So he'd been shopped to the Dutch, not that there had been much question about it. And not that he might not have been safer in French hands, the way everybody on this cursed planet thought he was a traitor to his real employers. Well, it wasn't fair; but Danny Pritchard had grown up a farmer, and no farmer is ever tricked into believing that life is fair.

The truck finally jolted to a stop. Gloved hands jerked the cover from Pritchard's eyes. He was not surprised to recognize the concrete angles of Haacin as men passed him hand to hand into a cellar. The attempt to hijack Barthe's powerguns had been an accident, an opportunity seized; but the crew which had kidnapped Pritchard must have been in position before the call from S-39 had intervened. "Is this wise?" Pritchard heard someone demand from the background. "If they begin searching, surely they'll begin in Haacin."

The two men at the bottom of the cellar stairs took Pritchard's shoulders and ankles to carry him to a spring cot. It had no mattress. The man at his feet called, "There won't be a search, they don't have enough men. Besides, the beasts'll be blamed—as they should be for so many things. If Pauli won't let us kill the turncoat, then we'll all have to stand the extra risk of him living."

"You talk too much," Mayor van Oosten muttered as he dropped Pritchard's shoulders on the bunk. Many civilians had followed the captive into the cellar. The last of them swung the door closed. It lay almost horizontal to the ground. When it slammed, dust sprang from the ceiling. Someone switched on a dim incandescent light. The scores of men and women in the storage room were as hard and fell as the bare walls. There were three windows at street level, high on the wall. Slotted shutters blocked most of their dusty glass.

"Get some heat in this hole or you may as well cut my throat," Pritchard grumbled.

A woman with a musket cursed and spat in his face. The man behind her took her arm before the gun butt could smear the spittle. Almost in apology, the man said to Pritchard, "It was her husband you killed."

"You're being kept out of the way," said a husky man— Kruse, the hothead from the hijack scene. His facial hair was pale and long, merging indistinguishably with the silky fringe of his parka. Like most of the others in the cellar, he carried a musket. "Without your meddling, there'll be a chance for us to . . . get ready to protect ourselves, after the tanks leave and the beasts come to finish us with their powerguns."

"Does Riis think I won't talk when this is over?" Pritchard asked.

"I told you—" one of the men shouted at van Oosten. The heavy-set mayor silenced him with a tap on the chest and a bellowed, "Quiet!" The rising babble hushed long enough for van Oosten to say, "Captain, you will be released in a very few days. If you—cause trouble, then, it will only be an embarrassment to yourself. Even if your colonel believes you were doing right, he won't be the one to bring to light a violation which was committed with—so you will claim—the connivance of his own officers."

The mayor paused to clear his throat and glower around the room. "Though in fact we had no help from any of your fellows, either in seizing you or in arming ourselves for our own protection."

"Are you all blind?" Pritchard demanded. He struggled with his elbows and back to raise himself against the wall. "Do you think a few lies will cover it all up? The only ships that've touched on Kobold in three months are the ones supplying us and the other mercs. Barthe maybe's smuggled in enough guns in cans of lube oil and the like to arm some civilians. He won't be able to keep that a secret, but maybe he can keep the Authority from proving who's responsible.

"That's with three months and preplanning. If Riis tries to do anything on his own, that many of his own men are going to be short sidearms—they're all issued by serial number, Lord take it!— and a blind Mongoloid could get enough proof to sink the Regiment."

"You think we don't understand," said Kruse in a quiet voice. He transferred his musket to his left hand, then slapped Pritchard across the side of the head. "We understand very well," the civilian said. "All the mercenaries will leave in a few days or weeks. If the French have powerguns and we do not, they will kill us, our wives, our children . . . There's a hundred and fifty villages on Kobold like this one, Dutch, and as many French ones scattered between. It was bad before, with no one but the beasts allowed any real say in the government; but now if they win, there'll be French villages and French mines—and slave pens. Forever."

"You think a few guns'll save you?" Pritchard asked. Kruse's blow left no visible mark in the tanker's livid flesh, though a better judge than Kruse might have noted that Pritchard's eyes were as hard as his voice was mild.

"They'll help us save ourselves when the time comes," Kruse retorted.

"If you'd gotten powerguns from French civilians instead of the mercs directly, you might have been all right," the captain said. He was coldly aware that the lie he was telling was more likely to be believed in this situation than it would have been in any setting he might deliberately have contrived. There had to be an incident, the French civilians *had* to think they were safe in using their illegal weapons . . . "The Portelans, say, couldn't admit to having guns to lose. But anything you take from mercs—us or Barthe, it doesn't matter—we'll take back the hard way. You don't know what you're buying into."

Kruse's face did not change, but his fist drew back for another blow. The mayor caught the younger man's arm and snapped, "Franz, we're here to show him that it's not a few of us, it's every family in the village behind . . . our holding him." Van Oosten nodded around the room. "More of us than your colonel could dream of trying to punish," he added naively to Pritchard. Then he flashed back at Kruse, "If you act like a fool, he'll want revenge anyway."

"You may never believe this," Pritchard interjected wearily, "but I just want to do my job. If you let me go now, it—may be easier in the long run."

"Fool," Kruse spat, and turned his back on the tanker.

A trapdoor opened in the ceiling, spilling more light into the cellar. "Pauli!" a woman shouted down the opening, "Hals is on the radio. There's tanks coming down the road, just like before!"

"The Lord's wounds!" van Oosten gasped. "We must—"

"They can't know!" Kruse insisted. "But we've got to get everybody out of here and back to their own houses. Everybody but me and him—" a nod at Pritchard "—and this." The musket lowered so that its round, black eye pointed straight into the bound man's face.

"No, by the side door!" van Oosten called to the press of conspirators clumping up toward the street. "Don't run right out in front of them." Cursing and jostling, the villagers climbed the ladder to the ground floor, there presumably to exit on an alley.

Able only to twist his head and legs, Pritchard watched Kruse and the trembling muzzle of his weapon. The village must have watchmen with radios at either approach through the forests. If Hals was atop the heap of mine tailings—where Pritchard would have placed his outpost if he were in charge, certainly—then he'd gotten a nasty surprise when the main gun splashed the rocks with Hell. The captain grinned at the thought. Kruse misunderstood and snarled, "If they *are* coming for you, you're dead, you treacherous bastard!" To the backs of his departing fellows, the young Dutchman called, "Turn out the light here, but leave the trapdoor open. That won't show on the street, but it'll give me enough light to shoot by."

The tanks weren't coming for him, Pritchard knew, because they couldn't have any idea where he was. Perhaps his disappearance had stirred up some patrolling, for want of more directed action; perhaps a platoon was just changing ground because of its commander's whim. Pritchard had encouraged random motion. Tanks that freeze in one place are sitting targets, albeit hard ones. But whatever the reason tanks were approaching Haacin, if they whined by in the street outside they would be well within range of his implanted transmitter.

The big blowers were audible now, nearing with an arrogant lack of haste as if bears headed for a beehive. They were moving at about thirty kph, more slowly than Pritchard would have expected even for a contact patrol. From the sound there were four or more of them, smooth and gray and deadly.

"Kruse, I'm serious," the Slammer captain said. Light from the trapdoor back-lit the civilian into a hulking beast with a musket. "If you—"

"Shut up!" Kruse snarled, prodding his prisoner's bruised forehead with the gun muzzle. "One more word, any word, and—"

Kruse's right hand was so tense and white that the musket might fire even without his deliberate intent.

The first of the tanks slid by outside. Its cushion of air was so dense that the ground trembled even though none of the blower's 170 tonnes was in direct contact with it. Squeezed between the pavement and the steel curtain of the plenum chamber, the air spurted sideways and rattled the cellar windows. The rattling was inaudible against the howling of the fans themselves, but the trembling shutters chopped facets in the play of the tank's running lights. Kruse's face and the far wall flickered in blotched abstraction.

The tank moved on without pausing. Pritchard had not tried to summon it.

"That power," Kruse was mumbling to himself, "that should be for us to use to sweep the beasts—" The rest of his words were lost in the growing wail of the second tank in the column.

Pritchard tensed within. Even if a passing tank picked up his implant's transmission, its crew would probably ignore the message. Unless Pritchard identified himself, the tankers would assume it was babbling thrown by the ionosphere. And if he did identify himself, Kruse—

Kruse thrust his musket against Pritchard's skull again, banging the tanker's head back against the cellar wall. The Dutchman's voice was lost in the blower's howling, but his blue-lit lips clearly were repeating, "One word . . ."

The tank moved on down the highway toward Portela.

". . . and maybe I'll shoot you anyway," Kruse was saying. "That's the way to serve traitors, isn't it? *Mercenary!*"

The third blower was approaching. Its note seemed slightly different, though that might be the Aftereffect of the preceding vehicles' echoing din. Pritchard was cold all the way to his heart, because in a moment he was going to call for help. He knew that Kruse would shoot him, knew also that he would rather die now than live after hope had come so near but passed on, passed on. . . .

The third tank smashed through the wall of the house.

The Plow's skirts were not a bulldozer blade, but they were thick steel and backed with the mass of a 150-tonne command tank. The slag wall repowdered at the impact. Ceiling joists buckled into pretzel shape and ripped the cellar open to the floor above. Kruse flung his musket up and fired through the cascading rubble. The boom and red flash were lost in the chaos, but the blue-green fire stabbing back across the cellar laid the Dutchman on his back with his parka aflame. Pritchard rolled to the floor at the first shock. He thrust himself with corded legs and arms back under the feeble protection of the bunk. When the sound of falling objects had died away, the captain slitted his eyelids against the rock dust and risked a look upward.

The collision had torn a gap ten feet long in the house wall, crushing it from street level to the beams supporting the second story. The tank blocked the hole with its gray bulk. Fresh scars brightened the patina of corrosion etched onto its skirts by the atmospheres of a dozen planets. Through the buckled flooring and the dust whipped into arabesques by the idling fans, Pritchard glimpsed a slight figure clinging left-handed to the turret. Her right hand still threatened the wreckage with a submachine gun. Carpeting burned on the floor above, ignited by the burst that killed Kruse. Somewhere a woman was screaming in Dutch.

"Margritte!" Pritahard shouted. "Margritte! Down here!"

The helmeted woman swung up her face shield and tried to pierce the cellar gloom with her unaided eyes. The tank-battered opening had sufficed for the exchange of shots, but the tangle of structural members and splintered flooring was too tight to pass a man—or even a small woman. Sooty flames were beginning to shroud the gap. Margritte jumped to the ground and struggled for a moment before she was able to heave open the door. The Plow's turret swung to cover her, though neither the main gun nor the tribarrel in the cupola could depress enough to rake the cellar. Margritte ran down the steps to Pritchard. Coughing in the rock dust, he rolled out over the rubble to meet her. Much of the smashed sidewall had collapsed onto the street when the tank backed after the initial impact. Still, the crumpled beams of the ground floor sagged further with the additional weight of the slag on them. Head-sized pieces had splanged on the cot above Pritchard.

Margritte switched the submachine gun to her left hand and began using a clasp knife on her captain's bonds. The cord with which he was tied bit momentarily deeper at the blade's pressure.

Pritchard winced, then began flexing his freed hands. "You know, Margi," he said, "I don't think I've ever seen you with a gun before."

The commo tech's face hardened as if the polarized helmet shield had slipped down over it again. "You hadn't," she said. The ankle bindings parted and she stood, the dust graying her helmet and her foam-filled coveralls. "Captain, Kowie had to drive and we needed Rob in the cupola at the gun. That left me to—do anything else that had to be done. I did what had to be done."

Pritchard tried to stand, using the technician as a post on which to draw himself upright. Margritte looked frail, but with her legs braced she stood like a rock. Her arm around Pritchard's back was as firm as a man's.

"You didn't ask Captain Riis for help, I guess," Pritchard said, pain making his breath catch. The line tanks had two-man crews with no one to spare for outrider, of course.

"We didn't report you missing," Margritte said, "even to First Platoon. They just went along like before, thinking you were in the Plow giving orders." Together, captain and technician shuffled across the floor to the stairs. As they passed Kruse's body, Margritte muttered cryptically, "That's four."

Pritchard assumed the tremors beginning to shake the woman's body were from physical strain. He took as much weight off her as he could and found his numbed feet were beginning to function reasonably well. He would never have been able to board the Plow without Sergeant Jenne's grip on his arm, however.

The battered officer settled in the turret with a groan of comfort. The seat cradled his body with gentle firmness, and the warm air blowing across him was just the near side of heaven.

"Captain," Jenne said, "what d'we do about the slopes who grabbed you? Shall we call in an interrogation team and—"

"We don't do anything," Pritchard interrupted. "We just pretend none of this happened and head back to . . ." He paused. His flesh wavered both hot and cold as Margritte sprayed his ankles with some of the apparatus from the medical kit. "Say, how did you find me, anyway?"

"We shut off coverage when you—went into your room," Jenne said, seeing that the commo tech herself did not intend to speak. He meant, Pritchard knew, they had shut off the sound when their captain had said, "Sal." None of the three of them were looking either of the other two in the eyes. "After a bit, though, Margi noticed the carrier line from your implant had dropped off her oscilloscope. I checked your room, didn't find you. Didn't see much point talking it over with the REMFs on duty, either.

"So we got satellite recce and found two trucks'd left the area since we got back. One was Riis', and the other was a civvie junker before that. It'd been parked in the woods out of sight, half a kay up the road from the buildings. Both trucks unloaded in Haacin. We couldn't tell which load was you, but Margi said if we got close, she'd home on your carrier even though you weren't calling us on the implant. Some girl we got here, hey?"

Pritchard bent forward and squeezed the commo tech's shoulder. She did not look up, but she smiled. "Yeah, always knew she was something," he agreed, "but I don't think I realized quite what a person she was until just now."

Margritte lifted her smile. "Rob ordered First Platoon to fall in with us," she said. "He set up the whole rescue." Her fine-fingered hands caressed Pritchard's calves.

But there was other business in Haacin, now. Riis had been quicker to act than Pritchard had hoped. He asked, "You say one of the infantry's trucks took a load here a little bit ago?"

"Yeah, you want the off-print?" Jenne agreed, searching for the flimsy copy of the satellite picture. "What the Hell would they be doing, anyhow?"

"I got a suspicion," his captain said grimly, "and I suppose it's one we've got to check out."

"Michael First-Three to Michael One," the radio broke in. "Vehicles approaching from the east on the hardball."

"Michael One to Michael First," Pritchard said, letting the search for contraband arms wait for this new development. "Reverse and form a line abreast beyond the village. Twenty-meter intervals. The Plow'll take the road." More weapons from Riis? More of

Barthe's troops when half his sector command was already in Portela? Pritchard touched switches beneath the vision blocks as Kowie slid the tank into position. He split the screen between satellite coverage and a ground-level view at top magnification. Six vehicles, combat cars, coming fast. Pritchard swore. Friendly, because only the Slammers had armored vehicles on Kobold, not that cars were a threat to tanks anyway. But no combat cars were assigned to this sector; and the unexpected is always bad news to a company commander juggling too many variables already.

"Platoon nearing Tango Sigma four-two, three-two, please identify to Michael One," Pritchard requested, giving Haacin's map coordinates.

Margritte turned up the volume of the main radio while she continued to bandage the captain's rope cuts. The set crackled, "Michael One, this is Alpha One and Alpha First. Stand by."

"God's bleeding cunt!" Rob Jenne swore under his breath. Pritchard was nodding in equal agitation. Alpha was the Regiment's special duty company. Its four combat car platoons were Colonel Hammer's bodyguards and police.

The troopers of A Company were nicknamed the White Mice, and they were viewed askance even by the Slammers of other companies—men who prided themselves on being harder than any other combat force in the galaxy. The White Mice in turn feared their commander, Major Joachim Steuben; and if that slightly built killer feared anyone, it was the man who was probably traveling with him this night. Pritchard sighed and asked the question. "Alpha One, this is Michael One. Are you flying a pennant, sir?"

"Affirmative, Michael One."

Well, he'd figured Colonel Hammer was along as soon as he heard what the unit was. What the Old Man was doing here was another question, and one whose answer Pritchard did not look forward to learning.

The combat cars glided to a halt under the guns of their bigger brethren. The tremble of their fans gave the appearance of heat ripples despite the snow. From his higher vantage point, Pritchard watched the second car slide out of line and fall alongside the Plow.

The men at the nose and right wing guns were both short, garbed in nondescript battle gear. They differed from the other troopers only in that their helmet shields were raised and that the faces visible beneath were older than those of most Slammers: Colonel Alois Hammer and his hatchetman.

"No need for radio, Captain," Hammer called in a husky voice. "What are you doing here?"

Pritchard's tongue quivered between the truth and a lie. His crew had been covering for him, and he wasn't about to leave them holding the bag. All the breaches of regulations they had committed were for their captain's sake. "Sir, I brought First Platoon back to Haacin to check whether any of the powerguns they'd hijacked from Barthe were still in civvie hands." Pritchard could feel eyes behind the cracked shutters of every east-facing window in the village.

"And have you completed your check?" the colonel pressed, his voice mild but his eyes as hard as those of Major Steuben beside him; as hard as the iridium plates of the gun shields.

Pritchard swallowed. He owed nothing to Captain Riis, but the young fool was his superior—and at least he hadn't wanted the Dutch to kill Pritchard. He wouldn't put Riis' ass in the bucket if there were neutral ways to explain the contraband. Besides, they were going to need Riis and his Dutch contacts for the rest of the plan. "Sir, when you approached I was about to search a building where I suspect some illegal weapons are stored."

"And instead you'll provide backup for the major here," said Hammer, the false humor gone from his face. His words rattled like shrapnel. "He'll retrieve the twenty-four powerguns which Captain Riis saw fit to turn over to civilians tonight. If Joachim hadn't chanced, *chanced* onto that requisition . . ." Hammer's left glove shuddered with the strength of his grip on the forward tribarrel. Then the colonel lowered his eyes and voice, adding, "The quartermaster who filled a requisition for twenty-four pistols from Central Supply is in the infantry again tonight. And Captain Riis is no longer with the Regiment."

Steuben tittered, loose despite the tension of everyone around him. The cold was bitter, but Joachim's right hand was bare. With it he traced the baroque intaglios of his holstered pistol. "Mr. Riis is lucky to be alive," the slight Newlander said pleasantly. "Luckier than some would have wished. But, Colonel, I think we'd best go pick up the merchandise before anybody nerves themself to use it on us."

Hammer nodded, calm again. "Interfile your blowers with ours, Captain," he ordered. "Your panzers watch street level while the cars take care of upper floors and roofs."

Pritchard saluted and slid down into the tank, relaying the order to the rest of his platoon. Kowie blipped the Plow's throttles, swinging the turreted mass in its own length and sending it back into the village behind the lead combat car. The tank felt light as a dancer, despite the constricting side street Kowie followed the car into. Pritchard scanned the full circuit of the vision blocks. Nothing save the wind and armored vehicles moved in Haacin. When Steuben had learned a line company was requisitioning two dozen extra sidearms, the major had made the same deductions as Pritchard had and had inspected the same satellite tape of a truck unloading. Either Riis was insane or he really thought Colonel Hammer was willing to throw away his life's work to arm a village— inadequately. Lord and Martyrs! Riis would have *had* to be insane to believe that!

Their objective was a nondescript two-story building, separated from its neighbors by narrow alleys. Hammer directed the four rearmost blowers down a parallel street to block the rear. The searchlights of the vehicles chilled the flat concrete and glared back from the windows of the building. A battered surface truck was parked in the street outside. It was empty. Nothing stirred in the house.

Hammer and Steuben dismounted without haste. The major's helmet was slaved to a loudspeaker in the car. The speaker boomed, "Everyone out of the building. You have thirty seconds. Anyone found inside after that'll be shot. Thirty seconds!"

Though the residents had not shown themselves earlier, the way they boiled out of the doors proved they had expected the summons. All told there were eleven of them. From the front door came a well-dressed man and woman with their three children: a sexless infant carried by its mother in a zippered cocoon; a girl of eight with her hood down and her hair coiled in braids about her forehead; and a twelve-year-old boy who looked nearly as husky as his father. Outside staircases disgorged an aged couple on the one hand and four tough-looking men on the other.

Pritchard looked at his blower chief. The sergeant's right hand was near the gun switch and he mumbled an old ballad under his breath. Chest tightening, Pritchard climbed out of his hatch. He jumped to the ground and paced quietly over to Hammer and his aide.

"There's twenty-four pistols in this building," Joachim's amplified voice roared, "or at least you people know where they are. I want somebody to save trouble and tell me."

The civilians tensed. The mother half-turned to swing her body between her baby and the officers.

Joachim's pistol was in his hand, though Pritchard had not seen him draw it. "Nobody to speak?" Joachim queried. He shot the eight-year-old in the right knee. The spray of blood was momentary as the flesh exploded. The girl's mouth pursed as her buckling leg dropped her face-down in the street. The pain would come later. Her parents screamed, the father falling to his knees to snatch up the child as the mother pressed her forehead against the door jamb in blind panic.

Pritchard shouted, "You son of a bitch!" and clawed for his own sidearm. Steuben turned with the precision of a turret lathe. His pistol's muzzle was a white-hot ring from its previous discharge. Pritchard knew only that and the fact that his own weapon was not clear of its holster. Then he realized that Colonel Hammer was shouting, *"No!"* and that his open hand had rocked Joachim's head back.

Joachim's face went pale except for the handprint burning on his cheek. His eyes were empty. After a moment, he holstered his weapon and turned back to the civilians. "Now, who'll tell us where the guns are?" he asked in a voice like breaking glassware.

The tear-blind woman, still holding her infant, gurgled, "Here!

In the basement!" as she threw open the door. Two troopers followed her within at a nod from Hammer. The father was trying to close the girl's wounded leg with his hands, but his palms were not broad enough. Pritchard vomited on the snowy street. Margritte was out of the tank with a medikit in her hand. She flicked the civilian's hands aside and began freezing the wound with a spray. The front door banged open again. The two White Mice were back with their submachine guns slung under their arms and a heavy steel weapons chest between them. Hammer nodded and walked to them.

"You could have brought in an interrogation team!" Pritchard shouted at the backs of his superiors. "You don't shoot children!"

"Machine interrogation takes time, Captain," Steuben said mildly. He did not turn to acknowledge the tanker. "This was just as effective."

"That's a little girl!" Pritchard insisted with his hands clenched. The child was beginning to cry, though the local anesthetic in the skin-sealer had probably blocked the physical pain. The psychic shock of a body that would soon end at the right knee would be worse, though. The child was old enough to know that no local doctor could save the limb. "This isn't something that human beings *do*!"

"Captain," Steuben said, "they're lucky I haven't shot all of them."

Hammer closed the arms chest. "We've got what we came for," he said. "Let's go."

"Stealing guns from my colonel," the Newlander continued as if Hammer had not spoken. The handprint had faded to a dull blotch. "I really ought to—"

"Joachim, shut it off!" Hammer shouted. "We're going to talk about what happened tonight, you and I. I'd rather do it when we were alone but I'll tell you now if I have to. Or in front of a court-martial."

Steuben squeezed his forehead with the fingers of his left hand. He said nothing.

"Let's go," the colonel repeated.

Pritchard caught Hammer's arm. "Take the kid back to Central's medics," he demanded.

Hammer blinked. "I should have thought of that," he said simply. "Some times I lose track of . . . things that aren't going to shoot at me. But we don't need this sort of reputation."

"I don't care cop for public relations," Pritchard snapped. "Just save that little girl's leg."

Steuben reached for the child, now lying limp. Margritte had used a shot of general anesthetic. The girl's father went wild-eyed and swung at Joachim from his crouch. Margritte jabbed with the injector from behind the civilian. He gasped as the drug took hold, then sagged as if his bones had dissolved. Steuben picked up the girl.

Hammer vaulted aboard the combat car and took the child from his subordinate's arms. Cutting himself into the loudspeaker system, the stocky colonel thundered to the street, "Listen you people. If you take guns from mercs—either Barthe's men or my own—we'll grind you to dust. Take 'em from civilians if you think you can. You may have a chance, then. If you rob mercs, you just get a chance to die."

Hammer nodded to the civilians, nodded again to the brooding buildings to either side. He gave an unheard command to his driver. The combat cars began to rev their fans.

Pritchard gave Margritte a hand up and followed her. "Michael One to Michael First," he said. "Head back with Alpha First."

Pritchard rode inside the turret after they left Haacin, glad for once of the armor and the cabin lights. In the writhing tree limbs he had seen the Dutch mother's face as the shot maimed her daughter.

Margritte passed only one call to her commander. It came shortly after the combat cars had separated to return to their base camp near Midi, the planetary capital. The colonel's voice was as smooth as it ever got. It held no hint of the rage which had blazed out in Haacin. "Captain Pritchard," Hammer said, "I've transferred command of Sigma Company to the leader of its First Platoon. The sector, of course, is in your hands now. I expect you to carry out your duties with the ability you've already shown."

"Michael One to Regiment," Pritchard replied curtly. "Acknowledged."

Kowie drew up in front of the command post without the furious caracole which had marked their most recent approach. Pritchard slid his hatch open. His crewmen did not move. "I've got to worry about being sector chief for a while," he said, "but you three can sack out in the barracks now. You've put in a full tour in my book."

"Think I'll sleep here," Rob said. He touched a stud, rotating his seat into a couch alongside the receiver and loading tube of the main gun.

Pritchard frowned. "Margritte?" he asked.

She shrugged. "No, I'll stay by my set for a while." Her eyes were blue and calm.

On the intercom, Kowie chimed in with, "Yeah, you worry about the sector, we'll worry about ourselves. Say, don't you think a tank platoon'd be better for base security than these pongoes?"

"Shut up, Kowie," Jenne snapped. The blond Burlager glanced at his captain. "Everything'll be fine, so long as we're here," he said from one elbow. He patted the breech of the 200mm gun.

Pritchard shrugged and climbed out into the cold night. He heard the hatch grind shut behind him.

Until Pritchard walked in the door of the building, it had not occurred to him that Riis' replacement was Sally Schilling. The words "First Platoon leader" had not been a name to the tanker, not in the midst of the furor of his mind. The little blonde glanced up at Pritchard from the map display she was studying. She spat cracklingly on the electric stove and faced around again. Her aide, the big corporal, blinked in some embarrassment. None of the headquarters staff spoke.

"I need the display console from my room," Pritchard said to the corporal. The infantryman nodded and got up. Before he had taken three steps, Lieutenant Schilling's voice cracked like pressure-heaved ice, "Corporal Webbert!"

"Sir?" The big man's face went tight as he found himself a pawn in a game whose stakes went beyond his interest. "Go get the display console for our new commander. It's in his room."

Licking his lips with relief, the corporal obeyed. He carried the heavy four-legged console back without effort.

Sally was making it easier for him, Pritchard thought. But how he wished that Riis hadn't made so complete a fool of himself that he had to be removed. Using Riis to set up a double massacre would have been a lot easier to justify when Danny awoke in the middle of the night and found himself remembering. . . .

Pritchard positioned the console so that he sat with his back to the heater. It separated him from Schilling. The top of the instrument was a slanted, 40 cm screen which glowed when Pritchard switched it on. "Sector Two display," he directed. In response to his words the screen sharpened into a relief map.

"Population centers," he said. They flashed on as well, several dozen of them ranging from a few hundred souls to the several thousand of Haacin and Dimo. Portela, the largest Francophone settlement west of the Aillet, was about twenty kilometers west of Haacin.

And there were now French mercenaries on both sides of that division line. Sally had turned from her own console and stood up to see what Pritchard was doing. The tanker said, "All mercenary positions, confirmed and calculated."

The board spangled itself with red and green symbols, each of them marked in small letters with a unit designation. The reconnaissance satellites gave unit strengths very accurately and computer analysis of radio traffic could generally name the forces. In the eastern half of the sector, Lieutenant Colonel Benoit had spread out one battalion in platoon-strength billets. The guard posts were close enough to most points to put down trouble immediately. A full company near Dimo guarded the headquarters and two batteries of rocket howitzers.

The remaining battalion in the sector, Benoit's own, was concentrated in positions blasted into the rocky highlands ten kays west of Portela. It was not a deployment that would allow the mercs to effectively police the west half of the sector, but it was a very good defensive arrangement. The forest that covered the center of the sector was ideal for hit-and-run sniping by small units of infantry.

The tree boles were too densely woven for tanks to plow through them. Because the forest was so flammable at this season, however, it would be equally dangerous to ambushers. Benoit was wise to concentrate in the barren high ground.

Besides the highlands, the fields cleared around every settlement were the only safe locations for a modern firefight. The fields, and the broad swathes cleared for roads through the forest. . . .

"Incoming traffic for Sector Chief," announced a radioman. "It's from the skepsel colonel, sir." He threw his words into the air, afraid to direct them at either of the officers in the orderly room.

"Voice only, or is there visual?" Pritchard asked. Schilling held her silence.

"Visual component, sir."

"Patch him through to my console," the tanker decided. "And son—watch your language. Otherwise, you say 'beast' when you shouldn't."

The map blurred from the display screen and was replaced by the hawk features of Lieutenant Colonel Benoit. A pick-up on the screen's surface threw Pritchard's own image onto Benoit's similar console.

The Frenchman blinked. "Captain Pritchard? I'm very pleased to see you, but my words must be with Captain Riis directly. Could you wake him?"

"There've been some changes," the tanker said. In the back of his mind, he wondered what had happened to Riis. Pulled back under arrest probably. "I'm in charge of Sector Two, now. Co-charge with you, that is."

Benoit's face steadied as he absorbed the information without betraying an opinion about it. Then he beamed like a feasting wolf and said, "Congratulations, Captain. Someday you and I will have to discuss the . . . events of the past few days. But what I was calling about is far less pleasant, I'm afraid."

Benoit's image wavered on the screen as he paused. Pritchard touched his tongue to the corner of his mouth. "Go ahead, Colonel," he said. "I've gotten enough bad news today that a little more won't signify."

Benoit quirked his brow in what might or might not have been humor. "When we were proceeding to Portela," he said, "some of my troops mistook the situation and set up passive tank interdiction points. Mines, all over the sector. They're booby-trapped, of course. The only safe way to remove them is for the troops responsible to do it. They will of course be punished later."

Pritchard chuckled. "How long do you estimate it'll take to clear the roads, Colonel?" he asked.

The Frenchman spread his hands, palms up. "Weeks, perhaps. It's much harder to clear mines safely than to lay them, of course."

"But there wouldn't be anything between *here* and Haacin, would there?" the tanker prodded. It was all happening just as Hammer's informant had said Barthe planned it. First, hem the tanks in with nets of forest and minefields; then, break the most important Dutch stronghold while your mercs were still around to back you up . . . "The spur road to our HQ here wasn't on your route; and besides, we just drove tanks over it a few minutes ago."

Behind Pritchard, Sally Schilling was cursing in a sharp, carrying voice. Benoit could probably hear her, but the colonel kept his voice as smooth as milk as he said, "Actually, I'm afraid there *is* a field—gas, shaped charges, and glass-shard antipersonnel mines—somewhere on that road, yes. Fortunately, the field was signal activated. It wasn't primed until after you had passed through. I assure you, Captain Pritchard, that all the roads west of the Aillet may be too dangerous to traverse until I have cleared them. I warn you both as a friend and so that we will not be charged with damage to any of your vehicles—and men. You have been fully warned of the danger; anything that happens now is your responsibility."

Pritchard leaned back in the console's integral seat, chuckling again. "You know, Colonel," the tank captain said, "I'm not sure that the Bonding Authority wouldn't find those mines were a hostile act justifying our retaliation." Benoit stiffened, more an internal hardness than anything that showed in his muscles. Pritchard continued to speak through a smile. "We won't, of course. Mistakes happen. But one thing, Colonel Benoit—"

The Frenchman nodded, waiting for the edge to bite. He knew as well as Pritchard did that, at best, if there were an Authority investigation, Barthe would have to throw a scapegoat out. A high-ranking scapegoat.

"Mistakes happen," Pritchard repeated, "but they can't be allowed to happen twice. You've got my permission to send out a ten-man team by daylight—only by daylight—to clear the road from Portela to Bever. That'll give you a route back to your side of the sector. If any other troops leave their present position, for any reason, I'll treat it as an attack."

"Captain, this demarcation within the sector was not a part of the contract—"

"It was at the demand of Colonel Barthe," Pritchard snapped, "and agreed to by the demonstrable practice of both regiments over the past three months." Hammer had briefed Pritchard very carefully on the words to use here, to be recorded for the benefit of the Bonding Authority. "You've heard the terms, Colonel. You can either take them or we'll put the whole thing—the minefields and some other matters that've come up recently—before the Authority right now. Your choice."

Benoit stared at Pritchard, apparently calm but tugging at his upper lip with thumb and forefinger. "I think you are unwise, Captain, in taking full responsibility for an area in which your tanks cannot move; but that is your affair, of course. I will obey your mandate. We should have the Portela-Haacin segment cleared by evening; tomorrow we'll proceed to Bever. Good day."

The screen segued back to the map display. Pritchard stood up. A spare helmet rested beside one of the radiomen. The tank captain donned it—he had forgotten to requisition a replacement from stores—and said, "Michael One to all Michael units." He paused for the acknowledgment lights from his four platoons and the command vehicle. Then, "Hold your present positions. Don't attempt to move by road, any road, until further notice. The roads have been mined. There are probably safe areas, and we'll get you a map of them as soon as Command Central works it up. For the time being, just stay where you are. Michael One, out."

"Are you really going to take that?" Lieutenant Schilling demanded in a low, harsh voice.

"Pass the same orders to your troops, Sally," Pritchard said. "I know they can move through the woods where my tanks can't, but I don't want any friendlies in the forest right now either." To the intelligence sergeant on watch, Pritchard added, "Samuels, get Central to run a plot of all activity by any of Benoit's men. That won't tell us where they've laid mines, but it'll let us know where they can't have."

"What happens if the bleeding skepsels ignore you?" Sally blazed. "You've bloody taught them to ignore you, haven't you? Knuckling under every time somebody whispers 'contract'? You can't move a tank to stop them if they do leave their base, and I've got 198 effectives. A battalion'd laugh at me, *laugh*!"

Schilling's arms were akimbo, her face as pale with rage as the snow outside. Speaking with deliberate calm, Pritchard said, "I'll call in artillery if I need to. Benoit only brought two calliopes with him, and they can't stop all the shells from three firebases at the same time. The road between his position and Portela's just a snake-track cut between rocks. A couple firecracker rounds going off above infantry strung out there—Via, it'll be a butcher shop."

Schilling's eyes brightened. "Then for tonight, the sector's just like it was before we came," she thought out loud. "Well, I suppose you know best," she added in false agreement, with false nonchalance. "I'm going back to the barracks. I'll brief First Platoon in person and radio the others from there. Come along, Webbert."

The corporal slammed the door behind himself and his lieutenant. The gust of air that licked about the walls was cold, but Pritchard was already shivering at what he had just done to a woman he loved.

It was daylight by now, and the frosted windows turned to flame in the ruddy sun. Speaking to no one but his console's memory, Pritchard began to plot tracks from each tank platoon. He used a topographic display, ignoring the existence of the impenetrable forest which covered the ground.

Margritte's resonant voice twanged in the implant, "Captain, would you come to the blower for half a sec?"

"On the way," Pritchard said, shrugging into his coat. The orderly room staff glanced up at him.

Margritte poked her head out of the side hatch. Pritchard climbed onto the deck to avoid some of the generator whine. The skirts sang even when the fans were cut off completely. Rob Jenne, curious but at ease, was visible at his battle station beyond the commo tech. "Sir," Margritte said, "we've been picking up signals from—there." The blue-eyed woman thumbed briefly at the infantry barracks without letting her pupils follow the gesture.

Pritchard nodded. "Lieutenant Schilling's passing on my orders to her company."

"Danny, the transmission's in code, and it's not a code of ours." Margritte hesitated, then touched the back of the officer's gloved left hand. "There's answering signals, too. I can't triangulate without moving the blower, of course, but the source is in line with the tailings pile at Haacin."

It was what he had planned, after all. Someone the villagers could trust had to get word of the situation to them. Otherwise they wouldn't draw the Portelans and their mercenary backers into a fatal mistake. Hard luck for the villagers who were acting as bait, but very good luck for every other Dutchman on Kobold . . . Pritchard had no reason to feel anything but relief that it had happened. He tried to relax the muscles which were crushing all the breath out of his lungs. Margritte's fingers closed over his hand and squeezed it.

"Ignore the signals," the captain said at last. "We've known all along they were talking to the civilians, haven't we?" Neither of his crewmen spoke. Pritchard's eyes closed tightly. He said, "We've known for months, Hammer and I, every damned thing that Barthe's been plotting with the skepsels. They want a chance to break Haacin now, while they're around to cover for the Portelans. We'll give them their chance and ram it up their ass crosswise. The Old Man hasn't spread the word for fear the story'd get out, the same way Barthe's plans did. We're all mercenaries, after all. But I want you three to know. And I'll be glad when the only thing I have to worry about is the direction the shots are coming from."

Abruptly, the captain dropped back to the ground. "Get some sleep," he called. "I'll be needing you sharp tonight."

Back at his console, Pritchard resumed plotting courses and distances. After he figured each line, he called in a series of map coordinates to Command Central. He knew his radio traffic was being monitored and probably unscrambled by Barthe's intelligence staff; knew also that even if he had read the coordinates out in clear, the French would have assumed it was a code. The locations made no sense unless one knew they were ground zero for incendiary shells.

As Pritchard worked, he kept close watch on the French battalions. Benoit's own troops held their position, as Pritchard had ordered. They used the time to dig in. At first they had blasted slit trenches in the rock. Now they dug covered bunkers with the help of mining machinery trucked from Portela by civilians. Five of the six antitank guns were sited atop the eastern ridge of the position. They could rake the highway as it snaked and switched back among the foothills west of Portela.

Pritchard chuckled grimly again when Sergeant Samuels handed him highmagnification off-prints from the satellites. Benoit's two squat, bulky calliopes were sited in defilade behind the humps of the eastern ridge line. There the eight-barreled powerguns were safe from the smashing fire of M Company's tanks, but their ability to sweep artillery shells from the sky was degraded by the closer horizon, The Slammers did not bother with calliopes themselves. Their central fire director did a far better job by working through the hundreds of vehicle-mounted weapons. How much better, Benoit might learn very shortly.

The mine-sweeping team cleared the Portela-Haacin road, as directed. The men returned to Benoit's encampment an hour before dusk. The French did not come within five kilometers of the Dutch village.

Pritchard watched the retiring minesweepers, then snapped off the console. He stood. "I'm going out to my blower," he said.

His crew had been watching for him. A hatch shot open, spouting condensate, as soon as Pritchard came out the door. The smooth bulk of the tank blew like a restive whale. On the horizon, the sun was so low that the treetops stood out in silhouette like a line of bayonets.

Wearily, the captain dropped through the hatch into his seat. Jenne and Margritte murmured greetings and waited, noticeably tense. "I'm going to get a couple hours' sleep," Pritchard said. He swung his seat out and up, so that he lay horizontal in the turret. His legs hid Margritte's oval face from him. "Punch up coverage of the road west of Haacin would you?" he asked. "I'm going to take a tab of Glirine. Slap me with the antidote when something moves there."

"*If* something moves," Jenne amended.

"When." Pritchard sucked down the pill. "The squareheads think they've got one last chance to smack Portela and hijack the powerguns again. Thing is, the Portelans'll have already distributed the guns and be waiting for the Dutch to come through. It'll be a damn short fight, that one . . ." The drug took hold and Pritchard's consciousness began to flow away like a sugar cube in water. "Damn short. . . ."

At first Pritchard felt only the sting on the inside of his wrist. Then the narcotic haze ripped away and he was fully conscious again.

"There's a line of trucks, looks like twenty, moving west out of Haacin, sir. They're blacked out, but the satellite has 'em on infrared."

"Red Alert," Pritchard ordered. He locked his seat upright into its combat position. Margritte's soft voice sounded the general alarm. Pritchard slipped on his radio helmet. "Michael One to all Michael units. Check off." Five green lights flashed their silent acknowledgments across the top of the captain's face shield display. "Michael One to Sigma One," Pritchard continued.

"Go ahead, Michael One." Sally's voice held a note of triumph.

"Sigma One, pull all your troops into large, clear areas—the fields around the towns are fine, but stay the hell away from Portela and Haacin. Get ready to slow down anybody coming this way from across the Aillet. Over."

"Affirmative, Danny, affirmative!" Sally replied. Couldn't she use the satellite reconnaissance herself and see the five blurred dots halfway between the villages? They were clearly the trucks which had brought the Portelans into then-ambush positions. What would she say when she realized how she had set up the villagers she was trying to protect? Lambs to the slaughter. . . .

The vision block showed the Dutch trucks more clearly than the camouflaged Portelans. The crushed stone of the roadway was dark on the screen, cooler than the surrounding trees and the vehicles upon it. Pritchard patted the breech of the main gun and looked across it to his blower chief. "We got a basic load for this aboard?" he asked.

"Do bears cop in the woods?" Jenne grinned. "We gonna get a chance to bust caps tonight, Captain?"

Pritchard nodded. "For three months we've been here, doing nothing but selling rope to the French. Tonight they've bought enough that we can hang 'em with it." He looked at the vision block again. "You alive, Kowie?" he asked on intercom.

"Ready to slide any time you give me a course," said the driver from his closed cockpit.

The vision block sizzled with bright streaks that seemed to hang on the screen though they had passed in microseconds. The leading blobs expanded and brightened as trucks blew up.

"Michael One to Fire Central," Pritchard said.

"Go ahead, Michael One," replied the machine voice.

"Prepare Fire Order Alpha."

"Roger, Michael One."

"Margritte, get me Benoit."

"Go ahead, Captain."

"Slammers to Benoit. Pritchard to Benoit. Come in please, Colonel."

"Captain Pritchard, Michel Benoit here." The colonel's voice was smooth but too hurried to disguise the concern underlying it. "I assure you that none of my men are involved in the present fighting. I have a company ready to go out and control the disturbance immediately, however."

The tanker ignored him. The shooting had already stopped for lack of targets. "Colonel, I've got some artillery aimed to drop various places in the forest. It's coming nowhere near your troops or any other human beings. If you interfere with this necessary shelling, the Slammers'll treat it as an act of war. I speak with my colonel's authority."

"Captain, I don't—"

Pritchard switched manually. "Michael One to Fire Central. Execute Fire Order Alpha."

"On the way, Michael One."

"Michael One to Michael First, Second, Fourth. Command Central has fed movement orders into your map displays. Incendiary clusters are going to burst over marked locations to ignite the forest. Use your own main guns to set the trees burning in front of your immediate positions. One round ought to do it. Button up and you can move through the fire—the trees just fall to pieces when they've burned."

The turret whined as it slid under Rob's control. "Michael Third, I'm attaching you to the infantry. More Frenchmen're apt to be coming this way from the east. It's up to you to see they don't slam a door on us."

The main gun fired, its discharge so sudden that the air rang like a solid thing. Seepage from the ejection system filled the hull with the reek of superheated polyurethane. The side vision blocks flashed cyan, then began to flood with the mounting white hell-light of the blazing trees. In the central block, still set on remote, all the Dutch trucks were burning as were patches of forest which the ambush had ignited. The Portelans had left the concealment of the trees and swept across the road, mopping up the Dutch.

"Kowie, let's move," Jenne was saying on intercom, syncopated by the mild echo of his voice in the turret. Margritte's face was calm, her lips moving subtly as she handled some traffic that she did not pass on to her captain. The tank slid forward like oil on a lake. From the far distance came the thumps of incendiary rounds scattering their hundreds of separate fireballs high over the trees.

Pritchard slapped the central vision block back on direct; the tank's interior shone white with transmitted fire. The Plow's bow slope sheared into a thicket of blazing trees. The wood tangled and sagged, then gave in a splash of fiery splinters whipped aloft by the blowers fans. The tank was in Hell on all sides, Kowie steering by instinct and his inertial compass. Even with his screens filtered all the way down, the driver would not be able to use his eyes effectively until more of the labyrinth had burned away.

Benoit's calliopes had not tried to stop the shelling. Well, there were other ways to get the French mercs to take the first step over the line. For instance—

"Punch up Benoit again," Pritchard ordered. Even through the dense iridium plating, the roar of the fire was a subaural presence in the tank.

"Go ahead," Margritte said, flipping a switch on her console. She had somehow been holding the French officer in conversation all the time Pritchard was on other frequencies.

"Colonel," Pritchard said, "we've got clear running through this fire. We're going to chase down everybody who used a powergun tonight; then we'll shoot them. We'll shoot everybody in their families, everybody with them in this ambush, and we'll blow up every house that anybody involved lived in. That's likely to be every house in Portela, isn't it?"

More than the heat and ions of the blazing forest distorted Benoit's face. He shouted, "Are you mad? You can't think of such a thing, Pritchard!"

The tanker's lips parted like a wolf 's. He could think of mass murder, and there were plenty of men in the Slammers who would really be willing to carry out the threat. But Pritchard wouldn't have to, because Benoit was like Riis and Schilling—too much of a nationalist to remember his first duty as a merc . . . "Colonel Benoit, the contract demands we keep the peace and stay impartial. The record shows how we treated people in Haacin for *having* power-guns. For what the Portelans did tonight—don't worry, we'll be impartial. And they'll never break the peace again."

"Captain, I will not allow you to massacre French civilians," Benoit stated flatly.

"Move a man out of your present positions and I'll shoot him dead," Pritchard said. "It's your choice, Colonel. Michael One out."

The Plow bucked and rolled as it pulverized fire-shattered trunks, but the vehicle was meeting nothing solid enough to slam it to a halt. Pritchard used a side block on remote to examine Benoit's encampment. The satellite's enhanced infrared showed a stream of sparks flowing from the defensive positions toward the Portela road: infantry on skimmers. The pair of larger, more diff use blobs were probably antitank guns. Benoit wasn't moving his whole battalion, only a reinforced company in a show of force to make Pritchard back off .

The fool. Nobody was going to back off now.

"Michael One to all Michael and Sigma units," Pritchard said in a voice as clear as the white flames around his tank. "We're now in a state of war with Barthe's Company and its civilian auxiliaries. Michael First, Second, and Fourth, we'll rendezvous at the ambush site as plotted on your displays. Anybody between there and Portela is fair game. If we take any fire from Portela, we go down the main drag in line and blow the cop out of it. If any of Barthe's people are in the way, we keep on sliding west. Sigma One, mount a fluid defense, don't push, and wait for help. It's coming. If this works, it's Barthe against Hammer—and that's wheat against the scythe. Acknowledged?"

As Pritchard's callboard lit green, a raspy new voice broke into the sector frequency. "Wish I was with you, panzers. We'll cover your butts and the other sectors—if anybody's dumb enough to move. Good hunting!"

"I wish you *were* here and not me, Colonel," Pritchard whispered, but that was to himself . . . and perhaps it was not true even in his heart. Danny's guts were very cold, and his face was as cold as death.

To Pritchard's left, a lighted display segregated the area of operations. It was a computer analog, not direct satellite coverage. Doubtful images were brightened and labeled—green for the Slammers, red for Barthe; blue for civilians unless they were fighting on one side or the other. The green dot of the Plow converged on the ambush site at the same time as the columns of First and Fourth

Platoons. Second was a minute or two farther off. Pritchard's breath caught. A sheaf of narrow red lines was streaking across the display toward his tanks. Barthe had ordered his Company's artillery to support Benoit's threatened battalion.

The salvo frayed and vanished more suddenly than it had appeared. Other Slammers' vehicles had ripped the threat from the sky. Green lines darted from Hammer's own three firebases, off-screen at the analog's present scale. The fighting was no longer limited to Sector Two. If Pritchard and Hammer had played their hand right, though, it would stay limited to only the Slammers and Compagnie de Barthe. The other Francophone regiments would fear to join an unexpected battle which certainly resulted from someone's contract violation. If the breach were Hammer's, the Dutch would not be allowed to profit by the fighting. If the breach were Barthe's, anybody who joined him would be punished as sternly by the Bonding Authority.

So violent was the forest's combustion that the flames were already dying down into sparks and black ashes. The command tank growled out into the broad avenue of the road west of Haacin. Dutch trucks were still burning— fabric, lubricants, and the very paint of their frames had been ignited by the powerguns. Many of the bodies sprawled beside the vehicles were smoldering also. Some corpses still clutched their useless muskets. The dead were victims of six centuries of progress which had come to Kobold prepackaged, just in time to kill them. Barthe had given the Portelans only shoulder weapons, but even that meant the world here. The powerguns were repeaters with awesome destruction in every bolt. Without answering fire to rattle them, even untrained gunmen could be effective with weapons which shot line-straight and had no recoil. Certainly the Portelans had been effective.

Throwing ash and fire like sharks in the surf, the four behemoths of First Platoon slewed onto the road from the south. Almost simultaneously, Fourth joined through the dying hellstorm to the other side. The right of way was fifty meters wide and there was no reason to keep to the center of it. The forest, ablaze or glowing embers, held no ambushes anymore.

The Plow lurched as Kowie guided it through the bodies. Some of them were still moving. Pritchard wondered if any of the Dutch had lived through the night, but that was with the back of his mind. The Slammers were at war, and nothing else really mattered. "Triple line ahead," he ordered. "First to the left, Fourth to the right; the Plow'll take the center alone till Second joins. Second, wick up when you hit the hardball and fall in behind us. If it moves, shoot it."

At one hundred kph, the leading tanks caught the Portelans three kilometers east of their village. The settlers were in the trucks that had been hidden in the forest fringe until the fires had been started. The ambushers may not have known they were being pursued until the rearmost truck exploded. Rob Jenne had shredded it with his tribarrel at five kilometers' distance. The cyan flicker and its answering orange blast signaled the flanking tanks to fire. They had just enough parallax to be able to rake the four remaining trucks without being blocked by the one which had blown up. A few snapping discharges proved that some Portelans survived to use their new powerguns on tougher meat than before. Hits streaked ashes on the tanks' armor. No one inside noticed.

From Portela's eastern windows, children watched their parents burn.

A hose of cyan light played from a distant roof top. It touched the command tank as Kowie slewed to avoid a Portelan truck. The burst was perfectly aimed, an automatic weapon served by professionals. Professionals should have known how useless it would be against heavy armor. A vision block dulled as a few receptors fused. Jenne cursed and trod the foot-switch of the main gun. A building leaped into dazzling prominence in the microsecond flash. Then it and most of the block behind collapsed into internal fires, burying the machine gun and everything else in the neighborhood. A moment later, a salvo of Hammer's high explosive got through the calliopes' inadequate screen. The village began to spew skyward in white flashes.

The Portelans had wanted to play soldier, Pritchard thought. He had dammed up all pity for the villagers of Haacin; he would not spend it now on these folk.

"Line ahead—First, Fourth, and Second," Pritchard ordered. The triple column slowed and reformed, with the Plow the second vehicle in the new line. The shelling lifted from Portela as the tanks plunged into the village. Green trails on the analog terminated over the road crowded with Benoit's men and over the main French position, despite anything the calliopes could do. The sky over Benoit's bunkers rippled and flared as firecracker rounds sleeted down their thousands of individual bomblets. The defensive fire cut off entirely. Pritchard could imagine the carnage among the unprotected calliope crews when the shrapnel whirred through them.

The tanks were firing into the houses on either side, using tribarrels and occasional wallops from their main guns. The blue-green flashes were so intense they colored even the flames they lit among the wreckage. At fifty kph the thirteen tanks swept through the center of town, hindered only by the rubble of houses spilled across the street. Barthe's men were skittering white shadows that burst when powerguns hit them point blank.

The copper mine was just west of the village and three hundred meters north of the highway. As the lead tank bellowed out around the last houses, a dozen infantrymen rose from where they had sheltered in the pit head and loosed a salvo of buzzbombs. The tank's automatic defense system was live. White fire rippled from just above the skirts as the charges there flailed pellets outward to intersect the rockets. Most of the buzzbombs exploded ten meters distant against the steel hail. One missile soared harmlessly over its target, its motor a tiny flare against the flickering sky. Only one of the shaped charges burst alongside the turret, forming a bell of light momentarily bigger than the tank. Even that was only a near miss. It gouged the iridium armor like a misthrust rapier which tears skin but does not pierce the skull.

Main guns and tribarrels answered the rockets instantly. Men dropped, some dead, some reloading. "Second Platoon, go put some HE down the shaft and rejoin," Pritchard ordered. The lead tank now had expended half its defensive charges. "Michael First-Three, fall in behind First-One. Michael One leads," he went on.

Kowie grunted acknowledgment. The Plow revved up to full

honk. Benoit's men were on the road, those who had not reached Portela when the shooting started or who had fled when the artillery churned the houses to froth. The infantry skimmers were trapped between sheer rocks and sheer drop-offs, between their own slow speed and the onrushing frontal slope of the Plow. There were trees where the rocks had given them purchase. Scattered incendiaries had made them blazing cressets lighting a charnel procession.

Jenne's tribarrel scythed through body armor and dismembered men in short bursts. One of the antitank guns—was the other buried in Portela?—lay skewed against a rock wall, its driver killed by a shell fragment. Rob put a round from the main gun into it. So did each of the next two tanks. At the third shot, the ammunition ignited in a blinding secondary explosion.

The antitank guns still emplaced on the ridge line had not fired, though they swept several stretches of the road. Perhaps the crews had been rattled by the shelling, perhaps Benoit had held his fire for fear of hitting his own men. A narrow defile notched the final ridge. The Plow heaved itself up the rise, and at the top three bolts slapped it from different angles.

Because the bow was lifted, two of the shots vaporized portions of the skirt and the front fans. The tank nosed down and sprayed sparks with half its length. The third bolt grazed the left top of the turret, making the iridium ring as it expanded. The interior of the armor streaked white though it was not pierced. The temperature inside the tank rose thirty degrees. Even as the Plow skidded, Sergeant Jenne was laying his main gun on the hot spot that was the barrel of the leftmost antitank weapon. The Plow's shot did what heavy top cover had prevented Hammer's rocket howitzers from accomplishing with shrapnel. The antitank gun blew up in a distance-muffled flash. One of its crewmen was silhouetted high in the air by the vaporizing metal of his gun.

Then the two remaining weapons ripped the night and the command blower with their charges.

The bolt that touched the right side of the turret spewed droplets of iridium across the interior of the hull. Air pistoned Pritchard's eardrums. Rob Jenne lurched in his harness, right arm burned away by the shot. His left hand blackened where it touched bare metal that sparked and sang as circuits shorted. Margritte's radios were exploding one by one under the overloads. The vision blocks worked and the turret hummed placidly as Pritchard rotated it to the right with his duplicate controls.

"Cut the power! Rob's burning!" Margritte was shrieking. She had torn off her helmet. Her thick hair stood out like tendrils of bread mold in the gathering charge. Then Pritchard had the main gun bearing and it lit the ridge line with another secondary explosion.

"Danny, our ammunition! It'll—"

Benoit's remaining gun blew the tribarrel and the cupola away deafeningly. The automatic's loading tube began to gang-fire down into the bowels of the tank. It reached a bright column up into the sky, but the turret still rolled.

Electricity crackled around Pritchard's boot and the foot trip as he fired again. The bolt stabbed the night. There was no answering blast. Pritchard held down the switch, his nostrils thick with ozone and superheated plastic and the sizzling flesh of his friend. There was still no explosion from the target bunker. The rock turned white between the cyan flashes. It cracked and flowed away like sun-melted snow, and the antitank gun never fired again.

The loading tube emptied. Pritchard slapped the main switch and cut off the current. The interior light and the dancing arcs died, leaving only the dying glow of the bolt-heated iridium. Tank after tank edged by the silent command vehicle and roared on toward the ridge. Benoit's demoralized men were already beginning to throw down their weapons and surrender.

Pritchard manually unlatched Jenne's harness and swung it horizontal. The blower chief was breathing but unconscious. Pritchard switched on a battery-powered handlight. He held it steady as Margritte began to spray sealant on the burns. Occasionally she paused to separate clothing from flesh with a stylus.

"It had to be done," Pritchard whispered. By sacrificing Haacin, he had mousetrapped Benoit into starting a war the infantry could not win. Hammer was now crushing Barthe's Company one on one, in an iridium vise. Friesland's Council of State would not have let

Hammer act had they known his intentions, but in the face of a stunning victory they simply could not avoid dictating terms to the French.

"It had to be done. But I look at *what* I did—" Pritchard swung his right hand in a gesture that would have included both the fuming wreck of Portela and the raiders from Haacin, dead on the road beyond. He struck the breech of the main gun instead. Clenching his fist, he slammed it again into the metal in self-punishment. Margritte cried out and blocked his arm with her own.

"Margi," Pritchard repeated in anguish, "it isn't something that human beings *do* to each other." But soldiers do. And hangmen.

TABLE OF ORGANIZATION AND EQUIPMENT, HAMMER'S REGIMENT

SEC I: HEADQUARTERS BATTALION

Except for Artillery and Replacement, all the support elements were grouped for administrative convenience in HQ Battalion. In practice, a large percentage of the strength of these units was parceled out to line companies according to need.

a) Headquarters Company—Colonel Hammer and his personal staff, including battalion officers; satellite launch and maintenance personnel; finance; and a security element. Total: 153 effectives.

b) Maintenance—Capable of handling anything short of full hull rebuilds and internal work on fusion units. Company included three tank and six combat car transporters, stretched-chassis vehicles with fans at either end; ACVs cannot, of course, be towed. Total: 212 effectives.

c) Communications—Included not only the staff of Command Central, but the staffs of local headquarters with area responsibilities. Total: 143 effectives.

d) Medical—Twenty-four first-line medics with medicomps linked to Central, and a field hospital with full life-support capability. Total: 60 effectives.

e) Supply—Included Mess and Quartermaster functions. Total: 143 effectives.

f) Intelligence—Order of Battle was performed mostly by computer. Imagery Interpretation, study of satellite recce, was in large measure still a human function. There were three mechanical interrogation (i.e., mind probe) teams. Total: 84 effectives.

g) Transport—312 men (heavily supplemented from Replacement Battalion) and 288 air-cushion trucks for local unit supply from spaceport or planetary logistics centers. True aircraft, flying above the nape of the earth, would have been suicidally vulnerable to powerguns.

h) Combat Engineers—Carried out bridging, clearing, mine-sweeping, and very frequently fighting tasks. Formed in three 16-man platoons, each mounted on a pair of tank-chassis Engineer Vehicles. Total: 50 effectives.

i) Recreation—Field brothels. The strength and composition of this unit varied from world to world. Generally, teams of 3–6 were put under the direct control of company supply personnel.

SEC II: COMBAT CARS

Eight combat car companies, each of a command section (one car) and four line platoons. Each platoon contained a command car and five combat cars, or six combat cars. Company total: 100 effectives.

SEC III: TANKS

Four tank companies, each of a command tank and four line platoons. Each line platoon contained four tanks. Company total: 36 effectives.

SEC IV: INFANTRY

Four companies, each of four platoons. Each platoon contained four 10-man line squads; two 2-man tribarrel teams (jeep-mounted); one 2-man 100 mm mortar team (jeep-mounted); and a command element. All but Heavy Weapons were on 1-man skimmers. Buzzbombs could be issued for special purposes; but in general, support from the armored vehicles allowed the Slammers' infantry to travel lighter than most pongoes. Company total: 202 effectives.

SEC V: ARTILLERY

Three batteries of self-propelled 200 mm rocket howitzers. Each battery contained six tubes; one command car; and two munitions haulers. Battery total: 37 effectives.

SEC VI: REPLACEMENT

The training and reserve component of the Slammers, normally totaling 1500 men (including cadre) with about ten tanks, twenty-five combat cars, and a hundred trucks. Because Hammer had no permanent base world, training had to be performed wherever the Regiment was located. Because men were more vulnerable than the armored vehicles they rode, and the vehicles were too valuable to run undercrewed or held out of service while replacements were trained, a pool of trained men had to be on hand to fill gaps immediately. Until they were needed in combat slots, they acted as extra drivers, loading crews, camp police, and firebase security.

Note: As personal weapons line infantry were issued 2 cm shoulder powerguns and grenades. Vehicle and Heavy Weapons crewmen carried 1 cm pistols (unless they had picked up shoulder arms on their own). Officers carried pistols or 1 cm submachine guns as they desired.

STANDING DOWN

"Look, I'm not about to wear a goon suit like that, even to my wedding," Colonel Hammer said, loudly enough to be heard through the chatter. There were a dozen officers making last-minute uniform adjustments in the crowded office and several civilians besides. "Joachim, where's Major Pritchard? I want him in the car with us, and it's curst near jump-off now."

Joachim Steuben was settled nonchalantly on the corner of a desk, unconcerned about the state of his dress because he knew it was perfect—as always. He shrugged. "Pritchard hasn't called in," the Newlander said. His fine features brightened in a smile. "But go ahead, Alois, put the armor on."

"Yes indeed, sir," said the young civilian. He was holding the set of back and breast armor carefully by the edges so as not to smear its bright chrome. Rococo whorls and figures decorated the plastron, but despite its ornateness, the metal/ceramic sandwich beneath the brightwork was quite functional. "Really, the image you'll project to the spectators will be ideal, quite ideal. And there couldn't be a better time for it, either."

Lieutenant Colonel Miezierk frowned, wrinkling his forehead to the middle of his bald skull. He said, "Yes Colonel. After all, Mr. van Meter's firm studied the matter very carefully and I think—" Joachim snickered; Miezierk's scalp reddened but he went on "—that you ought to follow his advice here."

"Lord!" Hammer said, but he thrust his hands through the arm-holes and let Miezierk lock the clamshell back.

Someone tapped on the door. A lieutenant was leaning over the front desk, combing his hair in the screen of the display console. He cursed and straightened so that the door could open to admit Captain Fallman. The Intelligence captain was duty officer for the afternoon, harried by the inevitable series of last-minute emergencies. "Colonel," he said, "there's a Mr. Wang here to see you."

"Lord curse it, Fallman, can wait till tomorrow! Hammer blazed, "He can wait till Hell freezes over. Miezierk, get this bloody can off me, it's driving the stylus in my pocket clear through my rib cage."

"Sir, we can take the stylus—" Miezierk began.

"Sir, he's from the Bonding Authority," Fallman was saying. "It's about President Theismann's—death."

Hammer swore, brushing the startled Miezierk's hands away. The room grew very silent. "Joachim, what's in the office next door?" Hammer asked.

"Dust, three walls, and some stains from the Iron Guards who decided to make a stand there," the Newlander replied.

"Bring him next door, Captain, I'll talk to him there," Hammer said. He met his bodyguard's eyes. "Come along too, Joachim."

At the door the colonel paused, looking back at his still-faced officers. "Don't worry," he said. "Everything's going to work out fine."

The closing door cut off the babble of nervous speculation from within.

A moment after Hammer and his aide had entered the side office, Captain Fallman ushered in a heavy Oriental. Joachim bowed to the civilian and closed the door, leaving the duty officer alone in the hallway.

An automatic weapon had punched through the outer wall of the office, starting fires which the grenade thrown in a moment later had snuffed. There was still a scorched-plastic afterstench mingling with that of month-dead meat. Joachim had been serious about the Iron Guards.

"I'm Hammer," the colonel said, smiling but not offering the Authority representative his hand for fear it might be refused.

"Wang An-wei," said the Oriental, nodding curtly. He held a flat briefcase. It seemed to be more an article of dress than a tool he intended to use this morning. "I was sent here as Site Officer when Councillor Theismann—"

"President Theismann, he preferred," interjected Hammer. He seated himself in feigned relaxation on a blast-warped chair.

Wang's answering smile was brief and as sharp as the lightning. "He was never awarded the title by a quorum of the Council," the Terran said. "As you no doubt are aware, Site Officers are expected to be precise. If I may continue?"

Hammer nodded. Steuben snickered. His left thumb was hooked in the belt which tucked his tailored blouse in at the waist, but his right hand dangled loose at his side.

"When Councillor Theismann hired you to make him dictator," Wang continued coolly. "Naturally I have been investigating the death of your late employer. There have been—and I'm sure you're aware of this—accusations that you murdered Councillor Theismann yourself in order to replace him as head of the successful coup."

The Site Officer looked at the men in turn. The two Slammers looked back.

"I started with the autopsy data. In addition, I have interrogated the Councillor's guards, both his personal contingent and the platoon of—White Mice—on security detail here at Government House." Wang stared at Hammer. "I assume you were informed of this?"

Hammer nodded curtly. "I signed off before they'd let you mind-probe my men."

"I used mechanical interrogation on all troops below officer rank involved," Wang agreed, "as your bond agreement specifies the Site officer may require." When Hammer made no reply, he continued: "The evidence is uncontroverted that Councillor Theismann, accompanied by you, Colonel—" Hammer nodded again "—stepped out onto his balcony and was struck in the forehead by a pistol bolt."

Wang paused again. The room was very tense. "The pistol must have been fired from at least a kilometer away. Because of the distance and the fact that fighting was going on at several points within the city, I have reported to my superiors that it was a stray shot, and that the Councillor's death was accidental."

Joachim's fingers ceased toying with the butt of the powergun holstered high on his right hip. "We were clearing some of van Vorn's people out of the Hotel Zant," he said. "Pistol and submachine gun work. There might have been a stray shot from that. It'd be very difficult to brain a man that far away with a pistol, wouldn't it?"

"Impossible, of course," Wang said. His gaze flicked to Steuben's ornate pistol, flicked up to the bodyguard's eyes. For the first time the Oriental looked startled. He looked away from Steuben very quickly and said, "Since the investigation has cleared you, and your employment has ended for the time, I'll be returning to Earth now. I wish you good fortune, and I hope we may do business again in the near future."

Hammer laughed, clapping the civilian on the shoulder with his left hand while their right hands shook. "That's all over, Mr. Wang. The Slammers're out of the merc business for good, now. But I appreciate your wishes."

Wang turned to the door, smiling by reflex. He looked at Joachim's face again: the Cupid grin and unlined cheeks; the hair which, though naturally graying, still fell across the Newlander's forehead in an attractive pageboy; and the eyes. Wang was shivering as he stepped into the hall.

Danny Pritchard stood outside the door watching the Site officer leave. He was dressed in civilian clothing.

Spaceport buses did not serve the cargo ships for the man or two they might bring, so Rob Jenne hiked toward the barrier on foot. At first he noticed only that the short man marching toward the terminal from the other recently landed freighter was also missing an arm. Then the other's crisp stride rang a bell in Jenne's mind. He shouted, "Top! Sergeant Horthy! What the hell're *you* doing here?"

Horthy turned with the wary quickness of a man uncertain as to any caller's interest. At Jenne's grin he broke into a smile himself. The two men dropped their bags and shook hands awkwardly, Jenne's left in Horthy's right. "Same thing you're doing, trooper," Horthy said. The Magyar's goatee was white against his swarthy skin, but his grip was as firm as it had been when Rob Jenne was Horthy's right wing gunner. "Comin' here to help the colonel put some backbone in this place. You don't know how glad I was when the call came, snake."

"Don't I though?" Jenne murmured. Side by side, talking simultaneously, the two veterans walked toward the spaceport barrier. There was already a line waiting at the customs kiosk. Jenne knew very well what his old sergeant meant. Seven years of retirement had been hard on the younger man, too. He hadn't lacked money—his pension put him well above the norm for the Burlage quarrymen to whom he had returned—but he was useless. To himself, to Burlage, to the entire human galaxy. Jenne had shouted for joy when Colonel Hammer summoned all pensioned Slammers who wanted to come. The Old Man needed supervisors and administrators, now. It didn't matter anymore that gaseous iridium had burned off Jenne's right arm, right eye, and his gonads; it was enough that Hammer knew where his loyalties lay.

A gray bus with wire-mesh windows and SECURITY stencilled on its side pulled up to the barrier. The faces and clothing of the prisoners within were as drab as the air-cushion vehicle's exterior. A guard wearing the blue of the civil police stepped out and walked to the barrier. His submachine gun was slung carelessly under his right arm.

Horthy nudged his companion. "It's a load a' politicals for the Borgo Mines," he muttered. "Bet they're bein' hauled out on the ship that brought me in. *And* I'll bet that bus'll be heading back to wherever the colonel is, just as quick as it unloads. Let's see if that cop'll offer us a ride, snake."

As he spoke, the Magyar veteran stepped to the waist-high barrier. The customs official bustled over from his kiosk and shouted in Horthy's face. Horthy ignored him. The official unsnapped the flap of his pistol holster. Other travellers waiting for entry scattered, more afraid of losing their lives than their places in line. Jenne, his good eye flashing across the tension, knowing as well as any man alive that his muscles were nothing to the blast of a powergun, cursed and closed the Magyar's rear.

A second bus, civilian in stripes of white and bright orange, pulled up behind the prison vehicle. The policeman turned and waved angrily. The bus hissed and settled to the pavement despite him. The policeman fumbled with his submachine gun.

A shot from the bus cut him down.

A man with a pistol swung to the loading step of the striped vehicle. He roared, "Just hold it, everybody. We got a load of hostages here. Either we get out of here with our friends or nobody gets out!"

The customs official had paused, staring with his mouth open and his fingers brushing the butt of the gun whose existence he had forgotten. Horthy, behind him, drew the pistol and fired. The rebel doubled over, his jacket afire over his sternum. Someone aboard the civilian bus screamed. Another gun fired. Horthy was prone, his pistol punching out windows in answer to the burst that had sawed the customs official in half.

Rob rolled over the barrier, coming up with the guard's automatic weapon.

The striped bus was moving, dragging the fallen gunman's torso on the concrete. The ex-tanker's mind raced in the old channels. The fans of the bus were not armored like those of a military vehicle. Rob aimed low. A powergun bolt sprayed lime dust over his head and shoulders. His own burst ripped across the plenum chamber. The driving fans disintegrated, flaying the air with steel like a bursting shell. The bus rolled over on its left side. Metal and humans screamed together. A gray-suited prisoner jumped from the door of the government bus. Horthy shot her in the face.

The ruptured fuel cell of the overturned vehicle ignited. The explosion slapped the area with a pillow of warm air. The screaming took a minute to die. Then there was just the rush of wind feeding the fire, and the nearing wail of sirens.

Jenne's cheek and shoulder-stub were oozing where the concrete had ground against them. He rose to his knees, keeping his eye and the submachine gun trailed on the gray bus. No one else was trying to get out of it. The police could sort through whatever had happened inside in their own good time.

Horthy stood, heat rippling from the barrel of the weapon he had appropriated. He glanced at the mangled customs official as if he would rather have spit on the body. "Oh, yes," the veteran said. "They need us here, trooper. They need people to teach 'em the facts of life."

"Pritchard, where the Hell have you been?" Hammer demanded, pretending that he did not understand the implications of his subordinate's business suit.

"I need to talk to you, Colonel," the brown-haired major said.

Hammer stood aside. "Then come on in. Joachim, we'll join the group next door in a moment. Wait for us there, if you will."

Pritchard took a step forward. He hesitated when he realized that Joachim was not moving. The Newlander had been as relaxed as a sunning adder during the interview with Wang An-wei. Now he was white and tense. "Colonel, he's a traitor to you," Joachim said. "He's going to walk out." His voice was quiet but not soft.

"Joachim, I told you—"

"You don't talk to traitors, Colonel. What you do to traitors—" The Newlander's hand was dipping to his gun butt. Hammer grappled with him. He was not as fast as his aide, but he knew Joachim's mind even better than the gunman did himself. The extra fraction of a second saved Pritchard's life.

The two men stood, locked like wrestlers or lovers. Pritchard did not move, knowing that emphasizing his presence would be the worst possible course under the circumstances. Hammer said, "Joachim, are you willing to shoot me?"

The bodyguard winced, a tic that momentarily disfigured his face. "Alois! You know I wouldn't . . ."

"Then do as I say. Or you'll have to shoot me. To keep me from shooting you."

Hammer stepped away from his aide. Joachim lurched through

the doorway, bumping Pritchard as he passed because his eyes had filled with tears.

Pritchard swung the door shut behind him. "I told you last week I was going to resign from the Slammers, sir."

Hammer nodded. "And I told you, you weren't."

Pritchard looked around at the dust and rubble of the room, the bloodstains. "I've decided there's been enough killing, Colonel. For me. We're going somewhere else."

"Danny, the killing's over!"

The taller man gave a short snap of his head. He said, "No, it'll never be over—not any place you are." He spread his hands, then clenched them. He was staring at his knuckles because he would not look at his commander. "Right now we're chasing van Vorn's guards like rabbits, shooting 'em down or sticking 'em behind wire where they're not a curse a' good to you or themselves or this planet."

He faced Hammer, the outrage bubbling out at a human being, not the colonel he had served for all his adult life. "And the ones we kill—doesn't every one a' them have a wife or a brother or a nephew? And they'll put a knife in a Slammer some night and be shot the same way because of it!"

"All right," said Hammer calmly. "What else?"

"How about the Social Unity Party, then?" Pritchard blazed. "Maybe the one chance to get this place a work force that *works* instead of the robots the Great Houses've been trying to make them. And does anybody listen? Hell, no! The Council tinkers with the franchise to make sure they don't get a majority of the Estates-General; van Vorn outlaws the party and makes their leaders terrorists instead of politicians. And you, *you* ship them off-planet to rot in state-owned mines on Kobold!"

"All right," Hammer repeated. He sat down again, his stillness as compelling as that of the shattered room around him. "What would you do?"

Pritchard's eyes narrowed. He stretched his left hand out to the wall, not leaning on it but touching its firmness, its chill. "What do you care?" he asked quietly. "I didn't say the Slammers couldn't keep you in power here the rest of your life. I just don't want to be a part of it, is all."

Without warning, Hammer stood and slammed his fist into the wall. He turned back to his aide. His bleeding knuckles had flecked the panel more brightly than the remains of the Iron Guards. "Is that what you think?" he demanded. "That I'm a bandit who's found himself a bolt hole? That for the past thirty years I've fought wars because that's the best way to make bodies?"

"Sir, I . . ." But Pritchard had nothing more to say or need to say it.

Hammer rubbed his knuckles. He grinned wryly at his subordinate, but the grin slipped away. "It's my own fault," he said. "I don't tell people much. That's how it's got to be when you're running a tank regiment, but . . . that's not where we are now.

"Danny, this is my *home*." Hammer began to reach out to the taller man but stopped. He said, "You've been out there. You've seen how every world claws at every other one, claws its own guts, too. The whole system's about to slag down, and there's nothing to stop it if *we* don't."

"You don't create order by ramming it down peoples' throats on a bayonet! It doesn't work that way."

"Then show me a way that *does* work!" Hammer cried, gripping his subordinate's right hand with his own. "Are things going to get better because you're sitting on your butt in some farmhouse, living off the money *you* made killing? Danny I *need* you. My *son* will need you."

Pritchard touched his tongue to his lips. "What is it you're asking me to do?" he said.

"Do you have a way to handle the Unionists?" Hammer shot back at him. "And the Iron Guards?"

"Maybe," Pritchard said with a frown. "Amnesty won't be enough—they won't believe it's real, for one thing. But a promise of authority . . . administrative posts in education, labor, maybe even security—that'd bring out a few of the Unionists because they couldn't afford not to take the chance. Most of the rest of them might follow when they saw you really were paying off."

The brown-haired man's enthusiasm was building without the hostility that had marked it before. "The Guards, that'll be harder because they're rigid, most of them. But if you can find some way to convince them there's nothing to gain by staying out, and—Hell, there'll be counter-protests, but work the ones who turn over their guns into the civil police. Not in big dollops, but scattered all over the planet. They'll feel more secure that way, and you can keep an eye on them easier anyhow."

Hammer nodded. "All right, bring me a preliminary assessment of both proposals by, say, 0800 Tuesday. No, make that noon, you're going to waste the rest of today watching a wedding from the front row. You'll have the backing you'll need, but these are *your* projects— I've got too much blood on my hands to run them." His eyes held Pritchard's. "Or don't you have the guts to try?"

The taller man hesitated, then squeezed Hammer's hand in return. "I rode your lead tank," he said. "I ran your lead company. If you need me now, you've got me." His face clouded. "Only, Colonel—"

Hammer tightened. "Spit it out."

"I'm not ashamed of anything. But I swore to Margritte I'd never wear another uniform or carry another gun. And I won't."

Hammer cleared his throat. "Right now I don't need a major as much as I do a conscience," he said. He cleared his throat again. "Now let's go. We've got a wedding to get to."

Cosimo Barracks was a fortress in the midst of estates which had belonged for three hundred years to the family of the late President van Vorn. The Slammers had bypassed Cosimo in the blitzkrieg which replaced van Vorn with Theismann, their employer. But now, a month after van Vorn had poisoned himself in Government House and three weeks after someone else had burst Theismann's skull with a powergun, the fortress still refused to surrender. Sally Schilling, leading a "battalion" made up of S Company and six hundred local recruits, was on hand to do something about the situation.

A burst of automatic fire combed the rim of the dugout, splashing

Captain Schilling with molten granite. "Via!" she snapped to the frightened recruit. "Keep your coppy head down and don't draw fire."

The sergeant who shared the dugout with Schilling and the recruit shook his own head in disgust. In her mind, Schilling seconded the opinion. To police a planet, Hammer needed more men than the five thousand he had brought with him. He wanted to give the new troops at least a taste of combat in the mopping-up operations. Schilling could understand that desire, but it was a pain in the ass trying to do her own job and act as baby-sitter besides.

She looked again through the eyepiece of her periscope. The machine gun had ceased firing, though cyan flickers across the perimeter showed someone else was catching it. The Iron Guards were political bullies rather than combat soldiers, but their fortress here was as tough as anything the Slammers had faced in their history. The fiber-optic periscope showed Cosimo Barracks only as a rolling knob. The grass covering the rock was streaked yellow in fans pointing back to hidden gunports. The ports themselves were easy enough targets, but the weapons within were on disappearing carriages and popped up only long enough to fire. The rest of the fortress, with an estimated five hundred Iron Guards plus enough food, water, and ammunition to last a century, was deep underground.

Schilling glanced down at her console. On it Cosimo Barracks showed as a red knot of tunnels drawn from plans found in Government House. "Sigma Battalion," she said, "check off." Points of green light winked on the screen, an emerald necklace ringing the fortress. Each point was a squad guarding nearly one hundred meters of front. That was adequate; the infantry was on hand primarily to prevent a breakout.

"Fire Central," Schilling said, "prepare Fire Order Tango-Niner."

"Ready," squawked the helmet.

"Ma'am," said the recruit, "w-why don't the tanks attack instead of us?"

"Shut it off, boy!" the sergeant snapped.

"No, Webbert, we're supposed to be teaching them," Schilling said. She gestured toward the knob. The recruit automatically raised his head. Webbert shoved him back down before another burst could decapitate him. The captain sighed. "Mines're as thick up there as flies on a fresh turd," she said, "and they've got more guns in that hill than the light stuff they've been using on us.

Besides, *we* aren't going to attack."

The recruit nodded with his mouth and eyes both wide open. He began to rub the stock of his unfamiliar powergun.

"Fire Central, execute Tango-Niner," Schilling ordered.

"On the way."

Nothing happened. After a long half-minute, the recruit burst out, "What went wrong? Dear Lord, will they make us charge—"

"Boy!" the sergeant shouted, his own knuckles tight on his weapon.

"Webbert!"

The sergeant cursed and turned away.

Schilling said, "The hogs're a long way away. It takes time, that's all. Everything takes time."

"Shot," said the helmet. Five seconds to impact. The sky overhead began to howl. The recruit was trembling, his own throat working as if to scream along with the shells.

The explosions were almost anticlimactic. They were only a rumbling through the bedrock, more noticed by one's feet than one's ears. Schilling, at the periscope, caught the spurts of earth as the first penetrator rounds struck. The detonations seconds later were lost in the shriek of further shells landing on the same points. Each tube's first shell ripped sod to the granite. The second salvo struck gravel; the third, sand. By the tenth salvo, the charges were bursting in the guts of Cosimo Barracks, thirty meters down. A magazine went off there, piercing earth and sky in a cyan blast that made the sun pale.

"Not an oyster born yet but a starfish can drill a hole through it," muttered Webbert. He had been a fisherman long years before when he saw one of Hammer's recruiting brochures.

"Sigma One, this is Sigma Eight-Six," said the helmet. "Our sensors indicate all three fortress elevators are rising."

With the words, circuits of meadow gaped. "Sigma Battalion,"

Schilling said as she rose and aimed over the lip of the dugout, "time to earn our pay. And remember— no prisoners!"

Because of the way the ground pitched, it was hard for the captain to keep her submachine gun trained on the rising elevator car. But there were eight hundred guns firing simultaneously at the three elevator heads. The bolts converged like suns burning into the heart of the hillside.

"They were sending up their families!" the recruit suddenly screamed. "The children!"

Sally Schilling slid a fresh gas cylinder in place in the butt of her weapon, then reached for another magazine as well. "They had three months to turn in their guns," she said. "Half the ones down there were troops we beat at Maritschoon and paroled. So this was the second time, and *I'm* not going to have my ass blown away because I gave somebody three chances to do it. As for the families, well . . . there's a couple thousand more of van Vorn's folks mooching around in the Kronburg, and they won't know it was an accident: when word of this gets around, the ones that're still out are going to think again."

The fortress guns had fallen silent as the elevator cars rose. Now a few weapons opened up again, but in long, suicidal bursts which flailed the world until the Slammers' fire silenced them forever.

President van Vorn's Iron Guards had planned to use the garage beneath Government House for a last stand; which in a manner of speaking was what they did. The political soldiers had naively failed to consider gas. The Slammers introduced KD7 into the forced ventilation system, then spent three days neutralizing the toxin before they could safely enter the garage and remove the bloated corpses. Now the concrete walls, unmarred by shots or grenade fragments, echoed to the fans of two dozen combat cars readying for the parade.

"There's three layers a' gold foil," the bald maintenance chief was saying as he rapped the limousine's myrmillon bubble. "That'll diffuse most of a two see-emma bolt, but the folks, they'll still be able to *see* you, you see?"

"What I don't see is my wife," Hammer snapped to the stiff-faced noble acting as the Council's liaison with their new overlord. "She's agreed, I've agreed. If you think that the Great Houses can back out of this now—"

"Colonel," interrupted Pritchard, pointing at the closed car which was just entering the garage. The armored doors to the mews slammed shut behind the vehicle, cutting off the wash of sunlight which had paled the glow strips by comparison. The car hissed slowly between armored vehicles and support pillars, coming to a halt beside Hammer and his aides. Two men got out, dressed in the height of conservative fashion. The colors of Great Houses slashed their collar flares. A moment later, a pair of women stepped out between them.

One of them was sixty, as tall and heavy as either of the men. Her black garments were as harsh as the glare she turned on Hammer when he nodded to her.

The other woman was short enough to be petite. It was hard to tell, however, because she wore a dress of misty, layered fabric which gave the impression of spiderweb but hid even the outline of her body. The celagauze veil hanging from her cap-brim blurred her face similarly. Before any of those around her could interfere, she had reached up and removed the cap.

"Anneke!" cried the woman in black. One of the escorting nobles shifted. Danny Pritchard motioned him back, using his left hand by reflex.

Anneke sailed the cap into the intake of a revving combat car. Shreds of white fabric softened the floor of the garage. "What, Aunt Ruth?" she asked. Her voice was clearly audible over the fans and the engines. "That's the idea, isn't it? Prove to the citizens that the Great Houses are still in charge because the colonel is marrying one of us? But then they've got to see who I am, don't they?"

Hammer stepped forward. "Lady Brederode," he said, repeating his nod. The older woman looked away as if Hammer were a spot of offal on the pavement. "Lady Tromp."

Anneke Tromp extended her right hand. She had fine bones and skin as soft as the lining of a jewelry box. The fingernails looked metallic.

The colonel knelt to kiss her hand, the gesture stiffened by his armor. "Well, Lady Tromp," he said, "are you ready?"

The woman smiled. Hammer became the commander again. He waved dismissingly toward his bride's aunt and escort. "I've made provisions for your seating at the church," he said, "but you'll not be needed for the procession. Lady Tromp will ride in my vehicle. We'll be accompanied by majors—that is, by Major Steuben and Mr. Pritchard."

Anneke nodded graciously to the aides flanking Hammer. Unexpectedly, Joachim giggled. His eyes were red. "Your family and I go back a long way, Lady," he said. "Did you know that I shot your father on Melpomone? Between the eyes, so that he could see it coming."

The colonel's face changed, but he grinned as he turned. He threw an arm around his bodyguard's shoulders. "Joachim," he said, "let's talk in the car for a moment." Steuben looked away, blazing hatred at everyone else in the room, but he followed his commander into the soundproofed compartment.

As the car door thudded shut, Anneke Tromp stepped idly to Pritchard's side. She was still smiling. Without looking at the limousine's bubble, she said, "That's a very jealous man, Mr. Pritchard. And jealous not only of me, I should think."

Danny shrugged. "Joachim's been with the colonel a long time," he said. "He's not an . . . evil . . . man. Just loyal."

"A razor blade in a melon isn't evil, Mr. Pritchard," the woman said, gesturing as though they were discussing the markings of the nearest combat car. "It's just too dangerous to be permitted to exist."

Pritchard swallowed. Part of his duties involved checking the roster of veterans returning to the colors. He was remembering a big man with an engaging grin—as good a tank commander as had ever served under Pritchard, and the lightest touch he knew on the trigger of an automatic weapon. "We'll see," Danny said without looking at the woman.

"When I was a little girl," she murmured, "my father ruled Friesland. I want to live to see my son rule."

The car door opened and both men got out. "Joachim has

decided to ride up front with the driver instead of with us in back," Hammer said with a false smile. He held the door. "Shall we?"

Pritchard sat on a jump seat across from Hammer and Lady Tromp. The armored bubble was cloudy, like the sky on the morning of a snowstorm. Hammer touched a plate on the console. "Six-two," he said. "Move 'em out."

Fans revved. The garage door lifted and began passing combat cars out into the mews. Hammer's driver slid the limousine into the line of cars waiting to exit. More armored vehicles edged in behind them. They accelerated up the ramp and into the Frisian sunlight. The whole west quarter of Government House had burned in the fighting, darkening the vitril panels there.

Pritchard leaned forward. "You don't really think that you can turn Friesland around, much less the galaxy?" he asked.

Hammer shrugged. "If I don't, they'll at least say that I died trying."

The limousine glided through the archway into Independence Boulevard. Tank companies were already closing either end of the block, eight tanks abreast. The panzers had been painted dazzlingly silver for the celebration. The combat cars aligned themselves in four ranks between the double caps of bigger vehicles, leaving the limousine to tremble alone in the midst of the waves of heavy armor. Hammer's breastplate was a sun-blazed eye in the center of all.

On the front bench beside the driver, Joachim was trying nervously to scan the thousands of civilians. He knew that despite the armored bubble, the right man could kill Hammer as easily as he himself had murdered Councillor Theismann. He wished he could kill every soul in the crowd.

Pritchard checked the time, then radioed a command. The procession began to slip forward toward the throngs lining the remaining three kilometers of the boulevard, all the way to the Church of the First Landfall.

"I've been a long time coming back to Friesland," said Hammer softly. He was not really speaking to his companions. "But now I'm back. And I'm going to put this place in order."

Anneke Tromp touched him. Her glittering fingernails lay like knife blades across the back of his hand. "*We're* going to put it in order," she said.

"We'll see," said Danny Pritchard.

"Hammer!" shouted the crowd.

"Hammer!"

"Hammer!"

"Hammer!"

M2A4F TANK

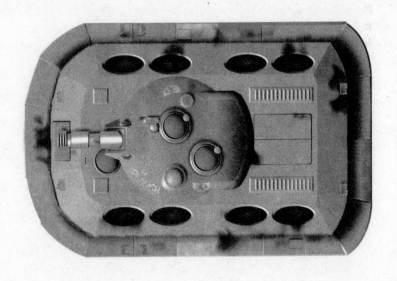

CODE-NAME FEIREFITZ

"Lord, we got one!" cried the trooper whose detector wand pointed toward the table that held the small altar. "That's a powergun for sure, Captain, nothing else'd read so much iridium!"

The three other khaki-clad soldiers in the room with Captain Esa Mboya tensed and cleared guns they had not expected to need. The villagers of Ain Chelia knew that to be found with a weapon meant death. The ones who were willing to face that were in the Bordj, waiting with their households and their guns for the Slammers to rip them out. Waiting to die fighting.

The houses of Ain Chelia were decorated externally by screens and colored tiles; but the tiles were set in concrete walls and the screens themselves were cast concrete. Narrow cul-de-sacs lined by blank, gated courtyard walls tied the residential areas of the village into knots of strongpoints. The rebels had elected to make their stand outside Ain Chelia proper only because the fortress they had cut into the walls of the open pit mine was an even tougher objective.

"Stand easy, troopers," said Mboya. The householder gave him a tight smile; he and Mboya were the only blacks in the room—or the village. "I'll handle this one," Captain Mboya continued. "The rest of you get on with the search under Sergeant Scratchard. Sergeant—" calling toward the outside door—"come in here for a moment."

Besides the householder and the trooper, a narrow-faced civilian named Youssef ben Khedda stood in the room. On his face was dawning a sudden and terrible hope. He had been Assistant Superintendent of the ilmenite mine before Kabyles all over the planet rose against their Arabized central government in al-Madinah. The Superintendent was executed, but ben Khedda had joined the rebels to be spared. It was a common enough story to men who had sorted through the ruck of as many rebellions as the Slammers had. But now ben Khedda was a loyal citizen again. Openly he guided G Company from house to house, secretly he whispered to Captain Mboya the names of those who had carried their guns and families to the mine. "Father," said ben Khedda to the householder, lowering his eyes in a mockery of contrition, "I never dreamed that there would be contraband *here*, I swear it."

Juma al-Habashi smiled back at the small man who saw the chance to become undisputed leader of as much of Chelia as the Slammers left standing and alive. "I'm sure you didn't dream it, Youssef," he said more gently than he himself expected. "Why should you, when I'd forgotten the gun myself?"

Sergeant Scratchard stepped inside with a last glance back at the courtyard and the other three men of Headquarters Squad waiting there as security. Within, the first sergeant's eyes touched the civilians and the tense enlisted men; but Captain Mboya was calm, so Scratchard kept his own voice calm as he said, "Sir?"

"Sergeant," Mboya said quietly, "you're in charge of the search. If you need me, I'll be in here."

"Sir," Scratchard agreed with a nod. "Well, get the lead out, daisies!" he snarled to the troopers, gesturing them to the street. "We got forty copping houses to run yet!"

As ben Khedda passed him, the captain saw the villager's control slip to uncover his glee. The sergeant was the last man out of the room; Mboya latched the street door after him. Only then did he meet the householder's eyes again. "Hello, Juma" he said in the Kabyle he had sleep-learned rather than the Kikuyu they had both probably forgotten by now. "Brothers shouldn't have to meet this way, should we?"

Juma smiled in mad irony rather than humor. Then his mouth slumped out of that bitter rictus and he said sadly, "No, we shouldn't, that's right." Looking at his altar and not the soldier, he added, "I knew there'd be a—a unit sent around, of course. But I didn't expect you'd be leading the one that came here, where I was."

"Look, I didn't volunteer for Operation Feirefitz," Esa blazed. "And Via, how was I supposed to know where you were anyway? We didn't exactly part kissing each other's cheeks ten years ago, did we? And here you've gone and changed your name even—how was I supposed to keep from stumbling over you?"

Juma's face softened. He stepped to his brother, taking the other's wrists in his hands. "I'm sorry," he said. "Of course that was unfair. The—what's going to happen disturbs me." He managed a genuine smile. "I didn't really change my name, you know. 'Al-Habashi' just means 'the Black,' and it's what everybody on this planet was going to call me whatever I wanted. We aren't very common on Dar al-B'heed, you know. Any more than we were in the Slammers."

"Well, there's one fewer black in the Slammers than before *you* opted out," Esa said bitterly; but he took the civilian's wrists in turn and squeezed them. As the men stood linked, the clerical collar that Juma wore beneath an ordinary jellaba caught the soldier's eye. Without the harshness of a moment before, Esa asked, "Do they all call you 'Father'?"

The civilian laughed and stepped away. "No, only the hypocrites like Youssef," he said. "Oh, Ain Chelia is just as Islamic as the capital, as al-Madinah, never doubt. I have a small congregation here . . . and I have the respect of the rest of the community, I think. I'm head of equipment maintenance at the mine, which doesn't mean assigning work to other people, not here." He spread his hands, palms down. The fingernails were short and the grit beneath their ends a true black and no mere skin tone. "But I think I'd want to do that anyway, even if I didn't need to eat to live. I've guided more folk to the Way by showing them how to balance a turbine than I do when I mumble about peace."

Captain Mboya walked to the table on top of which stood an altar triptych, now closed. Two drawers were set between the table legs. He opened the top one. In it were the altar vessels, chased brasswork of local manufacture. They were beautiful both in sum and in detail, but they had not tripped a detector set to locate tool steel and iridium.

The lower drawer held a powergun.

Juma watched without expression as his brother raised the weapon, checked the full magazine, and ran a fingertip over the manufacturer's stampings. "Heuvelmans of Friesland," Esa said conversationally. "Past couple contracts have been let on Terra, good products . . . but I always preferred the one I was issued when they assigned me to a tribarrel and I rated a sidearm." He drew his own pistol from its flap holster and compared it to the weapon from the drawer. "Right, consecutive serial numbers," the soldier said. He laid Juma's pistol back where it came from. "Not the sort of souvenir we're supposed to take with us when we resign from the Slammers, of course."

Very carefully, and with his eyes on the wall as if searching for flaws in its thick plastered concrete, Juma said, "I hadn't really . . . thought of it being here. I suppose that's grounds for carrying me back to a Re-education Camp in al-Madinah, isn't it?"

His brother's fist slammed the table. The triptych jumped and the vessels in the upper drawer rang like Poe's brazen bells. "Re-education? It's grounds for being burned at the *stake* if I say so! Listen, the reporters are back in the capital, not here. My orders from the District Governor are to *pacify* this region, not coddle it!" Esa's face melted from anger to grief as suddenly as he had swung his fist a moment before. "Via, elder brother, why'd you have to leave? There wasn't a man in the Regiment could handle a tribarrel the way you could."

"That was a long time ago," said Juma, facing the soldier again.

"I remember at Sphakteria," continued Esa as if Juma had not spoken, "when they popped the ambush and killed your gunner the first shot. You cut 'em apart like they weren't shooting at you, too. And then you led the whole platoon clear, driving the jeep with the wick all the way up and working the gun yourself with your right hand. Nobody else could've done it."

"Do you remember," said Juma, his voice dropping into a dreamy caress as had his brother's by the time he finished speaking, "the night we left Nairobi? You led the Service of Farewell yourself, there in the starport, with everyone in the terminal joining in. The faith we'd been raised in was just words to me before then, but you made the Way as real as the tiles I was standing on. And I thought 'Why is he going off to be a soldier? If ever a man was born to lead other men to peace, it was Esa.' And in time, you did lead me to peace, little brother."

Esa shook himself, standing like a centipede in his body armor. "I got that out of my system," he said.

Juma walked over to the altar. "As I got the Slammers out of my system," he said, and he closed the drawer over the powergun within.

Neither man spoke for moments that seemed longer. At last Juma said, "Will you have a beer?"

"What?" said the soldier in surprise. "That's permitted on Dar al-B'heed?"

Juma chuckled as he walked into his kitchen. "Oh yes," he said as he opened a trapdoor in the floor, "though of course not everyone drinks it." He raised two corked bottles from their cool recess and walked back to the central room. "There are some Arab notions that never sat very well with Kabyles, you know. Many of the notions about women, veils and the like. Youssef ben Khedda's wife wore a veil until the revolt . . . then she took it off and walked around the streets like the other women of Ain Chelia. I suspect that since your troops swept in, she has her veil on again."

"*That* one," said the captain with a snort that threatened to spray beer. "I can't imagine why nobody had the sense to throttle him—at least before they went off to their damned fortress."

Juma gestured his brother to one of the room's simple chairs and took another for himself. "Not everyone has seen as many traitors as we have, little brother," he said. "Besides, his own father was one of the martyrs whose death ignited the revolt. He was caught in al-Madinah with hypnocubes of Kabyle language instruction. The government called that treason and executed him."

Esa snorted again. "And didn't anybody here wonder who

shopped the old man to the security police? Via! But I shouldn't complain—he makes my job easier." He swallowed the last of his beer, paused a moment, and then pointed the mouth of the bottle at Juma as if it would shoot. "What about you?" the soldier demanded harshly. "Where do you stand?"

"For peace," said Juma simply, "for the Way. As I always have since I left the Regiment. But . . . my closest friends in the village are dug into the sides of the mine pit now, waiting for you. Or they're dead already outside al-Madinah."

The soldier's hand tightened on the bottle, his fingers darker than the clear brown glass. With a conscious effort of will he set the container down on the terrazzo floor beside his chair. "They're dead either way," he said as he stood up. He put his hand on the door latch before he added, pausing but not turning around, "Listen, elder brother. I told you I didn't ask to be assigned to this mop-up operation; and if I'd known I'd find you here, I'd have taken leave or a transfer. But I'm here now, and I'll do my duty, do you hear?"

"As the Lord wills," said Juma from behind him.

The walls of Juma's house, like those of all the houses in Ain Chelia, were cast fifty centimeters thick to resist the heat of the sun. The front door was on a scale with the walls, close-fitting and too massive to slam. To Captain Mboya, it was the last frustration of the interview that he could elicit no more than a satisfied thump from the door as he stamped into the street.

The ballistic crack of the bullet was all the louder for the stillness of the plateau an instant before. Captain Mboya ducked beneath the lip of the headquarters dugout. The report of the sniper's weapon was lost in the fire of the powerguns and mortars that answered it. "Via, Captain!" snarled Sergeant Scratchard from the parked commo jeep. "Trying to get yourself killed?"

"Via!" Esa wheezed. He had bruised his chin and was thankful for it, the way a child is thankful for any punishment less than the one imagined. He accepted Scratchard's silent offer of a fiber-optic periscope. Carefully, the captain raised it to scan what had been the Chelia Mine and was now the Bordj—the Fortress—holding approximately one hundred and forty Kabyle rebels with enough supplies to last a year.

Satellite photographs showed the mine as a series of neatly stepped terraces in the center of a plateau. From the plateau's surface, nothing of significance could be seen until a flash discovered the position of a sniper the moment before he dodged to fire again.

"It'd be easy," Sergeant Scratchard said, "if they'd just tried to use the pit as a big foxhole . . . Have Central pop a couple antipersonnel shells overhead and then we go in and count bodies. But they've got tunnels and spider holes—and command-detonated mines—laced out from the pit like a giant worm-farm. This one's going to cost, Esa."

"Blood and martyrs," the captain said under his breath. When he had received the Ain Chelia assignment, Mboya had first studied reconnaissance coverage of the village and the mine three kilometers away. It was now a month and a half since the rebel disaster at al-Madinah. The Slammers had raised the siege of the capital in a pitched battle that no one in the human universe was better equipped to fight. Surviving rebels had scattered to their homes to make what preparations they could against the white terror they knew would sweep in the wake of the government's victory. At Ain Chelia, the preparations had been damned effective. The recce showed clearly that several thousand cubic meters of rubble had been dumped into the central pit of the mine, the waste of burrowings from all around its five kilometer circumference.

"We can drop penetrators all year," Mboya said, aloud but more to himself than to the noncom beside him. "Blow the budget for the whole operation, and even then I wouldn't bet they couldn't tunnel ahead of the shelling faster than we broke rock on top of them."

"If we storm the place," said Sergeant Scratchard, "and then go down the tunnels after the holdouts, we'll have thirty percent casualties if we lose a man."

A rifle flashed from the pit-edge. Almost simultaneously, one of the company's three-barreled automatic weapons slashed the edge of the rebel gunpit. The trooper must have sighted in his weapon earlier when a sniper had popped from the pit, knowing the site would be reused eventually. Now the air shook as the powergun detonated a bandolier of grenades charged with industrial explosives. The sniper's rifle glittered as it spun into the air; her head was by contrast a ragged blur, its long hair uncoiling and snapping outward with the thrust of the explosion.

"Get that gunner's name," Mboya snapped to his first sergeant. "He's earned a week's leave as soon as we stand down. But to get all the rest of them . . ." and the officer's voice was the more stark for the fact that it was so controlled, "we're going to need something better. I think we're going to have to talk them out."

"Via, Captain," said Scratchard in real surprise, "why would they want to come out? They saw at al-Madinah what happens when they faced us in the field. And nobody surrenders when they know all prisoners're going to be shot."

"Don't say nobody," said Esa Mboya in a voice as crisp as the gunfire bursting anew from the Bordj. "Because that's just what you're going to see this lot do."

The dead end of Juma's street had been blocked and turned into the company maintenance park between the time Esa left to observe the Bordj and his return to his brother's house. Skimmers, trucks, and a gun-jeep with an intermittent short in its front fan had been pulled into the cul-de-sac. They were walled on three sides by the courtyards of the houses beyond Juma's.

Sergeant Scratchard halted the jeep with the bulky commo equipment in the open street, but Mboya swung his own skimmer around the supply truck that formed a makeshift fourth wall for the park. A guard saluted. "Muller!" Esa shouted, even before the skirts of his one-man vehicle touched the pavement. "What in the name of heaven d'ye think you're about! I told you to set up in the main square!"

Bog Muller stood up beside a skimmer raised on edge. He was a bulky technician with twenty years service in the Slammers. A good administrator, but his khakis were clean. Operation Feirefitz had required the company to move fast and long, and there was no way Muller's three half-trained subordinates could have coped with the consequent rash of equipment failures. "Ah, well, Captain," Muller temporized, his eyes apparently focused on the row of wall spikes over Esa's head, "we ran into Juma and he said—"

"He *what!*" Mboya shouted.

"I said," said Juma, rising from behind the skimmer himself, "that security in the middle of the village would be more of a problem than anyone needed. We've got some hotheads; I don't want any of them to get the notion of stealing a gun-jeep, for instance. The two households there—" he pointed to the entrances now blocked by vehicles, using the grease gun in his right hand for the gesture—"have both been evacuated to the Bordj." The half-smile he gave his brother could have been meant for either what he had just said or for the words he added, raising both the grease gun and the wire brush he held in his left hand: "Besides, what with the mine closed, I'd get rusty myself with no equipment to work on."

"After all," said Muller in what was more explanation than defense, "I knew Juma back when."

Esa took in his brother's smile, took in as well the admiring glances of the three Tech I's who had been watching the civilian work. "All right," he said to Muller, "but the next time clear it with me. And you," he said, pointing to Juma, "come on inside for now. We need to talk."

"Yes, little brother," the civilian said with a bow as submissive as his tone.

In the surprising cool of his house, Juma stripped off the gritty jellaba he had worn while working. He began washing with a waterless cleaner, rubbing it on with smooth strokes of his palms. On a chain around his neck glittered a tiny silver crucifix, normally hidden by his clothing.

"You didn't do much of a job persuading your friends to your Way of Peace," Esa said with an anger he had not intended to display.

"No, I'm afraid I didn't," the civilian answered mildly. "They were polite enough, even the Kaid, Ali ben Cheriff. But they pointed out that the Arabizers in al-Madinah intended to stamp out all traces of Kabyle culture as soon as possible . . . which of course was true. And we did have our own martyr here in Ain Chelia, as you know. I couldn't—" Juma looked up at his brother, his dark skin glistening beneath the lather—"argue with their *military* estimate, after all, either. The Way doesn't require that its followers lie about reality in order to change it—but I don't have to tell you that."

"Go on," said the captain. His hand touched the catches of his body armor. He did not release them, however, even though the hard-suit was not at the moment protection against any physical threat.

"Well, the National Army was outnumbered ten to one by the troops we could field from the backlands," Juma continued as he stepped into the shower. "That's without defections, too. And weapons aren't much of a problem. Out there, any jack-leg mechanic can turn out a truck piston in his back room. The tolerances aren't any closer on a machine gun. But what we didn't expect—" he raised his deep voice only enough to override the hiss of the shower—"was that all six of the other planets of the al-Ittihad al-Arabi—" for Arab Union Juma used the Arabic words, and they rasped in his throat like a file on bars— "would club together and help the sanctimonious butchers in al-Madinah hire the Slammers."

He stepped shining from the stall, no longer pretending detachment or that he and his brother were merely chatting. "I visited the siege lines then," Juma rumbled, wholly a preacher and wholly a man, "and I begged the men from Ain Chelia to come home while there was time. To make peace, or if they would not choose peace then at least to choose life—to lie low in the hills till the money ran out and the Slammers were off on somebody else's contract, killing somebody else's enemies. But my friends would stand with their brothers . . . and so they did, and they died with their brothers, too many of them, when the tanks came through their encirclement like knives through a goat-skin." His smile crooked and his voice dropped. "And the rest came home and told me they should have listened before."

"They'll listen to you now," said Esa, "if you tell them to come out of the Bordj without their weapons and surrender."

Juma began drying himself on a towel of coarse local cotton. "Will they?" he replied without looking up.

Squeezing his fingers against the bands of porcelain armor over his stomach, Esa said, "The Re-education Camps outside al-Madinah aren't a rest cure, but there's too many journalists in the city to let them be too bad. Even if the holdouts are willing to die, they surely don't want their whole families wiped out. And if we have to clear the Bordj ourselves—well, there won't be any prisoners, you know that. . . . There wouldn't be even if we wanted them, not after we blast and gas the tunnels, one by one."

"Yes, I gathered the Re-education Camps aren't too bad," the civilian agreed, walking past his brother to don a light jellaba of softer weave than his work garment. "I gather they're not very full, either. A—a cynic, say, might guess that most of the trouble-makers don't make it to al-Madinah where journalists can see them. That they die in the desert after they've surrendered. Or they don't surrender, of course. I don't think Ali ben Cheriff and the others in the Bordj are going to surrender, for instance."

"Damn you!" the soldier shouted, "The choice is *certain* death, isn't it? *Any* chance is better than that!"

"Well, you see," said Juma, watching the knuckles of his right hand twist against the palm of his left, "they know as well as I do that the only transport you arrived with was the minimum to haul your own supplies. There's no way you could carry over a hundred prisoners back to the capital. No way in . . . Hell."

Esa slammed the wall with his fist. Neither the concrete nor his raging expression showed any reaction to the loud impact. "I could be planning to put them in commandeered ore haulers, couldn't I?" he said. "Some of them must be operable!"

Juma stepped to the younger man and took him by the wrists as gently as a shepherd touching a newborn lamb. "Little brother," he said, "swear to me that you'll turn anyone who surrenders over to the authorities in al-Madinah, and I'll do whatever I can to get them to surrender."

The soldier snatched his hands away. He said, "Do you think I wouldn't lie to you because we're brothers? Then you're a fool!"

"What I think, what anyone thinks, is between him and the Lord," Juma said. He started to move toward his brother again but caught the motion and turned it into a swaying only. "If you will swear to me to deliver them unharmed, I'll carry your message into the Bordj."

Esa swung open the massive door. On the threshold he paused and turned to his brother. "Every one of my boys who doesn't make it," he said in a venomous whisper. "His blood's on your head."

Captain Mboya did not try to slam the door this time. He left it standing open as he strode through the courtyard. "Scratchard!" he roared to the sergeant with an anger not meant for the man on whom it fell. "Round up ben Khedda!" Mboya threw himself down on his skimmer and flicked the fans to life. Over their whine he added, "Get him up to me at the command dugout. Now!"

With the skill of long experience, the captain spun his one-man vehicle past the truck and the jeep parked behind it. Sergeant Scratchard gloomily watched his commander shriek up the street. The captain shouldn't have been going anywhere without the jeep, his commo link to Central, in tow. No point in worrying about that, though. The noncom sighed and lifted the jeep off the pavement. Ben Khedda would be at his house or in the cafe across the street from it. Scratchard hoped he had a vehicle of his own and wouldn't have to ride the jump seat of the jeep. He didn't like to sit that close to a slimy traitor.

But Jack Scratchard knew he'd done worse things than sit with a traitor during his years with the Slammers; and, needs must, he would again.

The mortar shell burst with a white flash. Seconds later came a distant *chunk!* as if a rock had been dropped into a trash can. Even after the report had died away, fragments continued ricocheting from rock with tiny gnat-songs. Ben Khedda flinched beneath the clear night sky.

"It's just our harassing fire," said Captain Mboya. "You rag-heads don't have high-angle weapons, thank the Lord. Of course, all our shells do is keep them down in their tunnels."

The civilian swallowed. "Your sergeant," he said, "told me you needed me at once." Scratchard stirred in the darkness at the other end of the dugout, but he made no comment of his own.

"Yeah," said Mboya, "but when I cooled off I decided to take a turn around the perimeter. Took a while. It's a bloody long perimeter for one cursed infantry company to hold."

"Well, I," ben Khedda said, "I came at once, sir. I recognize the duty all good citizens owe to our liberators." Firing broke out, a burst from a projectile weapon answered promiscuously by powerguns. Ben Khedda winced again. Cyan bolts from across the pit snapped overhead, miniature lightning followed by miniature thunder.

Without looking up, Captain Mboya keyed his commo helmet and said, "Thrasher Four to Thrasher Four-Three. Anybody shoots beyond his sector again and it's ten days in the glass house when we're out of this cop." The main unit in Scratchard's jeep purred as it relayed the amplified signal. All the firing ceased.

"Will ben Cheriff and the others in the Bordj listen to you, do you think?" the captain continued.

For a moment, ben Khedda did not realize the officer was speaking to him. He swallowed again, "Well, I . . . I can't say," he blurted. He began to curl in his upper lip as if to chew a moustache, though he was clean shaven. "They aren't friends of mine, of course, but if God wills and it would help you if I addressed them over a loudspeaker as to their true duties as citizens of Dar al-B'heed—"

"We hear you were second in command of the Chelia contingent at Madinah," Mboya said inflexibly. "Besides, there won't be a loudspeaker, you'll be going in person."

Horror at past and future implications warred in ben Khedda's mind and froze his tongue. At last he stammered, "Oh no, C-Captain, before G-God, they've lied to you! That accurst al-Habashi wishes to lie away my life! I did no more than any man would do to stay alive!"

Mboya waved the other to silence. The pale skin of his palm winked as another shell detonated above the Bordj. When the echoes died away, the captain went on in a voice as soft as a leopard's paw, "You will tell them that if they all surrender, their lives will be spared and they will not be turned over to the government until they are actually in al-Madinah. You will say that I swore that on my honor and on the soul of my house."

Ben Khedda raised a hand to interrupt, but the soldier's voice rolled on implacably, "They must deposit all their arms in the Bordj and come out to be shackled. The tunnels will be searched. If there are any holdouts, three of those who surrendered will be shot for each holdout. If there are any booby traps, ten of those who surrendered will be shot for every man of mine who is injured."

Mboya drew a breath, long and deep as that of a power lifter. The civilian, tight as a house-jack, strangled his own words as he waited for the captain to conclude. "You will say that after they have done as I have said, all of them will be loaded on ore carriers with sun-screens. You will explain that there will be food and water brought from the village to support them. And you will tell them that if some of them are wounded or are infirm, they may ride within an ambulance which will be air-conditioned.

"Do you understand?"

For a moment, ben Khedda struggled with an inability to phrase his thoughts in neutral terms. He was unwilling to meet the captain's eyes, even with the darkness as a cushion. Finally he said, "Captain—I, I trust your word as I would trust that of no man since the Prophet, on whom be peace. When you say the lives of the traitors will be spared, there can be no doubt, may it please God."

"Trust has nothing to do with it," said Captain Mboya without expression. "I have told you what you will say, and you will say it."

"Captain, Captain," whimpered the civilian, "I understand. The trip is a long one and surely some of the most troublesome will die of heat stroke. They will know that themselves. But there will be no . . . general tragedy? I must live here in Ain Chelia with the friends of the, the traitors. You see my position?"

"Your position," Mboya repeated with scorn that drew a chuckle from Scratchard across the dugout. "Your position is that unless you talk your friends there out of the Bordj—" he gestured. Automatic weapons began to rave and chatter as if on cue. "Unless you go down there and come back with them, I'll have you shot on your doorstep for a traitor, and your body left to the dogs. That's your position."

"Cheer up, citizen," Sergeant Scratchard said. "You're getting a great chance to pick one side and stick with it. The change'll do you good."

Ben Khedda gave a despairing cry and stood, his dun jellaba flapping as a lesser shadow. He stared over the rim of the dugout into a night now brightened only by stars and a random powergun bolt, harassment like that of the mortars. He turned and shouted at the motionless captain, "It's easy for you—you go where your colonel sends you, you kill who he tells you to kill. And then you come all high and moral over the rest of us, who have to make our own decisions! You despise me? At least I'm a man and not somebody's dog!"

Mboya laughed harshly. "You think Colonel Hammer told us how to clear the back country? Don't be a fool. My official orders are to cooperate with the District Governor and to send all prisoners back to al-Madinah for internment. The colonel can honestly deny ordering anything else—and letting him do that is as much a part of my job as co-operating with a governor who knows that anybody really sent to a Re-education Camp will be back in his hair in a year."

There was a silence in the dugout. At last the sergeant said, "He can't go out now, sir." The moan of a ricochet underscored the words.

"No, no, we'll have to wait till dawn," the captain agreed tiredly. As if ben Khedda were an unpleasant machine, he added, "Get him the hell out of my sight, though. Stick him in the bunker with the Headquarters Squad and tell them to hold him till called for. Via! but I wish this operation was over."

The guns spat at one another all through the night. It was not the fire that kept Esa Mboya awake, however, but rather the dreams that plagued him with gentle words whenever he did manage to nod off.

"Well," said Juma, scowling judiciously at the gun-jeep on the rack before him, "I'd say we pull the wiring harness first. Half the time that's the whole problem—grit gets into the conduits and when the fans vibrate, it saws through the insulation. Even if we're wrong, we haven't done anything that another few months of running on Dar al-B'heed wouldn't have required anyway."

"You should have seen him handle one a' these when I first knew him," said Bog Muller proudly to his subordinates. "Beat it to hell, he would, Via—bring her in with rock scrapes on both sides that he'd put on at the same time!"

The Kikuyu civilian touched a valve and lowered the rack. His hand caressed the sand-burnished skirt of the jeep as it sank past him. The joystick controls were in front of the left-hand seat. Finesse was a matter of touch and judgment, not sophisticated instrumentation. He waggled the stick gently, remembering. In front of the other seat was the powergun, its three iridium barrels poised to rotate and hose out destruction in a nearly continuous stream.

"You won't believe it," continued the technician, "but I saw it with my own eyes—" that was a lie—"this boy here steering with one hand and working the gun with the other. Bloody miracle that was—even if he did give Maintenance more trouble than any three other troopers."

"You learn a lot about a machine when you push it, when you stress it," said Juma. His fingers reached for but did not quite touch the spade grips of the tribarrel. "About men, too," he added, and lowered his hand. He looked Muller in the face and said, "What I learned about myself was that I didn't want to live in a universe that had no better use for me than to gun other people down. I won't claim to be saving souls . . . because that's in the Lord's hands and he uses what instruments he desires. But at least I'm not taking lives."

One of the younger techs coughed; Muller nodded heavily and said, "I know what you mean, Juma. I've never regretted getting into Maintenance right off the way I did. Especially times like today. . . But Via, if we stand here fanning our lips, we won't get a curst bit of work done, will we?"

The civilian chuckled without asking for an explanation of 'especially times like today.' "Sure, Bog," he said, latching open the left-side access ports one after another.

"Somebody dig out a 239B harness and we'll see if I remember as much as I think I do about changing one of these beggars." He glanced up at the truncated mass of the plateau, wiping his face with a bandanna. "Things have quieted down since the sun came up," he remarked. "Even if I weren't—dedicated to the Way—I know too many people on both sides to like to hear the shooting at the mine."

None of the other men responded. At the time it did not occur to Juma that there might be something about his words that embarrassed them.

"There's a flag," said Scratchard, his eyes pressed tight to the lenses of the periscope. "Blood and martyrs, Cap—there's a flag!"

"No shooting!" Mboya ordered over his commo as he moved. "Four to all Thrasher units, stand to but no shooting!"

All around the mine crater, men watched a white rag flapping on the end of a long wooden pole. Some looked through periscopes like those in the command dugout, others over the sights of their guns in hope that something would give them an excuse to fire. "Well, what are they waiting for?" the captain muttered.

"It's ben Khedda," guessed Scratchard without looking away from the flag. "He was just scared green to go out there. Now he's just as scared to come back."

The flag staggered suddenly. Troopers tensed, but a moment later an unarmed man climbed full height from the Bordj. The high sun threw his shadow at his feet like a pit. Standing as erect as his age permitted him, Ali ben Cheriff took a step toward the Slammers' lines. Wind plucked at his jellaba and white beard; the rebel leader was a patriarch in appearance as well as in simple fact. On his head was the green turban that marked him as a pilgrim to al-Meccah on Terra. He was as devotedly Moslem as he was Kabyle, and he—like most of the villagers—saw no inconsistencies in the facts. To ben Cheriff it was no more necessary to become an Arab in order to accept Islam than it had seemed necessary to Saint Paul that converts to Christ first become Jews.

"We've won," the captain said as he watched the figure through the foreshortened lenses. "That's the Kaid, ben Cheriff. If he comes, they all do."

Up from the hidden tunnel clambered an old woman wearing

the stark black of a matron. The Kaid paused and stretched back his hand, but the woman straightened without help. Together the old couple began to walk toward the waiting guns.

The flagstaff flapped erect again. Gripping it like a talisman, Youssef ben Khedda stepped from the tunnel mouth where the Kaid had shouldered aside his hesitation. He picked his way across the ground at increasing speed. When ben Khedda passed the Kaid and his wife, he skirted them widely as if he were afraid of being struck. More rebels were leaving the Bordj in single file. None of them carried visible weapons. Most, men and women alike, had their eyes cast down; but a red-haired girl leading a child barely old enough to walk glared around with the haughty rage of a lioness.

"Well, no rest for the wicked," grunted Sergeant Scratchard. Settling his submachine gun on its sling, he climbed out of the dugout. "Headquarters Squad to me," he ordered. Bent over against the possible shock of a fanatic's bullets, experienced enough to know the reality of his fear and brave enough to face it nonetheless, Scratchard began to walk to the open area between pit and siege lines where the prisoners would be immobilized. The seven men of HQ Squad followed; their corporal drove the jeep loaded with leg irons.

One of the troopers raised his powergun to bar ben Khedda. Scratchard waved and called an order; the trooper shrugged and let the Kabyle pass. The sergeant gazed after him for a moment, then spat in the dust and went on about the business of searching and securing the prisoners.

Youssef ben Khedda was panting with tension and effort as he approached the dugout, but there was a hard glint of triumph in his eyes as well. He knew he was despised, by those he led no less than by those who had driven him; but he had dug the rebels from their fortress when all the men and guns of the Slammers might have been unable to do so without him. Now he saw a way to ride the bloody crest to permanent power in Ain Chelia. He tried to set his flag in the ground. It scratched into the rocky soil, then fell with a clatter. "I have brought them to you," ben Khedda said in a haughty voice.

"Some of them, at least," said Mboya, his face neutral. Rebels continued to straggle from the Bordj, their faces sallow from more than the day they had spent in their tunnels. The Kaid had submitted to the shackles with a stony indifference. His wife was weeping beside him, not for herself but for her husband. Two of the nervous troopers were fanning the prisoners with detector wands set for steel and iridium. Anything the size of a razor blade would register. A lead bludgeon or a brass-barreled pistol would be ignored, but there were some chances you took in the service of practicality.

"As God wills, they are all coming, you know that," ben Khedda said, assertive with dreamed-of lordship. "If they were each in his separate den, many of them would fight till you blew them out or buried them. All are willing to die, but most would not willingly kill their fellows, their families." His face worked. "A fine joke, is it not?" If what had crossed ben Khedda's lips had been a smile, then it transmuted to a sneer. "They would have been glad to kill me first, I think, but they were afraid that you would have been angry."

"More fools them," said the captain.

"Yes . . ." said the civilian, drawing back his face like a rat confronting a terrier, "more fools them. And now you will pay me."

"Captain," said the helmet speaker in the first sergeant's voice, "this one says he's the last."

Mboya climbed the four steps to surface level. Scratchard waved and pointed to the Kabyle who was just joining the scores of his fellows. The number of those being shackled in a continuous chain at least approximated the one hundred and forty who were believed to have holed up in the Bordj. Through the clear air rang hammer strokes as a pair of troopers stapled the chain to the ground at intervals, locking the prisoners even more securely into the killing ground. The captain nodded. "We'll give it a minute to let anybody still inside have second thoughts," he said over the radio. "Then the search teams go in." He looked at ben Khedda. "All right," he said, "you've got your life and whatever you think you can do with it. Now, get out of here before I change my mind."

Mboya gazed again at the long line of prisoners. He was unable not to imagine them as they would look in an hour's time, after the

Bordj had been searched and their existence was no longer a tool against potential holdouts. He could not have broken with the Way of his childhood, however, had he not replaced it with a sense of duty as uncompromising. Esa Mboya, Captain, G Company, Hammer's Regiment, would do whatever was required to accomplish the task set him. They had been hired to pacify the district, not just to quiet it down for six months or a year.

Youssef ben Khedda had not left. He was still facing Mboya, as unexpected and unpleasant as a rat on the pantry shelf. He was saying, "No, there is one more thing you must do, as God wills, before you leave Ain Chelia. I do not compel it—" the soldier's face went blank with fury at the suggestion—"your duty that you talk of compels you. There is one more traitor in the village, a man who did not enter the Bordj because he thought his false god would preserve him."

"Little man," said the captain in shock and a genuine attempt to stop the words he knew were about to be said, "don't—"

"Add the traitor Juma al-Habashi to these," the civilian cried, pointing to the fluttering jellabas of the prisoners. "Put him there or his whines of justice and other words and his false god will poison the village again like a dead rat stinking in a pool. Take him!"

The two men stood with their feet on a level. The soldier's helmet and armor increased his advantage in bulk, however, and his wrath lighted his face like a cleansing flame. "Shall I slay my brother for thee, lower-than-a-dog?" he snarled.

Ben Khedda's face jerked at the verbal slap, but with a wave of his arm he retorted, "Will you now claim to follow the Way yourself? There stand one hundred and thirty-four of your brothers. Make it one more, as your duty commands!"

The absurdity was so complete that the captain trembled between laughter and the feeling that he had gone insane. Carefully, his tone touched more with wonder than with rage until the world should return to focus, the Kikuyu said, "Shall I, Esa Mboya, order the death of Juma Mboya? My brother, flesh of my father and of my mother . . . who held my hand when I toddled my first steps upright?"

Now at last ben Khedda's confidence squirted out like blood from a slashed carotid. "The name —" he said. "I didn't *know!*"

Mboya's world snapped into place again, its realities clear and neatly dovetailed. "Get out, filth," he said harshly, "and wonder what I plan for you when I come down from this hill."

The civilian stumbled back toward his car as if his body and not his spirit had received the mortal wound. The soldier considered him dispassionately. If ben Khedda stayed in Ain Chelia, he wouldn't last long. The Slammers would be out among the stars, and the central government a thousand kilometers away in al-Madinah would be no better able to protect a traitor. Youssef ben Khedda would be a reminder of friends and relatives torn by blasts of cyan fire with every step he took on the streets of the village. Those steps would be few enough, one way or the other.

And if in the last fury of his well-earned fear ben Khedda tried to kill Juma—well, Juma had made his bed, his Way . . . he could tread it himself. Esa laughed. Not that the traitor would attempt murder personally. Even in the final corner, rats of ben Khedda's stripe tried to persuade other rats to bite for them.

"Captain," murmured Scratchard's voice over the command channel, "think we've waited long enough?"

Instead of answering over the radio, Mboya nodded and began walking the hundred meters to where his sergeant stood near the prisoners. The rebels' eyes followed him, some with anger, most in only a dull appreciation of the fact that he was the nearest moving object on a static landscape. Troopers had climbed out of their gun pits all around the Bordj. Their dusty khaki blended with the soil, but the sun woke bright reflections from the barrels of their weapons.

"The search teams are ready to go in, sir," Scratchard said, speaking in Dutch but stepping a pace further from the shackled Kaid besides.

"Right," the captain agreed. "I'll lead the team from Third Platoon."

"Captain—"

"Where are the trucks, unbeliever?" demanded Ali ben Cheriff. His voice started on a quaver but lashed at the end.

"—there's plenty cursed things for you to do besides crawling down a hole with five pongoes. Leave it to the folks whose job it is."

"There's nothing left of this operation that Mendoza can't wrap up," Mboya said. "Believe me, he won't like doing it any less, either."

"Where are the trucks to carry away our children, dog and son of dogs?" cried the Kaid. Beneath the green turban, the rebel's face was as savage and unyielding as that of a trapped wolf.

"It's not for fun," Mboya went on. "There'll be times I'll have to send boys out to be killed while I stay back, safe as a staff officer, and run things. But if I lead from the front when I can, when it won't compromise the mission if I do stop a load—then they'll do what they're told a little sharper when it's me that says it the next time."

The Kaid spat. Lofted by his anger and the breeze, the gobbet slapped the side of Mboya's helmet and dribbled down onto his porcelain-sheathed shoulder.

Scratchard turned. Ignoring the automatic weapon slung ready to fire under his arm, he drew a long knife from his boot sheath instead. Three strides separated the noncom from the line of prisoners. He had taken two of them before Mboya caught his shoulder and stopped him. "Easy, Jack," the captain said.

Ben Cheriff's gaze was focused on the knife-point. Fear of death could not make the old man yield, but neither was he unmoved by the approach of its steel-winking eye. Scratchard's own face had no more expression than did the knife itself. The Kaid's wife lunged at the soldier to the limit of her chain, but the look Scratchard gave her husband dried her throat around the curses within it.

Mboya pulled his man back. "Easy," he repeated. "I think he's earned that, don't you?" He turned Scratchard gently. He did not point out, nor did he need to do so, the three gun-jeeps which had swung down the fifty meters in front of the line of captives. Their crews were tense and still with the weight of their orders. They met Mboya's eyes comprehendingly but without enthusiasm.

"Right," said Scratchard mildly. "Well, the quicker we get down that hole, the quicker we get the rest of the job done. Let's go."

The five tunnel rats from Third Platoon were already squatting at the entrance from which the rebels had surrendered. Captain

Mboya began walking toward them. "You stay on top, Sergeant," he said. "You don't need to prove anything."

Scratchard cursed without heat. "I'll wait at the tunnel mouth unless something pops. You'll be out of radio contact and I'll be curst if I trust anybody else to carry you a message."

The tunnel rats were rising to their feet, silent men whose faces were in constant, tiny motion. They carried detector wands and sidearms; two had even taken off their body armor and stood in the open air looking paler than shelled shrimp. Mboya cast a glance back over his shoulder at the prisoners and the gun-jeeps beyond. "Do you believe in sin, Sergeant?" he asked.

Scratchard glanced sidelong at his superior. "Don't know, sir. Not really my field."

"My brother believes in it," said the captain, "but I guess he left the Slammers before you transferred out of combat cars. And he isn't here now, Jack, I am, so I guess we'll have to dispense with sin today."

"Team Three ready, sir," said the black-haired man who probably would have had sergeant's pips had he not been stripped to the waist.

"Right," said Mboya. Keying his helmet he went on, "Thrasher to Club One, Club Two. Let's see what they left us, boys." And as he stepped toward the tunnel's mouth, without really thinking about the words until he spoke them, he added, "And the Lord be with us all."

The bed of the turbine driving Youssef ben Khedda's car was enough out of true that the vehicle announced its own approach unmistakably. Juma wondered in the back of his mind what brought the little man, but his main concentration was on the plug connector he was trying to reeve through a channel made for something a size smaller. At last the connector shifted the last two millimeters necessary for Juma to slip a button-hook deftly above it. The three subordinate techs gave a collective sigh, and Bog Muller beamed in reflected glory.

"Father!" ben Khedda wheezed, oblivious to the guard frowning over his powergun a pace behind, "Father! You've got to . . . I've got to talk to you. You must!"

"All right, Youssef," the Kikuyu said. "In a moment." He tugged the connector gently through its channel and rotated it to mate with the gun leads.

Ben Khedda reached for Juma's arm in a fury of impatience. One of the watching techs caught the Kabyle's wrist. "Touch him, rag-head," the trooper said, "and you better be able to grow a new hand." He thrust ben Khedda back with more force than the resistance demanded.

Juma straightened from the gun-jeep and put an arm about the shoulders of the angry trooper. "Worse job than replacing all the fans," he said in Dutch, "but it gives you a good feeling to finish it. Run the static test, if you would, and I'll be back in a few minutes." He squeezed the trooper, released him, and added in Kabyle to his fellow villager, "Come into my house, then, Youssef. What is it you need of me?"

Ben Khedda's haste and nervousness were obvious from the way his car lay parked with its skirt folded under the front from an over-hasty stop. Juma paused with a frown for more than the mechanical problem. He bent to lift the car and let the skirt spring away from the fan it was probably touching at the moment.

"Don't *worry* about that," ben Khedda cried, plucking at the bigger man's sleeve. "We've *got* to talk in private."

Juma had left his courtyard gate unlatched since he was working only a few meters away. Before ben Khedda had reached the door of the house, he was spilling the words that tormented him. "Before God, you have to talk to your brother or he'll kill me, Father, he'll kill *me!*"

"Youssef," said the Kikuyu as he swung his door open and gestured the other man toward the cool interior, "I pray—I have been praying—that at worst, none of our villagers save those in the Bordj are in danger." He smiled too sadly to be bitter. "You would know better than I, I think, who may have been marked out to Esa as an enemy of the government. But he's not a cruel man, my brother, only a very—determined one. He won't add you to whatever list he has out of mere dislike."

The Kabyle's lips worked silently. His face was tortured by the explanation that he needed to give but could not. "Father," he pleaded, "you *must* believe me, he'll have me killed. Before God, you must beg him for my life, you *must!*"

Ben Khedda was gripping the Kikuyu by both sleeves. Juma detached himself carefully and said, "Youssef, why would my brother want you killed—of all the men in Ain Chelia? Did something happen?"

The smaller man jerked himself back with a dawning horror in his eyes. "You planned this with him, didn't you?" he cried. His arm thrust at the altar as if to sweep away the closed triptych. "This is all a lie, your prayers, your *Way*—you and your butcher brother trapped me to bleed like a sheep on Id al-Fitr! Traitor! Liar! Murderer!" He threw his hands over his face and flung himself down and across a stool. The Kabyle's sobs held the torment of a man without hope.

Juma stared at the weeping man. There was something unclean about ben Khedda. His back rose and fell beneath the jellaba like the distended neck of a python bolting a young child. "Youssef," the Kikuyu said as gently as he could, "you may stay here or leave, as you please. I promise you that I will speak to Esa this evening, on your behalf as well as that of . . . others, all the others. Is there anything you need to tell me?"

Only the tears responded.

The dazzling sun could not sear away Juma's disquiet as he walked past the guard and the barricading truck. Something was wrong with the day, with the very silence. Though all things were with the Lord.

The jeep's inspection ports had been latched shut. The techs had set a pair of skimmers up on their sides as the next project. The civilian smiled. "Think she'll float now?" he asked the trooper who had grabbed ben Khedda. "Let's see if I remember how to put one of these through her paces. You can't trust a fix, you see, till you've run her under full load."

There was a silence broken by the whine of ben Khedda's turbine firing. Juma managed a brief prayer that the Kabyle would find a Way open to him—knowing as he prayed that the impulse to do so was from his mind and not at all from his heart.

"Juma, ah," Bog Muller was trying to say. "Ah, look, this isn't—isn't our idea, it's the job, you know. But the captain—" none of the four techs were looking anywhere near the civilian—"he ordered that you not go anywhere today until, until . . . it was clear."

The silence from the Bordj was a cloak that smothered Juma and squeezed all the blood from his face. "Not that you're a prisoner, but, ah, your brother thought it'd be better for both of you if you didn't see him or call him till—after."

"I see," said the civilian, listening to his own voice as if a third party were speaking. "Until after he's killed my friends, I suppose . . . yes." He began walking back to his house, his sandaled feet moving without being consciously directed. "Juma—" called Muller, but the tech thought better of the words or found he had none to say.

Ben Khedda had left the door ajar. It was only by habit that Juma himself closed it behind him. The dim coolness within was no balm to the fire that skipped across the surface of his mind. Kneeling, the Kikuyu unlatched and opened wide the panels of his altar piece. It was his one conscious affectation, a copy of a triptych painted over a millennium before by the Master of Hell, Hieronymus Bosch. Atop a haywain rode a couple. Their innocence was beset by every form of temptation in the world, the World. Where would their Way take them? No doubt where it took all Mankind, saving the Lord's grace, to Hell and the grave—good intentions be damned, hope be damned, innocence be damned. . . . Obscurely glad of the harshness of the tiles on which he knelt, Juma prayed for his brother and for the souls of those who would shortly die in flames as like to those of Hell as man could create. He prayed for himself as well, for he was damned to endure what he had not changed. They were all travelers together on the Way.

After a time, Juma sighed and raised his head. A demon faced him on the triptych; it capered and piped through its own blue snout. Not for the first time, Juma thought of how pleasant it would be to personify his own weakness and urgings. Then he could pretend that they were somehow apart from the true Juma Mboya, who remained whole and incorruptible.

The lower of the two drawers beneath the altar was not fully closed.

Even as he drew it open, Juma knew from the lack of resistance that the drawer was empty. The heavy-barreled powergun had rested within when ben Khedda had accompanied the search team. It was there no longer.

Striding swiftly and with the dignity of a leopard, Mboya al-Habashi crossed the room and his courtyard. He appeared around the end of the truck barricade so suddenly that Bog Muller jumped. The Kikuyu pointed his index finger with the deliberation of a pistol barrel. "Bog," he said very clearly, "I need to call my brother at once or something terrible will happen."

"Via, man," said the technician, looking away, "you know how I feel about it, but it's not my option. You don't leave here, and you don't call, Juma—or it's my ass."

"Lord blast you for a fool!" the Kikuyu shouted, taking a step forward. All four technicians backed away with their hands lifting. "Will you—" But though there was confusion on the faces watching him, there was nothing of assent, and there was no time to argue. As if he had planned it from the start, Juma slipped into the left saddle of the jeep he had just rewired and gunned the fans.

With an oath, Bog Muller grappled with the civilian. The muscles beneath Juma's loose jellaba had shifted driving fans beneath ore carriers in lieu of a hydraulic jack. He shrugged the technician away with a motion as slight and as masterful as that of an earth tremor. Juma waggled the stick, using the vehicle's skirts to butt aside two of the younger men who belatedly tried to support their chief. Then he had the jeep clear of the repair rack and spinning on its own axis.

Muller scrambled to his feet again and waited for Juma to realize there was not enough room between truck and wall for the jeep to pass. If the driver himself had any doubt, it was not evident in the way he dialed on throttle and leaned to bring the right-hand skirt up an instant before it scraped the courtyard wall. Using the wall as a running surface and the force of his turn to hold him there, Juma sent the gun-jeep howling sideways around the barricade and up the street.

"Hey!" shouted the startled guard, rising from the shady side of the truck. "Hey!" and he shouldered his weapon.

A technician grabbed him, wrestling the muzzle of the gun skyward. It was the same lanky man who had caught ben Khedda when he would have plucked at Juma's sleeve. "Via!" cried the guard, watching the vehicle corner and disappear up the main road to the mine. "We weren't supposed to let him by!"

"We're better off explaining that," said the tech, "than we are telling the captain how we just killed his brother. Right?"

The street was empty again. All five troopers stared at it for some moments before any of them moved to the radio.

Despite his haste, Youssef ben Khedda stopped his car short of the waiting gun-jeeps and began walking toward the prisoners. His back crept with awareness of the guns and the hard-eyed men behind them; but, as God willed, he had chosen and there could be no returning now.

The captain—his treacherous soul was as black as his skin—was not visible. No doubt he had entered the Bordj as he had announced he would. Against expectation, and as further proof that God favored his cause, ben Khedda saw no sign of that damnable first sergeant either. If God willed it, might they both be blasted to atoms somewhere in a tunnel!

The soldiers watching the prisoners from a few meters away were the ones whom ben Khedda had led on their search of the village. The corporal frowned, but he knew ben Khedda for a confidant of his superiors. "Go with God, brother," said the civilian in Arabic, praying the other would have been taught that tongue or Kabyle. "Your captain wished me to talk once more with that dog—" he pointed to ben Cheriff. "There are documents of which he knows," he concluded vaguely.

The noncom's lip quirked nervously. "Look, can it wait—" he began, but even as he spoke he was glancing at the leveled tribarrels forty meters distant. "Blood," he muttered, a curse and a prophecy. "Well, go talk then. But watch it—the bastard's mean as a snake and his woman's worse."

The Kaid watched ben Khedda approach with the fascination of a mongoose awaiting a cobra. The traitor threw himself to the ground and tried to kiss the Kaid's feet. "Brother in God," the unshackled man whispered, "we have been betrayed by the unbelievers. Their dog of a captain will have you all murdered on his return, despite his oaths to me."

"Are we to believe, brother Youssef," the Kaid said with a sneer, "that you intend to die here with the patriots to cleanse your soul of the lies you carried?"

Others along the line of prisoners were peering at the scene to the extent their irons permitted, but the two men spoke in voices too low for any but the Kaid's wife to follow the words. "Brother," ben Khedda continued, "preservation is better than expiation. The captain has confessed his wicked plan to no one but me. If he dies, it dies with him—and our people live. Now, raise me by the hands."

"Shall I touch your bloody hands, then?" ben Cheriff said, but he spoke as much in question as in scorn.

"Raise me by the hands," ben Khedda repeated, "and take from my right sleeve what you find there to hide in yours. Then wait the time."

"As God wills," the Kaid said and raised up ben Khedda. Their bodies were momentarily so close that their jellabas flowed together.

"And what in the blaze of Hell is *this*, Corporal!" roared Sergeant Scratchard. "Blood and martyrs, who told you to let anybody in with the prisoners?"

"Via, Sarge," the corporal sputtered, "he said—I mean, it was the captain, he tells me."

Ben Khedda had begun to sidle away from the line of prisoners. "Where the hell do you think *you're* going?" Scratchard snapped in Arabic. "Corporal, get another set of leg irons and clamp him onto his buddy there. If he's so copping hot to be here, he can stay till the captain says otherwise."

The sergeant paused, looking around the circle of eyes focused nervously on him. More calmly he continued, "The Bordj is clear. The captain's up from the tunnel, but it'll be a while before he gets here—they came up somewhere in West Bumfuck and he's borrowing a skimmer from First Platoon to get back.

We'll wait to see what he says." The first sergeant stared at Ali ben Cheriff, impassive as the wailing traitor was shackled to his right leg. "We'll wait till then," the soldier repeated.

Mboya lifted the nose of his skimmer and grounded it behind the first of the waiting gun-jeeps. Sergeant Scratchard trotted toward him from the direction of the prisoners. The noncom was panting with the heat and his armor; he raised his hand when he reached the captain in order to gain a moment's breathing space.

"Well?" Mboya prompted.

"Sir, Maintenance called," said Scratchard jerkily. "Your brother, sir. They think he's coming to see you."

The captain swore. "All right," he said, "if Juma thinks he has to watch this, he can watch it. He's a cursed fool if he expects to do anything *but* watch."

Scratchard nodded deeply, finding he inhaled more easily with his torso cocked forward. "Right, sir, I just—didn't want to rebroadcast on the Command channel in case Central was monitoring. Right. And then there's that rag-head, ben Khedda—I caught him talking to green-hat over there and thought he maybe ought to stay. For good."

Captain Mboya glanced at the prisoners. The men of Headquarters Squad still sat a few meters away because nobody had told them to withdraw. "Get them clear," the captain said with a scowl. He began walking toward the line, the first sergeant's voice turning his direction into a tersely radioed order. Somewhere down the plateau, an aircar was being revved with no concern for what pebbles would do to the fans. Juma, very likely. He was the man you wanted driving your car when it had all dropped in the pot and Devil took the hindmost.

"Jack," the captain said, "I understand how you feel about ben Khedda; but we're here to do a job, not to kill sons of bitches. If we were doing that, we'd have to start in al-Madinah, wouldn't we?"

Mboya and his sergeant were twenty meters from the prisoners.

The Kaid watched their approach with his hands folded within the sleeves of his jellaba and his eyes as still as iron. Youssef ben Khedda was crouched beside him, a study in terror. He retained only enough composure that he did not try to run—and that because the pressure of the leg iron binding him to ben Cheriff was just sharp enough to penetrate the fear.

A gun-jeep howled up onto the top of the plateau so fast that it bounced and dragged its skirts, still under full throttle. Scratchard turned with muttered surprise. Captain Mboya did not look around. He reached into the thigh pocket of his coveralls where he kept a magnetic key that would release ben Khedda's shackles. "We can't just kill—" he repeated.

"Now, God, *now!*" ben Khedda shrieked. "He's going to *kill me!*"

The Kaid's hands appeared, the right one extending a pistol. Its muzzle was a gray circle no more placable than the eye that aimed it.

Mboya dropped the key. His hand clawed for his own weapon, but he was no gunman, no quick-draw expert. He was a company commander carrying ten extra kilos, with his pistol in a flap holster that would keep his hand out at least as well as it did the wind-blown sand. Esa's very armor slowed him, though it would not save his face or his femoral arteries when the shots came.

Behind the captain, in a jeep still skidding on the edge of control, his brother triggered a one-handed burst as accurate as if parallax were a myth. The tribarrel was locked on its column; Juma let the vehicle's own side-slip saw the five rounds toward the man with the gun. A single two-centimeter bolt missed everything. Beyond, at the lip of the Bordj, a white flower bloomed from a cyan center as ionic calcium recombined with the oxygen from which it had been freed a moment before. Closer, everything was hidden by an instant glare. The pistol detonated in the Kaid's hand under the impact of a round from the tribarrel. That was chance—or something else, for only the Lord could be so precise with certainty. The last shot of the burst hurled the Kaid back with a hole in his chest and his jellaba aflame. Ali ben Cheriff's eyes were free of fear and his mouth still wore a tight smile. Ben Khedda's face would have been less of a study in virtue and manhood, no doubt, but the two bolts that flicked across it took the traitor's head into oblivion with his memory. Juma had walked his burst on target, like any good man with an automatic weapon; and if there was something standing where the bolts walked—so much the worse for it.

There were shouts, but they were sucked lifeless by the wind. No one else had fired, for a wonder. Troops all around the Bordj were rolling back into dugouts they had thought it safe to leave.

Juma brought the jeep to a halt a few meters from his brother. He doubled over the joystick as if he had been shot himself. Dust and sand puffed from beneath the skirts while the fans wound down; then the plume settled back on the breeze. Esa touched his brother's shoulder, feeling the dry sobs that wracked the jellaba. Very quietly the soldier said in the Kikuyu he had not, after all, forgotten, "I bring you a souvenir, elder brother. To replace the one you have lost." From his holster, now unsnapped, he drew his pistol and laid it carefully down on the empty gunner's seat of the jeep.

Juma looked up at his brother with a terrible dignity. "To remind me of the day I slew two men in the Lord's despite?" he asked formally. "Oh, no, my brother, I need no trinket to remind me of that forever."

"If you do not wish to remember the ones you killed," said Esa, "then perhaps it will remind you of the hundred and thirty-three whose lives you saved this day. And my life, of course."

Juma stared at his brother with a fixity by which alone he admitted his hope. He tugged the silver crucifix out of his jellaba and lifted it over his head. "Here," he said, "little brother. I offer you this in return for your gift. To remind you that wherever you go, the Way runs there as well."

Esa took the chain. With clumsy fingers he slipped it over his helmet. "All right, Thrasher, everybody stand easy," the captain roared into his commo link. "Two-six, I want food for a hundred and thirty-three people for three days. You've got my authority to take what you need from the village. Three-six, you're responsible for the transport. I want six ore carriers up here and I want them fast. If the first truck isn't here loading in twenty, that's two-zero mikes, I'll burn somebody a new asshole. Four-six, there's drinking water in drums down in those tunnels. Get it up here. Now, *move!*"

Juma stepped out of the gun-jeep, his left hand gripping Esa's right. Skimmers were already lifting from positions all around the Bordj. G Company was surprised but no one had forgotten that Captain Mboya meant his orders to be obeyed.

"Oh, one other thing," Esa said, then tripped his commo and added, "Thrasher Four to all Thrasher units—you get any argument from villagers while you're shopping, boys . . . just refer them to my brother."

It was past midday now. The sun had enough westering to wink from the crucifix against the soldier's armor—and from the pistol in the civilian's right hand.

COMBAT CARS AT SPEED

THE INTERROGATION TEAM

The man the patrol brought in was about forty, bearded, and dressed in loose garments—sandals, trousers, and a vest that left his chest and thick arms bare. Even before he was handed from the back of the combat car, trussed to immobility in sheets of water-clear hydorclasp, Griffiths could hear him screaming about his rights under the York Constitution of '03.

Didn't the fellow realize he'd been picked up by Hammer's Slammers?

"Yours or mine, Chief?" asked Major Smokey Soames, Griffiths' superior and partner on the interrogation team—a slim man of Afro-Asian ancestry, about as suited for wringing out a mountaineer here on York as he was for swimming through magma. Well, Smokey'd earned his pay on Kanarese. . . .

"Is a bear Catholic?" Griffiths asked wearily. "Go set the hardware up, Major."

"And haven't I already?" said Smokey, but it had been nice of him to make the offer. It wasn't that mechanical interrogation *required* close genetic correspondences between subject and operator, but the job went faster and smoother in direct relation to those correspondences. Worst of all was to work on a woman, but you did what you had to do. . . .

Four dusty troopers from A Company manhandled the subject,

247

still shouting, to the command car housing the interrogation gear. The work of the firebase went on. Crews were pulling maintenance on the fans of some of the cars facing outward against attack, and one of the rocket howitzers rotated squealingly as new gunners were trained. For the most part, though, there was little to do at midday so troopers turned from the jungle beyond the berm to the freshly snatched prisoner and the possibility of action that he offered.

"Don't damage the goods!" Griffiths said sharply when the men carrying the subject seemed ready to toss him onto the left-hand couch like a log into a blazing fireplace. One of the troopers, a noncom, grunted assent; they settled the subject in adequate comfort. Major Soames was at the console between the paired couches, checking the capture location and relevant intelligence information from Central's data base.

"Want us to unwrap 'im for you?" asked the noncom, ducking instinctively though the roof of the command car, cleared his helmet. The interior lighting was low, however, especially to eyes adapted to the sun hammering the bulldozed area of the firebase.

"Listen, me 'n my family *never,* I swear it, dealt with interloping traders!" the York native pleaded.

"No, we'll take care of it," said Griffiths to the A Company trooper, reaching into the drawer for a disposable-blade scalpel to slit the hydorclasp sheeting over the man's wrist. Some interrogators liked to keep a big fighting knife around, combining practical requirements with a chance to soften up the subject through fear. Griffiths thought the technique was misplaced: for effective mechanical interrogation, he wanted his subjects as relaxed as possible. Panic-jumbled images were better than no images at all; but only *just* better.

"We're not the Customs Police, old son," Smokey murmured as he adjusted the couch headrest to an angle which looked more comfortable for the subject. "We're a lot more interested in the government convoy ambushed last week."

Griffiths' scalpel drew a line above the subject's left hand and wrist. The sheeting drew back in a narrow gape, briefly iridescent as stresses within the hydorclasp readjusted themselves. As if the sheeting were skin, however, the rip stopped of its own accord at the end of the scored line. "What're you doing to me?"

"Nothing I'm not doing to myself, friend," said Griffiths, grasping the subject's bared forearm with his own left hand so that their inner wrists were together. Between the thumb and forefinger of his right hand he held a standard-looking stim cone up where the subject could see it clearly, despite the cocoon of sheeting still holding his legs and torso rigid. "I'm George, by the way. What do your friends call you?"

"You're drugging me!" the subject screamed, his fingers digging into Griffiths' forearm fiercely. The mountaineers living under triple-canopy jungle looked pasty and unhealthy, but there was nothing wrong with this one's muscle tone.

"It's a random pickup," said Smokey in Dutch to his partner. "Found him on a trail in the target area, nothing suspicious— probably just out sap-cutting—but they could snatch him without going into a village and starting something."

"Right in one," Griffiths agreed in soothing English as he squeezed the cone at the juncture of his and the subject's wrist veins. The dose in its skin-absorbed carrier—developed from the solvent used with formic acid by Terran solifugids for defense—spurted out under pressure and disappeared into the bloodstreams of both men: thrillingly cool to Griffiths, and a shock that threw the subject into mewling, abject terror.

"Man," the interrogator murmured as he detached the subject's grip from his forearm, using the pressure point in the man's wrist to do so, "if there was anything wrong with it, I wouldn't have split it with you, now would I?"

He sat down on the other couch, swinging his legs up and lying back before the drug-induced lassitude crumpled him on the floor. He was barely aware of movement as Smokey fitted a helmet on the subject and ran a finger up and down columns of touch-sensitive controls on his console to reach a balance. All Griffiths would need was the matching helmet, since the parameters of his brain were already loaded into the database. By the time Smokey got around to him, he wouldn't even feel the touch of the helmet.

Though the dose *was* harmless, as he'd assured the subject, unless the fellow had an adverse reaction because of the recreational drugs he'd been taking on his own. You could never really tell with the sap-cutters, but it was generally okay. The high jungles of York produced at least a dozen drugs of varying effect, and the producers were of course among the heaviest users of their haul.

By itself, that would have been a personal problem; but the mountaineers also took the position that trade off-planet was their own business, and that there was no need to sell their drugs through the Central Marketing Board in the capital for half the price that traders slipping into the jungle in small star-ships would cheerfully pay. Increasingly violent attempts to enforce customs laws on men with guns and the willingness to use them had led to what was effectively civil war—which the York government had hired the Slammers to help suppress.

It's a bitch to fight when you don't know who the enemy is; and that was where Griffiths and his partner came in.

"Now I want you to imagine that you're walking home from where you were picked up," came Smokey's voice, but Griffiths was hearing the words only through the subject's mind. His own helmet had no direct connection to the hushed microphone into which the major was speaking. The words formed themselves into letters of dull orange which expanded to fill Griffiths' senses with a blank background.

The monochrome sheet coalesced abruptly, and he was trotting along a trail which was a narrow mark beaten by feet into the open expanse of the jungle floor. By cutting off the light, the triple canopies of foliage ensured that the real undergrowth would be stunted—as passable to the air-cushion armor of Hammer's Slammers as it was to the locals on foot.

Judging distance during an interrogation sequence was a matter of art and craft, not science, because the "trip"—though usually linear—was affected by ellipses and the subject's attitude during the real journey. For the most part, memory was a blur in which the trail itself was the major feature and the remaining landscape only occasionally obtruded in the form of an unusually large or colorful hillock of fungus devouring a fallen tree. Twice the subject's mind—not necessarily the man himself—paused to throw up a dazzlingly sharp image of a particular plant, once a tree and the other time a knotted, woody vine which stood out in memory against the misty visualization of the trunk that the real vine must wrap.

Presumably the clearly defined objects had something to do with the subject's business—which was none of Griffiths' at this time. As he "walked" the Slammer through the jungle, the mountaineer would be mumbling broken and only partly intelligible words, but Griffiths no longer heard them or Smokey's prompting questions.

The trail forked repeatedly, sharply visualized each time although the bypassed forks disappeared into mental fog within a meter of the route taken. It was surprisingly easy to determine the general direction of travel: though the sky was rarely visible through the foliage, the subject habitually made sunsightings wherever possible in order to orient himself.

The settlement of timber-built houses was of the same tones—browns, sometimes overlaid by a gray-green—as the trees which interspersed the habitations. The village glowed brightly by contrast with the forest, however, both because the canopy above was significantly thinner and because the place was home and a goal to the subject's mind.

Sunlight, blocked only by the foliage of very large trees which the settlers had not cleared, dappled streets which had been trampled to the consistency of coarse concrete. Children played there, and animals—dogs and pigs, probably, but they were undistinguished shadows to the subject, factors of no particular interest to either him or his interrogator.

Griffiths did not need to have heard the next question to understand it, when a shadow at the edge of the trail sprang into mental relief as a forty-tube swarmjet launcher with a hard-eyed woman slouched behind it watching the trail. The weapon needn't have been loot from the government supply convoy massacred the week before, but its swivelling base was jury-rigged from a truck mounting.

At present, the subject's tongue could not have formed words more complex than a slurred syllable or two, but the Slammers had no need for cooperation from his motor nerves or intellect. All they needed were memory and the hard-wired processes of brain function which were common to all life forms with spinal cords. The subject's brain retrieved and correlated the information which the higher centers of his mind would have needed to answer Major Soames' question about defenses—and Griffiths collected the data there at the source.

Clarity of focus marked as the subject's one of the houses reaching back against a bole of colossal proportions. Its roof was of shakes framed so steeply that they were scarcely distinguishable from the vertical timbers of the siding. Streaks of the moss common both to tree and to dwelling faired together cut timber and the russet bark. On the covered stoop in front, an adult woman and seven children waited in memory.

At this stage of the interrogation Griffiths had almost as little conscious volition as the subject did, but a deep level of his own mind recorded the woman as unattractive. Her cheeks were hollow, her expression sullen, and the appearance of her skin was no cleaner than that of the subject himself. The woman's back was straight, however, and her clear eyes held, at least in the imagination of the subject, a look of affection.

The children ranged in height from a boy already as tall as his mother to the infant girl looking up from the woman's arms with a face so similar to the subject's that it could, with hair and a bushy beard added, pass for his in a photograph. Affection cloaked the vision of the whole family, limning the faces clearly despite a tendency for the bodies of the children to mist away rather like the generality of trees along the trail; but the infant was almost deified in the subject's mind.

Smokey's unheard question dragged the subject off abruptly, his household dissolving unneeded to the answer as a section of the stoop hinged upward on the end of his own hand and arm. The tunnel beneath the board flooring dropped straight down through the layer of yellowish soil and the friable rock beneath. There was a wooden ladder along which the wavering oval of a flashlight beam traced as the viewpoint descended.

The shaft was seventeen rungs deep, with a further gooseneck dip in the gallery at the ladder's end to trap gas and fragmentation grenades. Where the tunnel straightened to horizontal, the flashlight gleamed on the powergun in a niche ready to hand but beneath the level to which a metal detector could be tuned to work reliably.

Just beyond the gun was a black-cased directional mine with either a light beam or ultrasonic detonator—the subject didn't know the difference and his mind hadn't logged any of the subtle discrimination points between the two types of fuzing. Either way, someone ducking down the tunnel could, by touching the pressure-sensitive cap of the detonator, assure that the next person across the invisible tripwire would take a charge of shrapnel at velocities which would crumble the sturdiest body armor.

"Follow all the tunnels," Smokey must have directed, because Griffiths had the unusual experience of merger with a psyche which split at every fork in the underground system. Patches of light wavered and fluctuated across as many as a score of simultaneous images, linking them together in the unity in which the subject's mind held them.

It would have made the task of mapping the tunnels impossible, but the Slammers did not need anything so precise in a field as rich as this one. The tunnels themselves had been cut at the height of a stooping runner, but there was more headroom in the pillared bays excavated for storage and shelter. Flashes—temporal alternatives, hard to sort from the multiplicity of similar physical locations—showed shelters both empty and filled with villagers crouching against the threat of bombs which did not come. On one image the lighting was uncertain and could almost have proceeded as a mental artifact from the expression of the subject's infant daughter, looking calmly from beneath her mother's worried face.

Griffiths could not identify the contents of most of the stored crates across which the subject's mind skipped, but Central's data bank could spit out a list of probables when the interrogator called in the dimensions and colors after the session. Griffiths would do that, for the record. As a matter of practical use, all that was important was that the villagers had thought it necessary to stash the material here—below the reach of ordinary reconnaissance and even high explosives.

There were faces in the superimposed panorama, villagers climbing down their own access ladders or passed in the close quarters of the tunnels. Griffiths could not possibly differentiate the similar, bearded physiognomies during the overlaid glimpses he got of them. It was likely enough that everyone, every male at least, in the village was represented somewhere in the subject's memory of the underground complex.

There was one more sight offered before Griffiths became aware of his own body again in a chill wave spreading from the wrist where Smokey had sprayed the antidote. The subject had seen a nine-barreled powergun, a calliope whose ripples of high-intensity fire could eat the armor of a combat car like paper spattered by molten steel. It was deep in an underground bay from which four broad "windows"—firing slits—were angled upward to the surface. Preparing the weapon in this fashion to cover the major approaches to the village must have taken enormous effort, but there was a worthy payoff: at these slants, the bolts would rip into the flooring, not the armored sides, of a vehicle driving over the camouflaged opening of a firing slit. Not even Hammer's heavy tanks could survive having their bellies carved that way. . . .

The first awareness Griffiths had of his physical surroundings was the thrashing of his limbs against the sides of the couch while Major Soames lay across his body to keep him from real injury. Motor control returned with a hot rush, permitting Griffiths to be still for a moment and pant.

"Need to go under again?" asked Smokey as he rose, fishing in his pocket for another cone of antidote for the subject if the answer was "no."

"Got all we need," Griffiths muttered, closing his eyes before he took charge of his arms to lift him upright. "It's a bloody fortress, it is, all underground and cursed well laid out."

"Location?" said his partner, whose fingernails clicked on the console as he touched keys.

"South by southeast," said Griffiths. He opened his eyes, then shut them again as he swung his legs over the side of the couch. His muscles felt as if they had been under stress for hours, with no opportunity to flush fatigue poisons. The subject was coming around with comparative ease in his cocoon, because his system had not been charged already with the drug residues of the hundreds of interrogations which Griffiths had conducted from the right-hand couch. "Maybe three kays—you know, plus or minus."

The village might be anywhere from two kilometers to five from the site at which the subject had been picked up, though Griffiths usually guessed closer than that. This session had been a good one, too, the linkage close enough that he and the subject were a single psyche throughout most of it. That wasn't always the case: many interrogations were viewed as if through a bad mirror, the images foggy and distorted.

"Right," said Smokey to himself or the hologram map tank in which a named point was glowing in response to the information he had just keyed. "Right, Thomasville they call it." He swung to pat the awakening subject on the shoulder. "You live in Thomasville, don't you, old son?"

"Wha . . .?" murmured the subject.

"You're sure he couldn't come from another village?" Griffiths queried, watching his partner's quick motions with a touch of envy stemming from the drug-induced slackness in his own muscles.

"Not a chance," the major said with assurance. "There were two other possibles, but they were both north in the valley."

"Am I—" the subject said in a voice that gained strength as he used it. "Am I all right?"

Why ask us? thought Griffiths, but his partner was saying, "Of course you're all right, m'boy, we said you would be, didn't we?"

While the subject digested that jovial affirmation, Smokey turned to Griffiths and said, "You don't think we need an armed recce then, Chief?"

"They'd chew up anything short of a company of panzers," Griffiths said flatly, "and even *that* wouldn't be a lotta fun. It's a bloody underground fort, it is."

"What did I say?" the subject demanded as he regained intellectual control and remembered where he was—and why. "Please, please, what'd I say?"

"Curst little, old son," Smokey remarked. "Just mumbles— nothing to reproach yourself about, not at all."

"You're a gentle bastard," Griffiths said.

"Ain't it true, Chief, ain't it true?" his partner agreed. "Gas, d'ye think, then?"

"Not the way they're set up," said Griffiths, trying to stand and relaxing again to gain strength for a moment more. He thought back over the goosenecked tunnels; the filter curtains ready to be drawn across the mouths of shelters; the atmosphere suits hanging beside the calliope. "Maybe saturation with a lethal skin absorptive like K3, but what's the use of that?"

"Right you are," said Major Soames, tapping the consoles preset for Fire Control Central.

"You're going to let me go, then?" asked the subject, wriggling within his wrappings in an unsuccessful attempt to rise.

Griffiths made a moue as he watched the subject, wishing that his own limbs felt capable of such sustained motion. "Those other two villages may be just as bad as this one," he said to his partner.

"The mountaineers don't agree with each other much better'n they do with the government," demurred Smokey with his head cocked toward the console, waiting for its reply. "They'll bring us in samples, and we'll see then."

"Go ahead," said Fire Central in a voice bitten flat by the two-kilohertz aperture through which it was transmitted.

"Got a red-pill target for you," Smokey said, putting one ivory-colored fingertip on the holotank over Thomasville to transmit the coordinates to the artillery computers. "Soonest."

"Listen," the subject said, speaking to Griffiths because the major was out of the line of sight permitted by the hydorclasp wrappings, "let me go and there's a full three kilos of Misty Hills Special for you. Pure, I swear it, so pure it'll float on water!"

"No damper fields?" Central asked in doubt.

"They aren't going to put up a nuclear damper and warn everybody they're expecting attack, old son," said Major Soames tartly. "Of course, the least warning and they'll turn it on."

"Hold one," said the trooper in Fire Control.

"Just lie back and relax, fella," Griffiths said, rising to his feet at last. "We'll turn you in to an internment camp near the capital. They keep everything nice there so they can hold media tours. You'll do fine."

There was a loud squealing from outside the interrogators' vehicle. One of the twenty-centimeter rocket howitzers was rotating and elevating its stubby barrel. Ordinarily the six tubes of the battery would work in unison, but there was no need for that on the present fire mission.

"We have clearance for a nuke," said the console with an undertone of vague surprise which survived sideband compression. Usually the only targets worth a red pill were protected by damper fields which inhibited fission bombs and the fission triggers of thermonuclear weapons.

"Lord blast you for sinners!" shouted the trussed local. "What is it you're doing, you blackhearted devils?"

Griffiths looked down at him, and just at that moment the hog fired. The base charge blew the round clear of the barrel and the sustainer motor roared the shell up in a ballistic path for computer-determined seconds of burn. The command vehicle rocked. Despite their filters, the vents drew in air burned by exhaust gases.

It shouldn't have happened after the helmets were removed and both interrogator and subject had been dosed with antidote. Flashback contacts did sometimes occur, though. This time it was the result of the very solid interrogation earlier; that, and meeting the subject's eyes as the howitzer fired.

The subject looked so much like his infant daughter that Griffiths had no control at all over the image that sprang to his mind: the baby's face lifted to the sky which blazed with the thermonuclear fireball detonating just above the canopy—

—and her melted eyeballs dripping down her cheeks.

The hydorclasp held the subject, but he did not stop screaming until they had dosed him with enough suppressants to turn a horse toes-up.

M9A4 AMBULANCE

THE TANK LORDS

They were the tank lords.

The Baron had drawn up his soldiers in the courtyard, the twenty men who were not detached to his estates on the border between the Kingdom of Ganz and the Kingdom of Marshall—keeping the uneasy truce and ready to break it if the Baron so willed.

I think the King sent mercenaries in four tanks to our place so that the Baron's will would be what the King wished it to be . . . though of course we were told they were protection against Ganz and the mercenaries of the Lightning Division whom Ganz employed.

The tanks and the eight men in them were from Hammer's Slammers, and they were magnificent.

Lady Miriam and her entourage rushed back from the barred windows of the women's apartments on the second floor, squealing for effect. The tanks were so huge that the mirror-helmeted men watching from the turret hatches were nearly on a level with the upper story of the palace.

I jumped clear, but Lady Miriam bumped the chair I had dragged closer to stand upon and watch the arrival over the heads of the women I served.

"Leesh!" cried the Lady, false fear of the tanks replaced by real anger at me. She slapped with her fan of painted ox-horn, cutting me across the knuckles because I had thrown a hand in front of my eyes.

261

I ducked low over the chair, wrestling it out of the way and protecting myself with its cushioned bulk. Sarah, the Chief Maid, rapped my shoulder with the silver-mounted brush she carried for last-minute touches to the Lady's hair. "A monkey would make a better page than you, Elisha," she said. "A gelded monkey."

But the blow was a light one, a reflexive copy of her mistress' act. Sarah was more interested in reclaiming her place among the others at the windows now that modesty and feminine sensibilities had been satisfied by the brief charade. I didn't dare slide the chair back to where I had first placed it; but by balancing on tiptoes on the carven arms, I could look down into the courtyard again.

The Baron's soldiers were mostly off-worlders themselves. They had boasted that they were better men than the mercenaries if it ever came down to cases. The fear that the women had mimed from behind stone walls seemed real enough now to the soldiers whose bluster and assault rifles were insignificant against the iridium titans which entered the courtyard at a slow walk, barely clearing the posts of gates which would have passed six men marching abreast.

Even at idle speed, the tanks roared as their fans maintained the cushions of air that slid them over the ground. Three of the Baron's men dodged back through the palace doorway, their curses inaudible over the intake whine of the approaching vehicles.

The Baron squared his powerful shoulders with his dress cloak of scarlet, purple, and gold. I could not see his face, but the back of his neck flushed red and his left hand tugged his drooping moustache in a gesture as meaningful as the angry curses that would have accompanied it another time.

Beside him stood Wolfitz, his Chamberlain; the tallest man in the courtyard; the oldest; and, despite the weapons the others carried, the most dangerous.

When I was first gelded and sold to the Baron as his Lady's page, Wolfitz had helped me continue the studies I began when I was training for the Church. Out of his kindness, I thought, or even for his amusement . . . but the Chamberlain wanted a spy, or another spy, in the women's apartments. Even when I was ten years old, I knew that death lay on that path—and life itself was all that remained to me.

I kept the secrets of all. If they thought me a fool and beat me for amusement, then that was better than the impalement which awaited a boy who was found meddling in the affairs of his betters.

The tanks sighed and lowered themselves the last finger's breadth to the ground. The courtyard, clay and gravel compacted over generations to the density of stone, crunched as the plenum-chamber skirts settled visibly into it.

The man in the turret of the nearest tank ignored the Baron and his soldiers. Instead, the reflective face shield of the tanker's helmet turned and made a slow, arrogant survey of the barred windows and the women behind them. Maids tittered; but the Lady Miriam did not, and when the tanker's face shield suddenly lifted, the mercenary's eyes and broad smile were toward the Baron's wife.

The tanks whispered and pinged as they came into balance with the surroundings which they dominated. Over those muted sounds, the man in the turret of the second tank to enter the courtyard called, "Baron Hetziman, I'm Lieutenant Kiley and this is my number two—Sergeant-Commander Grant. Our tanks have been assigned to you as a Protective Reaction Force until the peace treaty's signed."

"You do us honor," said the Baron curtly. "We trust your stay with us will be pleasant as well as short. A banquet—"

The Baron paused, and his head turned to find the object of the other tanker's attention.

The lieutenant snapped something in a language that was not ours, but the name "Grant" was distinctive in the sharp phrase.

The man in the nearest turret lifted himself out gracefully by resting his palms on the hatch coaming and swinging up his long, powerful legs without pausing for footholds until he stood atop the iridium turret. The hatch slid shut between his booted feet. His crisp moustache was sandy blond, and the eyes which he finally turned on the Baron and the formal welcoming committee were blue. "Rudy Grant at your service, Baron," he said, with even less respect in his tone than in his words.

They did not need to respect us. They were the tank lords.

"We will go down and greet our guests," said the Lady Miriam, suiting her actions to her words. Even as she turned, I was off the chair, dragging it toward the inner wall of imported polychrome plastic.

"But, Lady . . ." said Sarah nervously. She let her voice trail off, either through lack of a firm objection or unwillingness to oppose a course on which her mistress was determined.

With coos and fluttering skirts, the women swept out the door from which the usual guard had been removed for the sake of the show in the courtyard. Lady Miriam's voice carried back: "We were to meet them at the banquet tonight. We'll just do so a little earlier."

If I had followed the women, one of them would have ordered me to stay and watch the suite—though everyone, even the tenants who farmed the plots of the home estate here, was outside watching the arrival of the tanks. Instead, I waited for the sounds to die away down the stair tower—and I slipped out the window.

Because I was in a hurry, I lost one of the brass buttons from my jacket—my everyday livery of buff; I'd be wearing the black plush jacket when I waited in attendance at the banquet tonight, so the loss didn't matter. The vertical bars were set close enough to prohibit most adults, and few of the children who could slip between them would have had enough strength to then climb the bracing strut of the roof antenna, the only safe path since the base of the West Wing was a thicket of spikes and razor ribbon.

I was on the roof coping in a matter of seconds, three quick hand-over-hand surges. The women were only beginning to file out through the doorway. Lady Miriam led them, and her hauteur and lifted chin showed she would brook no interference with her plans.

Most of the tankers had, like Grant, stepped out of their hatches, but they did not wander far. Lieutenant Kiley stood on the sloping bow of his vehicle, offering a hand which the Baron angrily refused as he mounted the steps recessed into the tank's armor.

"Do you think I'm a child?" rumbled the Baron, but only his pride forced him to touch the tank when the mercenary made a hospitable offer. None of the Baron's soldiers showed signs of wanting to look into the other vehicles. Even the Chamberlain, aloof if not afraid, stood at arm's length from the huge tank which even now trembled enough to make the setting sun quiver across the iridium hull.

Because of the Chamberlain's studied unconcern about the vehicle beside him, he was the first of the welcoming party to notice Lady Miriam striding toward Grant's tank, holding her skirts clear of the ground with dainty, bejeweled hands. Wolfitz turned to the Baron, now leaning gingerly against the curve of the turret so that he could look through the hatch while the lieutenant gestured from the other side. The Chamberlain's mouth opened to speak, then closed again deliberately.

There were matters in which he too knew better than to become involved.

One of the soldiers yelped when Lady Miriam began to mount the nearer tank. She loosed her dress in order to take the hand which Grant extended to her. The Baron glanced around and snarled an inarticulate syllable. His wife gave him a look as composed as his was suffused with rage. "After all, my dear," said Lady Miriam coolly, "our lives are in the hands of these brave men and their amazing vehicles. Of *course* I must see how they are arranged."

She was the King's third daughter, and she spoke now as if she were herself the monarch.

"That's right, milady," said Sergeant Grant. Instead of pointing through the hatch, he slid back into the interior of his vehicle with a murmur to the Lady.

She began to follow.

I think Lady Miriam and I, alone of those on the estate, were not nervous about the tanks for their size and power. I loved them as shimmering beasts, whom no one could strike in safety. The Lady's love was saved for other subjects.

"Grant, that won't be necessary," the lieutenant called sharply— but he spoke in our language, not his own, so he must have known the words would have little effect on his subordinate.

The Baron bellowed, "*Mir—*" before his voice caught. He was not an ungovernable man, only one whose usual companions were men and women who lived or died as the Baron willed. The Lady squeezed flat the flounces of her skirt and swung her legs within the hatch ring.

"Murphy," called the Baron to his chief of soldiers. "Get up there with her." The Baron roared more often than he spoke quietly. This time his voice was not loud, but he would have shot Murphy where he stood if the soldier had hesitated before clambering up the bow of the tank.

"Vision blocks in both the turret and the driver's compartment," said Lieutenant Kiley, pointing within his tank, "give a three-sixty-degree view at any wavelength you want to punch in."

Murphy, a grizzled man who had been with the Baron a dozen years, leaned against the turret and looked down into the hatch. Past him, I could see the combs and lace of Lady Miriam's elaborate coiffure. I would have given everything I owned to be there within the tank myself—and I owned nothing but my life.

The hatch slid shut. Murphy yelped and snatched his fingers clear.

Atop the second tank, the Baron froze and his flushed cheeks turned slatey. The mercenary lieutenant touched a switch on his helmet and spoke too softly for anything but the integral microphone to hear the words.

The order must have been effective, because the hatch opened as abruptly as it had closed—startling Murphy again.

Lady Miriam rose from the turret on what must have been a power lift. Her posture was in awkward contrast to the smooth ascent, but her face was composed. The tank and its apparatus were new to the Lady, but anything that could have gone on within the shelter of the turret was a familiar experience to her.

"We have seen enough of your equipment," said the Baron to Lieutenant Kiley in the same controlled voice with which he had directed Murphy. "Rooms have been prepared for you—the guest apartments alongside mine in the East Wing, not the barracks below. Dinner will be announced—" he glanced at the sky. The sun was low enough that only the height of the tank's deck permitted the Baron to see the orb above the courtyard wall "—in two hours. Make yourselves welcome."

Lady Miriam turned and backed her way to the ground again. Only then did Sergeant Grant follow her out of the turret. The two of them were as powerful as they were arrogant—but neither a king's daughter nor a tank lord is immortal.

"Baron Hetziman," said the mercenary lieutenant. "Sir—" the modest honorific for the tension, for the rage which the Baron might be unable to control even at risk of his estates and his life. "That building, the gatehouse, appears disused. We'll doss down there, if you don't mind."

The Baron's face clouded, but that was his normal reaction to disagreement. The squat tower to the left of the gate had been used only for storage for a generation. A rusted barrow, upended to fit farther within the doorway, almost blocked access now.

The Baron squinted for a moment at the structure, craning his short neck to look past the tank from which he had just climbed down. Then he snorted and said, "Sleep in a hog byre if you choose, Lieutenant. It might be cleaner than that."

"I realize," explained Lieutenant Kiley as he slid to the ground instead of using the steps, "that the request sounds odd, but Colonel Hammer is concerned that commandos from Ganz or the Lightning Division might launch an attack. The gatehouse is separated from every thing but the outer wall—so if we have to defend it, we can do so without endangering any of your people."

The lie was a transparent one; but the mercenaries did not have to lie at all if they wished to keep us away from their sleeping quarters. So considered, the statement was almost generous, and the Baron chose to take it that way. "Wolfitz," he said offhandedly as he stamped toward the entrance. "Organize a party of tenants—" he gestured sharply toward the pattern of drab garments and drab faces lining the walls of the courtyard "—and clear the place, will you?"

The Chamberlain nodded obsequiously, but he continued to stride along at his master's heel.

The Baron turned, paused, and snarled, "*Now*," in a voice as grim as the fist he clenched at his side.

"My Lord," said Wolfitz with a bow that danced the line between brusque and dilatory. He stepped hastily toward the soldiers who had broken their rank in lieu of orders—a few of them toward the tanks and their haughty crews but most back to the stone shelter of the palace.

"You men," the Chamberlain said, making circling motions with his hands. "Fifty of the peasants, *quickly*. Everything is to be turned out of the gatehouse, thrown beyond the wall for the time being. *Now. Move* them."

The women followed the Baron into the palace. Several of the maids glanced over their shoulders, at the tanks—at the tankers. Some of the women would have drifted closer to meet the men in the khaki uniforms, but Lady Miriam strode head high and without hesitation.

She had accomplished her purposes; the purposes of her entourage could wait.

I leaned from the roof ledge for almost a minute further, staring at the vehicles which were so smooth-skinned that I could see my amorphous reflection in the nearest. When the sound of women's voices echoed through the window, I squirmed back only instants before the Lady reentered her apartment.

They would have beaten me because of my own excitement had they not themselves been agog with the banquet to come—and the night which would follow it.

The high-arched banquet hall was so rarely used that it was almost as unfamiliar to the Baron and his household as it was to his guests. Strings of small lights had been led up the cast-concrete beams, but nothing could really illuminate the vaulting waste of groins and coffers that formed the ceiling.

The shadows and lights trembling on flexible fastenings had the look of the night sky on the edge of an electrical storm. I gazed up at the ceiling occasionally while I waited at the wall behind Lady Miriam. I had no duties at the banquet—that was for house servants, not body servants like myself—but my presence was required for show and against the chance that the Lady would send me off with a message.

That chance was very slight. Any messages Lady Miriam had

were for the second-ranking tank lord, seated to her left by custom: Sergeant-Commander Grant.

Only seven of the mercenaries were present at the moment. I saw mostly their backs as they sat at the high table, interspersed with the Lady's maids. Lieutenant Kiley was in animated conversation with the Baron to his left, but I thought the officer wished primarily to distract his host from the way Lady Miriam flirted on the other side.

A second keg of beer—estate stock; not the stuff brewed for export in huge vats—had been broached by the time the beef course followed the pork. The serving girls had been kept busy with the mugs—in large part, the molded-glass tankards of the Baron's soldiers, glowering at the lower tables, but the metal-chased crystal of the tank lords was refilled often as well.

Two of the mercenaries—drivers, separated by the oldest of Lady Miriam's maids—began arguing with increasing heat while a tall, black-haired server watched in amusement. I could hear the words, but the language was not ours. One of the men got up, struggling a little because the arms of his chair were too tight against those to either side. He walked toward his commander, rolling slightly.

Lieutenant Kiley, gesturing with his mug toward the roof peak, was saying to the Baron, "Has a certain splendor, you know. Proper lighting and it'd look like a cross between a prison and a barracks, but the way you've tricked it out is—"

The standing mercenary grumbled a short, forceful paragraph, a question or a demand, to the lieutenant who broke off his own sentence to listen.

"Ah, Baron," Kiley said, turning again to his host. "Question is, what, ah, sort of regulations would there be on my boys dating local women. That one there—" his tankard nodded toward the black-haired servant. The driver who had remained seated was caressing her thigh "—for instance?"

"Regulations?" responded the Baron in genuine surprise. "On *servants*? None, of course. Would you like me to assign a group of them for your use?"

The lieutenant grinned, giving an ironic tinge to the courteous shake of his head. "I don't think that'll be necessary, Baron," he said.

Kiley stood up to attract his men's attention. "Open season on the servants, boys," he said, speaking clearly and in our language, so that everyone at or near the upper table would understand him. "Make your own arrangements. Nothing rough. And no less than two men together."

He sat down again and explained what the Baron already understood: "Things can happen when a fellow wanders off alone in a strange place. He can fall and knock his head in, for instance."

The two drivers were already shuffling out of the dining hall with the black-haired servant between them. One of the men gestured toward another buxom server with a pitcher of beer. She was not particularly well-favored, as men describe such things; but she was close, and she was willing—as any of the women in the hall would have been to go with the tank lords. I wondered whether the four of them would get any farther than the corridor outside.

I could not see the eyes of the maid who watched the departure of the mercenaries who had been seated beside her.

Lady Miriam watched the drivers leave also. Then she turned back to Sergeant Grant and resumed the conversation they held in voices as quiet as honey flowing from a ruptured comb.

In the bustle and shadows of the hall, I disappeared from the notice of those around me. Small and silent, wearing my best jacket of black velvet, I could have been but another patch of darkness. The two mercenaries left the hall by a side exit. I slipped through the end door behind me, unnoticed save as a momentary obstacle to the servants bringing in compotes of fruits grown locally and imported from across the stars.

My place was not here. My place was with the tanks, now that there was no one to watch me dreaming as I caressed their iridium flanks.

The sole guard at the door to the women's apartments glowered at me, but he did not question my reason for returning to what were, after all, my living quarters. The guard at the main entrance would probably have stopped me for spite: he was on duty while others of the household feasted and drank the best quality beer.

I did not need a door to reach the courtyard and the tanks parked there.

Unshuttering the same window I had used in the morning, I squeezed between the bars and clambered to the roof along the antenna mount. I was fairly certain that I could clear the barrier of points and edges at the base of the wall beneath the women's suite, but there was no need to take that risk.

Starlight guided me along the stone gutter, jumping the pipes feeding the cistern under the palace cellars. Buildings formed three sides of the courtyard, but the north was closed by a wall and the gatehouse. There was no spiked barrier beneath the wall, so I stepped to the battlements and jumped to the ground safely.

Then I walked to the nearest tank, silently from reverence rather than in fear of being heard by someone in the palace. I circled the huge vehicle slowly, letting the tip of my left index finger slide over the metal. The iridium skin was smooth, but there were many bumps and irregularities set into the armor: sensors, lights, and strips of close-range defense projectors to meet an enemy or his missile with a blast of pellets.

The tank was sleeping but not dead. Though I could hear no sound from it, the armor quivered with inner life like that of a great tree when the wind touches its highest branches.

I touched a recessed step. The spring-loaded fairing that should have covered it was missing, torn away or shot off—perhaps on a distant planet. I climbed the bow slope, my feet finding each higher step as if they knew the way.

It was as if I were a god.

I might have attempted no more than that, than to stand on the hull with my hand touching the stubby barrel of the main gun—raised at a sixty-degree angle so that it did not threaten the palace. But the turret hatch was open and, half convinced that I was living in a hope-induced dream, I lifted myself to look in.

"Freeze," said the man looking up at me past his pistol barrel.

His voice was calm. "And then we'll talk about what you think you're doing here."

The interior of the tank was coated with sulphurous light. It was too dim to shine from the hatch, but it provided enough illumination for me to see the little man in the khaki coveralls of the tank lords. The bore of the powergun in his hand shrank from the devouring cavity it had first seemed. Even the 1 cm bore of reality would release enough energy to splash the brains from my skull, I knew.

"I wanted to see the tanks," I said, amazed that I was not afraid. All men die, even kings; what better time than this would there be for me? "They would never let me, so I sneaked away from the banquet. I—it was worth it. Whatever happens now."

"Via," said the tank lord, lowering his pistol. "You're just a kid, ain'tcha?"

I could see my image foreshortened in the vision screen behind the mercenary, my empty hands shown in daylit vividness at an angle which meant the camera must be in another of the parked tanks.

"My Lord," I said—straightening momentarily but overriding the reflex so that I could meet the mercenary's eyes. "I am sixteen."

"Right," he said, "and I'm Colonel Hammer. Now—"

"Oh Lord!" I cried, forgetting in my joy and embarrassment that someone else might hear me. My vision blurred and I rapped my knees on the iridium as I tried to genuflect. "Oh, Lord Hammer, forgive me for disturbing you!"

"Blood and *martyrs*, boy!" snapped the tank lord. A pump whirred and the seat from which, cross-legged, he questioned me rose. "Don't be an idiot! Me name's Curran and I drive this beast, is all."

The mercenary was head and shoulders out of the hatch now, watching me with a concerned expression. I blinked and straightened. When I knelt, I had almost slipped from the tank; and in a few moments, my bruises might be more painful than my present embarrassment.

"I'm sorry, Lord Curran," I said, thankful for once that I had practice in keeping my expression calm after a beating. "I have studied, I have dreamed about your tanks ever since I was placed in my present status six years ago. When you came I—I'm afraid I lost control."

"You're a little shrimp, even alongside me, ain'tcha?" said Curran reflectively.

A burst of laughter drifted across the courtyard from a window in the corridor flanking the dining hall.

"Aw, Via," the tank lord said. "Come take a look, seein's yer here anyhow."

It was not a dream. My grip on the hatch coaming made the iridium bite my fingers as I stepped into the tank at Curran's direction; and besides, I would never have dared to dream this paradise.

The tank's fighting compartment was not meant for two, but Curran was as small as he had implied and I—I had grown very little since a surgeon had fitted me to become the page of a high-born lady. There were screens, gauges, and armored conduits across all the surfaces I could see.

"Drivers'll tell ye," said Curran, "the guy back here, he's just along for the ride 'cause the tank does it all for 'em. Been known t'say that myself, but it ain't really true. Still—"

He touched the lower left corner of a screen. It had been black. Now it became gray, unmarked save by eight short orange lines radiating from the edge of a two-centimeter circle in the middle of the screen.

"Fire control," Curran said. A hemispherical switch was set into the bulkhead beneath the screen. He touched the control with an index finger, rotating it slightly. "That what the Slammers're all about, ain't we? Firepower and movement, and the tricky part—movement—the driver handles from up front. Got it?"

"Yes, My Lord," I said, trying to absorb everything around me without taking my eyes from what Curran was doing. The West Wing of the palace, guest and baronial quarters above the ground-floor barracks, slid up the screen as brightly illuminated as if it were daylight.

"Now *don't* touch nothin'!" the tank lord said, the first time he had spoken harshly to me. "Got it?"

"Yes, My Lord."

"Right," said Curran, softly again. "Sorry, kid. Lieutenant'll have my ass if he sees me twiddlin' with the gun, and if we blow a hole in Central Prison here—" he gestured at the screen, though I did not understand the reference "—the colonel'll likely shoot me hisself."

"I won't touch anything, My Lord," I reiterated.

"Yeah, well," said the mercenary. He touched a four-position toggle switch beside the hemisphere. "We just lowered the main gun, right? I won't spin the turret, 'cause they'd hear that likely inside. Matter of fact—"

Instead of demonstrating the toggle, Curran fingered the sphere again. The palace dropped off the screen and, now that I knew to expect it, I recognized the faint whine that must have been the gun itself gimbaling back up to a safe angle. Nothing within the fighting compartment moved except the image on the screen.

"So," the tanker continued, flipping the toggle to one side. An orange numeral **2** appeared in the upper left corner of the screen. "There's a selector there, too—" he pointed to the pistol grip by my head, attached to the power seat which had folded up as soon as it lowered me into the tank at Curran's direction.

His finger clicked the switch to the other side—**1** appeared in place of **2** on the screen—and then straight up—**3**. "Main gun," he said, "co-ax—that's the tribarrel mounted just in front of the hatch. You musta seen it?"

I nodded, but my agreement was a lie. I had been too excited and too overloaded with wonder to notice the automatic weapon on which I might have set my hand.

"And **3**," Curran went on, nodding also, "straight up—that's both guns together. Not so hard, was it? You're ready to be a tank commander now—and—" he grinned "—with six months and a little luck, I could teach ye t'drive the little darlin' besides."

"Oh, My Lord," I whispered, uncertain whether I was speaking to God or to the man beside me. I spread my feet slightly in order to keep from falling in a fit of weakness.

"*Watch* it!" the tank lord said sharply, sliding his booted foot to block me. More gently, he added, "Don't be touching *nothing*, remember? That—" he pointed to a pedal on the floor which I had not noticed "—that's the foot trip. Touch it and we give a little fireworks demonstration that nobody's gonna be very happy about."

He snapped the toggle down to its original position; the numeral disappeared from the screen. "Shouldn't have it live no how," he added.

"But—all this," I said, gesturing with my arm close to my chest so that I would not bump any of the close-packed apparatus. "If shooting is so easy, then why is—*everything*—here?"

Curran smiled. "Up," he said, pointing to the hatch. As I hesitated, he added, "I'll give you a leg-up, don't worry about the power lift."

Flushing, sure that I was being exiled from Paradise because I had overstepped myself—somehow—with the last question, I jumped for the hatch coaming and scrambled through with no need of the tanker's help. I supposed I was crying, but I could not tell because my eyes burned so.

"Hey, slow down, kid," called Curran as he lifted himself with great strength but less agility. "It's just Whichard's about due t'take over guard, and we don't need him t'find you inside. Right?"

"Oh," I said, hunched already on the edge of the tank's deck. I did not dare turn around for a moment. "Of course, My Lord."

"The thing about shootin'," explained the tank lord to my back, "ain't *how* so much's when and what. You got all this commo and sensors that'll handle any wavelength or take remote feeds. But *still* somebody's gotta decide which data t'call up—and decide what it means. And decide t'pop it er not—" I turned just as Curran leaned over to slap the iridium barrel of the main gun for emphasis. "Which is a mother-huge decision for whatever's downrange, ye know."

He grinned broadly. He had a short beard, rather sparse, which partly covered the pockmarks left by some childhood disease. "Maybe even puts tank commander up on a level with driver for tricky, right?"

His words opened a window in my mind, the frames branching and spreading into a spidery, infinite structure: responsibility, the choices that came with the power of a tank.

"Yes, My Lord," I whispered.

"Now, you better get back t' whatever civvies do," Curran said, a suggestion that would be snarled out as an order if I hesitated. "And *don't* be shootin' off yer mouth about t'night, right?"

"No, My Lord," I said as I jumped to the ground. Tie-beams between the wall and the masonry gatehouse would let me climb back to the path I had followed to get here.

"And thank you," I added, but varied emotions choked the words into a mumble.

I thought the women might already have returned, but I listened for a moment, clinging to the bars, and heard nothing. Even so I climbed in the end window. It was more difficult to scramble down without the aid of the antenna brace, but a free-standing wardrobe put that window in a sort of alcove.

I didn't know what would happen if the women saw me slipping in and out through the bars. There would be a beating—there was a beating whenever an occasion offered. That didn't matter, but it was possible that Lady Miriam would also have the openings crossbarred too straitly for even my slight form to pass.

I would have returned to the banquet hall, but female voices were already greeting the guard outside the door. I only had enough time to smooth the plush of my jacket with Sarah's hairbrush before they swept in, all of them together and their mistress in the lead as usual.

By standing against a color-washed wall panel, I was able to pass unnoticed for some minutes of the excited babble without being guilty of "hiding" with the severe flogging that would surely entail. By the time Lady Miriam called, "Leesh? *Elisha!*" in a querulous voice, no one else could have sworn that I hadn't entered the apartment with the rest of the entourage.

"Yes, My Lady?" I said, stepping forward.

Several of the women were drifting off in pairs to help one another out of their formal costumes and coiffures. There would be a banquet every night that the tank lords remained—providing occupation to fill the otherwise featureless lives of the maids and their mistress.

That was time consuming, even if they did not become more involved than public occasion required.

"Leesh," said Lady Miriam, moderating her voice unexpectedly. I was prepared for a blow, ready to accept it unflinchingly unless it were aimed at my eyes and even then to dodge as little as possible so as not to stir up a worse beating.

"Elisha," the Lady continued in a honeyed tone—then, switching back to acid sharpness and looking at her Chief Maid, she said, "Sarah, what *are* all these women doing here? Don't they have rooms of their own?"

Women who still dallied in the suite's common room—several of the lower-ranking stored their garments here in chests and clothes presses—scurried for their sleeping quarters while Sarah hectored them, arms akimbo.

"I need you to carry a message for me, Leesh," explained Lady Miriam softly. "To one of our guests. You—you do know, don't you, boy, which suite was cleared for use by our guests?"

"Yes, My Lady," I said, keeping my face blank. "The end suite of the East Wing, where the King slept last year. But I thought—"

"Don't think," said Sarah, rapping me with the brush which she carried on all but formal occasions. "And don't interrupt milady."

"Yes, My Lady," I said, bowing and rising.

"I don't want you to *go* there, boy," said the Lady with an edge of irritation. "If Sergeant Grant has any questions, I want you to point the rooms out to him—from the courtyard."

She paused and touched her full lips with her tongue while her fingers played with the fan. "Yes," she said at last, then continued, "I want you to tell Sergeant Grant oh-four hundred and to answer any questions he may have."

Lady Miriam looked up again, and though her voice remained mild, her eyes were hard as knife points. "Oh. And Leesh? This is business which the Baron does not wish to be known. Speak to Sergeant Grant in private. And never speak to anyone else about it— even to the Baron if he tries to trick you into an admission."

"Yes, My Lady," I said bowing.

I understood what the Baron would do to a page who brought

him the news—and how he would send a message back to his wife, to the king's daughter whom he dared not impale in person.

Sarah's shrieked order carried me past the guard at the women's apartment, while Lady Miriam's signet was my pass into the court-yard after normal hours. The soldier there on guard was muzzy with drink. I might have been able to slip unnoticed by the hall alcove in which he sheltered.

I skipped across the gravel-in-clay surface of the courtyard, afraid to pause to touch the tanks again when I knew Lady Miriam would be peering from her window. Perhaps on the way back . . . but no, she would be as intent on hearing how the message was received as she was anxious to know that it had been delivered. I would ignore the tanks—

"*Freeze*, buddy!" snarled someone from the turret of the tank I had just run past.

I stumbled with shock and my will to obey. Catching my balance, I turned slowly—to the triple muzzles of the weapon mounted on the cupola, not a pistol as Lord Curran had pointed. The man who spoke wore a shielded helmet, but there would not have been enough light to recognize him anyway.

"Please, My Lord," I said, "I have a message for Sergeant-Commander Grant?"

"From who?" the mercenary demanded. I knew now that Lieutenant Kiley had been serious about protecting from intrusion the quarters allotted to his men.

"My Lord, I . . ." I said and found no way to proceed.

"Yeah, Via," the tank lord agreed in a relaxed tone. "None a' my affair." He touched the side of his helmet and spoke softly.

The gatehouse door opened with a spill of light and the tall, broad-shouldered silhouette of Sergeant Grant. Like the mercenary on guard in the tank, he wore a communications helmet.

Grant slipped his face shield down, and for a moment my own exposed skin tingled—or my mind *thought* it perceived a tingle—as the tank lord's equipment scanned me.

"C'mon, then," he grunted, gesturing me toward the recessed

angle of the building and the gate leaves. "We'll step around the corner and talk."

There was a trill of feminine laughter from the upper story of the gatehouse: a servant named Maria, whose hoots of joy were unmistakable. Lieutenant Kiley leaned his head and torso from the window above us and shouted to Grant, his voice and his anger recognizable even though the words themselves were not.

The sergeant paused, clenching his left fist and reaching for me with his right because I happened to be closest to him. I poised to run—survive this first, then worry about what Lady Miriam would say—but the tank lord caught himself, raised his shield, and called to his superior in a tone on the safe side of the insolent, "All right, all right. I'll stay right here where Cermak can see me from the tank."

Apparently Grant had remembered Lady Miriam also, for he spoke in our language so that I—and the principal for whom I acted—would understand the situation.

Lieutenant Kiley banged his shutters closed.

Grant stared for a moment at Cermak until the guard understood and dropped back into the interior of his vehicle. We could still be observed through the marvelous vision blocks, but we had the minimal privacy needed for me to deliver my message.

"Lady Miriam," I said softly, "says oh-four hundred."

I waited for the tank lord to ask me for directions. His breath and sweat exuded sour echoes of the strong estate ale.

"Won't go," the tank lord replied unexpectedly. "I'll be clear at oh-three *to* oh-four." He paused before adding, "You tell her, kid, she better not be playin' games. Nobody plays prick-tease with *this* boy and likes what they get for it."

"Yes, My Lord," I said, skipping backward because I had the feeling that this man would grab me and shake me to emphasize his point.

I would not deliver his threat. My best small hope for safety at the end of this affair required that Lady Miriam believe I was ignorant of what was going on, and a small hope it was.

That *was* a slim hope anyway.

"Well, go on, then," the tank lord said.

He strode back within the gatehouse, catlike in his grace and lethality, while I ran to tell my mistress of the revised time.

An hour's pleasure seemed a little thing against the risk of two lives—and my own.

My "room" was what had been the back staircase before it was blocked to convert the second floor of the West Wing into the women's apartment. The dark cylinder was furnished only with the original stone stair treads and whatever my mistress and her maids had chosen to store there over the years. I normally slept on a chair in the common room, creeping back to my designated space before dawn.

Tonight I slept *beneath* one of the large chairs in a corner; not hidden, exactly, but not visible without a search.

The two women were quiet enough to have slipped past someone who was not poised to hear them as I was, and the tiny flashlight the leader carried threw a beam so tight that it could scarcely have helped them see their way. But the perfume they wore, imported, expensive, and overpowering—was more startling than a shout.

They paused at the door. The latch rattled like a tocsin though the hinges did not squeal.

The soldier on guard, warned and perhaps awakened by the latch, stopped them before they could leave the apartment. The glow lamp in the sconce beside the door emphasized the ruddy anger on his face.

Sarah's voice, low but cutting, said, "Keep silent, my man, or it will be the worse for you." She thrust a gleam of gold toward the guard, not payment but a richly chased signet ring, and went on, "Lady Miriam knows and approves. Keep still and you'll have no cause to regret this night. Otherwise . . ."

The guard's face was not blank, but emotions chased themselves across it too quickly for his mood to be read. Suddenly he reached out and harshly squeezed the Chief Maid's breast. Sarah gasped, and the man snarled, "What've they got that *I* don't, tell me, huh? You're *all* whores, that's all you are!"

The second woman was almost hidden from the soldier by the Chief Maid and the panel on the half-opened door. I could see a shimmer of light as her hand rose, though I could not tell whether it was a blade or a gun barrel.

The guard flung his hand down from Sarah and turned away. "Go on, then," he grumbled. "What do I care? Go *on*, sluts."

The weapon disappeared, unused and unseen, into the folds of an ample skirt, and the two women left the suite with only the whisper of felt slippers. They were heavily veiled and wore garments coarser than any I had seen on the Chief Maid before—but Lady Miriam was as recognizable in the grace of her walk as Sarah was for her voice.

The women left the door ajar to keep the latch from rattling again, and the guard did not at first pull it to. I listened for further moments against the chance that another maid would come from her room or that the Lady would rush back, driven by fear or conscience—though I hadn't seen either state control her in the past.

I was poised to squeeze between the window-bars again, barefoot for secrecy and a better grip, when I heard the hum of static as the guard switched his belt radio live. There was silence as he keyed it, then his low voice saying, "They've left, sir. They're on their way toward the banquet hall."

There was another pause and a radio voice too thin for me to hear more than the fact of it. The guard said, "Yes, Chamberlain," and clicked off the radio.

He latched the door.

I was out through the bars in one movement and well up the antenna brace before any of the maids could have entered the common room to investigate the noise.

I knew where the women were going, but not whether the Chamberlain would stop them on the way past the banquet hall or the Baron's personal suite at the head of East Wing. The fastest, safest way for me to cross the roof of the banquet hall was twenty feet up the side, where the builder's forms had left a flat, thirty-centimeter path in the otherwise sloping concrete.

Instead, I decided to pick my way along the trash-filled stone gutter just above the windows of the corridor on the courtyard side. I could say that my life—my chance of life—depended on knowing what was going on . . . and it did depend on that. But crawling through the starlit darkness, spying on my betters, was also the only way I had of asserting myself. The need to assert myself had become unexpectedly pressing since Lord Curran had showed me the tank, and since I had experienced what a man *could* be.

There was movement across the courtyard as I reached the vertical extension of the load-bearing wall that separated the West Wing from the banquet hall. I ducked beneath the stone coping, but the activity had nothing to do with me. The gatehouse door had opened and, as I peered through dark-adapted eyes, the mercenary on guard in a tank exchanged with the man who had just stepped out of the building.

The tank lords talked briefly. Then the gatehouse door shut behind the guard who had been relieved while his replacement climbed into the turret of the vehicle parked near the West Wing—Sergeant Grant's tank. I clambered over the wall extension and stepped carefully along the gutter, regretting now that I had not worn shoes for protection. I heard nothing from the corridor below, although the casements were pivoted outward to catch any breeze that would relieve the summer stillness.

Gravel crunched in the courtyard as the tank lord on guard slid from his vehicle and began to stride toward the end of the East Wing.

He was across the courtyard from me—faceless behind the shield of his commo helmet and at best only a shadow against the stone of the wall behind him. But the man was Sergeant Grant beyond question, abandoning his post for the most personal of reasons.

I continued, reaching the East Wing as the tank lord disappeared among the stone finials of the outside staircase at the wing's far end. The guest suites had their own entrance, more formally ornamented than the doorways serving the estate's own needs. The portal was guarded only when the suites were in use—and then most often by a mixed force of the Baron's soldiers and those of the guests.

That was not a formality. The guest who would entrust his life solely to the Baron's good will was a fool.

A corridor much like that flanking the banquet hall ran along the courtyard side of the guest suites. It was closed by a cross-wall and door, separating the guests from the Baron's private apartment, but the door was locked and not guarded.

Lady Miriam kept a copy of the door's microchip key under the plush lining of her jewel box. I had found it but left it there, needless to me so long as I could slip through window grates.

The individual guest suites were locked also, but as I lowered myself from the gutter to a window ledge I heard a door snick closed. The sound was minuscule, but it had a crispness that echoed in the lightless hall.

Skirts rustled softly against the stone, and Sarah gave a gentle, troubled sigh as she settled herself to await her mistress.

I waited on the ledge, wondering if I should climb back to the roof—or even return to my own room. The Chamberlain had not blocked the assignation, and there was no sign of an alarm. The soldiers, barracked on the ground floor of this wing, would have been clearly audible had they been aroused.

Then I did hear something—or feel it. There had been motion, the ghost of motion, on the other side of the door closing the corridor. Someone had entered or left the Baron's apartment, and I had heard them through the open windows.

It could have been one of the Baron's current favorites—girls from the estate, the younger and more vulnerable, the better. They generally used the little door and staircase on the outer perimeter of the palace—where a guard *was* stationed against the possibility that an axe-wielding relative would follow the lucky child.

I lifted myself back to the roof with particular care, so that I would not disturb the Chief Maid waiting in the hallway. Then I followed the gutter back to the portion of roof over the Baron's apartments.

I knew the wait would be less than an hour, the length of Sergeant Grant's guard duty, but it did not occur to me that the interval would be as brief as it actually was. I had scarcely settled myself again to wait when I thought I heard a door unlatch in the guest suites. That could have been imagination or Sarah, deciding to wait in a room instead of the corridor; but moments later the helmeted tank lord paused on the outside staircase.

By taking the risk of leaning over the roof coping, I could see Lord Grant and a woman embracing on the landing before the big mercenary strode back across the courtyard toward the tank where he was supposed to be on guard. Desire had not waited on its accomplishment, and mutual fear had prevented the sort of dalliance after the event that the women dwelt on so lovingly in the privacy of their apartment . . . while Leesh, the Lady's page and no man, listened of necessity.

The women's slippers made no sound in the corridor, but their dresses brushed one another to the door which clicked and sighed as it let them out of the guest apartments and into the portion of the East Wing reserved to the Baron.

I expected shouts, then; screams, even gunfire as the Baron and Wolfitz confronted Lady Miriam. There was no sound except for skirts continuing to whisper their way up the hall, returning to the women's apartment. I stood up to follow, disappointed despite the fact that bloody chaos in the palace would endanger everyone—and me, the usual scapegoat for frustrations, most of all.

The Baron said in a tight voice at the window directly beneath me, "Give me the goggles, Wolfitz," and surprise almost made me fall.

The strap of a pair of night-vision goggles rustled over the Baron's grizzled head. Their frames clucked against the stone sash as my master bent forward with the unfamiliar headgear.

For a moment, I was too frightened to breathe. If he leaned out and turned his head, he would see me poised like a terrified gargoyle above him. Any move I made—even flattening myself behind the wall coping—risked a sound and disaster.

"You're right," said the Baron in a voice that would have been normal if it had any emotion behind it. There was another sound of something hard against the sash, a metallic clink this time.

"*No*, My Lord!" said the Chamberlain in a voice more forceful than I dreamed any underling would use to the Baron. Wolfitz must have been seizing the nettle firmly, certain that hesitation or uncertainty meant the end of more than his plans. "If you shoot him now, the others will blast everything around them to glowing slag."

"Wolfitz," said the Baron, breathing hard. They had been struggling. The flare-mouthed mob gun from the Baron's nightstand—scarcely a threat to Sergeant Grant across the courtyard—extended from the window opening, but the Chamberlain's bony hand was on the Baron's wrist. "If you tell me I must let those arrogant outworlders pleasure *my* wife in *my* palace, I will kill you."

He sounded like an architect discussing a possible staircase curve.

"There's a better way, My Lord," said the Chamberlain. His voice was breathy also, but I thought exertion was less to account for that than was the risk he took. "We'll be ready the next time the—outworlder gives us the opportunity. We'll take him in, in the crime; but quietly so that the others aren't aroused."

"Idiot!" snarled the Baron, himself again in all his arrogant certainty. Their hands and the gun disappeared from the window ledge. The tableau was the vestige of an event the men needed each other too much to remember. "No matter what we do with the body, the others will blame us. Blame *me*."

His voice took a dangerous coloration as he added, "Is that what you had in mind, Chamberlain?"

Wolfitz said calmly, "The remainder of the platoon here will be captured—or killed, it doesn't matter—by the mercenaries of the Lightning Division, who will also protect us from reaction by King Adrian and Colonel Hammer."

"But . . ." said the Baron, the word a placeholder for the connected thought which did not form in his mind after all.

"The King of Ganz won't hesitate an instant if you offer him your fealty," the Chamberlain continued, letting the words display their own strength instead of speaking loudly in a fashion his master might take as badgering.

The Baron still held the mob gun, and his temper was doubtful at the best of times.

"The mercenaries of the Lightning Division," continued Wolfitz with his quiet voice and persuasive ideas, "will accept any risk in order to capture four tanks undamaged. The value of that equipment is beyond any profit the Lightning Division dreamed of earning when they were hired by Ganz."

"But . . ." the Baron repeated in an awestruck voice. "The truce?"

"A matter for the kings to dispute," said the Chamberlain offhandedly. "But Adrian will find little support among his remaining barons if you were forced into your change of allegiance. When the troops he billeted on you raped and murdered Lady Miriam, that is."

"How quickly can you make the arrangements?" asked the Baron. I had difficulty in following the words: not because they were soft, but because he growled them like a beast.

"The delay," Wolfitz replied judiciously, and I could imagine him lacing his long fingers together and staring at them, "will be for the next opportunity your—Lady Miriam and her lover give us. I shouldn't imagine that will be longer than tomorrow night."

The Baron's teeth grated like nutshells being ground against stone.

"We'll have to use couriers, of course," Wolfitz added. "The likelihood of the Slammers intercepting any other form of communication is too high . . . But all Ganz and its mercenaries have to do is ready a force to dash here and defend the palace before Hammer can react. Since these tanks *are* the forward picket, and they'll be unmanned while Sergeant Grant is—otherwise occupied—the Lightning Division will have almost an hour before an alarm can be given. Ample time, I'm sure."

"Chamberlain," the Baron said in a voice from which amazement had washed all the anger. "You think of everything. See to it."

"Yes, My Lord," said Wolfitz humbly.

The tall Chamberlain *did* think of everything, or very nearly; but he'd had much longer to plan than the Baron thought. I wondered how long Wolfitz had waited for an opportunity like this one; and what payment he had arranged to receive from the King of Ganz if he changed the Baron's allegiance?

A door slammed closed, the Baron returning to his suite and his current child-mistress. Chamberlain Wolfitz's rooms adjoined his master's, but my ears followed his footsteps to the staircase at the head of the wing.

By the time I had returned to the West Wing and was starting down the antenna brace, a pair of the Baron's soldiers had climbed into a truck and gone rattling off into the night. It was an unusual event but not especially remarkable: the road they took led off to one of the Baron's outlying estates.

But the road led to the border with Ganz, also; and I had no doubt as to where the couriers' message would be received.

The tank lords spent most of the next day busy with their vehicles. A squad of the Baron's soldiers kept at a distance the tenants and house servants who gawked while the khaki-clad tankers crawled through access plates and handed fan motors to their fellows. The bustle racks welded to the back of each turret held replacement parts as well as the crew's personal belongings.

It was hard to imagine that objects as huge and powerful as the tanks would need repair. I had to remember they were not ingots of iridium but vastly complicated assemblages of parts—each of which could break, and eight of which were human.

I glanced occasionally at the tanks and the lordly men who ruled and serviced them. I had no excuse to take me beyond the women's apartment during daylight.

Excitement roused the women early, but there was little pretense of getting on with their lace-making. They dressed, changed, primped—argued over rights to one bit of clothing or another—and primarily, they talked.

Lady Miriam was less a part of the gossip than usual, but she was the most fastidious of all about the way she would look at the night's banquet.

The tank lords bathed at the wellhead in the courtyard like so many herdsmen. The women watched hungrily, edging forward despite the scandalized demands of one of the older maids that they at least stand back in the room where their attention would be less blatant.

Curran's muscles were knotted, his skin swarthy. Sergeant Grant could have passed for a god—or at least a man of half his real age. When he looked up at the women's apartments, he smiled.

The truck returned in late afternoon, carrying the two soldiers and a third man in civilian clothes who could have been—but was not—the manager of one of the outlying estates. The civilian was closeted with the Baron for half an hour before he climbed back into the truck. He, Wolfitz, and the Baron gripped one another's forearms in leave-taking; then the vehicle returned the way it had come.

The tank lord on guard paid less attention to the truck than he had to the column of steam-driven produce vans, chuffing toward the nearest rail terminus.

The banquet was less hectic than that of the first night, but the glitter had been replaced by a fog of hostility now that the newness had worn off. The Baron's soldiers were more openly angry that Hammer's men picked and chose—food at the high table and women in the corridor or the servant's quarters below.

The Slammers, for their part, had seen enough of the estate to be contemptuous of its isolation, of its low technology—and of the folk who lived on it. And yet—I had talked with Lord Curran and listened to the others as well. The tank lords were men like those of the barony. They had walked on far worlds and had been placed in charge of instruments as sophisticated as any in the human galaxy—but they were not sophisticated *men*, only powerful ones.

Sergeant-Commander Grant, for instance, made the child's mistake of thinking his power to destroy conferred on him a sort of personal immortality.

The Baron ate and drank in a sullen reverie, deaf to the lieutenant's attempts at conversation and as blind to Lady Miriam on his left as she was to him. The Chamberlain was seated among the soldiers because there were more guests than maids of honor. He watched the activities at the high table unobtrusively, keeping his own counsel and betraying his nervousness only by the fact that none of the food he picked at seemed to go down his throat.

I was tempted to slip out to the tanks, because Lord Curran was on duty again during the banquet. His absence must have been his own choice; a dislike for the food or the society perhaps . . . but more probably, from what I had seen in the little man when we talked, a fear of large, formal gatherings.

It would have been nice to talk to Lord Curran again, and blissful to have the controls of the huge tank again within my hands. But if I were caught then, I might not be able to slip free later in the night—and I would rather have died than missed that chance.

The Baron hunched over his ale when Lieutenant Kiley gathered his men to return to the gatehouse. They did not march well in unison, not even by comparison with the Baron's soldiers when they drilled in the courtyard.

The skills and the purpose of the tank lords lay elsewhere.

Lady Miriam rose when the tankers fell in. She swept from the banquet hall regally as befit her birth, dressed in amber silk from Terra and topazes of ancient cut from our own world. She did not look behind her to see that her maids followed and I brought up the rear . . . but she did glance aside once at the formation of the tank lords.

She would be dressed no better than a servant later that night, and she wanted to be sure that Sergeant Grant had a view of her full splendor to keep in mind when next they met in darkness.

The soldier who had guarded the women's apartments the night before was on duty when the Chief Maid led her mistress out again. There was no repetition of the previous night's dangerous byplay this time. The guard was subdued, or frightened; or, just possibly, biding his time because he was aware of what was going to come.

I followed, more familiar with my route this time and too pumped with excitement to show the greater care I knew was necessary tonight, when there would be many besides myself to watch, to listen.

But I was alone on the roof, and the others, so certain of what *they* knew and expected, paid no attention to the part of the world which lay beyond their immediate interest.

Sergeant Grant sauntered as he left the vehicle where he was supposed to stay on guard. As he neared the staircase to the guest suites, his stride lengthened and his pace picked up. There was nothing of nervousness in his manner; only the anticipation of a man focused on sex to the extinction of all other considerations.

I was afraid that Wolfitz would spring his trap before I was close enough to follow what occurred. A more reasonable fear would have been that I would stumble into the middle of the event.

Neither danger came about. I reached the gutter over the guest corridor and waited, breathing through my mouth alone so that I wouldn't make any noise.

The blood that pounded through my ears deafened me for a moment, but there was nothing to fear. Voices murmured, Sarah and Sergeant Grant, and the door that had waited ajar for the tank lord clicked to shut the suite.

Four of the Baron's soldiers mounted the outside steps, as quietly as their boots permitted. There were faint sounds, clothing and one muted clink of metal, from the corridor on the Baron's side of the door.

All day I'd been telling myself that there was no safe way I could climb down and watch the events through a window. I climbed down, finding enough purchase for my fingers and toes where weathering had rounded the corners of stone blocks. Getting back to the roof would be more difficult, unless I risked gripping an out-swung casement for support.

Unless I dropped, bullet-riddled, to the ground.

I rested a toe on a window ledge and peeked around the stone toward the door of the suite the lovers had used on their first assignation. I could see nothing—

Until the corridor blazed with silent light.

Sarah's face was white, dazzling with direct reflection of the high-intensity floods at either end of the hallway. Her mouth opened and froze, a statue of a scream but without the sound that fear or self-preservation choked in her throat.

Feet, softly but many of them, shuffled over the stone flags toward the Chief Maid. Her head jerked from one side to the other, but her body did not move. The illumination was pinning her to the door where she kept watch.

The lights spilled through the corridor windows, but their effect was surprisingly slight in the open air: highlights on the parked tanks; a faint wash of outline, not color, over the stones of the wall and gatehouse; and a distorted shadow play on the ground itself, men and weapons twisting as they advanced toward the trapped maid from both sides.

There was no sign of interest from the gatehouse. Even if the tank lords were awake to notice the lights, what happened at night in the palace was no affair of theirs.

Three of perhaps a dozen of the Baron's soldiers stepped within my angle of vision. Two carried rifles; the third was Murphy with a chip recorder, the spidery wands of its audio and video pick-ups retracted because of the press of men standing nearby.

Sarah swallowed. She closed her mouth, but her eyes stared toward the infinite distance beyond this world. The gold signet she clutched was a drop from the sun's heart in the floodlights.

The Baron stepped close to the woman. He took the ring with his left hand, looked at it, and passed it to the stooped, stone-faced figure of the Chamberlain.

"Move her out of the way," said the Baron in a husky whisper.

One of the soldiers stuck the muzzle of his assault rifle under the chin of the Chief Maid, pointing upward. With his other hand, the man gripped Sarah's shoulder and guided her away from the door panel.

Wolfitz looked at his master, nodded, and set a magnetic key on the lock. Then he too stepped clear.

The Baron stood at the door with his back to me. He wore body armor, but he can't have thought it would protect him against the Slammer's powergun. Murphy was at the Baron's side, the recorder's central light glaring back from the door panel, and another soldier poised with his hand on the latch.

The Baron slammed the door inward with his foot. I do not think I have ever seen a man move as fast as Sergeant Grant did then.

The door opened on a servants' alcove, not the guest rooms themselves, but the furnishings there were sufficient to the lovers' need. Lady Miriam had lifted her skirts. She was standing, leaning slightly backwards, with her buttocks braced against the bed frame. She screamed, her eyes blank reflections of the sudden light.

Sergeant-Commander Grant still wore his helmet. He had slung his belt and holstered pistol over the bedpost when he unsealed the lower flap of his uniform coveralls, but he was turning with the pistol in his hand before the Baron got off the first round with his mob gun.

Aerofoils, spread from the flaring muzzle by asymmetric thrust, spattered the lovers and a two-meter circle on the wall beyond them.

The tank lord's chest was in bloody tatters and there was a brain-deep gash between his eyebrows, but his body and the power-gun followed through with the motion reflex had begun.

The Baron's weapon clunked twice more. Lady Miriam flopped over the footboard and lay thrashing on the bare springs, spurting blood from narrow wounds that her clothing did not cover. Individual projectiles from the mob gun had little stopping power, but they bled out a victim's life like so many knife blades.

When the Baron shot the third time, his gun was within a meter of what had been the tank lord's face. Sergeant Grant's body staggered backward and fell, the powergun unfired but still gripped in the mercenary's right hand.

"Call the Lightning Division," said the Baron harshly as he turned. His face, except where it was freckled by fresh blood, was as pale as I had ever seen it. "It's time."

Wolfitz lifted a communicator, short range but keyed to the main transmitter, and spoke briefly. There was no need for communications security now. The man who should have intercepted and evaluated the short message was dead in a smear of his own wastes and bodily fluids.

The smell of the mob gun's propellant clung chokingly to the back of my throat, among the more familiar slaughterhouse odors. Lady Miriam's breath whistled, and the bedsprings squeaked beneath her uncontrolled motions.

"Shut that off," said the Baron to Murphy. The recorder's pool of light shrank into shadow within the alcove.

The Baron turned and fired once more, into the tank lord's groin.

"Make sure the others don't leave the gatehouse till Ganz's mercenaries are here to deal with them," said the Baron negligently. He looked at the gun in his hand. Strong lights turned the heat and propellant residues rising from its barrel into shadows on the wall beyond.

"Marksmen are ready, My Lord," said the Chamberlain.

The Baron skittered his mob gun down the hall. He strode toward the rooms of his own apartment.

It must have been easier to climb back to the roof than I had feared. I have no memory of it, of the stress on fingertips and toes or the pain in my muscles as they lifted the body which they had supported for what seemed (after the fact) to have been hours. Minutes only, of course; but instead of serial memory of what had happened, my brain was filled with too many frozen pictures of details for all of them to fit within the real timeframe.

The plan that I had made for this moment lay so deep that I executed it by reflex, though my brain roiled.

Executed it by instinct, perhaps; the instinct of flight, the instinct to power.

In the corridor, Wolfitz and Murphy were arguing in low voices about what should be done about the mess.

Soldiers had taken up positions in the windowed corridor flanking the banquet hall. More of the Baron's men, released from trapping Lady Miriam and her lover, were joining their fellows with words too soft for me to understand. I crossed the steeply pitched roof on the higher catwalk, for speed and from fear that the men at the windows might hear me.

There were no soldiers on the roof itself. The wall coping might hide even a full-sized man if he lay flat, but the narrow gutter between wall and roof was an impossible position from which to shoot at targets across the courtyard.

The corridor windows on the courtyard side were not true firing slits like those of all the palace's outer walls. Nonetheless, men shooting from corners of the windows could shelter their bodies behind stone thick enough to stop bolts from the Slammers' personal weapons. The sleet of bullets from twenty assault rifles would turn anyone sprinting from the gatehouse door or the pair of second-floor windows into offal like that which had been Sergeant Grant.

The tank lords were not immortal.

There was commotion in the women's apartments when I crossed them. Momentarily a light fanned the shadow of the window bars across the courtyard and the gray curves of Sergeant Grant's tank. A male voice cursed harshly. A lamp casing crunched, and from the returned darkness came a blow and a woman's cry.

Some of the Baron's soldiers were taking positions in the West Wing. Unless the surviving tank lords could blow a gap in the thick outer wall of the gatehouse, they had no exit until the Lightning Division arrived with enough firepower to sweep them up at will.

But I could get in, with a warning that would come in time for them to summon aid from Colonel Hammer himself. They would be in debt for my warning, owing me their lives, their tanks, and their honor.

Surely the tank lords could find a place for a servant willing to go with them anywhere?

The battlements of the wall closing the north side of the court-yard formed my pathway to the roof of the gatehouse. Grass and brush grew there in ragged clumps. Cracks between stones had trapped dust, seeds, and moisture during a generation of neglect. I crawled along, on my belly, tearing my black velvet jacket.

Eyes focused on the gatehouse door and windows were certain to wander: to the sky; to fellows slouching over their weapons; to the wall connecting the gatehouse to the West Wing. If I stayed flat, I merged with the stone . . . but shrubs could quiver in the wrong pattern, and the Baron's light-amplifying goggles might be worn by one of the watching soldiers.

It had seemed simpler when I planned it; but it was necessary in any event, even if I died in a burst of gunfire.

The roof of the gatehouse was reinforced concrete, slightly domed, and as proof against indirect fire as the stone walls were against small arms. There was no roof entrance, but there was a capped flue for the stove that had once heated the guard quarters. I'd squirmed my way through that hole once before.

Four years before.

The roof of the gatehouse was a meter higher than the wall on which I lay, an easy jump but one which put me in silhouette against the stars. I reached up, feeling along the concrete edge less for a grip than for reassurance. I was afraid to leave the wall because my body was telling itself that the stone it pressed was safety.

If the Baron's men shot me now, it would warn the tank lords in time to save them. I owed them that, for the glimpses of freedom Curran had showed me in the turret of a tank.

I vaulted onto the smooth concrete and rolled, a shadow in the night to any of the watchers who might have seen me. Once I was *on* the gatehouse, I was safe because of the flat dome that shrugged off rain and projectiles. The flue was near the north edge of the structure, hidden from the eyes and guns waiting elsewhere in the palace.

I'd grown up only slightly since I was twelve and beginning to explore the palace in which I expected to die. The flue hadn't offered much margin, but my need wasn't as great then, either.

I'd never needed *anything* as much as I needed to get into the gatehouse now.

The metal smoke pipe had rusted and blown down decades before. The wooden cap, fashioned to close the hole to rain, hadn't been maintained. It crumbled in my hands when I lifted it away, soggy wood with only flecks remaining of the stucco which had been applied to seal the cap in place.

The flue was as narrow as the gap between window bars, and because it was round, I didn't have the luxury of turning sideways. So be it.

If my shoulders fit, my hips would follow. I extended my right arm and reached down through the hole as far as I could. The flue was as empty as it was dark. Flakes of rust made mouselike patterings as my touch dislodged them. The passageway curved smoothly, but it had no sharp-angled shot trap as far down as I could feel from outside.

I couldn't reach the lower opening. The roof was built thick enough to stop heavy shells. At least the slimy surface of the concrete tube would make the job easier.

I lowered my head into the flue with the pit of my extended right arm pressed as firmly as I could against the lip of the opening. The cast concrete brought an electric chill through the sweat-soaked velvet of my jerkin, reminding me—now that it was too late—that I could have stripped off the garment to gain another millimeter's tolerance.

It was too late, even though all but my head and one arm were outside. If I stopped now, I would never have the courage to go on again.

The air in the flue was dank, because even now in late summer the concrete sweated and the cap prevented condensate from evaporating. The sound of my fear-lengthened breaths did not echo from the end of a closed tube, and not even panic could convince me that the air was stale and would suffocate me. I slid farther down; down to the *real* point of no return.

By leading with my head and one arm, I was able to tip my collarbone endwise for what would have been a relatively easy fit within the flue if my ribs and spine did not have to follow after. The concrete caught the tip of my left shoulder and the ribs beneath my right armpit—let me flex forward minutely on the play in my skin and the velvet—and held me.

I would have screamed, but the constriction of my ribs was too tight. My legs kicked in the air above the gatehouse, unable to thrust me down for lack of purchase. My right arm flopped in the tube, battering my knuckles and fingertips against unyielding concrete.

I could die here, and no one would know.

Memory of the tank and the windows of choice expanding infinitely above even Leesh, the Lady's page, flashed before me and cooled my body like rain on a stove. My muscles relaxed and I could breathe again—though carefully, and though the veins of my head were distending with blood trapped by my present posture.

Instead of flapping vainly, my right palm and elbow locked on opposite sides of the curving passage. I breathed as deeply as I could, then let it out as I kicked my legs up where gravity, at least, could help.

My right arm pulled while my left tried to clamp itself within my rib cage. Cloth tore, skin tore, and my torso slipped fully within the flue, lubricated by blood as well as condensate.

If I had been upright, I might have blacked out momentarily with the release of tension. Inverted, I could only gasp and feel my face and scalp burn with the flush that darkened them. The length of a hand farther and my pelvis scraped. My fingers had a grip on the lower edge of the flue, and I pulled like a cork extracting itself from a wine bottle. My being, body and mind, was so focused on its task that I was equally unmoved by losing my trousers—dragged off on the lip of the flue—and the fact that my hand was free.

The concrete burned my left ear when my right arm thrust my torso down with a real handhold for the first time. My shoulders slid free and the rest of my body tumbled out of the tube which had seemed to grip it tightly until that instant.

The light that blazed in my face was meant to blind me, but I was already stunned—more by the effort than the floor which I'd hit an instant before. Someone laid the muzzle of a powergun against my left ear. The dense iridium felt cool and good on my damaged skin.

"Where's Sergeant Grant?" said Lieutenant Kiley, a meter to the side of the light source.

I squinted away from the beam. There was an open bedroll beneath me, but I think I was too limp when I dropped from the flue to be injured by bare stone. Three of the tank lords were in the room with me. The bulbous commo helmets they wore explained how the lieutenant already knew something had happened to the guard. The others would be on the ground floor, poised.

The guns pointed at me were no surprise.

"He slipped into the palace to see Lady Miriam," I said, amazed that my voice did not break in a throat so dry. "The Baron killed them both, and he's summoned the Lightning Division to capture you and your tanks. You have to call for help at once or they'll be here."

"Blood and martyrs," said the man with the gun at my ear, Lord Curran, and he stepped between me and the dazzling light. "Douse that, Sparky. The kid's all right."

The tank lord with the light dimmed it to a glow and said, "Which *we* bloody well ain't."

Lieutenant Kiley moved to a window and peeked through a crack in the shutter, down into the courtyard.

"But . . ." I said. I would have gotten up but Curran's hand kept me below the possible line of fire. I'd tripped the mercenaries' alarms during my approach, awakened them—enough to save them, surely. "You have your helmets?" I went on. "You can call your colonel?"

"That bastard Grant," the lieutenant said in the same emotionless, diamond-hard voice he had used in questioning me. "He slaved all the vehicle transceivers to his own helmet so Command Central wouldn't wake *me* if they called while he was—out fucking around."

"Via," said Lord Curran, holstering his pistol and grimacing at his hands as he flexed them together. "I'll go. Get a couple more guns up these windows—" he gestured with jerks of his forehead "—for cover."

"It's my platoon," Kiley said, stepping away from the window but keeping his back to the others of us in the room. "Via, *Via!*"

"Look, sir," Curran insisted with his voice rising and wobbling like that of a dog fighting a choke collar. "I was his bloody driver, I'll—"

"*You* weren't the fuck-up!" Lieutenant Kiley snarled as he turned. "This one comes with the rank, trooper, so shut your—"

"I'll go, My Lords," I said, the squeal of my voice lifting it through the hoarse anger of grown men arguing over a chance to die.

They paused and the third lord, Sparky, thumbed the light up and back by reflex. I pointed to the flue. "That way. But you'll have to tell me what to do then."

Lord Curran handed me a disk the size of a thumbnail. He must have taken it from his pocket when he planned to sprint for the tanks himself. "Lay it on the hatch—anywhere on the metal. Inside, t' the right a' the main screen—"

"Curran, *knot* it, will you?" the lieutenant demanded in peevish amazement. "We can't—"

"*I* don't want my ass blown away, Lieutenant," said the trooper with the light—which pointed toward the officer suddenly, though the pistol in Sparky's other hand was lifted idly toward the ceiling. "Anyhow, kid's got a better chance'n you do. Or me."

Lieutenant Kiley looked from one of his men to the other, then stared at me with eyes that could have melted rock. "The main screen is on the forward wall of the fighting compartment," he said flatly. "That is—"

"He's used it, Lieutenant," said Lord Curran. "He knows where it is." The little mercenary had drawn his pistol again and was checking the loads for the second time since I fell into the midst of these angry, nervous men.

Kiley looked at his subordinate, then continued to me: "The commo screen is the small one to the immediate right of the main screen, and it has an alphanumeric keypad beneath it. The screen will have a numeral two or a numeral three on it when you enter, depending whether it's set to feed another tank or to Grant's helmet."

He paused, wet his lips. His voice was bare of affect, but in his fear he was unable to sort out the minimum data that my task required. The mercenary officer realized that he was wandering, but that only added to the pressure which already ground him from all sides.

"Push numeral one on the keypad," Lieutenant Kiley went on, articulating very carefully. "The numeral on the visor should change to one. That's all you need to do—the transceiver will be cleared for normal operation, and we'll do the rest from here." He touched his helmet with the barrel of his powergun, a gesture so controlled that the iridium did not clink on the thermoplastic.

"I'll need," I said, looking up at the flue, "a platform—tables or boxes."

"We'll lift you," said Lieutenant Kiley, "and we'll cover you as best we can. Better take that shirt off now and make the squeeze easier."

"No, My Lord," I said, rising against the back wall—out of sight, though within a possible line of fire. I stretched my muscles, wincing as tags of skin broke loose from the fabric to which blood had glued them. "It's dark-colored, so I'll need it to get to the tank. I, I'll use—"

I shuddered and almost fell; as I spoke, I visualized what I had just offered to do—and it terrified me.

"Kid—" said Lord Curran, catching me; though I was all right again, just a brief fit.

"I'll use my trousers also," I said. "They're at the other—"

"Via!" snapped Lord Sparky, pointing with the light which he had dimmed to a yellow glow that was scarcely a beam. "What *happened* t'you?"

"I was a servant in the women's apartments," I said. "I'll go now, if you'll help me. I must hurry."

Lord Curran and Lieutenant Kiley lifted me. Their hands were moist by contrast with the pebbled finish of their helmets, brushing my bare thighs. I could think only of how my nakedness had just humiliated me before the tank lords.

It was good to think of that, because my body eased itself into the flue without conscious direction and my mind was too full of old anger to freeze me with coming fears.

Going up was initially simpler than worming my way down the tube had been. With the firm fulcrum of Lieutenant Kiley's shoulders beneath me, my legs levered my ribs and shoulder past the point at which they caught on the concrete.

Someone started to shove me farther with his hands.

"No!" I shouted, the distorted echo unintelligible even to me and barely heard in the room below. Someone understood, though, and the hands locked instead into a platform against which my feet could push in the cautious increments which the narrow passage required.

Sliding up the tube, the concrete hurt everywhere it rubbed me. The rush of blood to my head must have dulled the pain when I crawled downward. My right arm had no strength and my legs, as the knees cramped themselves within the flue, could no longer thrust with any strength.

For a moment, the touch of the tank lord's lifted hands left my soles. I was wedged too tightly to slip back, but I could no more have climbed higher in the flue than I could have shattered the concrete that trapped me. Above, partly blocked by my loosely waving arm, was a dim circle of the sky.

Hands gripped my feet and shoved upward with a firm, inexorable pressure that was now my only chance of success. Lord Curran, standing on his leader's shoulders, lifted me until my hand reached the outer lip. With a burst of hysterical strength, I dragged the rest of my body free.

It took me almost a minute to put my trousers on. The time was not wasted. If I had tried to jump down to the wall without resting, my muscles would have let me tumble all the way into the courtyard— probably with enough noise to bring an immediate storm of gunfire from the Baron's soldiers.

The light within the gatehouse must have been visible as glimmers through the same cracks in the shutters which the tank lords used to desperately survey their position. That meant the Baron's men would be even more alert . . . but also, that their attention would be focused even more firmly on the second-floor windows—rather than on the wall adjacent to the gatehouse.

No one shot at me as I crawled backwards from the roof, pressing myself against the concrete and then stone hard enough to scrape skin that had not been touched by the flue.

The key to the tank hatches was in my mouth, the only place from which I could not lose it—while I lived.

My knees and elbows were bloody from the flue already, but the open sky was a relief as I wormed my way across the top of the wall. The moments I had been stuck in a concrete tube more strait than a coffin convinced me that there were worse deaths than a bullet.

Or even than by torture, unless the Baron decided to bury me alive.

I paused on my belly where the wall mated with the corner of the West Wing. I knew there were gunmen waiting at the windows a few meters away. They could not see me, but they might well hear the thump of my feet on the courtyard's compacted surface.

There was no better place to descend. Climbing up to the roofs of the palace would only delay my danger, while the greater danger rushed forward on the air-cushion vehicles of the Lightning Division.

Taking a deep breath, I rolled over the rim of the wall. I dangled a moment before my strained arms let me fall the remaining two meters earlier than I had intended to. The sound my feet, then finger-tips, made on the ground was not loud even to my fearful senses. There was no response from the windows above me—and no shots from the East Wing or the banquet hall, from which I was an easy target for any soldier who chanced to stare at the shadowed corner in which I poised.

I was six meters from the nearest tank—Lord Curran's tank, the tank from which Sergeant Grant had surveyed the women's apartments. Crawling was pointless—the gunmen were above me. I considered sprinting, but the sudden movement would have tripped the peripheral vision of eyes turned toward the gatehouse.

I strolled out of the corner, so frightened that I could not be sure my joints would not spill me to the ground because they had become rubbery.

One step, two steps, three steps, four—

"Hey!" someone shouted behind me, and seven powerguns raked the women's apartments with cyan lightning.

Because I was now so close to the tank, only soldiers in the West Wing could see me. The covering fire sent them ducking while glass shattered, fabrics burned, and flakes spalled away from the face of the stone itself. I heard screams from within, and not all of the throats were female.

A dozen or more automatic rifles—the soldiers elsewhere in the palace—opened fire on the gatehouse with a sound like wasps in a steel drum. I jumped to the bow slope of the tank, trusting my bare feet to grip the metal without delay for the steps set into the iridium.

A bolt from a powergun struck the turret a centimeter from where my hand slapped it. I screamed with dazzled surprise at the glowing dimple in the metal and the droplets that spattered my bare skin.

Only the tank lords' first volley had been aimed. When they

ducked away from the inevitable return fire, they continued to shoot with only their gun muzzles lifted above the protecting stone. The bolts which scattered across the courtyard at random did a good job of frightening the Baron's men away from accurate shooting, but that randomness had almost killed me.

As it was, the shock of being fired at by a friend made me drop the hatch key. The circular field-induction chip clicked twice on its way to disappear in the dark courtyard.

The hatch opened. The key had bounced the first time on the cover.

I went through the opening head first, too frightened by the shots to swing my feet over the coaming in normal fashion. At least one soldier saw what was happening, because his bullets raked the air around my legs for the moment they waved. His tracers were green sparks; and when I fell safely within, more bullets disintegrated against the dense armor about me.

The seat, though folded, gashed my forehead with a corner and came near enough to stunning me with pain that I screamed in panic when I saw there was no commo screen where the lieutenant had said it would be. The saffron glow of instruments was cold mockery.

I spun. The main screen was behind me, just where it should have been, and the small commo screen—reading **3**—was beside it. I had turned around when I tumbled through the hatch.

My finger stabbed at the keypad, hit **1** and **2** together. A slash replaced the **3**—and then **1**, as I got control of my hand again and touched the correct key. Electronics whirred softly in the belly of the great tank.

The West Wing slid up the main screen as I palmed the control. There was a **1** in the corner of the main screen also.

My world was the whole universe in the hush of my mind. I pressed the firing pedal as my hand rotated the turret counterclockwise.

The tribarrel's mechanism whined as it cycled and the bolts thumped, expanding the air on their way to their target; but when the blue-green flickers of released energy struck stone, the night and the facade of the women's apartments shattered. Stones the size of a man's head were blasted from the wall, striking my tank and the other palace buildings with the violence of the impacts.

My tank.

I touched the selector toggle. The numeral **2** shone orange in the upper corner of the screen which the lofty mass of the banquet hall slid to fill.

"Kid!" shouted speakers somewhere in the tank with me. "*Kid!*"

My bare toes rocked the firing pedal forward and the world burst away from the axis of the main gun.

The turret hatch was open because I didn't know how to close it. The tribarrel whipped the air of the courtyard, spinning hot vortices smoke from fires the guns had set and poisoned by ozone and gases from the cartridge matrices.

The 20 cm main gun sucked all the lesser whorls along the path of its bolt, then exploded them in a cataclysm that lifted the end of the banquet hall ten meters before dropping it back as rubble.

My screen blacked out the discharge, but even the multiple reflections that flashed through the turret hatch were blinding. There was a gout of burning stone. Torque had shattered the arched concrete roof when it lifted, but many of the reinforcing rods still held so that slabs danced together as they tumbled inward.

Riflemen had continued to fire while the tribarrel raked toward them. The 20 cm bolt silenced everything but its own echoes. Servants would have broken down the outside doors minutes before. The surviving soldiers followed them now, throwing away weapons unless they forgot them in their hands.

The screen to my left was a panorama through the vision blocks while the orange pips on the main screen provided the targeting array. Men, tank lords in khaki, jumped aboard the other tanks. Two of them ran toward me in the vehicle farthest from the gatehouse.

Only the west gable of the banquet hall had collapsed. The powergun had no penetration, so the roof panel of the palace's outer side had been damaged only by stresses transmitted by the panel that took the bolt. Even on the courtyard side, the reinforced concrete still held its shape five meters from where the bolt struck, though fractured and askew.

The tiny figure of the Baron was running toward me from the entrance.

I couldn't see him on the main screen because it was centered on the gun's point of impact. I shouted in surprise, frightened back into slavery by that man even when shrunken to a doll in a panorama.

My left hand dialed the main screen down and across so that the center of the Baron's broad chest was ringed with sighting pips. He raised his mob gun as he ran, and his mouth bellowed a curse or a challenge.

The Baron was not afraid of me or anything else. But he had been *born* to the options that power gives.

My foot stroked the firing pedal.

One of the mercenaries who had just leaped to the tank's back deck gave a shout as the world became ozone and a cyan flash. Part of the servants' quarters beneath the banquet hall caught fire around the three-meter cavity blasted by the gun.

The Baron's disembodied right leg thrashed once on the ground. Other than that, he had vanished from the vision blocks.

Lieutenant Kiley came through the hatch, feet first but otherwise with as little ceremony as I had shown. He shoved me hard against the turret wall while he rocked the gun switch down to safe. The orange numeral blanked from the screen.

"In the *Lord's* name, kid!" the big officer demanded while his left hand still pressed me back. "Who told you to do *that?*"

"Lieutenant," said Lord Curran, leaning over the hatch opening but continuing to scan the courtyard. His pistol was in his hand, muzzle lifted, while air trembled away from the hot metal. "We'd best get a move on unless you figure t' fight a reinforced battalion alone till the supports get here."

"Well, get in and *drive*, curse you!" the lieutenant shouted. The words relaxed his body and he released me. "*No*, I don't want to wait around here alone for the Lightning Division!"

"Lieutenant," said the driver, unaffected by his superior's anger, "we're down a man. You ride your blower. Kid'll be all right alone with me till we join up with the colonel and come back t' kick ass."

Lieutenant Kiley's face became very still. "Yeah, get in and drive," he said mildly, gripping the hatch coaming to lift himself out without bothering to use the power seat.

The driver vanished but his boots scuffed on the armor as he scurried for his own hatch. "Gimme your bloody key," he shouted back.

Instead of replying at once, the lieutenant looked down at me. "Sorry I got a little shook, kid," he said. "You did pretty good for a new recruit." Then he muscled himself up and out into the night.

The drive fans of other tanks were already roaring when ours began to whine up to speed. The great vehicle shifted greasily around me, then began to turn slowly on its axis. Fourth in line, we maneuvered through the courtyard gate while the draft from our fans lifted flames out of the palace windows. We are the tank lords.

A21F JEEP

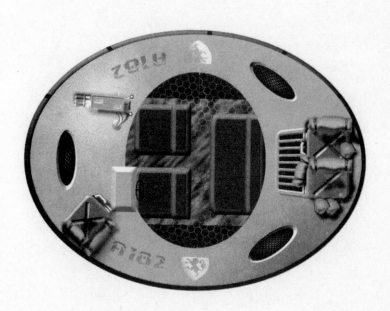

LIBERTY PORT

Commandant Horace Jolober had just lowered the saddle of his mobile chair, putting himself at the height of the Facilities Inspection Committee seated across the table, when the alarm hooted and Vicki cried from the window in the next room, "*Tanks!* In the street!"

The three Placidan bureaucrats flashed Jolober looks of anger and fear, but he had no time for them now even though they were his superiors. The stump of his left leg keyed the throttle of his chair. As the fans spun up, Jolober leaned and guided his miniature air-cushion vehicle out of the room faster than another man could have walked.

Faster than a man with legs could walk.

Vicki opened the door from the bedroom as Jolober swept past her toward the inside stairs. Her face was as calm as that of the statue which it resembled in its perfection, but Jolober knew that only the strongest emotion would have made her disobey his orders to stay in his private apartments while the inspection team was here. She was afraid that he was about to be killed.

A burst of gunfire in the street suggested she just might be correct.

"Chief," called Jolober's mastoid implant in what he thought was the voice of Karnes, his executive officer. "I'm at the gate and the new arrivals, they're Hammer's, just came right through the wire! There's half a dozen tanks and they're shooting in the air!"

Could've been worse. Might yet be.

He slid onto the staircase, his stump boosting fan speed with reflexive skill. The stair treads were too narrow for Jolober's mobile chair to form an air cushion between the surface and the lip of its plenum chamber. Instead he balanced on thrust alone while the fans beneath him squealed, ramming the air hard enough to let him slope down above the staircase with the grace of a stooping hawk. The hardware was built to handle the stress, but only flawless control kept the port commandant from upending and crashing down the treads in a fashion as dangerous as it would be humiliating.

Jolober was a powerful man who'd been tall besides until a tribarrel blew off both his legs above the knee. In his uniform of white cloth and lavish gold, he was dazzlingly obvious in any light. As he gunned his vehicle out into the street, the most intense light source was the rope of cyan bolts ripping skyward from the cupola of the leading tank.

The buildings on either side of the street enticed customers with displays to rival the sun, but the operators—each of them a gambler, brothel keeper, and saloon owner all in one—had their own warning systems. The lights were going out, leaving the plastic facades cold.

Lightless, the buildings faded to the appearance of the high concrete fortresses they were in fact. Repeated arches made the entrance of the China Doll, directly across the street from the commandant's offices, look spacious. The door itself was so narrow that only two men could pass it at a time, and no one could slip unnoticed past the array of sensors and guards that made sure none of those entering were armed.

Normally the facilities here at Paradise Port were open all day. Now an armored panel clanged down across the narrow door of the China Doll, its echoes merging with similar tocsins from the other buildings.

Much good that would do if the tanks opened up with their 20cm main guns. Even a tribarrel could blast holes in thumb-thick steel as easily as one had vaporized Jolober's knees and calves. . . .

He slid into the street, directly into the path of the lead tank. He would have liked to glance up toward the bedroom window for what he knew might be his last glimpse of Vicki, but he was afraid that he couldn't do that and still have the guts to do his duty.

For a long time after he lost his legs, the only thing which had kept Horace Jolober from suicide was the certainty that he had always done his duty. Not even Vicki could be allowed to take that from him.

The tanks were advancing at no more than a slow walk though their huge size gave them the appearance of speed. They were buttoned up—hatches down, crews hidden behind the curved surfaces of iridium armor that might just possibly turn a bolt from a gun as big as the one each tank carried in its turret.

Lesser weapons had left scars on the iridium. Where light powerguns had licked the armor—and even a tribarreled automatic was light in comparison to a tank—the metal cooled again in a slope around the point where a little had been vaporized. High-velocity bullets made smaller, deeper craters plated with material from the projectile itself.

The turret of the leading tank bore a long gouge that began in a pattern of deep, radial scars. A shoulder-fired rocket had hit at a slight angle. The jet of white-hot gas spurting from the shaped-charge warhead had burned deep enough into even the refractory iridium that it would have penetrated the turret had it struck squarely.

If either the driver or the blower captain were riding with their heads out of the hatch when the missile detonated, shrapnel from the casing had decapitated them.

Jolober wondered if the present driver even saw him, a lone man in a street that should have been cleared by the threat of 170 tonnes of armor howling down the middle of it.

An air-cushion jeep carrying a pintle-mounted needle stunner and two men in Port Patrol uniforms was driving alongside the lead tank, bucking and pitching in the current roaring from beneath the steel skirts of the tank's plenum chamber. While the driver fought to hold the light vehicle steady, the other patrolman bellowed through the jeep's loudspeakers. He might have been on the other side of the planet for all his chance of being heard over the sound of air sucked through intakes atop the tank's hull and then pumped beneath the skirts forcefully enough to balance the huge weight of steel and iridium.

Jolober grounded his mobile chair. He crooked his left ring finger so that the surgically redirected nerve impulse keyed the microphone implanted at the base of his jaw. "Gentlemen," he said, knowing that the base unit in the Port Office was relaying his words on the Slammers' general frequency. "You are violating the regulations which govern Paradise Port. Stop before somebody gets hurt."

The bow of the lead tank was ten meters away—and one meter less every second.

To the very end he thought they were going to hit him—by inadvertence, now, because the tank's steel skirt lifted in a desperate attempt to stop but the vehicle's mass overwhelmed the braking effect of its fans. Jolober knew that if he raised his chair from the pavement, the blast of air from the tank would knock him over and roll him along the concrete like a trashcan in a windstorm—bruised but safe.

He would rather die than lose his dignity that way in front of Vicki.

The tank's bow slewed to the left, toward the China Doll. The skirt on that side touched the pavement with the sound of steel screaming and a fountain of sparks that sprayed across and over the building's high plastic facade.

The tank did not hit the China Doll, and it stopped short of Horace Jolober by less than the radius of its bow's curve.

The driver grounded his huge vehicle properly and cut the power to his fans. Dust scraped from the pavement, choking and chalky, swirled around Jolober and threw him into a paroxysm of coughing. He hadn't realized that he'd been holding his breath—until the danger passed and instinct filled his lungs.

The jeep pulled up beside Jolober, its fans kicking up still more dust, and the two patrolmen shouted words of concern and congratulation to their commandant. More men were appearing, patrolmen and others who had ducked into the narrow alleys between buildings when the tanks filled the street.

"Stecher," said Jolober to the sergeant in the patrol vehicle, "go back there—" he gestured toward the remainder of the column, hidden behind the armored bulk of the lead tank "—and help 'em get turned around. Get 'em back to the Refit Area where they belong,"

"Sir, should I get the names?" Stecher asked.

The port commandant shook his head with certainty. "None of this happened," he told his subordinates. "I'll take care of it."

The jeep spun nimbly while Stecher spoke into his commo helmet, relaying Jolober's orders to the rest of the squad on street duty.

Metal rang again as the tank's two hatch covers slid open. Jolober was too close to the hull to see the crewmen so he kicked his fans to life and backed a few meters.

The mobile chair had been built to his design. Its only control was the throttle with a linkage which at high-thrust settings automatically transformed the plenum chamber to a nozzle. Steering and balance were matters of how the rider shifted his body weight. Jolober prided himself that he was just as nimble as he had been before.

—Before he fell back into the trench on Primavera, half-wrapped in the white flag he'd waved to the oncoming tanks. The only conscious memory he retained of *that* moment was the sight of his right leg still balanced on the trench lip above him, silhouetted against the crisscrossing cyan bolts from the powerguns.

But Horace Jolober was just as much a man as he'd ever been. The way he got around proved it. And Vicki.

The driver staring out the bow hatch at him was a woman with thin features and just enough hair to show beneath her helmet. She looked scared, aware of what had just happened and aware also of just how bad it could've been.

Jolober could appreciate how she felt.

The man who lifted himself from the turret hatch was under thirty, angry, and—though Jolober couldn't remember the Slammers' collar pips precisely—a junior officer of some sort rather than a sergeant.

The dust had mostly settled by now, but vortices still spun above the muzzles of the tribarrel which the fellow had been firing skyward. "What're you doing, you bloody fool?" he shouted. "D'ye *want* to die?"

Not anymore, thought Horace Jolober as he stared upward at the tanker. One of the port patrolmen had responded to the anger in the Slammer's voice by raising his needle stunner, but there was no need for that.

Jolober keyed his mike so that he didn't have to shout with the inevitable emotional loading. In a flat, certain voice, he said, "If you'll step down here, Lieutenant, we can discuss the situation like officers—which I am, and you will continue to be unless you insist on pushing things."

The tanker grimaced, then nodded his head and lifted himself the rest of the way out of the turret. "Right," he said. "Right. I . . ." His voice trailed off, but he wasn't going to say anything the port commandant hadn't heard before.

When you screw up real bad, you can either be afraid or you can flare out in anger and blame somebody else. Not because you don't know better, but because it's the only way to control your fear. It isn't pretty, but there's no pretty way to screw up bad.

The tanker dropped to the ground in front of Jolober and gave a sloppy salute. That was lack of practice, not deliberate insult, and his voice and eyes were firm as he said, "Sir. Acting Captain Tad Hoffritz reporting."

"Horace Jolober," the port commandant said. He raised his saddle to put his head at what used to be normal standing height, a few centimeters taller than Hoffritz. The Slammer's rank made it pretty clear why the disturbance had occurred. "Your boys?" Jolober asked, thumbing toward the tanks sheepishly reversing down the street under the guidance of white-uniformed patrolmen.

"Past three days they have been," Hoffritz agreed. His mouth scrunched again in an angry grimace and he said, "Look, I'm real sorry. I know how dumb that was. I just . . ."

Again, there wasn't anything new to say.

The tank's driver vaulted from her hatch with a suddenness

which drew both men's attention. "Corp'ral Days," she said with a salute even more perfunctory than Hoffritz's had been. "Look, sir, *I* was drivin' and if there's a problem, it's my problem."

"Daisy—" began Captain Hoffritz.

"There's no problem, Corporal," Jolober said firmly. "Go back to your vehicle. We'll need to move it in a minute or two."

Another helmeted man had popped his head from the turret—surprisingly, because this was a line tank, not a command vehicle with room for several soldiers in the fighting compartment. The driver looked at her captain, then met the worried eyes of the trooper still in the turret. She backed a pace but stayed within earshot.

"Six tanks out of seventeen," Jolober said calmly. Things *were* calm enough now that he was able to follow the crosstalk of his patrolmen, their voices stuttering at low level through the miniature speaker on his epaulet. "You've been seeing some action, then."

"Too bloody right," muttered Corporal Days.

Hoffritz rubbed the back of his neck, lowering his eyes, and said, "Well, running . . . There's four back at Refit deadlined we brought in on transporters, but—"

He looked squarely at Jolober. "But sure we had a tough time. That's why I'm CO and Chester's up there—" he nodded toward the man in the turret "—trying to work company commo without a proper command tank. And I guess I figured—"

Hoffritz might have stopped there, but the port commandant nodded him on.

"—I figured maybe it wouldn't hurt to wake up a few rear-echelon types when we came back here for refit. Sorry, sir."

"There's three other units, including a regiment of the Division Léégèère, on stand-down here at Paradise Port already, Captain," Jolober said. He nodded toward the soldiers in mottled fatigues who were beginning to reappear on the street. "Not rear-echelon troops, from what I've heard. And they need some relaxation just as badly as your men do."

"Yes, sir," Hoffritz agreed, blank-faced. "It was real dumb. I'll sign the report as soon as you make it out."

Jolober shrugged. "There won't be a report, Captain. Repairs to the gate'll go on your regiment's damage account and be deducted from Placida's payment next month." He smiled. "Along with any chairs or glasses you break in the casinos. Now, get your vehicle into the Refit Area where it belongs. And come back and have a good time in Paradise Port. That's what we're here for."

"*Thank* you, sir," said Hoffritz, and relief dropped his age by at least five years. He clasped Jolober's hand and, still holding it, asked, "You've seen service, too, haven't you, sir?"

"Fourteen years with Hampton's Legion," Jolober agreed, pleased that Hoffritz had managed not to stare at the stumps before asking the question.

"Hey, good outfit," the younger man said with enthusiasm. "We were with Hampton on Primavera, back, oh, three years ago?"

"Yes, I know," Jolober said. His face was still smiling, and the subject wasn't an emotional one anymore. He felt no emotion at all . . . "One of your tanks shot—" his left hand gestured delicately at where his thighs ended "—these off on Primavera."

"Lord," Corporal Days said distinctly.

Captain Hoffritz looked as if he had been hit with a brick. Then his face regained its animation. "No, sir," he said. "You're mistaken. On Primavera, we were both working for the Federalists. Hampton was our infantry support."

Not the way General Hampton would have described the chain of command, thought Jolober. His smile became real again. He still felt pride in his old unit—and he could laugh at those outdated feelings in himself.

"Yes, that's right," he said aloud. "There'd been an error in transmitting map coordinates. When a company of these—" he nodded toward the great iridium monster, feeling sweat break out on his forehead and arms as he did so "—attacked my battalion, I jumped up to stop the shooting."

Jolober's smile paled to a frosty shadow of itself. "I was successful," he went on softly, "but not quite as soon as I would've liked."

"Oh, Lord and Martyrs," whispered Hoffritz. His face looked like that of a battle casualty.

"Tad, that was—" Corporal Days began.

"Shut it *off*, Daisy!" shouted the Slammers' commo man from the turret. Days' face blanked and she nodded.

"Sir, I—" Hoffritz said.

Jolober shook his head to silence the younger man. "In a war," he said, "a lot of people get in the way of rounds. I'm luckier than some. I'm still around to tell about it."

He spoke in the calm, pleasant voice he always used in explaining the—matter—to others. For the length of time he was speaking, he could generally convince even himself.

Clapping Hoffritz on the shoulder—the physical contact brought Jolober back to present reality, reminding him that the tanker was a young man and not a demon hidden behind armor and a tribarrel—the commandant said, "Go on, move your hardware and then see what Paradise Port can show you in the way of a good time."

"Oh, that I know already," said Hoffritz with a wicked, man-to-man smile of his own. "When we stood down here three months back, I met a girl named Beth. I'll bet she still remembers me, and the *Lord* knows I remember her."

"Girl?" Jolober repeated. The whole situation had so disoriented him that he let his surprise show.

"Well, you know," said the tanker. "A Doll, I guess. But believe me, Beth's woman enough for *me*."

"Or for anyone," the commandant agreed. "I know just what you mean."

Stecher had returned with the jeep. The street was emptied of all armor except Hoffritz's tank, and that was an object of curiosity rather than concern for the men spilling out the doors of the reopened brothels. Jolober waved toward the patrol vehicle and said, "My men'll guide you out of here, Captain Hoffritz. Enjoy your stay."

The tank driver was already scrambling back into her hatch. She had lowered her helmet shield, so the glimpse Jolober got of her face was an unexpected, light-reflecting bubble.

Maybe Corporal Days had a problem with where the conversation had gone when the two officers started talking like two men. That was a pity, for her and probably for Captain Hoffritz as well. A tank was too small a container to hold emotional trouble among its crew.

But Horace Jolober had his own problems to occupy him as he slid toward his office at a walking pace. He had his meeting with the Facilities Inspection Committee, which wasn't going to go more smoothly because of the interruption.

A plump figure sauntering in the other direction tipped his beret to Jolober as they passed. "Ike," acknowledged the port commandant in a voice as neutral as a gun barrel that doesn't care in the least at whom it's pointed.

Red Ike could pass for human, until the rosy cast of his skin drew attention to the fact that his hands had only three fingers and a thumb. Jolober was surprised to see that Ike was walking across the street toward his own brothel, the China Doll, instead of being inside the building already. That could have meant anything, but the probability was that Red Ike had a tunnel to one of the buildings across the street to serve as a bolthole.

And since all the *real* problems at Paradise Port were a result of the alien who called himself Red Ike, Jolober could easily imagine why the fellow would want to have a bolthole.

Jolober had gone down the steps in a smooth undulation. He mounted them in a series of hops, covering two treads between pauses like a weary cricket climbing out of a well.

The chair's powerpack had more than enough charge left to swoop him up to the conference room. It was the man himself who lacked the mental energy now to balance himself on the column of driven air. He felt drained—the tribarrel, the tank . . . the memories of Primavera. If he'd decided to, sure, but . . .

But maybe he was getting old.

The Facilities Inspection Committee—staff members, actually, for three of the most powerful senators in the Placidan legislature—waited for Jolober with doubtful looks. Higgey and Wayne leaned against the conference room window, watching Hoffritz's tank reverse sedately in the street. The woman, Rodall, stood by the stairhead watching the port commandant's return.

"Why don't you have an elevator put in?" she asked. "Or at least a ramp?" Between phrases, Rodall's full features relaxed to the pout that was her normal expression.

Jolober paused beside her, noticing the whisper of air from beneath his plenum chamber was causing her to twist her feet away as if she had stepped into slime. "There aren't elevators everywhere, Mistress," he said. "Most places, there isn't even enough smooth surface to depend on ground effect alone to get you more than forty meters."

He smiled and gestured toward the conference room's window. Visible beyond the China Doll and the other buildings across the street was the reddish-brown expanse of the surrounding landscape: ropes of lava on which only lichen could grow, where a man had to hop and scramble from one ridge to another.

The Placidan government had located Paradise Port in a volcanic wasteland in order to isolate the mercenaries letting off steam between battles with Armstrong, the other power on the planet's sole continent. To a cripple in a chair which depended on wheels or unaided ground effect, the twisting lava would be as sure a barrier as sheer walls.

Jolober didn't say that so long as he could go anywhere other men went, he could pretend he was still a man. If the Placidan civilian could have understood that, she wouldn't have asked why he didn't have ramps put in.

"Well, what *was* that?" demanded Higgey—thin, intense, and already half bald in his early thirties. "Was anyone killed?"

"Nothing serious, Master Higgey," Jolober said as he slid back to the table and lowered himself to his "seated" height. "And no, no one was killed or even injured."

Thank the Lord for his mercy.

"It *looked* serious, Commandant," said the third committee member—Wayne, half again Jolober's age and a retired colonel of the Placidan regular army. "I'm surprised you permit things like that to happen."

Higgey and Rodall were seating themselves. Jolober gestured toward the third chair on the curve of the round table opposite him and said, "Colonel, your, ah—opposite numbers in Armstrong tried to stop those tanks last week with a battalion of armored infantry. They got their butts kicked until they didn't *have* butts anymore."

Wayne wasn't sitting down. His face flushed and his short, white mustache bristled sharply against his upper lip.

Jolober shrugged and went on in a more conciliatory tone, "Look, sir, units aren't rotated back here unless they've had a hell of a rough time in the line. I've got fifty-six patrolmen with stunners to keep order . . . which we do, well enough for the people using Paradise Port. We aren't here to start a major battle of our own. Placida needs these mercenaries and needs them in fighting trim."

"That's a matter of opinion," said the retired officer with his lips pressed together, but at last he sat down.

The direction of sunrise is also a matter of opinion, Jolober thought. It's about as likely to change as Placida is to survive without the mercenaries who had undertaken the war her regular army was losing.

"I requested this meeting—" requested it with the senators themselves, but he hadn't expected them to agree "—in order to discuss just that, the fighting trim of the troops who undergo rest and refit here. So that Placida gets the most value for her, ah, payment."

The committee staff would do, if Jolober could get them to understand. Paradise Port was, after all, a wasteland with a village populated by soldiers who had spent all the recent past killing and watching their friends die. It wasn't the sort of place you'd pick for a senatorial junket.

Higgey leaned forward, clasping his hands on the tabletop, and said, "Commandant, I'm sure that those—" he waggled a finger disdainfully toward the window "—men out there would be in better physical condition after a week of milk and religious lectures than they will after the regime they choose for themselves. There are elements—"

Wayne nodded in stern agreement, his eyes on Mistress Rodall, whose set face refused to acknowledge either of her fellows while the subject was being discussed.

"—in the electorate and government who would like to try that method, but fortunately reality has kept the idea from being attempted."

Higgey paused, pleased with his forceful delivery and the way his eyes dominated those of the much bigger man across the table. "If you've suddenly got religion, Commandant Jolober," he concluded, "I suggest you resign your current position and join the ministry."

Jolober suppressed his smile. Higgey reminded him of a lap dog, too nervous to remain either still or silent, and too small to be other than ridiculous in its posturing. "My initial message was unclear, madam, gentlemen," he explained, looking around the table. "I'm not suggesting that Placida close the brothels that are part of the recreational facilities here."

His pause was not for effect, but because his mouth had suddenly gone very dry. But it was his duty to—

"I'm recommending that the Dolls be withdrawn from Paradise Port and that the facilities be staffed with human, ah, females."

Colonel Wayne stiffened and paled.

Wayne's anger was now mirrored in the expression on Rodall's face. "Whores," she said. "So that those—*soldiers*—can disgrace and dehumanize real women for their fun."

"And kill them, one assumes," added Higgey with a touch of amusement. "I checked the records, Commandant. There've been seventeen Dolls killed during the months Paradise Port's been in operation. As it is, that's a simple damage assessment, but if they'd been human prostitutes—each one would have meant a manslaughter charge or even murder. People don't cease to have rights when they choose to sell their bodies, you know."

"When they're forced to sell their bodies, you mean," snapped Rodall. She glared at Higgey, who didn't mean anything of the sort.

"Scarcely to the benefit of your precious mercenaries," said Wayne in a distant voice. "Quite apart from the political difficulties it would cause for any senator who recommended the change."

"As a matter of fact," said Higgey, whose natural caution had tightened his visage again, "I thought you were going to use the record of violence here at Paradise Port as a reason for closing the facility. Though I'll admit that I couldn't imagine anybody selfless enough to do away with his own job."

No, you couldn't, you little weasel, thought Horace Jolober. But politicians have different responsibilities than soldiers, and politicians' flunkies have yet another set of needs and duties.

And none of them are saints. Surely no soldier who does his job is a saint.

"Master Higgey, you've precisely located the problem," Jolober said with a nod of approval. "The violence isn't a result of the soldiers, it's because of the Dolls. It isn't accidental, it's planned. And it's time to stop it."

"It's time for us to leave, you mean," said Higgey as he shoved his chair back. "Resigning still appears to be your best course, Commandant. Though I don't suppose the ministry is the right choice for a new career, after all."

"Master Higgey," Jolober said in the voice he would have used in an argument with a fellow officer, "I know very well that no one is irreplaceable—but *you* know that I am doing as good a job here as anybody you could hire to run Paradise Port. I'm asking you to listen for a few minutes to a proposal that will make the troops you pay incrementally better able to fight for you."

"We've come this far," said Rodall.

"There are no listening devices in my quarters," Jolober explained, unasked. "I doubt that any real-time commo link out of Paradise Port is free of interception."

He didn't add that time he spent away from *his* duties was more of a risk to Placida than pulling these three out of their offices and expensive lunches could be. The tanks roaring down the street should have proved that even to the committee staffers.

Jolober paused, pressing his fingertips to his eyebrows in a habitual trick to help him marshal his thoughts while the others stared at him. "Mistress, masters," he said calmly after a moment, "the intention was that Paradise Port and similar facilities be staffed by independent contractors from off-planet."

"Which is where they'll return as soon as the war's over," agreed

Colonel Wayne with satisfaction. "Or as soon as they put a toe wrong, any one of them."

"The war's bad enough as it is," said Rodall. "Building up Placida's stock of *that* sort of person would make peace hideous as well."

"Yes, ma'am, I understand," said the port commandant. There were a lot of "that sort of person" in Placida just now, including all the mercenaries in the line—and Horace Jolober back here. "But what you have in Paradise Port isn't a group of entrepreneurs, it's a corporation—a monarchy, almost—subservient to an alien called Red Ike."

"Nonsense," said Wayne.

"We don't permit that," said Rodall.

"Red Ike owns a single unit here," said Higgey. "The China Doll. Which is all he can own by law, to prevent just the sort of situation you're describing."

"Red Ike provides all the Dolls," Jolober stated flatly. "Whoever owns them on paper, they're his. And *everything* here is his because he controls the Dolls."

"Well . . ." said Rodall. She was beginning to blush.

"There's no actual proof," Colonel Wayne said, shifting his eyes toward a corner of walls and ceiling. "Though I suppose the physical traits are indicative . . ."

"The government has decided it isn't in the best interests of Placida to pierce the corporate veil in this instance," said Higgey in a thin voice. "The androids in question are shipped here from a variety of off-planet suppliers."

The balding Placidan paused and added, with a tone of absolute finality, "If the question were mine to decide—which it isn't—I would recommend searching for a new port commandant rather than trying to prove the falsity of a state of affairs beneficial to us, to Placida."

"I think that really must be the final word on the subject, Commandant Jolober," Rodall agreed.

Jolober thought she sounded regretful, but the emotion was too faint for him to be sure. The three Placidans were getting up, and he had failed.

He'd failed even before the staff members arrived, because it was now quite obvious that they'd decided their course of action before the meeting. They—and their elected superiors—would rather have dismissed Jolober's arguments.

But if the arguments proved to be well founded, they would dismiss the port commandant, if necessary to end the discussion.

"I suppose I should be flattered," Jolober said as hydraulics lifted him in the saddle and pressure of his stump on the throttle let him rotate his chair away from the table. "That you came all this way to silence me instead of refusing me a meeting."

"You might recall," said Higgey, pausing at the doorway. His look was meant to be threatening, but the port commandant's bulk and dour anger cooled the Placidan's face as soon as their eyes met. "That is, we're in the middle of a war, and the definition of treason can be a little loose in such times. While you're not technically a Placidan citizen, Commandant, you—would be well advised to avoid activities which oppose the conduct of war as the government has determined to conduct it."

He stepped out of the conference room. Rodall had left ahead of him.

"Don't take it too hard, young man," said Colonel Wayne when he and Jolober were alone. "You mercenaries, you can do a lot of things the quick and easy way. It's different when you represent a government and need to consider political implications."

"I'd never understood there were negative implications, Colonel," Jolober said with the slow, careful enunciation which proved he was controlling himself rigidly, "in treating your employees fairly. Even the mercenary soldiers whom you employ."

Wayne's jaw lifted. "I beg your pardon, Commandant," he snapped. "I don't see anyone holding guns to the heads of poor innocents, forcing them to whore and gamble."

He strode to the door, his back parade-ground straight. At the door he turned precisely and delivered the broadside he had held to that point. "Besides, Commandant—if the Dolls are as dangerous to health and welfare as you say, why are you living with one yourself?"

Wayne didn't expect an answer, but what he saw in Horace

Jolober's eyes suggested that his words might bring a physical reaction that he hadn't counted on. He skipped into the hall with a startled sound, banging the door behind him.

The door connecting the conference room to the port commandant's personal suite opened softly. Jolober did not look around.

Vicki put her long, slim arms around him from behind. Jolober spun, then cut power to his fans and settled his chair firmly onto the floor. He and Vicki clung to one another, legless man and Doll whose ruddy skin and beauty marked her as inhuman.

They were both crying.

Someone from Jolober's staff would poke his head into the conference room shortly to ask if the meeting was over and if the commandant wanted non-emergency calls routed through again.

The meeting was certainly over . . . but Horace Jolober had an emergency of his own. He swallowed, keyed his implant, and said brusquely, "I'm out of action till I tell you different. Unless it's another Class A flap."

The kid at the commo desk stuttered a "Yessir" that was a syllable longer than Jolober wanted to hear. Vicki straightened, wearing a bright smile beneath the tear streaks, but the big human gathered her to his chest again and brought up the power of his fans.

Together, like a man carrying a moderate-sized woman, the couple slid around the conference table to the door of the private suite. The chair's drive units were overbuilt because men are overbuilt, capable of putting out huge bursts of hysterical strength.

Drive fans and powerpacks don't have hormones, so Jolober had specified—and paid for—components that would handle double the hundred kilos of his own mass, the hundred kilos left after the tribarrel had chewed him. The only problem with carrying Vicki to bed was one of balance, and the Doll remained still in his arms.

Perfectly still, as she was perfect in all the things she did.

"I'm not trying to get rid of you, darling," Jolober said as he grounded his chair.

"It's all right," Vicki whispered. "I'll go now if you like. It's all right."

She placed her fingertips on Jolober's shoulders and lifted herself by those fulcrums off his lap and onto the bed, her toes curled beneath her buttocks. A human gymnast could have done as well—but no better.

"What I *want*," Jolober said forcefully as he lifted himself out of the saddle, using the chair's handgrips, "is to do my job. And when I've done it, I'll buy you from Red Ike for whatever price he chooses to ask."

He swung himself to the bed. His arms had always been long—and strong. Now he knew that he must look like a gorilla when he got on or off his chair . . . and when the third woman he was with after the amputation giggled at him, he began to consider suicide as an alternative to sex.

Then he took the job on Placida and met Vicki.

Her tears had dried, so both of them could pretend they hadn't poured out moments before. She smiled shyly and touched the high collar of her dress, drawing her fingertip down a centimeter and opening the garment by that amount.

Vicki wasn't Jolober's ideal of beauty—wasn't what he'd *thought* his ideal was, at any rate. Big blondes, he would have said. A woman as tall as he was, with hair the color of bleached straw hanging to the middle of her back.

Vicki scarcely came up to the top of Jolober's breastbone when he was standing—at standing height in his chair—and her hair was a black fluff that was as short as a soldier would cut it to fit comfortably under a helmet. She looked buxom, but her breasts were fairly flat against her broad, powerfully muscled chest.

Jolober put his index finger against hers on the collar and slid down the touch-sensitive strip that opened the fabric. Vicki's body was without blemish or pubic hair. She was so firm that nothing sagged or flattened when her dress and the supports of memory plastic woven into it dropped away.

She shrugged her arms out of the straps and let the garment spill as a pool of sparkling shadow on the counterpane as she reached toward her lover.

Jolober, lying on his side, touched the collar of his uniform jacket.

"No need," Vicki said blocking his hand with one of hers and opening his trouser fly with the other. "Come," she added, rolling onto her back and drawing him toward her.

"But the—" Jolober murmured in surprise, leaning forward in obedience to her touch and demand. The metallic braid and medals on his stiff-fronted tunic had sharp corners to prod the Doll beneath him whether he wished or not.

"Come," she repeated. "This time."

Horace Jolober wasn't introspective enough to understand why his mistress wanted the rough punishment of his uniform. He simply obeyed.

Vicki toyed with his garments after they had finished and lay on the bed, their arms crossing. She had a trick of folding back her lower legs so that they vanished whenever she sat or reclined in the port commandant's presence.

Her fingers tweaked the back of Jolober's waistband and emerged with the hidden knife, the only weapon he carried.

"I'm at your mercy," he said, smiling. He mimed as much of a hands-up posture as he could with his right elbow supporting his torso on the mattress. "Have your way with me."

In Vicki's hand, the knife was a harmless cylinder of plastic—a weapon only to the extent that the butt of the short tube could harden a punch. The knife was of memory plastic whose normal state was a harmless block. No one who took it away from Jolober in a struggle would find it of any use as a weapon.

Only when squeezed after being cued by the pore pattern of Horace Jolober's right hand would it—

The plastic cylinder shrank in Vicki's hand, sprouting a double-edged 15cm blade.

"Via!" swore Jolober. Reflex betrayed him into thinking that he had legs. He jerked upright and started to topple off the bed because the weight of his calves and feet wasn't there to balance the motion.

Vicki caught him with both arms and drew him to her. The blade collapsed into the handle when she dropped it, so that it bounced as a harmless cylinder on the counterpane between them.

"My love, I'm *sorry*," the Doll blurted fearfully. "I didn't mean—"

"No, no," Jolober said, settled now on his thighs and buttocks so that he could hug Vicki fiercely. His eyes peered secretively over her shoulders, searching for the knife that had startled him so badly. "I was surprised that it . . . How *did* you get the blade to open, dearest? It's fine, it's nothing you did wrong, but I didn't expect that, is all."

They swung apart. The mattress was a firm one, but still a bad surface for this kind of conversation. The bedclothes rumpled beneath Jolober's heavy body and almost concealed the knife in a fold of cloth. He found it, raised it with his fingertips, and handed it to Vicki. "Please do that again," he said calmly. "Extend the blade."

Sweat was evaporating from the base of Jolober's spine, where the impermeable knife usually covered the skin.

Vicki took the weapon. She was so doubtful that her face showed no expression at all. Her fingers, short but perfectly formed, gripped the baton as if it were a knife hilt—and it became one. The blade formed with avalanche swiftness, darkly translucent and patterned with veins of stress. The plastic would not take a wire edge, but it could carve a roast or, with Jolober's strength behind it, ram twenty millimeters deep into hardwood.

"Like this?" Vicki said softly. "Just squeeze it and . . .?"

Jolober put his hand over the Doll's and lifted the knife away between thumb and forefinger. When she loosed the hilt, the knife collapsed again into a short baton.

He squeezed—extended the blade—released it again—and slipped the knife back into its concealed sheath.

"You see, darling," Jolober said, "the plastic's been keyed to *my* body. Nobody else should be able to get the blade to form."

"I'd never use it against you," Vicki said. Her face was calm, and there was no defensiveness in her simple response.

Jolober smiled. "Of course, dearest; but there was a manufacturing flaw or you wouldn't be able to do that."

Vicki leaned over and kissed the port commandant's lips, then bent liquidly and kissed him again. "I told you," she said as she straightened with a grin. "I'm a part of you."

"And believe me," said Jolober, rolling onto his back to cinch up his short-legged trousers. "You're not a part of me I intend to lose."

He rocked upright and gripped the handles of his chair.

Vicki slipped off the bed and braced the little vehicle with a hand on the saddle and the edge of one foot on the skirt. The help wasn't necessary—the chair's weight anchored it satisfactorily, so long as Jolober mounted swiftly and smoothly. But it *was* helpful, and it was the sort of personal attention that was as important as sex in convincing Horace Jolober that someone really cared—*could* care—for him.

"You'll do your duty, though," Vicki said. "And I wouldn't want you not to."

Jolober laughed as he settled himself and switched on his fans. He felt enormous relief now that he had proved beyond doubt—he was sure of that—how much he loved Vicki. He'd calmed her down, and that meant he was calm again, too.

"Sure I'll do my job," he said as he smiled at the Doll. "That doesn't mean you and me'll have a problem. Wait and see."

Vicki smiled also, but she shook her head in what Jolober thought was amused resignation. Her hairless body was too perfect to be flesh, and the skin's red pigment gave the Doll the look of a statue in blushing marble.

"Via, but you're lovely," Jolober murmured as the realization struck him anew.

"Come back soon," she said easily.

"Soon as I can," the commandant agreed as he lifted his chair and turned toward the door. "But like you say, I've got a job to do."

If the government of Placida wouldn't give him the support he needed, by the Lord! he'd work through the mercenaries themselves.

Though his belly went cold and his stumps tingled as he realized he would again be approaching the tanks which had crippled him.

The street had the sharp edge which invariably marked it immediately after a unit rotated to Paradise Port out of combat. The troops weren't looking for sex or intoxicants—though most of them would have claimed they were.

They were looking for life. Paradise Port offered them things they thought equaled life, and the contrast between reality and hope led to anger and black despair. Only after a few days of stunning themselves with the offered pleasures did the soldiers on leave recognize another contrast: Paradise Port might not be all they'd hoped, but it was a lot better than the muck and ravening hell of combat.

Jolober slid down the street at a walking pace. Some of the soldiers on the pavement with him offered ragged salutes to the commandant's glittering uniform. He returned them sharply, a habit he had ingrained in himself After he took charge here.

Mercenary units didn't put much emphasis on saluting and similar rear-echelon forms of discipline. An officer with the reputation of being a tight-assed martinet in bivouac was likely to get hit from behind the next time he led his troops into combat.

There were regular armies on most planets—Colonel Wayne was an example—to whom actual fighting was an aberration. Economics or a simple desire for action led many planetary soldiers into mercenary units . . . where the old habits of saluting and snapping to attention surfaced when the men were drunk and depressed.

Hampton's Legion hadn't been any more interested in saluting than the Slammers were. Jolober had sharpened his technique here because it helped a few of the men he served feel more at home— when they were very far from home.

A patrol jeep passed, idling slowly through the pedestrians. Sergeant Stecher waved, somewhat uncertainly.

Jolober waved back, smiling toward his subordinate but angry at himself. He keyed his implant and said "Central, I'm back in business now, but I'm headed for the Refit Area to see Captain van Zuyle. Let anything wait that can till I'm back."

He should have cleared with his switchboard as soon as he'd . . . calmed Vicki down. Here there'd been a crisis, and as soon as it was over he'd disappeared. Must've made his patrolmen very cursed nervous, and it was sheer sloppiness that he'd let the situation go on beyond what it had to. It was his job to make things simple for the people in Paradise Port, both his staff and the port's clientele.

Maybe even for the owners of the brothel: but it was going to have to be simple on Horace Jolober's terms.

At the gate, a tank was helping the crew repairing damage. The men wore khaki coveralls—Slammers rushed from the Refit Area as soon as van Zuyle, the officer in charge there, heard what had happened. The faster you hid the evidence of a problem, the easier it was to claim the problem had never existed.

And it was to everybody's advantage that problems never exist.

Paradise Port was surrounded with a high barrier of woven plastic to keep soldiers who were drunk out of their minds from crawling into the volcanic wasteland and hurting themselves. The fence was tougher than it looked—it looked as insubstantial as moonbeams—but it had never been intended to stop vehicles.

The gate to the bivouac areas outside Paradise Port had a sturdy framework and hung between posts of solid steel. The lead tank had been wide enough to snap both gateposts off at the ground. The gate, framework, and webbing, was strewn in fragments for a hundred meters along the course it had been dragged between the pavement and the tank's skirt.

As Jolober approached, he felt his self-image shrink by comparison to surroundings which included a 170-tonne fighting vehicle. The tank was backed against one edge of the gateway.

With a huge *clang!* the vehicle set another steel post, blasting it home with the apparatus used in combat to punch explosive charges into deep bunkers. The ram vaporized osmium wire with a jolt of high voltage, transmitting the shock waves to the piston head through a column of fluid. It banged home the replacement post without difficulty, even though the "ground" was a sheet of volcanic rock.

The pavement rippled beneath Jolober, and the undamped harmonics of the quivering post were a scream that could be heard for kilometers. Jolober pretended it didn't affect him as he moved past the tank. He was praying that the driver was watching his side screens—or listening to a ground guide—as the tank trembled away from the task it had completed.

One of the Slammers' noncoms gestured reassuringly toward Jolober. His lips moved as he talked into his commo helmet. The port commandant could hear nothing over the howl of the drive fans and prolonged grace notes from the vibrating post, but the tank halted where it was until he had moved past it.

A glance over his shoulder showed Jolober the tank backing into position to set the other post. It looked like a great tortoise, ancient and implacable, maneuvering to lay a clutch of eggs.

Paradise Port was for pleasure only. The barracks housing the soldiers and the sheds to store and repair their equipment were located outside the fenced perimeter. The buildings were prefabs extruded from a dun plastic less colorful than the ruddy lava fields on which they were set.

The bivouac site occupied by Hammer's line companies in rotation was unusual in that the large leveled area contained only four barracks buildings and a pair of broad repair sheds. Parked vehicles filled the remainder of the space.

At the entrance to the bivouac area waited a guard shack. The soldier who stepped from it wore body armor over her khakis. Her submachine gun was slung, but her tone was businesslike as she said, "Commandant Jolober? Captain van Zuyle's on his way to meet you right now."

Hold right here till you're invited in, Jolober translated mentally with a frown.

But he couldn't blame the Slammers' officer for wanting to assert his authority *here* over that of Horace Jolober, whose writ ran only to the perimeter of Paradise Port. Van Zuyle just wanted to prove that his troopers would be punished only with his assent— or by agreement reached with authorities higher than the port commandant.

There was a flagpole attached to a gable of one of the barracks. A tall officer strode from the door at that end and hopped into the driver's seat of the jeep parked there. Another khaki-clad soldier stuck her head out the door and called something, but the officer pretended not to hear. He spun his vehicle in an angry circle, rubbing its low-side skirts, and gunned it toward the entrance.

Jolober had met van Zuyle only once. The most memorable thing about the Slammers' officer was his anger—caused by fate, but directed at whatever was nearest to hand. He'd been heading a company of combat cars when the blower ahead of his took a direct hit.

If van Zuyle'd had his face shield down—but he hadn't, because the shield made him, made most troopers, feel as though they'd stuck their head in a bucket. That dissociation, mental rather than sensory, could get you killed in combat.

The shield would have darkened instantly to block the sleet of actinics from the exploding combat car. Without its protection . . . well, the surgeons could rebuild his face, with only a slight stiffness to betray the injuries. Van Zuyle could even see—by daylight or under strong illumination.

There just wasn't any way he'd ever be fit to lead a line unit again—and he was very angry about it.

Commandant Horace Jolober could understand how van Zuyle felt—better, perhaps, than anyone else on the planet could. It didn't make his own job easier, though.

"A pleasure to see you again, Commandant," van Zuyle lied brusquely as he skidded the jeep to a halt, passenger seat beside Jolober. "If you—"

Jolober smiled grimly as the Slammers' officer saw—and remembered—that the port commandant was legless and couldn't seat himself in a jeep on his air-cushion chair.

"No problem," said Jolober, gripping the jeep's side and the seat back. He lifted himself aboard the larger vehicle with an athletic twist that settled him facing front.

Of course, the maneuver was easier than it would have been if his legs were there to get in the way.

"Ah, your—" van Zuyle said, pointing toward the chair. Close up, Jolober could see a line of demarcation in his scalp. The implanted hair at the front had aged less than the gray-speckled portion which hadn't been replaced.

"No problem, Captain," Jolober repeated. He anchored his left arm around the driver's seat, gripped one of his chair's handles with the right hand, and jerked the chair into the bench seat in the rear of the open vehicle.

The jeep lurched: the air-cushion chair weighed almost as much as Jolober did without it, and he was a big man. "You learn tricks when you have to," he said evenly as he met the eyes of the Slammers' officer.

And your arms get very strong when they do a lot of the work your legs used to—but he didn't say that.

"My office?" van Zuyle asked sharply.

"Is that as busy as it looks?" Jolober replied, nodding toward the door where a soldier still waited impatiently for van Zuyle to return.

"Commandant, I've had a tank company come in shot to *hell*," van Zuyle said in a voice that built toward fury. "Three vehicles are combat lossed and have to be stripped—*and* the other vehicles need more than routine maintenance—*and* half the personnel are on medic's release. Or dead. I'm trying to run a refit area with what's left, my staff of twenty-three, and the trainee replacements Central sent over who haven't ridden in a panzer, much less pulled maintenance on one. And you ask if I've got time to waste on you?"

"No, Captain, I didn't ask that," Jolober said with the threatening lack of emotion which came naturally to a man who had all his life been bigger and stronger than most of those around him. "Find a spot where we won't be disturbed, and we'll park there."

When the Slammers' officer frowned, Jolober added, "I'm not here about Captain Hoffritz, Captain."

"Yeah," sighed van Zuyle as he lifted the jeep and steered it sedately toward a niche formed between the iridium carcasses of a pair of tanks. "We're repairing things right now—" he thumbed in the direction of the gate "— and any other costs'll go on the damage chit; but I guess I owe you an apology besides."

"Life's a dangerous place," Jolober said easily. Van Zuyle wasn't stupid. He'd modified his behavior as soon as he was reminded of the incident an hour before—and the leverage it gave the port commandant if he wanted to push it.

Van Zuyle halted them in the gray shade that brought sweat to Jolober's forehead. The tanks smelled of hot metal because some of their vaporized armor had settled back onto the hulls as fine dust.

Slight breezes shifted it to the nostrils of the men nearby, a memory of the blasts in which it had formed.

Plastics had burned also, leaving varied pungencies which could not conceal the odor of cooked human flesh.

The other smells of destruction were unpleasant. That last brought Jolober memories of his legs exploding in brilliant coruscance. His body tingled and sweated, and his mouth said to the Slammers' officer, "Your men are being cheated and misused every time they come to Paradise Port, Captain. For political reasons, my superiors won't let me make the necessary changes. If the mercenary units serviced by Paradise Port unite and demand the changes, the government will be forced into the proper decision."

"Seems to me," said van Zuyle with his perfectly curved eyebrows narrowing, "that somebody could claim you were acting against your employers just now."

"Placida hired me to run a liberty port," said Jolober evenly. He was being accused of the worst crime a mercenary could commit: conduct that would allow his employers to forfeit his unit's bond and brand them forever as unemployable contract-breakers.

Jolober no longer was a mercenary in that sense; but he understood van Zuyle's idiom, and it was in that idiom that he continued: "Placida wants and needs the troops she hires to be sent back into action in the best shape possible. Her *survival* depends on it. If I let Red Ike run this place to his benefit and not to Placida's, then I'm not doing my job."

"All right," said van Zuyle. "What's Ike got on?"

A truck, swaying with its load of cheering troopers, pulled past on its way to the gate of Paradise Port. The man in the passenger's seat of the cab was Tad Hoffritz, his face a knife-edge of expectation.

"Sure, they need refit as bad as the hardware does," muttered van Zuyle as he watched the soldiers on leave with longing eyes. "Three days straight leave, half days after that when they've pulled their duty. But Via! I could use 'em here, especially with the tanks that're such a bitch if you're not used to crawling around in 'em."

His face hardened again. "Go on," he said, angry that Jolober knew how much he wanted to be one of the men on that truck instead of having to run a rear-echelon installation.

"Red Ike owns the Dolls like so many shots of liquor," Jolober said. He never wanted a combat job again—the thought terrified him, the noise and flash and the smell of his body burning. "He's using them to strip your men, everybody's men, in the shortest possible time," he continued in a voice out of a universe distant from his mind. "The games are honest—that's my job—but the men play when they're stoned, and they play with a Doll on their arm begging them to go on until they've got nothing left. How many of those boys—" he gestured to where the truck, now long past, had been "—are going to last three days?"

"We give 'em advances when they're tapped out," said van Zuyle with a different kind of frown. "Enough to last their half days—if they're getting their jobs done here. Works out pretty good.

"As a matter of fact," he went on, "the whole business works out pretty good. I never saw a soldier's dive without shills and B-girls. Don't guess you ever did either, Commandant. Maybe they're better at it, the Dolls, but all that means is that I get my labor force back quicker—and Hammer gets his tanks back in line with that much fewer problems."

"The Dolls—" Jolober began.

"The Dolls are clean," shouted van Zuyle in a voice like edged steel. "They give full value for what you pay 'em. And I've never had a Doll knife one of my guys—which is a curst sight better'n anyplace I been staffed with human whores!"

"No," said Jolober, his strength a bulwark against the Slammer's anger. "But you've had your men knife or strangle Dolls, haven't you? All the units here've had incidents of that sort. Do you think it's chance?"

Van Zuyle blinked. "I think it's a cost of doing business," he said, speaking mildly because the question had surprised him.

"No," Jolober retorted. "It's a major profit center for Red Ike. The Dolls don't just drop soldiers when they've stripped them. They humiliate the men, taunt them . . . and when one of these kids breaks and chokes the life out of the bitch who's goading him, Red Ike pockets the damage assessment. And it comes out of money Placida would otherwise have paid Hammer's Slammers."

The Slammers' officer began to laugh. It was Jolober's turn to blink in surprise.

"Sure," van Zuyle said, "androids like that cost a lot more'n gateposts or a few meters of fencing, you bet."

"He's the only source," said Jolober tautly. "Nobody knows where the Dolls come from—or where Ike does."

"Then nobody can argue the price isn't fair, can they?" van Zuyle gibed. "And you know what, Commandant? Take a look at this tank right here."

He pointed to one of the vehicles beside them. It was a command tank, probably the one in which Hoffritz's predecessor had ridden before it was hit by powerguns heavy enough to pierce its armor.

The first round, centered on the hull's broadside, had put the unit out of action and killed everyone aboard. The jet of energy had ignited everything flammable within the fighting compartment in an explosion which blew the hatches open. The enemy had hit the iridium carcass at least three times more, cratering the turret and holing the engine compartment.

"We couldn't replace this for the cost of twenty Dolls," van Zuyle continued. "And we're going to have to, you know, because she's a total loss. All I can do is strip her for salvage . . . and clean up as best I can for the crew, so we can say we had something to bury."

His too-pale, too-angry eyes glared at Jolober. "Don't talk to me about the cost of Dolls, Commandant. They're cheap at the price. I'll drive you back to the gate."

"You may not care about the dollar cost," said Jolober in a voice that thundered over the jeep's drive fans. "But what about the men you're sending back into the line thinking they've killed somebody they loved—or that they *should've* killed her?'

"Commandant, that's one I can't quantify," the Slammers' officer said. The fans' keening lowered as the blades bit the air at a steeper angle and began to thrust the vehicle out of the bivouac area. "First time a trooper kills a human here, that I *can* quantify: we lose him.

If there's a bigger problem and the Bonding Authority decides to call it mutiny, then we lost a lot more than that.

"And I tell you, buddy," van Zuyle added with a one-armed gesture toward the wrecked vehicles now behind them. "We've lost too fucking much already on this contract."

The jeep howled past the guard at the bivouac entrance. Wind noise formed a deliberate damper on Jolober's attempts to continue the discussion. "Will you forward my request to speak to Colonel Hammer?" he shouted. "I can't get through to him myself."

The tank had left the gate area. Men in khaki, watched by Jolober's staff in white uniforms, had almost completed their task of restringing the perimeter fence. Van Zuyle throttled back, permitting the jeep to glide to a graceful halt three meters short of the workmen.

"The colonel's busy, Commandant," he said flatly. "And from now on, I hope you'll remember that *I* am, too."

Jolober lifted his chair from the back seat. "I'm going to win this, Captain," he said. "I'm going to do my job whether or not I get any support."

The smile he gave van Zuyle rekindled the respect in the tanker's pale eyes.

There were elements of four other mercenary units bivouacked outside Paradise Port at the moment. Jolober could have visited them in turn—to be received with more or less civility, and certainly no more support than the Slammers' officer had offered.

A demand for change by the mercenaries in Placidan service had to be just that: a demand by *all* the mercenaries. Hammer's Slammers were the highest-paid troops here, and by that standard—any other criterion would start a brawl—the premier unit. If the Slammers refused Jolober, none of the others would back him.

The trouble with reform is that in the short run, it causes more problems than continuing along the bad old ways. Troops in a combat zone, who know that each next instant may be their last, are more to be forgiven for short-term thinking than, say, politicians; but the pattern is part of the human condition.

Besides, nobody but Horace Jolober seemed to think there was anything to reform.

Jolober moved in a walking dream while his mind shuttled through causes and options. His data were interspersed with memories of Vicki smiling up at him from the bed and of his own severed leg toppling in blue-green silhouette. He shook his head gently to clear the images and found himself on the street outside the Port offices.

His stump throttled back the fans reflexively; but when Jolober's conscious mind made its decision, he turned away from the office building and headed for the garish facade of the China Doll across the way.

Rainbow pastels lifted slowly over the front of the building, the gradation so subtle that close up it was impossible to tell where one band ended and the next began. At random intervals of from thirty seconds to a minute, the gentle hues were replaced by glaring, super-saturated colors separated by dazzling blue-white lines.

None of the brothels in Paradise Port were sedately decorated, but the China Doll stood out against the competition.

As Jolober approached, a soldier was leaving and three more—one a woman—were in the queue to enter. A conveyor carried those wishing to exit, separated from one another by solid panels. The panels withdrew sideways into the wall as each client reached the street—but there was always another panel in place behind to prevent anyone from bolting into the building without being searched at the proper entrance.

All of the buildings in Paradise Port were designed the same way, with security as unobtrusive as it could be while remaining uncompromised. The entryways were three-meter funnels narrowing in a series of gaudy corbelled arches. Attendants—humans everywhere but in the China Doll—waited at the narrow end. They smiled as the customers passed—but anyone whom the detection devices in the archway said was armed was stopped right there.

The first two soldiers ahead of Jolober went through without incident. The third was a short man wearing lieutenant's pips and the uniform of Division Léégèère. His broad shoulders and chest narrowed to his waist as abruptly as those of a bulldog, and it was with a bulldog's fierce intransigence that he braced himself against the two attendants who had confronted him.

"I am Lieutenant Alexis Condorcet!" he announced as though he were saying "major general." "What do you mean by hindering me?"

The attendants in the China Doll were Droids, figures with smoothly masculine features and the same blushing complexion which set Red Ike and the Dolls apart from the humans with whom they mingled.

They were not male—Jolober had seen the total sexlessness of an android whose tights had ripped as he quelled a brawl. Their bodies and voices were indistinguishable from one to another, and there could be no doubt that they were androids, artificial constructions whose existence proved that the Dolls could be artificial, too.

Though in his heart, Horace Jolober had never been willing to believe the Dolls were not truly alive. Not since Red Ike had introduced him to Vicki.

"Could you check the right-hand pocket of your blouse, Lieutenant Condorcet?" one of the Droids said.

"I'm not carrying a weapon!" Condorcet snapped. His hand hesitated, but it dived into the indicated pocket when an attendant started to reach toward it.

Jolober was ready to react, either by grabbing Condorcet's wrist from behind or by knocking him down with the chair. He didn't have time for any emotion, not even fear.

It was the same set of instincts that had thrown him to his feet for the last time, to wave off the attacking tanks.

Condorcet's hand came out with a roll of coins between two fingers. In a voice that slipped between injured and minatory, he said, "Can't a man bring money into the Doll, then? Will you have me take my business elsewhere, then?"

"Your money's very welcome, sir," said the attendant who was reaching forward. His thumb and three fingers shifted in a sleight of hand; they reappeared holding a gold-striped China Doll chip worth easily twice the value of the rolled coins. "But let us hold these till you return. We'll be glad to give them back then without exchange."

The motion which left Condorcet holding the chip and transferred the roll to the attendant was also magically smooth.

The close-coupled soldier tensed for a moment as if he'd make an issue of it; but the Droids were as strong as they were polished, and there was no percentage in being humiliated.

"We'll see about that," said Condorcet loudly. He strutted past the attendants who parted for him like water before the blunt prow of a barge.

"Good afternoon, Port Commandant Jolober," said one of the Droids as they both bowed. "A pleasure to serve you again."

"A pleasure to feel wanted," said Jolober with an ironic nod of his own. He glided into the main hall of the China Doll.

The room's high ceiling was suffused with clear light which mimicked daytime outside. The hall buzzed with excited sounds even when the floor carried only a handful of customers. Jolober hadn't decided whether the space was designed to give multiple echo effects or if instead Red Ike augmented the hum with concealed sonic transponders.

Whatever it was, the technique made the blood of even the port commandant quicken when he stepped into the China Doll.

There were a score of gaming stations in the main hall, but they provided an almost infinite variety of ways to lose money. A roulette station could be collapsed into a skat table in less than a minute if a squad of drunken Frieslanders demanded it. The displaced roulette players could be accommodated at the next station over, where until then a Droid had been dealing desultory hands of fan-tan.

Whatever the game was, it was fair. Every hand, every throw, every pot was recorded and processed in the office of the port commandant. None of the facility owners doubted that a skewed result would be noticed at once by the computers, or that a result skewed in favor of the house would mean that Horace Jolober would weld their doors shut and ship all their staff off-planet.

Besides, they knew as Jolober did that honest games would get them most of the available money anyhow, so long as the Dolls were there to caress the winners to greater risks.

At the end of Paradise Port farthest from the gate were two

establishments which specialized in the left overs. They were staffed by human males, and their atmosphere was as brightly efficient as men could make it.

But no one whose psyche allowed a choice picked a human companion over a Doll.

The main hall was busy with drab uniforms, Droids neatly garbed in blue and white, and the stunningly gorgeous outfits of the Dolls. There was a regular movement of Dolls and uniforms toward the door on a room-width landing three steps up at the back of the hall. Generally the rooms beyond were occupied by couples, but much larger gatherings were possible if a soldier had money and the perceived need.

The curved doors of the elevator beside the front entrance opened even as Jolober turned to look at them. Red Ike stepped out with a smile and a Doll on either arm.

"Always a pleasure to see you, Commandant," Red Ike said in a tone as sincere as the Dolls were human. "Shana," he added to the red-haired Doll. "Susan—" he nodded toward the blond. "Meet Commandant Jolober, the man who keeps us all safe."

The redhead giggled and slipped from Ike's arm to Jolober's. The slim blond gave him a smile that would have been demure except for the fabric of her tank top. It acted as a polarizing filter, so that when she swayed her bare torso flashed toward the port commandant.

"But come on upstairs, Commandant," Red Ike continued, stepping backwards into the elevator and motioning Jolober to follow him. "Unless your business is here—or in back?" He cocked an almost-human eyebrow toward the door in the rear while his face waited with a look of amused tolerance.

"We can go upstairs," said Jolober grimly. "It won't take long." His air cushion slid him forward. Spilling air tickled Shana's feet as she pranced along beside him; she giggled again.

There must be men who found that sort of girlish idiocy erotic or Red Ike wouldn't keep the Doll in his stock.

The elevator shaft was opaque and looked it from outside the car. The car's interior was a visiscreen fed by receptors on the shaft's exterior. On one side of the slowly rising car, Jolober could watch the games in the main hall as clearly as if he were hanging in the air. On the other, they lifted above the street with a perfect view of its traffic and the port offices even though a concrete wall and the shaft's iridium armor blocked the view in fact.

The elevator switch was a small plate which hung in the "air" that was really the side of the car. Red Ike had toggled it up. Down would have taken the car—probably much faster—to the tunnel beneath the street, the escape route which Jolober had suspected even before the smiling alien had used it this afternoon.

But there was a second unobtrusive control beside the first. The blond Doll leaned past Jolober with a smile and touched it.

The view of the street disappeared. Those in the car had a crystalline view of the activities in back of the China Doll as if no walls or ceilings separated the bedrooms. Jolober met—or thought he met—the eyes of Tad Hoffritz, straining upward beneath a black-haired Doll.

"*Via!*" Jolober swore and slapped the toggle hard enough to feel the solidity of the elevator car.

"Susan, Susan," Red Ike chided with a grin. "She will have her little joke, you see, Commandant."

The blond made a moue, then winked at Jolober.

Above the main hall was Red Ike's office, furnished in minimalist luxury. Jolober found nothing attractive in the sight of chair seats and a broad onyx desktop hanging in the air, but the decor did show off the view. Like the elevator, the office walls and ceiling were covered by pass-through visiscreens.

The russet wasteland, blotched but not relieved by patterns of lichen, looked even more dismal from twenty meters up than it did from Jolober's living quarters.

Though the view appeared to be panorama, there was no sign of where the owner himself lived. The back of the office was an interior wall, and the vista over the worms and pillows of lava was transmitted through not only the wall but the complex of rooms that was Red Ike's home.

On the roof beside the elevator tower was an aircar sheltered behind the concrete coping. Like the owners of all the other facilities comprising Paradise Port, Red Ike wanted the option of getting out fast, even if the elevator to his tunnel bolthole was blocked.

Horace Jolober had fantasies in which he watched the stocky humanoid scramble into his vehicle and accelerate away, vanishing forever as a fleck against the milky sky.

"I've been meaning to call on you for some time, Commandant," Red Ike said as he walked with quick little steps to his desk. "I thought perhaps you might like a replacement for Vicki. As you know, any little way in which I can make your task easier . . .?"

Shana giggled. Susan smiled slowly and, turning at a precisely calculated angle, bared breasts that were much fuller than they appeared beneath her loose garment.

Jolober felt momentary desire, then fierce anger in reaction. His hands clenched on the chair handles, restraining his violent urge to hurl both Dolls into the invisible walls.

Red Ike sat behind the desktop. The thin shell of his chair rocked on invisible gimbals, tilting him to a comfortable angle that was not quite disrespectful of his visitor

"Commandant," he said with none of the earlier hinted mockery, "you and I really ought to cooperate, you know. We need each other, and Placida needs us both."

"And the soldiers we're here for?" Jolober asked softly. "Do they need you, Ike?"

The Dolls had become as still as painted statues.

"You're an honorable man, Commandant," said the alien. "It disturbs you that the men don't find what they need in Paradise Port."

The chair eased more nearly upright. The intensity of Red Ike's stare reminded Jolober that he'd never seen the alien blink.

"But men like that—all of them now, and most of them for as long as they live . . . all they really need, Commandant, is a chance to die. I don't offer them that, it isn't my place. But I sell them everything they pay for, because I too am honorable."

"You don't know what honor is!" Jolober shouted, horrified at the thought—the nagging possibility—that what Red Ike said was true.

"I know what it is to keep my word, Commandant Jolober," the alien said as he rose from behind his desk with quiet dignity. "I promise you that if you cooperate with me, Paradise Port will continue to run to the full satisfaction of your employers.

"And I also promise," Red Ike went on unblinkingly, "that if you continue your mad vendetta, it will be the worse for you."

"Leave here," Jolober said. His mind achieved not calm, but a dynamic balance in which he understood everything—so long as he focused only on the result, not the reasons. "Leave Placida, leave human space, Ike. You push too hard. So far you've been lucky—it's only me pushing back, and I play by the official rules."

He leaned forward in his saddle, no longer angry. The desktop between them was a flawless black mirror. "But the mercs out there, they play by their own rules, and they're not going to like it when they figure out the game you're running on them. Get out while you can."

"Ladies," Red Ike said. "Please escort the commandant to the main hall. He no longer has any business here."

Jolober spent the next six hours on the street, visiting each of the establishments of Paradise Port. He drank little and spoke less, exchanging salutes when soldiers offered them and, with the same formality, the greetings of owners.

He didn't say much to Vicki later that night, when he returned by the alley staircase which led directly to his living quarters.

But he held her very close.

The sky was dark when Jolober snapped awake, though his bedroom window was painted by all the enticing colors of the facades across the street. He was fully alert and already into the short-legged trousers laid on the mobile chair beside the bed when Vicki stirred and asked, "Horace? What's the matter?"

"I don't—" Jolober began, and then the alarms sounded: the radio implanted in his mastoid, and the siren on the roof of the China Doll.

"Go ahead," he said to Central, thrusting his arms into the uniform tunic.

Vicki thumbed up the room lights but Jolober didn't need that, not to find the sleeves of a white garment with this much sky-glow. He'd stripped a jammed tribarrel once in pitch darkness, knowing that he and a dozen of his men were dead if he screwed up—and absolutely confident of the stream of cyan fire that ripped moments later from his gun muzzles.

"Somebody shot his way into the China Doll," said the voice. "He's holed up in the back."

The bone-conduction speaker hid the identity of the man on the other end of the radio link, but it wasn't the switchboard's artificial intelligence. Somebody on the street was cutting through directly, probably Stecher.

"Droids?" Jolober asked as he mounted his chair and powered up, breaking the charging circuit in which the vehicle rested overnight.

"Chief," said the mastoid, "we got a man down. Looks bad, and we can't get medics to him because the gun's covering the hallway. D'ye want me to—"

"Wait!" Jolober said as he bulled through the side door under power. Unlocking the main entrance—the entrance to the office of the port commandant—would take seconds that he knew he didn't have. "Hold what you got, I'm on the way."

The voice speaking through Jolober's jawbone was clearly audible despite wind noise and the scream of his chair as he leaped down the alley staircase in a single curving arc. "Ah, Chief? We're likely to have a, a crowd control problem if this don't get handled real quick."

"I'm on the way," Jolober repeated. He shot onto the street, still on direct thrust because ground effect wouldn't move him as fast as he needed to go.

The entrance of the China Doll was cordoned off, if four port patrolmen could be called a cordon. There were over a hundred soldiers in the street and more every moment that the siren—couldn't somebody cut it? Jolober didn't have time—continued to blare.

That wasn't what Stecher had meant by a "crowd control

problem." The difficulty was in the way soldiers in the Division Léégèère's mottled uniforms were shouting—not so much as onlookers as a lynch mob.

Jolober dropped his chair onto its skirts—he needed the greater stability of ground effect. "Lemme through!" he snarled to the mass of uniformed backs which parted in a chorus of yelps when Jolober goosed his throttle. The skirt of his plenum chamber caught the soldiers just above the boot heels and toppled them to either side as the chair powered through.

One trooper spun with a raised fist and a curse in French. Jolober caught the man's wrist and flung him down almost absently. The men at the door relaxed visibly when their commandant appeared at their side.

Behind him, Jolober could hear off-duty patrolmen scrambling into the street from their barracks under the port offices. That would help, but—

"You, Major!" Jolober shouted, pointing at a Division Léégèère officer in the front of the crowd. The man was almost of a size with the commandant; fury had darkened his face several shades beyond swarthiness. "I'm deputizing you to keep order here until I've taken care of the problem inside."

He spun his chair again and drove through the doorway. The major was shouting to his back, "But the bastard's shot my—"

Two Droids were more or less where Jolober had expected them, one crumpled in the doorway and the other stretched full length a meter inside. The Droids were tough as well as strong. The second one had managed to grasp the man who shot him and be pulled a pace or two before another burst into the back of the Droid's skull had ended matters.

Stecher hadn't said the shooter had a submachine gun. That made the situation a little worse than it might have been, but it was so bad already that the increment was negligible.

Droids waited impassively at all the gaming stations, ready to do their jobs as soon as customers returned. They hadn't fled the way human croupiers would have—but neither did their programming say anything about dealing with armed intruders.

The Dolls had disappeared. It was the first time Jolober had been in the main hall when it was empty of their charming, enticing babble.

Stecher and two troopers in Slammers' khaki, and a pair of technicians with a portable medicomp stood on opposite sides of the archway leading into the back of the China Doll. A second patrolman was huddled behind the three room-wide steps leading up from the main hall.

Man down, Jolober thought, his guts ice.

The patrolman heard the chair and glanced back. "*Duck!*" he screamed as Sergeant Stecher cried, "*Watch—*"

Jolober throttled up, bouncing to the left as a three-shot burst snapped from the archway. It missed him by little enough that his hair rose in response to the ionized track.

There *was* a man down, in the corridor leading back from the archway. There was another man firing from a room at the corridor's opposite end, and he'd just proved his willingness to add the port commandant to the night's bag.

Jolober's chair leaped the steps to the broad landing where Stecher crouched, but it was his massive arms that braked his momentum against the wall. His tunic flapped and he noticed for the first time that he hadn't sealed it before he left his quarters. "Report," he said bluntly to his sergeant while running his thumb up the uniform's seam to close it.

"Their officer's in there," Stecher said, bobbing his chin to indicate the two Slammers kneeling beside him. The male trooper was holding the female and trying to comfort her as she blubbered.

To Jolober's surprise, he recognized both of them—the commo tech and the driver of the tank which'd nearly run him down that afternoon.

"He nutted, shot his way in to find a Doll," Stecher said quickly. His eyes flicked from the commandant to the archway, but he didn't shift far enough to look down the corridor. Congealed notches in the arch's plastic sheath indicated that he'd been lucky once already.

"Found her, found the guy she was with, and put a burst into him as he tried to get away." Stecher thumbed toward the body invisible behind the shielding wall. "Guy from the Léégèère, an El-Tee named Condorcet."

"The bitch made him do it!" said the tank driver in a scream strangled by her own laced fingers.

"She's sedated," said the commo tech who held her.

In the perfect tones of Central's artificial intelligence, Jolober's implant said, "Major de Vigny of the Division Léégèère requests to see you. He is offering threats."

Letting de Vigny through would either take the pressure off the team outside or be the crack that made the dam fail. From the way Central put it, the dam wasn't going to hold much longer anyhow.

"Tell the cordon to pass him. But tell him keep his head down or he's that much more t'clean up t'morrow," Jolober replied with his mike keyed, making the best decision he could when none of 'em looked good.

"Tried knock-out gas but he's got filters," said Stecher. "Fast, too." He tapped the scarred jamb. "All the skin absorptives're lethal, and I don't guess we'd get cleared t' use 'em anyhow?"

"Not while I'm in the chain of command," Jolober agreed grimly.

"She was with this pongo from the Léégèère," the driver was saying through her laced fingers. "Tad, he wanted her so much, so fucking *much*, like she was human or something . . ."

"The, ah, you know. Beth, the one he was planning to see," said the commo tech rapidly as he stroked the back of the driver— Corporal Days—Daisy . . . "He tried to, you know, buy 'er from the Frog, but he wouldn't play. She got 'em, Beth did, to put all their leave allowance on a coin flip. She'd take all the money and go with the winner."

"The bitch," Daisy wailed. "The bitch the bitch the bitch . . ."

The Léégèère didn't promote amateurs to battalion command. The powerful major that Jolober had seen outside rolled through the doorway, sized up the situation, and sprinted to the landing out of the shooter's line of sight.

Line of fire.

David Drake

"Hoffritz, can you hear me?" Jolober called. "I'm the port commandant, remember?"

A single bolt from the submachine gun spattered plastic from the jamb and filled the air with fresher stenches.

The man sprawling in the corridor moaned.

"I've ordered up an assault team," said Major de Vigny with flat assurance as he stood up beside Jolober. "It was unexpected, but they should be here in a few minutes."

Everyone else in the room was crouching. There wasn't any need so long as you weren't in front of the corridor, but it was the instinctive response to knowing somebody was trying to shoot you.

"Cancel the order," said Jolober, locking eyes with the other officer.

"You aren't in charge when one of my men—" began the major, his face flushing almost black.

"The gate closes when the alarm goes off!" Jolober said in a voice that could have been heard over a tank's fans. "And I've ordered the air defense batteries," he lied, "to fire on anybody trying to crash through now. If you want to lead a mutiny against your employers, Major, now's the time to do it."

The two big men glared at one another without blinking. Then de Vigny said, "Blue Six to Blue Three," keying his epaulet mike with the code words. "Hold Team Alpha until further orders. Repeat, hold Alpha. Out."

"Hold Alpha," repeated the speaker woven into the epaulet's fabric.

"If Condorcet dies," de Vigny added calmly to the port commandant, "I will kill you myself, sir."

"Do you have cratering charges warehoused here?" Jolober asked with no emotion save the slight lilt of interrogation.

"What?" said de Vigny. "Yes, yes."

Jolober crooked his left ring finger so that Central would hear and relay his next words. "Tell the gate to pass two men from the Léégèère with a jeep and a cratering charge. Give them a patrol guide, and download the prints of the China Doll into his commo link so they can place the charge on the wall outside the room at the T of the back corridor."

De Vigny nodded crisply to indicate that he too understood the order. He began relaying it into his epaulet while Stecher drew and reholstered his needle stunner and Corporal Days mumbled.

"Has she tried?" Jolober asked, waving to the driver and praying that he wouldn't have to . . .

"He shot at 'er," the commo tech said, nodding sadly. "That's when she really lost it and medics had to calm her down."

No surprises there. Certainly no good ones.

"Captain Hoffritz, it's the port commandant again," Jolober called.

A bolt spat down the axis of the corridor.

"That's right, you bastard, *shoot!*" Jolober roared. "You blew my legs off on Primavera. Now finish the job and *prove* you're a fuck-up who's only good for killing his friends. Come on, I'll make it easy. I'll come out and let you take your time!"

"Chief—" said Stecher.

Jolober slid away from the shelter of the wall.

The corridor was the stem of a T, ten meters long. Halfway between Jolober and the cross-corridor at the other end, capping the T, lay the wounded man. Lieutenant Condorcet was a tough little man to still be alive with the back of his tunic smoldering around the holes punched in him by three powergun bolts. The roll of coins he'd carried to add weight to his fist wouldn't have helped; but then, nothing much helped when the other guy had the only gun in the equation.

Like now.

The door of the room facing the corridor and Horace Jolober was ajar. Beyond the opening was darkness and a bubble of dull red: the iridium muzzle of Hoffritz's submachine gun, glowing with the heat of the destruction it had spit at others.

De Vigny cursed; Stecher was pleading or even calling an order. All Jolober could hear was the roar of the tank bearing down on him, so loud that the slapping bolts streaming toward him from its cupola were inaudible.

Jolober's chair slid him down the hall. His arms were twitching in physical memory of the time they'd waved a scrap of white cloth to halt the oncoming armor.

The door facing him opened. Tad Hoffritz's face was as hard and yellow as fresh bone. He leaned over the sight of his submachine gun. Jolober slowed, because if he kept on at a walking pace he would collide with Condorcet, and if he curved around the wounded man it might look as if he were dodging what couldn't be dodged.

He didn't want to look like a fool and a coward when he died.

Hoffritz threw down the weapon.

Jolober bounced to him, wrapping the Slammers' officer in both arms like a son. Stecher was shouting, "Medics!" but the team with the medicomp had been in motion as soon as the powergun hit the floor. Behind all the battle was Major de Vigny's voice, remembering to stop the crew with the charge that might otherwise be set—and fired even though the need was over.

"I *loved* her," Hoffritz said to Jolober's big shoulder, begging someone to understand what he didn't understand himself. "I, I'd been drinking and I came back . . ."

With a submachine gun that shouldn't have made it into Paradise Port . . . but the detection loops hadn't been replaced in the hours since the tanks ripped them away; and anyhow, Hoffritz was an officer, a company commander.

He was also a young man having a bad time with what he thought was a woman. Older, calmer fellows than Hoffritz had killed because of that.

Jolober carried Hoffritz with him into the room where he'd been holed up. "Lights," the commandant ordered, and the room brightened.

Condorcet wasn't dead, not yet; but Beth, the Doll behind the trouble, surely was.

The couch was large and round. Though drumhead-thin, its structure could be varied to any degree of firmness the paying half of the couple desired. Beth lay in the center of it in a tangle of long black hair. Her tongue protruded from a blood-darkened face, and the prints of the grip that had strangled her were livid on her throat.

"She told me she loved *him*," Hoffritz mumbled. The commandant's embrace supported him, but it also kept Hoffritz from doing something silly, like trying to run.

"After what I'd done," the boy was saying, "she tells me she doesn't love me after all. She says I'm no good to her in bed, that I never gave her any pleasure at all. . . ."

"Just trying to maximize the claim for damages, son," Jolober said grimly. "It didn't mean anything real, just more dollars in Red Ike's pocket."

But Red Ike hadn't counted on Hoffritz shooting another merc. Too bad for Condorcet, too bad for the kid who shot him—

And just what Jolober needed to finish Red Ike on Placida.

"Let's go," Jolober said, guiding Hoffritz out of the room stinking of death and the emotions that led to death. "We'll get you to a medic."

And a cell.

Condorcet had been removed from the corridor, leaving behind only a slime of vomit. Thank the Lord he'd fallen face down.

Stecher and his partner took the unresisting Hoffritz and wrapped him in motion restraints. The prisoner could walk and move normally, so long as he did it slowly. At a sudden movement, the gossamer webs would clamp him as tightly as a fly in a spider-web.

The main hall was crowded, but the incipient violence facing the cordon outside had melted away. Judging from Major de Vigny's brusque, bellowed orders, the victim was in the hands of his medics and being shifted to the medicomp in Division Léégèère's bivouac area.

That was probably the best choice. Paradise Port had excellent medical facilities, but medics in combat units got to know their jobs and their diagnostic/healing computers better than anybody in the rear echelons.

"Commandant Jolober," said van Zuyle, the Slammers' bivouac commander, "I'm worried about my man here. Can I—"

"He's not your man anymore, Captain," Jolober said with the weary chill of an avalanche starting to topple. "He's mine and the

Placidan courts'—until I tell you different. We'll get him sedated and keep him from hurting himself, no problem."

Van Zuyle's face wore the expression of a man whipping himself to find a deity who doesn't respond. "Sir," he said, "I'm sorry if I—"

"You did the job they paid you t'do," Jolober said, shrugging away from the other man. He hadn't felt so weary since he'd awakened in the Legion's main hospital on Primavera: alive and utterly unwilling to believe that he could be after what happened.

"Outa the man's way," snarled one of the patrolmen, trying to wave a path through the crowd with her white-sleeved arms. "Let the commandant by!"

She yelped a curse at the big man who brushed through her gestures. "A moment, little one," he said—de Vigny, the Léégèère major.

"You kept the lid on good," Jolober said while part of his dazed mind wondered whose voice he was hearing. "Tomorrow I'll want to talk to you about what happened and how to prevent a repeat."

Anger darkened de Vigny's face. "I heard what happened," he said. "Condorcet was not the only human victim, it would seem."

"We'll talk," Jolober said. His chair was driving him toward the door, pushing aside anyone who didn't get out of the way. He didn't see them any more than he saw the air.

The street was a carnival of uniformed soldiers who suddenly had something to focus on that wasn't a memory of death—or a way to forget. There were dark undercurrents to the chatter, but the crowd was no longer a mob.

Jolober's uniform drew eyes, but the port commandant was too aloof and forbidding to be asked for details of what had really happened in the China Doll. In the center of the street, though—

"Good evening, Commandant," said Red Ike, strolling back toward the establishment he owned. "Without your courage, tonight's incident would have been even more unfortunate."

Human faces changed in the play of light washing them from the brothel fronts. Red Ike's did not. Colors overlay his features, but the lines did not modify as one shadow or highlight replaced another.

"It couldn't be more unfortunate for you, Ike," Jolober said to the bland alien while uniforms milled around them. "They'll pay you money, the mercs will. But they won't have you killing their men."

"I understand that the injured party is expected to pull through," Red Ike said emotionlessly. Jolober had the feeling that the alien's eyes were focused on his soul.

"I'm glad Condorcet'll live," Jolober said, too tired for triumph or subtlety. "But you're dead on Placida, Ike. It's just a matter of how long it takes me to wrap it up."

He broke past Red Ike, gliding toward the port offices and the light glowing from his room on the upper floor.

Red Ike didn't turn around, but Jolober thought he could feel the alien watching him nonetheless.

Even so, all Jolober cared about now was bed and a chance to reassure Vicki that everything was all right.

The alley between the office building and the Blue Parrot next door wasn't directly illuminated, but enough light spilled from the street to show Jolober the stairs.

He didn't see the two men waiting there until a third had closed the mouth of the alley behind him. Indonesian music began to blare from the China Doll.

Music on the exterior's a violation, thought the part of Jolober's mind that ran Paradise Port, but reflexes from his years as a combat officer noted the man behind him held a metal bar and that knives gleamed in the hands of the two by the stairs.

It made a hell of a fast trip back from the nightmare memories that had ruled Jolober's brain since he wakened.

Jolober's left stump urged the throttle as his torso shifted toward the alley mouth. The electronics reacted instantly but the mechanical links took a moment. Fans spun up, plenum chamber collapsed into a nozzle—

The attackers moved in on Jolober like the three wedges of a drill chuck. His chair launched him into the one with the club, a meter off the ground and rising with a hundred and eighty kilos of mass behind the impact.

At the last instant the attacker tried to duck away instead of swinging at Jolober, but he misjudged the speed of his intended victim. The center of the chair's frame, between the skirt and the saddle, batted the attacker's head toward the wall, dragging the fellow's body with it.

Jolober had a clear path to the street. The pair of knifemen thought he was headed that way and sprinted in a desperate attempt to catch a victim who moved faster than unaided humans could run.

They were in midstride, thinking of failure rather than defense, when Jolober pogoed at the alley mouth and came back at them like a cannonball.

But bigger and heavier.

One attacker stabbed at Jolober's chest and skidded the point off the battery compartment instead when the chair hopped. The frame slammed knife and man into the concrete wall from which they ricochetted to the ground, separate and equally motionless.

The third man ran away.

"Get 'em, boys!" Jolober bellowed as if he were launching his battalion instead of just himself in pursuit. The running man glanced over his shoulder and collided with the metal staircase. The noise was loud and unpleasant, even in comparison to the oriental music blaring from the China Doll.

Jolober bounced, cut his fan speed, and flared his output nozzle into a plenum chamber again. The chair twitched, then settled into ground effect.

Jolober's mind told him that he was seeing with a clarity and richness of color he couldn't have equalled by daylight, but he knew that if he really focused on an object it would blur into shadow. It was just his brain's way of letting him know that he was still alive.

Alive like he hadn't been in years.

Crooking his ring finger Jolober said, "I need a pickup on three men in the alley between us and the Blue Parrot."

"Three men in the alley between HQ and the Blue Parrot," the artificial intelligence paraphrased.

"They'll need a medic." One might need burial. "And I want them sweated under a psycomp—who sent 'em after me, the works."

Light flooded the alley as a team of patrolmen arrived. The point man extended a surface-luminescent area light powered from a backpack. The shadows thrown by the meter-diameter convexity were soft, but the illumination was the blaze of noon compared to that of moments before.

"Chief!" bellowed Stecher. "You all right? Chief!" He wasn't part of the team Central vectored to the alley, but word of mouth had brought him to the scene of the incident.

Jolober throttled up, clamped his skirts, and boosted himself to the fourth step where everyone could see him. The man who'd run into the stairs moaned as the side-draft spat grit from the treads into his face.

"No problem," Jolober said. No problem they wouldn't be able to cure in a week or two. "I doubt these three know any more than that they got a call from outside Port to, ah, handle me . . . but get what they have, maybe we can cross-reference with some outgoing traffic."

From the China Doll; or just maybe from the Blue Parrot, where Ike fled when the shooting started. But probably not. Three thugs, nondescripts from off-planet who could've been working for any establishment in Paradise Port *except* the China Doll.

"Sir—" came Stecher's voice.

"It'll keep, Sergeant," Jolober interrupted. "Just now I've got a heavy date with a bed."

Vicki greeted him with a smile so bright that both of them could pretend there were no tears beneath it. The air was steamy with the bath she'd drawn for him.

He used to prefer showers, back when he'd had feet on which to stand. He could remember dancing on Quitly's Planet as the afternoon monsoon battered the gun carriages his platoon was guarding and washed the soap from his body.

But he didn't have Vicki then, either.

"Yeah," he said, hugging the Doll. "Good idea, a bath."

Instead of heading for the bathroom, he slid his chair to the cabinet within arm's reach of the bed and cut his fans. Bending over, he unlatched the battery compartment—the knifepoint hadn't even penetrated the casing—and removed the powerpack.

"I can—" Vicki offered hesitantly.

"S'okay, dearest," Jolober replied as he slid a fresh pack from the cabinet into place. His stump touched the throttle, spinning the fans to prove that he had good contact, then lifted the original pack into the cabinet and its charging harness.

"Just gave 'em a workout tonight and don't want t' be down on power tomorrow," he explained as he straightened. Vicki could have handled the weight of the batteries, he realized, though his mind kept telling him it was ludicrous to imagine the little woman shifting thirty-kilo packages with ease.

But she wasn't a woman.

"I worry when it's so dangerous," she said as she walked with him to the bathroom, their arms around one another's waist.

"Look, for Paradise Port, it was dangerous," Jolober said in a light appearance of candor as he handed Vicki his garments. "Compared to downtown in any capital city I've seen, it was pretty mild."

He lowered himself into the water, using the bars laid over the tub like a horizontal ladder. Vicki began to knead the great muscles of his shoulders, and Lord! but it felt good to relax after so long . . .

"I'd miss you," she said.

"Not unless I went away," Jolober answered, leaning forward so that her fingers could work down his spine while the water lapped at them. "Which isn't going to happen any time soon."

He paused. The water's warmth unlocked more than his body. "Look," he said quietly, his chin touching the surface of the bath and his eyes still closed. "Red Ike's had it. He knows it, I know it. But I'm in a position to make things either easy or hard, and he knows that, too. We'll come to terms, he and I. And you're the—"

"Urgent from the gate," said Jolober's mastoid implant.

He crooked his finger, raising his head. "Put him through," he said.

Her through. "Sir," said Feldman's attenuated voice, "a courier's just landed with two men. They say they've got an oral message from Colonel Hammer, and they want me to alert you that they're coming. Over."

"I'll open the front door," Jolober said, lifting himself abruptly from the water, careful not to miskey the implant while his hands performed other tasks.

He wouldn't rouse the human staff. No need and if the message came by courier, it wasn't intended for other ears.

"Ah, sir," Feldman added unexpectedly. "One of them insists on keeping his sidearms. Over."

"Then he can insist on staying outside my perimeter!" Jolober snarled. Vicki had laid a towel on the saddle before he mounted and was now using another to silently dry his body. "You can detach two guards to escort 'em if they need their hands held, but *nobody* brings powerguns into Paradise Port."

"Roger, I'll tell them," Feldman agreed doubtfully. "Over and out."

"I have a fresh uniform out," said Vicki, stepping back so that Jolober could follow her into the bedroom, where the air was drier.

"That's three, today," Jolober said, grinning. "Well, I've done a lot more than I've managed any three other days.

"Via," he added more seriously. "It's more headway than I've made since they appointed me commandant."

Vicki smiled, but her eyes were so tired that Jolober's body trembled in response. His flesh remembered how much he had already been through today and yearned for the sleep to which the hot bath had disposed it.

Jolober lifted himself on his hands so that Vicki could raise and cinch his trousers. He could do it himself, but he was in a hurry, and . . . besides, just as she'd said, Vicki was a part of him in a real way.

"Cheer up, love," he said as he closed his tunic. "It isn't done yet, but it's sure getting that way."

"Good-bye, Horace," the Doll said as she kissed him.

"Keep the bed warm," Jolober called as he slid toward the door and the inner staircase. His head was tumbling with memories and images. For a change, they were all pleasant ones.

★ ★ ★ ★

The port offices were easily identified at night because they *weren't* garishly illuminated like every other building in Paradise Port. Jolober had a small staff, and he didn't choose to waste it at desks. Outside of ordinary business hours, Central's artificial intelligence handled everything—by putting non-emergency requests on hold till morning, and by vectoring a uniformed patrol to the real business.

Anybody who insisted on personal service could get it by hammering at the Patrol entrance on the west side, opposite Jolober's private staircase. A patrolman would find the noisemaker a personal holding cell for the remainder of the night.

The front entrance was built like a vault door, not so much to prevent intrusion as to keep drunks from destroying the panel for reasons they'd be unable to remember sober. Jolober palmed the release for the separate bolting systems and had just begun to swing the door open in invitation when the two men in khaki uniforms, neither of them tall, strode up to the building.

"Blood and Martyrs!" Jolober said as he continued to back, not entirely because the door required it.

"You run a tight base here, Commandant," said Colonel Alois Hammer as he stepped into the waiting room. "Do you know my aide, Major Steuben?"

"By reputation only," said Jolober, nodding to Joachim Steuben with the formal correctness which that reputation enjoined. "Ah— with a little more information, I might have relaxed the prohibition on weapons."

Steuben closed the door behind them, moving the heavy panel with a control which belied the boyish delicacy of his face and frame. "If the colonel's satisfied with his security," Joachim said mildly, "then of course I am, too."

The eyes above his smile would willingly have watched Jolober drawn and quartered.

"You've had some problems with troops of mine today," said Hammer, seating himself on one of the chairs and rising again, almost as quickly as if he had continued to walk. His eyes touched

Jolober and moved on in short hops that covered everything in the room like an animal checking a new environment.

"Only reported problems occurred," said Jolober, keeping the promise he'd made earlier in the day. He lighted the hologram projection tank on the counter to let it warm up. "There was an incident a few hours ago, yes."

The promise didn't matter to Tad Hoffritz, not after the shootings; but it mattered more than life to Horace Jolober that he keep the bargains he'd made.

"According to Captain van Zuyle s report," Hammer said as his eyes flickered over furniture and recesses dim under the partial lighting, "you're of the opinion the boy was set up."

"What you do with a gun," said Joachim Steuben softly from the door against which he leaned, "is your own responsibility."

"As Joachim says," Hammer went on with a nod and no facial expression, "that doesn't affect how we'll deal with Captain Hoffritz when he's released from local custody. But it does affect how we act to prevent recurrences, doesn't it?"

"Load file Ike One into the downstairs holo," said Jolober to Central.

He looked at Hammer, paused till their eyes met. "Sure, he was set up, just like half a dozen others in the past three months—only they were money assessments, no real problem.

"And the data prove," Jolober continued coolly, claiming what his data suggested but could *not* prove, "that it's going to get a lot worse than what happened tonight if Red Ike and his Dolls aren't shipped out fast."

The holotank sprang to life in a three-dimensional cross-hatching of orange lines. As abruptly, the lines shrank into words and columns of figures. "Red Ike and his Dolls—they were all his openly, then—first show up on Sparrow-home a little over five years standard ago, according to Bonding Authority records. Then—"

Jolober pointed toward the figures. Colonel Hammer put his smaller, equally firm, hand over the commandant's and said, "Wait. Just give me your assessment."

"Dolls have been imported as recreational support in seven

conflicts," said Jolober as calmly as if his mind had not just shifted gears. He'd been a good combat commander for the same reason, for dealing with the situation that occurred rather than the one he'd planned for. "There's been rear-echelon trouble each time, and the riot on Ketelby caused the Bonding Authority to order the disbandment of a battalion of Guardforce O'Higgins."

"There was trouble over a woman," said Steuben unemotionally, reeling out the data he gathered because he was Hammer's adjutant as well as his bodyguard. "A fight between a ranger and an artillery-man led to a riot in which half the nearest town was burned."

"Not a woman," corrected Jolober. "A Doll."

He tapped the surface of the holotank. "It's all here, downloaded from Bonding Authority archives. You just have to see what's happening so you know the questions to ask."

"You can get me a line to the capital?" Hammer asked as if he were discussing the weather. "I was in a hurry, and I didn't bring along my usual commo."

Jolober lifted the visiplate folded into the surface of the counter beside the holotank and rotated it toward Hammer.

"I've always preferred nonhumans for recreation areas," Hammer said idly as his finger played over the plate's keypad. "Oh, the troops complain, but I've never seen *that* hurt combat efficiency. Whereas real women gave all sorts of problems."

"And real men," said Joachim Steuben, with a deadpan expression that could have meant anything.

The visiplate beeped. "Main Switch," said a voice, tart but not sleepy. "Go ahead."

"You have my authorization code," Hammer said to the human operator on the other end of the connection. From Jolober's flat angle to the plate, he couldn't make out the operator's features— only that he sat in a brightly illuminated white cubicle. "Patch me through to the chairman of the Facilities Inspection Committee."

"'Senator Dieter?" said the operator, professionally able to keep the question short of being amazement.

"If he's the chairman," Hammer said. The words had the angry undertone of a dynamite fuse burning.

"Yessir, she is," replied the operator with studied neutrality. "One moment, please."

"I've been dealing with her chief aide," said Jolober in a hasty whisper. "Guy named Higgey. His pager's loaded—"

"Got you a long ways, didn't it, Commandant?" Hammer said with a gun-turret click of his head toward Jolober.

"Your pardon, sir," said Jolober, bracing reflexively to attention. He wasn't Hammer's subordinate, but they both served the same ideal—getting the job done. The ball was in Hammer's court just now, and he'd ask for support if he thought he needed it.

From across the waiting room, Joachim Steuben smiled at Jolober. That one had the same ideal, perhaps; but his terms of reference were something else again.

"The senator isn't at any of her registered work stations," the operator reported coolly.

"Son," said Hammer, leaning toward the visiplate, "you have a unique opportunity to lose the war for Placida. All you have to do is *not* get me through to the chairman."

"Yes, Colonel Hammer," the operator replied with an aplomb that made it clear why he held the job he did. "I've processed your authorization, and I'm running it through again on War Emergency Ord—"

The last syllable was clipped. The bright rectangle of screen dimmed gray. Jolober slid his chair in a short arc so that he could see the visiplate clearly past Hammer's shoulder.

"What is it?" demanded the woman in the dim light beyond. She was stocky, middle-aged, and rather attractive because of the force of personality she radiated even sleepless in a dressing gown.

"This is Colonel Alois Hammer," Hammer said. "Are you recording?"

"On *this* circuit?" the senator replied with a frosty smile. "Of course I am. So are at least three other agencies, whether I will or no."

Hammer blinked, startled to find himself on the wrong end of a silly question for a change.

"Senator," he went on without the hectoring edge that had been present since his arrival. "A contractor engaged by your government to provide services at Paradise Port has been causing problems. One of the Léégèère's down, in critical, and I'm short a company commander over the same incident."

"You've reported to the port commandant?" Senator Dieter said, her eyes unblinking as they passed over Jolober.

"The commandant reported to me because your staff stonewalled him," Hammer said flatly while Jolober felt his skin grow cold, even the tips of the toes he no longer had. "I want the contractor, a nonhuman called Red Ike, off-planet in seventy-two hours with all his chattels. That specifically includes his Dolls. We'll work—"

"That's too soon," said Dieter, her fingers tugging a lock of hair over one ear while her mind worked. "Even if—"

"*Forty-eight* hours, Senator," Hammer interrupted. "This is a violation of your bond. And I promise you, I'll have the support of all the other commanders of units contracted to Placidan service. Forty-eight hours, or we'll withdraw from combat and you won't have a front line."

"You *can't—*" Dieter began. Then all muscles froze, tongue and fingers among them, as her mind considered the implications of what the colonel had just told her.

"I have no concern over being able to win my case at the Bonding Authority hearing on Earth," Hammer continued softly. "But I'm quite certain that the present Placidan government won't be there to contest it."

Dieter smiled without humor. "Seventy-two hours," she said as if repeating the figure.

"I've shifted the Regiment across continents in less time, Senator," Hammer said.

"Yes," said Dieter calmly. "Well, there are political consequences to any action, and I'd rather explain myself to my constituents than to an army of occupation. I'll take care of it."

She broke the circuit.

"I wouldn't mind getting to know that lady," said Hammer, mostly to himself, as he folded the visiplate back into the counter.

"That takes care of your concerns, then?" he added sharply, looking up at Jolober.

"Yes, sir, it does," said Jolober, who had the feeling he had drifted into a plane where dreams could be happy.

"Ah, about Captain Hoffritz . . ." Hammer said. His eyes slipped, but he snapped them back to meet Jolober's despite the embarrassment of being about to ask a favor.

"He's not combat-fit right now, Colonel," Jolober said, warming as authority flooded back to fill his mind. "He'll do as well in our care for the next few days as he would in yours. After that, and assuming that no one wants to press charges—"

"Understood," said Hammer, nodding. "I'll deal with the victim and General Claire."

"—then some accommodation can probably be arranged with the courts."

"It's been a pleasure dealing with a professional of your caliber, Commandant," Hammer said as he shook Jolober's hand. He spoke without emphasis, but nobody meeting his cool blue eyes could have imagined that Hammer would have bothered to lie about it.

"It's started to rain," observed Major Steuben as he muscled the door open.

"It's permitted to," Hammer said. "We've been wet be—"

"A jeep to the front of the building," Jolober ordered with his ring finger crooked. He straightened and said, "Ah, Colonel? Unless you'd like to be picked up by one of your own vehicles?"

"Nobody knows I'm here," said Hammer from the doorway. "I don't want van Zuyle to think I'm second-guessing him—I'm not, I'm just handling the part that's mine to handle."

He paused before adding with an ironic smile, "In any case, we're four hours from exploiting the salient Hoffritz's company formed when they took the junction at Kettering."

A jeep with two patrolmen, stunners ready, scraped to a halt outside. The team was primed for a situation like the one in the alley less than an hour before.

"Taxi service only, boys," Jolober called to the patrolmen. "Carry these gentlemen to their courier ship, please."

The jeep was spinning away in the drizzle before Jolober had closed and locked the door again. It didn't occur to him that it mattered whether or not the troops bivouacked around Paradise Port knew immediately what Hammer had just arranged.

And it didn't occur to him, as he bounced his chair up the stairs calling, "Vicki! We've won!" that he should feel any emotion except joy.

"Vicki!" he repeated as he opened the bedroom door. They'd have to leave Placida unless he could get Vicki released from the blanket order on Dolls—but he hadn't expected to keep his job anyway, not after he went over the head of the whole Placidan government.

"Vi—"

She'd left a light on, one of the point sources in the ceiling. It was a shock, but not nearly as bad a shock as Jolober would have gotten if he'd slid onto the bed in the dark.

"Who?" his tongue asked while his mind couldn't think of anything to say, could only move his chair to the bedside and palm the hydraulics to lower him into a sitting position.

Her right hand and forearm were undamaged. She flexed her fingers and the keen plastic blade shot from her fist, then collapsed again into a baton. She let it roll onto the bedclothes.

"He couldn't force me to kill you," Vicki said. "He was very surprised, very . . ."

Jolober thought she might be smiling, but he couldn't be sure since she no longer had lips. The plastic edges of the knife Vicki took as she dressed him were not sharp enough for finesse, but she had not attempted surgical delicacy.

Vicki had destroyed herself from her toes to her once-perfect face. All she had left was one eye with which to watch Jolober, and the parts of her body which she couldn't reach unaided. She had six ribs to a side, broader and flatter than those of a human skeleton. After she laid open the ribs, she had dissected the skin and flesh of the left side farther.

Jolober had always assumed—when he let himself think about it—that her breasts were sponge implants. He'd been wrong. On the bedspread lay a wad of yellowish fat streaked with blood vessels. He didn't have a background that would tell him whether or not it was human normal, but it certainly was biological.

It was a tribute to Vicki's toughness that she had remained alive as long as she had.

Instinct turned Jolober's head to the side so that he vomited away from the bed. He clasped Vicki's right hand with both of his, keeping his eyes closed so that he could imagine that everything was as it had been minutes before when he was triumphantly happy. His left wrist brushed the knife that should have remained an inert baton in any hands but his. He snatched up the weapon, feeling the blade flow out—

As it had when Vicki held it, turned it on herself.

"We are one, my Horace," she whispered, her hand squeezing his.

It was the last time she spoke, but Jolober couldn't be sure of that because his mind had shifted out of the present into a cosmos limited to the sense of touch: body-warm plastic in his left hand, and flesh cooling slowly in his right.

He sat in his separate cosmos for almost an hour, until the emergency call on his mastoid implant threw him back into an existence where his life had purpose.

"All units!" cried a voice on the panic push. "The—"

The blast of static which drowned the voice lasted only a fraction of a second before the implant's logic circuits shut the unit down to keep the white noise from driving Jolober mad. The implant would be disabled as long as the jamming continued—but jamming of this intensity would block even the most sophisticated equipment in the Slammers' tanks.

Which were probably carrying out the jamming.

Jolober's hand slipped the knife away without thinking—with fiery determination not to think—as his stump kicked the chair into life and he glided toward the alley stairs. He was still dressed, still mounted in his saddle, and that was as much as he was willing to know about his immediate surroundings.

The stairs rang. The thrust of his fans was a fitful gust on the metal treads each time he bounced on his way to the ground.

The voice could have been Feldman at the gate; she was the most likely source anyway. At the moment, Jolober had an emergency.

In a matter of minutes, it could be a disaster instead.

It was raining, a nasty drizzle which distorted the invitations capering on the building fronts. The street was empty except for a pair of patrol jeeps, bubbles in the night beneath canopies that would stop most of the droplets.

Even this weather shouldn't have kept soldiers from scurrying from one establishment to another, hoping to change their luck when they changed location. Overhanging facades ought to have been crowded with morose troopers, waiting for a lull—or someone drunk or angry enough to lead an exodus toward another empty destination.

The emptiness would have worried Jolober if he didn't have much better reasons for concern. The vehicles sliding down the street from the gate were unlighted, but there was no mistaking the roar of a tank.

Someone in the China Doll heard and understood the sound also, because the armored door squealed down across the archway even as Jolober's chair lifted him in that direction at high thrust.

He braked in a spray. The water-slicked pavement didn't affect his control, since the chair depended on thrust rather than friction—but being able to stop didn't give him any ideas about how he should proceed.

One of the patrol jeeps swung in front of the tank with a courage and panache which made Jolober proud of his men. The patrolman on the passenger side had ripped the canopy away to stand waving a yellow light-wand with furious determination.

The tank did not slow. It shifted direction just enough to strike the jeep a glancing blow instead of center-punching it. That didn't spare the vehicle; its light frame crumpled like tissue before it resisted enough to spin across the pavement at twice the velocity of the slowly advancing tank. The slight adjustment in angle did save the patrolmen, who were thrown clear instead of being ground between concrete and the steel skirts.

The tank's scarred turret made it identifiable in the light of the building fronts. Jolober crooked his finger and shouted, "Commandant to Corporal Days. For the *Lord's* sake, trooper, don't get your unit disbanded for mutiny! Colonel Hammer's already gotten Red Ike ordered off-planet!"

There was no burp from his mastoid as Central retransmitted the message a microsecond behind the original. Only then did Jolober recall that the Slammers had jammed his communications.

Not the Slammers alone. The two vehicles behind the tank were squat armored personnel carriers, each capable of hauling an infantry section with all its equipment. Nobody had bothered to paint out the fender markings of the Division Léégèère.

Rain stung Jolober's eyes as he hopped the last five meters to the sealed facade of the China Doll. Anything could be covered, could be settled, except murder—and killing Red Ike would be a murder of which the Bonding Authority would have to take cognizance.

"Let me in!" Jolober shouted to the door. The armor was so thick that it didn't ring when he pounded it. "Let me—"

Normally the sound of a mortar firing was audible for a kilometer, a hollow *shoomp!* like a firecracker going off in an oil drum. Jolober hadn't heard the launch from beyond the perimeter because of the nearby roar of drive fans.

When the round went off on the roof of the China Doll, the charge streamed tendrils of white fire down as far as the pavement, where they pocked the concrete. The snake-pit coruscance of blue sparks lighting the roof a moment later was the battery pack of Red Ike's aircar shorting through the new paths the mortar shell had burned in the car's circuitry.

The mercs were playing for keeps. They hadn't come to destroy the China Doll and leave its owner to rebuild somewhere else.

The lead tank swung in the street with the cautious delicacy of an elephant wearing a hoopskirt. Its driving lights blazed on, silhouetting the port commandant against the steel door. Jolober held out his palm in prohibition, knowing that if he could delay events even a minute, Red Ike would escape through his tunnel.

Everything else within the China Doll was a chattel which could be compensated with money.

There was a red flash and a roar from the stern of the tank, then an explosion muffled by a meter of concrete and volcanic rock. Buildings shuddered like sails in a squall; the front of the port offices cracked as its fabric was placed under a flexing strain that concrete was never meant to resist.

The rocket-assisted penetrators carried by the Slammers' tanks were intended to shatter bunkers of any thickness imaginable in the field. Red Ike's bolthole was now a long cavity filled with chunks and dust of the material intended to protect it.

The tanks had very good detection equipment, and combat troops live to become veterans by observing their surroundings. Quite clearly, the tunnel had not escaped notice when Tad Hoffritz led his company down the street to hoo-rah Paradise Port.

"Wait!" Jolober shouted, because there's always a chance until there's no chance at all.

"Get out of the way, Commandant!" boomed the tank's public address system, loudly enough to seem an echo of the penetrator's earth-shock.

"Colonel Hammer has—" Jolober shouted.

"We'd as soon not hurt you," the speakers roared as the turret squealed ten degrees on its gimbals. The main gun's bore was a 20cm tube aligned perfectly with Jolober's eyes.

They couldn't hear him; they wouldn't listen if they could; and anyway, the troopers involved in this weren't interested in contract law. They wanted justice, and to them that didn't mean a ticket off-planet for Red Ike.

The tribarrel in the tank's cupola fired a single shot. The bolt of directed energy struck the descending arch just in front of Jolober and gouged the plastic away in fire and black smoke. Bits of the covering continued to burn, and the underlying concrete added an odor of hot lime to the plastic and the ozone of the bolt's track through the air.

Jolober's miniature vehicle thrust him away in a flat arc, out of the door alcove and sideways in the street as a powergun fired from a port concealed in the China Doll's facade. The tank's main gun demolished the front wall with a single round.

The street echoed with the thunderclap of cold air filling the track seared through it by the energy bolt. The pistol shot an instant earlier could almost have been a proleptic reflection, confused in memory with the sun-bright cyan glare of the tank cannon—and, by being confused, forgotten.

Horace Jolober understood the situation too well to mistake its events. The shot meant Red Ike was still in the China Doll, trapped there and desperate enough to issue his Droid's lethal weapons that must have been difficult even for him to smuggle into Paradise Port.

Desperate and foolish, because the pistol bolt had only flicked dust from the tank's iridium turret. Jolober had warned Red Ike that combat troops played by a different rulebook. The message just hadn't been received until it was too late. . . .

Jolober swung into the three-meter alley beside the China Doll. There was neither an opening here nor ornamentation, just the blank concrete wall of a fortress.

Which wouldn't hold for thirty seconds if the combat team out front chose to assault it.

The tank had fired at the building front, not the door. The main gun could have blasted a hole in the armor, but that wouldn't have been a large enough entrance for the infantry now deploying behind the armored flanks of the APCs.

The concrete wall shattered like a bomb when it tried to absorb the point-blank energy of the 20cm gun. The cavity the shot left was big enough to pass a jeep with a careful driver. Infantrymen in battle armor, hunched over their weapons, dived into the China Doll. The interior lit with cyan flashes as they shot everything that moved.

The exterior lighting had gone out, but flames clawed their way up the thermoplastic facade. The fire threw a red light onto the street in which shadows of smoke capered like demons. Drips traced blazing lines through the air as they fell to spatter troops waiting their turn for a chance to kill.

The assault didn't require a full infantry platoon, but few operations have failed because the attackers had too many troops.

Jolober had seen the equivalent too often to doubt how it was going to go this time. He didn't have long; very possibly he didn't have long enough.

Standing parallel to the sheer sidewall, Jolober ran his fans up to full power, then clamped the plenum chamber into a tight nozzle and lifted. His left hand paddled against the wall three times. That gave him balance and the suggestion of added thrust to help his screaming fans carry out a task for which they hadn't been designed.

When his palm touched the coping, Jolober used the contact to center him, and rotated onto the flat roof of the China Doll.

Sparks spat peevishly from the corpse of the aircar. The vehicle's frame was a twisted wire sculpture from which most of the sheathing material had burned away, but occasionally the breeze brought oxygen to a scrap that was still combustible.

The penthouse that held Ike's office and living quarters was a squat box beyond the aircar. The mortar shell had detonated just as the alien started to run for his vehicle.

He'd gotten back inside as the incendiary compound sprayed the roof, but bouncing fragments left black trails across the plush blue floor of the office.

The door was a section of wall broad enough to have passed the aircar. Red Ike hadn't bothered to close it when he fled to his elevator and the tunnel exit. Jolober, skimming again on ground effect, slid into the office shouting, "Ike! This—"

Red Ike burst from the elevator cage as the door rotated open. He had a pistol and eyes as wide as a madman's as he swung the weapon toward the hulking figure in his office.

Jolober reacted as the adrenaline pumping through his body had primed him to do. The arm with which he swatted at the pistol was long enough that his fingers touched the barrel, strong enough that the touch hurled the gun across the room despite Red Ike's deathgrip on the butt.

Red Ike screamed.

An explosion in the elevator shaft wedged the elevator doors as they began to close and burped orange flame against the far wall.

Jolober didn't know how the assault team proposed to get to the roof, but neither did he intend to wait around to learn. He wrapped both arms around the stocky alien and shouted, "Shut up and hold still if you want to get out of here alive!"

Red Ike froze, either because he understood the warning—or because at last he recognized Horace Jolober and panicked to realize that the port commandant had already disarmed him.

Jolober lifted the alien and turned his chair. It glided toward the door at gathering speed, logy with the double burden.

There was another blast from the office. The assault team had cleared the elevator shaft with a cratering charge whose directed blast sprayed the room with the bits and vapors that remained of the cage. Grenades would be next, then grappling hooks and more grenades just before—

Jolober kicked his throttle as he rounded the aircar. The fans snarled and the ride, still on ground effect, became greasy as the skirts lifted undesirably.

The office rocked in a series of dense white flashes. The room lights went out and a large piece of shrapnel, the fuze housing of a grenade, powdered a fist-sized mass of the concrete coping beside Jolober.

His chair's throttle had a gate. With the fans already at normal maximum, he sphinctered his skirts into a nozzle and kicked again at the throttle. He could smell the chair's circuits frying under the overload as it lifted Jolober and Red Ike to the coping—

But it did lift them, and after a meter's run along the narrow track to build speed, it launched them across the black, empty air of the alley.

Red Ike wailed. The only sound Horace Jolober made was in his mind. He saw not a roof but the looming bow of a tank, and his fears shouted the word they hadn't been able to get out on Primavera either: *"No!"*

They cleared the coping of the other roof with a click, not a crash, and bounced as Jolober spilled air and cut thrust back to normal levels.

An explosion behind them lit the night red and blew chunks of Red Ike's office a hundred meters in the air.

Instead of trying to winkle out their quarry with gunfire, the assault team had lobbed a bunker-buster up the elevator shaft. The blast walloped Jolober even though distance and the pair of meter-high concrete copings protected his hunching form from dangerous fragments.

Nothing in the penthouse of the China Doll could have survived. It wasn't neat, but it saved lives where they counted—in the attacking force—and veteran soldiers have never put a high premium on finesse.

"You saved me," Red Ike said.

Jolober's ears were numb from the final explosion, but he could watch Red Ike's lips move in the flames lifting even higher from the front of the China Doll.

"I had to," Jolober said, marvelling at how fully human the alien seemed.

"Those men, they're line soldiers. They think that because there were so many of them involved, nobody can be punished."

Hatches rang shut on the armored personnel carriers.

A noncom snarled an order to stragglers that could be heard even over the drive fans.

Red Ike started toward the undamaged aircar parked beside them on this roof. Jolober's left hand still held the alien's wrist. Ike paused as if to pretend his movement had never taken place. His face was emotionless.

"Numbers made it a mutiny," Jolober continued. Part of him wondered whether Red Ike could hear the words he was speaking in a soft voice, but he was unwilling to shout.

It would have been disrespectful.

Fierce wind rocked the flames as the armored vehicles, tank in the lead as before, lifted and began to howl their way out of Paradise Port.

"I'll take care of you," Red Ike said. "You'll have Vicki back in three weeks, I promise. Tailored to *you,* just like the other. You won't be able to tell the difference."

"There's no me to take care of anymore," said Horace Jolober with no more emotion than a man tossing his uniform into a laundry hamper.

"You see," he added as he reached behind him, "if they'd killed you tonight, the Bonding Authority would have disbanded both units *whatever* the Placidans wanted. But me? Anything I do is my responsibility."

Red Ike began to scream in a voice that became progressively less human as the sound continued.

Horace Jolober was strong enough that he wouldn't have needed the knife despite the way his victim struggled.

But it seemed like a fitting monument for Vicki.

M91A COMBAT CAR

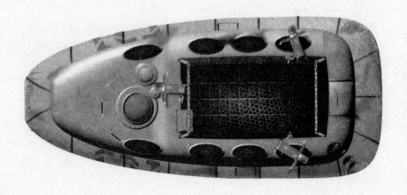

NIGHT MARCH

Panchin heard Sergeant-Commander Jonas swear softly as he tried to coax anything more than a splutter from the ionization-track communicator. The wind blew a hiss of sand against *Hula Girl*'s iridium armor.

On a map of any practical scale this swatch of desert would look as flat as a mirror, but brush and rocky knobs limited Reg Panchin's view to a hundred meters in any direction from the combat car's right wing gun. Night stripped the terrain of all color but grays and purple-grays. Panchin could have added false color to the light-amplified view through the face shield of his commo helmet, but that would have made the landscape even more alien—and Panchin more lonely.

"I'm curst if I know what they're fighting over," muttered the driver, Trooper Rita Cortezar, over *Hula Girl*'s intercom channel. "I sure don't see anything here worth getting killed over."

Frosty Ericssen chuckled from the left gun. "Did you ever see a stretch of country that looked much better than this does, Tits?" he asked. "At least after we got through blowing it inside out, I mean."

Panchin was a Clerk/Specialist with G Company's headquarters section. He rode *Hula Girl* during the change of base because the combat car was short a crewman and HQ's command car was overloaded. You had to know Cortezar better than he did to call her "Tits" to her face.

Hula Girl carried three tribarreled powerguns—left wing, right wing, and the commander's weapon mounted on the forward bulkhead to fire over the driver's head. Space in the rear fighting compartment was always tight, but the change of base made the situation even worse than it would have been on a normal combat patrol.

A beryllium fishnet hung on steel stakes a meter above the bulkheads. It was meant to catch mortar bombs and similar low-velocity projectiles before they landed in the fighting compartment, but inevitably it swayed with the weight of the crew's personal baggage. More gear was slung to the outside of the armor, and the deck of the compartment was covered with a layer of ammo cans.

"They're fighting about power, not territory," Panchin said. Spiky branches quivered as wind swept a hillock, then danced toward *Hula Girl* in a dust devil that quickly dispersed. "Everybody on Sulewesi's a Malay, but they came in two waves—original colonists and the batch brought in three generations afterwards. The first lot claims to own everything, including the folks who came later. Eventually the other guys decided to do something about it."

Reg Panchin wasn't so much frightened as empty: he'd never expected to be out in the middle of a hostile nowhere like this. He supposed the line troopers were used to it. Talking about something he knew didn't help Panchin a lot, but it helped.

"We're working for the old guys, right?" Frosty said.

"Right," Panchin said. "Hammer's Slammers support the Sulewesi government. The rebels have a Council. I don't guess there's a lot to choose except who's paying who."

Sergeant Jonas straightened and patted the communicator. "Well, this thing's fucked," he said in a conversational tone. "I can't get more than three words at a time from Scepter Base. If they've got a better fix on the missing column than we do, they can't send it so I hear it."

Hula Girl's crew knew exactly where they were. Sulewesi had been mapped by satellite before the war broke out, and the combat car's inertial navigation system was accurate to within a meter in a day's travel. That didn't tell the Slammers where the missing platoon of local troops was, though.

"So let's go home," Frosty said. He relaxed a catch of his clamshell body armor to scratch his armpit. "I'm not thrilled being out alone in Injun Country like this."

"It might be the transmitter at Scepter Base," Panchin said. He squeezed the edge of the bulkhead between thumb and forefinger to remind himself of how thick the armor was between him and hostile guns. "Goldman was working on it before the move. She said the traverse was getting wonky."

"Fucking wonderful," Cortezar said. "Just wonderful."

Long-distance communications for Hammer's Slammers on Sulewesi were by microwaves bounced off the momentary ionization tracks meteors drew in the upper atmosphere. The commo bursts were tight-beam and couldn't be either jammed or intercepted by hostile forces.

That same directionality was the problem now. Unless the bursts were precisely aligned, they didn't reach their destination. *Hula Girl*'s crew had been out of communication with the remainder of the force ever since Captain Stenhuber sent them off to find a column that had gotten separated from the main body during the change of base.

"Rita, ease us forward a half klick on this heading," Jonas said. "We'll check again there. If that doesn't work we'll head for the barn."

He gave Ericssen a gloomy nod, then lifted his commo helmet with one hand to rub his scalp with the other. The sergeant was completely bald, though his eyebrows were unusually thick for a man of African ancestry.

"That won't be too soon for me," Frosty muttered.

Cortezar switched on the fans and let them spin for a moment before she flared the blades to lift the car. Even on idle the drive fans roared as they sucked air through the armored intake vents. There was no chance of hearing the missing column while the fans were running, though the acoustics of a landscape baffled with gullies, knolls, and clumps of brush up to four meters high made sound a doubtful guide here.

Hula Girl lifted with a greasy shudder. Sand sprayed through the narrow gap between the ground and the lower edge of the steel skirts enclosing the air cushion on which the combat car rode. A fusion bottle powered the eight drive fans. They in turn raised the pressure in the plenum chamber high enough to support the vehicle's thirty tonnes on ground effect. A combat car couldn't fly, but it could dance across quicksand or bodies of still water because the bubble of air spread the car's weight evenly over any surface.

"What did the locals do before they had us for guide dogs?" Cortezar asked as she took *Hula Girl* down one of the channels winding though the desert. The car wasn't moving much faster than a man could walk.

Wind and the occasional flash flood scoured away the soil here except where it was bound by rocks or the roots of plants. The desert vegetation stood on pedestals of its own making.

"They used positioning satellites," Panchin said. "The whole constellation got blasted as soon as the shooting started."

He'd read up on the planet when the Slammers took the Sulewesi Government contract. Mostly the line troopers didn't bother with the briefing materials. The information usually didn't affect mercenaries enough to matter more than a poker game did, but Panchin was interested.

"That puts both sides in the same leaky boat, don't it?" Frosty asked. "You'd think they could've figured that out and left the satellites up so that we could get some sleep."

"In a few minutes we'll head for Scepter Base," Jonas said in a reasonable tone. "I'll see if I can't keep us off perimeter watch for tonight. What's left of it."

The sergeant obviously didn't like the situation either, but his rank kept him from grumbling about orders. Ericssen would have probably acted the same as Jonas if their positions had been reversed. Mercenary soldiering had never been the easiest way to earn a living. People who didn't know that when they signed on with the Slammers learned it quick enough thereafter.

Hula Girl's intakes made the brush to either side wobble toward the vehicle. Gossamer fuzz as long as a man's fingers hung from the branches. The tendrils sucked moisture from the air at night when the relative humidity rose, though the vegetation only flowered after a rain.

It might not rain here for years.

"If they'd left the satellites up to begin with," Panchin said, "then one side or the other would've knocked them down when they thought that gave them an advantage. Maybe before an attack, when they had their people in position already. We'd still be out here."

War is a costly business. Importing mercenaries and their specialist equipment from off-planet is devastatingly expensive, but at least in the short run it costs less than losing. Both sides on Sulewesi had hired a few of the best and most expensive troops in the human universe. Hammer's Slammers were paid by the government, while the rebels had three comparable armored battalions from Brazil on Earth.

Four or five thousand soldiers, no matter how well equipped, weren't enough to fight a war across the whole surface of a planet; locally raised forces could only be trained as mechanized infantry because time was so short. To bridge the gap between the general mass and the highly paid cutting edge, the government and rebels both used less-sophisticated mercenaries. The midrange troops provided weapons and communications of a higher order than those produced on Sulewesi, but at a tenth the cost of outfits like the Slammers and the Brazilians.

A tenth as effective, too, the Slammers thought; but a pipe gun throwing a chunk of lead was still enough to splash your brains across the deck of a tank if you happened to be in the wrong place. War didn't stop being a dangerous business just because you were good at it.

Cortezar goosed the fans to take *Hula Girl* onto a ridge whose rocks had resisted the wind better than the light soil to either side. The skirts rubbed stones, clanking and throwing sparks. Ball-shaped vegetation flattened and shivered away from the gale that squirted under the plenum chamber.

Panchin held firmly onto the twin spade grips of his tribarrel as the deck slanted beneath his boots. "I don't see why they had to split the Regiment up this way," he said. "You can't blame Captain Stenhuber sending us out alone when all he's got to work with is seven combat cars and the G Company command vehicle."

"Yeah," Frosty agreed. "If we were all together we'd go through everything else on this planet like a spike through an eyeball."

"You bet we would," Jonas said in grim disapproval. "And while we were doing that, the rebels'd smash the rest of the government army, putting a platoon or two of Brazilian armor on point each time. The people who hired us want to win the war, not just one battle."

"The odometer says this is half a kilometer, Sarge," Cortezar said with an edge in her voice. Reg Panchin felt alone, but really he was elbow to elbow with two fellow troopers. Cortezar sat by herself in the driver's compartment, and she was a meter closer to the most likely direction for a first shot besides.

"Yeah, all right," Jonas agreed. "I make Scepter Base forty-two degrees from here, but we'll want to dodge—"

A hand flare popped against the heavens and drained back to the desert floor as a shower of silver droplets. Panchin wasn't an expert at judging distances at night, but he didn't imagine the signal could have been launched from more than half a kilometer away.

"Bloody hell," said Ericssen. "We found them after all."

Jonas tilted the muzzles of his tribarrel skyward and tapped out three spaced rounds on the butterfly trigger between the grips. Each bolt of copper plasma lit the night cyan. Heated air cracked shut behind each hissing discharge.

"Head for the flare, Rita," the sergeant ordered. "But take it easy—I want to raise them with the laser communicator before we go barreling in."

Frosty nodded. "There's no such thing as friendly fire," he agreed. "And if they're not trigger happy, they ought to be with as many rebels as there are operating in this sandbox."

Three flares and at least a dozen bursts of automatic gunfire lofted skyward from the previous location northeast of *Hula Girl*. Distance thinned the muzzle blasts to a nervous rustling, like brushes stroking a drumhead. The tracers were the white used by local forces and a strobing pink that Panchin hadn't seen before.

He switched through the UHF and VHF bands on his commo helmet but only picked up static. He couldn't tell whether the problem was the helmet—even intercom was scratchy; this desert, where mineral deposits and temperature inversions played hell with everything in the electro-optical spectrum—or most likely, that nobody in the missing column was transmitting on any push that *Hula Girl's* crew had been given for the operation.

The combat car ambled toward the flares as Sergeant Jonas bent over the multifunction display fixed to the bulkhead beside his tribarrel. Panchin echoed the display for a moment on his face shield but cut back quickly to light amplification of his normal viewpoint. If he'd been in the Tactical Operations Center at Scepter Base where he belonged, it might have been interesting to watch blurs resolve into icons against a terrain map as the car processed sensor data on the column *Hula Girl* was approaching. Out here it might mean that Reg Panchin, right wing gunner, didn't see the hostile who was aiming a buzzbomb at *Hula Girl*.

Ericssen must have been thinking the same thing. He touched a button on the tribarrel's pintle. The barrel group rotated a third of a turn; a flat 2cm disk clucked from the ejection slot. The disk was a polyurethane matrix holding an alignment of copper atoms which, when stripped in a powergun's chamber, streamed downrange as a ravening cyan plasma. Frosty was checking—again—to make sure that his weapon was loaded and ready.

There was nothing on Panchin's side of the car. Nothing but wind and desert.

"Hold here, Rita," Jonas ordered. He started to raise the communications mast even before *Hula Girl* settled on idling fans.

Panchin helped set the bracing wires of the telescoping five-meter mast; this was something he'd done before. Jonas used a joystick to align the transceiver head and began to speak into the separate microphone. The lens on top of the mast directed his words over the intervening brush and sand to the local column in the form of a modulated laser beam.

After a moment the sergeant straightened. "All right, they're expecting us," he said. "Take us in, Rita."

To save time he collapsed the mast without undoing the wires; they wound like spiderweb across the fighting compartment. Panchin coiled them quickly on their spools, smoothing kinks with his left hand.

Hula Girl wallowed over another crest. The column they'd been searching for was halted in the broad gully below. That was probably part of the reason they'd been out of communications for so long. Panchin had been a soldier too long to be surprised that nobody'd had sense enough to drive one of the working vehicles onto a ridge for a better signal.

There were four Sulewesi-built six-wheeled armored personnel carriers and a command vehicle that was similar but slightly larger than the APCs; it had four axles instead of three. The recovery/repair vehicle with a crane and parts lockers used the longer chassis as well.

Besides the locals, the column contained three medium tanks with caterpillar tracks, ceramic armor, and a long coil gun in the hull. The tanks' turbine engines whined, but power for the coil guns must come from another source—probably magneto-hydrodynamic generators. A small cupola offset on the hull contained an automatic weapon.

One tank towed another. The third tank was towing an APC. The recovery vehicle towed a second APC; and, judging by the removed cover plates, the command vehicle had broken down also. Troops in a variety of uniforms stood around the vehicles. Some of them waved.

"Typical ratfuck," Jonas muttered. "Ninety klicks is too far for a change of base even when everybody knows what he's doing."

Hula Girl started down the slope. Cortezar deliberately broke away the gully rim to ease the angle. Sand and pebbles, some of them big enough to whang like bullets against the skirts, blasted ahead of the car in a spreading cloud.

"We going to be able to talk to these people?" Frosty asked. He had to use helmet intercom for Jonas to hear the question over the fan noise.

"The CO, Major Lebusan, spoke good Standard," Jonas said. "The rest of them, I dunno. Probably not."

Most rich people on Sulewesi were well educated and spoke Standard, the interstellar commercial language. Most rich people also managed to stay out of the military, at least the part of the military that might have to do some fighting. A few of the Slammers learned languages for fun, but nobody aboard *Hula Girl* knew more Malay than was necessary to ask for sex or a drink.

Cortezar slowed to a halt beside the command vehicle and cut the fans. A small man covered his face with a spotted bandanna until the dust had settled, then stepped forward. He wore a saucer hat with gold braid and his uniform was tailored; he'd probably been dapper some twenty hours earlier at the start of the march.

"I am Major Lebusan," the local said. "Can you fix my vehicle? That would be best."

"We're not mechanics, Major," Sergeant Jonas said. He swung a leg over the bulkhead.

"I've worked on diesels," Cortezar said as she climbed out of the driver's compartment.

"We'll take a look then," Jonas said. He jumped to the ground. "Frosty, you keep an eye on the sensors, will you?"

Panchin took that as clearance for him to leave *Hula Girl* also. The ground would feel good for a change, and it'd be nice to have more elbow room than there was in the fighting compartment.

A burly man with a full black beard walked over to Panchin. He wore a ripple-camouflaged uniform of a style Panchin hadn't seen before. The holster across the center of his chest held a heavy sidearm with a folding stock.

"I Dolgov," the man said, extending a big hand to Panchin. Panchin took it, expecting—correctly—that Dolgov would squeeze hard as they shook. "Zaporoskiye Brigade. Tanks!"

Dolgov pointed to the tank being towed. "Electrics all go out, poof! Kaput. These Sulewesi monkeys, they not real mechanics. Good for nothing monkeys!"

Panchin wondered how well the Zaporoskiye maintenance section would do with *Hula Girl* if she broke down. The range in sophistication was no greater. Of course, the locals didn't seem able to repair their own command vehicle. Aloud he said, "We'll guide you to the firebase. Somebody there can fix you up, right?"

"Yah, monkeys," Dolgov said, shaking his head morosely. He spat into the night.

Before Panchin could figure out whether that was a "yes" or a "no," Jonas called, "Hey Panchin! Get over here, will you?"

He nodded to Dolgov and joined the group around the command vehicle. Cortezar had stepped away and the locals were closing the engine compartment again. A gas lantern hanging from a cable hook on a fender threw white light across the ground and nearby personnel from their waists down.

"You double-checked the base coordinates, didn't you?" Jonas asked bluntly. "The major here says it's grid A27, 4-4-9, 1-3-0."

"Negative!" Panchin said, feeling cold inside. He *had* checked the coordinates in the TOC before *Hula Girl* left Trident Base, though. "A-2-7, that's a roger, but the block was 6-2-1, 5-2-5."

Major Lebusan took off his fancy hat and slapped it angrily against his thigh.

His uniform was green with a touch of mustard yellow. Though the major wore short-sleeved field kit except for the hat, an array of medal ribbons spilled from his left breast to his right.

"That is not right!" he said. "Look, I show you!"

He snapped his fingers. An aide handed him a clipboard holding a map covered in clear plastic. Panchin and the sergeant both bent to read it. The crayon markings on the plastic were in cursive Malay script, but the circle drawn over Knoll 45/13 on the printed map was clear enough.

"Sarge," Frosty said over the intercom, "I'll bet they're in one of the outlying companies. I never saw those tanks at any of the fire-bases we've operated out of."

"I'll bet he's right," Panchin said. He wasn't sure if Zaporoskiye was a place or just the name of a freelance unit raised on some Slavic planet.

Sergeant Jonas lifted his helmet and rubbed his bare scalp again. "All right," he said tiredly. "Scepter Base is ten klicks away. I wasn't willing to tow this pig—"

He nodded at the command vehicle.

"—that far. But I guess we can manage three. Panchin, give me a hand. We'll use our own towlines."

Under his breath to Panchin as they walked to *Hula Girl*, the sergeant added, "Because their bloody cables won't be worth any more than any of the other bloody equipment on this bloody planet!"

"And you will carry me in your tank, please," Major Lebusan called after them.

Major Lebusan's presence made *Hula Girl's* fighting compartment a little more cramped, but he was a small man and didn't wear body armor like the three Slammers. Panchin couldn't blame the major for riding with them. The broken-down command vehicle had no power for its communication devices, and *Hula Girl's* fans kicked a quite astounding amount of sand and dust over it besides.

The grip of the Sulewesan vehicle's wheels meant that sometimes it jerked *Hula Girl* unexpectedly, even though the combat car was heavier and had plenty of excess power for the tow. Friction with the soil was a more efficient means of braking than the vectored thrust of an air-cushion vehicle like *Hula Girl*.

For three kilometers it was bearable. There were rebels all over this stretch of desert. Abandoning a broken-down vehicle could mean making the other side a gift of it.

"Are there going to be any friendlies at this outpost?" Cortezar asked over the intercom. "Slammers, I mean."

"Negative," Panchin said. "I'd have handled their supply requests if there were."

That was his job: supply clerk for the 1st and 2nd Platoons of G Company, Hammer's Slammers; assigned to the government's Desert Dragons combat group, a motley assortment of locals and off-planet mercenaries in roughly regimental strength. The Slammers' combat cars had been perimeter security for the main body during the change of base. It was *Hula Girl's* bad luck that she was the nearest car to where the missing column was supposed to be; and Reg Panchin's bad luck that he happened to be riding her instead of another vehicle.

The column was echeloned back to the left of *Hula Girl* and her tow to avoid the worst of the dust. The personnel of broken-down vehicles were all packed onto others. A rebel ambush would mean a massacre; but again, Panchin understood why the weary locals wanted to escape choking discomfort even at the risk of their lives.

"Sarge, we ought to have a sight of them from the next rise," Cortezar said. Her compartment had a multi function display like the commander's, so she didn't have to echo the terrain map on her face shield as Panchin could have done.

"Right, I'm getting their signatures already," Jonas said. He sounded a little concerned. "Keep us hull down and I'll let the major talk us in on the laser. We don't have any of the codes for this laager."

Cortezar slowed *Hula Girl* carefully, then cut her steering yoke to the left so that the Sulewesan command vehicle didn't slam them from behind as it rolled off the last of its inertia. Flares were the only way to signal the remainder of the column, and Jonas wasn't willing to target *Hula Girl* that way. The other vehicles, local and Zaporoskiye alike, stopped anyway without command. Their crews didn't know how close the laager was, and they didn't want to be leading a trek through the desert. Both sides had troops scattered throughout the region.

Sergeant Jonas deployed the mast. Panchin stared at the desert, switching his face shield repeatedly from thermal viewing to light amplification and back again. He thought one enhancement technique might disclose something that he'd missed using the other. Rebels could be lurking just outside the laager, their electro-magnetic signatures hidden by those of the friendly vehicles; waiting to ambush late-comers like *Hula Girl* and the column she was shepherding in.

There was nothing but sand and bushes bending in the night wind. In the false-color thermal display, dew-gathering tendrils were a cool blue against the warmer orange of the branches from which they hung.

Major Lebusan talked animatedly on the communicator, waving his arms. Jonas watched the night ahead, his hands on his tribarrel's grip. The line troopers knew even better than a clerk like Panchin that this was a dangerous location.

Troops on the other halted vehicles called questions. When that brought no response, an officer in a less-ornate version of Lebusan's uniform jumped from the nearest APC and ran over to *Hula Girl*. He spoke in quick Malay beside the combat car. The skirts and bulkhead were so high that the small man close to the vehicle couldn't see the major in the fighting compartment.

Frosty Ericssen looked down from his gun. "We're talking to the laager, buddy," he said to the local in Standard. "Do you understand? Your friends are right over the hill there."

"Ah!" said the local. He ran back to the APC, chattering loudly.

Lebusan turned from the microphone fixed at the base of the mast. "Yes, yes, we're clear to enter," he said angrily to Jonas. "Where was I? they ask! They abandon me in the desert and they claim *I'm* at fault?"

Jonas telescoped the mast. Moving stresses would break the raised wand. Panchin helped the sergeant coil the braces as he had before.

An engine roared. The nearer APC started forward, spraying gravel from all six wheels. The remainder of the column followed a moment later. It was like watching the starting grid of a race. Two routes over the low ridge merged beyond a grove of shrubs with intertwined branches. Panchin expected to see a collision, but the recovery vehicle gave way at the last moment to the tank towing an APC.

Jonas shook his head in disgust as he locked the mast in place. "Take us in, Rita," he said. "I guess we eat dust for the last half klick."

Hula Girl accelerated slowly: a quick jerk against the inertia of the command vehicle would snap the tow cables. Dust from the rest of the column was almost a wall rather than a cloud. Panchin breathed through his helmet filters. An electrostatic charge was supposed to keep his face shield clear, but some of the grit was too large to be repelled. Lebusan covered his face with his bandanna again.

This ridge was a slightly lower step of Knoll 45/13. When *Hula Girl* topped it, the laager was in view just ahead. APCs and

Zaporoskiye tanks faced out from a circle so that their thicker bow armor and main weapons were toward a potential enemy.

There were many more vehicles than Panchin had expected to see.

"Via, Sarge!" Ericssen said. "That's the firebase, not an outpost. Did they give us the wrong coordinates?"

So quietly that his crew could barely hear him over the intercom, Sergeant Jonas said, "Those are Brazilian free-launch artillery vehicles. They aren't ours."

Major Lebusan bobbed his head enthusiastically. "I used to complain because the Council spent so much money on you Brazilians but didn't pay its own officers properly," he shouted through the bandanna. "Now I know you're worth the expense!"

Panchin looked over his shoulder. The locals still aboard the command vehicle were inside with the hatches closed; dust turned all the surfaces white, armor and vision blocks alike. Nobody could see what was happening aboard *Hula Girl*.

He smiled at Major Lebusan and kneed him in the groin.

The rebel officer doubled up with a squeal. His hat fell off. Ericssen chopped Lebusan on the back of the head with the butt of a grenade launcher.

Panchin felt cold and sick to his stomach. He had to consciously force his lips to straighten out of the frozen smile.

Ericssen tossed the rebel major over the side. Lebusan was a small man, but it was still an impressive one-handed lift by the gunner. Hysterical strength, very likely.

"Awaiting instructions!" Cortezar said urgently.

"Keep going," Sergeant Jonas said. He sounded calm. "We'll never get away if we turn around a hundred meters from them. We'll proceed till they notice us, then bull straight in and raise so much hell that maybe we'll be able to get out the other side."

"I make it four Brazilian launchers and a calliope," Cortezar said. Her voice was an octave higher than normal, but she didn't speak any faster than usual. "The rest of the hardware's local or Zaporoskiye like the folks in the column. That what you've got, too, Sarge?"

"There ought to be a second calliope with a battery of artillery," Jonas said. "Maybe it's deadlined, but don't count on that."

The Slammers depended on the 2cm tribarrels of their tanks and combat cars to sweep incoming shells and missiles from the sky. Most other high-end mercenary units used specialized equipment to protect themselves from artillery. Calliopes, eight- or nine-tube fixed powergun arrays, could blast incoming even if one or more of the individual guns jammed.

They could also shred a combat car the way a shark tears a man.

"Brigadier Vijanta's going to be pleased to know where to find the rebel main body," Ericssen said sourly. "If we get to Scepter Base to tell him, that is."

Panchin was suddenly thankful for the dust. His sweaty hands wouldn't slip from the grips of his tribarrel.

"Rita, when I give the word, break the tow lines," Jonas said. "We won't have time to do it any other way. Wing guns shoot at everything on your side. Try to get the launchers and any reload vehicles. Remember, we need to confuse them for long enough to get away."

The Slammers' own rocket howitzers fired individual rounds from a tube with a closed breech. The Brazilians launched from open troughs, a less efficient technique. In exchange for needing more fuel to reach a given range, the Brazilians were able to mount their artillery on much lighter chassis than the Slammers' massive Hogs.

Ericssen turned his head. "You okay with this, Panchin?" he asked.

Panchin nodded. "I'm okay," he said. His mouth was dry and his soul was already trying to squeeze free. He knew in a moment his body would be ripped and burned.

The rebels hadn't raised a dirt berm around the encampment for protection, but the air-cushion artillery vehicles were dug in hull deep. Soldiers were filling sandbags under artificial light. The layout was at least as professional as that of a government firebase.

A pair of female soldiers lounged against a sandbag bunker near the entrance, drinking from a bottle they passed back and forth.

They wore chameleon-weave uniforms whose fabric adjusted to match the background patterns.

One of the soldiers straightened and spoke to her companion. They both stared at *Hula Girl*, now only forty meters away.

"Hit it!" Sergeant Jonas shouted as his tribarrel lashed the night. His cyan bolts missed the Brazilian women, but he blew the side of the bunker in. The metal-plank roof buried the gun position.

Hula Girl lurched forward on the full thrust of her fans. The right tow cable parted. The combat car and the command vehicle whipsawed on the remaining cable. *Hula Girl* sideswiped the Zaporoskiye tank being towed by its fellow ahead of them. The impact helped Cortezar fight her controls straight. She continued to accelerate, pulling the command vehicle into the pair of tanks in a crash that finally broke the cable.

Panchin pressed his trigger with both thumbs, blinking reflexively. The barrel group spun at 500 rpm. Each stubby iridium tube fired with a *hissCRACK* when it rotated into the top position, then ejected the spent matrix from the port in a spurt of liquid nitrogen before loading a fresh round in the third station on the receiver.

He aimed at a parked APC but shot high, raking the roof of a tent in the center of the encampment. The sidewalls were heavily sandbagged, but the center pole shattered and dropped blazing canvas into the interior.

Frosty Ericssen's bolts glanced crazily from the turtle-backed hull of a Zaporoskiye tank. When the ceramic armor finally failed, the tank exploded in a mushroom of flame—fuel for the turbine and the main gun's MHD generator.

Hula Girl drove into the crowded firebase at 40 kph and still accelerating. Panchin squeezed the butterfly trigger, remembering to fire short bursts. His face shield blanked the bolts' intense blue-green glare to save his vision. He didn't hit what he aimed at— he was constantly behind his targets even though he tried to allow for the combat car's acceleration. He'd lowered his muzzles, and there were too many targets to miss everything.

When he shot at the three crew members running for a Zaporoskiye tank, his bolts slapped the flank of their vehicle instead.

The cyan reflection threw the men down anyway, their clothing afire.

Hula Girl skidded. Panchin aimed at the open rear hatch of an APC close enough to spit into but punched the side of a carrier twenty meters away. The steel armor burned white in the heat of the plasma; then the whole vehicle erupted. The commander's cupola spun out of the fireball.

Cortezar was dodging obstacles as best she could, but *Hula Girl* repeatedly brushed a vehicle or a sandbag wall. The skirts were sturdy, but they weren't a bulldozer blade. If the plenum chamber was too damaged to hold high-pressure air, the car became a sitting duck for everything a regimental firebase could throw at her.

An explosion with three distinct pulses hammered the camp. *Hula Girl* spun ninety degrees before Cortezar got her under control again. The quivering yellow flare threw the shadows of men and equipment a kilometer across the desert. Jonas or Ericssen had hit an artillery vehicle, detonating some of the ready ammo.

Metal clanged discordantly. Pink tracers clipped one of the stakes holding *Hula Girl*'s overhead screen and kicked smoldering dimples in the baggage.

Panchin tried to swing his tribarrel onto the Zaporoskiye tank firing at them with the automatic weapon in its cupola. Sergeant Jonas was faster, pounding the tank's mid-hull with a long burst that crumbled the ceramic. The tank didn't explode violently, but a red flash lifted all the hatches. The machine gun stopped firing.

Panchin shot at a supply truck and for once hit his target. Greasy flames enveloped the crates stacked on the bed. Men jumped off the other side of the vehicle and ran unharmed into the night.

Panchin's iridium barrels glowed so brightly that his face shield had to gray out their glare. The long burst Sergeant Jonas fired to destroy the tank had jammed his tribarrel. He tilted his weapon up to chip with a knife blade at the matrix material gumming his ejection port.

Cortezar swung *Hula Girl* hard left on the track within the outer ring of vehicles. Half a dozen rebel soldiers squatted behind their

APC and the sandbag wall they'd started for a sleeping bunker. They fired at *Hula Girl* with automatic rifles. Panchin slewed his gun toward them. A bullet whanged Jonas' weapon. The impact spun the tribarrel on its pintle. Like a white-hot baseball bat, the lower muzzle knocked the sergeant down.

A second artillery vehicle blew up. This time at least four rounds detonated simultaneously. The blast threw *Hula Girl* ten meters sideways into a heavy tractor with an earthmoving blade. The combat car rotated a half turn and stalled because Cortezar had dropped the controls when her helmet bounced off the side of her compartment.

Panchin screamed in fear and clamped his trigger. There was a sound like water dropped into an ocean of hot grease, and the center of his face shield became a shadow with cyan edges. The protective spot collapsed to show the ruin of an air-cushion vehicle, still glowing but no longer so bright that it could etch retinas.

"Drive!" Sergeant Jonas said. "Drive!"

Hula Girl shuddered, rose minusculy, and turned to lurch off the northern edge of the knoll between a pair of Sulewesan APCs. One burned sluggishly; the other was as still as a grave though apparently undamaged.

More Brazilian rockets exploded. *Hula Girl* pogoed twice even though this time high ground shielded them from the shockwave. Debris from a previous explosion must have set this one off because Frosty wasn't shooting and Panchin's tribarrel had jammed.

Hula Girl tore through the night. Tracers arched across the sky, but the rebel laager was out of direct sight. There was a risk that the car might hit a large boulder, but Cortezar was driving with a touch as deft as a brain surgeon's.

Panchin knelt with his hands clasped over the chestplate of his armor. He knew he ought to clear his tribarrel, but his whole body was shaking.

Ericssen worked on Sergeant Jonas' forearm. "It's just a bruise!" the sergeant said. His voice was tight with pain.

"So the medics at Scepter Base take the splint off," Ericssen said equably. "Where's the harm in that? Now, you just relax until the blue tab—" the analgesic injector built into Slammer's body armor, beside the red tab which injected stimulant "—kicks in."

The night behind them belched yellow again. The shockwave was a dull thump instead of a world-devouring roar when it reached *Hula Girl* several seconds later.

"I never thought it'd work," Panchin whispered.

"Hey, snake?" Ericssen said. "You did good to nail that second calliope before it waxed us. I didn't even see it till you lit the spics up."

"I'm glad," Panchin said. He closed his eyes, then opened them again very quickly. He'd throw up if he closed them.

"Blood and martyrs!" Cortezar said. "I don't get it. We were shaking *hands* with those bastards and we didn't even know they were the other side. And them too! It don't make sense that if everybody's the same they're all trying to kill each other."

The overhead net sagged. The bullet-damaged stake had bent and might break at any moment.

"Maybe in some universe there's got to be a difference before people kill each other," Panchin said to his clasped hands. "That's never been a requirement in the universe humans live in, though."

M9A4 COMMAND CAR

THE IMMOVABLE OBJECT

Hoodoo, the only one of the Slammers' gigantic tanks remaining on Ambiorix, hulked in the starlight beyond the barred window of the maintenance shed where the party was going on. Lamartiere looked at the gray bulk again, then tossed down the last of the drink he'd been nursing for an hour.

It wasn't quite time for him to act. Since Franciscus, the commander of the Company of Death, had sent the orders three days ago, Lamartiere had been worried sick over what he had to do. Now he just wished it was over, one way or the other.

Sergeant Heth tried to stand but toppled back onto a couch improvised from rolls of insulating foam. He was *Hoodoo*'s commander and the ranking mercenary on Ambiorix since the remainder of Hammer's Regiment had lifted during the past three weeks. Even though the stubby, dark-skinned mercenary had drunk himself legless, his gaze was sharp as he searched the crowd of Local Service Personnel to focus on Lamartiere.

"Hey, Curly!" he called. It was a joke: Lamartiere's straight blond hair was so fine that he looked bald in a strong light. "I want you to know that you were a good LSP, and I'd say that even if you hadn't just fed me the best whiskey I ever had in my life!"

"Yeah, Denis," said L'Abbaye, another of the LSPs. "I didn't know your folks had money. What're you doing in a job like this, anyhow?"

"Because of my faith," Lamartiere said simply. His mouth was dry, but oddly enough the question steadied him. "I thought the best way I could serve God was by serving the mercenaries who came here to fight the Mosite rebels. These refreshments are also a way of serving God."

That was quite true. The Company of Death, the special operations commando of the Mosite rebellion, had recruited Lamartiere from the ranks of ordinary guerrillas and ordered him to take this job. He came from the planetary capital, Carcassone, rather than the western mountains where the Mosite faith—Mosite *heresy*, the Synod of the Established Church would have it—was centered. Lamartiere had his father's fair complexion. Perhaps in compensation his sister Celine was darker than most pure-blood Westerners, but they both had their mother's faith. Lamartiere's technical education from the Carcassone Lyceum made him an ideal recruit to the Local Service Personnel whom the mercenaries hired for cleaning and fetch-and-carry during depot maintenance of their great war machines.

Heth prodded *Hoodoo*'s driver, Trooper Stegner, with a boot toe. "Hear that, Steg?" the sergeant said. "We're the Sword of God again. How many gods d'ye suppose we been the swords for, hey?"

"We ain't nobody's sword now," Stegner said, lying on his back on the floor with a block of wood for his pillow. His eyes were closed and the straw of an emergency water bottle projected into the corner of his mouth. "We been fired, cast into the outer darkness of space just because we want to be paid."

Before Stegner lay down on the concrete, he'd filled the water bottle with the whiskey Lamartiere brought to this farewell party for the two mercenaries. Though the trooper had seemed to be asleep, his Adam's apple moved at intervals as he sucked on the straw.

"You weren't fired, sir," said another of the LSPs. "You've won and can go home now."

Everyone in the shed except Lamartiere was drunk or almost drunk. For this operation, Franciscus had provided enough liquor to fill *Hoodoo*'s heat exchanger. The money to buy it had come from folk on whom the yoke of war and the Synod lay heavy; but they paid the tax, just as they paid in blood—for their Mosite faith.

"Home?" muttered Stegner. "Where's that?"

"We won the battles we fought, son," Sergeant Heth said, turning to the LSP who'd spoken. "The Slammers generally do. That's why people hire us. But don't kid yourself that the war's over. That's not going to happen until either you give your rebels a piece of the government or you kill everybody in the Western District."

"But they're heretics!" Fourche blurted. "We aren't going to allow Ambiorix to be ruled by heretics!"

Heth belched loudly. He stared at his empty class. Lamartiere filled it from the bottle he held.

"Well, that leaves the second way, don't it?" Heth said. "I don't think we'd be able to handle the job, not kill *all* of them, even if you had the money to pay us. And not to be unkind, son, but your National Army *sure* can't do it, which is why you hired us in the first place."

"Cast into the darkness . . ." Stegner mumbled. He started to laugh, choked, and turned his head away from the bottle to vomit.

It was time. Lamartiere stood, wobbly with adrenalin rather than liquor, and said, "We're getting low on whiskey. I'll fetch more."

"I'll give you a hand," volunteered L'Abbaye. He was a friendly youth but all thumbs on any kind of mechanical task. Lamartiere thought with grim humor that if the secret police came looking for Mosites among the LSPs, L'Abbaye's clumsiness could easily be mistaken for systematic sabotage.

Lamartiere handed him the present bottle. There was just enough liquor to slosh in the bottom. "You hold this," he said. "I'll be right back."

Lamartiere stepped outside, feeling the night air bite like a plunge into cold water. He was shivering. He closed the shed's sturdy door, then threw the strap over the hasp and locked it down with the heavy padlock he'd brought for the purpose.

He trotted to the sloped gray bow of *Hoodoo,* a vast boulder cropping out of the spaceport's flat expanse. Lamartiere had the feeling that the tank was watching him. Even now when it was completely shut down.

The mercenaries had used the spaceport of Brione, the major city of Ambiorix' Western District, as their planetary logistics base during operations against the Mosites in the surrounding mountains. The seventeen tanks of H Company provided base security during the Slammers' withdrawal at the end of their contract.

The withdrawal had gone so smoothly that the government in Carcassone was probably congratulating itself on the savings it had made by ceasing to pay the enormously high wages of the foreign mercenaries. Over a period of three weeks starship after starship had lifted, carrying the Slammers' equipment and personnel to Beresford, 300 light-years distant, where the dictator of a continental state didn't choose to become part of the planetary democracy.

The last transport was supposed to carry H Company. As the tanks headed for the hold, *Hoodoo*'s aft and starboard pairs of drive fans failed because of an electrical fault. This wasn't a serious problem or an uncommon one—vibration and grit meant wiring harnesses were almost as regular an item of resupply as ammunition. With the Regiment's tank transporters and dedicated maintenance personnel already off-planet, though, Major Harding—the logistics officer overseeing the withdrawal—had a problem.

Hoodoo's crew could repair the tank themselves as they'd done many times in the field, but the job might take anything up to a week. Harding had to decide whether to delay sixteen tanks whose punch was potentially crucial on Beresford, or to risk leaving *Hoodoo* behind alone to rejoin when Heth and Stegner got her running again.

For the moment Ambiorix seemed as quiet as if Bishop Moses had never had his revelation. Harding had chosen the second option and lifted with the remainder of H Company.

Hoodoo's crew spent the next thirteen hours tracing the fault through the on-board diagnostics, then six more hours pulling the damaged harness and reeving a new one through channels in armor thick enough to deflect all but the most powerful weapons known to man. Then and only then, they had slept.

It was four more days before the tramp freighter hired to carry *Hoodoo* to Beresford would be ready to lift, but Heth and Stegner could relax once they had the tank running again. *Hoodoo*'s speed, armor, and weaponry meant there was nothing within twenty light-years of Ambiorix to equal her.

And she was about to enter the service of the Mosite Rebellion.

A boarding ladder pivoted from *Hoodoo*'s hull, but Lamartiere walked up the smooth iridium bow slope instead like a real tanker. Local Service Personnel were taught to drive the Slammers' vehicles so that they could ferry them between maintenance and supply stations, freeing the troops for more specialized tasks.

Personal travel on Ambiorix, where roads were bad and often steep, was generally by air-cushion vehicle. A 170-tonne tank didn't handle like a 2-tonne van, but the principle was the same. Most of the LSPs were competent tank drivers, and Lamartiere flattered himself that he was pretty good—at least within the flat confines of the spaceport.

Lamartiere didn't need his stolen electronic key because the driver's hatch wasn't locked. He gripped the handle and slid the curved plate forward, feeling the counterweights move in greasy balance with the massive iridium forging.

He lowered himself into the compartment. The seat was raised for the driver to look out over the hatch coaming instead of viewing the world through the multifunction flat-plate displays that ringed his position.

Lamartiere took a deep breath and switched on *Hoodoo*'s drive fans.

The whine of the powerful impellers coming up to speed told everyone within a kilometer that the tank was in operation, but only the crew and the LSPs with them realized something was wrong. Lamartiere had cut the landlines into the building when he'd gone out earlier "to fetch another bottle".

The maintenance building had barred windows and heavy doors to safeguard the equipment within. Even if those partying inside had been sober, they wouldn't have been able to break out in time to affect the result. No one on base could hear their shouts over the sound of the adjacent tank. They were the least of Lamartiere's problems.

None of *Hoodoo*'s electronics were live, and that *was* a problem. Lamartiere realized what had happened as soon as he switched on: Heth and Stegner had disabled the systems while they were working on the wiring. They hadn't bothered to reconnect anything but the drive train to test it when they were done. There was probably a panel of circuit breakers in some easily accessible location, but Lamartiere didn't know where it was and he didn't have time to find it now in the dark.

He increased the bite of the fans so that instead of merely spinning they began to pump air into *Hoodoo*'s plenum chamber. The skirts enclosing the chamber were steel, not a flexible material like that used for lighter air-cushion vehicles. These had to support the tank's enormous mass while at rest. They couldn't deform to seal the chamber against irregularities in the ground, but the output of the eight powerful fans driven by a fusion generator made up for the leakage.

Hoodoo shivered as the bubble of air in the plenum chamber reached the pressure required to lift 170 tonnes. The tank hopped twice, spilling air beneath the skirts, then steadied as the flow through the fans increased to match the leakage. She was now floating a finger's breadth above the ground.

Lamartiere moved the control yoke forward. The fan nacelles tilted within the plenum chamber to direct their thrust rearward instead of simply down. *Hoodoo* moved at a sedate pace, scarcely more than a fast walk, through the shops area toward the spaceport's main gate.

Lamartiere shook violently in relief. He released the control yoke for the moment: the tank's AI would hold their speed and heading, which was all that was required now.

Using both hands, Lamartiere fumbled in a bellows pocket of his coveralls and brought out a hand-held radio stolen from government stores. He keyed it on the set frequency and said, "Star, on the way. Out."

He switched off without waiting for a response. He couldn't hear anything over the intake howl, and it really didn't matter. Whether or not Franciscus and the rest of the outside team were in position, Denis Lamartiere couldn't back out now.

The spaceport perimeter was defended, but the mines, fences, and guard towers were no danger to a supertank. At the main gate, however, was a five-story citadel containing the tactical control center and a pair of 25cm powerguns on dual-purpose mountings. Those weapons could rend a starship in orbit and when raised could bear on every route out of the port. A bolt from one of them would vaporize even *Hoodoo*'s thick iridium armor.

A spur from the four-lane Brione-Carcassone highway fed the spaceport. As Lamartiere drove slowly toward the gate, an air-cushion van and a fourteen-wheel semi turned onto the approach road from the other direction.

There was regular truck traffic to the port: a similar vehicle had just passed the checkpoint and was headed toward the warehouses. Guards at the gate waited for the oncoming semi, chatting and chewing wads of the harsh tobacco grown in Carcassone District.

Hoodoo's drive fans drew a fierce breeze past Lamartiere's face despite the tank's slow forward progress. He backed off the throttle even more. Without the tank's electronics Lamartiere had to keep his head out of the hatch to drive, so he couldn't afford to be too close when the semi reached the gate.

The small van pulled into the ditch beside the road and stopped. The semi accelerated past with the ponderous deliberation its weight made necessary.

Lamartiere watched as *Hoodoo* crawled forward, waiting for the driver to bail out. The truck continued to accelerate, but no one jumped from the cab. Had Franciscus decided to sacrifice himself, despite Lamartiere's loud refusal to be a part of a suicide mission?

It was too late to back out. If he met Franciscus in Hell, he could object then.

A machine gun on top of the citadel opened fire before any of the guards at the checkpoint appeared to understand what was happening. The gunner deserved full marks for reacting promptly, but his sparkling projectiles were aimed several meters high. A round flashed red when it cut one of the steel hoops supporting the trailer's canvas top, but none hit the cab. It was protected against small-arms anyway.

The driver was definitely going to stay with his vehicle. Lamartiere's stomach turned. Risk was one thing. No God Lamartiere worshipped demanded suicide of Her followers.

A siren called from the Port Operations Center in the center of the base. Half a dozen automatic rifles were firing from the roof and entranceway of the citadel. One of the guards at the checkpoint raked the truck from front to back as it swept past him. Most of his fellows had flung themselves down, though one stood in the guard kiosk and gabbled excitedly into the handset of the landline phone there.

The semi bounced over the shallow ditch—it was for drainage rather than protection—and wobbled across rough grass toward the citadel. The machine gun stopped firing because the target was too close for the gun to bear.

A guard leaned over the roof coping to aim a shoulder-launched antitank rocket but lost his balance in his haste. He bounced against the side of the building halfway down. From there to the ground he and the rocket launcher fell separately.

The semi bit the sloped glacis at the citadel's base.

Lamartiere lowered his seat, even though that meant he was driving blind. The disk of sky above Lamartiere flashed white. The pavement rippled, hitting the base of *Hoodoo*'s skirts an instant before an airborne shockwave twisted the tank sideways. It pounded Lamartiere brutally despite his protected location. *Hoodoo* straightened under the control of its AI. Lamartiere raised his seat and rocked the control yoke forward with the fans spinning at maximum power. The tank accelerated with the slow certainty of a boulder falling from a cliff .

A pillar of smoke and debris was still rising when Lamartiere lifted his head above the hatch coaming. It was nearly a kilometer high before it topped out into a mushroom and began to rain back on the surroundings. The citadel was a faded dream within the column, a hint of vertical lines within the black corkscrew of destruction.

The semi had vanished utterly. The Mosite Rebellion had never lacked explosives and people to use them expertly. The mines of the Western District had provided most of Ambiorix' off-planet exports in the form of hard coal with trace elements that made it the perfect culture medium for anti-aging drugs produced in the Semiramis Cluster. Ten-year-olds in the mountain villages could set a charge of slurry that would bring down a cliff face—or a two-meter section of it, if that was their intent.

The 25cm guns were housed in pits surrounded by a berm and protective dome, invulnerable until they came into action, but the control system was in the citadel. Eight tonnes of slurry exploding against the glacis wouldn't destroy the structure, but neither the gunnery computers nor their operators would be in working order for at least the next several minutes.

Nothing remained of the checkpoint or the troops who'd been firing from the top of the building. One of the objects spinning out of the mushroom might have been a torso from which the blast had plucked head and limbs.

Hoodoo hit a steel pole with a clang, one of the uprights from the perimeter fencing. The blast had thrown it onto the roadway. Lamartiere ducked without thinking. The reflex saved him from decapitation when a coil of razor wire writhed up the bow slope and hooked under *Hoodoo*'s main gun. A moment later the wire parted with a vicious twang at the end of its stretch, leaving a bright scar on the iridium.

The van that had guided the truck to its destruction now pulled out of the sheltering ditch. A figure hopped from the passenger side of the cab and ran into *Hoodoo*'s path, arms windmilling. *What fool was—*

Crossed bandoliers flopped as the figure gestured; he carried a slung rifle in addition to the submachine gun in his right had. Colonel Franciscus was identifiable even at night because of his paraphernalia.

If Franciscus was here, who had been driving the truck of explosives? Though that didn't matter, not really, except to the driver's widow or mother.

When Lamartiere realized Franciscus wasn't going to get out of his way, he swore and sank the control yoke in his belly, switching the nacelles' alignment from full rearward to full forward. Even so he was going to overrun the man. Halting the inertia of a 170-tonne mass with thrust alone was no sudden business.

"Idiot!" Lamartiere screamed as he spilled pressure from the vents on top of the plenum chamber. "Idiot!"

Hoodoo skidded ten meters in a dazzle of red sparks ground from the skirts by the concrete roadway. The bow halted just short of Franciscus. The shriek of metal was as painful as the blast a moment before and seemed equally loud.

Franciscus, his clothes smoldering in a dozen places from sparks—perhaps a just God had care of events after all—climbed aboard clumsily, grabbing a headlight bracket with his free hand. He waved the other until Lamartiere grabbed his wrist to keep from being slapped in the face with the submachine gun.

"I'll man the guns!" Franciscus shouted over the roar of the fans. He started climbing upward, this time grasping the muzzle of the stubby 20cm main gun.

"They don't work!" Lamartiere said. The vents slapped closed. He raised the yoke to vertical for a moment, building pressure before he started accelerating again. The air was harsh and dry with lime burned from the concrete by friction. "You should have stayed with the van!"

Franciscus couldn't hear him. He would have ignored the comment anyway, as he seemed to ignore everything but his own will and direct orders from Father Renaud, the spiritual head of the Company of Death.

Lamartiere needed to concentrate on his driving.

The van sprinted off now that Franciscus had boarded the tank. It had been supposed to pick up the semi's driver; there was no longer any reason for its presence.

The van's relatively high power-to-weight ratio allowed it to accelerate faster than *Hoodoo,* but air resistance limited the lighter vehicle's top speed to under a hundred kph. With the correct surface and time to accelerate, *Hoodoo* could easily double that rate.

Neither vehicle outsped gunshots, but the tank could shrug them off. If the government forces were even half-awake, for the van to wait while Franciscus played games had been a very bad idea.

Franciscus was shouting something about the hatch. It might be locked, but Lamartiere suspected the colonel was just trying to open it in the wrong direction, pushing it back instead of pulling it open. There was nothing the driver could do until—

Shells rang off *Hoodoo*'s rear hull. Rounds that missed sailed past, the tracers golden in the night air, and exploded in red pulses on the westbound lanes of the highway ahead.

If the tank's screens had been live, Lamartiere could have seen what was happening behind him without even turning his head. Now his choice was to ignore the pursuit or to swing the tank sideways so that he could see past the turret.

He twisted the yoke. The pursuers might have antitank missiles as well as automatic cannon, and even cannon could riddle the skirts and ground *Hoodoo* as surely as if they'd shot out her fan nacelles.

Two of the air-cushion vehicles that patrolled the perimeter fence had followed *Hoodoo* out of the spaceport. They had no armor to speak of, but they were fast and the guns in their small turrets had a range of several kilometers.

Because *Hoodoo* turned the next burst missed her, but red flashes ate across the back of the van. It flipped on edge and cartwheeled twice before the fuel cell ruptured. Lamartiere ducked as he drove through the fireball. He smelled flesh burning, but at least he couldn't hear the screams.

Franciscus must have opened the turret hatch because the flow past Lamartiere's chest and legs increased violently. The cross-draft cut off a moment later as Franciscus closed the cupola behind him.

Now that the colonel was clear, Lamartiere braked the tank at the end of the access road. Cannon shells crossed in front of him, then slapped both sides of the turret as the gunners adjusted. *Hoodoo* roared across the highway's eastbound lanes on inertia.

Lamartiere dumped pressure on the median, grounding in a gulp of yellow-gray soil far less spectacular than the sparks on the concrete. The tank pitched violently. Franciscus screamed in fury as he bounced around the fighting compartment, but Lamartiere had strapped in by habit.

He closed the vents and rotated *Hoodoo* clockwise. One of the patrol cars was trying to swing around their right side. It brushed the tank's bow and disintegrated as though it had hit a granite cuff. Building speed again, Lamartiere brought *Hoodoo* in line after the remaining government vehicle.

The minuscule bump might have been dirt, part of the patrol car, or the corpse of a government soldier. It made no difference after it passed beneath the tank's skirts.

They crossed the northern lanes of the highway, driving into the brush that grew on arid soil. If the car's driver had been thinking clearly, he'd have doubled back immediately and used his agility to escape. He'd panicked when he changed from hunter to hunted, though, and he tried to outrun the tank.

The gunner rotated his turret halfway, then gave it up as a bad job. A side door opened. The gunner jumped out, hit a thorn tree, and hung there impaled before *Hoodoo*'s skirts ran him under.

The tank was pitching because of irregularities in the surface, but brush thick enough to slow the patrol car had no effect on 170 tonnes. The driver looked back over his shoulder an instant before *Hoodoo* crushed car and driver both. Lamartiere had only a glimpse of staring eyes and the teeth that framed the screaming mouth.

There were no more immediate enemies. Lamartiere angled *Hoodoo*'s bow to the northwest. He should hit a road after a kilometer or so of brush busting. The mountains were within a hundred kilometers on this heading; Pamiers, his destination, was only another eighty kilometers beyond. He'd have *Hoodoo* under cover before government troops could mount a pursuit.

They'd won. He'd won.

In the fighting compartment behind Lamartiere, Franciscus swore in darkness. He was unable even to reopen the cupola hatch.

Pamiers had been shelled repeatedly since the start of the rebellion, and once a government column had taken out its frustration at recent sniping by burning every building in the village. Besides, a city resident like Lamartiere wouldn't have been impressed by the place on its best day.

The locals seemed happy, though. Children played shrilly on

the steep hillside. They'd wanted to stay beside the tank, but that would have given away *Hoodoo*'s location. Women chatted as they hung laundry or cooked on outdoor stoves. The flapping clothes made bright primary contrasts with the general coal-dust black of the landscape.

Hoodoo stood at the north side of a tailings pile, covered by a camouflage tarpaulin with the same thermal signature as bare ground. Lamartiere had heard reconnaissance aircraft twice this morning. If the government learned where *Hoodoo* was, they would come for her; but government troops only entered the mountains when they were in overwhelming force, and even that had a way of being risky.

"I'm not an engineer," Dr. Clargue muttered from the driver's compartment. "I'm a medical man. I should not be here!"

"You and I are what the rebellion has for a technical staff in Pamiers," Lamartiere said. He was in the turret and couldn't see the doctor. A narrow passage connected the two portions of the tank, but that was for emergency use only. "And we've *got* to figure out where the switches are. Without the guns and sensors, this is just scrap metal."

It was a good thing that Lamartiere needed to encourage Clargue: otherwise he'd have been screaming in frustration himself. Lamartiere had been in intimate contact with the mercenaries' armored vehicles for three months, learning every detail he could about them. It hadn't occurred to him that he'd need to know where the cut-off switches were, but without that information he might as well have waited to wave good-bye when the freighter lifted with *Hoodoo* tomorrow. At least that way Lamartiere would have his final pay packet to donate to the rebellion.

The fighting compartment darkened as Captain Befayt stuck her head in the cupola hatch. "How are you coming?" she asked. "Say, there really isn't much room in there, is there?"

"No," Lamartiere said, trying not to snarl. "And we don't even have the interior lights working, so while you're standing there I can't see anything inside."

Befayt commanded the company of guerrillas who provided

security for Pamiers. She had a right to be concerned since the tank was a risk to the community for as long as it remained here.

Besides that, Lamartiere liked Befayt. Too often in rebel communities the fighters ate and drank well while the civilians, even the children, starved. In Pamiers all shared, and anybody who thought his gun made him special found he had the captain to answer to.

Having said that, Lamartiere *really* didn't need to have the heavy-set woman looking over his shoulder while everything was a frustrating mess.

"Here, I'll come down with you," Befayt said. She lowered her legs through the hatch, then paused for a moment. Her boots dribbled dirt and cinders down on Lamartiere. After laying her equipment belt on top of the turret to give her ample waist more clearance, she dropped the rest of the way into the compartment.

Maybe Lamartiere *should* have snarled, though people pretty much heard what they wanted to hear. Befayt wanted a look at this wonderful, war-winning piece of equipment.

Twelve hours earlier, Lamartiere too had believed the tank was all those things. Now he wasn't sure.

The trouble was that there were so many marvelous devices packed into *Hoodoo*'s vast bulk that the breaker box Lamartiere was looking for was concealed like a grain of sand in the desert. If the electronics had been live, Dr. Clargue could have called up a schematic that would tell them where the switches were . . .

Befayt stood on the seat which Lamartiere had lowered to give himself more light within the fighting compartment. He and Clargue had handlights as well, but the focused beams distorted appearances by shutting off the ambiance beyond their edges.

Befayt peered around the turret in wonder. "Boy," she said with unintended irony, "I'm glad it's you guys figuring this stuff out instead of me. This the big gun?"

She patted what was indeed the breech of the main gun. Lamartiere had seen a 20cm weapon tested after armorers had replaced the tube. The target was a range of hills ten kilometers south of the firing point. The cyan bolt had blasted a cavity a dozen meters wide in solid rock.

"Yes," Lamartiere said shortly. "The round comes from the ready magazine in the turret ring, shifts to the transfer chamber—"

He slid back a spring-loaded door beside the breech. The interior was empty.

"—and then into the gun when the previous round's ejected. That way all but the one round's under heavy armor at all times."

"Amazing," Befayt said with a gratified smile. "Guess we'll be giving the Synod's dogs back some of what they been feeding us, right?"

"If we're given a chance to get the tank in working order, yes, we will!" Lamartiere said. To cover his outburst he immediately went on, "Say, Captain, I'd been meaning to ask you: Do you know where my sister Celine's gone? I thought she might be here to, you know, say hello when I arrived."

"She was until about a week ago," Befayt said, relaxing deliberately. The captain didn't want a pointless confrontation either. "Then she got a message and went back with the supply trucks to Goncourt. You might check with Franciscus when he comes back from there tonight."

"Yes, I'll do that," Lamartiere said. The only good thing about the past hours of failure were that Colonel Franciscus had gone on to Goncourt to confer with Father Renaud instead of staying to watch Lamartiere.

"Guess I'll get out of your way," Befayt said with a tight control that showed she knew she'd been unwelcome. She wasn't the sort to let that affect her unduly, but it wasn't something that anybody liked to feel. "Celine seemed chirpy as a cricket when I last saw her, though."

She braced her hands on the edges of the hatch.

"Here, let me raise the seat," said Lamartiere. He touched the button on the side of the cushion. It was hydraulic, not electrical, and worked off an accumulator driven directly by Number Four fan. "I know I shouldn't worry about her, but we're all each other has since—"

As the seat whined upward, Lamartiere saw the flat box attached to the base plate. It had a hinged cover.

"Clargue!" he shouted. "I found it! There's a breaker box on the bottom of the seat!"

He flipped the cover open. The seat had halted at midcolumn when Lamartiere took his finger off the control. Befayt, excited though uncertain about what was going on, squatted on the cushion and tried to look underneath without getting in the way.

Lamartiere aimed his handlight at the interior of the box. There was a triple row of circuit breakers. All of them were in the On position.

"Turn them one at a time!" Dr. Clargue said. "We don't want a surge to damage the equipment."

"They're already on, Doctor," Lamartiere said. He felt sandbagged. Were the electronics dead because of a fault, one the crew hadn't bothered to fix once they had *Hoodoo* mobile again? But Heth and Stegner wouldn't have relaxed until they had the tank's guns working, surely!

"Doctor!" Lamartiere said. "Check under your seat. Both crew members would have the cut-offs so they—"

"Yes, it's here!" said Clargue. "I've got it open . . ."

Lamartiere heard ventilation motors hum. The interior lights, flat and a deep yellow that didn't affect night vision, came on; then the 30cm gunnery screen above the breech of the main gun glowed.

Hoodoo rang with a violent explosion against the turret. Choking smoke swirled through the open hatch. The ventilation system switched to high speed.

Befayt jumped out of the hatch, moving quickly and without the awkwardness with which she'd entered. "What is happening?" Clargue shouted. The doctor's voice faded as he climbed out of the driver's compartment. "Are we attacked?"

Lamartiere tried to rotate the turret. It didn't move: that breaker was still off. He pulled himself into the open air. He couldn't do anything inside and he didn't choose to wait in the turret to be killed if that was what was going to happen.

The smoke was dissipating. The tarpaulin had been hurled up the tailings pile, but Lamartiere saw no other sign of damage. Dr. Clargue was coming around the front of the tank. Befayt stood on the back deck, staring in consternation at fresh scars on the side of the turret.

"My belt blew up," Befayt said. "May God cast me from Her if that's not what happened. My *belt* blew up."

The women and children who made up most of Pamiers' population were disappearing into the mouths of the mines that had sheltered them through previous attacks. The traverses weren't comfortable homes, but they were proof against anything the government could throw against them. Guerrillas had dived into fighting positions as quickly. Those in sight of their leader were looking toward her for direction.

"What?" said Clargue. "Did you have electrically primed explosives on your belt, Captain?"

"Well," said Befayt. "Sure, I—Oh, Mother God. You turned the radios on, didn't you?"

"Of course a tank like this has radios, you idiot!" the doctor screamed. His goatee wobbled. Clargue was a little man in his late sixties, unfailingly pleasant in all the encounters Lamartiere had had with him to this moment. "What did you mean bringing blasting caps here!"

"I . . ." Befayt said. She looked completely stupefied. Everyone in the district knew that a powerful radio signal generated enough current in the wires of an electrical blasting cap to detonate the primer. On reflection it was obvious that a tank would have radios; but Lamartiere hadn't thought of that, and neither had the guerrilla commander.

Clargue had scrambled back into the driver's compartment. "Doctor, I'm sorry!" Befayt called after him. "I'll warn the men. And I'll get the tarpaulin over you again."

She trotted toward the entrance of the mine which served as the village's command post. Her hand-held radio had been on the equipment belt.

Clargue reappeared. Lamartiere looked at him in dismay and said, "It was my fault. I should have warned her."

"No," said Clargue. "It was my fault for turning on the power without thinking of the radios. It's not only the blasting caps. We—

I—sent out a signal that the government listening posts almost certainly picked up. They know where we are now. They'll be coming."

He shook his head with an expression of miserable frustration. Lamartiere remembered Clargue looking the same way six months before, when a child who'd stepped on a bomblet died despite anything the doctor could do.

"I'll apologize to Captain Befayt," Clargue said. "I was angry with myself, but I blamed her."

"First we need to get *Hoodoo* working," Lamartiere said. Befayt was leading a group of guerrillas toward them to re-erect the camouflage cover. "So that when the government troops arrive, we're ready for them."

The villagers came out in the evening when they heard the truck approaching from Goncourt. They bowed low in the honor due a holy man on seeing that Father Renaud rode beside Franciscus in the cab. There wasn't, Lamartiere thought, much warmth in their greetings.

Father Renaud was a slim, deeply ascetic man with a fringe of white hair and a placid expression. He was personally very gentle, a man who would let an insect drink its fill of his blood rather than needlessly crush one of God's creatures.

But there was no compromise in the father's attitude as to what was owed God. He had blessed a young mother before she walked into a government checkpoint with six kilos of explosive hidden beneath the infant in her backpack.

Most people in the mountains respected Father Renaud and his faith. A man who spent so much of his time with God wasn't entirely safe for ordinary folk to be around, however.

The driver pulled up beside *Hoodoo* to let out Renaud and the colonel, then circled back to the center of the village to distribute the few crates of supplies which the Council in Goncourt could spare to Pamiers. The gardens planted in the rubble of burned-out buildings here couldn't support the population. Without some supplement the refugees would move to Goncourt, adding to the health and safety problems of what remained of the Mosites' alternative seat of government.

Befayt and several of her aides had started for *Hoodoo* when they heard the fans of the oncoming truck. The captain knelt and accepted the blessing from Father Renaud, but she and Franciscus exchanged only the briefest nods of greeting. There was no love lost between the Company of Death and local guerrilla units. As for rank—an officer could call himself anything he pleased, but in the field it came down to who accepted his orders.

In Pamiers, only Lamartiere took orders from Colonel Franciscus. Little as Lamartiere liked the man, he knew that local groups like Befayt's could never defeat the central government, though they might keep the mountains ungovernable indefinitely now that the mercenaries had left. In Lamartiere's opinion, decades of hungry squalor like this would be worse even than haughty repression by the government and Synod.

Franciscus waited impatiently for Lamartiere to take the blessing, then snapped, "Have you fixed the tank yet? I've told the Council that we can move on Brione as soon as they've concentrated our forces, but that I have to be in charge. The tank is crucial, and *I* command it."

"We have all the electronic systems working," Dr. Clargue said in a voice as thin as a scalpel. "The guns are not in operation yet because the magazines seem to be empty."

Clargue wasn't a member of any military body, but he was a Mosite believer and had been an expert on Ambiorix' most advanced medical computer systems before he left Carcassone Central Hospital for hands-on care of the folk of his home village. His presence was the reason the Council had picked Pamiers as an initial destination for the stolen tank.

"What do you mean?" Franciscus said. He turned on Lamartiere with all the fury of a terrier facing a rat. "Didn't you bring ammunition? Did you think we were going to stand on the turret and throw *rocks*?"

Lamartiere was taller than Franciscus, but the colonel was an athlete who went through a long exercise regimen every morning and who gloried in hand-to-hand combat. He didn't need his trappings of guns, bombs, and knives to be dangerous. He was physically capable of beating Lamartiere to death at this moment, and he was very possibly willing to do so as well.

"*Hoodoo* has a full load of ammunition, both 2cm and 20cm," Lamartiere said quietly, forcing himself not to flinch as Franciscus stepped toe to toe with him. "I drove the ammo trailer to her myself and watched Sergeant Heth load her. But the rounds are in storage magazines in the floor of the hull. The ready magazines in the turret are empty."

"You must understand," Clargue said, breaking in with an expression that implied he didn't care whether Franciscus understood how to breathe, "that this tank is a very complex system. As yet I haven't found the command that will transfer ammunition between locations or even the command set it belongs to. It doesn't seem to be part of the gunnery complex, as I would have expected."

He shrugged. His frustration was as great as Lamartiere's, but the doctor was better at hiding it. "We're working through the range of possibilities. It will take time."

Clargue knew, as Lamartiere did, that there might be very little time because of the RF spike when *Hoodoo*'s radios came on.

"Well look," said Befayt. She wore a new equipment belt, but this one didn't contain any of the electrically primed bombs that were a staple of the guerrillas' ambush techniques. "Why don't you move the disks by hand? I can supply the people if the weight's a problem."

"The storage magazines are sealed and locked," Lamartiere explained. *This* was something he knew about. "It takes a special fitting on the end of the ammo trailer to get into the tube. If there's dust on the rounds, they might explode when they're fired."

"We don't have time to be picky!" Franciscus said. He was a little off-balance around Clargue, perhaps because the doctor was so completely Franciscus' opposite in personality. "Blow open the magazines and load the turret by hand."

"No!" said Lamartiere and Clargue together.

"Like bloody Hell!" Befayt said, speaking directly to the colonel for the first time since he'd arrived. "I've looked at those fittings. Enough charge to blow one open and the best thing you're going to do is crush all the disks so they don't work. There's a better chance that you'll set one off and the whole lot gang fires. How does that help us, will you tell me, Mister Colonel?"

Franciscus looked as though he was going to hit her. Befayt's aides must have thought so too, because they backed slightly and leveled their weapons at the colonel: a pair of Ambiorix-made electromotive slug-throwers, and a 2cm powergun stolen or captured from the Slammers' stocks.

"Children," Father Renaud said with none of the sarcasm the word might have carried had it come from another mouth. "If we squabble among ourselves then we fail the Lord in Her time of need. There is no greater sin."

"Sorry, father," Befayt muttered. Franciscus gave her a sour look, then dipped his head to Renaud in a sign of contrition.

Renaud returned his attention to Clargue and Lamartiere. "Go on with your work," he said calmly. "Remember, have faith and She will provide."

Lamartiere bowed and turned to board the tank again. He mostly kept silent while Dr. Clargue methodically went over the software, but there was always the possibility that he would recognize something that the doctor had missed.

It hadn't happened yet, though. Working on the mercenaries' vehicles in depot didn't teach him anything about the way they operated in combat, and to ask questions on the subject would have compromised Lamartiere as surely waving a sign saying, I AM A MOSITE SPY!

The radio on Befayt's belt buzzed. She unhooked it and held it to her cheek, shielding the mouthpiece by reflex even in this company. When she lowered the unit, her face looked as though it had been hacked from stone.

"The government outposts at Twill, Lascade, and on Marcelline Ridge have just been reinforced," she said. "That's an anvil all around Pamiers. There's a mechanized battalion heading south out of the Ariege cantonment to be the hammer."

"It's because of my mistake," Dr. Clargue said in a stricken voice. "I shouldn't be involved in this. I'm not a man of war."

"Well, there's no problem," Franciscus said. "Just get the tank working and we'll wipe out this whole Synod battalion. The first battle will be in Pamiers instead of us having to go to them."

"I don't know how long I will need," Clargue said. "Finding the right command is like—"

He pointed to the sky. The sun had set and the first stars were appearing in the twilight.

"Like finding one star at random in all the heavens. How long is it before the enemy will attack?"

"It's forty klicks from Ariege," Befayt said uncomfortably. "I won't say they're going to have clear going, but after the way the villages on the route got ground up over the past five months I wouldn't expect a whole lot of resistance. Even though it's just government troops and not the mercenaries this time."

"Two hours," Lamartiere translated. "Less if they're willing to push very hard and abandon vehicles that break down."

"I can't guarantee success," Dr. Clargue said. His face wrinkled in misery. "I can't even expect success. There's no sign that I will ever find the right command."

"Well, then we have to move our tank to a new location," Franciscus said. He looked at Father Renaud, less for counsel than to indicate he wasn't attempting to give the priest orders. "Boukasset, I think? Even if they find us again, it'll take them days to mount an attack there. And even reinforced, none of those patrol posts can stop *us*."

He patted *Hoodoo*'s iridium flank with a proprietary gesture that made Lamartiere momentarily furious. He knew it was stupid to give in to personal dislike in a crisis like this, but he also knew human beings were much more than cold intellects in a body.

Aloud Lamartiere said, "We can break through, I'm pretty sure. But the villagers can't escape, and the government troops won't leave without doing all the damage they can. I'm afraid they'll blow up the mine entrances this time."

Befayt grimaced. "Yeah," she said. "I figure that, too."

She nodded toward *Hoodoo*. "They're scared of this thing. If they don't have it to fight after all, well, they'll find some other way to work off their energy."

"I'll get back to work," Clargue said simply. He put his hand on the boarding ladder.

"And I'll put my people in place at the crossing," Befayt said. "I don't know that we can slow them up much, not a battalion, but they'll know they been in a fight before they get across the Lystra."

"Wait," said Lamartiere. He pointed to the guerrilla carrying the powergun. "Captain, you've got several soldiers with 2cm guns, don't you? Give me all their ammunition. I can hand-feed it into the tribarrel's ready magazine and use the tanks gunnery system to aim and fire."

The guerrilla looked shocked at the thought he should surrender the weapon that gave him status in any gathering of fighters. Befayt nodded to him and said, "Yeah, do what he says, Aghulan. You can keep the gun. Just give him the ammo."

She smiled bitterly and added, "I'd say you could have it for your tombstone, but I don't guess there'll be enough of any of us left to bury in a couple hours."

The aide was a man in his sixties. He looked at the hills and said, "Well, I said I never wanted to leave this valley. Guess I'll get my wish."

He spat on the coal-blackened ground.

"Right," said Franciscus. "I'll man the tank's gun."

"No," said Lamartiere before Clargue could step away from the ladder. "I need the doctor with me. He understands the parts of the systems that I'll need but don't know anything about."

Clargue looked at Lamartiere in surprise. Both of them knew that was a lie.

Franciscus glared at Lamartiere and rang the edge of his fist angrily on *Hoodoo*'s skirt. "I should have infiltrated the base myself," he snarled, accepting the statement at face value. "Then we'd have somebody who knew what he was doing!"

Father Renaud looked at the colonel sharply. "Emmanuel," he said. "Glory will come to those who strive for the Lord, but neither glory nor martyrdom is an end in itself. Sometimes I fear that you forget that."

"Sorry, father," Franciscus muttered.

"And, Captain?" Lamartiere added as another idea struck him. The sky over the western hills was fully dark now. "Can your men make me up flash charges with about three meters of wire leads on each? As many as you can. And I'll need a clacker to set them off."

"Why?" Franciscus demanded. "What do you think you're going to do with them?"

If Franciscus hadn't spoken first, Befayt might have asked the same question. As it was, she gave the colonel a flat glare and said, "Yeah, I'll put a couple of the boys on it while the rest of us go wait at the crossing."

She looked at Renaud and added, "Father? I'd appreciate it if you'd bless us all before we go. It don't look like there'll be another chance."

There was a reconnaissance drone overhead. Darkness and altitude hid it, but the hum of its turbofan occasionally reached the ground.

"I'm going to button up," Lamartiere said over *Hoodoo*'s intercom. He grimaced to hear himself deliberately using jargon to prove he was a real tanker. "I'm going to close the hatches, I mean," he added. "Make sure you're clear of yours."

He touched the switch on the compartment's sidepanel; both hatches slid closed with cushioned thumps. One thing Lamartiere had proved he *wasn't*, was a tanker. The damage *Hoodoo*'s skirts had taken on the run from Brione suggested he wasn't much of a tank driver either, though he supposed he'd call himself adequate given haste and the condition of roads through the mountains.

"Denis, you know that I can't operate these weapons, don't you?" Dr. Clargue said. When the tank was sealed, the vehicle intercom was good enough for parties to hear one another even over the roar of the fans, though for greater flexibility on operations the mercenaries always wore commo helmets. Lamartiere had a momentary daydream of what he could do if he had all the equipment of Hammer's Regiment under his control.

He might not be able to do anything. Hardware was wonderful, but the training to use it was more wonderful still. He should have asked a few more questions when he worked for the mercenaries. He might have been exposed and shot, but at least the civilians of Pamiers would face less risk.

"I know that," Lamartiere said aloud. "We'll change places when we get to the crossing and I'll take over the gun. I just couldn't afford to have Franciscus in the turret. He doesn't know any more about the equipment than you do, and *he* wouldn't trade with me."

He started the fans, bringing the blades up to speed at a flat angle so that they didn't bite the air. The driver's compartment had two displays, one above the other. On default the lower screen was a 360-degree panorama with a keyboard overlay, while the upper one showed the view forward with system readouts overlying the right and left edges. By touching any gauge, Lamartiere could expand it to half the screen.

The fans and power system were within parameters. They shouldn't give any trouble on the three kilometers between here and the Lystra River.

The truck that had brought supplies was ferrying the last of the guerrillas to the defensive positions at the crossing. Befayt had allowed Franciscus to go with the first group. Tonight she wasn't about to turn away anyone with a gun and a willingness to die.

"You don't have to change places, you know," Clargue said. "Unless you want to, of course. You can control the weapons from your compartment by touching Star-Gee."

"What?" said Lamartiere, taking his hands off the control yoke. "I didn't know . . ."

He pressed *G on the keyboard. The display had no more give than the bulkhead, but the orange symbols of a gunnery screen replaced the center of the panorama. The crossed circle to the right of the display was a trigger.

"Oh . . ." Lamartiere whispered. For the first time he thought that the bluff he planned might actually work.

He checked the command bar on the left side of the display, chose seek, and raised the search area to ten degrees above the horizon. The tarpaulin covered the region selected, so for the moment neither the pipper on the screen nor the tribarrel in the cupola reacted.

"Hang on," he called to the doctor. "We're going to just move out a little ways."

Leaving the gunnery display set, Lamartiere adjusted fan angle with the right grip and slid *Hoodoo* onto clear ground. Dust and pebbles spun outward in the spray of air escaping beneath the edge of the plenum chamber.

Lamartiere let *Hoodoo* settle. The gunnery display appeared to scroll down past the pipper until vague motion quivered in the center of the crosshairs. In the turret Clargue exclaimed when the tribarrel also moved.

Lamartiere expanded his image. The target was a drone with long slender wings and a small engine mounted on a pylon above the fuselage. The default option was auto; Lamartiere switched to manual because he simply didn't have the ammunition to spare the burst a computer might think was necessary to make sure of the target. He tapped the trigger once.

In the closed-up tank, the 2cm weapon merely *whacked* as it sent a bolt of ionized copper skyward at light speed. The main display compensated automatically for the burst of intense light; unless set otherwise, the AI used enhancement and thermal imaging to keep the apparent illumination at 100 percent of local daylight.

There was a cyan flash on the gunnery display, though. The lightly built drone broke apart in a flurry of wing panels and a mist of vaporized fuel. There was no fireball. The drone had been operating at too high an altitude for atmospheric pressure to sustain combustion.

"It worked!" Clargue shouted. "You made it work!"

"Mother God!" Lamartiere said as he fumbled to modify the screen. He was shaking. After a moment's confusion he realized that *of course* Clargue had been able to echo the gunnery display on his own screens. "You understand this so much better than I do, Doctor."

"No," said Clargue. "And even if I did, you are a man of war, Denis. As I will never be."

Lamartiere reduced the image and switched from seek to protect. When the map display came up, he expanded the region from the default—a ten-meter fringe surrounding *Hoodoo*—to include the whole area of Pamiers.

He touched auto. The civilians were under cover, deep in the mines, but an incoming round might shatter rock and bring down a traverse on huddled forms. One of them might have been his sister Celine.

Taking the yoke in both hands again, Lamartiere drove toward the eastern exit from the valley at a sedate pace. He didn't need to rush to get into position, and high speed on this terrain would waste precious ammunition when the AI responded to incoming artillery.

Because he concentrated on his driving, Lamartiere heard the whine of the cupola before he noticed motion on the gunnery screen. The tribarrel fired: three rounds, two, three more. Cyan and the dull red light of high explosive quivered on the gunnery screen.

Hoodoo's sensors and AI permitted her to sweep shells from the sky when they were still so far away that the explosions couldn't be seen by the naked eye. Given a vantage point and enough 2cm ammunition, this tank could defend the whole area from horizon to horizon.

The sticking point now was the ammunition.

The second salvo came over just before *Hoodoo* reached the mouth of the valley. The shells were fired out of the northwest, probably from guns in the government base at Ariege. The tribarrel hummed and crackled, rotating barrels between rounds so that the polished iridium bores had a chance to cool. The powergun bolts detonated the shells when they were barely over the horizon.

Driving with one hand, Lamartiere adjusted the gunnery screen. He hoped the gunners wouldn't waste any more of their expensive terminally guided rounds. They didn't have direct observation of the results since the drone had been knocked down, but observers with the mechanized battalion would tell them their fire was fruitless.

"I'm setting the gun only to respond to shells aimed at us

from now on, Doctor," he explained to Clargue. He supposed he was trying to pass on the burden of the choice he'd just made. "We're down to seventy-seven rounds. If I keep covering the village, we'll use up all the ammunition and then we lose everything."

"Yes," Clargue said. He sounded cool; certainly not judgmental. "Rather like triage."

"Pardon?" Lamartiere said. "Triage?"

Driving *Hoodoo* with the electronics working was infinitely less wearing than the trip Lamartiere had made in the early hours of the morning, trying to pick his way over narrow, half-familiar roads in the dark. The screens showed the path as though in daylight, and the tank's microwave imaging ignored dust and the mist beginning to rise in low points where aquifers bled through the rocks.

"When there are many injured and limited medical facilities," Clargue explained, "you divide the casualties into three groups. You ignore the ones who aren't in immediate danger so you can concentrate on helping those who will survive only if they get immediate help. And you also ignore those who will probably die even if you try to help them."

He coughed to clear his throat. "It's a technique of setting priorities that was developed during wartime."

Hoodoo crested a rise and entered the floodplain of the Lystra River. Except in springtime, the Lystra ran in a narrow channel only a few hundred meters wide—though deep and fast-flowing. There was only one ford on the upper river, and the bridges that spanned it during peace had been blown early in the rebellion.

The ford was a dike of basalt intruding into the surrounding limestone, raising the channel and spreading it to nearly a kilometer in width. One of the bridges had been here. The abutments and two pillars still stood, but the tangle of dynamited girders had tumbled out of sight downstream last year when the snow melted.

Befayt's troops were hidden in fighting holes, covered with insulating blankets that dispersed their thermal signatures. They'd learned to be careful eight months before, when elements of the Slammers began accompanying government units who entered the mountains.

The guerrillas had been wary of the mercenaries' firepower. They'd quickly learned that the sensor suites of the vast iridium behemoths were even more of a threat.

Given a little time, Dr. Clargue could put those sensors in the hands of the rebels. Clargue—and *Hoodoo*—just had to survive this night.

Lamartiere found the spot he'd noticed on previous visits to Pamiers, a shallow draw that carried overflow from the channel during the spate. He took *Hoodoo* over the edge; gently, he thought, but bank broke away and the tank rushed to the bottom of gravel and coarse vegetation with a roar. A geyser of dust rose.

Hoodoo's skirts dug into the ground, sealing the plenum chamber for an instant before the pressure rose enough to pop the tank up like a cork from a champagne bottle. The plume of debris followed the breeze upstream, settling and dissipating while the echoes of Lamartiere's ineptitude slowly faded.

"Befayt's people must think I'm an incompetent fool," Lamartiere muttered. "And they're right."

"What they think," Dr. Clargue replied with his usual dispassion, "is that the most powerful machine on Ambiorix is on their side. And they are indeed right."

Lamartiere revved his fans. He took *Hoodoo* slowly back up the slope until the cupola and its sensors peeked over crest to view the ford. Then he shut down again and studied the display.

"Doctor?" he said, wishing he could see Clargue's face as he spoke. "I'm going to try to bluff the Synod troops into thinking *Hoodoo* has her full armament. A 2cm round doesn't have anything like the power of the main gun, but it's no joke. I'm hoping if there's a big flash here, they'll think whatever hits them is from the 20cm gun."

"Ah," said Clargue, quick on the uptake as always. "So these little bombs Lieutenant Aghulan put in the compartment with me are to make the flashes. You want me to throw them out one at a time for you to detonate when you fire the tribarrel."

"That's right," said Lamartiere, "but you'll have to detonate them yourself when I call, 'Shoot'. Do you know how to use a clacker?"

"Of course I know how to use a clacker," Clargue said with frigid disdain. "I was born in Pamiers, was I not? But have you forgotten how to turn on the radios, Denis? The timing will be more accurate if you do both things yourself; and as for the remaining blasting caps, the transfer chamber for the big gun will provide a Faraday cage to shield them."

"Mother God," said Lamartiere in embarrassment. "Yes, Doctor, that's a much better idea. I'm very sorry."

He heard the cupola hatch open. "I've placed the first bomb," Clargue said mildly. "You have a great deal to think about, Denis. You are doing well."

I wish I were a million light-years away, Lamartiere thought as he concentrated on his displays. But he wasn't, and the rebellion would have to make do with him for want of better.

Hoodoo's sensors indicated the government battalion had halted on the reverse slope of the ridge north of the Lystra River. Their commander had the same problem as a hunter who thinks he's trapped a dangerous animal in a deep cave: the only way to be sure is to go straight in.

If the rebels were going to defend Pamiers, the ford was the obvious location. On the other hand they might well have drifted higher in the mountains, leaving behind booby traps and snipers instead of trying to stop a force they knew was unstoppable. That had generally been the case in the past when the government focused its strength.

Besides, months of battering by government units supported by mercenaries had virtually eliminated the Mosites' ability to mass large forces of their own.

But now there was a tank, a devouring superweapon, which the rebels *might* have in operating condition. All the battalion from Ariege knew for sure was that they had been ordered to assault Pamiers and eliminate the stolen tank at all cost.

Lamartiere grinned despite himself as he considered his enemy's options. The government troops knew one other thing: they, and not the brass in Carcassone, would be paying that cost.

He could have felt sorry for them if he hadn't remembered the villages Synod troops had "cleansed" after a nearby ambush. Of course, there'd been the garrisons of overrun government bases left with their genitals sewn into their mouths. In the name of God. . . .

An 8-wheeled "tank" accelerated over the crest and bounced down the road to the crossing at too high a speed. The driver was afraid of a rebel ambush, but nothing the Mosites could do would be worse than flipping the 30-tonne vehicle to tumble sideways into the river.

The hidden rebels didn't respond.

The tank slowed, spraying gravel from its locked wheels. It pulled off the road at the end of a switchback and settled into a hull-down position from which its long 10cm coil gun could cover the crossing.

Three more tanks came into sight one after another, following the first without the initial panicked haste. They all took overwatch positions on the forward slope. They weren't well shielded—one of them was in a clump of spiny shrubs that wouldn't stop small arms, let alone a 20cm bolt—but at least there was psychological benefit for the crews.

The government tanks had good frontal protection and powerful electromotive guns that could throw either HE or long-rod tungsten armor-piercers. Local technology couldn't carry the gun, the armor, and the banks of capacitors which powered the weapon, on an air-cushion chassis of reasonable size, though.

The Slammers' 30-tonne combat cars, like their tanks, had miniaturized fusion powerplants. The Government of Ambiorix would have had to import fusion units at many times the cost of the gun vehicles as completed with locally manufactured diesels. The 8-wheeled chassis was probably the best compromise between economics and the terrain.

With the tanks in position, the remainder of the battalion came over the hill and headed for the river. Thirty-odd air-cushion armored personnel carriers made up the bulk of the unit. Each APC mounted an automatic cannon in a small turret and could carry up to sixteen troops in addition to its own crew.

To Lamartiere's surprise there was an air-cushion jeep in the middle of the column. It pulled out of line almost at once and vanished behind an outcrop too slight to hide a vehicle of any size.

A lightly loaded air-cushion vehicle can sail across water because its weight is spread evenly over the whole surface beneath the plenum chamber. Government APCs carried too high a density of armor and payload for that. They sank, but where the bottom was as shallow and firm as it was here they could pogo across without flooding their fans. Even so, the Lystra was dangerously high. Only a crisis could induce a battalion to force the crossing now instead of waiting for the load of melting snow to recede for another week.

Rather than driving straight into the water as Lamartiere expected, the APCs formed three lines abreast well short of the bank. Their turret guns nervously searched the hills across the river, and troops pointed personal weapons from the open hatches in the vehicles' top decks.

Four more tanks closed the battalion's line of march. They drove past their fellows in overwatch positions to halt at the river's edge. A pair of crewmen got out of each vehicle and erected a breathing tube over the engine vents. While they worked, the third crew member closed the coil gun's muzzle with a tompion.

The crews got back in their waterproofed tanks and drove slowly into the river. The initial drop-off brought water foaming over the tops of the big wheels, but the slope lessened. The vehicles were nearly at the Lystra's midpoint before their turrets went completely under, leaving only the snorkel tubes and occasionally the raised muzzle of a coil gun to mark their progress.

The first rank of APCs bounded into the river with a roar and wall of spray like that at the base of a waterfall. They had waited so that their boisterous passage didn't swamp the tanks while the latter were still in deep water.

"Here we go," Lamartiere warned Clargue. He fed power to the fans and lifted *Hoodoo* several meters higher up the swale, exposing her turret and main gun to view of the government forces.

The tanks across the river fired before *Hoodoo* came to rest. Two shells landed ringing hammer blows against the turret and a third exploded just short, flinging half a tonne of dirt over the bow slope. If Lamartiere had been looking out of his hatch, the blasts would have decapitated him.

The government vehicles had fired HE, not armor-piercing shot. That meant they hadn't really expected to meet the Slammers' tank here. They must be terrified already . . .

Lamartiere laid the pipper on the gun mantle of the tank on the left. *He* was too busy to be frightened now.

Befayt's guerrillas and the APCs were firing wildly. Government automatic weapons stitched the night together with golden tracers. Rebel coil guns showed only puffs of fluorescent mist, the ionized vestiges of the projectiles' driving bands.

Lamartiere tapped his trigger while his left index finger clicked the radios on and off. Light more brilliant than the shell bursts lit *Hoodoo*'s turret. Remnants of the copper leads bled blue-green across the flash of aluminized slurry. Simultaneously the tribarrel's bolt struck at the base of the target's electromotive gun, cratering the armor and stripping insulation from the tube's windings.

"Another charge!" Lamartiere screamed.

The guerrillas were concentrating on tank snorkels and the APCs which had entered the stream. A line of bullets tore out the side of an APC's skirts. The vehicle rolled over on its back, spilling soldiers through the open hatches. The weight of their gear sucked them down.

The government tanks fired again. The tank Lamartiere had damaged dissolved in a sizzling short circuit. The current meant to accelerate a kilo of tungsten to 4000 kph instead ate metal. Everything flammable in the interior ignited, including the flesh of the crew.

The other three rounds missed *Hoodoo*. The gunners had switched to AP, but in their haste they'd forgotten to correct for the much flatter trajectory of the high-velocity shot.

"Ready!" Clargue called. Lamartiere hit the second tank exactly where he'd nailed the first. A 2cm bolt couldn't penetrate the government tanks' frontal armor, but accurately used it put paid to their armament. This time, the hatches flew open and the crew bailed out as soon as the bolt hit.

The government command vehicles carried hoop antennas that set them apart from the ordinary APCs. A guerrilla hit one with a shoulder-launched buzzbomb. The shaped-charge warhead sent a line of white fire through the interior and triggered a secondary explosion that blew the turret off.

In his triumph the rebel forgot the obvious. He reloaded and rose again from the same location. At least a dozen automatic cannon chewed him to a fiery memory.

Lamartiere laid his pipper on the third target. He didn't have time to shoot: the crew was already abandoning their untouched vehicle.

The APCs of the first wave were mostly bogged in the Lystra, though one had managed to wallow back to dry land with riddled skirts. An air-cushion vehicle could move with a leaking plenum chamber, but the fans shed their blades if they tried to push water.

Three of the fording tanks were only ripples on the surface of the river. The fourth had started to climb the south bank. Its bow and turret were clear, but the engine compartment was still under water when rebels had shot the breathing tube away. The bodies of the three crewmen lay halfway out of their hatches.

Lamartiere settled his pipper on the last of the overwatching tanks. The government driver backed and turned sharply, trying to retreat the way he had come. Lamartiere hit the vehicle in the middle of the flank, blowing the thin armor into the capacitor compartment. This time the short circuit was progressive rather than instantaneous as with the first victim, but the tank's ultimate destruction was no less complete.

The surviving APCs roared up the north slope of the valley, going back the way they'd come. Some of them had reversed their turrets and were spraying cannon shells southward, but they no longer made a pretense of aiming. Several vehicles stood empty, though without magnification Lamartiere couldn't see any signs of damage.

There were a dozen brush fires on the south side of the river, and almost that many burning vehicles on the north. It had been a massacre.

Guerrillas sniped at soldiers who were still moving, but some of Befayt's people were already splashing into the water to gather loot from the nearest tank. There was a cable bridge slung underwater a kilometer upstream. Organized parties of guerrillas would cross to sweep the northern bank in a few hours.

The jeep Lamartiere had forgotten suddenly accelerated out of cover, heading uphill. Lamartiere slapped his pipper on it for magnification rather than in a real attempt to shoot.

The vehicle jinked left and vanished before he *could* have shot. He was almost sure from the brief glimpse that the two figures aboard were wearing Slammers' uniforms.

Lamartiere heard the tribarrel whine under the AI's guidance. It began firing short bursts: the artillery in Ariege was shelling again. The gunners hadn't had enough warning to support the crossing with the concentrations they must have prepared in case of rebel resistance.

"They could have crushed us, Doctor," Lamartiere said in wonder. "They could have gone right through except they panicked. We won because we frightened them, not because we beat them."

"In my proper profession," Clargue said, "a cure is a cure. I don't see a distinction between the psychological effect of a placebo and the biological effect of a real drug—so long as the beneficial effect occurs."

He paused before adding, "I find it difficult to view this destruction as beneficial, but I suppose it's better than the same thing happening to Pamiers."

The last of the surviving APCs had crossed the ridge to safety, leaving behind a pall of dust and the wreckage of their fellows. The tribarrel continued to fire. The gunners no longer had the site under observation, but they were making noise for much the same reason as savages beat drums when the sun vanishes in eclipse.

"I'm going back to Pamiers," Lamartiere said. He was extraordinarily tired. "There's some damage to the skirts—" rips from fragments of the shells that hit the turret in the first salvo "—that needs to be repaired. Then we have to get out of here."

Franciscus jumped onto the bow slope. Lamartiere hadn't

seen him approaching; there'd been more on his mind than his immediate surroundings.

"We won!" the colonel shouted. "By God, the Council'll know who to give charge of the war to now! We won't stop in Brione, we'll take Carcassone!"

The cupola hatch was open because Dr. Clargue had been throwing the flash charges out of it. Franciscus climbed up and said, "I'll ride inside on the way back."

Lamartiere heard the hatch thump closed. Franciscus shouted in anger.

Lamartiere drove *Hoodoo* up and onto the road. Neither he nor the doctor spoke on the way back to Pamiers.

Lamartiere shut off the fans in the center of Pamiers. He opened his hatch.

Franciscus looked down at him. He wasn't wearing a shirt so the bomb-heavy bandoliers wobbled across the curly hair of his chest. He hadn't been around when Befayt provided the reminder about blasting caps and radios. Lamartiere didn't comment.

Despite the consciously heroic pose, the colonel looked vaguely unsure of himself. Being closed out of *Hoodoo* on the drive back had caused him to consider Lamartiere as something more than a pawn for the colonel to play. He asked, "Why didn't you put us under cover?"

"Because all it covers now," Lamartiere said as he got out, "is our sensors' ability to see any shells the Synod sends over. They know from the drone where we were hiding, so it's a fixed target for them. This way *Hoodoo* protects herself."

Of course there were only thirty-seven rounds left in the tribarrel's loading tube. Maybe Dr. Clargue would be able to find the transfer command in the respite he and *Hoodoo*—and Denis Lamartiere, for all Lamartiere felt a failure—had won. But the first order of business was to repair the tank and get *out* of here.

Lamartiere slid down the bow and walked toward the pit where Pelissier had his workshop. Civilians ran to the tank, some of them carrying lanterns. They cheered and waved yellow Mosite flags. Lamartiere tried to smile as he brushed his way through them.

A child handed him a garland of red windflowers. Lamartiere took it, but the streaming blooms made him think of blood in water. The Lystra's current would have carried the carnage kilometers downstream by now. . . .

Franciscus stood, using the tank as a podium. He began to tell the story of the battle in a loud, triumphant voice. Lamartiere didn't look back.

Pelissier had been only a teenager when he lost both legs in a mine accident. Since that time he'd served as Pamiers' machinist, living in an increasingly ornate house during peacetime and at the entrance of a disused mine since rebellion had destroyed the village.

Pelissier had a chair mounted on a four-wheeled tray. The seat raised and lowered, and there was an electric motor to drive him if required. For the most part, the cripple trundled himself around his immediate vicinity by hand. He never went far from his dwelling.

Pelissier and his old mother doffed their caps as Lamartiere approached. "So," the machinist said. "I congratulate you. But you have learned that no matter how powerful a machine may seem to be, it still can break. That is so?"

"I worked in the depot at Brione, Pelissier," Lamartiere said. "I never doubted that tanks break. Now I need you to weld patches over holes in the skirts so that I can get *Hoodoo* away from here. Otherwise she'll draw worse down on you."

Madame Pelissier spat. Her son looked past Lamartiere toward the ruined houses and said, "Worse? But no matter. Can I get within the chamber? The patches should be made from inside. That way pressure will hold them tighter."

"There's access ports in the skirts," Lamartiere said. He knew better than to suggest the cripple would be unable to use an opening made for a man with legs.

Pelissier nodded. "Bring your great machine up here, then, so that we don't have to move the welder through this wasteland."

He spun his tray back toward the entrance and his equipment. Over his shoulder he said, "I cannot fight them myself, Lamartiere. But to help you, that I can do."

Lamartiere walked back toward *Hoodoo*. He'd have to move the crowd away before he started the fans: pebbles slung under the skirts could put a child's eye out.

He still held the garland. He was staring at the flowers, wondering how he could decently rid himself of an object that made him feel queasy, when he realized that Father Renaud was standing in his path.

Lamartiere stopped and bowed. "I'm sorry, Father," he said. "I wasn't looking where I was going."

"You have much on your mind," Renaud said. "I wouldn't bother you merely to offer praise."

The priest's lips quirked in a tiny smile. "Glory is in God's hands, not mine, but I have no doubt that She will mete out a full measure to you, Denis."

Renaud's face sobered into its usual waxlike placidity. "I know I'm thought to be hard," he continued. "Perhaps I am. But I feel the loss of every member of my flock, even those I know are seated with God in heaven. You have my sincere sympathy for the loss of your sister."

"Loss?" said Lamartiere. He wasn't sure what he'd just heard. "Celine is . . .?"

Father Renaud blinked. He looked honestly shocked for the first time in the year Lamartiere had known him. "You didn't know?" he said. "Oh, my poor child. Celine drove the truck into the gate so that you could escape from Brione. I think she did it as much for your sake as for God's, but God will receive her in Her arms nonetheless."

Lamartiere hung the garland around his neck. Some child had picked the flowers as the only gift she could offer the man she thought had saved her. It would please that child to see him wearing them.

"I see," Lamartiere said. He heard his voice catch, but his mind was detached, dispassionate. "Celine wasn't the sort to refuse when called to duty, Father. She would have sacrificed herself as quickly for faith alone as for me. As I would very willingly have sacrificed myself for her."

He bowed and stepped past Renaud.

"Denis?" Renaud called. "If there is anything I can offer. . . ?"

"Your faith needs *Hoodoo* in working order, Father,"

Lamartiere said without looking around. "I'm going to go take care of that now."

Hundreds of civilians crowded around the tank; the vast metal bulk dwarfed them. The superweapon, the machine that would win the war. . . .

"Let me through!" Lamartiere said. People stepped aside when they saw who was speaking. "I have to get the tank repaired immediately. Everyone get back to the tunnels!"

Franciscus stood on *Hoodoo*'s turret. He called something; Lamartiere couldn't hear him over the crowd noise. The colonel was everything a military hero needed to be: trim, armed to the teeth, and willing to sacrifice anything to achieve his ends.

Dr. Clargue sat nearby on a man-sized lump of tailings, rubbing his temples. He looked as tired as Lamartiere felt.

Lamartiere climbed up *Hoodoo*'s bow slope. "Doctor," he called. "Get everyone out of here. It's very dangerous to be here!"

"Lamartiere!" Franciscus said. "I want you to teach me how to operate the guns. We can start right now, while the repairs are being done."

"Yes, all right," said Lamartiere, slipping into the driver's compartment. He threw the switch closing the cupola hatch before Franciscus could get in.

"Sorry, wrong button," he called over the colonel's angry shout. "Just a moment. Let me start the fans and I'll open it."

He didn't want Franciscus inside *Hoodoo*'s turret. Lamartiere still owed something to the rebellion; and Celine had, after all, sacrificed herself for the purpose of stealing the tank.

The civilians were drifting away, but some were still too close. Lamartiere revved the fans with the blades flat. They made a piercing whine as unpleasant as fingernails on a blackboard.

Children shrieked, holding their hands over their ears. They and their mothers scampered away. Clargue chivied them with a fierceness that suggested he guessed what was about to happen.

Franciscus shouted, "You idiot, what are you trying to do?"

Lamartiere looked up at the man on the turret. "Good-bye, Colonel," he said. "Give my love to Celine if you meet her."

He closed the driver's hatch over himself. He wasn't doing this for Celine, because Celine was already dead; but perhaps he was doing it so that Colonel Franciscus wouldn't create any more Celines.

Lamartiere switched on *Hoodoo*'s radios. The simultaneous blast of the six bombs on Franciscus' bandoliers barely made the tank shudder.

M2A4 TANK

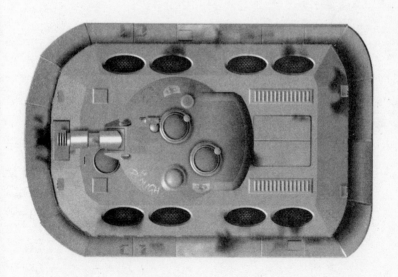

THE IRRESISTIBLE FORCE

Lamartiere sat in the driver's compartment of the supertank *Hoodoo*, which he'd stolen from Hammer's Slammers as the mercenaries left Ambiorix for Beresford and another contract. The tank's 20cm main gun could smash mountains; the fully automatic 2cm tribarrel in the cupola defended her against incoming artillery as well as packing a sizable punch in its own right. She was the most powerful weapon within twenty light-years.

In theory, at least. *Hoodoo*'s practical value to the sputtering remnants of the Mosite Rebellion would have to wait until Lamartiere and Dr. Clargue figured out how to transfer ammunition from the tank's storage magazines in the hull to the ready magazines in the turret.

"The reconnaissance drone has turned east," Clargue said over the intercom. "The AI predicts it's completed its search pattern, but I suppose we should wait a short time to be sure."

"Right," Lamartiere said, wondering if he'd fall asleep if he closed his eyes for a moment. "We'll wait."

Even with *Hoodoo* at rest in a narrow gorge, her internal systems and the hum of the idling drive fans made her noisy. It would have been difficult to shout directly through the narrow passage between the fighting compartment and the driver's position in the bow. The Slammers would have used commo helmets to cut off the ambient noise, but Lamartiere hadn't bothered with frills the night he drove *Hoodoo* out of the spaceport at Brione.

The Government of Ambiorix had decided the Mosite Rebellion was broken, so they'd terminated the mercenaries' contract to save the cost of paying for such sophisticated troops and equipment. *Hoodoo* was the last piece of Slammers' hardware on the planet. An electrical fault had held it and its two-man crew back when the rest of the regiment lifted for Beresford, 300 light-years away.

Those planning the operation on behalf of the Mosite Council in Goncourt had claimed that *Hoodoo* would win the war. With a single supertank the Council could force the Carcassone government to grant autonomy to the Western District where the Mosite faith predominated.

Lamartiere had been at the sharp end, infiltrating Brione as one of the mercenaries' Local Service Personnel—cheap local labor who did fetch and carry for the Slammers' skilled service technicians. He hadn't thought beyond completion of the operation, and even that only in the moments when he had enough leisure to think more than half a second ahead. If asked, though, he'd have said that *Hoodoo*'s enormous power would restore military parity between Mosite forces and the government.

Maybe, just maybe, that would have been true—if he and Clargue could use *Hoodoo*'s armament properly. As it was, with luck and fewer than a hundred rounds of 2cm ammunition gleaned from the local militia, they'd been able to smash a government mechanized battalion at the Lystra River.

It wouldn't work that way again, though. By now the government would have analyzed the wreckage of the previous battle and realized that *Hoodoo*'s main gun wasn't working, though they might not guess why. A powerful force would attack *Hoodoo* again as soon as Carcassone learned where she had fled. This time Lamartiere's trickery wouldn't be enough to win.

In addition to the government, the tank's mercenary crew, Sergeant Heth and Trooper Stegner, had stayed on Ambiorix instead of rejoining the regiment. They might or might not be actively helping the government forces, but in any case they contributed to the aura of overhanging doom Lamartiere had felt ever since his triumph at stealing *Hoodoo* had worn off.

"The drone hasn't returned," Clargue said in his usual mild tone. The doctor was as tired and frustrated as Lamartiere, but you never heard that in his voice.

"Sorry," Lamartiere said. "I was daydreaming." Daydreaming in the middle of the night, with the stars above jewels in the desert air. It was thirty-six hours since Lamartiere had last slept.

He raised the drive fans from idle speed to full power, then broadened the angle of the blades so that they pushed the atmosphere instead of simply cutting it. *Hoodoo* rose on the bubble of air trapped within her steel-skirted plenum chamber, then slid out of the gully in which Lamartiere had hidden her when the government drone came over the horizon. With the nacelles tilted forward to retard the tank's rush down the slope, *Hoodoo* entered the Boukasset.

Most of Ambiorix' single large continent was organized in districts under administrators appointed by Carcassone. The sparsely settled Boukasset, the rocky wasteland in the rain shadow of the mountains forming the Western District, had always been ignored as a poor relation. Since the Western District had rebelled when the Synod of the Established Church attempted to put down what it described as the Mosite Heresy, the Boukasset's connection to Carcassone had become even more tenuous.

Hoodoo squirmed out of the mountains and into a broad river basin, dry now but a gushing, foaming torrent once every decade or so when cloudbursts drenched the Boukasset. The bottom was carpeted with vegetation that survived on groundwater dribbling beneath the sand. The coarse brush flattened beneath a 170-tonne tank with the power of a fusion bottle to drive it, then sprang up again to conceal all traces of *Hoodoo*'s passage.

Lamartiere pulled his control yoke back, increasing speed gradually. The AI overlaid a recommended course on the terrain display and steered the tank along it as long as Lamartiere permitted it to do so.

Their intended destination was the Shrine of the Blessed Catherine. If Lamartiere fell asleep now, *Hoodoo* would roar past the site in three hours and forty-nine minutes according to the countdown clock at the top of the display.

Giggling and aware that he wasn't safe to drive, Lamartiere pulled the yoke back a hair farther. The Estimated Time of Arrival dropped to three hours and twenty-four minutes.

Nowhere on Ambiorix was safe for Lamartiere until he and Clargue got *Hoodoo*'s guns working. He wouldn't be safe then either, but at least he could fight back.

Maury, the rebel commander in the Boukasset, dealt with off-planet smugglers who slipped down in small vessels. *Hoodoo*'s tribarrel used the same ammunition as the 2cm shoulder weapons of the Slammers' infantry and others who could afford those smashingly effective weapons. Maury had some of the guns, so he could supply the tank if he chose to.

If. . . .

"What do you know about Maury, Doctor?" Lamartiere asked, partly to keep himself awake. "He seems to have held the government out of his region, which we couldn't do in the mountains."

Great trees overhung the riverbed. The pinlike leaves of their branches shivered as the tank slid past. The trees' taproots penetrated the buried aquifer, but their trunks were clear of the flash floods that periodically scoured the channel.

"There's nothing in the Boukasset that the government wanted badly enough to commit Hammer's mercenaries to get it," Clargue said. "Nomadic herdsmen and small-scale farmers using terraces and deep wells. Our mines in the Western District were Ambiorix' main source of foreign exchange before the rebellion."

Clargue was a small, precise man in his sixties; a doctor who'd left the most advanced hospital in Carcassone to serve the sick of his home village of Pamiers in the mountains. Because of his experience with medical computers as complex as the systems of this tank, the Council had chosen him to help Lamartiere make *Hoodoo* operational. He'd tried despite his distaste for the war that had wrecked his home and Ambiorix as a whole, but he hadn't been able to find a way to access the ammunition Lamartiere *knew* was stored in *Hoodoo*'s hull.

"As for what I know of Maury," Clargue continued, "nothing to his credit. At the best of times leaders in the Boukasset have been one step removed from posturing thugs. 'Posturing thug' would be a kind description of Maury if half the rumors one hears are true."

"Beggars can't be choosers, I suppose," Lamartiere muttered. His yoke twitched in his hands as the AI guided *Hoodoo*.

He had a bad feeling about this, but he'd had a bad feeling about the operation almost from the beginning. He'd bloodied the government badly both when he escaped from Brione with the tank and at the Lystra River. But Pamiers had received a hammering by artillery and perhaps worse because *Hoodoo* had hidden there, and at Brione Lamartiere's sister Celine had died while driving a truck-load of explosive into the main gate of the base.

So long as the war went on, everybody lost. If *Hoodoo* became fully operational, she could extend the war for years and maybe decades.

"Beggars have no power," Clargue said. He sniffed. "A man like Maury understands no language but that of power. The Council must be fools to send us into the Boukasset with that message."

Lamartiere sighed. "Yeah," he said. "But we already knew that, and we're here anyway. We'll see what we can work out."

The dry riverbed lost itself among the plains. The skirts began to ring on rocks, the heavy debris dumped here at the last spate and not yet covered by sand. Lamartiere edged *Hoodoo* northward to where the ground was smoother. The AI reconfigured the course slightly; the ETA changed again.

Hoodoo roared through the starlit night, heading at speed toward the next way-station on a road to nowhere.

It was an hour past dawn. The low sun deepened the color of the red cliffs and the red sand into which those cliffs decayed. By midday the sun would turn the sky brassy and bleach every hue to a ghost of itself.

The shrine was in the Boukasset where four generations ago Catherine had given birth to the child who became Bishop Moses, to whom God revealed the foundations of the Mosite faith. The site had been a pilgrimage center during peacetime, but Lamartiere hadn't been religious in that fashion.

Since Lamartiere learned what had happened to his sister Celine, he hadn't been religious in any way at all; but now there was no way out of the course he'd chosen in the days when he could believe in a future.

The first sign of habitation was the line of conical shelters, two or three abreast, which wound across the plain. Low hills lay in the distance to east and west, and a jagged sandstone slope rose immediately north of the site.

The shrine itself was a fortress walled in the russet stone of the overlooking cliff. It was built on a lower slope where the rise could be accommodated by a single terrace, but the gullied rock behind it rose at 1:2 or even 1:1.

The spire of a church showed above the enclosure's ten-meter sidewalls. A bell there rang when *Hoodoo* appeared out of the east, trailing a great plume of dust.

Lamartiere disengaged the AI and began slowing the tank by turning the fan nacelles vertical instead of tilting them to the rear. *Hoodoo*'s enormous inertia meant control inputs had to be added well in advance.

"They grow lemon trees in those shelters," Dr Clargue said. He sounded puzzled at something. "The plantings are laid out over an underground aquifer, but without protection the wind would scour the leaves and even bark off the trees."

He paused, then added, "There weren't nearly as many trees when I came here twelve years ago. Only a handful of Brothers tended to the shrine then."

Lamartiere guided the tank past the cones straggling as they followed a seam in the bedrock. Overlying sand kept the water from evaporating. He knew that lemons from the Boukasset had a reputation for flavor, but because he'd never visited the region he hadn't wondered how terrain so barren could grow citrus fruit.

Hoodoo had slowed to a crawl when she was still a hundred meters from the high walls of the shrine. Lamartiere cut his fan speed but angled the nacelles sternward again. The tank slid the remainder of the way forward under perfect control.

Lamartiere ruefully congratulated himself on his skill. He was probably the only person in the Boukasset who knew how difficult it was to drive a 170-tonne air-cushion vehicle.

He slid open his hatch. What looked from a distance like the shrine's entrance had been closed by sandstone blocks many years in the past. A woman leaned over the battlements. Beside her, a basket hung on a crane extending from the wall. A great geared wheel within raised and lowered it. The basket was apparently the only way in and out of the shrine.

"Tell your leader that we need help to spread the camouflage cover over this tank," Lamartiere called to the woman. "Otherwise we'll be spotted if the government overflies us."

Men and women were approaching from the lemon orchard, though the sprawled extent of the plantings meant it would be half an hour before the more distant folk reached the shrine. There were hundreds of people, far more than Lamartiere had expected.

"The Brothers have been sheltering refugees," Clargue realized aloud. He sat on the edge of his hatch, his legs dangling down the turret's smooth iridium armor.

Lamartiere looked up at his companion and hid a frown. The doctor had always seemed frail. Now he was skeletal, worn to the bone by strain and the frustration of not being able to find the command that would transfer ammunition and permit *Hoodoo* to use her devastating weaponry.

"Go away!" the woman shouted. Her left hand was bandaged. "Go back to the hell you came from and leave us alone!"

An old man in black robes and a pillbox hat appeared on the battlements beside her. He and the woman held a brief discussion while Lamartiere kept silent.

The woman unpinned the gearwheel, letting the basket wobble down. The man held his hat on with one hand as he bent forward. "Please," he said. "If you gentlemen will come up, it will be easier for us to discuss your presence."

Lamartiere looked at Clargue. "One of us should stay with . . ." he said.

The doctor smiled. "Yes, of course," he said, "but you should carry out the negotiations. I wouldn't know what to say to them."

"And you think I do?" Lamartiere said; but he knew Clargue was right. The doctor was smarter and older and better educated; but this was war, and Clargue was utterly a man of peace.

Denis Lamartiere was . . . not a man of peace. He and Clargue were operating in a world at war, now, however much both of them might hate it.

Lamartiere got into the basket. He let the sway of it ratcheting upward soothe his tension.

The basket was still several feet below the stone coping when the pulley touched the fiber cage connecting the rim to the draw rope. The old man helped Lamartiere onto the battlements. Normally Lamartiere would have scrambled over easily by himself, but his head was swaying with fatigue even though the basket was steady again.

The old man wore a clean white tunic with a red sash under the black robe. Though his beard was gray, not white, his face bore the lines of someone much older than Lamartiere would have guessed from a distance.

"Sorry, ah, Father?" Lamartiere said. "You're in charge of the shrine?"

"I'm Father Blenis," the old man said. "We try to work cooperatively here in the presence of the Blessed Catherine, but because of my age the others let me speak for us all."

"It's not your age!" the woman said. She'd pinned the ratchet, locking the wheel so that a breeze didn't send the basket hurtling down uncontrolled. She looked at Lamartiere and continued: "Father Blenis is a saint. He's taken us in after your kind would have let us all die—once you'd stolen everything we had."

"Marie," Father Blenis said. "This gentleman—"

He looked at Lamartiere and raised an eyebrow.

"Lamartiere, Denis Lamartiere," Lamartiere said. "Dr. Clargue and I won't stay any longer than we need to, ah, do some work on *Hoodoo*. On our tank."

Three of the people coming in from the field were nearing the base of the walls. A thin younger man was pushing ahead of a woman while a much larger fellow clumped along close behind.

"It's the job of whoever last comes up the walls to lift the next person," Marie said with a challenging glare at Lamartiere. He first guessed she was well into middle age, but she might be considerably younger. Hunger and hard use could have carved the lines in her face.

And anger. Anger was as damaging to a woman's appearance as a spray of acid.

"Yes, all right," Lamartiere said. He was a little steadier now. Just getting out of the tank and its omnipresent vibration had helped, though he knew he was both weak and desperately tired.

He removed the pin and lifted the ratchet pawl, controlling the basket with his other hand on the crank. "Don't you have any power equipment here?"

"You should ask!" Marie spat. Pus had seeped through the bandage on her left hand; it needed to be changed again. "When it's your kind who stole it!"

"Marie," Father Blenis murmured. He put his own frail hands on the crank beside Lamartiere's, silently rebuking the woman for her lack of charity.

"We'd ordered a winch and solar power unit for it, Mr. Lamartiere," he explained, "but it didn't arrive. In general the parties who rule the region allow us to trade unhindered so long as we pay taxes to them—"

"I'll handle it, Father," Marie said contritely. She patted both Blenis and Lamartiere away from the winch. The process of moving hundreds of people in and out of the fortress must be a very time-consuming one, though having each person lift the next one kept it from being an unbearable physical burden.

Blenis stepped aside, gesturing Lamartiere with him. Lamartiere would have protested, but he was suddenly so dizzy that he sat down in order not to fall.

"When we order something that looks particularly enticing, though," Blenis went on, "it may not arrive. By living simply here we avoid such problems for the most part."

He grinned. "Another example of how those who follow God's tenets avoid temporal concerns," he said. It took Lamartiere a moment to realize that he was joking.

There was angry shouting at the base of the walls. Concern wiped the smile from the Father's face. He leaned over to see what was happening.

"It's not taxes," Marie muttered to Lamartiere. "It's pure theft, and by both sides. But what can *we* do since you have the guns, eh?"

"Rasile, Louise," Father Blenis called. His voice had penetrating volume when he chose to use it. Living in this windswept wasteland would teach a man to speak with authority. "Let Pietro come up first, then he can lift both of you together. Let us leave struggle outside our community."

"I haven't robbed anybody," Lamartiere said. He'd killed. Some of those he'd killed had probably been civilians as innocent as the refugees here at the shrine, but even in his present exhausted state it made him angry to be accused of things he hadn't done.

He shook his head, trying to clear it of the hot white fuzz that clogged his thoughts. "You pay taxes to the government, then?" he said. "I didn't know Carcassone had officials in the Boukasset nowadays."

Marie grunted with the effort of hauling up the first of the civilians below. Before she could catch her breath to speak, Father Blenis said, "There aren't regular officials, or regular troops either. The government sent a group of former rebels, Ralliers, into the Boukasset under a Captain de Laburat."

He smiled again. The Father's consistent good humor was a shock to Lamartiere. For years most of the people he'd been around were soured by war and fury.

"I'm not sure whether the government was trying to impose its will or merely hoping to prevent Maury from having things all his own way." Blenis continued. "In any case, Maury's band and the Ralliers under de Laburat decided to cooperate rather than fight. A model for the whole planet, wouldn't you say?"

The heavyset man got out of the basket. Lamartiere had seen more obvious signs of intelligence on the faces of sheep. Marie stepped away from the crank.

"Pietro," Father Blenis said, "bring up Rasile and your sister, please."

To Lamartiere he went on, "Pietro's strength has been a great help to our community since he and Louise arrived last month."

Marie turned and sniffed. Her good hand played with the stained dressings of the other.

"Look, Father," Lamartiere said. He spoke toward his hands in his lap because he was too tired to raise his eyes as he knew he should. The rhythmic squeals of the winch were starting to put him to sleep. "I don't mean to disturb your peace, but we have to stay here until we get in touch with Maury."

He shook his head again. It didn't help him think. "Or with the Council in Goncourt if they've got a better idea," he said. "We're going to need food and water, and if you don't help us get *Hoodoo* under cover you're going to learn how much the government cares for your neutrality as soon as the first drone comes over."

With Pietro's strength on the crank, the basket had already reached the battlements. The slim man and the woman, Louise, got out on opposite sides with the tense hostility of rival dogs. They looked remarkably fit in contrast to Marie, but neither was a person Lamartiere would have chosen to know in peacetime. He supposed that pimps and hard-faced whores sometimes became refugees also.

"Carcassone doesn't fly anything over the Boukasset," Rasile said. Lamartiere blinked in surprise to hear so throaty and pleasant a voice coming from the rat-faced civilian. "If they do, Maury shoots them down. Or de Laburat does it himself."

Marie stepped forward. "Look, you don't belong here!" she said harshly to Lamartiere. "We'll give you water, and you can have food, too. I suppose you'll like the taste even better because you're snatching it out of the mouths of widows and orphans, won't you? But take your tank and your war away from us—or die, that would be fine. That would be even better!"

"Marie," Father Blenis said. His tone was sharper than Lamartiere had heard from him previously, though it was still mild after the rasping anger of the others who'd been speaking. "Mr. Lamartiere has come as a distressed traveler. You can see how tired he is. The Blessed Catherine has never turned such folk away in the past, as you well know."

"He's a soldier!" she said. "He came in a tank!"

"We won't let him bring weapons within the walls," Blenis replied. With the gentle humor Lamartiere was learning to recognize, he added, "Especially his tank. But he and his companion are welcome to the hospitality we offer to anyone passing by."

Houses two and three stories high were built around the interior of the shrine. The rooms had external staircases and windows opening onto the central courtyard where an herb garden grew. Lamartiere could see two well copings and, at the upper end of the courtyard, a stone trough into which water trickled from an ancient bronze pipe.

Several younger women holding infants stood in the doorways, watching the group around the winch. All of them had the same worn look that Lamartiere had noticed in Marie. A woman alone—and worse, a woman with small children—would have had a tough time crossing a wasteland ruled by rival gangs. There were, quite literally, fates worse than death, because the dead didn't wake from a screaming nightmare before every dawn.

The basket was tight against the pulley. Pietro still held the crank, possibly because nobody'd told him to do otherwise. Someone shouted from below. Pietro looked at Louise, who snapped, "Yes, yes, bring the next one up. For God's sake!"

"Louise?" Blenis said.

The woman grimaced. She might have been attractive once, but the glint of her eyes was a worse disfigurement than the old scar on her right cheek. "Sorry, Father," she said. "I'll watch my language."

Lamartiere tried to stand. He didn't belong in a place where people worried about taking the name of God in vain.

"Look, the hell with you," he said. He was furious because of frustration at his inability to accomplish anything he could feel good about. "We'll go, just get us water."

The world went white. Lamartiere was lying on the stone battlements. He didn't remember how he got there. "We'll leave you alone," he tried to whisper.

"Marie, make a bed for Mr. Lamartiere here," Father Blenis murmured through the buzzing white blur. "Later on we can consider the future."

Lamartiere awoke to see Father Blenis rearranging a slatted screen so that the lowering sun didn't fall on the sleeper's face. The rattle and flickering light had brought Lamartiere up from the depths to which exhaustion had plunged him. Near the winch a young woman nursed her infant while an older child played at her feet.

"Oh God, help me," Lamartiere groaned. There was nothing blasphemous in the words. His every muscle ached and his head throbbed in tune with his heartbeat, though the haloes of light framing objects settled back to normal vision after a few moments.

"I'm sorry, I didn't mean to wake you," Blenis said. "Can you drink something, or. . . ?"

"Please," Lamartiere said. He sat up, ignoring the pain because he *had* to get moving. He had no traumatic injury, just the cumulative effects of a day and a half spent as a component of a tank.

Hoodoo's metal, seals, and insulation became worn in the course of service. A bearing in Number 7 drive fan would be repacked if the vehicle were in Brione for depot maintenance, and the lip of the skirts needed recontouring if not replacement.

The crew needed downtime also, but they wouldn't have gotten it in the field any more than the tank itself would. Heth and Stegner would have gone on until the mission was accomplished or something irretrievably broke.

Lamartiere was in the same situation, except that by now he was quite certain his mission—defeat of the Carcassone government— could never be accomplished. The only question was whether he or *Hoodoo* fell to ruin first.

Father Blenis held out a gourd cup. Lamartiere took it from the old man and drank unaided. The contents were milk, not water; goat's milk, he supposed, since he'd seen goats scrambling about the hillsides nearby. It was hard to imagine that the Boukasset had enough vegetation even for goats. No doubt they, like the shrine's human residents, had simple tastes.

Lamartiere looked over the wall coping. The camouflage tarp was stretched between poles and hooks hammered into wall crevices, so from this angle only *Hoodoo*'s bow was visible. The fabric provided a radar barrier and a sophisticated matrix which mimicked the thermal signature of the materials to either side. Aerial reconnaissance would show only a blotch of rock against the wall of the shrine.

Most of the residents were at work again in the orchard, either picking ripe lemons or building additional drystone shelters. The latter work was performed by gangs of refugees, but a black-robed Brother oversaw each group.

A few civilians sat or stood near *Hoodoo*'s bow. Dr. Clargue was in the driver's hatch, draining the sore on a child's shin while the mother looked on. A slightly older girl stood on a headlight bracket and, with a self-important expression, held the exiguous medical kit Clargue had brought with him from Pamiers. The equipment would have slipped down the bow slope if the doctor had laid it directly on the armor.

"I've got to go down and spell Clargue," Lamartiere said. "Has he been awake all the time?"

"In a moment," Father Blenis said. He smiled. "Your companion has been a godsend. We've never had a doctor in residence here, and some of the distressed folk coming for shelter recently have needed help beyond what I and the other Brothers are trained to provide. Regrettably, medical supplies don't reach us here."

Lamartiere scowled. He got carefully to his feet by bracing himself on the stone. As he slept the residents had slid a blanket-wrapped mattress of springy brush beneath him. It was the best bed that Lamartiere had had since he thundered out of Brione in the stolen tank.

Lamartiere's discomfort came from being shaken for over a day in the strait confines of *Hoodoo*'s driving compartment. Dr. Clargue understood the tank's software better than Lamartiere could ever hope to do, but driving a tank was a specialized skill that Clargue had never learned. They couldn't switch positions during the high-speed run into the Boukasset.

Lamartiere paused; he'd intended to climb into the basket, but his body wasn't quite ready. "You're in regular touch with the rest of Ambiorix, then?" he asked.

"A truck comes every week to pick up our lemons and bring us the things we've ordered with the proceeds," Blenis explained. "An aircraft would be better but as Rasile said, no one flies in the Boukasset. Maury and de Laburat both import very sophisticated weaponry, much of it by starship. Not medical supplies, though; at least not to share with us."

He shook his head. "I'm not complaining," he said. "God has poured Her bounty over us with great generosity. We give thanks daily that She allows us to help so many of Her afflicted."

"I'll go down now and send the doctor up," Lamartiere said. "He needs sleep at least as much as I did."

He stepped into the basket. The woman moved the slung infant to her right hip so that she could grip the crank.

"You know, all people really need is peace," Father Blenis said. "I regret that this isn't understood more widely. Ambiorix would be a better place."

Lamartiere walked to *Hoodoo*'s bow, feeling stronger with each step. He wasn't looking forward to getting inside again, but perhaps he wouldn't have to if he stayed close to the hatch.

Dr. Clargue was rebandaging Marie's hand. "The dry air is an advantage," he said, pitching his voice to greet Lamartiere as well as speaking to his patient. "Germs don't find it any more attractive than I do. Though I'd prefer to have a greater supply of antibiotic cream as well."

Rasile, Louise, and the woman's dimwitted brother—if Pietro really was her brother—loitered near the tank. Unlike Marie, none of them had any obvious medical problems.

"You three," Lamartiere ordered harshly. Whatever they were doing, it wasn't together: Louise and Rasile liked each other as little as Lamartiere liked either one of them. "Get out of here. Either out in the orchard or inside the shrine, I don't care which."

Pietro was in a different category. You couldn't dislike him any more than you could dislike a rock, though a rock could be dangerous enough in the wrong circumstances.

"Who do you think you are, giving me orders?" Rasile said.

"The guy who's going to be testing *Hoodoo*'s drive fans in a moment," Lamartiere said as he hopped onto the bow slope. "If you're within a hundred meters when I crank up, there won't be anything left of you but a smear by the time I shut down again. Just a friendly warning."

If trouble started, Lamartiere needed to be in the driver's seat. He wished Clargue weren't there now, but the doctor wouldn't have been able to work on his patients from the cupola.

The refugees drifted toward the orchard instead of pushing matters. Louise and Pietro walked together, while Rasile stayed twenty meters distant in space and a lot farther away in spirit.

Lamartiere supposed they'd been hoping to steal equipment. Tanks in the field were generally festooned with gear, but Heth and Stegner had stripped *Hoodoo* to be loaded on a starship before Lamartiere drove her out of the base. He and Clargue had only the clothes they stood in, but Lamartiere still didn't want the likes of those three rummaging around inside the tank.

Clargue got out of the compartment very stiffly. "I'm sorry, Denis," he said. "I should have been working on the software, but I found I was a doctor before I was a tank crewman."

"Go get a bath and some sleep, Doctor," Lamartiere said. "There's plenty of water here, for our purposes anyway."

He gripped Clargue's hand to permit him to negotiate the iridium slope under control. "You did just what you should've done. I wish I could say the same."

Clargue trudged toward the basket, carrying his medical kit. Marie still stood close to the tank. "I'll leave in a moment," she said. "I wanted to apologize for what I said when you arrived. Dr. Clargue is a good man, and he tells me that you are, too."

Lamartiere snorted. "Then he knows something I don't," he said. He squatted on the edge of the hatch instead of lowering his body inside. The driver's seat had almost infinite possible adjustments, but at the end of the long run there was no part of Lamartiere's body that hadn't been rubbed or pounded.

"Look," he said, "I'm sorry we're here. I'm sorry about a lot of things, though I know that doesn't make them any better. If Maury can get us ammo, then we'll go back across the mountains to where we can maybe do something about the war. Or whatever the Council decides it wants."

"Maury won't give you anything unless there's advantage in it for him," the woman said. "The last thing he wants is for the war to end. He and de Laburat are making too good a thing about being the only authorities in the Boukasset."

Despite Marie's initial comment, she didn't show any sign of wanting to leave. Lamartiere was glad of her company.

"They manufacture drugs, you know," Marie said. She glared at Lamartiere as though he was responsible for the situation. "Most of the output goes off planet, but I suppose there's enough left over for Ambiorix as well."

"I wasn't aware of that, no," Lamartiere said evenly. It made sense, though.

He should have wondered what Maury traded to the smugglers in exchange for his gang's weaponry. Goat-hair textiles or even the subtly flavored lemons of the Boukasset didn't buy many powerguns and antiaircraft missiles.

"I was at one of the factories for three months," Marie said. Her tone was harsh, but Lamartiere now saw the misery in her eyes. "Not as staff—they have off-planet technicians for that. As entertainment. Until they raided some other family of refugees and replaced me with someone who was in better shape. I came to the shrine instead of dying in the desert."

"I'm responsible for the things I've done," Lamartiere said. He deliberately met the woman's fierce glare. "I won't apologize for things other people have done. However much I may regret them."

Marie nodded. Her expression relaxed slightly. "I just wanted you to know the sort of people you'll be dealing with," she said. "And don't misunderstand me: de Laburat's gang ran the factory where I was held. But they're both the same. They and all their men are demons."

The sun was almost on the rim of the western hills. The shrine's residents were coming back from the lemon orchard, carrying their tools. Some of them were even singing.

Over the southern horizon roared a score of vehicles, both

wheeled and air-cushion. They bristled with weapons. Dust mounted in a pall that turned blood red in the light of the lowering sun.

The rulers of the Boukasset were paying a call on *Hoodoo*.

Lamartiere slid into the driver's hatch. His body no longer ached. He switched on the fans and checked the readouts. All were within parameters except Number 7, and that bearing wasn't of immediate concern. He blipped the throttle once, then let the blades drop to a humming idle.

A blast of fine grit sprayed beneath the skirt at the pressure spike in the plenum chamber. It staggered Marie as she backed away from the vehicle. Lamartiere was sorry, but he didn't have a lot of time. Worse things were likely to happen soon anyway.

The vehicles approaching in line abreast were already within a klick of the shrine. Even without magnification Lamartiere could tell that they were overloaded, wallowing over irregularities in the desert's surface.

He brought up the gunnery controls on the lower of the compartment's two displays. It was impossible for one person to drive and handle *Hoodoo*'s armament simultaneously, but though he was prepared to move the tank Lamartiere didn't expect to need to.

He hoped he wouldn't be shooting either, not when he had only seven 2cm rounds in the tribarrel's ready magazine and no ammunition at all for the main gun.

In the middle of the oncoming vehicles was a three-axle truck which flew a pennant of some sort. The windshield was covered with metal plates; the driver could only see through a slit in his armor. That was just barely better than driving blindfolded. If Lamartiere had been in either of the adjacent vehicles, he'd have given the truck at least fifty meters clearance to avoid a collision.

The truck's bed was armored with flat slabs of concrete, a makeshift that would stop small arms but not much more. Three launching tubes were bracketed to either side; Lamartiere couldn't tell whether they held antitank missiles or unguided bombardment rockets. On top was a turret that must have come from a light military vehicle: it mounted an automatic cannon and a coaxial machine gun, both of them electromotive weapons.

The remainder of the vehicles were similar though smaller: four- and six-wheeled trucks, massively overloaded with men, weapons, and armor, as well as half a dozen air-cushion vehicles of moderate capacity. The latter weren't armored or they wouldn't have been able to move. The wheeled vehicles' panoply of mild steel and concrete was next to valueless anyway.

Lamartiere had fought among the guerrillas of the Western District before the Council picked him to steal a tank for the rebellion. The rebels had tried to convert civilian trucks into armored fighting vehicles, but they'd immediately given up the practice as a suicidal waste. In combat against purpose-built military equipment, makeshifts were merely tombs for their crews. They were good for nothing but to threaten civilians and rival groups of undisciplined thugs.

Which was obviously what these were being used for.

Well, Denis Lamartiere was neither of those things. He rested his hands on the control yoke. His index finger was a centimeter away from the firing control on the screen in front of him. To his surprise, he was smiling.

The vehicles halted near the base of the shrine, disgorging men and a few women. Their clothing was a mixture of military uniforms, the loose robes of the Boukasset, and tawdry accents of Carcassone finery. A band of pirates, Lamartiere thought; about two hundred of them all told.

The residents still at a distance either stopped where they were or returned to the orchard which provided concealment if not shelter. Civilians who'd already reached the shrine squeezed against the walls, their eyes on the armed gang.

The basket was descending; Dr. Clargue was in it, doing what he saw as his duty. Lamartiere wished the doctor had stayed safe in the fortress, but there was no help for it now.

The big truck pulled up twenty meters from *Hoodoo*. Grit sprayed from beneath the tires, but the breeze carried it back away from the tank.

A man nearly two meters tall and broad in proportion got out of the door set in the concrete armor of the bed. He wore a blue and gold uniform—a military uniform, Lamartiere supposed, though he couldn't imagine what military force wore something so absurdly ornate. There was even a saber in a gilded sheath dangling from a shoulder belt.

"My name's Maury!" he called to Lamartiere. He put his hands on his hips. "I own everything in the Boukasset, so I guess I own you, too."

"No," said Lamartiere. He spoke through the conformal speakers in *Hoodoo*'s hull. His voice boomed across the desert, echoing from the cliffs and tall stone walls of the shrine. "You don't own us."

Maury laughed cheerfully. Lamartiere's amplified voice had made some members of the gang flinch or even hit the ground, but their leader seemed unafraid. "I like a boy with spirit," he said. "Come down out of that thing and we'll talk about how we can all win this one."

"We can discuss anything we need just like we are," Lamartiere replied. "You might say I've gotten used to being in the driver's seat."

The big man chuckled again. He sauntered toward *Hoodoo*.

"I said we're fine like we are!" Lamartiere repeated. "I can hear anything you've got to say from where you're standing."

Maury had fair hair and the pale complexion that goes with it. His expression didn't change, but a flush climbed his cheeks like fluid in a thermometer on a hot day.

"I got a message from the Council that they'd like me to give you a hand, boy," he said. "I don't take orders from Goncourt but I'm willing to be neighborly. Thing is, the way you're acting don't put me in a very neighborly frame of mind."

The rest of the gang didn't know how to take what was going on. The thugs seemed more nervous than angry. A 170-tonne tank was impressive even if it were shut down. When purring and under the control of someone who sounded unfriendly, it was enough to frighten most people.

"I was told you might help me with supplies," Lamartiere said.

He kept the emotion out of his voice, but the tank's speakers threw his words like the judgment of God. "Now that I'm here, I get the impression that any help you gave me would come at a price I wouldn't be willing to pay. Why don't you go back where you came from before there's an accident?"

Maury laughed again. His heart wasn't in it, but even as bravado it took courage. Most of his gang were festooned with weapons—there were at least a dozen 2cm powerguns whose ammo would have filled *Hoodoo*'s ready magazine if Lamartiere had dared ask for it—but Maury himself wore only the saber.

"We haven't even talked price," the big man said, almost cajoling. "Believe me, you'll do fine with your share. The Boukasset may not look like much—"

He gestured broadly. The gold braid on his cuff glowed in the sun's last ruddy light.

"—but my friends don't lack for anything. Anything at all!"

There was a commotion near the wall of the shrine. Lamartiere risked a quick glance sideward. He could drop his seat into the driver's compartment and button the hatch up over himself, but that would give Maury the psychological edge.

One of Maury's men had backed a woman against the stone. She shouted and tried to move sideways. The man caught her arm and lifted it, drawing her closer to him.

"Let go of her!" Dr. Clargue said as he stepped toward the pair. The gangster shoved the woman violently toward Clargue, then stepped back and unslung a submachine gun.

"Freeze!" Lamartiere said. His shout made dust in the air quiver.

"Let her go, Schwitzer," Maury said. His bellow was dwarfed by the echoes of Lamartiere's amplified voice. "For now at least. This is just a neighborly visit."

He turned to Lamartiere again and continued, "But let's say for the sake of discussion that you *did* want to make something out of this, kid—just how did you plan to do that? Because I know from Goncourt that you don't have any ammo for those pretty guns of yours."

Cursing under his breath the *idiots* on the Council who'd given this man a hold over him, Lamartiere slid the targeting pipper onto Maury's face in the gunnery display. The turret whined, bringing the 20cm main gun squarely in line with the self-styled chief of the Boukasset.

"I can't swear on my sister's grave," Lamartiere said, "because she doesn't have one. But by her soul in the arms of God, I swear to you that *Hoodoo* carries ten thousand rounds for the tribarrel and two hundred for the main gun. Shall I demonstrate for the rest of your men?"

The main gun's barrel was a polished iridium tunnel. Maury was no coward, but what he saw staring at him was not merely death but annihilation. After a frozen moment's indecision he turned his back. He took off his stiff cap and slammed it into the ground.

"Mount up!" Maury snarled. "We're moving out!"

He stalked to the armored truck. His men obeyed with the disorganized certainty of pebbles rolling downhill. One of them scuttled over to retrieve the cap, then dropped it again and ran off when he made the mistake of looking up at the 20cm bore.

Maury halted at the door. Drivers were starting their engines: turbines, diesels, and even a pair of whining electrics. Maury pointed an arm the size of a bridge truss at Lamartiere and said, "Maybe you'll come to talk to me when you've thought about things. And maybe we'll come to you again first!"

He got in and his motley squadron started to pull away from the shrine. The air-cushion vehicles merely swapped ends, but those with wheels turned awkwardly or even backed and filled. The bolted-on armor interfered both with visibility and their turning circles.

Dr. Clargue walked over to the tank's bow. He looked wobbly. Lamartiere himself felt as though he'd been bathed in ice water. He was shivering with reaction and had to take his hands away from the controls to keep from accidentally doing something he'd regret.

The gang vehicles headed south in a ragged line, looking like survivors from a rout. The leaders continued to draw farther ahead of the others. Maury's own overloaded truck wobbled in the rear of the procession.

"Doctor," Lamartiere said. He'd switched off the speakers, so he had to raise his voice to be heard over *Hoodoo*'s idling fans. "There's self-defense strips just above the skirts. They're supposed to blast pellets into incoming missiles, but I don't know if they're live. Can you check that for me?"

"Yes," Clargue said. "I'll do that now."

Lamartiere reached out a hand to help the doctor clamber up the bow slope. Before he got into the turret Clargue paused and said, "I worried when I stood watch alone, Denis, because I wasn't sure I'd be able to use a weapon. I was trained to save lives, as you know. But I think I can do that, too, if I must."

"I know what you mean," Lamartiere said. "Look, keep looking for the transfer command so we can use the ammo in the storage magazines if we have to. *When* we have to. Maury'll decide to call my bluff before long."

"Yes, I'll keep looking," the doctor said in a weary tone.

"I wish to God I was in a different place," Lamartiere whispered. "I wish to God I was in a different *life*."

The stars shone through the dry air in brilliant profusion. *Hoodoo*'s displays careted movement, but Lamartiere had already heard the winch squeal. He focused the upper screen on the descending basket, using light enhancement at 40:1 magnification.

"It's Marie," he said to Clargue. "She's carrying a couple buckets on a pole across her shoulders."

"Ah," said the doctor without noticeable interest. The turret's yellow, low-intensity lighting was on as Clargue searched the database for the command that would turn *Hoodoo* from a vehicle into *a fighting* vehicle.

Lamartiere was letting the screens' own dim ambiance provide the only illumination for the driver's station. He could have slept beside the tank if he'd wanted to, setting an audible alarm to warn him of motion; but so long as Clargue was working, Lamartiere preferred to be alert also.

He got out of the hatch and slid to the ground. The smooth iridium hull reflected starlight well enough to show him in silhouette. Marie stepped from the basket and said, "I brought you some food and water. Bread and vegetable stew—we're vegetarians here. But it's fresh and hot."

Lamartiere took the pole from her. He'd eaten as much as he wanted earlier in the evening. The pounding drive had left him too run down to be really hungry, and it was even an effort to drink though he knew his body needed the fluids.

"Hot food, Doctor," he called. "Want to come out, or shall I bring it in to you?"

"Perhaps in a while, Denis," replied Clargue's voice with a hint of irritation. "I will run this sequence before I stop, if God and the world permit me."

Lamartiere set the buckets on the ground and squatted beside them; the tank's armor slanted too sharply to use it as a ledge. "Thanks," he said to Marie as he took one of the pair of bottles from the left-hand basket. The loaf in the other one smelled surprisingly good.

"Government radio says they're launching an attack on Goncourt," Marie said as she sat across from him. "I don't know whether that's true or not."

The bottle contained water with just enough lemon juice to give it flavor. Lamartiere drank, let his stomach settle, and drank more.

"The other is goat's milk," Marie said. "I've come to enjoy the taste."

"I didn't know about Goncourt," Lamartiere said as he lowered the bottle. "I didn't think to listen to the commercial bands. That would explain why nobody's contacted us the way they were supposed to. To tell us what the fuck we're supposed to do!"

"What *are* you going to do?" the woman asked quietly.

Lamartiere shrugged. He broke off a piece of bread and dipped it into the stew. "We won't stay here much longer," he said. He wished he had a real answer to the question, but he wished a lot of things.

"We have our own garden inside the walls," Marie said. "We buy the grain for the bread, though. It's the main thing we do buy."

"We're just making things worse," Lamartiere said. He was glad for someone to talk to, to talk *at*. "The government was wrong and *stupid* to say that unless you did what the Synod said you weren't a citizen, you were only a taxpayer. But this war has made things so much worse. Me stealing *Hoodoo* has . . . got a lot of people killed that didn't have to be. Including my sister."

Marie shrugged. "I don't know who's right," she said. "I never did. It's easier to see who's wrong, and in the Boukasset that's pretty much everybody with a gun. Pretty much."

She stood. "I'll take back the containers in the morning," she said. "People like you and me can't change anything."

To her back Lamartiere said, "I changed things when I stole this tank, Marie. I changed things when I drove it here and put you all in danger. I want to start changing things for the better!"

Hoodoo's warning chime sounded. Lamartiere was climbing the bow slope before he was really aware of his movement. Consciously he viewed the tank more as Purgatory than as shelter, but he'd dived into the driver's compartment so often recently that reflex sent him there at the first hint of danger.

He brought up the fans before he checked to see what movement the sensors had found; he brought up the gunnery screen also, even though the weapons were more easily controlled from the fighting compartment where Dr. Clargue was. Clargue was the rebellion's best hope to decipher *Hoodoo*'s coded systems, but Denis Lamartiere was far the better choice to use the tank's weaponry.

An air-cushion jeep carrying a single person was coming out of the hills three kilometers west of the shrine. Its headlights were on.

So far as Lamartiere could tell, neither the vehicle nor the driver carried a weapon. He was using 100:1 magnification, as much as he trusted when coupled with light enhancement. Anything higher was a guess by the AI, and Lamartiere preferred his own instincts to machine intelligence when his life depended on it.

"What do you want me to do?" Clargue asked over the intercom.

"Close your hatch and warn me if anything happens," Lamartiere said. "This guy is too harmless to be out at night if he didn't have a hell of a lot lined up behind him."

"There's no one else in the direction he came from," Clargue reported. "I'll continue to monitor the sensors, but otherwise I'll not interfere with your business."

After a brief mental debate, Lamartiere raised his seat to await the visitor with his head out of the hatch. Clargue would warn him if *Hoodoo*'s electronics showed a danger that unaided eyes would miss.

After hesitating again, he cut the drive fans back to their minimum speed. A normal idle sent ringing harmonics through the surrounding air. To talk over that level of background noise, the parties would have had to shout. Shouting triggered anger and hostility deep in people's subbrains, even if consciously they would have preferred to avoid it.

If there'd been two figures in the jeep, Lamartiere would have guessed they were Heth and Stegner, *Hoodoo*'s original crew. He'd seen the mercenaries at the Lystra River, observing the battle from a similar vehicle. He supposed they were hoping to steal back their tank.

At this point he'd have rather that they'd driven *Hoodoo* aboard a starship and lifted for Beresford, 300 light-years distant, the way they'd planned to do. Then Lamartiere wouldn't have had to make decisions when all the alternatives seemed equally bad. It was too late to go back, though.

The jeep halted ten meters from *Hoodoo*'s bow. The driver shut off his turbine and stood. "May I approach you, Mr. Lamartiere?" he asked. His voice was cultured but a little too high-pitched. "Or is it Dr. Clargue?"

"I'm Lamartiere," Lamartiere said. "And you can come closer, yeah."

The man walked to the tank, moving with an easy grace. Lamartiere heard the winch squeal once more, then stop. Marie must have reached the battlements, but he didn't look up to be sure.

"My name is Alexis de Laburat," the man said. He was a slim, pantherlike fellow with a strikingly handsome face. His left cheek bore a serpentine scar and there was a patch over that eye. "I've come alone and unarmed to offer you a business proposition."

"I've heard about your business," Lamartiere said, more harshly than he'd intended. He was remembering what Marie had told him. "No thanks. And I think you'd better go now."

"I was born a Mosite and fought in the rebellion," de Laburat said. "I rallied to the government and fought for it when I saw the rebellion was doomed to fail; so did the other men under my command. But what I'm offering now, Mr. Lamartiere, is peace."

De Laburat's fingers toyed with the tip of his neat moustache. "As well as enough money to keep you and the doctor comfortably on any world to which you choose to emigrate. Obviously you can't stay on Ambiorix unless you join me, which I don't suppose you'd care to do."

"I told you, we have no business with you!" Lamartiere said.

The Rallier shook his head. "Think clearly," he said. "I know you're a clever man or you'd never have gotten this far. The Council wouldn't be able to use this tank, even if you were able to get ammunition for it. The rebellion is *over*. Goncourt will fall within the week. Though the Council will probably relocate to some cave in the hills, they'll control nothing at all."

De Laburat smiled. "You're the cause of that, you know," he said. He was trying to be pleasant, but his voice scraped Lamartiere's nerves to hear. "The attack on Goncourt has been very expensive. The government probably wouldn't have had the courage to attempt it except that they were afraid to let the embers of the rebellion smolder on when the Mosites had this superweapon. As they thought."

"You're not part of this war," Lamartiere said. "You've made that clear, you and Maury both. I am. You came unarmed so I won't hurt you—but you'd better leave now or you'll have to walk back, because I'll have driven *Hoodoo* over your jeep."

"Listen to me!" de Laburat said. He had to look up because Lamartiere was in the vehicle. He still gave the impression of a panther, but a caged one.

"*I'll* protect the Boukasset," de Laburat said. "The government knows I'm no threat to it. They won't come here to chase me, and the Synod won't try to impose its definition of heresy here while I have this tank!"

"Protect the Boukasset under yourself," Lamartiere said.

De Laburat chuckled. "You've met Maury," he said. "He has a strong back and about enough intellect to pull on his boots in the morning. Would you entrust the Shrine of the Blessed Catherine to him? And even if you did, one of his own men will shoot him in the back in a few weeks or months, as surely as the sun rises tomorrow."

"Go away," Lamartiere said. In sudden fury he repeated, "Go away, or by God I'll kill you now so that I can say there's one good deed to balance against all the harm I've done in this life!"

De Laburat nodded with stiff propriety. "Good day, Mr. Lamartiere," he said. "I hope you'll reconsider while there's still time."

Lamartiere watched the Rallier drive back across the desert the way he'd come. The jeep's headlights cut a wedge across the rocks and scrub, disappearing at last through a cleft in the low hills.

"What do we do now?" Dr. Clargue asked quietly.

"I wish I knew," Lamartiere said. "I wish to God I knew."

He slept curled up on the floor of the driver's compartment. He continued to hear the purr of *Hoodoo*'s computers late into the night as Clargue worked on a problem that neither he nor Lamartiere now believed they would ever solve.

The warning chime awakened Lamartiere. After a moment of blurred confusion—he was too tired and uncomfortable for panic— he realized what the problem was.

"It's all right, Doctor," he said. "I left the audible alarm on, and it's registering the locals leaving to go to the orchard."

It wasn't dawn yet, but the sky over the eastern mountains was noticeably lighter than in the west. Two hundred kilometers into those mountains was Goncourt, where Lamartiere supposed shell bursts had been glaring all night

"Ah," said Clargue. They'd seen very little of one another despite having been no more that a meter or two apart during most of the past week. Crewing *Hoodoo* was like being imprisoned in adjacent cells.

"Go get a bath and some breakfast," Lamartiere said. He cleared his throat and added, "I think we may as well move out today, even if we don't hear anything from the Council. Otherwise we're going to bring something down on these people that they don't deserve."

"Yes," said Clargue. "I'm afraid you're right"

He didn't ask Lamartiere where he intended to go. The only possible answer was *away*. They needed to go some place where there wasn't anybody else around to be harmed by what *Hoodoo* attracted.

Residents were coming down by pairs in the basket. Even so the process would take at least an hour. The Shrine of the Blessed Catherine hadn't been intended for its present population, at least not in the years since the ground-level gate had been blocked. The walls were little defense against heavy weapons, but they protected the handful of Brothers from the small arms and banditry of the Boukasset during normal times.

Hoodoo could turn the shrine into a pile of rubble in a matter of seconds. Not that anyone would bother to do so . . . except, perhaps, as a whim along the lines of pulling the wings off flies.

Clargue slid clumsily down the bow and walked toward the basket. Civilians coming in the other direction murmured greetings to the doctor. Everyone here was glad of his presence.

Indeed, most of them probably thought of *Hoodoo* herself as protection for the shrine and themselves. They were wrong. Even if Lamartiere could have used the ammunition he *knew* was in the storage magazines, the tank was sure to summon increasing levels of violence until everything in its vicinity was shattered to dust and vapor.

Lamartiere supposed he was dozing in the hatch, though his eyes were open. He wasn't consciously aware of his surroundings until Dr. Clargue said, "I will watch now, Denis," and Lamartiere realized direct sunlight stabbed across the plain through the notch in the hills by which *Hoodoo* had entered.

"Right," Lamartiere said, trying to clear his brain. He crawled out of the hatch, bitterly aware that he was in terrible shape. He supposed it didn't matter. The best option he could see now was to drive *Hoodoo* fifty kilometers out into the desert, and the AI could handle that once he got her under way.

De Laburat had been right about one thing. Dr. Clargue might be able to return to helping the sick in a village lost in the mountains, but there was no longer any place on Ambiorix for Denis Lamartiere. Like *Hoodoo* herself, he was a valuable resource: a tank crewman, to be captured if possible but otherwise killed to prevent another faction from gaining his expertise.

He stepped into the basket as a mother and her twins got out. The woman nodded while the children whispered excitedly to one another. They'd been close enough to the soldier to *touch* him!

The basket jogged its way up the wall of the shrine. His shadow sprawled across the hard sandstone blocks.

Below Lamartiere, most of the residents were trudging toward the orchard. Parties of the healthiest refugees were loading two-man cradles with blocks crumbled from the cliff face. Ordinary wheelbarrows would be useless on this terrain of sand and irregular stone. Human beings were more adaptable than even the simplest of machines.

Rasile was on the winch, somewhat to Lamartiere's surprise, but Marie sat nearby. She was embellishing a piece of canvas with a Maltese cross in needlepoint, holding the frame against her thighs with her left wrist and using her good right hand to direct the needle. The pattern of tight, small stitches was flawless so far as Lamartiere could tell.

"Will you lower Mr. Rasile to the ground?" Marie said to Lamartiere. "Or are you still—"

"I'm healthy enough," Lamartiere said. "Tired, is all."

And so frustrated that he felt like kicking a hole in the battlements, but neither fact would prevent him from turning a crank.

Children played within the courtyard, their voices shrilly cheerful. Lamartiere saw a pair of them momentarily, chasing one another among the rows of pole beans. The shrine wasn't really the Garden of Eden; but it was closer to that, and to Paradise, than most of the refugees could have hoped to find.

"I'm not going down," Rasile said. "I have permission from Father Blenis to read my scriptures here today."

He reached into the knapsack at his feet and brought out a

fabric-bound volume. It was probably the *Revelations of Moses,* though Lamartiere couldn't see the title. Despite the book in his hand, Rasile looked even more like a pimp—or a rat—than usual.

"What?" Marie said, both angry and amazed.

"I have permission!" Rasile said. "I'm not shirking. It's hard work to bring people up in the basket!"

"I wouldn't know that?" said the woman. "Father Blenis's so gentle he'd give you permission to carry off all the communion dishes, but we're not all of us such innocent saints here, Rasile!"

Lamartiere turned his head away as he would have done if he'd stumbled into someone else's family quarrel. Only then did he see the six-wheeled truck driving up from the south. It had an open cab and cargo of some sort in the bed under a reflective tarp, but there were no signs of weapons. The driver was alone.

"What's that?" Lamartiere said sharply. Marie and Rasile instantly stopped bickering to stare over the battlements. Fear made the woman look drawn and a decade older than she'd been a moment before; Rasile's expression was harder to judge, but fear was a large part of it also.

"It's just the provisions truck," Marie said. She sighed in relief. "It's a day early, but it seems . . ."

The driver parked near the wall and pulled the tarp back to uncover his cargo. He was carrying several hundred-kilo burlap grain sacks and a number of less-definable bags and boxes. It all looked perfectly innocent.

The residents who were still close to the shrine gathered around the truck. Others, including a pair of black-robed Brothers, were on their way back from the orchard.

Lamartiere noticed with approval that Dr. Clargue had closed the tank's hatches and was even aiming his tribarrel at the truck. Some of the shrine's residents sprawled away in panic when the weapon moved, but the driver didn't seem to care. If the fellow made this trip across the Boukasset regularly, he must be used to having guns pointed at him.

Rasile said, "Ah!" with a shudder. He'd dropped the book in his haste, but he'd grabbed the knapsack itself and was holding it in front of him. It was a sturdy piece of equipment and apparently quite new.

"I was hoping to wash up before we go," Lamartiere said quietly to the woman. "We'll be leaving soon. And I'd like to thank Father Blenis for his hospitality."

"He's usually in the chapel till midday," Marie said with a nod. "I'll get you some breakfast. You can draw the water yourself now, can't you?"

"Yes, I—" Lamartiere said.

Hoodoo's siren began to wind. Lamartiere looked down. The tank's turret gimbaled southward, pointing the guns at the line of vehicles racing toward the shrine.

Maury was returning.

"Let me down!" Lamartiere said. He stepped toward the basket, wondering if he could reach the tank before the armed band arrived.

Rasile backed away, fumbling inside his knapsack. His right hand came out holding a bell-mouthed mob gun. The weapon fired sheaves of aerofoils that spread enough to hit everyone in a normal-sized room with a single shot. As close as Lamartiere was to the muzzle, the charge would cut him in half.

"Don't either of you try to move!" Rasile screamed.

An oncoming vehicle fired its automatic cannon. Lamartiere suspected that the gunner had intended to shoot over the heads of the people streaming back from the orchard, but it was hard to aim accurately from a bouncing vehicle. Several shells exploded near the civilians. A woman remained standing after those around her had flung themselves to the ground. She finally toppled, her blood soaking the sand around her back.

The truck firing had dual rear wheels and an enclosure of steel plates welded onto the bed. The gun projected through a slot in the armor over the cab. *Hoodoo*'s tribarrel hit the vehicle dead center. The bolts of cyan plasma turned the steel into white fire an instant before the truck's fuel tank boomed upward in an orange geyser.

One round would have been enough for the job. Dr. Clargue fired all seven, emptying the loading tube. Lamartiere supposed that was a waste, but he saw where the woman sprawled on a flag of her own blood and he couldn't feel too unhappy. At least the short-term result was good.

Maury's surviving vehicles bounced and wallowed toward the shrine. None of them shot at *Hoodoo*, demonstrating a level of discipline Lamartiere wouldn't have expected of the gang. Several of the band were firing in the air, though. Their muzzle flashes flickered in the sunlight.

"Don't move or I'll kill you!" Rasile said, squeaking two octaves up from his normal voice. He waggled the mob gun.

Maury's agent in the shrine was as high as a kite either from drugs he'd taken to nerve himself up, or from simple adrenaline. Lamartiere guessed there was a radio in Rasile's knapsack. He'd signaled his master when Lamartiere was out of the tank. Dr. Clargue was the better of the two men in *Hoodoo*'s crew, but he wasn't a danger to Maury's plans.

Maury's vehicles pulled up in a ragged semicircle around the shrine's southern wall. *Hoodoo* and the provisions truck were within the arc, but the gang had cut most of the residents off from the structure.

If Lamartiere had been in *Hoodoo*, he'd have driven straight through one or more of the gang's vehicles: not even the heavy truck was a real barrier to a tank's weight and power. Clargue didn't think in those terms; and anyway, he couldn't drive the tank.

Most of the gangsters got out of their vehicles. Today Maury wore expensive battledress of chameleon fabric which took on the hues of its surroundings. He carried a submachine gun, but that was no more his real weapon than the saber of the previous day had been. Maury may have been a thug to begin with, but now he'd risen to a level that he ordered people killed instead of having to kill them himself.

"I'll be his chief man after this," Rasile said. A line of drool hung from the corner of his mouth. "I'll have all the women I want. Any woman at all."

Maury glanced up to make sure Lamartiere was out of the way. He waved the submachine gun cheerfully, then spoke to two henchmen. They grabbed an old man who'd been standing nearby.

One gangster twisted the victim's hands behind his back while the other put a pistol to his temple.

The driver of the provisions truck got up from where he'd lain beside his vehicle while the shooting was going on. He also looked toward Lamartiere, lifting his cap in a casual salute.

The driver was Sergeant Heth, *Hoodoo*'s commander until Lamartiere stole the tank from Brione.

"Come on out, Doctor!" Maury said in a voice loud enough for those on the battlements to hear. "We're going to start killing these people. We'll kill every one of them unless you give us the tank!"

Lamartiere opened his mouth but remained silent because he didn't know what advice to give Clargue. He didn't doubt that Maury would carry out his threat, and since the doctor couldn't drive *Hoodoo*—

The gangster fired. Ionized plasma from the projectile's driving skirt ignited a lock of the hair it blew from the victim's scalp. Hydrostatic shock fractured the cranial vault, deforming the skull into softer lines.

The shooter laughed. His partner flung the body down with a curse and wiped spattered blood from his face.

Hoodoo's hatches opened. Dr. Clargue climbed out of the cupola, bent and dejected. He might have been planning to surrender the tank anyway. Maury's men had acted before he'd really had a chance to make up his mind.

Rasile cackled in triumph. "Any woman—" he said.

Lamartiere caught a flicker of movement in the corner of his eye. An antitank missile hit the side of Maury's big armored truck. The warhead blew the slab of concrete into pebbles and a worm of reinforcing mesh twisted away.

The blast threw everyone within twenty meters to the ground. Dr. Clargue lost his grip and bounced down *Hoodoo*'s flank. He lay still on the ground. Ammunition inside the stricken vehicle went off in a series of red secondary explosions like a string of firecrackers, reducing to blazing junk whatever the warhead had left .

Rasile stared disbelievingly at the destruction. Lamartiere

twisted the mob gun's broad muzzle skyward, then punched the smaller man at the corner of the jaw.

Rasile toppled over the battlements. For a moment he kept his grip on the butt of the pistol whose barrel Lamartiere held. Marie leaned forward and jabbed her needle into the back of Rasile's hand. His screams as he fell were lost in the sudden ripping destruction below.

Two more missiles hit, each destroying its target with a blast intended to gut purpose-built armored vehicles. A shockwave flipped the provisions truck onto its back; Lamartiere didn't see what had happened to Sergeant Heth.

Even before the third warhead exploded, automatic cannons firing from the hills west of the shrine began to rake Maury's other vehicles. Three kilometers was well within their accurate range.

Maury's air-cushion vehicles disintegrated like tissue paper in a storm. The steel armor of some wheeled trucks wasn't thick enough to stop the shells, and the concrete slabs protecting the others fractured at the first impact. Following shells passed through unhindered, igniting cataclysms of fuel and stored ammunition.

"Let me down!" Lamartiere said as he jumped into the basket. He should have waited. Marie had to struggle with the locking pin because Lamartiere's weight was already on the winch, but she jerked it loose before he realized the problem. The basket wobbled downward.

Still shooting, the attacking vehicles drove out of the hills where they'd waited in ambush. There were three of them, air-cushion armored personnel carriers of the type used by government forces.

Each thirty-tonne APC could carry a platoon of troops behind armor thick enough to stop small-arms projectiles. The small turret near the bow carried a light electromotive cannon as well as a launching rail on the left side for an antitank missile. The hatches on the APCs' back decks opened. Troops leaned out, aiming rifles and submachine guns.

The men in the APCs wore government uniforms, though with cut-off sleeves and flourishes of metal and bright fabrics. Maury had played his card; now de Laburat's Ralliers were trumping the hand.

The gangs' alliance of convenience had broken down under the weight of loot that couldn't be shared and which gave the party owning it an overwhelming advantage over the other. In this at least, *Hoodoo*'s presence had benefited the other inhabitants of the Boukasset.

Most of Maury's men had thrown themselves to the ground or were running toward the rocks behind the shrine, the only available cover. Their leader stood and emptied his submachine gun at the oncoming vehicles.

The APCs' turrets were stabilized to fire accurately on the move. Two of the automatic cannon shot back simultaneously. Maury's head and torso disintegrated in white flashes. An arm flew skyward; the legs below the knees remained upright for an instant before toppling onto the sand.

Lamartiere was halfway to the ground when a Rallier noticed the mob gun and took him for one of Maury's gang. Chips of sandstone flew from the wall close enough to cut Lamartiere's arm: the shooter was either lucky or better than any man had a right to be when firing from a moving platform.

Lamartiere saw a cannon tracking toward him. The ground was still five meters below but there was no choice. Cradling the mob gun to his belly and hoping it wouldn't go off when he hit, he jumped. A burst of shells devoured the basket as he left it, stinging his back with fragments of casing and stone.

He knew to flex his knees as he hit, but his feet flew backward and he slapped the ground hard enough to knock his breath out and bloody his chin. He'd dropped the mob gun. He snatched it up again, then staggered toward *Hoodoo* with knife-blade pains jetting from two lower ribs.

The APCs closed to within thirty meters of the burning vehicles and flared broadside to a halt. The Ralliers wanted to stay beyond range of a hand-thrown bomb as they finished off the survivors of Maury's band. Bullets sparkled on the APCs' sides; a Rallier sprawled, bleeding down the sloping armor. Gunfire from the vehicles was twenty to one compared to what they received.

Lamartiere grabbed a headlight bracket with his left hand.

Behind him a woman's voice shrilled, "Stop him, Pietro!" through the roar of gunfire.

Lamartiere swung his right leg up. Pietro closed a hand like a bear trap on his ankle and jerked him back. With the muzzle of the mob gun tight against the giant's body, Lamartiere pulled the trigger.

Recoil bashed the gun butt hard against Lamartiere's ribs. He doubled up. Pietro stepped back with a look of blank incomprehension on his face. There was a hole two centimeters in diameter just above his navel. His tunic was smoldering.

Pietro pivoted and fell on his face. The cavity in his back was bigger than a man's head. Sections of purple-veined intestine squirmed out of the general red mass.

Louise stood behind her brother's body. "You bastard!" she cried and drew a small pistol from the bosom of her blouse.

Lamartiere hesitated a heartbeat, but there was no choice. Louise and her brother were combatants, agents working for de Laburat just as Rasile had worked for Maury—and she was about to kill him.

He pulled the trigger. Nothing happened. Excessive chamber pressure when he'd fired with the muzzle against Pietro's chest had ruptured the cartridge case. The mob gun was jammed.

Sergeant Heth grabbed the woman's wrist from behind, spun her, and broke her elbow neatly over his knee. The mercenary had lost the loose robe he'd worn for a disguise, and his left arm and shoulder were black with oil or soot.

"You drive, kid!" he shouted. He used *Hoodoo*'s toolbox as a handhold and a patch welded on the side skirt for a step to lift himself up the tank's side. "I'll take care of the rest!"

Lamartiere climbed the bow slope and dropped into the driver's compartment. He switched the fans on and closed the hatch above him.

De Laburat must have ordered his troops not to fire at the tank since its capture undamaged was the whole purpose of the attack, but now a dozen shells exploded against the side of the turret. They were as harmless as so many raindrops.

Fan speed built smoothly; only the ragged line of Number 7's readout reminded Lamartiere that there was a problem. *Hoodoo*'s systems were coming alive all around him. There were hums and purrs and the demanding whine of a hydraulic accumulator building pressure.

Some of the sounds were unfamiliar. With a sudden leap of his heart, Lamartiere realized that the rhythmic *shoop-shoop-shoop* from deep in the hull must be ammunition rising from the storage magazines.

Out of nervousness he coarsened blade pitch too fast. The fans threatened to bog, but Lamartiere rolled back on the adjustment in time. Adding power with his right handgrip and pitch with the left, he brought *Hoodoo* to hover in place.

The driver's compartment felt more comfortable to him without a gunnery display in the center of the lower screen. He'd regularly driven tanks during the months he'd worked as one of the Slammers' Local Service Personnel, but he'd never *seen* a gunnery display until Dr. Clargue went over *Hoodoo*'s systems in Pamiers.

Dozens of Ralliers were blazing away at *Hoodoo* with rifles and submachine guns, a dangerous waste of ammunition. Somebody with a better notion of utility jumped down from his APC and ran forward, swinging a satchel charge for a side-armed throw. A bullet ricocheting from the tank tore his face away as he released the satchel.

The bomb flew toward *Hoodoo* in a high arc. A section of self-defense strip fired, making the tank ring. Tungsten pellets shredded the satchel into tatters of cloth and explosive, flinging it back the way it had come. It didn't detonate.

Lamartiere eased his control yoke forward and twisted left to move the tank away from the shrine. There were too many civilians nearby. Shots that couldn't damage *Hoodoo* would kill and maim people who'd only looked for peace.

The APCs were driving away. Ralliers who'd gotten out to finish off Maury's men on foot ran along behind the vehicles, shouting and waving their arms. One of the gunners depressed his cannon as his APC turned, intending to rake *Hoodoo*'s skirts. If the plenum chamber was holed badly enough, the tank's fans couldn't build enough pressure to lift her off the ground.

Blue-green light sparkled on the APCs turret as a dozen bolts from *Hoodoo*'s 2cm weapon hit it. The tribarrel's rotation was an additional whirr in the symphony of the tank at work. In the driver's compartment, the plasma discharges were scarcely louder than peanuts cracking.

The turret flew apart like steam puffed into a stiff breeze. The APC's armor was a sandwich of ceramic within high-maraging steel: the steel burned white while glassy knives of the core ripped in all directions. The torso of a Rallier trying to climb back aboard the vehicle vanished in bloody spray.

Lamartiere crawled through the chaos. The ground in front of the shrine was littered with bodies and debris. Residents who'd been caught in the fighting lay intermixed with Maury's gang. Some of them might still be alive.

Above Lamartiere the tribarrel spat short bursts. Sergeant Heth was picking off dismounted Ralliers instead of firing at the fleeing vehicles. Some of de Laburat's men turned to run for shelter in the rocks when they saw the APCs weren't going to stop for them. None of them made it, and the ones who threw themselves down to feign death didn't survive either.

It was easy to tell dead Ralliers from those shamming. At short range a 2cm bolt tore a human body apart. When several hit the same target, the result was indistinguishable from a bomb blast.

Lamartiere drove over the wreckage of a truck that had been hit by an antitank missile. Lubricant and the synthetic rubber tires burned with low, smoky flames. *Hoodoo*'s skirt plowed a path through the skeletal frame, whipping the blaze higher with the downdraft from the plenum chamber.

The main gun fired.

The tribarrel had so little effect inside the tank that Lamartiere was merely aware that Heth was shooting. The 20cm weapon's discharge rocked *Hoodoo* backward despite the inertia of her 170 tonnes. Air clapped to fill the vacuum which the jolt of plasma had burned through its heart. Lamartiere shouted in surprise.

The leading APC, by now nearly a kilometer distant, burst as though a volcano had erupted beneath it. The bolt transferred its megajoules of energy to the vehicle, vaporizing even the ceramic armor. A fireball forty meters in diameter bloomed where the APC had been; bits of solid matter sprayed out of it, none of them bigger than a man's thumbnail.

The gun cycled, ejecting the spent round into the fighting compartment. Heat and stinking fumes flooded *Hoodoo*'s interior even though the ventilation fans switched to high speed. Lamartiere's eyes were watering and the back of his throat burned.

"Thought I'd wait till we were clear of the civilians," Sergeant Heth explained over the intercom in a conversational voice. "Sidescatter from the big gun can blister bare skin if you're anywhere nearby."

He fired the 20cm weapon again. This time the *clang* and the way the tank bucked weren't a surprise to Lamartiere, though his head wobbled back and forth in response to the hull's motion.

The second APC was making a skidding turn to avoid running through the flaming ruin that had exploded before it. The cyan bolt hit the vehicle at a slant, perfectly centered, and devoured it as completely as its fellow. The fire-ball dimmed to a ghost of its initial fury, but brush ignited by debris ignited hundreds of meters away.

The last Rallier vehicle fled at over 100 kph despite the broken terrain. It was drawing away because *Hoodoo*'s mass took so long to accelerate despite the tank's higher top speed. Lamartiere concentrated on driving, avoiding knobs of rock too heavy to smash through and crevices that would spill air from the plenum chamber and ground *Hoodoo* shriekingly.

He heard the turret gimbal onto its target. A Rallier stood on the deck of the APC and jumped. The man hit the ground and bounced high, limbs flailing in rubbery curves. He'd broken every bone in his body and was obviously dead.

But then, so were his fellows.

The main gun slammed. The third APC vanished in a smear of fire across the desert floor. The sun was high enough to pale the flames, but the pall of black smoke drifted west with the breeze.

"Go back to the fort, kid," Heth ordered. "Stegner's heading there in our jeep."

The mercenary chuckled, then started coughing. The ozone and matrix residue from the main gun burned his throat also. "We planned that Steg'd set off some fireworks on the hills. While everybody was looking that way I'd hop into *Hoodoo*. The locals made a better job of fireworks than we ever thought of, didn't they? Bloody near did for me, I'll tell the world!"

Lamartiere braked the tank with the caution its mass demanded. Unlike the driver of a wheeled vehicle, he didn't have the friction of tires against the ground to slow him unless he dumped air from the plenum chamber and deliberately skidded the skirt.

There was no need now for haste. Lamartiere wasn't in a hurry to face what came next.

He opened his hatch, thinking the draft would clear fumes from the tanks interior faster than the filtered ventilation system. The hatch rolled shut again an instant later; Sergeant Heth had used the commander's override.

"Not just yet, kid," he said. "The guy in charge of this lot, de Laburat . . . Did you ever meet him?"

"Yes," Lamartiere said. "I'd sooner trust a weasel."

"Yeah, that's the guy," the mercenary said. "But he's a smart sonuvabitch. He saw the way things were going before any of his people did. He bailed out and ran into the rocks right away. I didn't have the ready magazines charged yet, so I couldn't do anything about it."

"You mean de Laburat got away?" Lamartiere said in horror.

The main gun fired. The unexpected *CLANG/jerk!* whipsawed Lamartiere's head again. Fumes seeped through the narrow passage from the fighting compartment, but both hatches opened before he had time to sneeze. The wind of *Hoodoo*'s forward motion scoured Lamartiere's station.

This time the bolt had struck at the base of the cliff a hundred meters west of the shrine. Rock shattered in a blue-green flash.

The slope bulged, then slid downward with a roar. A plume of pulverized rock settled slowly, displaying an enormous cavity in the cliff. Below the crater was a pile of irregular blocks which in some cases were larger than a man. The mass was still shifting internally, giving it the look of organic life.

Civilians who'd been returning from the orchard, some of them running to check on loved ones, flattened again to the ground. They had no way of telling what had just happened.

"He got away for a while," Heth said with satisfaction. "But then he stuck his head up outa the crevice where he was hiding to see what was going on. He didn't get a very long view, did he?"

Heth's laughter changed again to coughing, though with a cheerful undercurrent. Because the fumes escaped via the cupola, the turret took longer to clear than the driver's compartment.

Father Blenis was on the battlements, standing as straight in his robes as age would permit him. He was alone. He hadn't flinched when the 20cm gun fired, even though he was closer to the bolt's crashing impact than any of the other civilians.

A jeep was racing across the desert from the foothills to the east, trailing a pennant of ruddy dust. Lamartiere wondered if Heth was armed. Probably not. The gangs searched the provisions truck, so one or the other of them would have confiscated any weapon the mercenary had tried to bring with him.

It didn't matter. Lamartiere had run as far as he was going to. The tank he'd stolen with such high hopes had brought disaster to everyone around him.

Hoodoo was nearing Maury's vehicles. Black smoke still poured out of the carcasses. Lamartiere swung his fan nacelles vertical, lifting the tank for an instant to spill air from the plenum chamber. *Hoodoo* pogoed, touching several times as she slowed. The impacts were too gentle to damage the skirts.

They nosed through the gap they'd plowed in pursuit of the Ralliers. Lamartiere drove carefully; there were civilians moving behind the smoke. He didn't see anyone holding a weapon, though there were plenty of guns strewn across the ground. Dr. Clargue squatted near the walls, bandaging a child's leg.

"Sir?" Lamartiere asked.

"I'm no fucking officer, kid," Heth said, at least half-serious.

"Anyway, 'Sarge' was good enough when you were an LSP at the base, wasn't it?"

"That was a long time ago, Sarge," Lamartiere said. Five calendar days, and a lifetime. "Anyway, I was wondering what the command was to transfer ammo to the ready magazines. Dr. Clargue's searched the data banks up, down, and crosswise and he can't find it. Couldn't find it."

Heth laughed himself into another fit of coughing. "Oh, blood and martyrs, was *that* the problem? Steg and me knew there must be something going on why you didn't use the main gun, but we couldn't on our lives figure out what it was!"

Lamartiere nestled the tank against the shrine. He shut down the fans. The jeep with Trooper Stegner was still a minute or two distant. "Well, what was it then?" he said sharply. There were worse things happening than Heth laughing at him, but it was still irritating.

The sergeant had cocked the turret to the side; the 20cm barrel was no longer glowing, but heat waves still distorted the air above the iridium. He climbed out of the cupola and slid down beside the driver's hatch. Lamartiere raised his seat, but for the moment he was too exhausted to get out of the vehicle.

"Hey, simmer down," Heth said. "I'm just laughing because of how lucky we were. Not that I'm not going to have some explaining to do about why *Hoodoo*'s late joining the regiment on Beresford, but at least you didn't turn Carcassone inside out with the main gun."

The jeep wound between a pair of truck chassis. The open flames had died down, though the wreckage still smoldered. Stegner, a tall man with wispy hair and a face like a rabbit's, waved to them.

"Transfer isn't a software process," Heth went on. "It's hardwired. There's a thumb switch on the firing lever. To recharge the ready magazines you roll it up for the tribarrel and down for the main gun."

"Oh," Lamartiere said. "Yeah, that explains why the doctor couldn't find the command."

He put a boot on the seat and lifted himself out of the compartment. Heth steadied him till he'd settled on the open hatch.

"Kid," the sergeant said. "There's maybe three million parts in one of these suckers. How were you supposed to know what every one of them is, and you not even through proper training?"

He patted *Hoodoo* with an affectionate hand. "You did plenty good enough with what you had. I watched you chew up that mechanized battalion at the Lystra, remember? I'll tell the world!"

The sergeant's torso was badly scraped besides being half-covered in oil, but apart from occasionally rubbing his elbow he showed no signs of discomfort. Lamartiere's chest hurt badly, particularly where the mob gun had recoiled into his ribs when he fired, but he thought the damage was probably limited to bruising.

"Did you see the holes in the skirt, Sarge?" Stegner called as he stood scowling at *Hoodoo*'s flank. "Must be about a hundred of 'em. Nothing very big but I don't want to drive back to Brione with her mushing like a pig."

"She sagged left," Lamartiere said. "I had to tilt the nacelles to keep her straight, but it wasn't as bad as the damage we took at the Lystra."

"Probably the warhead that flipped my truck over on me," Heth said judiciously. "Well, we can use the truck's bed for patching. Do they have a welder here, kid?"

Half the residents had returned to the shrine. They were crying in amazement and horror at the carnage. Many others still hid among the stone shelters of the orchard, waiting to be sure that it was safe to show themselves. Lamartiere couldn't blame them for their fear.

"I doubt it," he said. He thought for a moment. "There's mastic, though. I saw some where they're tiling the chapel entryway. It'll work for a patch on the inside of the skirts, since air pressure tightens the seal."

"Yeah, that'll work," said Stegner approvingly. He walked to the overturned truck and kicked it, judging the thickness of the body metal by the sound.

"Sergeant Heth," Lamartiere said, looking at the stone wall of the shrine. "Are you going to hand me over to the government, or . . .?"

He turned and gestured toward the body of the old man Maury's thugs had shot as a warning to Dr. Clargue—a few moments before they and all their fellows died also.

"Hey, we don't work for the government of Ambiorix anymore, kid," Heth said. "The only reason Steg and me are still on the planet is we *really* didn't want to explain to Colonel Hammer how we managed to lose one of his tanks. Do you have any idea what one of these costs?"

He patted *Hoodoo* again.

Marie's body lay at the foot of the wall. Her upturned face was peaceful and unmarked, but there was a splotch of blood on her upper chest. Lamartiere supposed a stray bullet had hit her. There'd been enough of them flying around.

"I know what it costs," he said. "I know what it cost these people."

"Yeah, that's so," Heth agreed. "And I'm not arguing with you. But you might remind yourself that things may be a little better for the folks here now that the gangs are out of the way. I don't say it will, mind you; but it may be."

He spat accurately onto the corpse of one of Maury's men; the one who'd held the hostage for his partner to shoot, Lamartiere thought.

"I don't work for the government, like I told you," Heth said quietly. "But sometimes I do things on my own personal account. War isn't a business where there's a lot of obvious good guys, but sometimes the bad guys are pretty easy to spot."

Lamartiere put a hand on Heth's shoulder so that the mercenary would look him straight in the eye. "Sergeant," Lamartiere said, "am I free to go? Is that what you're telling me?"

Heth shrugged. "Sure, if you want to," he said. "But Steg and me was hoping you might like to join the Slammers. The colonel's always looking for recruits."

Stegner morosely rubbed a dimple in the hull surrounded by a halo of bright radial scratches. A high-explosive shell had burst there against the armor. "If we bring you along," he said, "maybe we can get a few of these extra dings passed off as training accidents, you know?"

"And you might like to be someplace there wasn't a price on your head," Heth said, rubbing the armor with his thumb. "Nobody at the port's going to think twice if there's three of us boarding a ship for Beresford along with *Hoodoo,* here."

Lamartiere looked toward the battlements. Father Blenis knelt in prayer. A pair of young women, one of them holding an infant, were with him. At the base of the wall three laymen and a Brother worked with focused desperation to jury-rig a platform in place of the shattered basket.

"I guess I don't have a choice," Lamartiere said.

Trooper Stegner looked up from the side of the tank. "Sure you got a choice," he said in a hard, angry voice. Lamartiere had thought of the trooper as a little slow, but invariably good-humored. "There's always a choice. I coulda stayed on Spruill sniping at Macauleys till one of the Macauleys nailed me!"

"For me," said Sergeant Heth, "the problem was her father and brothers. I decided that joining the Slammers was better than the rest of my life married to Anna Carausio."

He smiled faintly in reminiscence. "I still think I was right, but who knows, hey?"

Lamartiere nodded. "Yeah, who knows?" he said.

He looked at Marie's silent body. Maybe she was in the arms of God; maybe Celine was there, too, and all the others who'd died since Denis Lamartiere stole a tank. It would be nice to believe that.

Lamartiere didn't believe in much of anything nowadays; certainly not in the Mosite Rebellion as a cause to get other people killed in. But one thing he did believe.

"Ambiorix'll be a better place if I'm off-planet," he said to the mercenaries. "And just maybe I'll be better off, too. I'll join if you'll have me."

Heth stuck out his hand for Lamartiere to shake. "Welcome aboard, kid," he said.

Stegner kicked *Hoodoo*'s skirt. "Now let's get this poor bitch patched up so we get the hell out of here, shall we?"

WHITE MICE COMBAT CAR

A DEATH IN PEACETIME

The brothel was too upscale to have an armored street entrance, but the doorman was a wall of solid muscle beneath a frock coat in the latest style. He frowned when the nondescript aircar hummed to a halt in front of the door.

Four hard-looking men got out. Hesitating only long enough to press the button warning those upstairs to keep an eye on the closed-circuit screen, the doorman stepped into the street. "I'm sorry, gentlemen," he said, "but we're closed tonight for a private party. Perhaps—"

"We're the party, buddy," one of the men said, placing himself alongside the doorman while his partner took the other side. The other two men faced the street in opposite directions. All four wore short capes which concealed their hands and whatever they might be holding.

A fifth man, small and dapper, followed the others out of the car. His suit was exquisitely tailored. The fabric had tawny dappling on the shoulders which faded imperceptibly into the gray undertone as one's eye travelled downward.

The man nodded pleasantly toward the doorman and started toward the stairs. Movement lifted the tail of his jacket enough to disclose the pistol holstered high on his right hip.

"I'm sorry, sir!" the doorman said. "We don't allow guns—"

He tried to step in front of the little man. The guards to either side of him— they were obviously guards—shoved him back against the wall.

"You're making an exception tonight," the little man said. His shoes touched the stair treads with the *tsk-tsk-tsk* of a whisk broom sweeping up ashes; the men who'd initially stayed with the car followed him. "I promise I won't tell anybody."

Madame opened the upper stairway door to let the little man into the parlor. Straight-backed and dressed in severe black, she was the only woman in the establishment. In the muted lighting which the mirrors diffused rather than multiplied, she might've been anything from forty years old to twice that age.

Her face was stony and her tone coldly furious. "You have no business here!" she said. "We have all our licenses. Everything is perfectly legal!"

Six youths had been reclining on couches of plush and dark wood. They'd sprung to their feet when the doorman gave the alarm. Though Madame had gestured them back to their places, they still had the look of startled fawns.

The barman and waiter had retreated into their small lounge off the parlor. The usher had slipped into the back hallway so recently that the door was still swinging shut.

All three had the size and hard features of the doorman. The waiter in particular looked upset at being ordered away, but Madame had reacted instantly when she recognized the visitor in the closed-circuit image from the street door. No matter how badly things went, she knew she'd make things worse if she used force.

It was possible that things were going to go *very* badly.

"Everything legal?" the little man said. He giggled. "Oh, I very much doubt that, my dear. I suspect that we wouldn't have to search very hard to find drugs that're illegal even in these unsettled times, and . . ."

He stepped past Madame and traced his left index finger along the jawline of a youth as slim as a willow sapling. The boy didn't flinch away, but when the finger withdrew he shuddered. His head was a mass of gleaming black ringlets; all other hair had been carefully removed from his nude body.

" . . . I'm *quite* sure that some of your staff is under age."

He turned and faced Madame. "That's why I'm here, you see. I've come on your business, not mine, and I assure you my money's good."

The boy he'd caressed looked like an ivory carving against the red velvet upholstery. His expression was unreadable. "You're Joachim Steuben," he said.

"Rafe!" said Madame in a harsh, desperate whisper.

"You kill people," Rafe said. He didn't seem to have heard Madame. His eyes were locked with the little man's. "You killed thousands of people other places, and now you're on Nieuw Friesland."

"Rafe, if you don't—" Madame said.

"I'll quiet him!" the waiter said. He stepped out of the lounge, his fists bunched.

The little man made a barely perceptible gesture. One of the guards who'd come up with him clipped the waiter behind the ear with the edge of his hand, dropping him in a boneless heap.

"I don't know about 'thousands', Rafe," the little man said without glancing back at the waiter. "I'm Joachim Steuben, though."

He giggled. "And perhaps thousands, yes. One loses track, you know."

Rafe rose in an eel-like wriggle. Joachim held out his hand, but the boy slipped past and through the door into the back hall.

Madame stood transfixed, her mouth open, then closing again. Touching her lips with her tongue she said at last, "Sir, I'll bring him back if you'll permit me. Rafe's new here, you see, and a little. . . ."

She didn't know how to end the phrase, so her voice trailed off.

Another boy rose as if to follow. He was black-haired also, but his skin was darker and he was probably several years older.

"Felipe," Madame said, gesturing urgently but continuing to watch Joachim.

Felipe sat down again reluctantly. "Rafe's brother was killed last month so he had to come here," he said to Joachim. "He's a sweet boy, please?"

"My name's Sharls, Baron Steuben," said the muscular youth on the next couch. His naturally blond hair was so fine that it clung to his scalp like a halo. "I won't run away from you."

Joachim glanced at Sharls' erection. "Indeed," he said. "Well, we'll see how things develop."

The waiter began to groan. The guard who'd slugged him gestured. The barman came out warily, gripped the waiter by collar and belt, and dragged him into the lounge. His eyes never left the grinning guard.

"Can I get you some refreshment, Baron Steuben?" Madame said, raising an eyebrow. "Or something for the gentlemen with you?"

She'd recognized her guest instantly, though she'd have preferred that he remain formally incognito. If Steuben's name hadn't been spoken, they could all pretend afterwards that this evening had never occurred.

"Those gentlemen are working," Joachim said. He seated himself on the couch Rafe had vacated. His movements were so supple that they appeared relaxed to a casual observer. "I'll have some light wine while I consider the rest of the evening, though."

Steuben had been the bodyguard and enforcer of Colonel Alois Hammer while the latter was a mercenary leader. Hammer, originally from Nieuw Friesland himself, had returned in the pay of one of the contenders in a presidential race turned violent. When his employer had been killed, supposedly by a stray pistol shot, Hammer himself had become president of Nieuw Friesland.

At Hammer's inauguration the former Major Joachim Steuben had become Baron Steuben, Director of Security for Nieuw Friesland. Joachim remained, as anyone who looked into his eyes could tell, the same sociopathic killer he'd been since birth.

"Of course, sir," said Madame, turning toward the barman with birdlike quickness. "Some Graceling, Kedrick! Red Seal, mind you."

He was already reaching beneath the bar. The nearer guard watched the barman's movements intently, but he rose cradling a fat, fluted bottle.

"Come here, Felipe dearest," Joachim said, smiling as he

crooked a finger toward the black-haired boy. "You can help me drink my wine."

A panel concealed as a pilaster between two mirrors opened. Rafe stood in the doorway, still nude but pointing a heavy service pistol in both hands at Joachim.

"You bastard!" he screamed. "You killed my brother!"

Rafe's head exploded in a cyan flash. The *whack!* of the shot that killed him was echoed an instant later as the boy's finger spasmed on the trigger of his own weapon. It blasted a similar bolt of copper plasma into the molding above where Joachim had been sitting. Rafe's body thrashed into the center of the parlor.

The air was hazy. Plaster dust, ozone from the pistol bolts, and the stench of Rafe's voided bowels combined to grip the guts of those who breathed it. A red-haired youth with the face of a cherub looked stricken. He tried to cover his mouth with his hands but only succeeded in deflecting the surge of vomit back over himself.

Joachim stood with his back to the wall, his pistol raised at a slight angle. Its iridium muzzle glowed white; he wouldn't be able to holster it again until it cooled. Not even the guards, crouching horror-struck with their submachine guns openly displayed, had seen him draw and shoot.

He looked at Rafe and giggled. "And now I've killed you, too," he said.

The 1cm plasma bolt had hit the boy between the eyes. At this short range, its energy had turned the boy's brain to steam and ruptured the skull.

Joachim gently toed the pistol from Rafe's hand. "Where do you suppose he got this?" he said. "It's standard military issue, but he scarcely seems a soldier."

One of the guards snatched Rafe's pistol up in his left hand and wheeled to put his submachine gun in Madame's face. "Where did he get it, bitch?" he shouted. "I'll kill you anyway, but you get to decide if it's fast or slow!"

"Calm down, Detrich," Joachim said. "There's no harm done, after all. But—"

He looked pointedly around the room. Even before the shooting his eyes had continually flicked from one side to the other, never resting.

"—I *do* need to know where the weapon came from."

Joachim's pistol had cooled below red heat, but he still didn't holster it. It was similar to Rafe's weapon, but the receiver was carved and filled with golden, silvery, and richly purple inlays.

"Rafe's brother was captain of Baron Herscholdt's bodyguards," the boy Felipe said unexpectedly. "Rafe lived with him. Rafe *loved* his brother."

"I'll check the serial number," said the guard holding the pistol, calm and professional again. He dropped the weapon into a side pocket attached to the armored vest he wore under his cape.

"Sir . . ." Madame said. Her legs slowly buckled; she looked like she was kneeling to pray, but her posture may simply have been the result of weakness. "Sir, I beg you, I didn't know. I didn't have any idea . . ."

"You're a monster," Felipe said. He'd gotten to his feet when Joachim summoned him. He remained where he'd been at the moment of the shot, one foot advanced. "You'll burn in Hell."

Madame turned to look over her shoulder. "Felipe," she said. "For *God's* sake, shut up!"

"You've never done a decent thing in your life!" Felipe said, his face distorted in a rictus of fear and loathing. Tears ran down his cheeks, but his eyes were open and staring. "Not one thing!"

"*Felipe!*" Madame shouted.

The guard who'd been watching Madame when Rafe opened the door behind him now muttered, "Punk *bastard.*" He stepped forward, raising his submachine gun to smash the butt of it down on the boy's face.

"Painter, I'll handle this," Joachim said. He didn't raise his voice, but the guard jerked back as though he'd been struck.

Felipe's lips moved, but the words had stopped coming out. Joachim walked closer.

"You're too sure of me on short acquaintance," he said, tracing the curve of the boy's jaw with the tip of his left index finger. He giggled again. "But you may be right at that."

"Baron . . ." Sharls said. He hadn't moved during the shooting. "Take me, Baron. Take me *now*."

Joachim looked at the blond youth without expression, then let his eyes travel over Madame and each of her boys in turn. "I could kill you all," he said. "Nobody would even care. I could kill almost anyone and nobody'd say a word. But tonight I don't think I will."

He put his left hand, as delicate as a woman's, on Felipe's shoulder. "Come along, boy," he said. "I prefer to transact our business in privacy."

As Joachim walked into the back hallway, his fingers on the boy's pale flesh, he holstered his pistol. The motion was as smooth and graceful as that of a lizard snatching a fly.

Whitey Bernsdorf jiggled the earthenware brandy bottle; it made a hollow rattle. He set it back on the workbench they were using for a table and said morosely, "We just about killed it, Spence, and Sally's going to be closed by now. Via, she'll be asleep."

"Then we'll wake her up, won't we?" Spencer growled. "Bloody hell, Whitey. It's not like we don't have real problems that you have to borrow more!"

Someone knocked on the sliding back door of the garage; not loud, but sharply. The men looked up, momentarily very still. "Go the hell away!" Spencer called.

The door opened. The man who stepped in wore a distortion cape which blurred his face and torso into a smoky haze.

Whitey got up and walked across the shop to his toolchest, moving with quick economy. Spencer remained seated, but he picked up the brandy bottle by the neck. He was balding and heavy, but much less of his weight was fat than a stranger might've guessed.

"You've come to the wrong place, buddy," Spencer said. "Go rob somebody else."

"I'm here to offer you money, not rob you," the figure said. The voice was male; the cape concealed even the sex. "I want you to kill a man for me."

The toolchest's lower right-hand drawer slid open when Whitey thumbed the lock, but he didn't pick up the pistol nested in foam within. Instead he glanced at Spencer, the first time his eyes had left the stranger.

Spencer laughed harshly and set the bottle down. "We're outa that business," he said. "I bought this garage with my retirement bonus. Come back in the morning and see our grand opening. We'll get your aircar running the way it ought to."

"I'm his wrench," Whitey said proudly. He hesitated, then closed the drawer over the gun. "I never could keep two trissies rubbing together in my pocket, but I'll balance your fans so you think it's a new car."

"You'll be sold up before the year's out, Sergeant Spencer," the stranger said calmly. "It'll take six months to build your clientele, and your suppliers will keep you on cash terms for at least that long. You've spent your entire savings buying the operation, so you don't have a cushion to see you through."

Spencer stood, gripping the bottle again. "Look, buddy," he said. "I told you to stay out, and now I'm telling you to *get* out. I won't tell you again."

"You know it's the truth," the stranger said. "That's why you're getting drunk tonight. The money I'll pay you will see you through."

Whitey stared at the blurred shape, then frowned and said to his partner, "Seems like we could talk to him, Spence. Right?"

Spencer's knuckles mottled as he squeezed the earthenware; then he relaxed and set the bottle down. "This is political?" he said in a challenging voice.

"Not for me," said the stranger. "It's purely personal. For somebody else it might be political, though."

His shrug beneath the cape looked like watching fog swirl. "I'll pay you a hundred thousand thalers for the job," he added in the same cool tone as everything else he'd said since he entered the garage.

"Are you crazy?" Whitey said. "Or is this some bloody game? There's so many guns around now that you can get a man killed for three hundred, not a hundred *thousand*!"

"Not this man," the stranger said. His left hand came out from under his cape with a holochip which he set on the table. He wore a pale gray glove, so thin that it could've been a second skin.

He squeezed the chip to activate it, then withdrew his hand. The two ex-soldiers stared at the image in disbelief.

"It's a trap, Spence!" Whitey said. He reached for the toolchest again, but he couldn't find the print-activated lock with his thumb. "He's setting us up for the chop!"

The stranger turned. "You little fool," he said. The cape concealed his features, but his tone of poisonous scorn was unmistakable. "How do you think you're worth setting up? If you were worth killing, you'd have been shot out of hand. *He* would've shot you himself!"

Whitey banged the heel of his hand on the toolchest and scowled. "It's still crazy!" he said, but his voice had dropped from a shout to an embarrassed mutter.

Spencer prodded the holochip with a thick, hairy index finger, then looked up at the stranger's smoky face. "Why do you want him dead?" he said. His voice was suddenly husky and soft, as though he'd just awakened.

"I told you," said the stranger. He shrugged. "Personal reasons."

"It happens I've got personal reasons, too," Spencer said. "He shot a buddy of mine on Dunderberg for thinking there was better use for a warehouse of good liquor than burning it. That was twelve years ago; hell, fourteen. But it's a good reason."

"Robbie shouldn't have gone for his gun, Spence," Whitey said sadly. "He'd been into that whiskey already or he'd have known better."

"Did I ask your opinion?" Spencer said. "Just belt up, Whitey! D'you hear me? Belt up!"

"Sorry, Spence," the mechanic said in a low voice. He pretended to study the travelling hoist latched against the wall of the garage.

"Anyway," Spencer said, his voice harsh again, "it don't matter what your reasons are, or mine either. It can't be done. Not without taking out a couple square blocks, and even then I wouldn't trust the bastard not to wriggle clear. I don't care how much money you promise."

"I'll guarantee you a clean shot at the target," the stranger said. He made a sound that might have been meant for laughter. "You won't be close, but you'll have a clear line of sight. Then it's just a matter of whether you're good enough."

"I don't believe it," Whitey said. "I don't *believe* it."

The stranger shrugged. "I'll give you a day to think about it," he said. "I'll be back tomorrow."

He paused in the doorway and looked back at them. "He has to die, you know," he said in his soft, precise voice. "*Has* to."

Then he was gone, sliding the door closed behind him.

Spencer lifted the bottle to his lips and finished it in a gulp. "I'm good enough, Whitey," he said. "But bloody *hell*. . . ." They stared at the fist-sized image of Joachim Steuben projected by the holochip.

Danny Pritchard stood at the balcony railing, looking out over Landfall City. A few fires smudged the clear night, and once his eye caught the familiar cyan flash of a powergun bolt somewhere in the capital's street. Those were merely incidents of city life: the real fighting had been over for nearly a month.

Danny'd been born on Dunstan, a farming world where everybody was pretty much equal: equally in debt to the Combine of off-planet merchants who bought Dunstan's wheat and shipped it to hungry neighboring worlds at a fat profit. Nobody on Dunstan would've known what a baron was except as a name out of a book, so for that whimsical reason Danny'd refused the title of Baron when President Hammer offered it to him. He was simply Mister Daniel Pritchard, Director of Administration for Nieuw Friesland.

Danny hadn't been back to Dunstan since he left thirty-odd standard years before. His homeworld was a peaceful place. It didn't need soldiers, and until he took off his uniform on the day Colonel Hammer became President Hammer, Danny Pritchard had been a soldier.

Nobody on Dunstan could've afforded to pay Hammer's Slammers anyway. The Slammers weren't cheap, but in cases where victory was the difference between having a future or not . . . well, what was life worth?

"Danny?" Margritte said, coming out onto the balcony with him. She'd put a robe over her nightgown. He hadn't bothered with clothing; the autumn chill helped bring his thoughts into perfect clarity.

That didn't help, of course. When there's no way out, there's little pleasure in having a clear view of your own doom.

"Just going over things," Danny said, smiling at his wife. He wished that she hadn't awakened. "I didn't mean to get you up, too."

Margritte had been as good a communications officer as there was in the Slammers, and as good a wife to him as ever a soldier had. There was nothing she could do now except give him one more problem to worry about.

Danny chuckled. No, when you really came down to it, he had only one real problem. Unfortunately, that one was insoluble.

"You're worried about Steuben, aren't you," Margritte said. The words weren't a question.

"Joachim, yes," Danny said, following the path of a low-flying aircar. It was probably a police patrol. The repeal of the ban on private aircars in Landfall City wouldn't come into effect till the end of the month, though a few citizens were anticipating it.

They were taking more of a risk than they probably realized. There were still military patrols out, and the Slammers' motto wasn't so much "Preserve and Protect" as "Shoot first and ask questions later."

Danny grinned faintly. Troops blasting wealthy citizens out of the sky would make more problems for the Directorate of Administration, but relatively minor ones. A number of Nieuw Friesland's wealthy citizens had been gunned down in the recent past—the former owners of this palace among them.

He had a breathtaking view from this balcony. The palace was a rambling two-story structure, but it was built on the ridge overlooking Landfall City from the south. It'd belonged to Baron Herscholdt, the man who'd regarded himself as the power behind President van Vorn's throne though he stayed out of formal politics.

Herscholdt was out of life, now; he and his wife as well, because she'd gotten in the way when a squad of White Mice, the security troops under the direct command of Major Steuben, came for the baron.

Danny was used to being billeted in palaces. He was even used to the faint smell of burned flesh remaining even after the foyer'd been washed down with lye. What he wasn't used to was owning the palace; which he did, for as long as he lived. It was one of the perquisites of his government position.

For as long as he lived.

"Steuben has to go," Margritte said, hugging herself against more than the evening chill. "Can't the colonel see that? There's no place for him anymore."

"Joachim's completely loyal," Danny said. He tried to put an arm around his wife. Now she flinched away, too tense for even that contact. "He won't permit the existence of anything that threatens the colonel."

Danny sighed. "That works in a war zone," he said, letting out the words that'd spun in his mind for weeks. "We go in and then we leave. The people who hired us can blame everything that happened on us evil mercenaries. Then they can get on with governing without the bother of the folks who'd have been in opposition if we hadn't shot them."

Margritte shook her head angrily. "Maybe it'll work here too," she said. Her voice was thick, and Danny thought he caught the gleam of starlight on a tear. He looked away quickly.

"President Hammer isn't leaving this time," he explained quietly. "Shooting everybody who might be a threat will only work if you're willing to kill about ninety percent of the population."

He barked a laugh of sorts. "Which Joachim probably is," he added. "But it isn't *possible*, which is something else entirely."

"Steuben isn't stupid," Margritte said. She suddenly reached for Danny's hand and gripped it between hers; she still wouldn't turn to look at him. "He's . . . I don't think he's human, Danny, but I believe he really does love the colonel. Can't he see that unless he steps aside, the colonel's government can't survive?"

"There're fish that have to keep swimming to breathe," Danny said—to Margritte; to himself; to the night. "For Joachim, retirement would mean suffocating. He won't retire, and the colonel—"

He grimaced. He was trying to remember that Alois Hammer was no longer a mercenary leader and that Danny Pritchard was no longer his adjutant.

"And President Hammer," he went on, "won't force him out. The colonel—"

Again!

"—is loyal too. And besides, he *needs* a Director of Security. He knows as well as I do that there's nobody better at it than Joachim. Nobody. The problem is that Joachim's only willing to go at the job in one way, and that way's going to be fatal to the civil government."

Danny shook his head. "Maybe he *can* only go at it one way," he said. "I've known Joachim for half my life, but I won't pretend I understand what goes on in his head."

"He's a monster!" Margritte said to the night in sudden, fierce anger. She turned and glared at her husband. "Danny?" she said. "If he won't leave but he has to go . . . ?"

Danny laughed. He gave Margritte a quick hug, but that was to permit him to ease back and look toward the city before speaking.

"Sure," he said. "I've thought about killing Joachim. Having him killed. It'd be possible, though it might take a platoon of tanks to make sure of him."

He looked at his wife, his face hard in the starlight. Danny Pritchard was only a little over average height, but there were times—this one of them—that he seemed a much bigger man.

"And I could get a platoon of tanks for the job, sure," he said harshly. "If this was a war, I'd do just that. I've done it, done worse, and we both know it. But that's the whole point, it's not a war: it's the civil government of the planet where I'm going to spend the rest of my life. Unlike Joachim, I won't try to preserve that government by means that I know would destroy it."

Margritte hugged herself again. "What is there to do then, Danny?" she said. "What are we going to do?"

Danny reached out and hugged her with real affection. "We're going to deal with the situation as it develops, I suppose," he said softly, stroking his wife's hair. She cut it short to fit under a commo helmet, but it retained a springy liveliness that always thrilled him. "War gives you a lot of experience in doing that, and war's been my whole life."

He kissed Margritte's forehead. "Now," he said with mock sternness. "Go back to bed and let me stand here for a little while more, all right?"

She kissed him passionately, then stepped away. "All right, Danny," she said as she went back into the bedroom. "I know you'll find a way."

I wish I *knew that*, thought Danny Pritchard, looking down on the nighted city. *I* sure *don't*.

All he knew was that if he stood here alone, an assassin wouldn't kill anybody besides his intended target. Joachim Steuben certainly realized that the Director of Administration was a potential danger to him, which he'd read as meaning a danger to President Hammer.

And Joachim didn't have Danny Pritchard's compunctions about how to deal with a threat.

They were expecting the knock on the back door, but even so Whitey's hand jerked the bottle; brandy splashed onto the work-bench, beading on the oil-soaked wood.

Spencer said, "Bloody *hell*, Whitey." Then, louder and with the anger directed at the real cause, he said, "Come in then, curse it!"

The shop's harsh overhead lights were on. The stranger's distortion cape was a deeper pool of shadow than it'd been in the light of the small table lamp the night before. He closed the door and said, "How was your first day's business, then?"

Spencer didn't speak. "It was fine," Whitey said, a trifle too loudly. "Anyway, things'll pick up."

"What have you decided about my proposition?" the stranger said. His voice was like the paw of a cat playing with a small animal; it was very delicate, but points pressed through its softness.

Whitey looked at his partner. Spencer took the holochip from his pocket, activated the image of Joachim Steuben, and tossed it onto the bench.

"All right," he said in a challenging tone. "We'll do it on one condition: you pay us *all* the money up front."

"Every thaler!" Whitey said. His index finger had been drawing circles in the spilled brandy. When he realized what he was doing, he jerked his hand into his lap.

"Yes, that's reasonable," the stranger said. His gloved left hand slipped from beneath his cape, this time holding a small bag of wash leather. He placed it on the bench, then withdrew his hand. "I think you'll find the full amount there."

"What the hell is this?" Spencer muttered. After a moment's general silence he tugged open the drawstring closure and spilled the bag's contents, several dozen credit chips, onto the wood.

"A hundred thousand thalers in one chip," the stranger said mildly, "might present you with difficulties. But the total is correct."

Spencer began rotating the semiconductor wafers so that the amounts printed on the edges faced him. Whitey picked one up. His lips moved; then he read aloud, "Four . . . four-thousand-one-hunnert-forty-nine."

"Most of the chips range from three to five thousand thalers," the stranger said. "One's for eleven thousand, but you shouldn't have any trouble banking it if you build up a pattern of deposits over the course of a month."

"What the hell," Spencer repeated, scowling at the chips and then looking up at the stranger. "You agreed just like that?"

The shadow rippled in a shrug. "It was a reasonable condition," the stranger said. "You have no reason to trust me, after all. And as for me trusting you . . ."

He gave a chittering laugh. "You may fail, Sergeant Spencer," he said, "but you won't try to cheat me."

"No, I don't guess we will," Spencer said grimly. "But just how are *you* so sure of that, buddy?"

The gloved hand pointed to the holochip image. "Because if you did, he'd learn that you took money to kill him," the stranger said. "What do you think would happen next?"

"We'll do the bloody job," Spencer said, pushing the credit chips back into the bag. He hadn't counted them; at this point the money wasn't the most important thing. "We'll do it *if* we get a clear shot."

He glowered at the stranger's blurred face. "How d'ye plan to arrange it?" he demanded. "Because I'll tell you, nothing *I* know about that bastard makes me think you can do it."

The stranger put a small data cube beside the image of Joachim Steuben. "This will run in your inventory reader," he said. "It contains the full plan. I suggest you take the machine off-line before you view it, though. It's unlikely that the Directorate of Security would be doing key-word sweeps detailed enough to pick up the contents, but—"

His laugh was like bats quarrelling.

"—it would only take once, wouldn't it? So better safe than sorry."

"How are you going to manage it?" Whitey demanded, angry because he was so nervous. He's been shot at many times; he knew how to handle himself in a firefight. The thing that was happening now made him feel as though the ground was streaming away beneath his feet. "You say 'here's the plan', but what d'you know about this kinda job? You think it's easy?"

Spencer looked at the stranger's smoky features, pursed his lips, and said to his partner, "Whitey, we'll take a look at it—"

He prodded an index finger in the direction of the cube.

"—and make our go, no-go on what we think."

He shifted his gaze back to the stranger. "That's how Whitey and me've always worked, buddy," he said, raising his voice slightly. "If we don't like the mission, we don't take it. We figure we're not paid to commit suicide, we're paid to kill other people. And we're *bloody* good at it!"

"I know, Sergeant," the stranger said; there was more real humor in his voice now than there had been in his previous cracklings of laughter. "That's why I'm here."

His blurred visage turned to Whitey. Occasionally his eyes glinted through the polarizing fabric.

"Next week there'll be privy council meeting in the Maritime

Commission building on Quetzal Point, Trooper Bernsdorf," the stranger said. "There's a knoll three kilometers west of the building. When the meeting breaks up, the sergeant will have a shot."

The distortion cape rippled as he gestured through it toward the data cube.

"The details are in there. If you decide there's anything else you need—a tribarrel, for example, or perhaps a vehicle—hang a white rag on your rear doorlatch. I'll come back to get the details."

Spencer rose and walked to the degreasing tank in which air bubbled through a culture of petroleum-eating bacteria. "I don't need a tribarrel," he said, reaching into the tank and coming out with a long, sealed tube. "You want to knock down a wall, a tribarrel does the job a treat. But if you're just trying to drop one man—"

He twisted the top off the container and slid a shoulder-stocked powergun onto the workbench. It should've been turned in when Spencer retired from the Slammers. An unassigned weapon, picked up in the bloody shambles that'd been an Iron Guard barracks, had gone into the armory in its place.

"—this old girl has always done the job for me."

Spencer shook his head as he lifted the weapon. The stubby iridium barrel's 2cm bore channeled plasma released from precisely aligned copper atoms in the breech. The bolts were as straight as light beams and remained lethal to a human at any range within the curvature of a planet's surface.

"I don't remember how many times I've rebarreled her," Spencer said affectionately. "She never let me down."

"Five-hunnert-an-three kills," Whitey said proudly. "Planned shots, I mean, not firefights where you never know who nailed what."

"I'll use a sandbag rest," Spencer said, facing the hidden figure. "Whitey'll spot for me and pull security, like always. I don't see any bloody thing but what's in my sight picture when I'm waiting, and at three klicks that's not very much. If there's a shot, I'll take it."

He was a different man with the big weapon cradled in his arms. The change wasn't so much that Spencer projected confidence as that he'd become an utterly stable *thing*: a boulder or a tree with centuries of growth behind it.

"All right, Sergeant," the stranger said. "That appears satisfactory. I don't suppose I'll be seeing you again."

He touched the vertical door handle, then reached back beneath the cape and did something hidden. When his gloved hand came out again, it held a coin of gold-colored crystal that'd been pierced for a chain. He dropped it on the bench between the sack of credit chips and the image of Joachim Steuben.

"This is my lucky piece," he said. He chuckled. "If you ever get to Newland I suppose it's still worth a hundred wreaths, but I think you're going to need the luck more than you will the money."

He closed the door behind him, a shadow returning to the night's other shadows.

Whitey carried the data cube to the inventory computer in the service port between the work bay and the front office. "If he gets you a clear line of sight, you don't need luck, Spence," he said.

Spencer didn't reply. He was sliding a twenty-round tube of ammunition into the butt-well of his weapon.

President Hammer rested his elbows on the top of the table and massaged his forehead with the fingers of both hands. He muttered something, but the words were lost in his palms. The meeting had been going on since dawn, and it was now late in the afternoon.

"We really need to settle this quickly, sir," said Danny Pritchard, seated to the right of Hammer at the head of the table. "Every day there's another hundred people being added to the camps. Releasing them won't gain us back nearly the amount of good will we lose by arresting them in the first place. And there's too many being shot during arrest, too."

"There's always going to be a few fools who think they can outrun a powergun bolt," said Joachim Steuben with a grin. "I think we're benefiting the race by removing them from the gene pool. And as for the ones who choose to shoot it out with *my* men, well, that's simply a form of suicide."

Joachim was in a khaki uniform, identical except for the lack of rank tabs to those he'd worn during his years in the Slammers. Instead of a normal uniform's tough, rip-stopped synthetic and utilitarian fit, Joachim's was woven from natural fabrics and tailored with as much skill as a debutante's ball gown. He'd always dressed that way. Strangers who'd met Joachim for the first time had often mistaken him for Hammer's lover instead of his bodyguard and killer.

He didn't wear body armor; he rarely had except on battlefields where shell fragments were a threat. He said that armor slowed him down and that his quickness was better protection than a ceramic plate. Thus far he'd been right.

Hammer lowered his hands and looked at the twelve officials—nine men and three women—seated at the table with him. No aides were present within the temporary privacy capsule erected within the volume of the large conference room.

"We're not going to decide this today," Hammer said. His voice was raspy and his face had aged more in a month as president than it had in the previous five years of combat operations. "I've had it for now."

"Then we'll settle it tomorrow?" Danny said in a carefully emotionless tone.

"Blood and martyrs!" said Hammer. "Not tomorrow. Maybe next week. I don't want to hear about it tomorrow."

"Sir," said Danny, "no decision is a decision, and it's the wrong one. We've—"

Hammer lurched up from the table and slammed the heel of his right fist down on the resin-stabilized wood. "This meeting is over!" he said. "Mister Pritchard, Baron Steuben—remain with me for a moment. Everyone else leaves *now*."

Council members got to their feet and moved quickly to the capsule's exit. Guards stationed there opened the doors of the room itself onto the corridor. Aides waited there with additional guards and a number of the people who ordinarily worked in the building.

The locations of privy council meetings were kept secret from all but the attendees and were never held in the same place twice in succession. The first the staff of the site knew what was happening was when workmen arrived an hour ahead of time to erect the privacy capsule that sealed the meeting from the eyes and ears of non-participants.

Half the councillors dressed in civilian clothes; the other half were in uniform, either Slammers khaki or the blue-piped gray of the Frisian Defense Forces. Hammer himself wore a civilian tunic and breeches, but he'd deliberately had them tailored in the style that'd been popular when he left Nieuw Friesland half a lifetime ago.

Hammer's wife Anneke, nee Tromp, was present as the Director of Social Welfare. "Shut the door!" he called to her as she went out.

Anneke turned, met her husband's eyes, and walked on through to the corridor without responding. A guard swung the panel closed, sealing the capsule again.

Hammer sighed. "Now listen, both of you," he said in a voice that didn't hold the same key from word to word. "I'll make a decision on the detention policy when I'm ready to. Nobody—neither of you—will say another word to me on the subject till then. Do you *hear* me?"

"As you wish, Alois," said Joachim Steuben.

Danny Pritchard grimaced. "Yes sir, I hear you," he said.

"Pritchard, I mean it!" Hammer said in sudden fury.

"I've never doubted your word, Colonel," Danny said, letting his anger show also. "Don't you start doubting mine now!"

"Via, I'm not getting enough sleep," Hammer muttered. He put his left hand over Danny's right, squeezed it, and stepped out of the capsule.

Danny made a wry face and gestured to the exit. "After you, Baron," he said.

Joachim grinned and walked out ahead of the other man. Without turning he said, "I wouldn't shoot you in the back, Mister Pritchard."

Danny laughed. Workmen moved into the meeting room behind him to tear down the privacy capsule for use in another few days or a week. It was simply a framework with an active sound-cancellation system between two layers of light-diffusing membrane.

"Joachim, we've known each other too long for nonsense," Danny said. It was battlefield humor, but this was surely a battle-field. "You'd shoot me any way you felt like at the moment."

Joachim giggled. They'd reached the hallway, but guards had formed a bubble of space around them without being directed to.

Margritte had been standing with the rest of the aides and clerks. They'd gone off with the remaining council members, leaving her alone. She was as still-faced as a statue in a wall niche.

"If I thought it was necessary, I suppose I would at that," Joachim said. "As you would do in similar circumstances. Wouldn't you, Daniel?"

Danny looked at the shorter man. They'd known each other for such a long time . . .

Aloud he said, "If you mean, 'Would I shoot you if I thought that was necessary to bring an end to policies that I'm sure will destroy the government?' then the answer is apparently, 'No.' Even though I believe that if I don't kill you, nobody in that council meeting is going to die in bed. *None* of us."

"You have your beliefs," Joachim said, shrugging. "I have mine. I don't believe that I should wait to see if a man who threatens the president is really serious; or if maybe he'll change his mind before acting; or if he's simply too incompetent to carry through with that threat."

"Joachim . . ." Danny said. He and the other man were so focused on one another that the bustle of the hallway could have taken place on another planet. "You know I'm right. You can follow a chain of consequences as far as anybody I've ever met."

"Yes, Daniel," Joachim said. "And so can you, which is why you know that *I'm* right also."

He giggled. "A pity that we can't run the experiment both ways before we make our decision, isn't it?" he said. "Well, perhaps in another universe Nieuw Friesland is being governed according to other principles. For now . . . well, go to your wife, Daniel. The only thing *I* know about is killing."

Danny opened his mouth, then closed it and smiled. He said, "That's been our job for a long time, Joachim. Maybe you're right and it still is. If so, the Lord help us."

Joachim frowned. "I left my hat," he said, stepping back into the meeting room.

"Watch it!" a workman shouted as he and his partner swung one of the last panels of the privacy capsule out of its frame. When the fellow looked over his shoulder and saw who he'd spoken to, the panel slipped from his hands.

Joachim ignored him and bent to retrieve the saucer hat on the frame bracing the chair legs. He turned with a smile and called to Danny, "You have to remember, Daniel, that dying in bed has never been a goal of mine."

One of the west-facing windows shattered in a cyan flash. The bolt caught Joachim between the shoulder blades. His body fluids flashed into steam, flinging his trim figure in a somersault that landed him face-up at Danny's feet. The shot had torn the right arm from his torso, but his cherubic face was still smiling.

Mister Daniel Pritchard wasn't carrying a gun, but his reflexes were still in place. He threw himself to the floor, snatched the pistol from the cutaway holster on Joachim's right hip, and rose. He fired three times out the window through which the shot had come.

Danny didn't expect to hit anything but empty sky, but he'd gotten to be a veteran by learning that you *always* shot back instantly. At the worst it wasn't going to do their aim any good, and every once in a while you might nail the bastard.

People were shouting and running. The meeting room's other high vitril windows cascaded in splinters as guards smashed them out with gun butts. They began raking shots along the distant hills.

Danny lifted himself into a crouch to get a better view. A trooper wearing body armor, one of Joachim's White Mice, landed on his back and flattened him again.

"Keep the fuck down, sir!" she shouted. "We already lost the major!"

"Roger!" Danny said, trying to breathe against the weight of the trooper protecting him with her own body. "I'll stay down!"

The guard got up and scuttled to join her fellows as they fired into the distance. Danny didn't have commo, so he could only hope that the captain commanding the security detail was doing something more useful than the nearest personnel were.

"What happened?" said a voice nearby. He looked back, expecting to see Margritte. She was in the corridor under a guard twice her size.

President Hammer hunched at Danny's side. In one hand he held the pistol he'd worn in a shoulder holster, but the fingers of the other traced Joachim's cheek with a feather-light touch.

"A two-see-em bolt through the window," Danny said, gesturing with his pistol. The inlays winked festively, reminding him whose weapon it'd been. "One round only, so the shooter was either really good or really lucky."

He set the gun down. A floor tile *crack*ed, broken by the glowing iridium barrel.

"Joachim wouldn't have given him more than one round," Hammer whispered. His face was set, but tears ran down his cheek. "I never thought I'd see this. Never."

Hammer holstered his own pistol and rose to his knees. The guards had stopped shooting. Under a sergeant's bellowed orders they backed away from the windows and stood shoulder to shoulder, a living wall between the direction of the shot and the men they were here to protect.

The bolt had blown the remainder of Joachim's tunic away. His chest was as white and hairless as an ivory statue.

"Where's his lucky piece?" Hammer said.

"What?"

Hammer looked at Danny, his expression suddenly blank and watchful. "Joachim always wore a coin from Newland around his neck," Hammer said. "That was the only thing he'd brought from home. He said it was his luck."

"Colonel?" Danny said harshly. He got to his feet. "I'm not behind this. I don't care if you believe me, but it's the truth anyway. However, this is the best piece of luck you and the whole planet could've gotten."

Joachim's corpse smiled at him from the floor.

AFTERWORD

ACCIDENTALLY AND BY THE BACK DOOR

1.

Some people decide at an early age that all they want to be is a writer. A high school classmate of mine was like that, actively Gathering Material while the rest of us were basically being kids. His career never got off the ground—he sold a couple fillers to *Reader's Digest*—but Robert E. Howard and my late friend Karl Edward Wagner had the same attitude and were extremely successful in their time.

I wasn't like that: I was going to be a lawyer. I intended to write and sell at least one story, but writing was only a hobby so far as I was concerned. This distinction affects everything that comes after.

2.

I sold two horror stories to Arkham House before I was drafted in 1969, and sold two more in 1970–1. The fourth sale came after I got back to the World and reentered Duke Law School. Then August Derleth, the proprietor of Arkham House, died and left me without a market.

There were very few professional outlets for fantasy stories at the time, and the fan press didn't pay at all. The modern fantasy/horror small press really started when Stu Schiff began paying a penny a word for stories in *Whispers* in 1973 (at my instigation, I'm proud to say). I had no luck selling the professional markets my fantasies using backgrounds from ancient history, and I scorned the notion of giving stories away to fanzines.

My friends Manly Wade Wellman and Karl Edward Wagner suggested that I use Viet Nam settings. Nothing else was working, so I tried that, with some success, selling a fantasy to *F&SF* and an SF story to *Analog*. The fantasy involved letting loose a monster from an ancient tomb; the SF story dealt with a tank company finding a UFO.

3.

Then I decided that I'd write an SF story using my background with the 11th Armored Cavalry Regiment in Viet Nam (and Cambodia, for a couple months) instead of interjecting a fantasy or SF element into a real-world setting. That is, I'd write about a future armored unit fighting a future war. What I'd done before was simply to use the 11th Cav as background, the way New York City or the French Revolution could be backgrounds for stories.

I made the unit a mercenary company, as Kuttner and Moore had done in *Clash by Night* in 1943 and Gordy Dickson had done in 1958 with *Dorsai!* (in both cases in *Astounding*). I called the unit Hammer's Slammers, following as much as anything the practice of Robert Heinlein in *Starship Troopers*, where unit designators include the commanding officer's name.

4.

I couldn't sell the story—*The Butcher's Bill*—to save my life. This was remarkably frustrating, since the sales to *F&SF* and *Analog* demonstrated that I was capable of doing professional-quality work. I couldn't understand what the problem was.

One of the rejections, by Ben Bova of *Analog*, was particularly maddening. Ben was well disposed toward me: he'd bought one story of mine already and would later buy two more (none of them in the Hammer series). Ben commented that *The Butcher's Bill* was a good story, but he had Jerry Pournelle and Joe Haldeman already and he didn't think *Analog* needed a third series of the same sort.

From thirty years on, the notion Jerry's Falkenberg series and Joe's *Forever War* were the same is even more ludicrous than it appeared to me at the time, and what I was doing was a third thing yet. That wasn't obvious from the outside, not at the time.

5.

What I now think was going on in the early '70s is this. Jerry, Joe, and I were similar in one important fashion: we'd all been at the sharp end of war (Korea in Jerry's case, Viet Nam for Joe and me). Our work therefore shared a sort of realism which Kuttner, Dickson, and Heinlein lacked (for all their enormous strength as writers).

At that point we diverged. Jerry was writing something not greatly different in theme from the Military SF of past decades. His soldiers were saving civilization from the barbarians, despite the scorn and disgust with which they were regarded by many of the civilians whom they preserved. At the time (remember, the Vietnam War was still going on), the conservative *Analog* was probably the only place Jerry's stories could've appeared.

Joe's stories focused on confusion, hopelessness, and mutual distrust at every level of society, particularly within the military itself. They were a reflection of what he saw in Viet Nam and during the '60s more generally. In the context of this essay it's important to note that Joe is one of the finest prose writers of his (our) generation. His choice to write for *Analog* rather than *The New Yorker* was just that, a choice.

In my case, *The Butcher's Bill* showed a group of pretty ordinary people who were members of an elite armored unit which'd been given the job of defeating an enemy unit. They did so, and in the course of doing their job they completely destroyed the architectural marvel that the two sides were fighting over.

That's exactly what the 11th ACR had done to Snuol, Cambodia, in April of 1970. The only fiction in the background is that Snuol was a pretty ordinary market town rather than a unique ancient site; but if the NVA'd had their headquarters in Angkor Wat, our tanks would've gone through the same way they did at Snuol.

Clearly Hammer's Slammers weren't saving civilization. Neither were they hopeless, alienated people: they were individually good at their jobs, and they trusted the other members of their unit implicitly. It's also important that I do not and certainly did not deserve the critical respect that's rightly accorded to Joe. I fell between two stools, and I wasn't a polished enough craftsman to build a place for myself.

6.

If I'd been trying to build a writing career, at this point I'd have gone back to writing the sort of standard stories which I'd sold in the past. Instead I wrote another Hammer story, *Under the Hammer*. Fred Pohl had commented while rejecting *The Butcher's Bill* that military matters were too much in the fabric of the story for a general reader to understand it. I addressed the criticism by making the viewpoint character a new recruit to whom everything had to be explained, thus explaining it for the reader as well.

After the fact, I don't think that was a real problem: both the Viet Nam-setting stories I'd sold previously assumed equally extensive knowledge of the military. In any case, everybody rejected *Under the Hammer* also.

7.

Then the editor of *Galaxy*, one of the many who'd rejected the Hammer stories, was fired and replaced by his assistant, Jim Baen. Jim had recommended purchase of the stories and been overruled. Now that he was in charge, he called my agent and bought the stories after all (for *Galaxy*). He published them and asked for more in the series.

But—and this is very important—Jim neither understood nor liked the Hammer stories at the time he bought them (as he admitted to me later). He bought them simply because they were written with a higher degree of literacy than most of what was submitted to *Galaxy*, a magazine which paid poorly and late. *Under the Hammer* and *The Butcher's Bill* filled pages which would otherwise have contained stories which would've required heavy editing to bring up to minimum standards of English usage.

The Hammer stories were written with a flat affect, describing cruelty and horror with the detachment of a soldier who's shut down his emotional responses completely in a war zone . . . as soldiers always do, because otherwise they wouldn't be able to survive. Showing soldiers behaving and thinking as they really do in war was unique at the time and extremely disquieting to the civilians who were editing magazines.

8.

I mentioned that Jim asked for additional Hammer stories. I wrote three more, and Jim rejected two of them. No reasonable person thinking of a career in writing would've deliberately written stories which were not only hard to sell but which when they did sell were purchased by an editor who turned his eyes away when he bought them.

The reason *I* continued with the series is that the Hammer stories provided me with a form of therapy, a socially acceptable way of dealing with Viet Nam. (I didn't know that at the time. I came to the conclusion much later, when I was cool enough and sane enough to really analyze what'd been going on.)

9.

The funny—and wholly unexpected—thing is that after the Hammer stories were published, they gained a following. Though the magazine editors were civilians, SF readers included a number of veterans and serving members of the military. My stories were the first ones they'd seen which showed war the way they knew it. The comments Jim got on *The Butcher's Bill* and later stories in the series were positive; so much so that when he was hired to take over the SF program at Ace Books, he asked me to do a Hammer collection.

The collection, my first book, was the eighth book down on a list of eleven books from Ace in April, 1979. Short story collections are notoriously difficult to sell, as are authors' first books; *Hammer's Slammers* had both strikes against it. It sold over ninety percent of the first printing and went through eight more printings at Ace before I transferred the rights to Baen Books, Jim's new publishing line. The stories have never been out of print since their first book publication.

Not coincidentally, I became a full-time freelance writer in 1981 and have remained one since. *The Butcher's Bill* very directly gave me a career that I hadn't been looking for.

10.

Don't read things into the above account that aren't there. I'm not telling you that you have to believe in yourself in order to succeed: I didn't believe in myself (as a writer or as much of anything else).

I'm also not telling you that if you keep at it long enough you'll find an editor who believes in you. Jim bought my stories because they saved him editing time, not because he believed in them or me at the time he took them.

I *am* specifically saying that if I'd put my writing career first, I wouldn't have a writing career. I know many writers, some of them very good writers, about whom that isn't true.

But I'm saying one thing more: I believed in the truth of the vision I portrayed in the Hammer series. I followed that vision of truth to the exclusion of all other considerations in writing the stories.

And I don't believe any writer can have real success unless he follows his own truth.

7/22/15

DATE DUE			
SEP 0 9 2015			
FEB 0 9 2016			
AUG 0 6 2019			